The Lunar Trilogy

By Jerzy Zulawski

Translated by Elzbieta Morgan

ZMOK
BOOKS

Zmok Books

The Lunar Trilogy by Jerzy Zulawski
Cover by Michael Nigro
Translated by Elzbieta Morgan
This edition published in 2020

Zmok Books is an imprint of

Winged Hussar Publishing, LLC
1525 Hulse Rd, Unit 1
Point Pleasant, NJ 08742

Bibliographical References and Index
1. Science Fiction. 2. Alternate History. 3. Adventure

This publication has been supported by the © POLAND Translation Program

BOOK INSTITUTE
©POLAND

Jerzy Żuławski

Editor's Note:

We are very happy to present the complete Lunar Trilogy by Jerzy Zulawski. This is one of the early works of science fiction that influenced writers such as Stanislaw Lem, but surprisingly has not been published in English until today.

In some ways it was (and is) ahead of its time, using the latest information on astronomy and science combined with a healthy dose of Jules Verne and H.G. Wells to provide an interesting tale of adventure and humanity. It should be read on several levels – it is a product of its time in that the early part of the book shows a male dominated society, that will seem brutal. Over time it also develops strong female characters who take control of sectors of society on their own. There are devices anticipating some of the technology of today, while other aspects of technology might have been advances for that time, but might seem quaint by our standards today

The book examines the role of classes in society, how civilization transmits knowledge and questions that knowledge is used. It is a book of hope and of disappointment. The author tells you a story, then shows how history has interpreted that history over the years, and usually for the benefit of those in charge of society.

In its soul it is also a Polish book. The author was a Polish patriot at a time when Poland was still partitioned amongst three powers. Many of the characters in the story and the places featured on Earth are Polish. They were there to remind the readers of the early 20th century that Poland was still around them. Where possible we have retained the Polish spellings for names and places.

As was the style of the time, these books were published in serial format in different magazines. The first book – *On the Silver Globe* – was published in 1903 and it wasn't until 1910 that the second book, *The Conqueror* (though it could be translated as The Victor or The Redeemer) was serialized. Luckily, the third book, *The Old Earth*, was published in 1911. Although this series was not available in English, it has influenced western science fiction by osmosis, through the writings of eastern science fiction writers, and now it is available to you.

On the Silver Globe

Jerzy Żuławski

I. A MANUSCRIPT FROM THE MOON...

Almost fifty years have passed since that double expedition, the craziest that Man had ever undertaken and performed, and all of it had almost been forgotten until that article in the local K... daily. The article, signed by an assistant from a small local observatory, reminded us of it again. Its author claimed that he had indisputable information about the fate of those madmen launched to the Moon fifty years earlier. The whole story eventually led to unrest although it wasn't treated seriously at first. Those who had heard or read about it before, knew that those daring adventurers had perished. So, they shrugged their shoulders at the news that, those long believed to be dead, were not only alive but were even sending messages from the Moon.

The observatory assistant stood firmly by his statement, and to those who were interested, he even showed an iron cone like object forty cm tall that supposedly contained a manuscript created on the Moon. He would let you see and admire the intricately crafted and hollow interior of the object, which was covered with a thick layer of rust and slag, but he wouldn't be persuaded to show the manuscript itself to anybody. He claimed it was merely a stack of charred papers that he was still deciphering with the help of artificial photographs taken with the utmost effort and caution. Such secrecy evoked suspicions since the assistant still didn't disclose how he had come into possession of that object in the first place, and the curiosity kept building up. While we were waiting for the promised explanations, albeit with some degree of skepticism, the available contemporary writings helped us remember the history of the whole expedition.

Suddenly people started to wonder how they could have forgotten about the expeditions so soon... After all, wasn't it true that from the beginning of the expedition and especially after that improbable and unheard-of accident, all the daily newspapers, weekly and monthly magazines, devoted a few columns to those dubious events for several years in a row? Before the launch of the expedition itself, they all reported on the preparations and status updates. Almost every screw was examined in the "vehicle", that was to travel through the interplanetary space and drop off those daring madmen on the Moon. So far, the surface of the Moon had only been known from the excellent photographs taken over many years at the Licke-Observatory. All the details of the expedition were discussed. The travelers' portraits and their biographies were at the headlines of newspapers. Then, news about one of them backing out of the expedition at the last moment, two weeks before the designated "launch", generated much confusion and anxiety. The very same people who were throwing thunder on the expedition as being a ridiculously adventurous and reckless plan, calling its participants fools who should be sent to a mental institution, were now outraged with this quitter's "apostasies and cowardice". They wouldn't abide with the man who openly said that he expected to have an equally peaceful grave on Earth like those brave ones, but much later than they would.

However, the appearance of a new daredevil coming forward to take the vacated spot caused the utmost curiosity. It was commonly believed that the expedition participants wouldn't accept him on their team. There wasn't enough time for him to participate in the necessary training taken by the others who in doing so had achieved unheard-of results. Stories were told about their learning how to bear forty degrees below zero and forty degrees above zero temperatures in light clothes. They were supposedly able to survive for days without water and breathe air much thinner than Earth's atmosphere in the high mountains without ill effect. That's why there was a great disaffection that those generally called "lunatics" accepted him. Meanwhile, the newspaper reporters were in despair as they couldn't learn anything about this mysterious adventurer. He didn't let any reporter get close despite their insistence. Bah! He didn't even send his photograph to any of the dailies or answer their letters. Other participants of the expeditions also kept silent about him. Only two days before the expected launch of the expedition, some quite fantastic news surfaced. After much effort, one of the reporters managed to see the new participant of the expedition and immediately spread the rumor that it was a woman disguised as a man. However, the rumor wasn't taken too seriously, and there was not enough time to pay much attention to it. The decisive moment was approaching. The feverish expectation grew into madness. The Congo river estuary, where the expedition was to "start on their journey", swarmed with people arriving from all parts of the world.

Jules Verne's fantastic idea was finally to become a reality – a hundred years after its author's death.[1]

On the shore of Africa, twenty kilometers away from the Congo river estuary, one could see a huge hole in the ground, much like a well, with a lining of poured steel. In several hours, it would be ready to launch the first "missile" to the Moon with the five daredevils locked inside it. For one more time a separate committee hastily checked all those convoluted calculations; for one more time the inventory and

---

[1]On the Silver Globe was written in 1903 and Verne died in 1905.

tools were checked: everything was fine, everything was ready.

On the next day just before sunrise, the horrendous bang of an explosion was heard for hundreds of kilometers away and served to tell the world that the journey had started.

According to extremely complex and accurate calculations, the missile was to circle a giant parabola from west to east. It would use the explosive force calculated by orthogonal projection to escape Earth's formidable attraction and momentum forces, acquired by Earth's rotation around its axis. It would later enter the influence of the Moon's gravitational forces, and at the designated point, and at the designated time, fall almost vertically on the center of the Moon's surface facing Earth near Sinus Medii. The missile course observed by hundreds of telescopes at different locations on Earth turned out to be quite correct. Those watching it had an impression that the missile was moving backward in the sky from east to west, first slower than the Sun, and then faster and faster while moving away from Earth. That movement supposedly was the result of Earth's rotation and the missile lagging.

It was being watched for a long time until it got closer to the Moon after which even the strongest telescopes were no longer capable of seeing it anymore. All the while, communication with the daredevils locked inside the missile and Earth didn't stop, even for a moment, for quite some time. Besides other equipment, the travelers carried a superb device for wireless telegraphy with them that according to calculations should have functioned even at a distance of three hundred eighty-four thousand kilometers between the Moon and Earth. However, those calculations failed. The last telegram received by astronomic stations came from the distance of two hundred sixty thousand kilometers.

Whether due to insufficient power to create the broadcast waves or the defective construction of the device, telegraphing over a greater distance wasn't possible. However, the last message was encouraging: "Everything OK, no need to worry".

Following the earlier agreement, the second expedition was sent six weeks later. This time only two people occupied the missile as they were carrying a much bigger supply of food and necessary tools. Their telegraph equipment was much stronger than the one on the first expedition. There was no doubt that it would be enough to send messages from the Moon. Unfortunately, no telegram ever came from there. The travelers sent their last message within proximity of their destination, but well before their intended fall to the lunar surface. The message wasn't optimistic. For some unknown reason, the missile deviated slightly from its course. Now, it was expected that instead of falling perpendicularly on the surface of the Moon, it would fall diagonally, at a sharp angle. As the missile wasn't built for this kind of a fall, the travelers were afraid that the crash would kill them. They were probably right, as that was the last telegram ever received.

Because of that situation, subsequent planned expeditions were never carried out. There was no doubt about the fate of those unfortunate souls, why add more useless sacrifices? The feelings of regret and shame spread among people. The greatest supporters of "the interplanetary communication" became silent. The expeditions were eventually referred to as madness and to some, it was simply a crime. A few years later all was forgotten, for a long time.

Once again, the whole episode was remembered thanks to the article by a previously unknown assistant from a minor astronomical laboratory. From that moment on, every week brought something new. The assistant was slowly sharing his secret, and though there was no shortage of skeptics it started to gain more serious consideration. The sensational news spread all over the civilized world. Finally, the assistant explained how he had acquired that precious manuscript, and how he had deciphered it. He even let some professionals look at the charred remains and their miraculous photocopies.

So, this is what happened to the spheroid with the conical appendage and the manuscript:

"One afternoon" – said the assistant – "when I was busy recording my daily meteorological observations, a servant working for the observatory informed me that a young man wanted to see me. He was a good friend of mine who owned a nearby village. Although he lived close by, I rarely saw him as he infrequently came into town. So, I asked him to wait while I hurried up with finishing my work. Moments later I joined him in the room where he was waiting for me with visible impatience. After our greetings, he informed me that he was a deliverer of some information that would make me very happy. Knowing about my keen involvement in studies on meteorites, he came to tell me that a few days earlier, a meteor of considerable size had fallen close to his village. The rock couldn't be found because it had probably penetrated quite deep into the swamp, but if I wanted to get it, he would give me a few workers to dig it out from there. Sure, I wanted to have that rock, so I took a few days off from the observatory and went to the impact location alone. However, in spite of hard work and digging in what was thought to be the right spot, we still couldn't find the rock. Instead, we found a big piece of machined iron shaped like a cannon ball. It was a surprising discovery for that location. When I started hav-

ing doubts about the benefit of further searching and was about to cancel the effort, my friend called my attention to that spherical object. It
surely looked strange. Its surface was covered with slag found on iron
meteoritcs created when entering Earth as friction while penetrating
the atmospheric makes them simmer. Could that sphere possibly be
the fallen meteorite?

Suddenly, I had a Eureka moment. I remembered the expedition of fifty years earlier, the history of which I knew so well. I should
add here, that I never shared in the belief of the unfortunate loss of
those travelers, even in spite of the hopeless telegram they had sent to
Earth. Since it was too early to be guessing now, I took the object and
carefully carried it home. Its small weight led me to guess that it was
hollow inside. Thus, I was almost positive that it might contain some
clues about the lost ones.

After getting home, I started working on it with the utmost secrecy. I didn't doubt that if I found any papers inside, they would have
to be charred because of the iron annealing in Earth's atmosphere. That
is why the sphere had to be carefully opened in a manncr that wouldn't
destroy any potential contents if I had any hope for a chance of them
being deciphered.

I worked extremely hard because I didn't want to ask anybody
for help. It was too early to publicize my uncertain or fantastic theories.

On the top of the sphere, I noticed a big sort of plug that could
possibly be unscrewed. I placed the sphere in a big vice to protect
its content from shaking and got to work. The plug was indeed like
a screw, but it was rusty and didn't want to budge. After several attempts, I managed to make it move. I remember the first rasping noise
of the screw as if finally started to turn. It gave me shivers of joy and
anxiety at the same time. I had to stop turning it as my hands were
shaking. I resumed my work after an hour with my heart still pounding in my chest.

The screw was moving slowly when I heard a strange whistle. At first, I couldn't tell what caused it. Almost without thinking,
I moved the screw in the opposite direction and the whistle stopped
instantly. It returned a little weaker when I turned it a little more. I
understood it then! The inside of the sphere was a complete vacuum!
Loosening of the screw created a fissure in the seal and allowed air to
get to the inside, causing the whistling.

That discovery confirmed my belief that absence of air inside
the sphere might have saved the papers it supposedly contained from
total destruction when the sphere annealed while plummeting through
Earth's atmosphere! A few minutes later my guess proved to be cor-

7

rect. After removing the screw, I saw that the sphere was lined with a layer of burnt clay, and yes, yes there was a scroll of charred but not totally burnt papers. I removed them with the utmost care and ... was overcome with a despair. The letters on the charred paper were hardly visible, and the paper so fragile that it was almost falling apart.

It wouldn't stop me from attempting to decipher the content of the manuscript. I spent a few days thinking about how to get started. In the end, I decided to use X rays. I assumed, and was later proved to be right, that the ink used could contain mineral ingredients. Maybe the areas blackened with ink would provide a stronger resistance to the X rays than the charred paper. So, I was carefully gluing each page of the manuscript on a thin film stretched in a frame to take their pictures. This is how I created film plates, which after transferring the images on paper resulted in creating something like palimpsests. In this case, letters written on both sides of the paper appeared as being joined. That made them difficult to read, but it was still possible.

After a few weeks of working on deciphering the manuscript, I had gotten far enough not to keep it a secret any longer. So, I wrote the first article informing about the accident. Today, I have the whole manuscript in front of me. It has been deciphered, organized and copied. I had no doubts that it was written on the Moon and sent by one of the original five travelers aboard the first launch."

As for the rest – the manuscript itself will tell "all ".

Before publishing of the manuscript text, the assistant added an explanation about the history of the expedition.

He reminded us that an Irish astronomer, O'Tamor, was the author of the idea of an expedition to the Moon. Peter Varadol, a young Portuguese engineer, famous in Brazil, became its first ardent supporter who believed in bringing the whole thing to life. They recruited a third companion, a Pole - Jan Korecki. He sponsored them with significant amounts of money to help them bring their clearly written plan to fruition.

They began presenting their plans to academics and scientists and invited other expert authorities to work out the details. The ideas evoked quite unexpected recognition and excitement. Very soon not only was this nascent group of individuals involved, but the whole civilized world joined in. Everybody wanted to send their representatives to the Moon to learn more about it. In response to requests of academies and astronomy institutes, governments of many countries hurriedly ventured forth with financial help. That, together with the substantial resources provided by private donations, would suffice to finance not one expedition but many more. So that was the plan, but as you already know, only two of them were finalized.

The first missile was to have a crew of five people including the three authors of that project. An Englishman, Thomas Woodbell – a physician, was to be its fourth member, and Braun, the German who backed out at the last moment, was to be the fifth one. He was replaced by that unknown volunteer.

The second missile carried two French brothers Remonger.

After presenting that short historical background, the assistant moved on to a detailed description of the technical aspect of that enterprise. He provided a detailed explanation of the process of constructing of a gigantic canon fashioned out of a well in the ground and lined with steel. He talked about the structure of the canon's projectile, a sort of missile, which after reaching the airless surface of the Moon would be converted into a hermetically sealed steel vehicle, powered by a separate electric engine.

He described the security devices that were to protect the travelers from getting crushed at the moment of launching and the rapid descent to the surface upon reaching the Moon. He also listed all parts of the furnishing and equipment of the "mobile room".

The Moon isn't a hospitable environment. Astronomers have known about it for a long time, although they knew it only from far away, and unfortunately from one-sided. A significant improvement in optical devices in the twentieth century still didn't help with diminishing the distance to the Moon to an extent that would allow anyone to examine all the details of its surface. A lens with a thousand times enlargement power reduces the distance of its orbit around Earth from a distance of three hundred eighty-four thousand kilometers to three hundred eighty-four kilometers, but it is still too far. Stronger lens wouldn't help either in its studying. The high obscurity of Earth's atmosphere would make the image so blurry, that you couldn't recognize the mountains seen through weaker lens.

What's more, only one hemisphere of the Moon sphere is visible during its twenty-seven-day, forty-three minute and eleven seconds long orbit around Earth. During all this time, the Moon rotates around its axis only once, so it is always facing Earth with the same side of its surface. It is not an accidental phenomenon. The Moon isn't a perfect sphere, but it looks more like a slightly elongated egg. Earth's gravity makes this egg face it with its sharp tip and orbit it as if attached without a possibility to rotate on its axis.

What the astronomers had known about the lunar surface so far completely took away any possibility of hope for those dreaming about inhabiting other than Earth like worlds. This surface of our satellite, two times bigger than Europe, is seen in telescopes as waterless desert upland covered with a countless number of ring-like mountains. Those mountains resemble enormous craters often spanning several hundred kilometers in diameter with edges rising to a thousand meters above surrounding them plains. On the northern side of its hemisphere that faces Earth, you can see rows of circular planes called seas by early selenographers. The plains with steep edges created by enormous mountain ridges are carved by a multitude of crevices running in different directions. Astronomers have always wondered about the origin of these crevices since there is nothing like that on Earth.

We should remember that its surface has no atmosphere, and that "the lunar day", lasting fourteen days, is its summer with enormous heat. If we realize that its fourteen-day night is its winter, with temperatures lower than those found at our poles, we wouldn't readily consider it for a "permanent stay location". That's why those brave people deserved to be admired for the great sacrifice they were ready to make. Risking their lives, they went to that globe with the sole goal of increasing humanity's knowledge with true information about the heavenly body closest to Earth.

The travelers expected to pass through this inhospitable hemisphere as soon as possible and reach the other side not seen from Earth, as they expected to find bearable living conditions there. Although most of the scientists writing about the Moon claimed that the atmosphere there was also too thin to be breathable, it didn't discourage O'Tamor. Based on many years of studies and calculations, he claimed that he would find there not only the air thick enough to sustain life, but water and plants fit as nutrition as well. Those brave people were ready to die to uncover that secret for mankind. The telegraph device they carried with them boosted their courage. They believed their sacrifice wouldn't be in vain for sure if they could use that thing to share their observations with Earths inhabitants. Perhaps – they sometimes dreamed, drunk with the greatness of their enterprise, just perhaps - on that mysterious side of the Moon, they would find a magical and strange paradise. Perhaps, it would be different from the Earthly one, but hospitable? Then, they were dreaming about calling other volunteers eager to travel through hundreds of thousands of kilometers to the Moon. They thought about starting a new society there, a new humankind …. perhaps happier…perhaps…

At the same time, they had to consider the necessity of passing through a hilly, airless, and waterless desert elevation covering the Moon's whole hemisphere that faced Earth. It was quite a challenge. The Moon has a circumference of almost eleven thousand kilometers.

The plan was to fall in the middle of its surface visible from Earth. It would mean covering at least three thousand kilometers before reaching the area where they hoped to be able to breathe and live.

The missile, a cylinder like shape finished with a cone at one of its ends, was constructed in a way that enabled its conversion into a closed automobile. It was also provided with a supply of condensed air, water, food, and fuel for five people sufficient to last them for a year. It was considered more than that needed to reach the other side of the Moon.

Apart from the above, the travelers took a significant number of all kinds of tools with them, a small collection of books and… a female dog, a beautiful hound with two pups. She belonged to Thomas Woodbell, and before the trip, they all agreed to name her Selena.

The purpose of all those details referred to in the observatory assistant's memorial was to clarify the manuscript that was to be published soon after.

The manuscript itself was written on the Moon in Polish by Jan Korecki, a participant of the first expedition, and had three parts. They were written at different times but formed an organic whole. It was a history of the strange fate and experiences of a cast away on a land suspended in the blue sky three hundred eighty-four million meters above Earth.

Here is the exact reprint of the first issue of that manuscript prepared by the assistant from the observatory in K…

The Northern Hemisphere of the Moon (from the first edition)

II. THE MANUSCRIPT, PART ONE: TRAVEL DIARY

On the Moon, date ...

Oh, God! What date shall I put here? That dreadful explosion used to throw us out from Earth, tore apart the thing believed to be the most permanent of all existing things. It burst and destroyed time. It is awful to even think that where we are right now, neither years, months nor days exist - not even our lovely Earth days... My watch says that more than forty hours have passed since we fell here; we fell at night, before the sunrise. We expect to see the sun in twenty something hours. It will rise and walk lazily through the sky nine times slower than on Earth. It will shine over our heads for three hundred fifty-four hours, and then the night will come. That too will also last three hundred fifty-four hours. It will be followed by yet another day, the same as the previous one, then night again, and day – and so without end, without change, without seasons, with no years or months....

If we survive...

We are sitting idly, locked in our missile waiting for the sun. Oh! This terrible yearning for the sun!

The night here isn't very dark, it's much brighter than full moon nights on Earth. The huge half circle of Earth is hanging still on the black sky above us and floods the scary emptiness around us with a white light... That white light makes everything around us look mysterious and lifeless. And the frost... Oh! How awful is the frost! We miss the sun! Sun please!

Since the fall, O'Tamor hasn't regained consciousness. Woodbell, although also injured, isn't leaving him alone for a moment. He thinks it is a concussion and cannot promise anything. He says he could save him on Earth, but not here in this loathsome frost where our only nutrition is artificial protein and sugar, where we must economize on the supplies of air and water.

It would be awful to lose O'Tamor, especially him, as he is the soul of our expedition!...

Varadol, Marta and I, and even Selena with both cubs are healthy. Martha seems not to understand or feel anything. Worried by Woodbell's injuries, she watches his every movement. Lucky Thomas! She loves him so much!

Oh! That frost! It feels like the missile changes into an ice block with us locked inside. The pen is slipping out from my frozen fingers. Oh, when, oh when will the sun finally rise?

The same night 27 hours later

Tamor's condition is getting worse. He's in agony, no doubt about it. While watching over him, Thomas forgot about his own injuries and he got so weak that he had to lie down. Martha took his place at the sick bed. How does this woman find all that strength? Since she recovered from the first daze after our fall, she is the most active among us all. I don't think she has slept at all.

Oh! The frost! Varadol is sitting dejected and silent with Selena rolled into a ball on his lap. He says they both feel warmer this way. We put the cubs on the bed next to Thomas.

I was trying to fall asleep, but I cannot. The frost and that ghostly light of Earth above us won't let me fall asleep. Only a bit more than half of its surface is still visible which means the sun would rise soon. We don't know how to calculate the exact time yet because we don't know on which point of the surface of the Moon we are. O'Tamor would have easily calculated it from the location of the stars, but he is unconscious. Varadol will have to take his place in this kind of work, and I don't understand why he is not doing it yet.

According to earlier calculations, we should have fallen on Sinus Medii, but only God knows where we really are. The sun should be already shining on Sinus Medii. We must have fallen further towards the part of the Moon called "the East", but not too far from the Moon's center as the sun will soon be setting here with Earth being in its zenith.

I am bombarded with so many new, strange impressions that I can neither gather them nor organize them. Most surprising is the feeling that I have lost the feeling of lightness… We knew on Earth that the Moon, forty-nine times smaller and eighty-one times lighter, would pull us six times less even if we were closer to its center. However, it is one thing to know about something, but another to feel it. We have been on the Moon for seventy hours, and we still cannot get used to it. We haven't learned to adjust the effort of our muscles to the reduced weight of things, or even our bodies. I get up quickly from my seat and jump almost a meter up, although I only wanted to stand up. A few hours ago, Varadol wanted to bend a thick wire hook fastened to the wall of our house. He grabbed it with his palm, and he lifted himself up. He forgot that instead of over seventy kilograms, he now weighs less than thirteen! Every now and then, one of us throws something when trying to move it. Putting a nail in the wall becomes totally impossible because a hammer weighing two pounds on Earth weighs a little more than one hundred seventy grams! I cannot feel the weight of the pen I am writing with.

A moment ago, Martha said she felt like a ghost devoid of a weighted body. It is a very good description as there is really something eerie in this feeling of strange lightness... You could believe you are a ghost especially with Earth shining in the sky like a moon but fourteen times bigger and lighter than the one we know. I know that it is all true, but I seem to be dreaming or watching a strange show in a theater. I cannot stop thinking that in a moment, the curtain will go down, and the decorations will disappear like a dream.

Before beginning our expedition, we knew that Earth would shine above us like a huge, motionless lamp suspended from the sky. I keep repeating it to myself, that it is such a simple thing. Since the Moon travels around Earth facing it always with its one side, so if you look at Earth from the Moon, it must look still. Yes, it is a normal thing, but I am haunted by this shiny glass apparition of Earth that has been stubbornly staring at us for seventy hours from the same zenith!

I see it through a glass window in the wall of the missile turned up, and even with the naked eye, I can tell the difference between the darker seas and lighter land surfaces. They are slowly moving in front of me, one by one emerging from the shade: Asia, Europe, America. They become narrower at the end of the shiny globe and disappear to return after twenty-four hours.

Earth seems to have changed into an open, merciless and cautious eye that is stubbornly staring at us, surprised at our running away from it with our bodies, the first of its children to do so.

Soon after our fall, when we regained consciousness and unscrewed the iron covers of the windows of our house, we saw it already straight above us. We almost saw it in full. Then, it resembled an eye wide open as if in shock; now an eyelid of shade is slowly sliding over this awful still pupil. So, when the Sun, not preceded by the dawn, explodes from behind the rocks like a fairy ball with no rays, that eye will be half squinted, and it will close completely when the Sun stands above us perpendicularly.

Three hours later.

I stopped the writing that kept me occupied during those hours of waiting and went to O'Tamor. We would have never thought that we could be left without him. We were ready for death but ours not his, but there is no chance to save him... Thomas is lying down in fever and needs care, so Marta is taking care of both while Peter and I are standing there helpless.

O'Tamor hasn't regained consciousness and won't ever. He lived on Earth for over sixty years just to...No, no! I cannot even say this word! It is awful, that he! At the very beginning!...

We are here so terribly alone in this long, bone freezing night.

A few hours earlier, Martha, as if overcome by that feeling of vast emptiness and loneliness, threw herself at us with hands in a prayer, shouting:

"Let's go back to Earth! Let's go back!," and started to cry. Then she shouted again:

"Why aren't you sending a telegram to Earth?! Why aren't you letting them know?! Look, Thomas is sick!

Poor girl! – What could we tell her?

She knows as well as we do that our telegraph device stopped working at over twenty million meters before the Moon...So finally Peter had to remind her of that. Then, as sending a message could somehow save us, she started insisting on firing the canon which we brought with us to use in case of a telegraph malfunction.

That shot was now the only means of communication we had with those left there. Varadol and I gave in and mustered our courage to step out of the missile.

I must admit that I was scared to death to take such a step. Outside of those walls protecting us, there was almost total vacuum...The barometer showed the existence of atmosphere with a density smaller than three hundredths of Earth. The fact that there was the presence of any atmosphere at all, even so diluted, is optimistic. We can hope for finding a less diluted and more livable one on the other side of the Moon.

Oh! How much fluttering of our hearts accompanied sticking out the barometer for the first time after our fall a few tens of hours ago! First, the mercury level dropped so suddenly that all we saw was zero. Terrible cold fear clutched our throats. It meant an absolute vacuum, and death, no doubt! But soon after finding the bottom, the mercury began climbing to 2.3 mm. We sighed with relief, although you couldn't breathe with this kind of air!

Now, we had to step outside to set up the cannon in this vacuum. We put our "pressure" suits on and after setting the containers with condensed air above our necks, we stood in an alcove built into the wall of the missile. Marta closed the door from the inside not to let the precious air escape. Then we opened the outside cover...

We stepped onto the lunar surface and were suddenly surrounded by an awful solitude. Looking out through the glass of my face mask, I saw Peter's lips moving. I guessed that he was saying something, but I didn't hear a word. The air there was too thin to carry a human voice.

I picked up a piece of rock and dropped it. It fell very slowly, much slower than on Earth, and without an impact. I stumbled as if drunk; I thought I was already in the world of ghosts. We had to communicate with gestures. Shining, Earth that once fed us was helping us communicate.

We took out the cannon and a can with powder which were stored in a wall compartment accessible from an outside opening. It wasn't difficult as the cannon weighed one sixth of its Earth weight!

Now, we needed to ram it exactly vertically placing a piece of paper in the hollowed ball. Due to the lightness of materials on the Moon, the strength of the explosion was quite enough to carry it in a straight line to Earth. But that was something we couldn't do the horrible, merciless frost grabbed our chests with its iron claws. We forgot that the sun hadn't shone here for over three hundred hours, and the thin atmosphere couldn't maintain the warmth of rocks burning hot during the day.

So, we returned inside, and the missile felt like delightful, warm paradise even with our economizing on the fuel! It was impossible to try another walk out before the sunrise that would warm this world up.. And the sun is staying hidden forever! When will it appear, and what will it bring us?

70 hours and 46 minutes after our landing on the Moon.
O'Tamor has died.

First lunar day, 3 hours after the sunrise.
There are only four of us now. We will be getting on our way in a moment. Everything is ready. After fastening the wheels to our missile and adjusting its motor, it was converted into a vehicle which will carry us through the desert and to the area where life is possible… O'Tamor will stay here….

We escaped from Earth, but Death, that powerful queen of earth tribes traveled through space with us. It reminds us so soon that it is always with us, so merciless and so victorious. We felt its presence, its closeness and omnipotence so realistically as never on Earth. We are looking involuntarily at each other: who will be next?…

It was still night, when Selena jumped out from the corner where she had been sleeping for a few hours. Pointing her snout at the crescent of Earth shining through the window, she started howling terribly. We all jumped as if we were being launched upward by some inner force.

"Death is coming!," screamed Martha.

Woodbell, feeling better and standing at O'Tamor's bed, turned slowly towards us, and said:

"It has already come".

We carried the body outside. It wasn't possible to dig a grave in that rocky ground. The Moon doesn't want to welcome our dead, how will it treat us, the living?

We put the body on its back on that hard-lunar rock. Then we started collecting stones, scarcely scattered on the plain to make a grave. We surrounded the body with a low wall but couldn't find a bigger piece to cover it. Then Peter, using the line connecting us and enabling our communication, said:

"Let's leave him just as he is … Don't you see that he is looking at Earth?"

I looked at the body. He was on his back and he truly seemed to be looking, with his glassy wide-open eyes, into eye of Earth. It seemed to be incessantly squinting against the light of the still invisible Sun that was to rise soon…

Ok, let's do it…

For a cross, we used two iron bars from the damaged scaffolding that saved us from a crash while landing. We fastened it above O'Tamor's head in the stone wall of his makeshift crypt.

Then, just as we had finished that sad task and were about to return to the missile, something really strange happened. The mountain peaks looming in the ghostly light of Earth, suddenly became blood red for a moment. Then, they flamed with a white glow within the foreground of an evenly black sky. Because of the contrast of the lighting, the mountain peaks became darker and were now almost invisible. Only their tops, whitened from the heat, seemed to be hanging above us and getting bigger and bigger. Due to the lack of the atmospheric perspective, which allows making estimates of distances on Earth, their black peaks seemed to be hanging among the stars in the sky yet somehow separated from their rocky foundation which appeared to be lost in the greyness. We were afraid to stretch out our hands in fear of touching that intense light.

The illusion of peaks still growing in front of our eyes, created an impression that they were approaching us with slow but steady movement. They filled our eyes and seemed to be just a step ahead…. We backed off instinctively, forgetting in the moment that those peaks were hundreds or thousands of meters away.

Suddenly, Peter looked back and screamed. I turned my head too, and my body became petrified as I looked upon an eerie vision in the east.

The pale, silver pole of the zodiac light was sparkling above the black jagged teeth of a mountain ridge. Forgetting the deceased, we were gazing at it. Then a little above the horizons edge, at the bottom of that pole, we saw tiny, jumping red flames forming a crown.

It was the sunrise, at last! The eagerly awaited, life-giving sun O'Tamor would never see!

We cried like children.

At this moment, this sun is shining over the horizon, bright and white. Those previously observed red flames must have been pro-tuberances, huge eruptions of glowing gases. They shot out from the solar sphere in all directions. On Earth such flames are shaded by the atmosphere and can only be seen during a complete solar eclipse. Here without the air, they announced the appearance of the sun. They will be announcing it daily for a long time, casting for a moment a bloody glare at the mountains before they become aglow in the fullness of the daylight.

Gradually, after over an hour, the agile crown of flames was replaced with the white slice of Sun's disc appearing over the horizon. The rest of the Sun needed another whole hour to fully emerge from behind those rocks in the east.

All the while, despite the freezing cold, we were preparing for our travel. Every moment counted. We couldn't delay it. Now, every-thing is ready.

The sunrise warmed us up. The sun's rays, even at the least angle, heat with their full strength. They don't get weakened by the atmosphere absorbing them like it happens on Earth. Strange view…

The sun burns like a bright, ray less sphere, resting on the mountains like on a huge, black pillow. There are only two colors here: black and white, and their contrast is extremely tiresome for our eyes. The sky is black and even if it is daytime, it is still filled with count-less multitudes of stars. The landscape around us is empty, wild, ter-rifying, without mitigation, without half shadows. One half is shiny and white from the sunshine, the other half is completely black in the shade. There is no atmosphere here, which on Earth serves to color the sky with that wonderful blue tint. There, as it becomes saturated with light, the atmosphere melts in the stars before the sunrise. It creates dawns and dusks, paints pink dawns, saddens with clouds, crosses it with a rainbow and creates delicate transitions from light to darkness.

No! Our eyes are definitely not made for this light and this landscape. We are on a vast plain of solid rock. Here and there, it is scratched with small crevices or blown into oval humps with low, elongated mounds stretching in the north-west direction. In the west (the east and west of our world according to the true state of things, so contrary to what we see on Earth maps of the Moon), we can see small, but extremely steep hills. The ragged saw like edge of a peak towers over them on their north-west side. In the north, the ground raises to a seemingly considerable elevation. In the east, there are plenty of crevices, humps, gaps and small dales resembling artificially dug out holes. An impenetrable visage for eyes stretches towards the south.

Based on hasty measurements of the position of Earth in the sky, Varadol states that we are really on Sinus Medii, where we were supposed to fall according to calculations. I don't think so, because what we see here doesn't correspond to the known maps of peaks surrounding that plain. The height and placement of these peaks is different than that of Mosting, Sommering, Schroter, Bode and Pallas, but it doesn't matter! We set out towards the west to move along the equator as according to maps the ground seems to be the flattest. We want to circumvent the lunar sphere and reach its other side.

In a moment – there will be nothing left behind us beside the grave and the cross. They will for eternity mark the spot where the first people landed on the Moon.

Farewell then to our companion's grave, to our first construction in this new world! Goodbye friend, our dear and mean father who led us out of Earth, and then abandoned us at the start of the new life! That cross stuck in your grave is like a banner or proof that victorious Death, arriving here with us, has claimed possession of this new country…We are running away from it, but you will stay here more at peace than we are. With the cross that you believed in at your head, you will be gazing forever at the still Earth which gave life to you.

First lunar day, 197 hours after the sunrise. Mare Imbrium, 110 west longitude, 17021' north lunar latitude.

I can finally collect my thoughts! What a terrible and mercilessly long day! What a terrible fire breathing sun, scorching us from that bottomless black sky! Twenty hours have passed since noon, and it is still standing almost perpendicularly above our heads. It is surrounded by a cloud of dim stars, next to the black circle of the new Earth hemmed with a fiery ring of atmosphere saturated with light. So strange is this sky above us! Everything around us has changed, and only the constellations of stars are the same ones we saw from Earth. Without the diffusing effect of Earth's atmosphere, however, many more of them are visible to the naked eye, and the entire sky seems to be sown with them like sand. Double stars glisten like colored dots, green, red or blue, not merging with white as on Earth. Here, the sky, devoid of a colorless background of air, is not a smooth hollow dome. I feel its immeasurable depth. No calculations are needed to know which star is further away and which is closer. Looking at the Big Dipper, I sense a huge and deeper spatial disparity between some of its stars compared to those appearing closer, while on Earth it looked like seven studs, driven into a smooth ceiling. The Milky Way is not a streak here, but a lumpy snake slithering its way through the black abyss. I feel like I am looking at the sky through a wonderful stereoscope.

Even stranger is the fact, that the sun among the stars, so fiery and scary, is not eclipsing any of them.

The heat is insufferable; the rocks, it seems, will soon begin to melt like ice on our rivers on a beautiful March day. Recently we missed so much sun and warmth, and now we had to run away from it to save our lives. We have been standing for a dozen or so hours at the bottom of a deep crack, stretching from the feet of jagged Eratosthenes crags along the Apennine and in the Sea of Rains. Only here, a thousand meters below the surface, we found shade and some cool.

Hiding here, we slept, overwhelmed by weariness, for over a dozen hours without a break. I dreamed that I was still on Earth, in some green and cool groves, where a clear, trickling stream murmured among the fresh turf. White clouds were walking in the blue sky, I heard birds singing and the buzzing of insects, and the voice of people returning from the fields.

Selena's barking woke me up. She wanted food.

I opened my eyes but still dreamy, I couldn't understand yet where I was and what was happening. I couldn't understand the meaning of this closed vehicle and what those rocks around me so wild and empty meant. Finally, I understood everything, and unspeakable grief grasped my heart. Meanwhile, Selena, seeing that I was awake, came to me, put her snout on my knee and started looking at me with her intelligent eyes. I saw in her look mute reproach … I patted her head in silence, and she started to whine pitifully, looking back at her cubs playing freely in the corner. Those pups, Zagraj and Leda, are the only cheerful creatures here. Not true! Sometimes Martha is also as cheerful as a young animal, but only when her still ailing Woodbell extends his hand to touch her long, lush, dark brown hair. Then a smile lights up her swarthy face, and her big eyes flame up with endless love when gazing at her lover's manly and beautiful face. She does everything to cheer him up. With her every movement, every look, she tries to tell him that she loves him and that she is happy even here where it is difficult to be happy. I can't refrain from painful jealousy when I see her moving her full, cherry like passionate lips over his gaunt face, arm, and neck, as she kisses the eyelids of his cold steel eyes. I can not divert my gaze when, taking his head in her hands, she hugs it like a baby to her breasts with their flawless lines and sings those strange, incomprehensible songs to him. He probably heard them at the Malabar coast, and now when he hears them again, he must be dreaming about those swaying palm trees and the sounds of the blue sea lap. This woman smuggled for him, in her soul, the world that is lost to us forever. I will never forget the day when we saw her for the first time. It was just after we found out that Braun was backing out. The four of us were sitting in a hotel room in Marseille, windows looking out on the bay, and we were talking about our companion's defection that moved us so much. Then we were notified that a woman wanted to immediately see us. We were not sure if we wanted to let her in, when she let herself in. She was dressed like the daughters of rich men in the South of India. Her face was exceptionally beautiful and had a half frightened half firm expression. We all stood up surprised. Thomas paled and was looking at her closely. She stopped at the door with her head down.

"Martha! You are here!"- Woodbell finally exclaimed.
She stepped forward and lifted her head. Her face had no trace of earlier uncertainty but was beaming with passionate love. Her eyelids dropped heavily on her flaming, black pupils, her lips slightly parted, and her chin pushed forward. She stretched her arms towards Thomas and looking into his eyes, she answered:

"I followed you and will even follow you to the Moon!"
Woodbell was as pale as a corpse. He grabbed his head with his hands and moaned,

"It is impossible!"

Then she looked at us, and judging by our ages, she figured out that O'Tamor was our leader, so she fell to his feet so suddenly that he couldn't back out.

"Sir! – She shouted grabbing at his clothes, - "sir, take me with you! I am your companion's lover! I abandoned everything for him. Don't let him abandon me now! When I found out that you are short one person, I came here from India! Take me with you! I will be your servant! I am rich, very rich, so I will give you as much gold and pearls as you want. My father was a raj in Travancore on the Malabar Coast and left me a great treasure. I am strong, look!".

Saying that she extended her swarthy, naked, and round arms. Varadol snorted:

"This is not a voyage from Travancore to Marseille on a steamer! One must be prepared!"

Then, she started telling us, that keeping it a secret from Thomas, she was doing the same exercises as we were doing, hoping that she would succeed in persuading us to take her with us. She was taking advantage of the present opportunity to put her earlier plan into being. She knew that you may find death there on the Moon, but she didn't want to live without Thomas! And she pleaded again.

Then, O'Tamor, silent before, turned to Thomas asking if he wanted to take her with him. When Woodbell unable to utter a word nodded, he placed his hand on the girl's luxuriant hair and slowly and seriously said:

"You will come with us daughter. Perhaps God has selected you to be the Eve of a new generation, hopefully a happier than the one on Earth.!" That scene is still vivid in my memory....

But Martha is calling me. Thomas is feverish again. We need to give him quinine.

Two hours later.

The heat doesn't cease and somehow even intensifies. We've gone deeper into the crevice to avoid it. Until it passes, you can't even think about going on. Fear overwhelms me when I remember that we have to do nearly three thousand kilometers before we reach our destination ... Who will guarantee that we can live there? Only O'Tamor didn't doubt it, but he isn't with us anymore...

The gauge on our vehicle shows that we have already covered one hundred sixty-seven kilometers. If one considered the time it's taken us one hour to travel one kilometer, we were moving relatively fast. We left four hours after the sunrise heading straight towards the west. If we are on Sinus Medii, we wanted to reach the plain among the Sommering and Schroter mountains. From there, while circling Sommering from the south and west. Assuming that we would get closer to the equator and move straight toward the Gambart Mountain ring, and the higher one, further west towards Landsberg seated on the equator.

The ground was extremely even, almost without cracks, so the vehicle was moving quickly. Hope was with us and excitement entered our hearts; we felt warm and light, and only the memory of O'Tamor shadowed our merriment. Thomas was feeling better, and Martha seeing that was beaming with joy.

We began to make delightful plans again. The road seemed short to us without great hardships. We were enjoying the incredible wild beauty of the dead landscape or trying to guess ahead, with the map spread out before our eyes, what fantastic views awaited us. Varadol began to remember all O'Tamor's research and contentions, according to which, the other side of the Moon was not only to have appropriate living conditions but would be extremely interesting and beautiful.

"Indeed" – we were saying to ourselves, if there are the same mountains that we see now on the horizon, and there is also greenery and water, then it is worthwhile to travel three hundred eighty-four thousand kilometers to see such land!".

We were talking with excitement. Thomas and Martha were snuggling and dreaming up optimistic plans for their life on this land. Even Selena, hearing animated voices, started to bark joyfully and jump all over with her playful puppies.

Three hours passed like that, and we covered about thirty kilometers, when suddenly Varadol, whose turn was to stand at the motor helm, stopped the vehicle.

Ahead of us, we saw a low, rounded rocky embankment, stretching from south to northwest. The embankment could be easily traveled, but now we had to decide on the exact direction in which we should move. In the north-west there were some jagged, sky-high crags that formed the tops of Sommering Crater. According to astronomers, that crater rises only to one thousand four hundred meters above the nearby plain. While these crags seemed to be much higher, we attributed it to an easy-to-explain optical illusion. Still, such an assumption was valid as our missile fell in the southwest part of Sinus Medii onto a plain open to the Flammarion half circle, so now there is a crater called Mosting, which is 2.8 kilometers deep, on our right. In any case, we needed to circle this mountain if we didn't want to change our earlier plan. Woodbell recommended repeating the astronomic measurements to mark the spot where we were right then, but not to waste time, we postponed this task to a time when we would have to stop because of too much heat.

Then we directed our vehicle straight north. The road became more and more tedious. The ground was rising slowly up. Here and there we encountered fissures that we had to avoid, or entire fields of solid rock, like gneiss, covered with loose boulder debris. We were moving slower and slower and with great difficulty. In several places we had to put on our pressure suits to leave the vehicle and clear a path by rolling the blocking boulders away. Then we were blessing the small gravitational force of the Moon that allowed us to move or remove those huge boulders with ease. That work was amusing at first. Each of us, moving those huge boulders, must have looked like a giant. Even Martha was helping. Only Thomas stayed in the vehicle at the helm as he was too weak. The wounds stopped hurting, but the fever kept returning every now and then.

We were moving like that for over a dozen kilometers from the point where we turned south. On our right, there were numerous, small, but unusually steep hills with huge crags behind them. In front of us, the ground was constantly rising and forming a huge ridge with one peak sticking out from it. On the right towards the west, we saw a range of higher and higher mountains. Twenty-four hours had passed since the sunrise when we reached a smooth plane of solid rock where moving fast was easy. We decided to stop there to rest. At the same time, we were getting more worried by a strange layout of the land-scape.

We were all almost certain, that we were in a different part of the Moon, and not Sinus Medii. We had to take exact measurements to establish the lunar longitude and latitude of our whereabouts.

After a quick meal, we got to work. Peter set the astronomic instruments. The center of the Earth's spherical surface was inclined from the zenith by six degrees to the east and two degrees to the north; we were at six degrees west longitude and two degree south lunar lat-itude, that is, at the edge of Sinus Medii, next to the Mosting Crater. There could be no doubt about that, the measurements were accurate.

So, we decided to continue our way without a change in direc-tion.

We were about to start, when Varadol shouted:

"Our cannon! We left our cannon!"

Indeed, only now we remembered that the cannon with the bul-let, our only and last way of communicating with Earth inhabitants was still at O'Tamor's grave. When leaving that place, we were still in a such daze because of his death and funeral that we forgot to take that precious cannon with us. It was an irreparable loss, even more severe given the loss of telegraphic connection, as now it was the only thread connecting us to Earth. We suddenly felt so terribly alone, as if we add-ed hundreds of kilometers more to the distance from the globe, which is already hundreds of thousands of kilometers away from us.

Our first thought was to return and pick up the abandoned cannon. Woodbell insisted on doing just that, stating that we had to tell Earth to stop further expeditions until we let them know if we found some living conditions here.

"If we are to perish here," he said – "why should others perish too… You know that the Remonger brothers are ready to leave. They are waiting for a telegram from us, but our device isn't working. We need to have them postpone their departure even for some time."

However, returning there wasn't easy. Above all, in view of the tremendous journey we had before us, every hour was precious to us. Further, in the event of more and repeated delays, our food and air supply may become totally depleted, and then we would be doomed to inevitable death. Meanwhile, we still had to take a long break because of O'Tamor's illness, and we knew that either heat or frost would stop our march for many hours. Secondly, which of us could be sure that we would find the spot where we had left the cannon.

Varadol was trying to remove Thomas's scruples.

"After all,", he said, "they wouldn't leave without a message from us. Moreover, it is hard to tell if the bullet we shot to Earth would fall in a location where someone would find it. So, it is possible that our message won't get into the right hands."

We remembered that the cannon was designed exclusively for a vertical shot. It meant; we could only use it close to the center of the lunar spherical surface where Earth is in its zenith over us. The strength of the bullet wouldn't be sufficient for a parabolic shot. Even if it were enough, we had no way to set the cannon exactly enough to be sure that the bullet traveling on the curve, wouldn't bypass Earth altogether. On the other hand, if that shot stopped other expeditions, and if we found livable conditions, we wouldn't be able to call for new travelers to join us. This would sentence us to eternal loneliness. At the same time, if it happened that Remonger brothers would arrive anyway, they would bring stronger telegraph equipment, and thus we could get more companions and a way for continuous communication with Earth.

All these reasons supported not wasting time searching for a cannon, which was of little use to us. After a short delay, we started our journey.

Twenty-four hours passed again, and we already covered about one hundred and thirty kilometers. The sun was already twenty-eight degrees above the horizon, and the heat was rising steadily. We noticed an interesting phenomenon. While the wall of our vehicle illuminated by the sun was so hot that it could burn, the side turned away from the sun was as cold as ice. We also experienced the feeling of frost every time we entered the shadow of a rock promontory, which we passed more and more on the way. These sudden switches from heat and cold here are caused by the absence of atmosphere which reduces the strength of sun rays on Earth. At the same time, the atmosphere distributes the heat evenly and thus prevents the fast loss of heat through radiation.

For the same reason, every shadow here is like the night. The light not scattered in the thin atmosphere only reaches those places exposed directly to sunlight. If it weren't for the reflection of the mountains, lit up in the sun and the light from Earth, we would have to light electric lanterns every time we entered the shade.

We have already gone through this sloping, smooth surface and began to turn west to circle the supposed Mosting crater. The road was getting harder and harder and only with a great difficulty, we were able to move forward very slowly.

We were in a mountainous and very inhospitable area. The landscape here didn't resemble that of the Alps on Earth. There, among the mountain ridges connecting the peaks, there are valleys carved by water for thousands of years, but there is no trace of it here. The whole ground is folded and raised, covered with lots of unconnected deep valleys, round, with protruding edges, or smooth, completely loose kicks, sometimes reaching considerable heights. Valleys are replaced with deep crevices stretching for miles and resembling mountains split by a huge axe. I don't doubt even for a moment that these are the cracks of the Moon's congealing and shrinking crust. However, we have never found a trace of water, so powerful on Earth. I think that this land never had water.

That's why, we were surprised by the plenitude of loose rocks scattered on the rocky ground. A few dozen hours later, when the heat intensity reached its impossible limits, we understood what crushed these rocks as powerfully as water. We were just passing by a high rock, stone somewhat similar to our marble, when in front of our eyes, a boulder about a dozen meters in diameter detached from its top and collapsed into the abyss, breaking into thick scree. It all happened in a sudden and terrifying quietness. Due to the lack of air, we didn't hear a bang, only the ground under our vehicle quivered. The Moon swayed in its bearings.

The Sun's furious tooth bit off a piece of this rocky world. The rocks, squeezed at night by frost like an iron rim, expand during the searing heat on the side facing the scorching rays. Since it is still cool in the shade, the expansion of solid blocks must cause their cracking and crumbling.

Meanwhile, this sharp scree, covering huge spaces, took its toll on us. We were going through places where the vehicles wheels couldn't turn at all. There, we put "paws" on the vehicle and functioning just like animal paws, we bounced on, breaking through boulders or climbing the steep slopes.

Even with all the testing we performed converting the missile into a vehicle on Earth, we never imagined how hard such traveling would be, especially if it lasted longer. I believe now, that if the Moon's gravitational force were stronger, resulting in a huge increase in weight, we might have died, stuck among those rocks with no possibility to budge.

The third earthly day has already passed since the sunrise, and we have moved only twenty-two kilometers forward. The heat was getting unbearable again. In the stuffy and hot air of the vehicle, still shaken by its movements, Woodbell's fever returned. The injuries suffered at the fall started hurting him again. I still shiver at the memory of that terrible impact!

First, stillness in the skies; a muted explosion of mines attached to the bottom of the missile for the purpose of reducing the velocity of the fall; and then protective scaffolding pushed out with one pressing of a button and… No, it isn't possible to describe it! At the last moment, I saw Marta, suspended in her hammock press her lips to Thomas's lips.

O'Tamor shouted," Here we are!," and I passed out.

When I opened my eyes, I saw O'Tamor and Woodbell covered with blood, Varadol and Martha unconscious…Later, we used parts of the crashed scaffolding for a cross on O'Tamor's grave.

Our chronometers showed ninety hours past the sunrise when, totally exhausted, we noticed that we were approaching the top of the elevation that we had scaled with so much effort. During the last four days, equal to about the fourth of a lunar "day", we slept very little, and so, we decided to stop for some rest. Woodbell especially needed sleep and quiet.

We stopped the vehicle near a rock which protected us from getting baked by the unbearable sunlight and lied down to sleep. I awoke well rested after two hours. The others were still sleeping and since I didn't want to wake them up, I put on the pressure suit and stepped out of the vehicle to check out the surroundings. In an instant, I felt like I was inside smelting ironworks. It wasn't just hot. The heat was pouring from the sky, and the ground was burning my feet even through the thick heels of the pressure suit. I had to stop myself from going back to the vehicle.

We were in a shallow depression in the rock separating two heaped hills or mounds of solid boulder and a mountain pass ending among them. As far as I could see from where I was standing, the sunken formation staggered into a plane beyond those mounds westward.

The mounds also blocked my view from the north and south. Only towards the east I could see the road we had just crossed. I looked at the rocky fields, full of valleys, breaches, crevices and peaks - and I could not believe my eyes nor the fact that we managed to get through that terrain with our large and heavy vehicle. Such feat wouldn't be attainable on Earth with the weight six times greater.

At this moment, I felt somebody's touch. Varadol was standing behind me and was gesturing something desperately. He was also wearing a pressure suit, but he didn't bring his speaking pipe with him, so we couldn't talk. I saw that he was very pale and somehow abashed. I thought Thomas felt worse and ran back towards the vehicle, and he followed me there.

As soon as we got inside and took the pressure suits off, Varadol leaning over towards me, said:

"Don't wake the others and listen. Something terrible happened. I made a mistake."

"What?", I shouted, not understanding what he was talking about.

"We didn't fall on Sinus Medii."

"So, where are we?"

"Under Eratosthenes, on a pass connecting this crater with the lunar Apennine."

It got dark before my eyes. I remember from the photographs of the Moon surface taken from Earth that the mountain range we were on at that moment suddenly breaks off almost perpendicularly towards an immense plain, the Mare Imbrium.

"How will we get down!," I cried in terror.

"Be quiet. God only knows. My fault. We fell on Sinus Aestum. Look…", he showed me some pages with rows of numbers.

"Are you sure?," I said.

"Unfortunately, I am right this time! And my other measurements were exact as well. I only forgot at the time that; Earth could be in zenith over the center of the Moon's surface. You must know that the Moon during its rotation around its axis has some fluctuations called librations. Because of that, Earth doesn't seem to be immobile, but encircles a small ellipse. So, I forgot to make a correction for its deviation from the zenith and that's why according to its location, I falsely marked the lunar longitude and latitude of the spot where we were. Now, we may pay with our lives for this mistake!"

"Calm down!," I said, although I was shivering all over. "Perhaps, we will manage to save ourselves."

Then we began to re-check the calculations. This time there was no doubt. After making the necessary correction, we saw that we had fallen on Sinus Aestum at lunar coordinates seven degrees, thirty-five minutes west longitude, thirteen degrees, eight minutes north latitude. All that time, we were traveling along the steep hills at the foot of Eratosthenes heading towards a nameless crater stuck in the main part of the Apennine range. Our present location was eleven degrees west longitude, fifteen degrees, fifty-one minutes lunar north latitude marked this location on the map of the Moon. According to the map, the pass in front of us rises nine hundred sixty-two meters above the level of Mare Imbrium.

It is amazing that Earth astronomers can easily calculate the height of any lunar mountain using a telescope, from a distance of hundreds of thousands of kilometers, by measuring the length of the shadow that it casts. Whereas we, being on this mountain, had to rely on the help of a map drawn up on Earth to know what its elevation was. There being no atmosphere also had to be considered because lack of it prevented barometric altitude measurements. The change, we noticed in the barometer indicated the mercury in the tube had fallen so that it was almost level with the surface of the liquid in the vessel. At the height where we were, there was an almost absolute vacuum.

Soon Thomas and Martha woke up, and we couldn't hide the truth from them anymore, so I told them as gently as I could. Their reaction was quite subdued as well. Thomas only frowned and bit his lips, but based on Martha's behavior, I could see that she didn't understand the seriousness of our situation.

"So, what?," she said. "If we managed to ride up, we will ride down as well, or we will go back."

Oh, God! We will go down in the same way as we got up here! After all, finding the road that brought us here was a coincidence! And go back? After all this hardship and so much wasted time?...

Finally, we decided to get to the pass to see if we could lower ourselves down to the Mare Imbrium plain. After several minutes, we found ourselves above the abyss opening in front of us.

The rock ended at our feet almost perpendicularly, and down there, a thousand meters below, the impassive plain of Mare Imbrium stretched out beyond, with its peaks scattered everywhere. Lack of air perspective meant that the mountains, even very distant, were clearly visible to our eyes. Reflection of their incredible glistening whiteness from the completely black background of the starry sky created a truly magical sight. For a moment, we even forgot about our terrifying situation.

On the horizon towards north, four hundred kilometers away and seven thousand feet high, was the majestic Timocharis crater, sticking out from that endless plain like an island in a sea.

On Earth, mountains visible from far away appear bluish because of the opacity of the air. Here in the sun, that peak looked like white sweltering steel with thick, black shadow bands and shimmering red veins of darker rocks. Slightly toward the west, we could see the lower and more distant Lambert crater. From the very west, the horizon was limited by numerous small elevations and rocks, connecting to the core of the Carpatus mountains, a much closer lunar range bordering Mare Imbrium from the south.

Behind that range stretching in our view, far away, we could see the incredibly high Copernicus crags, almost the highest of mountains on the Moon which were resting on lower hills. If I used the word sweltering steel for Timocharis, then I don't have a word to describe the light radiating from that range of ninety kilometers diameter!

The peaks of the Archimedes circle were towering behind numerous elevations in an endless distance from the north east. The view east and west were blocked from one side by the sky-reaching range of the lunar the Apennine and from the other by the precipitous Eratosthenes connected to Apennine by the pass we were standing on. The Sea of Rains was among them. That name, invented by Earth astronomers, seemed to be a cruel irony! They gave that name to a cruel desert, dry, cold gray, plowed here and there with monstrous crevices, hollowed out in light, oblong humps, extending from the great Timocharis on the horizon towards Eratosthenes. There was no trace of life or a bit of greenery! Only in the sun, at the feet of huge, distant craters, great, similar to strands of expensive stones, like yellow, red, and steel blue veins of some deposit layers were glistening...

We looked ahead in silence, not knowing which path to take. Having reached the plane of the Sea of Rains, we would have a space in front of us where we could move briskly, but the problem was how to get there, how to come down a perpendicular wall a thousand meters high?

After a short conference, we set out on foot towards the south hoping that we would manage to find a way down the slope of the Eratosthenes crater. We were walking on a narrow path, pressed between a rock and the abyss opening towards Mare Imbrium. In one place, the passage was so narrow that we wanted to turn back, doubting that we would manage to get here with our vehicle. Fortunately, Marta, who went with us, reminded us that we had a supply of mines that could easily be used to light up the small rock barrier blocking our way. We

31

pressed forward then, squeezing over the dizzying abyss, and went on. Now the mountain ridge, significantly widened and flat, rose slowly upwards. We were still walking south, in between the monstrous rings of the Eratosthenes piled up to the left and to the right of us.

Half an hour after circling the rocky barrier, we had to stop suddenly before a new chasm that opened under our feet. Peter who was walking in the front, covered his eyes and was the first to climb up on the barrier. He then jumped back with a cry of fear. Indeed, it is difficult to imagine something more terrible than the view that was unfolding before us.

Still walking south, we unknowingly got into a deep gap carved in Eratosthenes ridge. To the right and to the left we saw jagged crags, one of which glistening white in the sunny glow, the other almost black in the shade. And before us ... no! Who can describe - the abyss ahead of us! That bottomless and unspeakable abyss, so monstrous, and so predatory in its incredible majesty of terror, enormity and deadness that now the thrill of paralyzing fear grabs me when I remember it!

The inside of the Eratosthenes crater was in front of us.

A huge mountain ridge, bristling with peeks like a saw blade, formed a closed circle of tens of kilometers creating a vast valley of the worst terrain one could imagine. The crags, rising over four thousand meters above the bottom of that abyss, were falling towards it almost vertically. The valley, about two thousand meters below the Mare Imbrium plain, seemed to be even deeper because of the huge mountains surrounding it and the eerie thick shadows it was filled with. A few separated, cone like peaks that were about half the height of the surrounding walls were sticking out from its bottom. From time to time, a few of them exploded into small clouds of dark gray smoke, which was falling and spreading flat at their feet in an ash heap because of the lack of atmosphere. There was no doubt that we still had some active volcanoes in front of us.

The vivid contrast of light and shadows increased the feeling of dread. Its east edge was sinking in a thick blackness while its west edge was sparking in the sun with its white wall etched with a multitude of dark spires visible against the background of black shade. From the south, the embankment seemed even lower because of the distance and the spiked gate of this terrible abyss. We were looking at a dizzying gulf at our feet.

And over all this, a fiery, ray less sun was walking across the black sky sown with non-shimmering stars. It was closer and closer to the sharp sickle like crest of Earth suspended over this valley with its dead glow like an omen of death.

Involuntarily, I remembered Dante's words:

> Vero i che in su la proda mi trovai
> Della valle d abisso dolorosa…[2]

Recollection of those words brought a vision of a Dante's hell to my tired, hot and frightened brain. At that moment, I thought that hell couldn't be more frightening than the one I was looking at now. The smoke of the volcanoes looked like rows of damned spirits twirling around the horrible shape of Lucifer taken upon by one of the volcano cones. There are numerous spirits meandering everywhere in a long procession of damned souls, omnipresent along the rocky slopes of the abyss. They are flowing in a huge wave, sliding deeper into the gully, overturning, rolling over, and crowding. Some want to rise, into the world, into the sun so they break away from the bottom with whole clouds and fall again like lead into the place of eternal torture…

And all this was going on in that awful silence. My head started spinning, and I felt like I was about to faint.

Then I heard someone crying. I was so stunned that first, I thought that I heard the voices of those condemned creatures…But it wasn't just a vision… I could really hear a cry though the pipe connecting the heads of our pressure suits.

I gathered my senses and looked around. Woodbell was pale with his back against a rock and looking down, while Varadol was pacing around like a wild animal on a chain because of the pipes connecting us. He was looking around as if trying to find a way out. Martha with her head on her knees was kneeling on the ground and shaking, sobbing upset and scared.

Overwhelmed with extreme pity, I approached her and placed my hand slowly on her shoulder. Then with some childlike complaint, as in that memorable long night before O'Tamor's death, she began to cry.

"I want to go back to Earth! To Earth!"

The despair in her voice was so deep, so penetrating, that I couldn't find words to cheer her up. How could I when our situation seemed so hopeless. I turned to Varadol:

"What will we do now?" Peter shrugged his shoulders.

"I don't know … death. It isn't possible to get down from here.

"How about going back," I interrupted,

"Oh, yes! Go back! Go back," sobbed Martha.

---

[2]It was true that I found myself up
the painful abyss of a valley …

Varadol seemed not to hear her cry. He looked ahead for a moment, and then answered me:

"Go back… waste a lot of so precious time only to encounter an obstacle like this one.

Look!" He turned his face north and gestured towards the vast plain of Mare Imbrium in front of us.

If only we could get there, we would have an almost even road ahead, but we won't get there…unless perhaps by falling on our heads…"

I looked in the indicated direction. The Sea of Rains, lit by sun, seemed extremely beautiful compared to the terrible interior of Eratosthenes. It was almost at our feet, just a jump to find ourselves there at that plain. In truth, one thousand meters of a vertical rock separated us from it and made it totally impossible!

We stood close together and looked with an unspeakable desire at the space that could save us. We didn't feel weariness or even the burning sun although half of it had already looked out from behind the rock edge above us.

Peter repeated it again:

"We won't get there…"

Martha, unable to control herself any longer started crying again.

Varadol snorted impatiently:

"Silence!," he shouted grabbing her shoulder, "or I will knock you down from here! We have enough trouble!"

Then Thomas suddenly stepped forward:

"Stop it" …and you don't cry? We will get to Mare Imbrium. Let's go back for the vehicle."

There was so much firmness and confidence in these calmly, though clearly said words, that we turned on the spot to carry out the order, not daring to oppose nor ask.

Woodbell stopped us.

"Look," he said pointing at the outer slopes of Eratosthenes descending towards the Sea of Rains, "Can you see that ridge, fifty meters below this cliff? If I am right, it slopes quite gently towards the plain, we will use it to get down…"

"But this wall…," I whispered, looking at the vertical torn off rock separating us from the wide ridge that we didn't see before.

"A trifle! We are good at rock climbing! We will easily go around it. And the vehicle? …We will push it forward tied on ropes. Don't forget, that we are on the Moon. Things are six times lighter, and the fall from the height of fifty meters means the same as eight meters on Earth!"

We followed Thomas's recommendation. One hundred and nine hours after the sunrise, we started descending Eratosthenes's steep slope to get to Marc Imbrium. Descending into the valley beneath our feet took us three Earth days. We walked most of that distance in the merciless sun, staggering from tiredness and effort.

We ended up lowering the vehicle on ropes into the abyss several tens meters down. It didn't damage it, but the dogs locked inside got badly bruised in spite of all our precautions. We stopped a few times thinking we wouldn't make it down alive. The ridge wasn't as even as it looked from above. Strewn with shelves and chasms, it forced us to turn and make laps. It was even more difficult because we had to drag the vehicle everywhere with us or to lower it on the ropes. We were often overwhelmed with despair. It was Woodbell, although weakened with fever, who showed the most consciousness and will power. We really owe him our lives.

I don't know if we slept more than twelve hours during those three days. We had to search for shaded places as much as possible to protect ourselves from baking alive in the rays of the sun. At times, the heat almost made us unconscious.

It was just at lunar noon, with the sun vertically above our heads, when totally exhausted we finally reached the plain.

The heat was so hideous that it took our breath away, and blood covered our eyes and pounded at our temples. Even the shadows gave no protection! Glowing rocks breathed fire everywhere like a pit of a metallurgical furnace.

Selena panted quickly with her tongue hanging out. The pups were wining pitifully spread motionless in the back of the vehicle. Every now and then someone fainted; it seemed that death was waiting for us at the entrance to the desired plain!

We had to run away from the sun - but where?

Then Martha remembered that while walking down, we saw a deep crevice hidden from us by the unevenness of the ground. We set off in the indicated direction, and indeed after a quick drive, which seemed like a year, we came across the crevice. It was a vertical wall fissure, formed by a crack in the Moon's crust, about a thousand meters deep, and a few hundred meters wide, not unlike Earth's gorges and ravines.

It was stretching for tens of kilometers parallel to the Apennine range. It wasn't marked on maps of the Moon. Astronomers must have missed it because of its closeness to the mountains and being hidden in their shade.

That crevice saved us. When we found its beginning, we descended into its depth, about a thousand meters below Mare Imbrium, and found some cool there…

The sleep refreshed us beautifully. Only Thomas, whose will power kept him going, now got more feverish again. He is so weak that he cannot move, However, we will be leaving in about twenty hours. The sun begins to tilt westwards from the zenith. There, the heat on the plain must still be terrible, but in any case, not like it was a few dozen hours ago. Anyway, after this rest, it will be easier to bear it.

After some consideration, we changed our travel plan. Instead of west, we will go straight towards north, toward the lunar pole. It will be a double advantage. First, we have about one thousand meters of even road across the plain of Mare Imbrium, which should speed up our traveling. Second, going towards the Pole, we will reach the area where the sun isn't so high over the horizon during the day, and it doesn't go so low under the horizon at night. That meant more bearable temperatures. If we experienced one more noon like the last one, we would die.

On Mare Imbrium 340 hours after the sunrise.

It is almost the end of the day. Soon, in about fourteen and a half hours, the sun will set. It's hanging over the hills in the west, just a few degrees over the horizon. All terrain unevenness, every rock, all small elevations cast long motionless shadows that cut this huge plain in one direction. Everywhere you look, there is only this deadly desert without an end. Far on the horizon, you can still see the higher spears of the mountains that we saw from Eratosthenes.

As we are going away from the equator, the glass Earth above us leans from the zenith towards the south. It now completes its first quarter and shines brightly - like seven full moons. There, where the fading glow of the sun does not reach, its ghostly glow is silvery. We have two blue lights, one of which is stronger by yellow contrast and the other by blue. The whole world is half bright yellow and half gray. When I look east, the desert turns yellow and the distant peaks of the lunar Apennine turn yellow; from the west, under the diamond sun, everything is cold, blue, and dark. Then, over the two-colored desert, it is still a sky of black velvet, full of colorful, precious stones, infused with a fabulous cloud of fine golden sand…

The night is approaching. It has sent forward the only herald it keeps in this world devoid of dusk and evening dawn… Night is preceded by the chill walking in front of it through the desert. It crouches in every crack, in every shade, waiting patiently for the slow Sun to crawl from the sky and skid from the desert. Then the night and the chill will despotically reign over it all…

We all feel much better because the inside of our vehicle isn't so stuffy and hot anymore. Varadol is full of hope and spinning new plans or playing with the puppies and their mother. Woodbell, much healthier and standing at the helm, is talking to Martha. When I raised my eyes from the paper, I see them both. I see Martha clearly. She is standing sideways to me and laughing now. She laughs strange. Her mouth takes on such a shape, as if it were full of air. When she is smiling her smile fills her eyes, and her breasts rise in small, quick movements. During the heat, her bosom was exposed. It was too hot even for her with her Indian suntan. Now she is covered up to her neck. I don't know why my eyes keep searching for those delicious, dark, and so warm in color breasts. I miss something when I don't see her. I shouldn't be thinking so often about this woman, but she is everywhere. Since Death stepped away from our vehicle, its small space is filled with Martha. Even Varadol, playing with the dogs, looks at her surreptitiously. It upsets me. Why isn't Thomas paying attention to it. But why should I care?

We have been on the road for sixty hours. The vehicle is constantly moving forward. We take turns sleeping, so now I am writing on the go. We stopped briefly to charge the batteries of our engine. To save on the fuel we will need during the night's frost, we set the machine in motion with the help of expanding condensed air. We must conserve the batteries charge, because with fast driving, batteries alone will not be enough.

We are moving as fast as possible on this kind of surface. Significant land unevenness didn't allow us to turn north for some time after leaving the Crevice of Salvation (This is what we called the hole whose coolness saved us from death). At twelve degrees west longitude we came across one of those streaks of light that circle the Copernicus crater. Visible even through weaker earth telescopes, these streaks have always surprised astronomers. Here, seeing them from a close distance, we now know that they are several kilometers wide bands of mountain that had been volcanically melted into a glass like glaze. I cannot explain the origin of these strange creations.

By and large, there are many puzzling objects around us. What was the origin of the plain we are traveling on? How were these huge mountainous circles of tens or hundreds of kilometers in diameter created? How did this ridge of a few thousand meters height come into being? It is certain that they are not extinct craters of volcanoes like the astronomers once thought. We peeked into the interior of Eratosthenes and we saw the volcano cones, very similar to those on Earth, but its round ring had never been a crater! Its dreadful dimensions and the kind of rock it was built from speak against such a theory. The depth and concavity of its bottom below the surrounding plains and other details also add to such contradiction.

It seems to me that to try to understand these wondrous formations, one should go back to ancient times when the Moon was still a liquid, burning ball, only just then congealing its surface in those cold interstellar spaces. Then those monstrous and impossible to imagine gas explosions, swallowed by that liquid mass, were inflating the still flexible surface, and creating those huge bubbles. Those bubbles were cooling and hardening then cracking before flowing into the surrounding plain. Those mountainous rings are the remains of those times. The sun bit at those ridges and tore them apart, while volcanic forces blew up their insides into cone like craters. That's how we see them now. They aren't eroded by the forces of the water leveling everything on Earth. They remained as proof of the creative might of the universe for which the lumps of planets and fiery balls of suns were only the obedient material in the pot of eternal coming into being.

All those small and big mountains and the valleys encountered on our way tell their story very vividly. When I look at that landscape, I have a feeling that those boulders, yellow from the sun, are a part of this liquid, glowing almost live mass. I imagine, that in a moment all this plain will start heaving, bending, swelling, rising, bulging and that under the pressure of the interior gases, it will splatter lava up in the black sky and they will cool down into enormous rings of mountains.

How many centuries have passed since those times! The Moon's shell has frozen and cracked while continually shrinking. Some mysterious fire forces burned huge radiant streaks of vitrified stone into its shell, and now here, where once struggling creative forces unleashed, silence reigns and the deadness is so terrible and so final, that we are embarrassed to be alive...

Until now, we have been moving along the bright streak created by that glass vein started at Copernicus. It makes a comfortable and even route. Its north-east direction works great for us, as it will bring us straight to the plain between Archimedes and Timocharis that we must pass. We cannot see Archimedes yet from the plain we are on. The side, where we expect to see it, is blocked from our view by small, steep hills ahead of us, like a mountainous island among the sea. It is probably a group of "craters" rising from eleven degrees West longitude and nineteen degrees North lunar latitude. We hope to pass it before the sunset, and then we will continue moving further north to get as far as possible from the place that, not only does the ominous Earth crescent hang straight above our heads, but is accompanied by the murderous Sun. This is not our earthly, life-giving sun, this lazy white and radiant sphere! It is a greedy and mocking god, a destroyer and devourer, and the four of us are the only living sacrifices it sees on this plane of death! We have to get away from it before it reaches the black, gold embroidered shroud of the firmament for the second time.

I stop writing. Varadol, who took the helm over from Thomas, is calling from the motor that it is my turn now to stand at the helm. The others are already sleeping, and Martha, with her head on the chest of the only happy person among us!

First lunar day, 4 hours past the sunset, on Mare Imbrium ten degrees West longitude and twenty degrees, twenty-eight minutes North lunar latitude.

Then the long lunar night had already begun, long because earth days are much shorter compared to what the Moon consumes in earthly nights. Earth, still tilting to the south, shines above us like a big bright clock. By looking at the movement of the shadow on its spherical surface, we can easily mark the time. It was after sunset in the first quarter, at midnight it will be full and again in the quarter at sunrise. Sections of the world play the part of the minute hand on this blue clock. After setting them in the shadows, we can guess the hours, which are like minutes to our seven hundred and eighty-nine-hour day.

After the sunset, it became very cold in an instant, and we had the feeling that we jumped from a steam bath into a pool of icy water. Still the sunset surprised us very nicely. Instead of the instant night that we expected, for some time, we experienced a strange glow competing with Earth's brightness and similar to our dusks.

The glass streak, that led us for over a hundred kilometers away from those small craters, has ended now. Driving north, we were approaching the twentieth parallel when the sun's circle, unblemished by the sunset, still bright and glittering as in the daytime, began to slowly sink into the horizon. We were suddenly overwhelmed by a terrible longing for this disappearing sun, which we will not see again for fourteen days. We stood next to each other at the west window of our vehicle. Martha raised her hands towards the setting star, and in her melodious voice, started to recite Indian hymns of the fakirs saying goodbye to their fair god. Woodbell was answering her with some incomprehensible sentences from the holy books. He probably remembered similar moments spent in Travancore when the sun was sinking in the shoreless ocean.

Meanwhile, the sun, wrapped within a part of its circle, seemed to be standing on the horizon and waiting. Its glow lit up the girl's stretched palms and sparked on her white teeth visible in her parting scarlet lips. I was under the impression that the two of them were talking, this girl and this sun.

In half an hour, only a piece of its circle was still visible. As the patch of white brightness faded, the stone desert blackened as if it had turned into a sea of ink. Here and there only smooth boulders gleamed, reflecting Earth's blue light. Martha finished her hymns and was standing with her head leaning on Thomas's shoulder staring at the desert.

Then strange sadness overwhelmed us all. Even Peter, the least prone to emotions, grew gloomy with his lips moving as if he were talking to his thoughts or memories. And I...Hey! How fast did my life pass on Earth.! I had a strange dance of phantoms and memories in my eyes. I was dreaming about the Vistula plains and cloudy crags of the Tatra Mountains - and all of them populated with such a countless retinue of friends, dear and farewell forever … Forever!...

Suddenly the Sun went dark. The red protuberances, like tiny flames flickered for a moment over the horizon, but those vanished as well, and the suddenly the falling twilight was so unexpected that we involuntarily pressed our bodies to each other. But it wasn't night yet, just a twilight. At that very moment, when the last piece of the sun sank, a pillar of brightness flew in the west topped with a dome, and similar to a fabulous fountain of light dust.

The Zodiac light glowed in front of us in a splendor never seen on Earth. We stared long, dumbfounded, at this glowing pole, tilting slightly from vertical towards the south, and diffused with the colorful cosmic dust of stars orbiting the sun and now reflecting its light in our face at its sunset.

Now, it all has gone away and only Earth and the stars, recessed in the black sky, shine over us. The stars look strange as they are colorful, and they don't flicker. That variety of colors not filtered by an atmosphere makes us wonder. I still cannot get used to it, although I saw them during the long lunar day.

Earth sends us so much light that we can use it to travel without a break. It is an auspicious situation for us as we don't need to waste time and can get so far north that on the next day, we won't be suffering from the sunlight directly overhead. However, thinking about the night frost scares us a lot.

On Mare Imbrium seven degrees, forty-five minutes West longitude and twenty-four degrees, one-minute North lunar latitude, first hour of the second lunar day.

The midnight has passed, and we almost don't remember what the sun looks like. We cannot understand why we complained about its heat. For the last one hundred eighty hours separating us from the sunset, we suffer such unheard-of freezing, that our very thoughts seem to freeze in our brains. Our heaters are working at maximum strength, and we, huddled next to them, are still shaking from the cold. Writing, I leaned on the stove. The skin on my back burns, and at the same time I feel my blood freeze and coagulates. The dogs force themselves on our laps and howl without a stop. We start feeling insane. We are looking at each other in silence with a strange hatred, as if someone here was the cause of the sun not shining and not heating here for three hundred fifty-four and a half hours.

I wanted to force myself to jot down a few impressions of our travel after the sunset, but I am not able to associate even the simplest images. My brain is frozen, stiff as a machine made of ice. Loose images and some desperate flashes that I cannot understand move through my mind. Sometimes I feel as if I were sleeping awake. I see Martha, Thomas, the dogs, Peter, the furnace, but I don't know what it all means. I don't know who I am, how I got here, and why…

Indeed, why?

I would like to think about that, remember that, but I cannot. There must have been a reason why I left Earth with these people…. I cannot remember. Thinking tires me.

I think we're standing. I can't hear the motor hissing. One has to go and see what happened, but I know that neither I, nor they will do it. We would have to step away from the heater.

What a hideous frost!

I see some rocks through the window that Earth illuminates brightly. These rocks must be the reason why we aren't moving… It is all very strange and all indifferent to me…

What am I writing? Am I really becoming insane? I am terribly sleepy, but I know that if I fall asleep, I will freeze and won't wake up again… I need to shake it off, I must come to consciousness…

It is strange, but we didn't have such frost during our first night on Sinus Aestum. Perhaps there are some volcanic veins underneath which warm that area.

Let's write, let's write not to fall asleep, because sleep means death.

Since the sunset, we were continuously moving westward towards the stronger and stronger light of Earth approaching its full phase and with it the increasing frost. At seven degrees West longitude and twenty-one North lunar latitude we conquered the low ridges that were blocking our way. We didn't change our direction, instead of straight North pushing North West towards the mountains stretched around the ring of Archimedes, in hope of finding an active crater and warmth. We are on the border of this mountainous land, but everything is dead and cold. We entered the middle of a strange crescent created by amphitheatrically stacked rocks. Varadol was taking astronomical measurements to mark the location of these mountains. According to his measurements, it is an elevation marked on astronomical maps with the letter E, seven degrees, forty-five minutes West longitude and twenty-four degrees, one-minute, North lunar latitude. Frost, frost, frost…, but I must force myself to stay awake. We cannot sleep! Sleep equals death! This death must be waiting somewhere near here. People on Earth should paint death as sitting on the Moon as it is its kingdom…

Why aren't we moving? Ah, right! I don't care!

Yes, we must overcome it. What was I writing about? Ah! These mountains… A strange amphitheater about four kilometers wide and open towards the south. Earth is hanging over it like a lamp. The highest peak in the north, straight ahead. It is probably about one thousand two hundred meters high. Yes, it all looks grotesque like a theater for giants, for monstrous skeleton giants. I wouldn't be surprised if I saw, in the light of Earth, crowds of giant skeletons entering slowly to occupy the seats for spectators. The huge skulls of those sitting at the top would shine white among the stars on the background of the black sky. I seem to see it all. The skeletons of the giants are sitting and talking to each other:

"What time is it? It's midnight. Earth, our huge and bright clock is in its full phase. Time to start."

And then to us:" It's time to start, die then; we are watching…"

I shiver suddenly.

Paulus Putredinis, the bottom of a crevice, seven-degree, thirty-six minutes West longitude and twenty-six degrees North lunar latitude. Second day 62 hours after midnight.

So, it happened. We are sentenced to death without hope for a rescue. We have known it for sixty hours so that's enough time to get used to this idea. But still, it is death. Stay calm. Stay calm, after all, it cannot be helped. Besides, it isn't quite unexpected. Starting that voyage, still there on Earth, we knew we were risking death. But why hasn't death hit us unexpectedly? Why has it appeared ahead of us and it is coming closer to us so slowly that we can calculate its every step, and we'll know when it starts grabbing our throats with its cold hand and suffocate us…

Yes, suffocate. We will all suffocate. The supply of condensed air will barely last us for three hundred hours even with economizing. And then…well, we should prepare ahead of time for what will happen later. For the next three hundred hours everything will be like it has been so far. We will be breathing, eating, sleeping, and moving… During that time our only remaining container with the condensed air will empty out. It will happen in three hundred hours in the afternoon… The sun would still be quite high. It will be light and warm, even hot, maybe too hot. For a while, for a few hours, everything will be all right. Then we will slowly start feeling some heaviness, buzzing in the head, stronger heartbeat… The air in our vehicle, not refreshed with oxygen that we don't have, will be saturated with exhaled carbon dioxide. Now, we are removing it artificially, but then why should we continue it when we don't have any more oxygen to replace it. Then that carbon dioxide will poison us… Blood flushing, heaviness, dyspnea, drowsiness…Yes, drowsiness, overpowering drowsiness. We will lie down in our hammocks to wait for death. As usual, Martha will lean out of her hammock and will rest her head on Thomas's chest. Then we all will start dreaming…Earth, our countries, meadows, air – plenty, plenty of air, the whole blue, beautiful and clean sea! In that dream we will feel the strangling, awful nightmares in our chests. I seem to feel it now. It is pressing on my ribs, choking my throat, and squeezing my heart. The fear sweeps over me. I would like to shake it off, get up, run away…Then the dreams will end. There on the Moon, on the infinite Mare Imbrium plain, there will be four corpses in a locked vehicle.

No! Not this way! At that moment, when we run out of the fresh air, we will open wide the door of the vehicle. In one second, we will find ourselves in a vacuum. Blood will gush out through mouths, ears, eyes, noses. A few spasmodic, desperate chest movements, a few furious heartbeats will follow, and – the end.

Why am I writing it all? Why am I writing at all? It doesn't make sense. There is no purpose for it all. I will die in three hundred hours.

An hour later.

I have returned to writing. I have to keep myself busy with something as thinking about this imminent death is dreadful. We walk around in our vehicle, we smile at each other vacuously, and talk about meaningless topics. A moment ago, Varadol was telling us about the Portuguese way of preparing a sauce from chicken livers with capers.

While listening, we were all, including him, thinking that we would die in hundred ninety hours.

As a matter of fact, death isn't so terrible at all. Why do we fear it so much? After all…Oh! How miserable is all this philosophizing about death! My pocket watch ticks louder than the voices of all those Greek philosophers recommending staying calm before dying. I hear quiet, small, metallic beats and I know that these are the steps of impending death. It will arrive before the sunset of this approaching long day. It even won't come an hour late.

Then, when we had still been among those semi circled rocks, numb from the frost, Varadol, accidentally looked at the manometer hand of one of the containers with the condensed air and uttered a terrifying scream. We all jumped as electrified, looking at what speechless Peter was pointing at.

I got hot in a moment as the manometer wasn't showing any pressure. Then, I thought that because of that dreadful frost, the air in the container got more condensed. I opened the valve – the container was empty. The same for the second, third, fourth and fifth. Only the sixth one, the last one, had air.

We all went insane. Not even thinking about the puzzling cause of the containers emptying of air, or about what we were doing, what should be done, or if anything could be done, we all jumped to the motor. We didn't feel the cold, weariness or drowsiness anymore. We were frenzied with one thought: run, run, as if escaping this death was possible.

The vehicle was ready to move in a few minutes. Having left the plain surrounded by the rocks, we were rushing at full power without stopping through the small hills spreading from Archimedes circle and covering the whole western part of the Rot Swamp bordering the Sea of Rains. The terrain was extremely uneven, so the vehicle was jumping, shaking, rising or collapsing, tossing us mercilessly, but we did not care. We pushed forward hoping in a terrible paroxysm of fear and despair that we will be able to get over to the other side of the Moon before we run out of our modest supply of air!
What a funny thought! Between us and the lunar pole, there is a distance of at least two thousand kilometers. Half of that area is mountainous and inaccessible, and our air will only last us three hundred hours.

The frost was solidifying the blood in our veins and we couldn't breathe, but we ignored it, continually bursting through the mountains silvering in Earth light. We were dashing through black valleys, through fields of scree, just farther and farther. No one thought about drowsiness anymore.

In this infernal ride as futile as it was crazy, a sudden obstacle stopped us. Riding forward blindly, we came across a crevice like our Crevice of Rescue at Eratosthenes, but this one was much wider and deeper. We spotted it almost at the last moment, a moment later we would have fallen into it with the vehicle.

Our vehicle stopped - and suddenly we were overcome with terrible apathy. The energy of despair that rushed us for so many hours, disappeared as quickly as it appeared, giving way to an unspeakable, overwhelming depression. At once everything became completely indifferent to us. Why bother and strain when it is pointless. We must die.

We sat at the heater idly and in silence. The frost nagged us more and more, but we didn't care anymore. Indeed, it doesn't matter if you die from frost or suffocation. Some time passed. We would have probably frozen to death if it weren't for Woodbell who recovered first and started to push us to seriously consider our situation.

"Let's look for a way out, a way of saving ourselves", he was saying. "Even if we don't find it, we will at least have something to occupy our thoughts with and turn them away from that death nightmare".

Sure, it was a good suggestion, but we were so exhausted and chilled that we accepted it with a total indifference without an answer. I remember that I was looking at Thomas and saw that he was saying something else, but I couldn't understand a word. The only thing that I was interested in was: How will he look after his death?

With obsessed stubbornness, I was staring at his moving jaws and was stripping them of their flesh in my thoughts, then I moved to his skull, ribs and other bones. Looking at the man, I saw his skeleton that seemed to say to me with a mean grimace: "You will all look like that soon."

Seeing that talking to us was pointless, Thomas took the helm, and we were soon moving along the edge of the crevice. After half an hour we reached its end. Varadol noticed it, and with a new energy, he rushed to the engine, screaming madly:

"We can circumnavigate this crevice and drive further north, towards the pole where we can find the air!"

He was laughing and jumping like crazy, and when he tried to grab the helm, Thomas pushed him away gently, and said curtly but firmly:

"We won't be circumnavigating it, but we will go through it."

Peter looked at him stupefied for a moment, and then suddenly in a fit, he threw himself towards Thomas and grabbed his throat.

"You murderer!," he roared. "You are a strangler! You want to kill us, waste us, but I want to live! I want to live! Can you hear me?! To the north, to the north, to the pole, there is air there!"

He was foaming with rage and yelling, and since he was stronger than Thomas, he knocked him over and pressed him down with his knees before we could stop him. Martha and I jumped to overpower the madman, and a scuffle started accompanied by barking of the frightened dogs. When we finally grabbed his shoulders, he suddenly flexed himself in our arms, shouted and sagged limply. Thomas was picking himself from the floor tired and pale when our vehicle suddenly tilted. I felt a sudden shock and fainted. When I regained consciousness, I realized that I was in my hammock, and Thomas was leaning over me and rubbing ether into my temples. Martha and Varadol were sitting beside me silent and gloomy.

Thomas is really a brave man. During his scuffle with Peter, the vehicle having no helm ran into a rock. Thrown by the shock, I hit the wall with my head and fainted. Thomas and Martha weren't hurt, and neither was Varadol though he was unconscious on the floor. When Thomas saw what happened, he and Martha put us in our hammocks, and backed off the vehicle, turned it around, and drove into the crevice. Only here, according to his assumption, it wasn't as cold as on the surface, so he could try to wake us up. Peter woke up first without any memory of his madness. I woke up soon after.

For now, there was no threat of freezing to death, as the frost in this crevice wasn't so bad. Apparently, the interior of the Moon, like the interior of Earth, is not yet completely devoid of its own heat, although being forty-nine times smaller than Earth, must submit to freezing much sooner. Thomas expected it, and that was why he drove the vehicle into the crevice to use it as protection from the direct danger of freezing our brains and to enable us to have a peaceful consultation.

We started our consultation. I had an idea that perhaps we could use a pump to condense the outside air to use it for refreshing our diminishing supply. That idea looked promising, so we all went about testing it, after an hour of hard work, we found out that it wasn't doable. The Moon's atmosphere is so thin, that when the piston in the pump is completely closed, it does not expand to the point that it can overcome the air pressure in our vehicle and open output port. Thinking the port was not functioning, we then tried to compress the air with a pump from one of the empty tanks, whose gap we had previously sealed not to let the air escape before, but it also turned out to be impossible.

Discouraged and exhausted, we gave up that pointless work. Thomas tried to comfort us that perhaps we would find a thicker atmosphere further north that would work with our pump, but I knew that he himself didn't believe it. The atmosphere on the whole of the Mare Imbrium would be equally thin, meaning almost nonexistent, so we would run out of air before we passed that space, and then the inevitable will happen. We will die in two hundred hours.

Nonetheless, we were determined to leave this crevice and head north at dawn as soon as it became a little warmer. It wouldn't solve all our problems, but neither would us staying in one place. Or maybe, just maybe, we will find a little thicker atmosphere somewhere … there.

The same location, 10 hours past midnight.

We have finally discovered the reason for the loss of our stored air. The containers were damaged while we were sliding down Eratosthenes's slope. Some sharp boulder on the road, scratched them deeply, and the internal gas pressure did the rest. The cracks are visible. Two things amaze me in all of this: one is that the pressure of the condensed air in the tanks didn't tear apart the damaged copper tanks, and the other that we didn't notice that loss earlier. I am racking my brain, trying to solve this puzzle as if it could somehow change our situation.

I cannot think about anything else as I only have the vision of death. The worst thing is that the knowing that we will die soon doesn't stop us from feeling healthy. It adds up to the terror of this terrible event awaiting us. Thomas is the calmest of all of us, but I can see in his behavior towards Martha that he cannot stop thinking about it either. He moves his hand through her hair with a gentle, almost feminine movement and looks at her as if he wants to ask forgiveness. She kisses his hand, telling him with this caress and her eyes: "Don't worry, Tom, everything is fine, after all, we will die together…"

The thought of dying together may give them some consolation, but I must admit that sharing this kind of fate with others doesn't reduce its horror. I feel so agitated that such reflections don't have any impact. I think intelligibly about everything, and I see everything clearly. I repeat to myself a hundred times that I will be dying with these people as a voluntary sacrifice of that all-powerful desire for knowledge. A desire that tore us all away from Earth and dropped us on this inhospitable globe. I tell myself that I should come to terms with fate and remain calm in this inevitable necessity, but despite all these beautiful reflections I still feel one thing: fear, boundless, desperate fear!

This is so inexorable and it is approaching so slowly...

I cannot understand, why we shouldn't think about a quick solution to this problem? Don't we have the power to shorten this life ... which isn't a life at all, but rather a mockery, a nightmare, a burden...?

An hour later.

No! I can't do it! I don't know what is stopping me, but I cannot. Perhaps it is a childish yearning for the sun, a godly day star that is to rise soon. Or perhaps, it is a funny feeling of an almost animal attachment to life, regardless how long it would be. Or is it what remained of that stupid, unfounded hope.

I know that nothing will save us, but I desperately want to live, and I am ... scared to death ... I don't care! Whatever will be, will be...!

I am so weary. May it finally come - inevitable! At each breath I take, I think I have one breath less. It does not matter! ...

At sunrise.

We are leaving in an hour. The western edge of the crevice is already shining above us in the sunlight. One more time, we will drive through the vast desert to see the sun, the stars, and the peaceful, brightly lit Earth so quiet on this black sky, one more time...And we will drive north. Why? Let it finally come - inevitable! I think I have one breath less with each breath. Does it matter? I don't know. None of us knows, but we will go. Death may accompany us through the rocky fields, through mountains and valleys, but when the manometer shows zero, it will enter our vehicle.

We aren't talking. There is nothing to talk about. We are trying to occupy ourselves with whatever, more out of embarrassment than for entertainment. How can work occupy a person who knows that everything he does is pointless?

So, let's go and meet our fate!

The second lunar day, fourteen hours past noon. On Mare Imbrium, eight degrees, fifty-four minutes West longitude and thirty-two degrees, sixteen minutes North lunar latitude, among the craters c-d...

We are saved! Our salvation came so suddenly, so surprisingly and in such an awful way, that I still cannot recover, even if twelve hours have passed since the moment when, Death, following us for two earth weeks, suddenly turned around and left.

It left, but not without a booty... Death never leaves without a booty. If for whatever reason it lets someone live with its mark, then it picks a random booty wherever it finds it, without a choice...

At sunrise we set off on the road, more out of habit rather than from a necessity. We were sure that we would not live till the evening of this long day. We were riding in silence aware of the death accompanying us and quietly waiting for the time when it could embrace us and snuff us out. We could feel its presence so realistically, as if it was a tangible and noticeable creature, and we were looking around surprised that we couldn't see it.

Now, it is all a memory, yet it was the most dreadful reality. I cannot understand how we could survive in this disabling, helpless fear with that inexorable spectrum for three hundred and several tens hours! It is not an exaggeration to say that we were dying every hour, thinking that we were inevitably going to die. Nobody expected to be saved, and especially not in the way it happened.

Now, it all seems to me like an awful dream, and I must summon all my senses to help me believe that it really happened.

I don't remember the details of the road we took. Hours dragged with our vehicle heading north quickly while we were looking at the passing landscapes like in a sleep. I feel now that all those impressions melted into one with the dominating impression of that inevitable death. I cannot untangle that chaos now. Everything I remember from that road was dreadful. At first, we were riding on the border between Palus Putredinis and Mare Imbrium, passing a mountainous and wild area on the right. To the left, towards the west, we saw a vast plain that changed into the low, rolling hills parallel to our direction of travel in the distance. Beyond these hills, we saw the shine of distant Timocharis peaks lit by direct sunlight.

I still remember my terror, strangely combined with the unimaginable richness of colors in the landscape we were passing.

The highest spires of the crater were white, but from them downwards streaks and circles played with all the colors of the rainbow. I don't know how to explain it. Was it possible that Timocharis, with a mountain ridge as big as Eratosthenes, was once an active volcano that is now a gigantic crater? Could those be the colors of calcites, trachyte, sulfur and ash settling on the craters? I cannot solve this puzzle today, but then I wasn't even thinking about it. I only had the impression of something unbelievable, something that made me think of fairy tales about magical countries and mountains built of expensive stones. Staring at those sunlit peaks, seemingly comprised of piles of topazes, rubies, amethyst and diamonds, I felt at the same time their lifelessness, and a chill overcame me. There was something mercilessly ferocious and unyielding in that sharp shimmer of colorful boulders.

Nothing dimmed or softened the intensity of that shimmer, not even the air... Splendor ...... splendor of death radiated from those mountains.

Fifteen hours past the sunrise, still looking at the peaks of Timocharis, we came into the shade of the not so tall Beer crater. Having passed it, we traveled along the foot of the shorter Feuillee crater and entered an immense plain stretching for about six hundred kilometers up to the northern end of Mare Imbrium. Facing north, we passed the peaks of Timocharis, and we soon saw on the horizon, the distant Archimedes embankment shrouded in shade.

I had a sudden feeling that we were entering a huge gate, open wide towards the plain of death. Boundless, choking fear gripped me again. Almost involuntarily, I wanted to stop the vehicle and turn it towards the rocks we passed so as not to enter this vast plain, which - I knew - we would not leave alive. It seems that it wasn't just my apprehension; the three of them were also looking darkly at the rocky desert in front of us.

Gloomy, Woodbell, with his head bowed and pressed lips, seemed to measure the infinite plain with his eyes, and then slowly moved his gaze to the manometer attached to the last container with the condensed air. I involuntarily followed his example and looked. The manometer tip in a small brass drum was constantly going down, slowly but without a stop.

Then, I had a sudden but dreadful idea There isn't enough air for four, but perhaps there would be enough for one. One person could get to the place where the Moon's atmosphere would be thick enough to be used for breathing with the help of a pump. That thought scared me before it even took shape, and I tried to chase it away, but it was stronger than my will, so it kept coming back. I couldn't take my eyes away from the manometer, and I kept hearing: not enough for four, but for one... I looked guardedly at my companions, and it was heartrending, but I read the same thought in their excited eyes. We understood each other. For a moment a depressing, agonizing silence took over.

Finally, Thomas rubbed his forehead with his hand and said:

"If we have to do it, it must be done quickly before the supply gets too low..."

We knew what he was talking about; Varadol nodded silently; a corrosive blush tightened my face, but I did not deny it.

"Shall we draw lots?," Thomas asked, visibly forcing himself to say those words. "But" ...his voice trembled then and broke down, taking on a soft, pleading tone – "but ... I would like to ... ask you to let Martha live ...too."

Dead, depressing silence fell again. Then Peter mumbled:

"There isn't enough for two..."

Thomas jerked his head back in a proud movement.

"Okay, let it happen this way! It is better."

Saying this, he took four matches, broke off the head of one of them, and hiding them in his hand so that only the ends could be seen, reached out his hand to us.

During that whole conversation, Martha was standing aside and didn't hear anything. She joined us at the moment when we were extending our fingers for those lots and asked in a quiet voice:

"What are you doing?"

And then to Thomas:

"Show me what you have in your hand..."

She took those matches from his hand that were to be a death sentence for the three of us so the fourth one could live. It all happened so quickly and unexpectedly that we couldn't stop her. We blushed ashamed. We understood that this woman caught us in the act of committing a disgusting murder of selfishness, pettiness and cowardice. We looked at each other, and we suddenly started hugging each other, breaking into a spasmatic, long muffled cry.

There was no way we could draw lots then. Because of the reaction, which is the fundamental law of the human soul, mutual envy, caused by the closeness and inevitability of death hanging above us, has now turned into a feeling of warmth and hearty exuberance. There was a strange, boundless relief. We sat close to each other. Martha still cuddled on Thomas's chest, and we started talking heartily with muted voices about lots of little things, that were once important for us on Earth. Each memory, each detail was gaining importance now. We felt that this conversation was a farewell to life. At the same time, the vehicle was racing north through the deadly plain.

Earth hours and days were passing with the manometer tip constantly falling, but we were at peace having accepted our fate. We talked, ate, and even slept, as if nothing had happened. I only felt a strange, unpleasant pressure in my throat and heart like people who suffered a great loss and cannot forget about it.

At about noon, we had come to the thirty-one - thirty-two parallel. The heat, although significant didn't bother us as much as previously, given that at this lunar latitude, the sun rises barely to sixty degrees over the horizon. Earth, suspended since noon at the same height, was still in the new phase, when the ray less Moon's surface, touching the flaming ring of its atmosphere, started going behind it slowly.

We were about to have a solar eclipse lasting about two hours and presenting itself to the inhabitants of Earth as a lunar eclipse. When the Sun touched Earth, the luminous ring of its atmosphere became like a wreath of bloody lightning surrounding a huge black spot, the only place in the sky where the stars did not shine. The Sun needed almost an hour to go behind that black circle surrounded by flames. At the same time, the wreath was becoming wider and more, and bloodier. As soon as the Sun disappeared, the light was already so strong, that contours of the landscape could be seen in an orange light. Earth's black shape looked like a gaping hole of a hideous well drilled in the starry sky. It was surrounded by a fringe of blood red flames that gradually turned into red, orange and yellow light of a widely spread circle, and finally vanishing on the black background with a weak, whitish after-glow. From behind this fiery wreath, two sheaves of rays shot out, two fountains of golden light dust. It was the zodiacal light, visible during the eclipse, just like after sunset.

At the same time, the light on the Moon changed from orange into red, and it looked like someone poured blood on the dark desert in front of us. We had to stop then as we couldn't see the road in this bloody and weak light. The shade was accompanied by an awful cold after the Sun disappeared. Wrapping ourselves, we cuddled together waiting for the Sun to reappear. A horned luminous wreath of multi-colored flames was still burning above us in a never-before-seen gorgeousness, when the dogs started howling, first softly, and then louder and more desperately. That howling made us shiver, reminding us the night before O'Tamor's death. Selena was howling like that, greeting the death entering our vehicle. Suddenly, surrounded by that magnificence in the sky, we felt again the whole boundless, terrible plight of our situation. It seemed as of those fires were started there, as a sneer over the heads of those dying, who didn't deserve the sunlight. The supply of the air in the container would only last us for twenty more hours.

After two hours, the Sun started to emerge on the west side of the black Earth circle while the light aureole became narrow and slowly faded. The sight of the Sun somehow surprised me quite unexpectedly. I had already gotten used to this bloody night, accepting it as an omen of the eternal night that would envelope us in the Sun's absence. Now, the dawn was something incomprehensible, and somehow the Sun's appearance uplifted my spirit to the level of a belief in a miracle.

"We will live!," I shouted suddenly and with so much faith, that everybody's eyes turned to me with a look of a question and hope.

Then an astounding thing happened. Some kind of a rattle came from the box in which the useless telegraph camera was stored. At first, we could not believe our ears, but the prattle could be heard more clearly. We rushed to the back: after opening it, we saw that the camera was knocking, as if it were receiving a message sent from somewhere. However, we tried in vain to understand the content of the message. Something was broken or mixed up, we could only catch a few broken words:

"The Moon….in an hour… from the center of the surface… at an angle… let … France… the others… and if… death… "

We were shocked. Varadol jumped to the device and telegraphed:

"Who is speaking?"

We waited for some time, No answer. Peter repeated his question several times but with no answer. The telegraph went silent and the rattle wasn't repeated. Half an hour passed, and we started thinking that it all was an illusion.

The sun came out from behind Earth and stood in the sky next to it. The heat was rising again.

Then something zoomed and flashed before us in the sunlight, and at the same time the ground shook like a wall hit by a cannonball. We shouted in fear and amazement. Rushing to the window, we saw a mass with a metallic shine which bouncing from the Moon surface made a huge arc in space and hit the ground again and bounced again and again rushing in dreadful jumps towards north west.

We were silent in awe as we couldn't understand what was happening when Peter suddenly shouted:

"Remonger brothers are arriving!"

Now everything became clear. Six earth weeks have passed since our fall at midnight on the lunar surface. It was the date when the second expedition was to follow ours. Our telegraph device was knocking because of the message sent by Remonger brothers from the Moon's vicinity. Though weaker, it could have knocked before, but since the equipment was locked in that box, we didn't hear it. Occupied with their preparation for the fall, Remonger brothers didn't see our telegram.

All these thoughts flashed through my mind when we started the engine moving our car in a hurry. A few moments later, we were already rushing in the direction where their space vehicle disappeared from our eyes. We were all possessed by one thought, more powerful at the moment than everything else: "Remonger brothers have brought air with them!"

In half an hour we reached the spot where their missile had fallen after several bounces. It was a dreadful sight. We saw two bloodied and smashed corpses among the remains of the crashed vehicle. We quickly put on our pressure suits and filling them with the rest of our air supply, we left our vehicle. We were moved by a possible damage to their air supply more than the death of our friends.

Two cracked and empty containers were lying on the ground among broken metal plates, but other four were intact. We were saved! For a moment we were engulfed by a mad joy, so out of place with what was around us, but we had been dying for three hundred fifty hours to find out now that we would live!

Having ascertained that fact, we could think about what happened to Remonger brothers. It seems like the same circumstances that saved us must have caused their death. A coincidence causing some miscalculations made them fall in front of us instead of at the very center of the lunar circle a thousand kilometers away from here. The same coincidence provided us with the supply of air but killed them. Because falling here, they didn't fall perpendicularly on the lunar surface but at an angle. That's why the missile hit the hard surface with its side that wasn't protected by a protective scaffolding, and those bounces must have smashed it. We trembled at the thought that it could've happened to us as well...

After carefully burying the corpses among the rocks, we went about checking out our inheritance. We picked everything that could become useful for us starting from those preciouses for us air containers. We moved them to our vehicle first, and then we carried in the food, water supply and some less damaged tools. Trembling, we searched for their telegraph device hoping to be able to communicate with Earth inhabitants. Alas, it broke in the crash, and so did most of the astronomic instruments. We took their motor although it was seriously damaged. How lucky we are, that at least those copper containers with air survived that dreadful catastrophe!

After collecting Remonger brothers' property, we immediately set off north, for the heat, interrupted by the cold during the solar eclipse, was rising rapidly again, and we needed to find an elevation that could lend us some shade. So, we stopped here among small craters.

These cones, sharp, almost touching each other at the bases, are undoubtedly of volcanic descent. The whole area, covered with sulfur, turns yellow in the dazzling sunlight. Deep gullies covering the crater slopes from the top to the bottom, give us a perfect refuge from the burning heat.

We are saved, but it is no relief from the gloom that we feel at the memory of those mutilated corpses of Remonger brothers. We were not the cause of their death, but I feel a kind of a remorse. After all we were saved by their death…

I am tired after all these experiences and all this writing. I need to lie down and rest before the further travel, as it isn't the end of all the hardships and dangers ahead of us.

I have just looked at Selena playing with her pups which have grown so much in those few weeks…Isn't it strange, that when we were threatened with a death by suffocation, we never thought about killing the dogs? …All that time we were ready to sacrifice the lives of the three of us to save the fourth, but we never thought that since they were using some of this air, killing them could prolong our time. Wouldn't it be awful, if sacrificing one of us, we would have let them live by forgetfulness?

After all the danger has passed for now, and it is better that the dogs are alive. Their animal ease reminds us of Earth better than any of us could do. I am looking at these animals with tenderness… We are so lonely and so torn away from Earth. It sent two people after us, but we only saw their corpses. We were hoping that with Remonger brothers' arrival, we would gain more companions together with the way for communication with Earth. Meanwhile, they saved our lives, but instead we are sentenced to an eternal loneliness.

On Mare Imbrium, nine degrees west longitude, thirty-seven degrees north lunar latitude, second day, one hundred fifty-two hours since noon.

For almost one hundred hours that is close to four earth days, we have been crawling through this endless plain. As far as the eye can see, there is nothing: no elevation, no summit that could attract your eyesight. The terrible sameness of the landscape overwhelms us and is boring. I was once traveling through the Sahara, but indeed now that desert seems to me to be a beautiful, diversified land compared to this emptiness that surrounds us here. In the Sahara, you still find some chains of rocks and some wavy sand hill with the green tops of palm trees growing in delightful oases beyond them. Above the Sahara, there is the blue sky, which silvers at dawn, brightens up at noon, blushes at daybreak, or fills with stars at night. Winds stroll on that dessert and by disturbing that sandy sea give a proof of life, and all that is absent here. We see only stone covered ground, ploughed in deep furrows, weathered on the surface from the heat of the sun, same, terrible, like the sky above us, almost unchanged in over three hundred forty hours! Wind, azure, greenery, water, life; all that seems to us to be a nice, beautiful, but improbable fairy tale that we had heard of or experienced long ago in our youth. According to Earth clock, we have been on the Moon for less than two months, but it seems to us like the whole century has passed since we left Earth. We are slowly getting used to the new living conditions. We are no longer surprised with our surroundings. We are more surprised by our memories of our growing up in a country so different from this one, somewhere on that bright sphere suspended among the stars on the black sky hundreds of thousand kilometers above us, and so delightful, so very delightful!...

Oh! People don't appreciate the beauty of Earth! If they came where we are, they would love it as we do now, lost to us forever. Like we do now, they would dream about it in feverish, restless dreams full of painful longing…Ah! How weary are those dreams! I wake up after a few hours and see that the Sun is standing in the sky almost in the same place, where it stood before I fell asleep. I see that our vehicle, despite its constant movement, is still in the same desert, equally distant from the horizon. I begin to suppose that there is no time or space, infinite eternity!

Not to lose our minds in this emptiness, and for entertainment, we share various, long, and sometimes childish stories or read the books we brought with us. We have some natural history works, an extensive history of civilization, several top poets, and the Bible. We especially often read the Bible. Woodbell usually opens that book and in a melodious, clear voice reads chapters from Genesis or Evangelias…

We listen to the story of how God created Earth for man to walk upon it, and the Moon that Earth would have its night light, as he ordered night after day, as he banished Adam from a flourishing paradise into an empty and unloving country. We hear that the Savior came into the world to redeem the human tribe, how he walked with faithful crowds on the fragrant meadows and green hills of Galilee, how he suffered and died. We listen to it all, looking at Earth like a silver sickle on the black velvet of the sky while we are traveling through those empty, dreadful fields under the Sun that is moving lazily and forgetting to mark the hours and days for us…

Martha is immersed in those stories with her whole soul, and when Thomas is finished, she asks him various or strange questions… She connects them to our present situation… Not long ago, she said to Thomas:

"The two of us are here like Adam and Eve"

Indeed, the two of them are the first couple banished from Earth to the desert, like they were expelled from the paradise, but what about Peter and me? Who are we? There is something inhuman in our present existence. There is a reason for Thomas and Martha existence, but we, why are we alive?

I remember what we were saying on Earth while planning that expedition. We were coming here for knowledge. Now, I see that the knowledge itself doesn't give you satisfaction if you cannot preserve it and pass it onto others. We see wonders that no man has seen since the creation of the World, but it doesn't matter to us because we have nobody to share that with. This is the reason why we don't investigate what we could or should…Oh, if only we had a way of communicating with Earth! Without it, our life doesn't have sense. Thomas and Martha are so lucky! They live for each other!

Woman Love. Recluse. Knowledge. Man

Looking at them or thinking about them gives me an awful fever. While living on Earth for thirty-six years I belonged to a group of those - I must say-madmen who had only one love: love of knowledge, and one longing: truth. Now I am beginning to feel longing for that secret of the eternal life that a woman carries, and for that holy madness being the expression of that secret – love…

Ha! Ha! The sentence above looks so funny! I am alone, and I will remain alone until death will take me away together with all this knowledge as useless as a spring among those inaccessible and infertile rocks.

Martha… I don't know why I have written her name here. Why should I care about that wild Malabar woman, as beautiful as a young animal who was pushed here not by yearning for knowledge but a common, stupid love for a man?

Sure, I don't care about it, but I stubbornly keep thinking about her and it hurts. There are three strong and smart men here, but none of us can carry a human here, only that stupid slender woman. Only the one among us she has chosen has some value…

The two of us are meaningless, we can only serve those two with our brains like the working animals serve with their muscles. It is unfair. Why he, why only he, why just he…On Earth, asking us to take her to the Moon, Martha said: "I will be your slave".

In truth, we are her slaves even if she doesn't order us, or if we don't try to serve her. We are her slaves for that extremely simple thing. We serve her involuntarily in various ways for one reason as only she can create new humans here.

Hey! Where is my thinking taking me! I have hardly freed myself from the specter of death, and with the old human habit, I am already thinking about the future that may never happen. Humanity, new humanity, and we are surrounded by a desert, a land with no air, water, and lifeless. The Moon hasn't given us anything yet, we are alive thanks to the tiny part of Earth we brought here with us! We don't even have any data to confirm that we will find living conditions here. We have traveled a few hundred kilometers and haven't noticed any changes in the configuration of the land surface or atmosphere density. The air is so thin here that it can neither dim the stars during the day nor paint the black sky blue. There are no traces of water existence here ever.

And we are still hopeful. Almost each of our conversation starts from that optimistic phrase: "And when we finally get to that side…" How will that side look like?" We still know as little about it as we knew leaving Earth for this expedition, meaning, we know nothing.

Under Three head, seven degrees, forty minutes western longitude, forty-three degrees, six minutes of lunar north latitude, before midnight of the second day.

We are at the foot of a mountain in the northern part of Mare Imbrium and different from all the elevations that we have encountered. The light of Earth raised only a little more than forty degrees over the horizon, falls diagonally at the rocks like a huge Gothic temple or a fairy tale castle for giants. The night glow here is much weaker than when Earth shone over us in its zenith, but we can see some contours. The first is the mountain, which does not have the form of an annular crater. It looks rather like the remains of such a ring ruin, damaged by some terrible cataclysm of nature or the slow operation of water.

Yes, we are already saying: the effect of water, and although this is only a weak guess, we feel such a thrill of joy, as if it were true … Because if water had been here, then we could expect that there is water on the other side as well. If there is water, then there must be air with a satisfactory density for us to breathe. Despite the frost that although weaker, is still quite oppressive, we left our vehicle briefly and with Earth diagonal light we were investigating the surrounding us area looking for traces confirming our assumption. We don't know anything for sure, but there is no doubt that there were other causes for creation of this mountain so different from those ring-like elevations. We are facing now an almost perpendicular wall with three huge peaks resembling bastions that we named Three Heads. The wall stretches in the north east direction, and we see its black unlit side. Only its peaks whiten with their surfaces leaning towards Earth and look like three silver helmets on black heads. The whole mountain differs from its sky background only by not having stars on its blackness that the sky is covered with. We can tell its shape in the same way as you would see at night a cloud against the dark but starry sky.

We are engulfed in absolute night as the mountain is blocking Earth from us. We light the road in front of us with electric lanterns. This makes travel extremely difficult. Every elevation casts a long shadow here, and we must be careful not to get trapped in the unevenness of the ground or the shallow cleft, which we encounter more and more here. It seems that we won't travel very far before the sunrise especially because the frost intensifying at the end of a night, will probably make us to take a longer break in one spot. We would like to reach a mountain called Pico before sunrise. According to the map, it is seventy kilometers away from us towards north, and we have already learned that it is usually warmer near mountains than on the plains. We think that this phenomenon is related to the volcanic origin of these mountains, or there must be underground veins of internal fire near them.

After a taking a short break to take care of the engine, we set off again. I must stop writing as it is almost impossible to think about it moving though that uneven terrain. That and numerous shadows thrown by the light of Earth leaning towards the horizon make it very dangerous and we all must be on guard all the time. We schedule sleep without stopping our vehicle, so only one person sleeps, and the three others keep watch. Now, Martha is sleeping. I can hear her even, calm breathing, her face peering from the pile of furs by the light of the dim lantern. Her lips are slightly parted, as if to smile or kiss ... What is she dreaming about now?

Ah! Foolishness! We get going.

Third day, thirty hours past midnight on Mare Imbrium nine degrees, fourteen minutes, western longitude, forty-three degrees, fifty-eight minutes lunar north latitude

I see something strange, very strange…

It was almost midnight when we set off from Three Heads. The road was terribly arduous, especially since we were frequently falling into the shadow of small elevations. A few times during an hour, we had to stop to examine the terrain in our electric light or take measurements altitude of stars that were our only guides. The area is carved by shadows resembling clusters of clouds slightly silvering on the top. It is impossible to see more than general contours. And still… maybe that's why…

In the last thirty hours we have only covered forty some kilometers. We finally reached a strange gray strip resembling a sandbar. It stretches with a slightly bent arch for a long distance towards north west with its lighter color from the dark background of the rocky desert. As far as I can see in Earth light, it ends at a group of rocks resembling the fantastic shape of a castle or a city from this distance. A city?..

We travel along that strip as it doesn't take us too far from the planned route and is more even than the dessert covered with boulders... We are moving quite fast, and we see that group of rocks more and more clear. Now we can distinguish all those boulders fantastically stacked and creating an illusion of ruin of towers and buildings. I don't know what to think about it. I am trying to understand it... No, no! It is too strange, indeed! Some almost superstitious fear overwhelms me... Could that be...?

Third day, thirty-six hours on Mare Imbrium

Damn! Damn! If we lose Thomas... He was emaciated so terribly by the first fever, and now again...Oh God! Please save him, as we already... This city of corpses...

Fifty-nine hours past midnight on Mare Imbrium near Pico, nine degrees, twelve minutes, west longitude, forty-five degrees, twenty-seven minutes lunar north latitude.

I am collecting my thoughts..... It is necessary to write about it.

I remember, I just stood up from this journal and looking at those inconceivable ruins or piled boulders, I involuntarily shouted:

"But it really looks like a city!"

Thomas, who had been standing at the window and watching those rocks with an increasing interest, turned quickly at my words. His face showed emotion.

"You may be right,"- he said seriously in a slightly trembling voice. – "It may really be a city...

"What?"

We all jumped towards the window and grabbed at the binoculars. Even Peter stopped the vehicle and left the steer to have a better look at this wonder. Thomas stretched his hand:

"Look to the right," he said, "After all aren't these the ruins of a stone gate. You can see both pillars there, and there is a piece of an arch on the top...What about that object behind, is it a half-wrecked tower? And there, look, a spacious building, with a low colonnade at the front and two truncated pyramids on the sides. I swear this kind of gorge, buried with lots of boulders now, was once a street ... Now it is fallen and dead... City of corpses."

I cannot describe what I felt then.

The longer I was looking, the more I inclined I was to believe that he was right. I could clearly see more and more towers, arches, columns, pieces of crumbled walls and streets covered with rubble of buildings. Earth light was silvering those fantastic ruins and their ruins were emerging from the shade like phantoms. A shiver came over me. Lunar Pompeii or Herculaneum but not dug out from sand, but changing into sand, horrible, bigger, and deathlier in this monstrous abandonment and in this strange light...Varadol shrugged his shoulders and mumbled:

Yes, these rocks look like rubble...But there was never a live being here.

"Who can tell", answered Thomas. "Today this side of the Moon doesn't have air or water, but it could have had it ages ago or thousands of ages ago, when the lunar globe was rotating faster and when Earth used to rise and set on its sky..."

"It's possible," I whispered contemplating it.

"We haven't come across any traces of erosion, and it is a proof that there was never neither water nor air here so there was no life." Said Peter.

Woodbell smiled and stretched his arm to point at the ground under our vehicle.

"And what about this sand? What about Three Heads that we recently passed. Didn't they look like a remnant of a mountain washed out by water. Perhaps only the eternal effect of frost and the heat of the sun blurred and destroyed what it had built ..."

There was silence for a moment among us, then Woodbell said suddenly.

"It seems to me that we have the most interesting puzzle we could have come across on the Moon that need to be solved."

"What do you mean?", I asked.

"Well, we will drive up to those ruins and check them out..."

I don't know why, the cold chilled me through the bones. It wasn't fear, but something very similar to it. These rumbles of buildings or rocks looked like white corpses on the infinite desert.

Peter shrugged his shoulders in distaste again:

"Strange tl Looking at the rocks, which in Earth light have some resemblance to buildings nothing else, is a waste of time.

Still we turned the vehicle in that direction. Martha was looking at them with anxiety.

"But if it is a city of the dead and built by the dead." She whispered when only two kilometers separated us from the arcade being the entrance to that strange place.

"The city of the dead...for sure", said Thomas smiling, "but believe me it must have once been built by the living."

"Or by the forces of nature", added Peter and at the same time suddenly stopped the vehicle on the spot. The sand bar had just ended, and in front of us there was a field so strewn with large boulders that there could be no question of getting through it closer to the city with our vehicle. Having noticed that, Thomas cried:

"I will walk there!"

At first, we tried to stop him from acting upon that intention not even realizing why. Could it be a hunch of what it was to happen? In the end, he got his way. Peter cursed under his nose and said that only a total madman would waste time and step out in the terrible frost for an illusion. I offered to accompany Thomas, but when he insisted on going out by himself, I didn't insist. Until now, I don't know what stopped me. Was it a fear of the cold or perhaps a fear of that corpse like city…? So, I stayed in the vehicle, and that was a mistake…

After stepping out of the vehicle, Thomas set out straight in the direction of the fantastically stacked up rumbles. Standing at the window, we could clearly see him in the light of Earth. He was moving slowly, bending frequently as if checking out the ground. For a moment, he disappeared in the shadow of a small boulder, and then we saw him again much further. Suddenly, something strange happened. Woodbell, after having walked perhaps one third of the way straightened up, stopped dead in his tracks, suddenly turned and started running back to our vehicle in big leaps.

We were looking at his moves puzzled. Suddenly, a few steps away from us, he stumbled and fell. As he wasn't getting up, we ran out to help him after a necessary delay caused by having to put on our pressure suits. When we got to him, he was unconscious, so we brought him inside immediately.

When we tore the pressure suit off him, we saw a terrible sight. His face was swollen and bruised and blue, covered with all blood leaking from the mouth, nose and eyes. There were also thick drops of blood on his swollen hands and neck, though we could not see a wound anywhere.

Martha screamed wildly at such a sight, and Varadol had to struggle to stop her from throwing herself at the body and calm her down, when I was trying to revive Thomas. At first, we thought it was an apoplectic attack, but when we examined his pressure suit, we discovered the real reason of his fainting. We noticed that the glass in the mask of the pressure suit got cracked probably when Thomas stumbled and fell. Before, he realized what happened, the air escaped from the pressure suit. When we got to him, his air container was almost empty. It caused the blood explosion and fainting, but we didn't know why he was running.

After some time, we managed to revive him. The first sign of his returning consciousness was taking a deep contractile breath followed by a spurt of blood from his mouth. Then his eyes opened, and breathing quickly, he started looking around bemused, as if not understanding what was happening to him. Suddenly he shouted terribly, reaching out as if pushing something away, and fainted again. We tried to revive him again, but he did not regain consciousness. A fever appeared which seemed to be a warning of a long illness. Arranging the patient as carefully as possible in his hammock, we continued our travel. Nobody thought about the mysterious city anymore. We were so upset by that terrible accident and couldn't wait to leave that menacing area. After twenty some hours, we finally reached the Pico slopes. We will be parked here till the morning.

Woodbell's condition is still critical. Although the bleeding has stopped, the fever continues to rise. Sometimes he bolts straight up and throws his body forward as if he wanted to run away. Then he hallucinates and shouts out incomprehensible sentences often repeating the names of those unlucky Remonger brothers. After such outbursts, his body becomes totally limp, and he looks so pale as if he didn't have a drop of blood left in his body.

We are deeply concerned by all of this. Martha is almost losing her mind out of despair and fear but tries to control it understanding that he needs her help. We are trying to console her as much as we can and to hide our own fears…

There is a puzzle in this awful accident. I cannot understand what could have caused Thomas's crazy escape that became a reason of this misfortune. It is obvious that his mask broke only when he fell. I regret now that it didn't occur to me to step out of our vehicle to check the route he had walked. Perhaps it would have helped with solving this puzzle…Something must have happened there! Thomas, with his normal presence of mind in the worst situations, would not have let fear get the best of him. But what scared him so much? What could have scared him in this generally lifeless world?… He hadn't even covered half of the distance to the gate of that alleged city of corpses…

At Pico, one hundred forty-eight hours after midnight.

We can finally breathe more easily. It seems that we may manage to keep Thomas alive. Now, he has fallen asleep, and it is a sign that the breakthrough moment of illness is over. We behave and move as quietly as possible. We even speak in a whisper so as not to wake him up. Maybe this sleep will save him.

We are afraid the dogs' barking could wake him up and that could kill him. That's why we are constantly next to them watching. If any of them makes a sound, we will kick it out of the vehicle. Fortunately, they are quiet. Selena, his favorite, is sitting next to his hammock as on guard and doesn't take her eyes away from her sick master. I am convinced that this intelligent animal is aware of the state he is in. There is so much sorrow and anxiety in her eyes ... When one of us approaches the patient, she growls quietly, as if warning that she is watching and will not let anyone hurt him, but then she wags her tail to let us know that she believes in our good intentions and appreciates our taking care of him.

Martha is sitting at the other end of the hammock. She has hardly spoken for the last hundred hours. She only says something when she needs to communicate something regarding the care of the sick. I cannot even imagine a greater anguish. She neither cries nor complains. She is even calm, but her calmness, her pressed lips and her dry, wide open eyes are awful enough to break your heart. We have admired her and her pain. We would like to encourage her, give her comfort and love, but we really don't dare to approach her or speak to her. She looks at us with such an indifference. It is obvious that we only matter if we help her save Thomas. We don't even exist apart from that.

At Pico before the third day sunrise.

The highest summit of Pico has already glowed in the sunlight. In three or four hours the day will come down here as well. All night long, we saw the silver wall of this mountain in Earth light. Now, this wall became gray and dark as a contrast to its peak sparkling in the sunlight.

Like the Three Heads, Pico isn't a crater but rather an immense ruble of a damaged mountain ring. We are standing near its highest peak sticking out in the north west. It suddenly ends here perpendicularly towards the valley. You can get dizzy at the sight of this immense height, even the more prominent against the smooth plain stretching around it. Its peak rises over it two and a half thousand meters up.

It is hard to guess what could have caused crumbling of this mountain ring it originated from. Perhaps, changes in temperature crumbled its soft rock, or perhaps it was water? We are making this assumption for the second time. It is more probable as we don't see rock shards here which would be the result of the sun and frost biting action. In the place of probable top of the ring, there is a small smooth elevation looming faintly in Earth shimmer. Despite terrible cold, Peter stepped outside to check out the ground. He couldn't stay there long, but he brought a piece of rock remarkably similar to those settling from water…

Thomas has been sleeping for over thirty hours. We are a bit more relaxed, but on the other hand such a long sleep begins to bother us. It is scary to look at his face so pale. His eyes are closed, his sunken cheeks are covered with yellow, almost transparent stretched skin, his lips are burned and bloodless. He lies motionless and only his ribs rise a little with his weak breathing. I am sometimes under an illusion that I am looking at a corpse not a living person, and I would like him to wake up.

Martha, still silent, doesn't leave his bedside for a moment. Overcome with fatigue, she falls asleep sitting, but it doesn't last long. She soon wakes up and stares at the patient with her wide-open eyes as if she wanted to heal him with her eyesight. I'm becoming really concerned about her health. Her getting sick would be unacceptable. It is very difficult to make her eat something.

I am worried that Woodbell won't wake up before the sunrise. We would like to start moving, but we are afraid to interrupt his sleep. Originally, we were planning to turn east from Pico to circumnavigate the Alps range forming the north-east end of the Mare Imbrium, but now we decide to head north straight towards the huge Platon ring. After thorough checking of the maps, Peter claims that we will manage to get through that ring straight to Mare Frigoris. The mountainous terrain behind him stretches up to the pole, so that would be a significant shortcut.

On Mare Imbrium, ten degrees western longitude, forty-seven degrees lunar north latitude, twenty hours after the sunrise of the third day.

We are finally approaching the end of the vast Sea of Rains that took us two months of travel that equal two lunar days, but meanwhile there on Earth, the Moon changed twice, fully glowed twice, and became new twice.

For over a dozen hours we have been facing the powerful ridge of Platon ring. Its western part is shining in the sun like a huge white wall against the dark sky. Its western side is still enveloped by night and only its peaks burn like torches. It is indeed the most magnificent and powerful view, we have come across so far but worried about Thomas's health, we don't pay attention to our surroundings.

Thomas woke up at sunrise. He looked at us in amazement for a moment and then tried to sit up in his hammock, but his strength failed him, and he fell back limply so Martha lifted him and helped him sit. I ran to him to ask if he wanted something while Peter stood at the steer.

At first, Thomas was surprised that it was day. He didn't remember his illness or the day before it. I hinted it to him so he was thinking for a moment, probably looking for it in his memory, and then he paled, if getting paler than he was could even be possible. Covering his eyes with his hands, he started repeating with fear:

"It was terrible, terrible!" He shivered.

After a while he calmed down a bit, and I tried to carefully find out what frightened him and caused this fatal escape, but all my attempts failed. He remained silent or gave me a run around with unrelated answers, so that I finally gave up the pointless questions, noting that I was just boring and tormenting him. Instead, I had to tell him with all the details about the condition we had found him in and about his illness. He was listening carefully sometimes pronouncing Latin medical names in a low voice. He was asking about the slightest details and symptoms and having listened to all of that, he turned to me and said calmly with a slight smile:

"You know, it looks like I am going to die."

I denied it lively and flatly, but he only nodded:

"I am a physician and now when I am conscious, I am looking at my illness consciously. I am surprised that I am still alive. You've said, that when I fell, the glass in the mask of the pressure suit got broken. I didn't die there because you had got to me before the air in the container managed to escape through the opening. Based on what you are telling me, the air in the pressure suit was already very thin so because of my higher inner blood pressure, I started bleeding not only through the nose and mouth but also through my skin. If you came a few seconds later, you would have found a bloodless corpse. It is strange that despite such a blood loss, I have managed to survive so many days of fever…Perhaps it wasn't so strong .. with lack of blood and such weak heartbeat. But in the end I survived the fever and I am alive, but it doesn't necessarily mean that I will continue to live. I don't have blood. Look, almost no pulse; touch my chest: can you feel my heartbeat? You can hardly feel it. I would perhaps come out of it on Earth, but we don't have the right conditions…"

He stopped tired and close his eyes. I thought he was falling asleep again, but his half-closed eyes were following Martha busy with preparing the medicine that he himself prescribed. Unheard off, profound sorrow was in his eyes. He moved his lips a few times, and then looking me into the eye, he quietly said:

"Will you be good for her? Okay?"

A painful cramp gripped my heart, and at the same time it seemed to me that some insolent, hideous voice was whispering in my ear: "When Thomas dies, one of you will get Martha, perhaps it will be you…". I lowered my eyes in shame at myself, but he seemed to have read the thought in my face, though I testify to God that it lasted less than the fastest blink of an eye!

He smiled with immense pain and, reaching out to me with his skeleton hand full of dark blue veins under yellow skin, he added:

"Don't fight over her. Leave it to her… respect… respect…"

He couldn't finish. Only after a moment, taking a breath, he said curtly, suddenly changing his tone:

"I may live after all. There is no necessity for me to die. I started to eagerly assure him that he would live, even if I doubted it myself."

A dozen or so hours have passed since that conversation, but his condition isn't improving in any way, indeed, it seems to be even worse. Fast heartbeats, shortness of breath and fainting are constantly recurring. I don't know how it will go from here. He became extremely irritable and demanding. Martha cannot leave him for a minute. He looks at us as at enemies.

A few more times I tried to find out about the reason of his mysterious escape, but each time I asked, he got silent again, and his eyes showed so much fear that I couldn't torment him with questions. Why do I care about it? It's enough that misfortune happened and let it be the last one.

The third lunar day, sixty-six hours after the sunrise at Platon on the way east.

Varadol's assumption proved to be completely wrong. It is totally impossible to get through the center of the ring. We have to go around the Alps range what will significantly extend our travel, but it cannot be helped. Not more than thirty hours have passed since the sunrise, when we got to Platon's crags after covering a distance of almost one hundred kilometers on an exceptionally smooth terrain. Huge Platon ring with an over ninety kilometers diameter is a part of the northern edge of Sea of Rains. The range of lunar Alps stretches from its south east up to Palus Nebularus which connects Mare Imbrium with Mare Serenitatis. The range is broken only once by a transverse valley, probably the only one of this side of the Moon. It leads towards Mare Frigoris that we need to cross on our way to the pole. To the west of Platon, there is a high steep edge forming a half circle with Bay of Rainbows being its part. The Platon range is formed from a mountain embankment encircling its interior plain for about seven thousand five hundred km. The highest summits in the eastern part of the embankment measure up to three hundred thirty-three meters of the elevation.

Having checked it all very thoroughly on the map, we noticed that in Platon's northern embankment, near a small crater stuck there, the ridge gets lower and flatter thus forming a wide pass. According to Peter's plan, to shorten our travel, we wanted to use this pass to the middle plain and moving north find the way to the elevation with its gentle slope towards Mare Frigoris.

After reaching Platon slopes, we had no problem locating the spot found on the map. The soaring crater protruding over the pass helped us with this. The road to the pass did not seem too difficult as the ground was rising slowly, and there were no bumps. Still, we didn't dare to drive there straight away. We had to first see if it was possible to drive this way.

Having left Woodbell in Martha's care, Peter and I walked forward leaving our vehicle behind. We walked around a crater in Platon's root, climbing up, but the route wasn't as easy as we had thought. We came at stony fields and cliffs that we had to omit. Nevertheless, we were sure that our vehicle would manage to travel this route. We were both in the best moods. The sun shining not far above the horizon, warmed us, we were warm and light, and there were wonderful views all around us! The slopes of the mountains, black as tar, shone in the blinding sun with a whole symphony of wonderful rainbow colors. We were treading on treasures that you could use to pay for kingdoms and crowns on Earth. Among cracked boulders, we saw dark rubies. Glowing malachite veins looked like lawns with onyx and topaz flowers on them. Sometimes when a ray of sun got into a crack, a fountain of light suddenly rainbowed out, a real orgy of light, split in huge prisms of rock crystal. Such unheard off wealth, gathered in one place by some extravagance of nature, dazed and blinded us at first. However, we soon got used to that view of useless for us treasures, so we treaded on them like on common flint rocks.

That magical environment had a great impact on our moods. We were joyful. We forgot about Thomas's illness and other troubles, about experienced difficulties, and mishaps, about dangers still awaiting us and about our uncertain future. The beautiful morning and the gorgeous views have made us as happy as children. We have got used to the uncomfortable pressure suits, and despite Woodbell's recent accident, we didn't want to think about the danger of the surrounding us vacuum. Taking advantage of the lightness of our bodies on the Moon with enhanced muscle strength, we were leaping over huge boulders or jumping from high cliffs.

However, such explosions of good spirits were trimmed by the thoughts about the necessity to rush. We have taken enough air and food to last us forty hours so that wasn't a lot, taking into consideration unforeseen circumstances that would make us stop on the way.

We got to the pass in less than ten hours and now were looking into Platon's mysterious interior. From almost one hundred kilometers, we saw the northern wall of the ring that looked like a huge saw with the peaks as its teeth. Until that end, the plain was smooth, dark gray, like a frozen and silent sea. Here and there, we saw slightly brighter, wide strips with low craters scattered on them like shallow valleys. At our feet, the rock rapidly ended, and there was no chance for our vehicle to go this way.

This sea of death emanated a hopeless sadness. It is hard to imagine a landscape with more peace and more inertia. Even the rocks are slowly flowing down towards the depths, the summits are rising sleepily, huge and so grim in the sunlight. Our earlier gaiety has disappeared without a trace.

It's strange how a landscape can affect human hearts! I was looking for a long time in silence, unable to take my eyes off that emptiness, and I felt a growing regret. I do not know for what and for whom ... I became so indifferent and tedious, and not worth the effort, and Death – the soother suddenly became very alluring to me. I cannot believe that I was so afraid of it not so long ago. I felt that this view was killing me, but I couldn't take my eyes away from it. It took a great effort to look away, so I turned my face towards the south and the sickle of Earth shining in the sky .

I saw Sea of Rains above the peaks of the crater that had served as our guidepost and was now behind and below us. We have passed this huge, huge plain! I was looking at it in the same way as I once did from the pass near Eratosthenes, but then it was still in front of me as an unknown path to an unknown longed-for country, and now I had it behind ...Like then it was gray, lifeless and spacey but instead of burning in the sun summits of Timocharis and Lambert, I was looking at the dark, enveloped in shadow spires of Pico first, and further east Piton.

The sickle of Earth was hanging above this sea closer now to the horizon than to the top of the sky. So now this whole plain appeared to me as a wide road originating from Earth. How awful, how difficult and how long it was! Before we got here, the sun passed over us twice, like a glaring and vivid flame. We were overwhelmed with frosty long shadows twice. And how many hardships, how many adventures and how much suffering! When descending from Eratosthenes, we struggled with deadly noon swelter, then unrelenting frost, and the again the spectrum of Death accompanied us for so many hours! Those were followed by the death of Remonger brothers and Thomas's accident and illness. Our road started from O'Tamor's death and traveling on it isn't over yet.

These gloomy thoughts and some sudden, just awaking but compelling longing for Earth totally absorbed me, when Varadol's cry woke me up from my wistfulness. I turned quickly thinking that another mishap happened, but Peter was standing next to me looking alright and pointing towards the distant northern Platon embankment. I looked in that direction and saw something like a wan cloud. No! Barely a faint shadow of a cloud, obscuring the foothills of the mountains clearly visible just a moment ago...

I trembled at the sight, as if it wasn't a cloud moving, but the mountains themselves moved and were walking in front of us. At the same time, Peter was shouting through the pipe:

"A cloud! So, there is atmosphere, there is air! We will be able to breathe there!" A crazy joy sounded in those words overflowing with hope.

Indeed, finally the first flame of life appeared to us over that "valley of death" as I called it. This cloud doesn't mean at all that a man can breathe with that atmosphere. Still, there is no doubt that the air is thicker there than in the areas we have passed so far if the clouds can appear there and stay close to the ground. The smoke from craters outside of Eratosthenes fell immediately like sand on the ground.

Encouraged with this discovery that strengthened our hope for finding air on the other side of the Moon or even earlier, we started our return descent towards Mare Imbrium in higher spirits. Descending, we were talking about the main goal of our trip that was finding a passage through Platon ring. Since we hadn't succeeded in that plan, now we were thinking about other options. Perhaps in the west of Platon, we could find a spot from which we could get to the top of the elevation, but it is impossible to dare something like this. If we didn't succeed in that, we would have to circumnavigate the edge of Mare Imbrium from the west what would amount to several thousand-kilometer travel. It is much safer to turn straight east. Maybe it will be possible to cross the earlier mentioned valley in the Alps, and even if it turned out to be an impossible, then, going around the entire chain, we will not add too much to the road.

We descended with the great news and this decision into the valley, but we were met with a shocking discovery. Our vehicle wasn't where we left it. At first, we thought that we got lost, but no, everything was the same including the same boulders where we had parked it.

Despite our exhaustion, we ran towards them, still not believing our own eyes, but it wasn't there. We tried to find traces of its wheels to guess in which side we should look for it, but there were none left on the rocky ground. A despair overcame us. The food we took with us was already eaten, we had only some leftover water and only a supply of air only for a dozen or so hours. Varadol began to call as he forgot that I was the only creature who could hear his cry, connected to him with a speaking tube!

We went searching. We walked all over the whole area, wasting six hours and found no trace. When after fruitless search, we returned to our original parking spot, we were very hungry, had no water and the air supply was almost finished. We fell to the ground feeling so helpless to wait for death. Varadol was cursing loudly, and I was trying to figure out what could have made them leave before our return.

Suddenly, I thought that Thomas overcome by a sick jealousy ran from us on purpose to allow us to die.

I noticed this jealousy when he was talking about his expected death and about Martha. Rage enveloped me. I got up and wanted to run, chase him, take revenge, kill him – but then ...

Then, I saw Martha not far from us. She was walking towards us slowly. We both jumped to her shouting with indignation and joy. Martha was calmly starring at our lips, and when we finally stopped hoarse and stunned with our own shouting, she gestured to us that she didn't hear us. We forgot that because of the lack of air, she couldn't hear our shouts. Anger has left us suddenly, and we gestured to her that we wanted to go back to our vehicle. When she took us there, we couldn't believe our eyes, it was so close hidden behind a huge boulder.

There, we finally found out what had happened. Soon after our departure, the sun set behind the boulder and our vehicle was left in a complete shade. When Woodbell started shivering from the cold, Martha moved the vehicle to the south of the boulder where the sun gave enough warmth to keep the patient warm. When we didn't see them, we started looking for them far, but it didn't occur to us to check under the boulder so close to us. Martha saw us from the vehicle but thought that we were walking away to examine that part of our surroundings and was patiently waiting for our return. Only when we came back for the second time and were keeping our distance, she came out to find what kept us away. It didn't occur to her that we couldn't see our vehicle. The whole incident ended happily with laughter, although it could have become dangerous for us.

Woodbell's condition was relatively good, and he fainted only four times during our absence. Now, he is much calmer and says that he is much better. We don't see it in his very pale and gaunt face, but please God, let it be true. We've had enough victims at the start. We set out again with a new plan. For the time being, we are moving towards east, still close to the Platon crags towering higher and higher. We will soon reach the Alps range.

Thomas's health condition dictates the greatest hurry. The sooner we reach a place where he will be able to get out of the closed vehicle, move freely and breathe, the more likely will be his rescue. We'll be racing day and night further from this desert and closer to the pole where we will likely find areas with air and water.

Under the Alps, three degrees western longitude, fort-seven degrees, thirty minutes lunar northern latitude, one hundred sixty-one hours past the sunrise of the third day.

We are losing hope in our ability to keep Thomas alive. We are racing like crazy as much as the terrain allows it, but the pole is still far away, and Thomas is fading away before our eyes. We shiver with anxiety and impatience, and to top it all off, the Alps, blocking our way, force us to stick to the south-west direction so instead of approaching the desired pole, we are moving away from it for now. Soon, in a dozen or so hours, we will reach the mouth of Transverse Valley with hope of being able to turn north from it. Until that time, we still have the vertical walls of the Alps on the left, where our vehicle looks like an insect under a wall of a huge fortress. We are longing for the moment when we reach a gate out of this wall, and that it will open a rock corridor over one hundred fifty kilometers long that will lead us to Mare Frigoris. We are passing, detached smaller steep boulders at the throat of the valley, being a sign that we are getting closer.

Woodbell keeps asking how far it is. He would like to get to the pole as soon as possible, but we haven't even covered half of the distance from Sinus Aestuum! Fear overwhelms me when I think about it! He must have forgotten about these distances! He is longingly talking about the polar area, the air and water like they were things that we will find tomorrow. Meanwhile, the lunar tomorrow, even so remote, won't bring anything like that yet. The weaker Thomas becomes, the stronger he believes in his recovery. He is making plans for the future and already making his life with Martha… I don't like his faith. They say on Earth, that it is a bad omen for a sick person. Martha listens to that with her usual sad smile. How much she must be suffering! It is impossible she doesn't see that he is dying.

In Traverse Valley, eighty-two hours past noon.

An internal voice tells me it's all for nothing. Despair overwhelms me because I want him to live, I want it even more because I feel a hideous, disgusting viper in my brain that whispers in my will: If he dies, one of you will get Martha, it may be you…No, he must live! He must, because if he dies, Martha will follow him for sure. And then what? What then? Why will we stay here? For what?… I was once complaining that we both serve those two, but now I feel that such servitude is the only purpose of our existence here. Our dying will start with their death as we won't be able to create anything from ourselves. Our life and our work will serve neither us nor anybody else. What for? Why?

But if Martha didn't die after his death, then one of us would get her. Perhaps she would put her arms around his neck perhaps mine, or cling with her mouth to my mouth like to Thomas's now … I feel as if a hot air ball has broken in my chest, blocking my breath, and pouring heat in my veins… Away with such thoughts! After all, Varadol could be the chosen one!… No! It would be better without a woman between us! I feel that I involuntarily want Thomas's death, and that I am beginning to hate Varadol… And she is sitting calmly, staring at his dying lover's face…

Woodbell doesn't want to die. He is fighting the death off in despair. Every now and then, he says that he will live and wants us to confirm it, so we do it insincerely. Only Martha nods her head with conviction, and repeats with her low, melodious voice: "Yes, you will live …you my…"

At the same time, her eyes will keep her in some fog of pleasure and intoxication … Can she really delude herself that this dried dead body without strength, without a drop of blood in his veins can live? And yet what would I give for him to live!

We didn't stop at noon. First of all, the heat was not as great as the previous days because of the significant lunar latitude, and second because of Thomas, we needed to hurry. We have covered a large distance since leaving Platon's slopes. We are in the middle of the Traverse Valley, and we should reach the Sea of Frost before the sunset.

Around noon, passing small, scattered rock outcroppings, we suddenly found ourselves at the wide mouth of the valley. The vertical wall of the Alps curves here and withdraws towards east broken up with the throat of a huge ravine. The Mare Imbrium plain goes in here with a wide half-circle becoming narrower towards the proper valley with its entrance blocked with a circular at first, and then changing into a huge, a few hundred meters high deck. On the other side of this half-circle, the lunar Mont Blanc, with its summit rising about four thousand meters, sticks out above this plain majestically. Its deck scared us, and we hesitated before entering the valley. If we encounter more of them, our trip will get extended again as it will make us climb steep slopes again.

Varadol took out the photographs of the Moon again. They mislead us before, and on Platon as well, but there was no better way to orient ourselves. After a short consideration, we decided to venture into the valley. That decision was influenced by Thomas who like a maniac insisted that extending our travel to omit the Alps and going through Palus Nebularum would definitely kill him.

What has the disease done to this man! Once firm, present and calm, full of prudence and adamant will, he is now whimsical and stubborn. He scolds us about anything, and then again apologizes or begs to save him ... However, we prefer it to periods of complete collapse in his strength, when he lies on his back for many hours, more like a corpse than a living man. He is talking a lot now as if he wanted to use his voice for ensuring himself that he is still alive. Only when one of us accidentally hints upon that unfortunate accident, he goes silent again and starts trembling in an utmost fear. I am fruitlessly racking my brain to figure out the nature of his secret…

It was already noon when we reached that deck blocking the entrance to the valley. With a great difficulty we managed to find a way to get onto that deck. From that height, we looked behind us to see Mare Imbrium for the last time ever. Despite all the hardships, suffering and despair that we experienced on it, I was leaving it with a dose of sadness…The human heart is so strange. It took us two months to get through it from one lunar noon to the other, and all that time, we were only praying to cross it as soon as possible, so why this nostalgia now?

We move through the valley quite quickly and relatively easily. We don't encounter wide decks anymore, and the smaller elevations which don't occupy the entire width of the valley, can be omitted. Now the sun stands in the sky so that it illuminates both edges. We see two huge embankments about four thousand meters high. The valley starting from over a dozen kilometers width on that deck narrows towards north east. It looks as if its formidable walls were getting closer to each other to squeeze us more and more. We feel like we were traveling through a huge carved in rocks very straight corridor. When we look ahead, we see a distant exit of this corridor similar to a tiny and deep recess among white rocks, filled with a big piece of the sky. I don't know if it is an illusion, but it seems that the sky there isn't as dark as here and the stars on it seem less numerous and less shiny. It could mean that the atmosphere above Mare Frigoris is thicker...Our barometer is slowly rising as well. It makes us more hopeful for delivering Thomas still alive to the area where there is enough air for his lungs.

The Transverse Valley, one hundred sixty-eight hours past noon, third lunar day.

Since the sunrise, we have covered over five hundred kilometers, and we are approaching the outlet of the valley. The spacey rocky throat is becoming narrower and the walls of its both sides get lower. We clearly see the exit from the ravine to Mare Frigoris, and it seems to get bigger the closer we get to it. At sunset, we will reach a plain again, let's hope, we will all do...

Oh! Oh, what a Golgote has today been for us. For dozens of hours, we have been trembling with each rustle and looking at Woodbell's hammock – is it now?... It's no doubt, he's in agony. He has become very silent and calm. He is only looking at us with begging eyes which show that he wants to live so badly but we cannot help him at all.

The recent shocks during crossing the gap have damaged his bones. We traveled almost two-thirds of the way, when in at thirty degrees east longitude, we came across an obstacle that almost made us go back to Mare Imbrium. The sun already low above the horizon, and the entire west side of the valley was hidden in impenetrable shade, lit only here and there by Earth's oblique low light. We had to travel close to the foothill of the western embankment to avoid getting lost at night. Here this embankment reaches its greatest height and rises perpendicularly above us similarly to that perpendicular edge of the Alps that we traveled before noon.

So just then a few hundred steps ahead of us, we noticed a black streak crossing our road on its whole width. When we got closer, we saw that it was a crevice cutting across both embankments and the bottom of the valley. Thick shade filled it up to its edges so we couldn't even guess its depth. Those thousands of meters high rocks were torn by it down to their bottom. We stopped helpless in front of this new obstacle.

We saw that crevice cutting across the upland separating Mare Imbrium from Mare Frigoris on a map, but we didn't expect it to be so deep to also cut the bottom of Transverse Valley situated two or three thousand meters lower than the surrounding elevations stretched behind these embankments.. When I saw that abyss in front of us, sweat broke out on my forehead, and Peter started cursing.

Meanwhile, Thomas, disturbed by our behavior and the fact that our vehicle wasn't moving, started asking questions. We were afraid to tell him the truth, but he, apparently disbelieving our maneuvers, having gathered the last of his strength, stood up and looked out the window. He stared for a moment, then lay down calmly and seemingly indifferent. It only popped of his mouth:

"They don't want me to live…"

"Who?," I asked surprised.

"Remonger brothers," he answered and went silent, squinting his eyes as if awaiting death.

I didn't speak to him more and didn't have time to think about the meaning of his strange words as Peter and I had to discuss what to do next. We were even thinking about returning to Mare Imbrium, when Peter had a brilliant idea to use our reflector to illuminate the bottom of the crevice to learn how deep it was. We came close to the very edge and directed a ray of electric light at the shade. The crevice, quite narrow in this place, was not deep either. The bottom was completely covered with debris, among which huge fragments of stone stuck out. It was like the dry bed of a huge mountain stream. Could it be a bed for water flowing here using this crevice created by other forces?

The reflector light was moving over those black desultorily stacked boulders, shone over the sides of the higher ones and disappeared in irregular chasms, and we are staring at all that not being able to decide. Then Martha came to us.

"Why aren't we leaving?" She asked in a voice that sounded like an order.

And then added, pointing her head at Thomas:

"I have to live for him… you don't have to be concerned about me…"

We looked at her surprised. What has happened to her? She has never spoken to us like that. Her eyes were shining strangely, there was some new majesty in her words and movements, and confidence. Oh! How beautiful and desirable this woman was! Varadol stared at her with fiery eyes, and I got suddenly furious with him. I grabbed him violently by the arm and shouted seething:

"Don't you see that we have no time to waste? Are we going forward or back?"

Peter turned suddenly to me, and we were staring at each other ready to attack.

Suddenly, we heard Martha's soft, scornful and contemptuous laughter. I felt as if I fell on a porcupine. We both dropped our eyes embarrassed, and she walked away shrugging her shoulders. I felt, I was beginning to hate her.

Finally, we decided to drop ourselves to the bottom and travel on those boulders. It was easier said than done. When we found a diagonal ledge under the eastern wall, we used it to start to carefully slide our vehicle to the bottom. However, our hardest task was at the bottom. The light of Earth didn't reach there, so we found ourselves in an absolute night there. I cannot even tell how difficult getting through a few hundred meters there was. Our reflector illuminated only a narrow strip in front of us, so it was very difficult to see enough. We took turns, and one of us walked forward while the other remained at the helm. The vehicle was constantly tilting, bouncing, bumping against boulders, or dropping, and once it even got stuck so that we doubted if we could get it out. Finally, we reached the opposite edge of the crevice. Fortunately, the ground slid there creating an incline that we were able to ascend with the help of special "claws".

In the middle of the incline, we suddenly got into the sunlight that blinded me, and I had to squint my eyes. It happened so suddenly that I had to look behind at that difficult passage which seemed like a dream now.

Having emerged to the level of Transverse Valley, we stopped for a moment to remove the "claws" and check on the condition of our vehicle. Everything was all right, everything but Thomas's health. All that commotion and shaking made him weaker so for a few hours he had been lying like a corpse moaning from time to time.

We have traveled quite a distance when Thomas suddenly sat up in his hammock with fever burning in his eyes. Peter was busy with the helm, but Martha and I ran up to him. For a moment, he stared at us vacantly, and then he suddenly cried out:

"Martha! I will die!"

Martha went pale and bent over him:

"No, you will live." She said it quietly but firmly, and she blushed all over.

Thomas shook his head weakly, but bending even lower, she started saying something to him in Malabar. I didn't understand her words but saw that they made a great impression on Thomas. First his face brightened, then he smiled sadly, and his eyes filled with tears. He started kissing her hair resting on his chest.

After that, he stayed quiet for some time holding Martha's hand in his dried up and sweaty hands. However, he soon started to spring and sit up, as he was struggling to breathe.

"Martha! I will die!," he was repeating in an utmost fear, but she kept responding like before:

"You will live."

He usually went quiet after her answer like a crying child calmed by its mother's hand. Now, hearing her words, he answered:

"So, what, if I don't make it till then…" And then, he added…

"They won't let me live… Remongers…

I couldn't control my curiosity any longer, so I asked him directly about the connection of Remonger brothers to his disease.

He hesitated for a moment, and at last he said:

"It doesn't matter anymore…I will tell you everything now…"

And he began to speak slowly, in a quiet voice interrupted by faster heartbeat and shortness of breath.

"Do you remember," he said, "that corpse city on the desert after Three Heads? Even today it's still looming ahead of me with it towers in ruins and with these semi-broken gates… I know I will die, but I still regret that I didn't visit it. But, that's what happened…When I left the gorge, I had to climb on piled up rocks what resembled a ruined Roman road somewhere in Switzerland or in the Italian Apennines…I had finally got to a more even surface. I could see the city clearly. I could clearly see the huge half-arch gate and the huge pillars, when suddenly…

He grabbed our hands and lifted himself from his bedding. His eyes were wide open, and his face turned from corpse pale to green.

"I know," he continued, "you all believe and I myself used to believe …once… that the only truth is the knowledge…based on experience which can be put in mathematical formulas, but there are things that are inconceivable and strange…You may laugh at me, but it won't change anything… We still know so little for sure, so very little."

He fell silent for a moment and looked at us, as if checking if we were sneering at him in our thoughts, but we sat silent and thoughtful. He took a deep breath and continued his interrupted story:

"Then I …suddenly saw two shadows, no, not shadows! Two people or two corpses or maybe ghosts stepped out from under the gate and were walking straight towards me…My knees buckled. I closed my eyes hoping that delusion would disappear, but it didn't. I saw them four steps away from me! They were the Remonger brothers. They were standing there holding their hands. They looked like we found them awful, swelled, and bloody, and they were looking through me so horribly…You know me, I am not fearful and not prone to hallucination, but I am telling you, they were just standing there, and I turned into an ice block from fear. I couldn't move or turn away…

78

Then they began to speak, yes speak and I could hear them as I can hear you although there was no air!...

"And what were they saying?" I asked involuntarily.

"You don't need to know it." He said. "It's enough that I heard it. Oh! More than enough, enough! They told me how I would die, and how the two of you would die...They set the day and the time. They also told me that there was no leaving Earth without a punishment and no impunity for peeking into secrets hidden from people. They said that it would have been better for us to die there on Mare Imbrium than prolong our lives for torments, only torments by stealing air from them the dead...

"We followed you," they were saying, I heard them, "and you are responsible for our death, but you..." They were saying it with an envious twinkle in their whitened eyes and a smirk on their swollen lips. Then I saw O'Tamor standing behind them, so pale, so white and so dried up... He didn't smile or say anything but was sad and looked at me as if with pity ... I cried out in terror and gathering all my will-power tore my frozen feet away from the ground and started to run. I forgot the city and everything. I stumbled and fell. I wanted to pick myself up and run, but I couldn't breathe, and I lost consciousness. He stopped exhausted, and we felt overwhelmed with depression."

I was deeply convinced that it was all an illusion as much as that city was a product of our imagination inspired by that strange grouping of rocks, but I didn't dare to tell him that. Whatever! Who knows? There are so many puzzles and secrets. People came on this already congealed globe and brought Death with them. Perhaps Something else, something unknown accompanied the people and their inseparable companion, Death. That Something had for ages defied all knowledge, all research and all experiments on Earth.

After that story, Thomas fell asleep for half an hour. When he woke up, he wanted to know where we were. I told him we were approaching the end of Transverse Valley, and that we would soon arrive at Mare Frigoris. He was listening as if he didn't understand what I was saying.

"Oh yes" He finally said. "Yes, yes, I was dreaming that I was on Earth." Then he turned to Martha:

"Martha, tell me how it is on Earth."

So Martha started speaking:

"There is blue air on Earth, followed by clouds. There is a lot, lots of water on Earth, the whole huge sea. On the coast of the sea there is a lot of sand and shells of different colors, and then there are meadows where such fragrant, sweet, moist flowers bloom ... Behind the meadows, there are forests again, full of various animals and singing birds. When the wind blows, the sea roars loudly, the forests hum, and the grass rustles."

She was saying it all with a childish simplicity, and we were listening to her words as if that was the most beautiful, magic fairy tale. Thomas moved his lips as if he was repeating after her, "and forests hum, and the grasses rustle...

"We won't ever be there again", he finally said aloud.

It was answered with Martha's sudden sobbing. She couldn't stop herself any longer. She rested her forehead on the edge of the hammock, and she was trembling all over in desperate and inconsolable cry.

"Quiet, quiet." Said Thomas lightly touching her hair, but fear began to overwhelm him as well.

He turned his face to us and started speaking in a broken voice as if having difficulty with getting his voice out of his chest:

"Save me! Have mercy! Save me! I don't want to die here! Not here! It is so awful here! Save me! I want... to live, live ... some more... Martha..."

He cried like a woman and crying he was stretching his thin hands pleading. What were we to say to him? How could we save him?

We are getting closer to the valley outlet, and we can already see the plain of Sea of Frosts. I have a painful awareness that we will go through it alone, without Thomas!

On Mare Frigoris, third solar day, twenty-three hours past the sunset.

I am checking out my last words written during that day: they came true. We entered Mare Frigoris plain alone. Thomas Woodbell has died at the sunset today.

What an emptiness! Our numbers are continually decreasing; only three of us are left...

I cannot stop thinking about Thomas's quiet but so terrible death.

The solar disc had already touched the lower edge of the horizon, when we finally left the rock corridor after a week. A smooth, gilded surface stretched before us with the last rays of the sun. I say: gilded, because the sun, which we did not notice in previous sunsets, bowed to the horizon, turned yellowish and brightened the circle of black sky around it. It is an undoubtedly sign that the atmosphere here is denser. We noticed another optimistic sign: Mare Frigoris is all covered with sand. Obviously, this plain was once the bottom of a true sea.

It improved our spirits, especially as Thomas seemed to feel better. We were beginning to feel joyful. We began to believe that we would fly over that plain like birds, and that before the sunrise we would get to the Country of Life with Thomas. We would feel the winds, hear the murmur of water and see the green…, but it didn't happen like that.

As soon as we had driven over a dozen meter of the plain, Thomas asked us to stop our vehicle. Even the slightest movement extremely exhausted him …

"I want to rest," he said in a weakening voice "and look at the Sun before it sets."

So, we stopped, and he started to look at the Sun pouring its last gold glows on his face. He looked at it for a moment not moving, but then he spoke to Martha:

"Martha, how does it go? Sun, you fair God – what is next?"

And Martha, like at our first sunset seen from the Moon, stood up in its full shine, stretched her arms and lifting her eyes full of tears towards the fading light, started half sing her strange hymn floating in wavy rhythms:

"Sun, you fair god, you are leaving us for the lands unknown to us!

Sun, your heavenly light, you pleasure of Earth, leaving, you leave our eyes in sadness to shine on those who have already been freed from their bodies … On those already liberated of their bodies already who did not yet take new ones, like slaves who were released for a moment, so that they could have peace and quiet before returning to the slaughter and chains.

He is good, the Eternal, Unspeakable and Inconceivable is good as he made the Day of Silence among battles and trials …

He is the source and outlet of all things, in Him are the melted souls of those who have already completed the fight, returning to the place from where they came centuries ago …

Oh, Sun, you fair god, you go to His feet and leave our longing eyes in sorrow…"

Woodbell was listening and seemed to be falling asleep, but he suddenly opened his eyes:

"Martha! Did O'Tamor die?"

"Yes, he did."

"Did the Remongers die?"

"Yes, they did."

"I will die, too… and they …they will die as well … he pointed his eyes at us."

"They will die, but you will live." She answered with that strange conviction.

"Oh, yes...," he whispered, "but what is in it for me..."

A silence fell for a moment. Selena climbed with her front paws to the hammock and was licking his hanging hand. He looked at her and moved his hand as if he wanted to pet her, but he was apparently too weak even for that...

"My, my dog" he only whispered.

Then he said that he wanted to look at Earth. We turned him in the way that he could see it. It was just standing in quarter over the rocks from the south. He was looking for a long time stretching his hands with a great longing towards that shining half circle in the sky. The shadow of the Indian Ocean with a bright triangle of India was just passing over it.

"Look, look! That's Travancore" called Thomas.

"That's Travancore." Martha repeated quietly.

"We were happy there..."

"Yes, so very happy..."

The patient started to fret again.

"Martha! Will I go there… after death?... You see, I don't want to … to wander here … on this desert… in that city of the dead… Martha, will I go there?"

Martha was silent bending her head, but Thomas insisted again.

"Martha! Will I go there… after death? …to Earth?

A painful spasm distorted the girl's face, but she controlled it and answered quietly in a tearful voice...

"You will go there for a short time, for a day of silence…and then you will return to me."

His eyes stayed fixed and his limp hands were blue and cold. He shuddered again and barely audible whispered:

"Martha, how is it there on Earth?"

Martha started to tell him about the sea, about meadows, about flowers, and a painful but peaceful smile was settling on his lips and his eyes were slowly closing. He opened them for a moment, looked at Earth and the sun shining only with its narrow edge over the desert, he sighed lightly and died with the last flash of the fading away day. Suddenly Martha's frantic cry rang out in the falling darkness. We dug the grave in the dark and poured some sand on his eyes.

We have been on the road again for almost twenty hours. We are traveling on the even sandy desert. At the outlet of Transverse Valley, we passed the fiftieth parallel. Earth is raised only forty degrees above the horizon, but fortunately for us there are no elevations here which could throw shadows, if possible, we will be driving all night…

We are saddened by a deep sorrow. Martha is sitting overwhelmed, wild from pain, and Selena, at her feet, is howling for her deceased master. We are trying to silence her by feeding her, but she doesn't want to eat. She was used to be always hand fed by Thomas.

On Mare Frigoris zero degrees, six minutes eastern latitude fifty-five degrees lunar northern latitude, after midnight, beginning of the fourth day.

We are turning towards the north pole. For over one hundred seventy hours, meaning since Woodbell's death, we have been moving in the northwest direction. Now, his grave is so far, far behind us…A week has passed on Earth since we buried him. All this week sand is sifting through the wheels of our vehicle, and only the motor's hiss interrupts the constant silence. Martha isn't crying any more but sitting mute with pressed lips and wide-open eyes with dried up tears. Selena is dead.

After Thomas's death, she didn't want to eat but was howling for hours and was sniffing all his things or those he once had touched. In the end, she lied down in a corner weakened and gloomy, growling dangerously at anybody trying to come near her. We were afraid she would develop rabies, and so although with great regret, we had to kill her. I am sure that she wouldn't live much longer after all.

So, our vehicle is awfully silent, as Peter and I have nothing to say to each other. A terrible thing has happened. Thomas's death was not only a person's death, but also a loss of a brave, faithful and dear friend. It was a disaster and a terrible irony suddenly throwing the woman we both desire between us. I can't look at her without a shiver of lust, and at the same time I feel all the horrible shame…sacrilege against our friend's fresh grave. I imagine Thomas's spirit is still close by spitting into my heart over this kind of thoughts, but I cannot stop them, I cannot resist them! Fever eats up my brain, blood rushes furiously in all my veins, and my eyes are so full of her that even when I close my eyes, I still see her in front of me with an unheard-of clarity.

I am struggling to hold back those thoughts, but they are like a bunch of wild dogs which want to break of the leash and attack her. They all brazenly peel off her dresses, fawn and rub against her every part of her shape, snake around her body and mess it with their hideous mouths. Then seeing that she is still indifferent and cold, they start to bark and whack at her with their teeth and bite and tuck… Oh, these mean thoughts of mine. How tormenting they are!

Varadol is going through the same; I know, feel and see it. He also knows what I am going through. That's the reason for this deep-seated, fierce hatred between us. What's the point of trying to deceive ourselves? Why should we try to give it a pretty name? We are both villains because she is between us. There are only two of us in this empty world, and that's one too many. We neither speak nor look each other into the eye. I sometimes catch Varadol's look, and I see a glow of death in it.

Am I scarred of him? No! No! Not at all, even if I know that he might kill me quite involuntarily. He can attack from the back and kill me now, when I am bent over my writing... A shiver goes through me, but I do not turn back, I do not want to catch one of those glances in which I see my own meanness as in a mirror. Anyway, I am not afraid of this sudden and unexpected death that may happen to me. Death is extremely scary only when it is approaching slowly but surely. I fear only one thing, I fear the thought that he could take this woman that I am equally entitled to have. It scares me to think that his kisses could make bring blushes to her face and that he not I could make her breast sigh quickly with passion. No! I just cannot think of it!

We are spying on each other so much, that as both of us are alive, she is safe between us. Still, sometimes madness fills me up. I want to spit in my face, and then face him, and say to him: "Let's fight, let's bite each other like two wolves would fight over a female. We are unsure of tomorrow, unsure of our lives, outcasts in this world, but let's fight over our deceased friend's lover. Let's see who can get this so contemptuously indifferent to us woman. Let's fight over her today, before our tomorrow death!"

I am too much of a hypocrite and coward to do it...Oh! How much I despise myself! And I despise and hate her! There are moments that I could pounce on her and make her sad, silent lips scream, and then smother that scream with life. Perhaps it would be better... We would be left to ourselves and to life without a purpose. We would die willingly then, but at least this wouldn't be between us...

Why is she still alive? What is holding her? How can she continue to live, if she loved him so much, if he really meant the world to her, and if everything ended for her with his death? We are mean, but she is mean too. Selena, the dog, showed more attachment and refused to live without her master who had reared her. He showed her much less love than he gave to this woman, but she can still live without him... Who knows? Perhaps despite her sorrow, perhaps despite her eyes still filled with the picture of the deceased, her brain is already dictating her to choose one of us? Perhaps she is already thinking about picking one of the living to fulfill a woman's eternal role?...

Perhaps, there is something primal, spontaneous, inserted into our beings by nature, and therefore holy a desire for existence and creation that does not look at anything. Perhaps, it does not care about the past or the future of thought, but for me in this moment, it's so disgusting, so hideous and monstrous!

Oh! Why is this woman still alive? Oh! No! I am sure, I wouldn't bear her death!

On Mare Frigoris, zero degrees, thirty minutes eastern longitude, sixty-one degrees lunar northern latitude, fourth day, one hundred seventy-two hours past midnight.

Martha was right telling Thomas: "You will live!".

Oh! Why didn't I understand it then?

Three-fourth of the night had passed, when sitting at the helm, I noticed that Peter was still hanging around me with a look on his face as if he wanted to start a conversation. Until then, we had limited ourselves to exchanging only necessary words, so I was surprised, but also pleased. I felt it was time to finally shed this unbearable, crushing bind and clarify our relationship.

I asked him as politely as I could:

"What can I do for you?"

"Yes, indeed" he eagerly joined in, sitting next to me, "I wanted to talk to you."

I noticed that he was forcing a smile, but his face twitched tightly. Despite my will, I looked at his hands. He, as if understanding my fleeting gaze, blushed and, taking his hands out of his pocket, put them on his knees. After a while he began, stuttering a bit:

"Yes, yes, you see, I wanted to …I think we don't have to stop tonight, as the frost isn't too bad, and the road is even, and it is quite bright although Earth is low above the horizon. You will agree, we must hurry, so …"

I wasn't taking my eyes off him, and he was getting more exasperated.

Suddenly, changing his tone, he shouted impetuously:

"Oh, hell! We are traveling north without a break, aren't we?"

"Yes." I confirmed, trying to stay calm.

There was a moment of embarrassing silence again. Varadol began to walk anxiously. I knew exactly what was happening to him, I knew what he wanted to talk to me about. Because he was jabbering and couldn't speak the word that brought us face to face with things that needed to be settled. For a moment I felt a malicious joy at his torment, and then, but suddenly, I felt sorry for him. There was a moment when I wanted to embrace him and… I don't know… swear on our old friendship, give her to him, or ask him to agree to her death…I don't know. I controlled myself immediately as it wouldn't do anything at all. On the other hand, I felt that it was impossible to postpone a serious talk.

"Is that all what you wanted to talk to me about?," I asked him suddenly.

He paused, apparently surprised by the kindness in my voice, and looked into my eyes enquiringly. Then he smiled sadly and ran his trembling hand over his forehead.

"Yes, indeed, I also wanted to…"

He suddenly stopped and looked at Martha. He hesitated for a moment, and then he frowned and in a broken, dry voice, he spoke in German so she couldn't understand him:

"What will we do with this woman?"

I expected those words, and yet I felt them as a hammer blow to the head. I braked the car abruptly, because my blood hit my brain and blinded me. My heart was beating rapidly, and I felt unpleasant dryness in my mouth. The decisive moment had arrived.

I looked at Varadol. He was facing me as pale as a corpse and was staring into my eyes. I will remember this look forever. There was anxiety and mean doglike begging and a terrible threat at the same time.

Without a word, I pushed him impulsively aside without realizing what I was doing, I went straight towards Martha who sat bending upon some sewing.

"Why are you still alive, woman?," I asked suddenly in a tone fitting a tragedy and probably funny, but then I didn't feel like laughing!

"I am waiting for Thomas's return…"

A rage came over me.

"Enough of this stupid prattle!," I shouted and tore the sewing out of her hands. I don't know what would have happened next if I didn't look at the piece of cotton. It was a baby shirt.

I suddenly understood everything. Unable to say a word I stretched my hand to show the shirt to Peter. He shouted lightly and went to the helm.

So that's why she was firm saying to dying Thomas: "You will live!," and that's why she didn't follow him!

After all, according to her people's beliefs, a baby born after father's death gets his soul. So, she is waiting for Thomas to come back to her as a baby? First, his soul will visit Earth he had missed so much at his agony. Did she share this "joyful news" with him, and the promise that she would be waiting for him when she was speaking to him in Malabarian? All this flashed through my mind now like lightning.

I looked at her; she was crying softly with her face hidden in that little shirt cut out from Thomas's undershirt.

Suddenly something strange happened to me. I felt as if something had broken in my heart, something like an unbearable ulcer, and at the same time the scales fell from my eyes. I saw Martha in a new light. I was looking at her surprised as if I saw her for the first time. This wasn't a woman I was ready to fight about with my friend and my only companion in this world. This was a mother of a new generation who was winning over death through a great mystery of life and love.

Unspoken gratitude filled my heart. Now, I was grateful to her for the cloud of maternity that would hide her from us, and we, we the blind ones, only saw her as an inheritance after the deceased. I bent unaware and kissed her hand.

She budged, but apparently, she understood my kiss, because at that moment she raised her face in tears, but now proud of her new and recognized dignity.

Human nature is so strange! All this doesn't solve anything, but postpones it for some time, but we are both at peace now, as it was all solved. We believe now that this woman doesn't belong to any of us living but to the one who died, and we respect her, not even thinking that time will come again…

But no! No! I don't want to think about it now! Let's go north now, only north!

Under Timaeus, after the sunrise of the fourth solar day.

None of the previous sunrises made us as happy as this one. It was preceded by dawn a phenomenon we hadn't seen on the Moon before. The night had just ended, and we expected the peak of the mountain looming in front of us to suddenly shine with the first rays of the rising sun. However, before it happened, we noticed that the black sky in the east was getting a little brighter as if covered by milk-opal fog. First, we thought it could be a zodiac light seen before the sunrise in the areas close to the equator and appearing at the sixtieth parallel that we had just passed. But no! It wasn't the zodiac light! The sky over the horizon got slightly silvered, and the stars glimmered in a whitish rim. Soon, Timaeus's peaks – the crater we were approaching, flamed in the sun, but they amazingly bloomed like blushing roses at the background of the night.

It was impossible to doubt it any longer! This dawn and this light heralded the fact that the air was already thick enough to be illuminated by the rays that sift through it and flushing their color white.

Sweet, great joy took over me. I smiled at Peter with his whole soul still staring at this phenomenon, and then I turned to Martha.

"Look!", I cried, "Your baby will be born there where we can breathe like we did on Earth!"

She lifted her head and looked towards the east that was changing its color to golden that was spilling over the horizon in the same way as the hope for a new life spilled in our hearts.

The Sun was rising slowly, much slower than on previous days because it wasn't going straight up, but it was moving along an arch leaning towards south and low over the horizon of Earth suspended there. When it all came up, we saw it in the sky in a circle of whitish fog changing into blue and disappearing in the black background around it. We couldn't see stars near it. They still shone in the further part of the firmament, but their multicolor disappeared. Now, they look like those twinkling flickers on the night blue sky seen from Earth.

In two or three lunar days, we will be able to leave our vehicle and for the first time take a deep breath of the lunar air.

Last night we covered a great distance. The night frost at the pole is much lighter than at the equator as the sun doesn't fall so deeply under the horizon, so we didn't stop at all. At the sunset, we entered Mare Frigoris, and now have left it behind us. We see the beginning of a mountainous area in the west, and we are passing its border pillar, Timaeus. A plane stretches before us, to the north, and it carves a wide bay in the foothill. According to the maps, it reaches the sixty-eighth parallel. This plane isn't as even as Sea of Frosts. It is undulated by low and parallel hills, which, however, do not hinder us because they have very gentle slopes. We should go through it before the day ends, so we will spend the next night in the mountains. We will still have to cover six hundred kilometers before we reach the pole…but what does six hundred kilometers mean in comparison to the distance we have covered so far?

We feel optimistic and peaceful with all the misunderstandings and nightmares left in the past. We are encouraged by the blessed thought that we are bringing a new bud to our dream destination. This thought brings with it such good feelings, such peace that at times that we don't regret abandoning Earth.

Oh, why isn't Thomas with us here? He shared in our torments. I wish so much that he could share our hope for life with him!

Jerzy Żuławski

The fourth lunar day, seventy-eight hours past the sunrise, zero degrees, two minutes eastern longitude, sixty- five northern lunar latitude.

A strange sadness has overcome me now. I don't know where it has come from and what it wants from me? Our journey is passing quite briskly. The sky above us slowly draws in dark blue, through which the earlier indifferent stars begin to flicker. All that announces nearness of the "promised land" where we will finally rest after all those hardships that have already taken four months, but instead of joy, I feel more and more sad.

What is the reason of my sadness? Is it the thought that Earth we are still looking at here will disappear from our view forever in several hundred hours? Or is it the memory of the graves that we left behind us? Or is it the result of all that recent internal turmoil that made my soul so exhausted? Could it be the thinking about the deceased's baby that is to be born in an unknown country for an unknown fate?

I am peaceful, but I can't bear this sadness and this exhaustion! Our eyes are blinded by this sharp sunlight. I am tired of constant looking at wild infinite plains and those precipitous mountains sticking out above us... Oh, how I long for even a small pond, a twig, or a blade of grass!...

This area looks like a huge cemetery. We are riding on the bottom of a sea that had dried up ages ago. It is covered with crumbled settlement calcium benches with the remains of washed away ring rocks sticking out above them.

What happened to this sea which once waved here? Its shore only stands above the dry valley, steep, huge, eaten by the impact of waves that no longer exist ... The winds dispelled its crumbs, and now the winds are no longer here. Emptiness and deadness. I really cannot wait to get to the country where I finally see the life! I need it to happen as soon as possible as I may not have much strength left...

Martha is the most patient among us, but well, her world is inside her now! It seems that she thinks more about this new world more than about her deceased lover. I often see her dropping her hands with her sewing and her eyes looking somewhere in the future and bringing smile to her lips. I am sure that she is already imagining the little pink baby stretching its little hands to her. But at times, a deep sigh chases that blissful smile of her face and fills her eyes with tears. This must be the memory of Thomas who won't see his child. Still her smile soon returns because she knows that if he hasn't died, his soul wouldn't be able to return to her in their baby. She is always busy with her thought and doesn't talk to us, but once she said to me:

"It was good that I followed Thomas here because I will give him a new life…" Now wonder she feels happy as she can say that.

The fourth day, seventeen hours past noon, on the elevation before Gold-schmidt, one degree, three minutes eastern longitude, sixty-nine degrees, three minutes northern solar latitude.

No more plains, we are in the mountains stretching until the pole. It's an elevation sown with loose ring-like hills. Vast and high mountain rings stick out above them like this huge Goldshmidt in front of us or the higher Barrow. Now, a thought strikes me that it is very strange that we encounter mountains and lands never touched by human feet named by people… A funny thought.

Today at noon, we were on the bordering peak of this elevation. When we looked behind, we saw the new Earth low above the horizon of the desert. It was obscured by a slight fume of air. The ring of its light atmosphere shone from behind that curtain even bloodier than on previous days. Just behind it, almost rubbing against its black sphere the Sun stood in a small circle of rays.

I am under an impression that during these four months Earth fell from the zenith towards the horizon, but in truth, we escaped from under it getting closer to the pole. The climate here is completely different. The afternoon sun, slightly above the horizon, does not strike us with heat, does not blind us with glare. Here the sun seems as sad and weary as we are…The elevation around us is full of long shadows. The sky in the north is more and more blue without stars that we can still see in the south shining around Earth and the Sun with a bland whitish glow.

I feel excessive fatigue. Despite the lightness of our bodies, I feel that my head, arms and legs are made of lead. I'm afraid that I may get sick. This journey seems so infinitely long that, despite the signs of the approaching end of the road, I am beginning to doubt whether we will ever reach our destination…Well – destination? Where? What destination? Oh, how everything is tiresome and depressing.

Martha is extremely good. If it weren't for her, I wouldn't want to move my hand or turn the vehicle steer towards the pole that we are so laboriously traveling to… she sees my exhaustion, and she knows how to encourage me with a holy word and add to my strength. How have I deserved all her goodness? Do I deserve it despite all the harm of my thoughts and my lust? I am so tired, that I don't care about anything anymore except for this woman's happiness. I would like to live and be useful to her…but who knows if I live…

We see large, steep mountains ahead of us, and we must go through them. These and other, and again different, because the pole is still far away ... I have no more strength. I cannot even continue writing. My words don't make sense together as I keep forgetting what I wanted to say. I would like to stretch in my hammock and watch Martha with half closed eyes. She is always smiling at her thoughts about her baby. Happy!

On the pass between Goldshmidt and Barrow, one hundred sixty-one hours past noon of the fourth lunar day.

I 'm struggling with weariness that is always overwhelming me. I feel sick and I'm afraid of it. How will they do together without me? The road is getting worse, and the night, long night is approaching. Will I live till its end? Is this my turn after O'Tamor and Woodbell? Haven't they predicted this? It would be a pity to die now. I would like to see the baby that is to be born here. I would like to take a deep breath. Oh!

When will this travel end? According to the map, the mountains we are passing are the last obstacle separating us from the pole. After we descend from the pass we are on right now, using the wide ravine, we will turn west. Next, we will continue along the northern slopes of Goldschmidt, and after turning north, we will pass Challis and Main rings. Then, we will circle Gioja ring from the west traveling on its narrow limb stretched towards the parallel, and we will get to a plain separated from the pole only by a narrow range of mountains.

This is what we see on the map. Still maps of these areas poorly visible from Earth are very inaccurate. What's more, we will have to travel this distance at night even without the light of Earth that the mountains will obscure from us. From this height here, you can see a piece of the world in front of us, but only the tops of the mountains glisten in the sun, the black sea of shade floods everything below. When we get there, the stars will be our only guides.

Something has broken up or disconnected in my head. It takes an enormous effort to think straight. Every now and then I see half dreams - half dreads. Is this a fever? I am biting on my fingers to wake up, but it doesn't help either. All the images are swinging in front of my eyes; I see the dark sea with the bloody mountain peaks floating on it. Our vehicles seem to be a ship that we may knock off into the abyss any moment now. I am so exhausted. Where are we sailing on this black ocean? Ah, right! We left Earth behind us, so far in the blue skies, and we will never go back there. Never. I hear awful noise in my head. I think I have fever.

After the sunset in ravines among mountains.

I've dragged myself out of my hammock. Martha told me to lie down, but what does she know? I was supposed to do something or write something, but I don't know what. I must remember what it was. Why is it so dark here? A bomb must have exploded in my head. It must have done it because I feel my head swelling and growing to the size of the Moon...

Isn't it funny that we are on the Moon? Oh, perhaps it's just a dream! How would the dogs get here? Where is Woodbell?... Something happened to him, but I cannot remember... His name was Thomas...

Someone is standing next to me and telling me to lie down because I have fever. So, what! Why can't I have fever? Am I not allowed to have it?... The pen is getting so heavy... but my fingers are heavy too. I don't know what it all means. I hear two voices next to me, I cannot anymore...

III. THE SECOND PART OF THE MANUSCRIPT. ON THE OTHER SIDE.

I

I will never forget the feeling I experienced when I opened my eyes af-

ter the long illness which left me unconscious at the end of that horrific journey through waterless and airless lunar desert. Today, as I begin to write more about our further adventures on this globe, those feelings, come to life in my memory as if only a dozen hours had passed since then. If I count the lunar days, I see that eleven years have passed on Earth since we fell on the Moon's surface. Ten years have passed since we stepped out of our vehicle after being imprisoned inside it for almost half a year. Now, we can breathe freely under a sky equal to the Earths blue sky. We live on the shore of a wavy sea and look at forests full of strange and quite improbable plants, but also full of life. The Sun has circled this world in our eyes, and we have almost gotten used to it. Our hair is getting gray, and a new generation is growing next to us. It is a generation of people who will in time treat our history of coming here from Earth as a myth. Only the more curious ones may venture to the end of that airless desert, may see that shiny sphere over the horizon there. That rarely seen sky light will be an interesting phenomenon, but for us, it is the mother whom we had abandoned forever. We cannot see it, but we are still connected to it by the last but very strong thread of longing.

In several dozen lunar days, we who came here from Earth will die, and the new generation reading my journal in the future will probably value it for a long time as a holy book like "Exodus". But sometime later a critic will appear and prove, that the legend about their origin of being from Earth, is only a childish fantasy.

I think of it as something quite natural. After all, much of what I have experienced myself seems to be only a fantastic dream. The illness, that kept me unconscious for the whole lunar day, created a strange interruption in my life. Later it was difficult for me to connect, what had been happening before it, to what I saw when I came around. I couldn't tell the difference between reality and feverish hallucinations. Indeed, my awakening was strange.

I opened my eyes and couldn't understand what was happening around me. When I just looked around me, I realized that I was on a vast meadow among the hills, covered with vividly fresh, fluffy greenery. The whole area was flooded with soft light resembling Earth mornings when the sun is only emerging from behind the horizon. Only the bare peaks of the high mountains burned in their full red glow. The sky above them was pale blue and slightly foggy. I looked for a long time as I was unable to realize exactly where I was. Then, on that meadow, I saw two people slowly walking and bending every now and then as if looking for something. They were accompanied by two dogs jumping around them and barking joyfully.

First, I thought I was on Earth in some unknown land and was wondering how I had got there. Then, I remembered our expedition to the Moon and a long travel in a closed vehicle through the lunar deserts. I looked around one more time as much as I could without lifting my head which felt like it was filled with lead. Where is our vehicle? Where are those wild sceneries seen through its windows that I still remembered so well? I wanted to call out to the people nearby, but I was suddenly so overwhelmed with fatigue that I couldn't get my voice out. Anyway, I began to suspect that all of these incredible adventures were only a dream. I was supposed to organize an expedition to the Moon, but fell asleep on a meadow, and who knows how long I slept. I was dreaming that I got there, and that I was fighting with some horrible people, lost companions, risked my life ... but it is strange that I don't know this area.

Then I started to recall something about my illness. I must have had a powerful fever and was wandering on the Moon during my hallucinations. In the end, I am happy to be done with them. The thought that it was just dream, and that I am on Earth and won't ever need to leave it, gave me great relief. I felt a strange bliss and fell asleep again.

When I woke up again, I saw the same people I noticed earlier, speaking in soft voices. I seemed to hear the word "sleeping," and the second person's response to it: "He will live". I was surprised by that, but I didn't want to let them know that I was awake. Still motionless and with half-closed eyelids, I started studying the people standing beside me. Although I understood that I must have been sleeping a long time, the lighting of my surroundings hadn't changed much, so I couldn't recognize those faces bending over me because of the weak light. After some time, as my eyes adjusted to the light, I realized I knew those people but couldn't remember their names. I slowly moved my eyes away from them to the mountains visible on the horizon. Their peaks were still lit in the same way, but I noticed now that the light was coming from a different place.

At that moment, something above the peaks caught my attention. A huge gray-white circle stood over the deep pass between two high mountains, leaning halfway out of the horizon. I was gazing at it for some time, and I suddenly understood. It was Earth shining there in the sky!

The awareness, that I am really on the Moon, has come back now and made me shiver. I screamed loudly and sat up on my bed. Peter and Martha, the people I saw earlier, running to me clearly very happy, but my head spun again, and I fainted.

It was my last fainting during that long illness. After regaining consciousness, I started my slow recovery process. More than one hundred hours had passed before I was able to get up and walk by myself. Meanwhile, Peter and Martha were caring for me with mother-like patience. Since I was still too weak to talk or ask questions, I was thinking about my surroundings. I already learned that during my illness, we had arrived at the land with air and plants we had longed for so much. I couldn't understand that it all had happened quite naturally. It was difficult for me to believe that I had been unconscious for the whole Earth month, and that our vehicle kept moving for several hundred miles after I fell sick, and we finally reached the pole.

We were indeed on the very lunar north pole. It is a strange land of constant light and constant murk at the same time with no sunsets, sunrises, noon's, or midnights. The lunar axis is almost perpendicular to the ecliptic plane, so the sun doesn't fall under the horizon here and doesn't rise in the sky but seems to be constantly rolling on the horizon. If you climb any of these mountains near here, you may see the fiery red sphere of the Sun lazily crawling close to the horizon. These mountains have always been blazing in a pink glow lighting them everywhere from different angles, and there has been no night here since the creation of the world. The green valleys at their feet have never seen the sun. They are forever shrouded in the shadow of the hills as there is a perpetual dusk or perpetual dawn here. Their only light are the flares of naked, sun-flushed peaks like a huge wreath of pale roses thrown on the grass. Only sometimes, once in a few Earth months, due to the Moon's librations, the Sun rises a few degrees over the horizon and will shine on the deep gap between the rocks. Then a huge river of light flows through the ravine, falls from the rocks in cascades, and marks the dark meadow with a broad, golden-red streak. A few hours pass, the sun hides again behind the mountains, and the soft twilight returns to flood the silent valley.

At times, a strange and weak glow like an agile pale rainbow comes over the mountains. It is the Moon's polar dawn very much like the dream about Earth dawn, and like in a dream beautiful, clean, and sad.

There is something amazingly mysterious in the weak light of those polar lands of the Moon. I remember that looking at them, I felt a dream had taken me to some enchanted Elysian Fields. Light misty fumes roam the spotless greenery like ghosts. No voice interrupts the enormous, intoxicating silence. In addition, there is always a cool and sunny spring here. We have lived here for over half a year, and only once we saw clouds on the light blue sky. It almost never rains, and that's why there are no springs, streams or water to be seen. However, the air is so saturated with water vapor that the moisture is sufficient for the development of vegetation. Our Earth grasses, trees and flowers would certainly dry of thirst here, but the lands at the lunar pole have a different, specific flora for such conditions.

Strangely juicy moss like plants form the meadows here. Like other plants, they have the ability to suck moisture out of the air but to a much larger degree. They collect and retain so much water inside them that we were able to use them to get enough water for all our needs. So, this was easy, but getting food was a big problem. We found a few edible plant species and many interesting creatures which looked like our snails without shells, but we had nothing to cook them in. Our fuel supply brought from Earth ran out, and we couldn't find any substitute for it nearby. Even the woodier moss branches were so saturated with water that we couldn't use them to start a fire. Drying them in this virtual steam room was impossible. Peat, which we found in great volume, also dripped with water when it was squeezed.

As I was feeling better and was leaving our makeshift tent to take walks, we became seriously concerned about the lack of fuel. We had long deliberations on this subject and made various tests that were always unsuccessful. Peter came up with an idea of carrying the thicker squeezed out branches and peat to the top of the mountain with a hope of them drying easier in the sun there. However, even there the warmth of the sun was still too weak. After some time, the peat merely re-absorbed enough water from the air to make our efforts futile.

So, having sacrificed all the wooden equipment we could do without, we lit a huge, last bonfire, attempting to dry the combustible material collected in the area. If we could do it, we could keep the eternal fire fueled with new dried fuel. But unfortunately, this attempt also failed us. We burned everything that could be burned, and we received only a tiny handful of dry twigs and peat in return. We learned that to dry some stuff, we had to burn three times as much. Our "eternal fire" expired after only a score of hours. Its only benefit was that we managed to set our machine in motion for charging the battery in our vehicle.

Then, we had to go without fire. We didn't feel cold, because the air was well saturated with steam which always equally distributed the scarce sun heat very well, but it was difficult to go without cooked meals. For traveling, we decided to save the rest of our supply of artificial protein and sugar which was very suitable for our digestion. We haven't given up our plan of getting to the center of the hemisphere of the Moon opposite to the side facing Earth. For the time being, there were three circumstances which were stopping us from that expedition. First, I was still too weak after my illness to survive the hardships of travel. Second, Martha expecting the birth of Thomas's baby soon couldn't take such a risk ... Additional concern was the fear of how we would fare with the long freezing night as we moved away from the pole with no fuel.

In spite of all those shortages and fears, I remember those months on the lunar pole as the nicest of my life on the Moon. We set up the canvas tent brought from Earth exactly on the lunar pole, so that the Dragon constellation was exactly above our heads where the Moon's polar star shone. Frankly speaking we saw this star, which was our guide for so long, only once during the sun eclipse as we were about to continue our travel. Here you never see the stars, which are visible day and night from the airless desert, unless the Sun goes behind Earth, and a short night envelops the land of eternal dawn.

We only slept in the tent and spent most of our time under the open sky enjoying the landscape. Although we got used to it, we still enjoyed its mild and poignant charm. Everything there is strangely harmonious and generally tuned up to a very peaceful tone: greenery, pink mountains, pale sky over us, and fresh, cool air saturated with the balsamic scents of those herbs. All of that fills your soul with peace ... and the warm cordiality prevailed in our small group. All the resentments, passions, and misunderstandings were as far away from us as those terrible deserts traveled, the memory of which still made us shiver.

The time was passing unnoticeably when we were talking for hours about Earth, whose sliver edge we could sometimes spot over the horizon. We remembered our dear friends now sleeping in those silent desert graves. We guessed at the unknown future ahead of us and about the baby which was about to arrive. We were talking about the lands we were about to see and about everything else except for one. We never talked about the matter that had almost caused an explosion between Peter and me earlier meaning who Martha would belong to in the future. Strange, but it seems to me that we did not even think about it at that time. At least I didn't. After all, today, years later, when everything has long been decided and done, I can confess to myself ... I loved this woman, I loved her more than I can describe, but it was a strange love ...

When I looked at her delicate and gaunt face, with the ever present half sad half dreamy smile, at her small and pale hands always busy with something, she seemed completely different from that Martha from before. This was not the same beautiful, passionate, confident and sometimes contemptuous woman I once knew. My heart was full of infinite tenderness for this so good and so poor creature. I felt like moving my hand slowly and lightly in her hair and telling her that I was ready to do everything in my power, to give up everything I could ask for myself, just so she would be a little happier and for all of that, out of gratitude, that I could see her.

Such love would be ridiculed on Earth, but when I think about it, it only makes me sad. I see that it would mean nothing to her even if I made the greatest sacrifice I could.

I owe her my life. When I succumbed to that fever at Barrow pass, only her care returned me to health, and today thinking about her keeps me alive. It was a painful thought, but while at the pole, that pain was far away from me. I had no idea how everything would play out, and that's why I can say that it was the nicest period of my life on the Moon. I still had her close to me. When I was ill, she took care of me. When I recovered, we took trips to the valley together looking for snails for dinner or picking up fragrant herbs that she used to ornament the inside of our tent.

When I fully recovered my strength, Peter and I were climbing the mountains to see the Sun and Earth in the sky or peek at the unknown and mysterious lands never seen by people, we would travel on. Martha stayed in the tent because in her condition climbing could be harmful.

During one of such trips to the mountains, Peter showed me the road that had brought us here and told me about the difficulties he had to overcome that mountainous and impenetrable night, having me unconscious and Martha still in pain after losing Thomas.

"There were times when I had to do everything myself," he told me, "and there were moments when I was succumbing to despair. Several times I lost my way among those rocks. On other occasions, I had to back our vehicle from the ravines without an exit and was afraid we would die there. In those moments of doubt, I was comforted by the sight of the barometer, which was rising constantly. A certain hope finally dawned on me as we got to the plain behind Gioja. The Earth astronomers, who picked that name for the mountain, couldn't predict what meaning it would have for us. Who could tell that after all the hardships and suffering, we finally would experience a real joy there?

The night had already brightened. We were so close to the pole, and the light of the sun not hidden deep beneath the horizon or scattered in the dense atmosphere, created a kind of gray twilight, allowing me to distinguish objects. There, I braved leaving the vehicle without a pressure suit for the first time. At first my head spun, since the atmosphere was still thinner, and it was difficult but possible to breathe. I will never forget the feeling of joy that overcame me with my first gulp of lunar air".

Then he told me about the difficulties while traveling through the last range of the mountains separating the Gioja plain from the Polar Land. He couldn't count on Martha's help as she was constantly busy with taking care of me. He had to drive the vehicle by himself on the slope covered with weathered rocks when there was hardly enough light to see anything. Eighty some hours past midnight, he reached the pass from where he had a view of the Polar Land.

"It seemed to me," he said "that I was looking at the promised land. My eyes, already used to wild mountains and deserts, were looking at this vast and green plain. Joy took my breath away, and I felt tears in my eyes. So, through tears, I looked at the dark meadows and the red sun visible from above us although it was still far away from the time of its sunrise on this parallel".

As he was saying that we involuntarily looked towards the Sun. It was lying down on the horizon on the side of this world that used to be our north, but from now on it would be our south. It was already day on that Moon's hemisphere that couldn't be seen from Earth.

Then, for the first time, I was overwhelmed by the desire to learn about the mysterious countries over which the Sun was standing. Coming down the mountain, it was all I could think about, so after returning to the tent, I started making plans for the continued journey.

Peter shared my opinion that we needed to go south towards the middle of the unknown hemisphere:

"We are fine here," he said, "and we could live the rest of our lives here. Though we could have lived better lives on Earth, we came to the Moon to investigate its secrets, and that's what we should do."

Our new expedition was already decided upon, but we weren't leaving yet because of Martha. Waiting for her readiness for further travel, we started our preparations and organized our supplies.

We started by transforming our vehicle since we didn't need such a heavy machine any longer. Originally, we wanted to remove its top half which would make it look like a boat on wheels. However, the thought of arriving at colder areas where we would need its warmth, stopped us from that idea. So, we only removed the rear part as it was originally used for storage and easy to unscrew. We closed the new opening with an aluminum plate, which was used before to protect our storage from the outside. In addition, we removed all metal parts used for reinforcing the walls but not needed anymore. We also fixed the engine that we had taken away from the unlucky Remonger brothers. We would keep it in case ours broke. All this preparation and organizing of the supply of food and water, which had to be squeezed out of the mosses, took us more than three months. Finally, everything was ready.

On the fifth full earth day since our arrival at the polar plain, upon my return from a solitary hiking trip, I heard a baby cry in the tent. No voice would move me as much as this weak cry of a creature that was coming into this world to increase our numbers and cheer us up. Having heard it, I dropped the armful of edible moss I was carrying and rushed into the tent. Pale and tired Martha was lying in bed radiating with joy. She seemed not to notice my arrival as all her attention was devoted to the little creature wrapped in shawls and screaming.

"My Tommy, my Tommy, my beautiful, my beloved! Son!," she was whispering through tears with her weak voice.

At her bedside, both dogs spun around and tried to sniff at that noisy unknown creature. I looked around for Peter and was surprised with his behavior. He was sitting in the corner of the tent grim and wistful, but I didn't have time to think about it then. I rushed to Martha to tell her how happy I was about her baby, that I wanted to bless her for that gift of life, but I couldn't say a word.

I just grabbed her tiny skinny hand and mumbled something unintelligible. She looked at me as if she had just noticed me. I felt a painful prick in my heart because her eyes told me that she was completely indifferent towards me. Sudden sadness overcame me, and she must have noticed it, because she smiled at me as if to diminish the pain, she involuntarily caused me and said:

"Look, Thomas has returned, my, my Thomas…"

I understood at that moment, neither Peter or I could ever win her heart, which would always beat for this child, who she would love not only because he came from her own body and her own blood, but her dead lover's soul as well. In silence, I started preparing food and drink for Martha. Peter joined me outside of the tent.

"What do you think about all that?," he asked me. I didn't know how to answer him,

"Oh, well, Thomas's son arrived…", I muttered after a while.

"Yes, Thomas's son", Peter repeated and became thoughtful.

I didn't want to ask him about anything as I knew what he was thinking.

After that, as if to avoid a touchy subject, we only talked about the upcoming travel. Since Martha was quickly regaining her strength and little Thomas was doing fine, we decided to set off before the first Earth quarter. It was the best time, as the day would be starting on the middle parallel and we would have two weeks of light ahead of us. If we didn't find better living conditions there, we would have enough time to return to the Polar Land.

Meanwhile, two weeks since Tommy's birth, we experienced our first new Earth rising, and then our second Sun eclipse on the Moon. We saw Earth rising over the desert, but we were overwhelmed by the fear of death and didn't even pay attention to it. Now, we wanted to take better advantage of the opportunity to study it. So, we packed our astronomical tools in a small cart pulled by the dogs and climbed the hill that was the closest to the pole where we could see both Earth and the Sun.

The show was spectacular, but our studies didn't fare so well. The low position of Earth above the horizon made taking exact measurements impossible and interfered with our observations. That's why a few minutes after the Sun hid behind Earth's disc, we dropped our tools in favor of admiring the enchanted play of light in the sky. We were looking at Earth surrounded by a huge, black half circle. The wide sky around it darkened further and became spread with stars. It seemed as if the glow of a great fire was dancing on the night's horizon, or like a twinkling polar light that glows on Earth near the poles, somehow with great effort transferred itself here and then grew stiff and froze in front of us.

To this day, I have an indelible memory of this sight. It seemed I was looking at the blackened corpse of Earth. There was something terrible and bothering about it. Today, when I think of Earth, it stands before my eyes in such a terrible black form. That is how I saw it at the time, and I have to strain my imagination to present it as a silver shining disc.

I couldn't bear this unusually wonderful but painful sight any longer, and I turned my gaze to the stars that I had not seen for several months. They glowed all over my head and sparkled as they sometimes did on Earth on winter nights. I looked at them with affection, like seeing a good old friend. I searched for constellations known to me since childhood and asked them in my thoughts what was happening on my native globe, the one now lying in front of me like slag on a fiery glow.

I suddenly noticed that the stars were getting darker. I rubbed my eyes thinking that my tears shaded my view, but it didn't help, as the stars were getting less and less visible. Peter noticed it too. We were concerned as we couldn't understand the reason of this phenomena. Meanwhile the stars continued to dim, and the dawn in that place where the Sun had gone behind Earth, was becoming less and less clear and even looked blurry. A few minutes later a starless night enveloped us, and only some reddish light was left on the south side of the sky. At the same time, we felt a strong blast of wind that we hadn't experienced in this area before. Startled, we didn't dare to make a move.

Finally, the eclipse ended, and the Sun peaked out from behind the circle of Earth. We figured it was just the returning day, because despite the brightness we could see neither the sun nor the area. Everything was sinking in a thick, milky white fog.

Now, we understood it all. There are no clouds and no rain in the Polar Land because the air is always evenly heated, so there is no reason for evaporation. This is true in normal conditions but during the eclipse, a sudden cooling happened creating wind and condensation of the steam.

Such a natural explanation of this unexpected phenomena calmed us down, but our situation was quite vexing. We were very cold but couldn't even dream of finding our way to our tent in the valley in that fog. I was also worried about Martha, but nothing could be done. We just had to sit down and wait for the fog to clear.

Surely enough, the fog started rising soon. In half an hour, we could already see our valley and only the peaks of higher mountains were still enveloped by the fog. It was obvious that the rain was coming so without wasting any time, we started down our hill. Before descending half the distance, lightning flashed over us, and the resulting thunder was accompanied by a deluge. In a few seconds we were soaked to the skin. We couldn't see a thing through the stream of water pouring from the heaven and lightning and thunder never stopped.

It lasted for two hours, through which, cold and wet, we cuddled with the dogs under some protruding rocky outcropping though it gave us only weak protection. As soon as the rain stopped, we immediately ventured back on the road. However, we barely looked out from our shelter when we stopped, terrified of the view that unfolded before us. The green valley at our feet was replaced by a wide lake.

My first thought was what happened to Martha and her baby. The site of our tent was probably flooded. I ran towards the lake not minding Peter's attempts to stop me. Having reached the water, I started fording. It wasn't deep at first, but soon the water reached my waist. I hesitated for a moment not sure whether to keep going or go back. It gave Peter an opportunity to jump in the water, grab my hand and make me return to the shore.

My situation was horrible. The dreadful worry about Martha's fate covered my forehead with droplets of sweat, but I had to admit that Peter was right. I would risk my life fording through the lake, but it wouldn't help her at all.

"If Martha noticed the flood in time" he said "and climbed up the hill, she doesn't need our help. We will have enough time to find her when the water settles down, but if she didn't, it is too late to help her."

He was saying it calmly but with some cruel tone which gave me shivers. I looked into his eyes, and I seemed to read in them a horrible jealous thought: "Let her die, if she were to be yours ever …".

"All the same," I shouted "I will still go to help them."

"Go." He answered and sat quietly at the shore.

I really wanted to go, but it is easier said than done. Where could I go? Could I go to the middle of that lake and look for them under water?

Desperate and angry, I sat next to Peter, and started staring at the water stubbornly. Here and there broken branches of mosses floated on its surface, even though it was even and smooth; no breeze rippled the surface. I was thinking, how could so much water be poured out of the atmosphere in such a short time … and how much time would pass before this sea would dry up, and we could look for the corpses of our companion and her baby. I was sure they perished, when I suddenly noticed that all those branches were heading rather fast in one direction. They were obviously carried by a current that meant that the water had found an outlet from the valley. That realization made me incredibly happy as it also meant that we wouldn't have to wait very long for the water to recede. To make sure that I was right, I ran along the shore in the direction of the current.

After a few kilometers, I came to a bay I was able to ford. Soon I was certain that there was an outlet. I could see higher spots emerging from the water like flat green islands.

All this made the view extremely beautiful and interesting, especially since the smooth glass of water among the green islands reflected the faces of the coastal bald mountains illuminated pink again by the sun. At that time, however, thinking only about Martha, I paid little attention to the landscape. Perhaps then, for the first time, I realized how much I cared about this woman, and how devastating her death would be for me ... I couldn't come to grips with such a dreadful thought. I couldn't imagine how she could have saved herself, but deep in my soul I harbored the desperate hope that she was still alive. So, I ran forward faster as if her rescue depended on my reaching that outlet sooner than later!

I was too excited to think logically. Only one thought dominated my actions. I couldn't live without that woman and, although not mine, that child. Nothing else matters, and I would give up having her for myself, if that could save her ... Who knows, perhaps fate eavesdrops on us and our pledges sometimes ...

Twelve hours had passed since I left Peter when I was stopped by a river created by the water flowing through a wide gorge we had not discovered before. Not knowing what to do, I sat down at the shore exhausted and hungry.

Now I realized the pointlessness of racing. Discouraged, I lied down on the still wet moss and without will or thoughts was staring at the sky. It was as peaceful and pale as before that menacing sun eclipse.

Suddenly I heard someone calling my name. I jumped to my feet listening carefully. I heard that voice again more clearly now. It was coming from the other side of the river flooded gorge, and that was where I saw Martha with the baby in her arms. I saw her signaling to me, and I became so filled with joy that disregarding the danger, I forded across and was soon standing next to her. The joy was choking my voice, so I started kissing her hands, and she wasn't resisting the flood of my emotions.

"My friend, my good, dear friend," her pale but already smiling lips kept repeating.

When we both calmed down a little, she started telling me what happened to her. When she noticed the water coming into the tent, she grabbed the baby and the most precious things from the tent and carried them to our vehicle standing nearby. That saved her as the tightly closed vehicle, much lighter now, could float on the top of rising waters. Like Noah's ark, it was drifting on those waves in the stormy harshness of lightning and thunder, and just like the ark, it saved humans from death.

Martha was still not out of the woods yet. Not being able to steer that improvised boat, she was hostage to the waves and winds carrying her towards the unknown. Her fright was multiplied by her fear about our fate and the anxiety in trying to guess the outcome of it all. When the rain stopped, and the waters stopped rising, she noticed that the vehicle was following a certain direction. She guessed that it was being carried by the current of the water flowing away, but that scared her even more. Carried to whatever outlet, the vehicle might fall into a crevice or at best be trapped in a remote area, so that it would be difficult for us to find it.

Martha felt some relief after several hours, when she noticed some hills emerging from the receding water, and she tried to steer her boat to one of them but couldn't. She could already hear the water that was escaping through the gorge. She expected that the vehicle and she would be carried to an unknown land, when luckily the vehicle stopped at a cape formed from a protruding rock above the outlet of the gorge. She took advantage of that opportunity, opened a window, and threw a line at a boulder, securing the vehicle from being carried further by the current. I arrived when the danger was over since the water had receded enough for the vehicle to rest on a dry spot. A score of hours later, only small puddles looking like glass panes were left among the greenery of the valley. We waited a while for Peter to find us. The dogs found my trail. Upon arrival, he checked us out with suspicion but without a word, he started examining the rescued supplies and tools in the vehicle. He is a strange person! I have lived with him for eleven earth years, but in several circumstances, I cannot evaluate his character correctly. It is a mix of courage, sacrifice and firmness with passion, tendency to selfishness, envy, secrecy and dispirited. I know for sure that he can be unpredictable.

The catastrophe caused us a lot of damage. We lost many needed things forever and had to search for others in the vast valley. At first, we couldn't find our tent carried away by the water. We were lucky to have stored most of our stuff in the vehicle during our preparations for traveling. The flood also happened to be advantageous to us as the direction of flowing water showed us the way south that we would follow.

Our rationale was quite simple. If the water disappeared so quickly, it meant that the gorge was leading towards lower areas where we could most probably find a big reservoir of water like a lake or even a sea. Such areas would be sprinkled with rain, so it would surely have life.

We were ready well ahead of the planned departure time. Our vehicle was ready and waiting at the very outlet of the gorge that opened itself to us like a gate for a new world. Now, we had to start the engine with the help of batteries that were charged when we still had fire.

We even explored a large distance along the way into the gorge on foot. It was not a beaten track, especially since the last waters carved deep trenches in places. Still one could go without risking extraordinary hardships. We were just waiting for the right time to follow the waters that flowed south to the unknown land of strange wonders, and whose nights are never exposed to the silver ring of Earth illuminating the deserts.

II

We left forty hours before the beginning of Earths' first quarter. It was still night on the unknown hemisphere of the Moon we were heading for, but the Sun was about to shine over those lands soon.

We were leaving the polar land with sadness and anxiety. We came to know it, and knew what we could expect from it, but everything ahead of us was a mystery and a supposition. We would be exposed to long days of the burning sun and endless nights of frost. We would travel again through gorges, mountains and perhaps deserts on the way to a land we knew nothing about, and we didn't know if it would embrace and sustain us. We were seriously worried about the lack of fuel and afraid that we would drain the batteries before we found something for starting a fire and could charge them again! Would we manage to return to the Polar Land before the night, so much more dangerous for us now since we wouldn't have fire to protect ourselves from the cold? Soon after we set off, we wanted to return to this moss-covered polar meadow and spend the rest of our lives there. We knew that we could be warm in those weak scattered sun rays and eat those raw snails and lichen. The hesitation didn't last long however as curiosity and hope won out. The food supply would last us for a long time. We also took some pressed peat with us hoping to be able to sufficiently dry it in the sunlight and use it to start a fire. Besides, in the worst case, we planned to return to the Polar Land after running out of half the batteries charge.

Nothing interesting happened in the first several dozen hours. The gorge ended and we traveled through a plain like the polar one but much bigger. We saw traces of a recent flood on it. Here and there vast, shallow puddles glistened in the rays of the rising sun. We were surprised to find different flora although we were only a few dozen kilometers away from the pole. The lichens we already knew were much scarcer than the ones on the pole and had a sallow color. Among them some dry stalks protruded from the ground, sparsely scattered and curled in a spiral like young fern leaves. The chill was strong after the night, which these regions already had. We guessed that since the sun was only a few degrees below the horizon, it would be like dusk. We were warming ourselves rubbing our hands when Martha had a bright idea to break some of those stalks and try to start a fire with them.

We got busy right away, but to my surprise, the first stalk I grabbed started first to open and then shrink like a live creature. I dropped it with an involuntary cry of fear. Having recovered from that first impression, I started to examine those peculiar plants. I cut one of them with a knife and saw that it had big, elongated, and fleshy leaves. They were doubly rolled up, first curled then looking like a snail. They resembled English tobacco rolls with brown outer shells built from tiny woody scales.

The light green inside was covered with scattered numerous pink veins. The whole plant, while alive, was endowed with the ability to move, as did our mimosa. What interested me the most, however, was that all these curled leaves were much warmer than their surroundings. Apparently, their body, generated a great amount of heat through some chemo-biological processes, which it lacked during long nights. All that was very interesting, but our hope for starting a fire vanished. We were looking longingly at the red sun waiting for its weak rays to warm up that area.

Besides our concern about cold, a new problem surfaced. We didn't know which road to choose. Our plan was to follow the direction of the flowing water, but it was difficult to recognize on the completely flooded plain. While we were wondering what to do, Peter noticed a big white object not far away. Curious, we went towards it and found our tent which the flood carried to a small hill. Its recovery made us doubly happy. First, it was our only tent, and we needed it. Second, finding it there helped us to figure out the direction the waters had flowed. The tent got here through the gorge that we had just traveled through, and so by line of sight from the outlet of the gorge to the place we found it, indicated the direction of the current of the flowing water. This line ran across the plane to the south with a slight diversion to the west. Moving in that direction, we found a narrow and curved mountain gorge. Then, after passing a small dale, we arrived at a broad green valley stretched straight towards the south. Both its sides were lined with high mountain ranges with craters sticking out from their slopes like the ones we had encountered on the airless lunar hemisphere. The peaks of those mountains were covered with snow which must have fallen at night and could still be seen in some places of the valley. The

Sun's rays, slightly higher above the horizon, were melting the snow there and changed it into fast running and curvy streams. We decided to stop in that valley for some time to avoid traveling so early in the severe cold in those areas with a greater difference between the average day and night temperatures.

When we started again, the sun had already covered a third of its daily travel. It was warm and bright. The snow in the valley had completely disappeared. Those rolled up stalks which prevailed here over lichen, started to quickly bloom under the solar heat. We were looking at huge, different shades of green painted leaves. They had various shapes. Some looked like huge fans finished with moving fringe. Others were mottled with various colors, among which red and dark blue prevailed, and they resembled some fabulous peacock feathers. There were those that had edges cut into the form of an acanthus leaf and bristling with spikes. Others curled at the bottom to form funnels. Some were smooth and shiny or covered with long, yellow-green hair, falling on both sides down to the ground. All those various shapes were alive, agilely writhing at the slightest touch. The bank of the stream was covered with long algae looking like rusty green snakes with snow white rings hanging from them and dispersing a powerful intoxicating scent. In other places, where the water spread more broadly and the current stopped, delicate eyelashes developed on the algae in the form of balls, in which they survived the frost of the night, covering the current with a fleeting and trembling mesh, similar to the finest lace of violet and green silk.

We were enchanted by the amazing splendor of those plants. With every step, something new and interesting caught our attention. Strange creatures resembling long lizards but with one eye and many legs started to emerge from the thicket. They were staring at us with interest but scurried away when our vehicle got closer. The dogs chased one of them and caught it, but when we took it away from them, the animal was already dead, so we could only examine its carcass, so different from earth animals. Its skeleton was limited to a big ring built of moving vertebrae placed on both sides under the skin. The skull was made of strong jaws, the brain was under its back inside the ring. What we believed to be legs were really two rows of elastic boneless tentacles with which the animal crawled along the ground at unusual speed.

Much later we found more amazing creatures on the Moon, but none interested us as much as these first examples of this local fauna. By and large, our whole travel through that valley was like an enchanted dream full of fantastic images. Hours passed quickly filled with looking at the constantly changing views. In some places, the valley narrowed, creating rocky inlets. We had to struggle through the banks of the stream, which has already grown into a large humming river. Again, we entered the extensive, circular plains where the deep water poured into wide lakes with thicket overgrown banks or sandy ones. We saw more and more animals. Deep waters were filled with all kinds of small monsters and there were flying lizards in the air which looked like birds with thick necks and long tails. Strange, that all those animals on the Moon were mute. There are no countless voices of life like those sounds among earthly meadows and forests. Only when the wind blows, the rustle of huge leaves of local plants and the murmur of the stream interrupt the perpetual solitude.

The lush vegetation was hindering our moving forward. We had to stop every now and then to free the axles of our wheels from branches. We weren't happy about those delays, as we also had to stop either to check out the environment or to search for food or fuel. Our dogs helped us a lot with locating fleshy plants or tasty mollusks, but fuel was still a big problem. The peat collected in the Polar Land dried and burnt well, but we had to save it as we didn't bring a big supply. We couldn't find anything else that could help us with making fire in the future. There are no trees here and those broad leaves are so juicy that they boil instead of burning. That issue worried us a lot, as we left the peat areas far behind us. The lunar noon was approaching, and we had to decide if we were to move on or return to the Polar Land before the night. We were leaning towards the second choice. Martha was pushing for returning, being afraid of the impact of the night frost on the baby, and she had my support, but Peter firmly resisted.

"Returning now", he said "would equal a life sentence in that polar area. Now, when our batteries are still charged, and we can make it back, but what then? If we ever wanted to travel to other areas of the Moon, how will we charge these batteries again without a fire?"

"But traveling south doesn't help us with anything.", I observed. "We'll only expose ourselves to the night frost, and we may not survive without fire …"

"We might find fuel before the night …"

"We might not find it either."

"Yes, it is an assumption, but we know it for sure that we will never find it on the pole. We have some peat left. We can survive with what we have and spend the next day searching"

We couldn't refute Peter's arguments, so we moved towards the equator. A dozen hours past noon, the sky filled with clouds and heavy rain followed. It was very welcome as it refreshed the hot and muggy air. As soon as it ended and the sun peaked from behind the clouds, we heard a strong murmur.

First, we thought it was an overflowing stream, but we soon discovered the reason for this phenomenon. We were just in the place, where the upper valley, collapsing westward, formed a knee so we couldn't see the rest of it. However, when we got to the bend, a wide and magnificent view opened to us.

A few hundred feet ahead of us, the valley suddenly ended and was falling with wide slopes towards an endless plain stretching till the end of the horizon. The stream was rolling down through those terraces with foamy cascades, creating ponds on each of them until it reached the last of them at the level of the plain and flew through it with a curved silver ribbon disappearing somewhere far, far away. Everywhere we looked, we saw the even and flat land, except for the foothills of the bordering mountains. There we could see scarce ringed hills looking like goblets filled with water. We saw more of these small lakes on the whole plain where silver streams or even rivers were slithering among them.

We stepped out of the vehicle. And standing on the edge of the terrace, we were silently looking at that strange land ahead of us. Martha spoke first:

"Let's go there. It's so beautiful there! ..."

Indeed, the view was beautiful, but will it be good for us? We were asking ourselves this question, preparing for the descent down the steep slopes to the plain below.

As soon as we got there, we left our vehicle on a bank of a stream and went to search for some combustible material. We went all the way in and out in a radius of several kilometers, we dug deep pits in the soil hoping to find some peat or a vein of coal. We picked various plants, trying to see if they could be used as fuel, but all in vain. The Sun was to set in a dozen of hours, when exhausted and discouraged, we stopped further search and experiments.

Our situation was very unpleasant, and we started regretting our frivolous departure from the Polar Land. We were afraid of the approaching night. We had very little peat and had to use it very sparingly to make it last the whole night. When we checked our supply, we only had a handful of it to fill our small mobile heater for the whole night.

"But we will all freeze, heating so economically!" Martha yelled, when we showed her the prepared portions. Peter shrugged his shoulders:

"Burning more, we will freeze for sure when the peat is finished. We just have to cover ourselves better"

110

"Why have we left the Polar Land, Martha lamented, "Tommy won't survive the cold, such a poor little baby."

"Ah! Tommy!" Peter whispered dismissively through his teeth.

I noticed then that each mention of the baby irritated him beyond words. It upset me in two ways. First, I fell in love with the delightful child. Second, I was upset for Martha. With her love and devotion to her son, she felt hurt by Peter's dislike of the infant. On several occasions, I saw her looking at him with reproach and instinctive apprehension. I also noticed that she never left the child with Peter when she had to do something, but she often trusted him to me.

"Tommy isn't the most important person here" Peter kept muttering, "so even if he froze to …

Martha usually endured such comments in silence, but this time she jumped to her feet and jumped to Peter with sparkling eyes.

"Listen, you", she shouted in muffled voice, "Tommy is the most important person here, and he won't freeze to death, because I will kill you first and use your bones for fuel!"

Saying that, she flashed a small Indian dagger which probably had a poisoned tip, before his eyes. We had no clue she had such weapon on her. Peter backed off involuntarily. He tried to smile, but the Malabar's voice and eyes were filled with such a scary inexorable threat that he paled and struggled to cover up his abashment.

I laughed loudly though with constraint to appease the situation.

"Martha cares for her little boy, no doubt about it", I shouted. "Peter let's go and think how to protect ourselves form the night freeze without sacrificing our bones!"

I had a simple plan. We dug a big deep hole to fit our vehicle in and after rolling it in there, we covered its top with frozen leaves and dirt. All that would protect it from losing too much warmth, and it would be easier to heat.

The sun had already set before we finished that job, but we didn't want to go back to our vehicle just yet. After a long day, the air outside was warm and pleasant. The wide, red evening dawn was still illuminating the plain with its lakes glistening like goblets of live silver, or if you looked under the dawn, they would look like filled with blood.

We sat together on a hill near our vehicle but didn't feel like talking. The last incident had an impact on everybody. After a few loosely made comments, we fell silent. The silence was only broken by the noise of nearby cascades and Martha's singing her doleful Indian songs to her baby. I listened to this song thoughtfully, looking at the lake's glass like surface that was dying out in the darkness when Peter's light shout interrupted my musings. I looked at him with a question, and he stretched his arm toward the plain:

"Look, look!"

Something lively was happening there. As the sky darkened, Earth grew brighter. At first, a handful of small, blue sparks scattered over the banks of a stream. Later, more and more sparks appeared; flashed to the right, to the left, in front of us, everywhere. Half an hour later the whole plain was glowing, as if overcast with a cloud of bluish, starry fog. The lakes looked like black spots on it. Martha stopped singing and was looking at this magic view with us.

Only sometime later I found out that all this was caused by the phosphorescence of those strange leafy plants that covered a large area here. Their inside surface glistened like rotted wood in our forests.

It didn't last long. We hardly had enough time to enjoy that unusual view, when the lights started disappearing one by one. The chill made the leaves close and roll for a two-week sleep. Abundant dew started falling, and it was time for us to hide in our well secured vehicle.

The night was freezing but we fared quite well thanks to our supplies of peat and additional protection. We didn't leave the vehicle, even for a minute, so as not to lose any heat. We couldn't look through the windows and see what was going on around us because of the tight cover of dirt and weeds. So, for two weeks we were completely cut off from the world.

When our calendar clocks showed it was time for sunrise, I dared to step out. To protect myself from the cold, I put on my pressure suit because its thick material had enough insulation. After leaving the vehicle, I found out that such precaution was more than necessary.

Having looked at the plain in the first moments of the sunrise, I couldn't recognize it. A thick layer of snow sparkling with the frost covered the whole world. The lakes were partly lost under the snow and partly shone with frosted ice panes. It seemed to me that I was suddenly transferred to some Arctic country.

I returned quickly inside with the news that we shouldn't go outside yet. The winter made us gloomy as the supply of peat was almost depleted. We didn't have to suffer the cold as much during this night, as we would for three more earth days while we waited for the beginning of the day, or "spring", and making do without a fire. After seventy hours of struggle with the frost, the Sun finally won.

The melted snow streamed down, the lakes emerged from the shore, and all the streams were rising. When we finally emerged and looked at the dripping plain, we saw that the huge, multiform leaves had already unfolded into the sun. Only the tops of the mountains were still covered by a white shroud.

We had to postpone further travel until the ground would dry a little. Meanwhile we started looking for a source of fuel. During one of such excursions undertaken in all possible directions, we encountered one of the pits we dug out during the previous lunar day with the hope of finding peat or coal. It was completely filled with water now. I passed it indifferently, but Peter stopped by it as if struck by something unusual and started staring at it. I had already walked further away when Peter's voice reached me:

"Jan!," he called gesturing to me to return, "Come, come quickly and look!"

I found him kneeling and supporting himself with one arm on the edge of the pit and gesturing to me with the other. His face showed emotion as bent over the pit.

"What has happened?" I called.

Instead of an answer, he used his palm to draw some of the water which had a peculiar, dirty yellow color and let me smell it.

"Petroleum!", I shouted with joy smelling the familiar sharp smell.

Peter nodded with a triumph smile. To make sure that it wasn't an illusion, I soaked my handkerchief in the liquid and put a match to it. It burst into a bright red flame, and we both looked at it like at a rainbow heralding a new life to us.

We rushed to Martha to share the good news with her.

Finding the source of petroleum was a tremendous event for us. Now, we could either travel further south or remain there without the fear of freezing nights or lack of cooked food. We devoted a few scores of hours to collect as much as possible of that blessed liquid. We dug a few more deep holes and before noon collected the oil into all possible containers we could find. Then we held a council about what to do next. Remaining near the oil sources would be the most practical decision, but we couldn't resist the temptation of moving further towards the sea that shouldn't be too far away. Besides curiosity, our other motivation for the travel, was the fact that on the coast the climate would be significantly milder due to the influence of a large water reservoir and less subjected to daytime fluctuations, even though would be closer to the equator. We had a sufficient supply of the fuel to even make this one a test trip. We were sure that, in the event of finding unfavorable circumstances there, we could easily return to the petroleum sources, if we followed our path back upstream.

We spent that day and the next night in the same location on the Plain of Lakes as we named that area. We postponed our travel till the next day in a belief that it would be easier for us to have more than three hundred hours of sun ahead of us during which we wouldn't have to interrupt our travel on account of the night and great frost. As soon as the first daylight made the snow blush, we left without waiting for the sunrise even though the frost was still aggravating.

The morning found us, or perhaps better said, spring floods found us almost one hundred kilometers away from where we departed six Earth weeks earlier. First, the thaws worried us a lot because the softened ground made traveling on it next to impossible. However, soon enough, we remembered that we had an ability to change our vehicle into a ship after substituting the wheels with special paddles and attaching a special steering device. Since then, floods were not a problem but rather an advantage, as we could travel on the waves of a swollen stream. It was a lucky turn of events, as the stream became the thread that would lead us to the sea. We were also saving the fuel, as the fast current was carrying us so quickly that we didn't need to use those paddles to make us move faster.

We spent the whole lunar day on those waves only seldom docking either to rest or to explore an interesting area near the shores. Before the flooding was over, we got so far that the stream changed into a big river deep enough for our tiny ship.

The sights and character of the landscape constantly changed along the way as we traveled. For some time, we sailed among the vast and apparently, quite dry savanah covered with small and fragile vegetation, very unlike the magnificent deciduous shrubs growing above the stream. There was something extremely sad about the monotonous view of this area.

We left the ringed hills, filled with water up to their edges, far behind us. We also passed among some heaving hills with rocky edged round lakes slightly raised above the level of the water we floated upon. We continued our travel along rusty green plains on both sides. Only scarcely it was interrupted with either small meadows of tiny violet like flowers or yellow sand bars on slight elevations. The river spilled wide and was flowing very slowly so we had to use the paddles to speed up the movement of our ship.

It was already past noon when we approached a range of rocky hills closing that savanah from the south. Here the river was narrowed by rocks on both its sides and sailing on it was becoming more dangerous. The current often grabbed us and knocked the ship against rocky pilings, but thanks to the strong structure of the missile now changed into a ship, we survived.

Soon after passing through that narrow gate, the river spilled into a big lake. Its shores were created by small hills, covered with abundant plant life and interrupted by numerous bays, resulting in one of the most pleasant views we had come across on the Moon.

We hardly sailed onto the lake, when suddenly the clear sky was covered with dark clouds. First, we welcomed that change, as we were fed up with the unbearable heat, but soon we started to worry, sensing an approaching storm. First, there was a distant, powerful thunder, and then the sky in the south was brightened frequently with bloody lightnings. We barely had enough time to turn towards shore and hide in a small bay, hidden by hills, when the storm started raging for real.

I knew of tropical storms on Earth, but I couldn't imagine anything as monstrous as this storm. Deafening thunder merged into one constant roar, lightning constantly flashed before our eyes, like the strings of a fiery harp densely strung between the sky and the ground. Rain...no! It wasn't rain! The flood of water falling from the clouds changed the whole atmosphere into a hanging lake torn by furious winds.

The air, mixed with the rain and the waves splashing under the wind, was so saturated with electricity that it sometimes flashed on its own, and then there was a fiery, hellish spectacle before our eyes. Under the blood colored clouds, there was an atmosphere made of transparent fire, full of drops as big as a fist, similar to dripping melted metal.

The storm sometimes calmed down suddenly, and the clouds moved away opening the view of blue sky and the sun. However, after giving us a break, the sky darkened again and attacked like a scary hurricane, bringing more roaring thunder and water splashing down from the clouds.

It lasted close to forty hours. We tied the ship to some roots, sticking out from the shore, to protect it from being thrown to the middle of the lake where wind and waves would have its way with it. Tired, scared, and confused, we were looking at that nasty struggle of fire, water, and air.

At last, everything became silent, and the sky brightened, and only swollen streams splashed among the hills, bloating the still rocking surface of the lake.

The waters rose quickly. We had to wait more than twenty hours for them to subside enough to make further travel possible. We were sailing much faster now since the current of the swollen river increased significantly. On the way, we saw massive traces of havoc everywhere: whole areas of dirt washed away, strange huge plants earlier creating thick forests were lying down now torn into shreds. Cascades of murky water were spurting from every crevice. There were shallow puddles on the plains with gatherings of various reptile like animals around them.

Today, since we have finally become used to living on the Moon, we know that such fierce storms are virtually an everyday phenomenon. They happen because of the incredible heat in the afternoon, and they are a blessing to this world despite their horror. They refresh the atmosphere and the drying ground, and if it wasn't for them, life would be impossible here.

I won't be describing our afternoon travel as it continued without interruptions. The landscape was constantly changing, and so did the plants. However, it's worth mentioning that due to the lack of climate zones, the flora here is much more monotonous than on Earth.

It was almost evening when we reached the place where the river slowed down, and started spilling wide and created numerous sand bars, making sailing extremely difficult. We realized that meant its estuary was close.

"We'll see the sea." We were saying as we turned our eyes toward the sun, as if to make sure that we would have enough daylight to reach that longed for destination. Meanwhile, sailing was becoming more and more difficult. After getting stranded on those sand bars several times, we decided to convert the ship back into our land vehicle and continue our travel.

The sunset found us at the foot of a low, barely covered with grass-like sand dunes. We sensed that the sea was close behind them. We even seemed to hear the great muffled crash of waves and almost feel the sharp smell of sea water in the air. That is why, impatient, we didn't stop our journey despite the falling night.

When we finally got to the top of those sand dunes, the darkness thickened so much that although we strained our eyes to see the sea, we couldn't tell what we were looking at. We only saw a glimmering surface covered with creepy phosphorescent plants. One could hear some gibbering and something like the sound of gushing water from the east. Everything was enveloped in thick white mists or vapors, drifting like ghosts, roaming over the luminous meadows. When we were pondering, whether we should spend the night on that elevation or descend, a wind suddenly picked up and dispelled the vapors. Then, in front of us, we saw a small creek dripping down rocky ledges into small pools arranged into rows of stairs. We saw it only for a moment as a thick mist covered it all again, and we could only hear splashing and gibbering. We were wondering about the unusual density of that mist, so we proceeded towards those pools. Soon we found ourselves in a thick warm fog. The wheels of our vehicle were now clanging on the rocks.

When the wind dispelled the fog again, we saw that we were close to the edge of one of the pools. A warm and moist whiff dabbed at our faces.

"Hot!," Springs!," both Varadol and I cried simultaneously.

Indeed, there must have been hot springs nearby because the water, flowing away in a stream and spilling over the pools, was some twenty-plus degrees Celsius. The dark was not the time to explore the area, so we decided to take advantage of our good fortune and spend a frosty night over this water, which would provide us with a significant amount of heat.

That night was rather restless. Four earth days after the sunset, it snowed heavily and frosty wind was so strong that to protect ourselves from the cold, we pushed our vehicle onto the warm water of the pool. The darkness was impenetrable. Only at times, when the wind dispelled the constantly rising vapors over the water, we could see the shining stars over us.

Then, in the south, a wide strip of blue light appeared along the edges of the horizon. We were surprised by this phenomenon, because it did not disappear for some time into the night, unlike the phosphorescent plants that had folded their blooms long ago. That interesting glow dimmed only well after midnight when the frost, far away from these springs, must have been extremely strong.

Before it happened, something else concerned us. Around midnight we felt a strong turbulence that was accompanied by a deafening ground thunder. Almost simultaneously, we noticed through the fog in the east a growing bloody blaze. It went out a few hours later only to fire up again. It repeated like that with small breaks for four earth days. It was like a scary hellish ghost appearing in the foggy night over the snowy desert.

The temperature of the water, swirling in the pool with the ground shakes, rose enough for us to complain more of the heat than of the cold. While, observing that disquieting or even scary phenomenon, we guessed that there was a volcano whose eruption we were observing. The presence of such hot springs was also typical for volcanic areas. The approaching day confirmed our speculations. At first, in spite of the daylight, we couldn't see much as we were still in the lake waiting for the temperature to rise, and the fog obstructed our view. Only forty hours after the sunrise, we docked our vehicle on a stony shore and were able to step outside. We took a few steps in the fog and then suddenly, as if with the rise of a magic curtain, a wide view opened up before us.

We stopped dead in our tracks, filled with wonder and joy. A dozen or so meters below, at a distance of two to three kilometers from the place where we were standing, there it was - the sea. Its waves, glowing with tiny creatures, kept shining long into the night through fog and shadows. Now, we could see it clearly. Boundless, still frozen at the shore, but wavy and busy a little further out, the sun-gilded surface stretched from our feet to beyond the horizon.

In the first moments, we were so enchanted with that longed-for view, that we couldn't take our eyes away from it. Only after some time, having filled our eyes with this kind of majestic view never seen since our leaving Earth, we started checking out our surroundings. From the west, among the vast plains, there was a glistening wide-spread river on whose waves we made the greater part of our trip the previous day. Its estuary was interrupted here by numerous bars of sand. From the east, the landscape was extremely wild and varied. It was dominated by the skyrocketing snow covered tip of the volcano no further than a few scores of kilometers away from us. It was surrounded by rocky hills whose slopes, headed towards the sea, were covered with thick forests. Those forests were made of nicely tangled deciduous shrubs and vines, which were just waking up from night sleep to life. Closer to us, gushing among numerous fantastically piled up boulders and small smoking lakes, enveloped in a cloud of white fog, there were the geysers. The brook, flowing away from them, was jumping onto the terraces, swaggering in the pools, and dripping down the boulders lower again, until it finally got lost among the thicket of bushes while heading for the sea.

This was to be the end of our odyssey.

III

Ten earth years have passed since our arrival at the seashore where we are still living today. Little has changed since then. The sea is roaring as it did then, and every night it shines with the same sparkling waves. The eruptions of the volcano O'Tamor, named by us in memory of our dear friend, repeat from time to time. The geysers spout in the same way and so does the brook murmur on the stones. The only difference is a house on stilts over one of the pools that we use as our winter home. There is also a hut near the seashore that we use as our summer place. Four children are playing, collecting shells, and picking flowers or playing with the dogs born here on the Moon. We have gotten used to this world and we are not surprised by the long freezing nights or the days with the lazily crawling sun breathing fire on us. We are not scared by the terrible afternoon storms regularly visiting us every seven hundred and nine hours. We look without surprise at the wild fantastic landscape and plants different from those on Earth. We accept the monstrous but clumsy animals as well known and natural … On the other hand, Earth, in our memories, has become something of a dream that has passed and left behind, only an elusive and full of longing, dreamy trail in our memory.

We sometimes sit at the seashore and talk about it for long, long hours … We are telling stories about short Earth days, about forests, birds, people, and countries in which they live, and about a lot of other important things, not something fantastic and heard of only in fairy tales. Tom is already quite big and intelligent, and he listens to all this as if listening to a fairy tale. He has never been to Earth …

In the end, we have crafted a quite comfortable life for ourselves here. At the foot of O'Tamor, we found a creeping plant whose thick and strong roots are a good material which can substitute for wood. Big leaves, dried and cleaned of woody scales, strong and durable, replace leather, and we use fibers of other plants to weave a thick and soft cloth. After long searching, we found a lode of brown coal on the plain behind the river. We also found sources of oil much closer to us than the first ones. There is an abundance of iron, silver, copper, sulfur, and calcium here. The sea supplies us with a multitude of useful shells and red amber.

We fish for food in the sea full of varied edible mollusks and other creatures looking like a mix between fish and lizards which are tasty and nutritious. Besides that, we find eggs in the sand or in the bushes. None of the local creatures are born alive. They all lay eggs very resistant to frost but begin hatching fast in the heat of the sun. We also make tasty and nutritious dishes from several types of abundant plants here. In the beginning, we missed meat, but we have gotten used to it now. All animals here have leathery and stinking meat, so we don't eat it, but the dogs aren't so picky.

It took us several lunar days to become domesticated. We started with finding a building material and fuel. Then we built a house on stilts made from strong roots. We built the winter house in the same hot springs pond where we spent our first night here. After completing those most important projects, we started taking long trips on foot to explore our surroundings. The dogs, which are our only working animals here, pulled the cart with tools. The only lunar animals that we breed are big, winged lizards, laying big and tasty eggs.

We sometimes went sailing along the seashores. The west coast is flat and sandy, but in the east, there are numerous capes formed from volcanic mountains, separated by deep bays, cutting far into the country from the shoreline. We benefited from almost every such trip whether by water or land. We found something new that could be useful to us, or we learned more about this area and its secrets where we would live in until death.

After thirteen lunar days, or one Earth year of our living at this seashore, we knew its surroundings well enough, and we had built much more than just a house. We had a workshop, a small steelwork, warehouse, a dog barn, pretty much everything that we needed to live here. The period of feverish, strenuous activity ended and boredom and a longing for the abandoned Earth descended slowly upon us. These were terrible times for us. I remember we couldn't cope. During the day we explored the area, wandering around the mountains, or dealt with fairly easy food gathering, but in the long nights we were overwhelmed with despair. Locked in a small house above the surface of a warm pond, idle and lazy, we just tried to sleep as much as possible.

However, we didn't always succeed. During those times, we sat silent, bored, and longing, obsessed and unfriendly to each other. One of the most undoubted truths is that nothing deters people towards each other as much as suffering and boredom. Unfortunately, I had the opportunity to observe it several times.

It was possible to take care of this and that, make some improvements, think about the future, but the thought that we were all sentenced to extinction here made us unable to do anything. People on Earth don't even know that they work not only for themselves but also for those who will come after them. Man wants to live, that's all. Meanwhile, the inexorable death stands before his eyes. If he hadn't found a way to deceive it, or maybe only himself, I do not believe that any thought other than this terrible and paralyzing one: 'I will die," could figure in his head! There are various medicines: there is faith in the immortality of the soul, there is faith in the immortality of humans and human deeds... Man extends his own existence with his deeds, because if he sometimes thinks about time, when he is no longer around, he imagines that there will still be a trace of his work. Then, in his own thoughts, he becomes present in that which his eyes won't see. But for this he needs to know that there will be people after him who, if they do not mention his name, at least, without knowing it, will use his work. This is a necessary condition for his deeds to have life. Human deeds are like people: they live or die. A deed that causes no change in anyone's consciousness is dead. Such observations are simple and natural, but I only came to such conclusions on the Moon during those long, idle and hopeless days in the beginning of our life by the sea.

I sometimes thought it would be good to investigate the borders of this great water, travel around this land, check out its mountains and rivers, make maps, write about the plants and animals here, but then a thought would stop me. Whom will it serve? Indeed, who would benefit from this, I thought, to whom would I tell what I would learn, to whom would I leave what I was writing? Tom? Little Tom will die in the same way as I will, though a little later, but it won't change anything. He will be the last human in this world where we are now. Everything will end with him ...

This awareness had a paralyzing impact on all my present actions and my great plans for the future like building a stronger house, starting new workshops, gardens, a zoo or just improving the quality of our life.

Then Peter and I decided that we had to give a start to new people here, and we looked at Martha. I try to excuse myself for that today because I know it was a crime and selfishness. At the time I knew it, but ... but ... Man - wants to live, at any price and whatever, but live - that's all! There was something terrible in our resolution, especially since it was sober and cold, at least in my case ...

I became attached to Martha with a great but quiet and affectionate love, but the time when I coveted her for myself, for my senses and for happiness, was long gone, and I thought it would never come back. I didn't even know why it'd passed ... I sometimes think that since I had gotten to genuinely love her, I also knew that she did not love me and would never love me. She would always love the dead one who was reborn in her son.

No, I didn't think about Martha then but mostly about children, about little girls who would grow up and whom Tom could marry when they grow up giving a beginning to new people. I was dreaming about it like the biggest happiness, and so all our work wouldn't be for nothing. New generations that would live could use the fruit of our labor and our discoveries.

I won't say that those dreams were not personal at all. On the contrary, in thinking about the children, I involuntarily imagined them to be my children. Imagining their happy smiling faces, I saw in them a quiet and good Martha, my Martha... These were exhausting and painful dreams because they seemed to me so impossible to come true....

Then I reproached myself again. After all, considering this lunar world, inhospitable and not suited for people ... What will be the fate of these future people, recklessly created by us, just for giving our lives a purpose and meaning? I knew the conditions on this globe well enough to understand that people would never develop here in the same way as on Earth. Man will always be a visitor and an intruder here who came uninvited, and...too late. Yes, it is too late. After all, the Moon is a withering globe.

Looking at the life occupying such a small part of the surface of this globe, at the plants, seemingly magnificent and lush but much less vital than those on Earth, and those strange, dwarfed and clumsy animals, I cannot stop myself from thinking that I am looking at the magnificence of a sunset. Life here has stopped in its development. It is mature or even overripe and waiting for its end. So here, nature, having worked incomparably more than ours on Earth, for the Moon, (as the smaller of the two had cooled first and thus became the first "world"), hadn't managed to evolve an intelligent creature. Even if it did, its time has irrevocably passed. It is the best proof that this globe isn't fit for such creatures. Man will always feel miserable and cramped here.

I often had such reflections. Since for people, feeling is always stronger than the abstract thought, I wished with all my heart that people would come after us. I was sometimes deceiving myself and trying to disguise this selfish yearning I was telling myself that I wanted people to save Tom from that most horrible fate of being the last very lonely person. No, that wasn't true. I wanted that new generation for myself.

I don't know what Peter was thinking, feeling or reasoning, but I am sure he was overcome by the same desire. It was quite a long time before we started talking to each other about it. I remember somehow, it was around the sunset. Martha, with Tom in her arms, went towards the hot springs, and we were sitting in silence on the seashore.

Peter was watching her for some time, and then he started counting the lunar days we had lived.

"Twenty-third sunset," he finally said.

"Yes," I answered thoughtlessly." Twenty-third, if we count the days spent on the pole although we didn't have sunsets there.

"And what next?," asked Peter. I shrugged my shoulders:

"Nothing. A dozen and some sunsets or several dozen or several hundred and it will be over. Tom will be left alone.

"I am not talking about Tom," he said. After a moment, he added: "Anyway, it is bad" We were thinking for a long time, then Peter started again:

"Martha..."

"Oh, yes, Martha," I repeated.

"Do we need to decide something?"

I seemed to hear in his voice that note again, a memory I had from our horrible journey through Mare Frigoris after Woodbell's death. As a silent rebellion surfaced in me, I looked him in the eye and said emphatically:

"We do."

He smiled strangely yet said nothing, and that day, we didn't return to this conversation.

The long night passed in silence and boredom. Tom was a little sickly, and Martha worriedly busied herself only with him. While watching her boundless maternal tenderness, we came up with an obnoxious plan of taking advantage of her love for the child to make her give in to our wishes. Anyway, that empty and boring night convinced us that we had to "decide something".

On the following morning, Peter and I went to the forests at the feet of O'Tamor. During that trip, we finally discussed the matter. One of us would marry Martha, and the other would never get in his way.

"One of us!", I repeated those words with a longing and painful anxiety.

They sounded like a threat in Peter's lips, or so it seemed to me. We were to leave the choice to Martha, but if she completely didn't want to make such a choice, we were to draw lots. Peter insisted that we should leave it to fate right away as Martha wouldn't want to choose, but I firmly objected and made him agree to ask Martha's opinion first. He reluctantly accepted it and finally said 'yes', but he had a mysterious smile on his lips and glitteringly bad flashes in his eyes. After coming home, we waited a long time for a decisive conversation, sure of Martha's objection to our plan. As we waited Peter was walking around, thoughtful and gloomy, pretending to be doing something, while I wandered around at the seashore with a heart full of unexplained fear. That day, the fate of all of us would be settled.

Finally, a stuffy and hot noon came. The sun, shining in the sky for over a hundred and a few score hours, was scorching the whole area with unbearable heat, from which the plants withered, waiting for refreshing rains. Thick clouds were gathering by the sea from the south-east side where the sun had already passed the equator. At small intervals, during which the air hung above us, hardened and heavy, a crazy, short-lived wind rose. It beat the shore with sea waves, disheveled the forests, broke the pearly geyser fountains and howled among the rocks announcing the time for the daily storm.

As usual on such an occasion, we left our summer cottage and moved to a cavern near the geysers that provided good shelter during storms. The three of us were sitting at its entrance. Little Tom was trying to walk holding on to his mother's knees, when Peter looked at me pointedly, and turned to Martha with an expression of a sudden decision.

I felt an increase in my heartbeat along with a choking sensation in my throat. The approach of a storm always had an exciting effect on us. On that day, the effect was doubled by a peculiar irritation, caused by the thought of a close and important conversation with Martha. It affected Peter even more than me. His dilated pupils gleamed uneasily, he was breathing quickly and unevenly, and blood rose to his cheeks. I almost held my breath when he asked her without even the slightest preamble.

"Martha, which of us do you prefer?"

Surprised by this question, Martha looked first at him and then at me in surprise, not understanding what he meant, and shrugged her shoulders with contempt.

Peter repeated:

"Martha, which of us do you prefer?"

His eyes, fixed on her, must have told her more than his question, as she suddenly understood everything. She paled and jumped up from her seat with a slight shout. The knife, she once threatened Peter with, flashed in her hand.

"You two? Neither!," she yelled. Peter made a step towards her.

"Still you have to choose and … make a choice." He said with emphasis.

Her eyes fluttered in silent despair and filled with terror. It seemed to me that for a moment, for a short fleeting moment, her gaze stopped on my face with a pleading hesitation or thought, but no, I must have imagined it, because a moment later, she defensively raised her hand with the dagger, and said firmly:

"I won't be choosing, and I am curious which of you will dare to come close to me! I want neither of you!"

I remember that again it seemed to me, her last word somehow softened on her lips, and her eyes met mine, but it was an illusion, no doubt. I was so excited then…Holy God! I wanted to believe that it was only an illusion!

When Martha got up, Tom sat on the ground, and now he was watching the whole scene with an interest. Peter touched his head, and Martha noticed it.

"Stay away!," she yelled with fear. "Stay away! Don't touch him. He is mine!"

Peter didn't budge. Still touching the boy's head, he was persistently looking at Martha with a sneer.

"What will happen to Tom?," he finally asked. Martha hesitated.

"With Tom? What will happen to Tom?," she repeated almost unwittingly.

"Oh, yes, when we die, and he will be left alone ..."

Those words struck her like a lightning. Her eyes opened widely as if she suddenly saw an abyss she hadn't seen before. She sighed deeply and sat down feeling weak.

"Yes, what will happen to Tom ...", she was repeating in whisper looking at the child with helpless despair.

Then Peter started to explain to her, that she had to choose one of us for the love of Tom. Would she want to sentence her beloved son to a horribly lonely death, and before that, an even more horrible lonely life? What will he do with himself after our death? Abandoned, sad, wild, he will wander alone through these mountains and on this seashore. He will be the only person on this globe, and he will be thinking about the only certain thing, his death.

The time will come when he will curse his mother for giving him such a life. Since he will have nobody to talk to, he will forget how to speak. He will be losing the words learned from us, one by one. Maybe he will finally remember the last few useless words whose sounds will caress him for a long time, though they will probably be terrible words expressing terror, loneliness, abandonment, and sadness. Nobody will soothe his despair and nobody will help him in need. If he gets sick, only the phantom hunger of death will be sitting at his bedside. Then, even the dogs, happier than him, will leave him. They will be happy because they will be able to procreate. They will leave him when he is not able to give orders. Perhaps one, that was his companion and friend, will stay longer with him, and even howl with morning at his death. Then the other dogs will return to feast on the still warm body of the last man on the Moon.

He continued like that for a while and painting a picture of all the horrors Tom will face after our deaths, and I, Oh! Help me God! I was helping him with tormenting her, and I was convincing her that she should pick one of us for Tom's sake.

Martha was listening to all this without a word, and only her face reflected surprise at first and after that: fear, despair, depression and finally resignation.

The first distant thunders of the approaching storm could be heard from the south. Martha was sitting silent. When we finally finished, and Peter asked her if she agreed to marry one of us, she seemed not to hear his question. Only when he repeated it, she budged and lifted her head as if awaken from sleep. She looked at us, and then spoke dully pronouncing her words with difficulty:

"I know you don't care about Tom, but it doesn't matter … You are right … I will do … everything … for him …" She sighed spasmodically and went silent.

"Bravo" Peter exclaimed. "It is wise! And so," bending towards her, "which of us do you prefer?"

I was standing on the side looking at Martha. She stepped back involuntarily as if with sudden disgust, but she controlled it and looked at us. And again, again, for the third time, it seemed to me that her gaze stopped at me for a moment. There was the look of a poor doe surrounded by dogs, asking for mercy.

All the blood rushed from my distressed heart to my brain, and Peter must have noticed it too because he suddenly paled and turned to me with a ferocious look on his face.   At this moment, Martha burst into tears. She was crying violently as if a dam, stopping her from crying before, was suddenly breached. Throwing herself to the ground, she started lamenting with despair:

"Thomas! My Thomas! My good, beloved Thomas!" She was calling the dead as if he could save her from the living.

Peter snorted impatiently. "No point in talking or waiting," he said. "Let's draw lots."

I wanted to protest. I felt terrible and almost claustrophobic. Clouds covered half of the sky and dazzling lightnings were flying over the sea. Tommy, seeing his mother crying, started crying as well.

I made a step towards Martha.

"Martha…"

"Martha", I repeated touching her shoulder lightly.

"Go away! Go away!," she yelled "you are both disgusting!" …

"Let's draw lots," urged Peter.

I looked behind. He was standing behind me holding a handkerchief in a closed palm.

"The one who draws the knot will get her." He nodded with his head at Martha still lying on the ground. Something scary was happening to me. There was a strange clarity in my head, I was even calm, but I was short of breath. I felt as if a whole mountain fell on my chest. I was looking at the two corners of the handkerchief sticking out from Peter's hand. First, I noticed a slightly torn hem ... Then, I remembered another scene on Mare Imbrium, where we were also going to draw lots - then for death ... now ... for love!

Peter was getting impatient.

"Draw!," he yelled.

I looked at him. His face was crookedly contorted with eyes fixed on me. I understood it all. If I draw the knot, I will have to kill this man right away otherwise he will kill me. I involuntarily put my hand into my pocket looking for my gun. However, at that moment, I thought what would happen if Peter was the lucky one. What would happen then? Will I have enough strength to give up the beloved woman, knowing that a stupid knot would decide it for me? Wouldn't I revolt against it?

Drops of sweat covered my forehead. If only I knew that Martha preferred me, that she had at least more heart for me than for Peter I wouldn't leave it to fate ...

But now ... Didn't she say a moment ago that we were both disgusting? Both of us! Should I force myself upon her and also kill a man... or should I bow my head to chance before ...

I looked at Martha. She stopped crying and was sitting quietly and looking at the distant sea as if not being aware of our close presence. I felt a terrible, bottomless and painful pity overcome me for this woman.

It all lasted only a second, but I was already involuntarily putting my hand in my jacket and touching the handle of my gun. My eyes moved wildly among the four of us including Tommy and picking the one to kill first.

However, it all soon passed. After a moment of a tremendous tension, everything relaxed in me. Only indifference and pride remained. I released my grip on the gun.

"Draw!," hissed Peter with a choked voice.

"No!" I answered with a sudden resolve.

"What?"

"We won't be drawing lots."

He still couldn't understand. He slipped his hand quickly into his pocket, and I heard the sound of the revolver being cocked. So, I was right. He was prepared. As fast as a lightning I grabbed both his hands. He bent and curled up in my iron grip with horror in his eyes.

I heard Martha's piercing scream. First, I seemed to hear something like joy in it, but I immediately realized that she might be scared of Peter. I looked at him. He was looking down with a powerless, desperate fury. It looked like he was expecting death. I smiled and shook my head.

"No. Not this. You can take her," I said and let go of him.

First, he was dumbfounded with amazement. He looked at me hazily, and then he smiled forcefully:

"You are very noble. Yes, thank you ... Admittedly, I am younger, then it is right ... But," he lowered his voice here "can you promise that you'll never ... never ...?"

He pointed at Martha with his head again. I looked him in the eye.

"Yes, I know, I don't need to... Thank you, you are ...," he said quickly.

I felt indescribable revulsion. Peter hesitated for a moment, but he soon turned away and went towards Martha. I looked at her as well, and our eyes met again, but now hers were full of bottomless contempt or hatred, I couldn't tell which. She turned away when she realized I was looking at her.

"Martha, I am to be your husband," said Peter.

"I know that," she answered with a complete indifference.

"Martha ..."

"What?"

"The storm is approaching ..."

"I see it ..."

Peter sighed nervously.

"Come. Let's hide in the cavern."

An awful animal excitement was smoldering in his eyes. His tightened jaws made it difficult to speak, and he was shivering like he had a fever.

I didn't dare to look at Martha. I heard her muffled, indifferent voice:

"Okay. I am coming."

Peter hesitated again:

"Martha, first give me your dagger."

She threw it on the stones with a loud sound and without looking back entered the cavern. Peter picked Tom up and ran after her into the cavern.

At that moment, a blinding lightning flashed across the black sky and a deafening prolonged roar of thunder echoed to announce the beginning of the storm. Heavy rain began to fall cooling the parched and dried soil.

My head spun then, and I fell to the ground bursting into a terrible non-manly sobbing. Constant thunder was roaring over me, and the whole world was obscured by the raging storm. This is how we made our life on the Moon.

IV

Then my life alone started. My relationship with Peter was never cordial. Now, I couldn't make myself behave in the same way as before towards Martha. Something happened between us, some kind of two-sided regret and shame … I don't know. She also changed unrecognizable. She got thin, pale and less beautiful. She seemed to avoid me and was always withdrawn. She spent hours and hours only with Tom. Only his presence made her face light up with a smile of happiness. Her son was everything for her, and she only thought about him. She often sat him on her lap and caressed him long and with passion or told him various strange stories he was too young to understand. She told him about the Earth left behind, far, far away in the sky, about his father in a grave on a dreadful desert, and about herself…

Peter was very jealous. He was averse to the child before, and now he sometimes looked at him with such an expression that I was afraid he could hurt him. He was jealous about me as well, although I avoided giving him any reasons for that. In the beginning I wouldn't be alone with Martha and didn't talk to her a lot in his presence either. Still, each time I said a word to her, I felt his anxious and predatory eyes on me.

My life and Martha's life were hard, but he was possibly the most unhappy among the three of us. At least Martha could find comfort in her child. While I had the noble, though poor, satisfaction of making a voluntary sacrifice, he, tormented by jealousy and desire for a woman wholly indifferent to him, didn't have any support. I involuntarily separated myself from him. Martha, though always agreeable and submissive to his wishes, always let him feel that he was only a tool for providing her son with human companionship on the Moon. I never heard her speak warmly to him when he was kissing her hand or face. She didn't protest, but she was sitting frigid and apathetic and only her eyes were sometimes showing weariness and … disgust.

Still, he loved her in his own way and did whatever he could to force her reciprocity, as if something like that was possible. There were times when he threatened her and tried to show his dominance, but then she looked at him calmly, indifferent, not afraid, but didn't want to object. She did what he ordered without any resistance but without a smile, in the same way as she did when he asked her for something. It made him desperate. I saw that he sometimes wanted to cause her rebellion and hatred, just to eliminate this terrible indifference. He bullied Tom, although he didn't dare to do it in my presence. I told him that if he hurt Tom in any way, I would shoot him, and he knew I always had my gun on me, but he hit Tom when I wasn't around. I found out about it much later and only by accident ... Martha didn't say a word or explode, but she just threatened him with the dagger that I returned to her after she had thrown it away. On other occasions, as a last resort, he would fall at her feet and ask for mercy.

I once witnessed such a scene, unnoticed. I was just returning from my solitary trip to some remote springs when approaching home, I first heard Peter's raised voice and then his cry. Martha was sitting on a bench in the garden on a hill. There was an amazing view of the mountains and the sea from there. Peter was lying on the sand at her feet with his hands resting at her knees folded as in prayer, because he was praying. He was praying to her with his face, eyes and his voice.

"Martha," he said, "Martha please have mercy on me! Don't you see what's happening to me? This is terrible! I am crazy about you, and you ... you ..."

"What do you want from me Peter?," she asked after a moment.

"I want your love!"

"You are my husband ..."

"Love me!"

"Ok. I love you"

She said it all slowly, calmly and with such terrible indifference that it gave me shivers.

Peter jumped to his feet:

"Woman! Don't annoy me!," he hissed.

"Ok," I won't be annoying you."

Peter's face pinched in helpless rage, and he grabbed her shoulders with both hands. I involuntarily pulled out the gun. My heart was beating rapidly, but I felt my hand would be steady.

"Do you want to beat me, Peter? Martha asked in the same tone as if she was saying: "Do you want to have some water?"

"Yes, I will beat you, murder you until ... until ..."

"Ok", beat me Peter ..." He moaned and staggered as if drunk."

I approached them to put a stop to this horrible scene.

Martha's constant sadness and Peter's terrible internal struggle were very unpleasant and depressing, and they both avoided me for different reasons. For those reasons, I spent the long lunar days in a total solitude, and I slowly got used to it. Anyway, I could think of the future and fill the emptiness and boredom that I voluntarily condemned myself to. Indeed, I imagined the marriage of "one" of us with Martha quite differently. I dreamed of some serene, quiet, but still full of longing sadness. I visualized a new, hearty union, long conversations conducted in hushed voices. Our life would be filled, with care and happiness and comfort, for those who are to come after us. So even though reality all these beautiful dreams seemed completely destroyed, it still gave me a priceless treasure to indulge in them: hope for a new generation.

I already loved those unborn children even if they wouldn't be mine. For them, I was gathering supplies, exploring the area, and making observations. For them, I dusted off and organized the small collection of books brought from Earth. I also made bricks and burned lime to build a brick house and a small astronomical observatory. I smelted iron from ore or forged different household objects from the abundant silver here. I even made paper and glass and other materials needed for civilized people. I was so happy with the idea of those children yet to be born! I believed that their arrival would definitely change things for the better. I hoped that their smile and babbling would finally dispel the stuffy atmosphere we lived in.

I didn't wait too long. In less than a year, Martha gave birth to twin girls. They were born at night. I was sitting with Tom in another room when I heard their weak cries. I jumped to my feet with a crazy joy. At the same time a pain, so terrible and so insatiable, squeezed my heart, that I began to bite my fingers to suppress the sobs, but tears rolled down my cheeks.

Tom was looking at me with surprise listening to the noises heard from the other room.

"Uncle," he finally said to me. "Uncle, what is crying there, is it Mother?"

"No, child. This is not your Mom's cry, but a little baby is crying there, similar to you but much smaller."

Tom made a serious face and started thinking.

"Where is the child from? What for?" He asked again.

I didn't know how to answer him, and he was watching me closely.

"Uncle why are you crying?," he suddenly asked.

Indeed, why was I crying?

"Because I am stupid." I answered peevishly.

The child nodded his head with an unusual seriousness.

"It is not true! I know that Uncle isn't stupid. Mother didn't say so. She said that Uncle is good, very good, only … only …"

"Only what? What did your Mother tell you?"

"I forgot."

The door opened at that moment, and Peter stood in the doorway. He was pale and emotional. He smiled at me bitterly but sincerely, for the first time in a year, and said,"

"Two daughters …," and he added right away:

"Jan, please, Martha wanted you to bring Tom in."

I went in the room where the patient was lying. Seeing her son, she stretched her arms to him.

"Tom! Come here and look! You have two little sisters, two at once! They are for you! You will forgive me, won't you? Forgive me … But they're for you, my dearest, only, beloved son!" She was saying in a broken voice, pressing him to her chest.

Tom thought about it for a moment.

"Mom, what will I do with these sisters?"

"Whatever you want, my darling. You will beat them, love them, scratch them, hug them, anything that you like. And they will listen to you and work for you when they grow up, you see?"

"Martha! What are you saying!," shouted Peter. "Martha, they are my children!"

She looked at him coldly:

I know Peter; they are your children …"

Peter made a move as if he wanted to pounce at her but controlled it, and coming closer to the bed, he said as softly as he could.

"Martha, they are our children. Don't you have anything else to say to me? Nothing? …"

"Sure. Thank you."

Then she resumed caressing and excitedly kissing her son's fair head: "My Tom, my beloved, golden son …"

Peter ran out mad, and I felt difficulty breathing. There was something monstrous in such exclusive mother's love.

Contrary to our expectations, the birth of those two baby girls, Lili and Rose didn't change our lives that much. Peter and Martha's relationship stayed the same. I felt compassion for Martha before, but now, I also felt deep sorrow over this man's fate.

He grew gloomy and each of his words showed tremendous, utter tiredness and depression. Younger by a few years than me, he stooped and turned gray. His sunken eyes burned with an unhealthy glow. I would never have thought that just a year of life would manage to break this inexhaustible body, which managed to victoriously survive, better than the rest of us, the incredible hardships of traveling through the desert. Although Martha was the cause of it, I couldn't blame her … She loved the first one who died. Besides him and his son, there was no room in her heart for anybody else, and that's the whole tragedy.

I think she didn't love her daughters, either. She took good care of them, but it was obvious that she was doing it for Tom's sake. They meant nothing more to her than valuable toys for her son, that shouldn't be damaged. She treated them as some rare animals that needed attention and care as losing them would be irrevocable. Even the way she spoke about them confirmed that. She always referred to them as "Tom's girls". Peter looked helpless and became more and more gloomy.

At any rate, the girls caused Martha a lot of trouble and took a lot of her time in their first months of life, so it resulted in my baby-sitting Tom all the time. I gained a companion. The child was very intelligent and mature above his age. He kept asking questions and talking to me like an adult. After some time, I became so attached to him that it was impossible for me to do without his company. During several lonely lunar days, I had got used to constant wandering. I began taking Tom along with me on all of them, even the long ones. Martha entrusted him to me willingly, knowing that he was safe with me, even safer than at home where his stepfather couldn't stand him.

I built a cart and taught our six strong dogs how to pull it. Due to our light weight on the Moon, they could easily transport us from place to place. We sometimes went on trips lasting two or three lunar days. Then because of night frost, I took the tightly covered cart powered by a motor and heated. I rebuilt our vehicle significantly reducing its size. Besides Tom and I, two dogs and considerable supplies of food and fuel could fit in it.

Traveling in this way, Tom and I visited almost all the north coast of the central lunar sea and got so far east and west that we reached the thinning atmosphere closer to the borders of the desert, and we had to back off. Mare Humboldtian, a valley situated almost at the same lunar latitude as Mare Frigoris was the farthest point west we reached. During favorable librations of the Moon, it is sometimes visible from Earth. It can be spotted as a small dark cloud in the very right edge of the top part of its circle.

That's where we saw Earth, emerging from beneath the horizon. I stayed there for a two-week long lunar night to feast my eyes on the view of that, long not seen and much earlier abandoned, native world.

At sunrise Earth was full … (we were on the 90th meridian constituting the western border of the Moon's visible hemisphere). When I saw that glistening, slightly blushed disc and noticed the light contours of Europe moving on it, I was overwhelmed by an unutterable, insurmountable emotion. I couldn't cope with the longing evoked in me by that globe shining in the sky. I felt like Adam must have felt when, after being expelled from paradise, he saw its gold reflection when looking back from afar. I stretched out my hands towards it with an irrational, naive, ominous, but unrestrained desire to get there again, even … after death. However, at the same moment I remembered Earth as I saw it for the last time in the Polar Land. It looked blackened and dead against a background of a bloody conflagration, and suddenly a great sadness came over me.

All misfortunes, all bad sentiment and human vices haunting people for ages, came with us to this previously untroubled globe, including the worst of all suffering – relentless death. Man won't be happy anywhere because he carries the germ of misfortune with him …

Tom's voice interrupted my gloomy reverie. He stood beside me, just awakened from a long sleep, and looked at the unknown, luminous circle in the sky.

"Uncle, what is that?," he finally said pointing with his hand.

"Don't you remember? It is Earth. I told you many times that I would bring you here where we could see it, and show it to you … After all, you saw it when we came here, don't you remember?"

"No, I haven't seen this Earth. The other one was different. It was horned on one side, and this one is round."

"Child, this is the same Earth."

Tom was thinking for a while.

"Uncle …"

"What?"

"I know. It probably has grown or opened in the morning like those big leaves."

I tried to explain to him the reasons for changes in the shape of Earth the best I could. He was listening absentmindedly, obviously not understanding what I was saying. Then he interrupted me again:

"Uncle, and what is this Earth?"

Then I kept telling him perhaps for the hundredth time, that there are mountains, lands and rivers like on the Moon, but they are much more beautiful than here. I told him that there were a lot of houses, built next to each other, which are called cities, and that lots and lots of adults and children lived in those cities. I said we had come to the Moon from there: his mother, and Peter, and also his deceased father, and even those two old dogs, Zagraj and Leda he liked to play with.

When I finished, Tom, listening to my story with a great interest, made a playful face, and said stroking my face:

"I already know this, but now Uncle, stop joking, and tell me the truth, what is this Earth?"

Both dogs were standing next to us and tilting their heads gazing at this shiny circle with interest.

About a dozen or more hours after the sunrise we started on our way back. In the daylight, Earth looked like a gray circular cloud sticking out from behind the horizon.

On another occasion we went on a long trip south. The sea coast, running in a broken line roughly between the fiftieth and sixtieth parallel, then retreats around ninety degrees east lunar latitude towards the equator. It created a few kilometer-wide peninsula or isthmus connecting the lands of the southern hemisphere. I wanted to find out if it was so, and explored along that outcropping, but I couldn't get any further than to the thirtieth parallel. Further south, I was held back by an unbearable climate. Despite close vicinity to the seas, the nights were as freezing as those in the airless hemisphere. During the terrible daytime heat, monstrous hurricane like storms never stopped. The ground was rocky, volcanic and completely bare. There were no plants, no life, nothing, only a dreadful dead desert between two vast seas. Two volcanic islands with two steep peaks often enveloped in a smoke cloud or bloody fire glow were sticking out between them.

There were moments during that trip that made me regret bringing Tom with me as I was afraid, we both might perish. Because of the steep mountains, we were unable to move in the middle of this strip of land. So, we kept to the east coast, where a wide low plain stretched a few hundred meters at the foot of the wild and fantastic rocks. Around noon, the tide caused by the attraction of the sun usually slow here, but quite significant, raised the sea so that its surface was almost level with the coast. Being afraid of this place becoming flooded, I started looking for a higher rock to climb for protection, when suddenly a hurricane like storm arrived. Huge waves started jumping to the shore. One of them hit our cart and threw it a few dozen steps back, straight under a rock promontory. There was no time to lose. After locking our cart very tightly, I attached it to a boulder with a big chain and started climbing up the rocks carrying Tom on my shoulders. It was the greatest fear I had experienced in my life at the time. Clinging to weathered boulders with my legs and one hand, in the other I was holding the little boy trembling with fear. I had a raging, furious, foaming sea right underneath, and a cloud of spitting rain and thunder above us. Fortunately, a rock mass was blocking me from the direct attack of the hurricane, otherwise I would have undoubtedly fallen into the abyss along with the boulders that, ripped off by a whirlwind at the top, were hailing around my head. Our terrible situation was worsened by my increasing concern for our cart that I had left below. If the breakers ripped off the chain and carried the cart away or threw it against the rocks, we wouldn't have a chance of returning home on foot without food and protection from the cold. As soon as I climbed to a safer place, I fastened Tom under a boulder, so the wind wouldn't knock him off and covered him well, and I returned to the cart to fasten it better. After several attempts, I finally managed to drag it into a cleft, where it was protected from the impact of the billows.

Tom and I sat under that boulder for a few hours waiting for the storm to end. The scared child was cuddling up to me and asking through tears why we had come here. I couldn't answer him as I couldn't answer my own question about why we had come to the Moon at all ...

After this experience, I was much more careful on the way back and selected roads more distant from the sea. Still it was the only dangerous situation we faced. All our other expeditions were enjoyable and without such adventures.

We also had a big and strong boat. Peter and I had repaired the motor, the one the unfortunate Remonger brothers were to use, and attached it to the boat to move its propeller. We used that boat for our fishing expeditions, or when I was taking Tom out to sea when it was calm in the morning or afternoon.

During one such trip, I discovered an interesting island whose shape looked very strange from far away. All the other islands I had discovered before, were either volcanoes pushed above the sea, or peaks of the ring mountains flooded with water. As for this one, I immediately thought it looked like the remains of the land swallowed by the sea. It was spacious and fairly flat, and only in the southwestern part of it, there was a range of low mountains crumbled by the eternal action of winds and rains. Its shores were steep and probably eaten by the impact of billows as the sea around it was shallow and full of sand bars, making docking our boat there difficult.

It was a remarkable land and quite different from any other familiar to us. First, I was surprised by its completely different vegetation. Less lush than elsewhere, it had an incomparably greater variety of species. On those few square meters of land, I noticed only three or four bushes familiar to me from other places, and a plenitude of plants I hadn't seen anywhere else at all. However, they were misshapen and dwarfed. Looking at them, I couldn't stop myself from thinking that they were remnants of an extinct generation, pushed out from everywhere else. They survived here miraculously and are proof of life on the Moon many centuries earlier when this area was land, and this sea was somewhere else.

Looking at the animals living on this strange island supported my train of thought. There were not many of them, but they were quite different from all the animals I was familiar with so far. There was something senile about their looks and behavior. Clumsy and dwarfed monsters were crawling out from their dens as we were walking by and looking at me smartly but without fear. Only the dog that I took with me filled them with fear. They were hiding themselves from his assault, half-angry, half-pathetic wheezing, which was the only voice they could make.

As usual, Tom was there with me. He was wondering at everything and kept stopping to look at some colorful pebble or shell, or a fragrant plant whose leaf arrangement resembled those of Earth flowers. I have just walked several steps away from him when I heard his calling me:

"Uncle! Uncle! Come and look at these nice sticks!"

I returned to him and saw that the boy was sitting among long thin bones. I don't know an animal on the Moon with such bones. When I bent down, I noticed a striking object among them. It was a thick piece of copper metal worn out on one side whose shape resembled a wide knife. My heart skipped a beat at this sight. If I was right and this object was made, it meant that intelligent creatures had lived on the Moon long before our arrival …

I remembered the City of the Dead that we saw on Mare Imbrium years ago, memorable because of the accident that caused Woodbell's death. We had rushed away from those rocks that resembled ruins of a place that might have once teemed with life. We never found out if it was a strange work of nature, or a phantom city that had died ages before. Now, I was looking at an object that could be proof that intelligent creatures had lived here long before our arrival.

I started a thorough search. I investigated the whole island along and across and went inside rocky caverns at the feet of a hilly range but found nothing to confirm my theory. Indeed, here and there, I noticed traces of something that could have been a planned labor. At the edge of a pond, I found a few pieces of a fossilized root with traces of cuts, and a dam making the stream pour into a pond seemed to have been artificially built. At another site, boulders were stacked as if on purpose and could be a part of a crumbled wall, but that could also be accidental or done by creative though not intelligent animals. After all, beavers also erect interesting structures on Earth …

Although I didn't solve the most important puzzle, my exploration confirmed my earlier supposition that the island is a remnant of a bigger land that had sank in the sea. As such, it gives us an approximate image of the lunar world and the development of the life on it in ancient times before our civilization.

I named that land Cemetery Island. I often liked to dock there and look from the top of the hill at the sun silvered sea stretching around it and think about the rest of the land that had probably disappeared under it, and life, who knows how strange and how rich?

The peaks of distant volcanoes could be seen from there with the huge dark cone of O'Tamor almost always glowing and dominating over all of them. The sea was lapping, swelling up with the tide towards the sun as it was lazily creeping across the sky. Cradled by its sound, a sound you could associate with the buzz of wings passing over eons or with the sound of a human soul, I was half asleep and half awake. I was dreaming about what had happened here, lost forever perhaps without an intelligent witness …

When did life start here? Did it start when the surface of Earth, suspended in freezing space was beginning to cool, and possibly due to the faster rotation of the lunar mass, the sun moved more briskly over the local lands and seas. It meant lush, waking days and short nights, quickly following one another, without frost and without unbearable heat. So, if Earth wasn't just hanging over that dreadful desert of death, and instead circulated in the lunar sky, rising, and setting … So perhaps then, there was no desert as well, airless and devoid of water? Today, we believe that the Moon was a desert since the beginning of the world, but Thomas had a different theory. This could have been a globe, like ours, before it turned towards Earth for good, and lost air and water as well. Could long centuries of deadness obliterate the traces of past life so much that it changed into a total desert?

I was closing my eyes and imagining that, among the continuous and monotonous sea rumbling, I could hear the sounds of that primary life. Forests made of exuberant and slender trees, that don't need to bend and fold against the night frost, are roaring and swaying in the wind. Huge and strong animals, antecedents of those dwarfed ones, are bursting through the thicket. The wings of powerful flying lizards are flapping in the branches … It is evening and the wind dies down for a moment and a huge, bloody and shiny Earth orb rises above the fogs of the bogs.

Could intelligent eyes be looking at this rising light from the walls and towers of huge cities? Didn't some intelligent beings, when interrupted in their labor, stretch their hands towards it to greet that silver guardian angel brightening those long nights? Who knows, perhaps they were guessing that intelligent creatures were living on that globe suspended in the sky. Did they guess how we looked or lived?

Then involuntarily my imagination turned away from the Moon and like a bird freed from a cage, soared further away, hundreds of thousands of kilometers into the sky, further away to that Earth, beautifully and magically painted by my longing in the same way the sunset paints mountain tops covered by snow.

My dreams on the Cemetery Island were usually interrupted by Tom, exasperated by my long silence. Then we returned home, where Martha was awaiting the boy impatiently, and he didn't belong to me any longer. His mother, heart aching through the long separation, caught him in her arms and after countless passionate hugs and kisses, sat with him on the doorstep and repeated a tale of the young, handsome and good Englishman, his father, whom she had followed to the Moon ... She was telling that story to him, or more to herself, as her hot thick tears kept falling on the child's head.

Peter, broken and gloomy was doing jobs around the house or taking care of his baby girls. Since nobody needed me, I withdrew somewhere to think or keep myself busy with something.

Hour after hour passed, the sun rose and set, earth years, counted with difficulty in lunar days, passed. Tom was growing and the girls were running after him on the meadows, but nothing changed for me. As before, I was wandering across entirely empty land and spending long hours on Cemetery Island. When I came home, I always saw a sad and silent Martha, and Peter resembling a phantom more than a living person. My longing for Earth kept rising in my chest and grew even more with the years until it became an unbearable and overwhelming heaviness. To defend myself against the threat of pain, I focused on thinking about the new generation or kept myself occupied with different jobs. However, whenever I fell to the ground, tired and weary, my longing returned victoriously to show me the pale faces of my companions here and dreams about those I had left forever ...

V

Seven earth years have passed since our arrival on the Moon when Martha realized she was pregnant again. She was awaiting the third baby with impatience, expecting a son that would be Tom's servant. She didn't make her plans a secret and as soon as she had made this discovery, she said to us:

"I can finally be at peace now as I will provide Tom with a servant and slave." She was talking about it with indifference as one speaks about something quite natural, but I heard a more complicated tone in her voice …

It was something like an exultation over such a dearly paid triumph, that it almost ceased to be a triumph. It was more like the sigh of a worker, who throws off a voluntarily carried burden with disgust, but also with joy that he carried it where he had intended and did not fall or didn't drop it earlier.

Peter, completely broken, had calmly given in to Martha's cruelty, wounding him with every word, every deed, so slightly and inexorably, as if she did it unconsciously, being only a tool of some terrible fatality. However, at her words now, he looked at her with dimmed eyes, laughed with irony, and stretched out his hand to Tom. He pulled him closer by his arm and started to examine him. Tom was very mature for his age, but he looked rather frail for his age. Peter pushed up Tom's sleeve and showed tiny arm, slightly slapped the boy's shoulders with his hand, felt his thigh, knocked at his chest, and with his hand on the head of the scared boy, he smiled with a sneer, and with his eyes fixed on Martha, drawling his words, he said:

"Yes, Tom is strong enough to dominate over girls, but his brother could be stronger."

Martha paled and looked anxiously at the boy, but her anxiety didn't last long. In the boy's shiny eyes, she must have seen what all creators of a new order have in theirs, as she smiled and answered:

"Tom will be stronger even if the other one is bigger."

Indeed, even at the age of six, Tom showed a great mental acuity and energy. He was developing very quickly and in a special way somehow different from the development of children there on Earth. He learned to be independent quite early and his practical sense surprised all of us. Unlike Earth children, he didn't show any tendency for daydreaming so typical and charming in Earth children, and a proof of artificial mental exuberance. Tom was serious, so terribly serious, that my heart ached when I looked at that fair-haired head in which thoughts, uninterrupted and not tangled with unruly dreams, flowed in such a calm and tight row, as if under an old man's bald skull. Still, the boy had a good heart. He loved his mother dearly and got attached to me, but he couldn't stand Peter. He was always self-confident and conscious like his father, but in Peter's presence he was apprehensive and perplexed. No, I don't even know if I have an appropriate vocabulary to describe what must have been going on in the child's soul in the presence of his stepfather. He kept silent so stubbornly, that it looked as if he would rather take a beating than open his mouth. His eyes would just shift restlessly. There was some fear in his behavior, but there was obstinacy, ferocity, hatred, and disgust … Peter felt and saw it, and I think even then he was afraid of this strange child.

Martha was right about Tom. He wasn't made for listening to anybody. There was too much of the firm, dominating English spirit and fiery blood of the proud raj's from Travancore. That's why I was sure that if the new baby were a boy, even if he were bigger and stronger than him, it wouldn't matter. He would also follow him everywhere and look humbly into Tom's eyes like the two little girls Lili and Rose.

Tom didn't get a brother, but instead another sister whom we named Ada. Martha greeted her birth without joy or excitement.

"Tom," she said several hours later when following her wish we brought the boy to her bed. "Tom, so you won't have a brother, but you have three sisters instead. They will have to do as your wives, companions and servants …"

This time Tom didn't ask questions, about what he would do with this sister, like he had at the birth of the twins. Instead, he simply looked back at Lili and Rose. The girls were standing there holding their hands and gazing at the boy with eyes full of love and admiration. He lightly touched the tiny, screaming, new creature with his finger and nodding seriously said:

"They will do, Mom, they will do…"

"Tom," I spoke, unpleasantly shaken by Martha's behavior and the boy's answer, "you have to be good to them."

"What for?," he asked naively.

"So, they will love you." I answered.

"They love me anyway …"

"Yes, we love Tom very much." The girls said almost simultaneously.

"See, Tom," I continued in a preacher tone, "they are better than you are because they love you even if you don't always deserve it. But the little one may not love you …"

Tom didn't say anything, but I noticed that he looked at the baby with aversion, frowning. In the end, perhaps it was better that Tom didn't get a brother as he would either be his slave or his enemy.

As I left that room, and later as well, I kept thinking about the awful irony of the human existence which followed us from Earth to the Moon. Then I remembered O'Tamor, poor, noble dreamer! He was dreaming that Martha and Thomas's children, freed from the influence, especially the bad influence of Earth's "civilization" would be the beginning of an ideal generation. Their children would not have the same vices and wouldn't know the differences of such things being the cause of those eternal misfortunes on Earth! I am looking at these children, and I see that old, noble dreamer O'Tamor, forgot that human offspring would always carry in their genetic makeup, the abominations of all earth generations. Isn't it the most terrible irony that man carries his enemy with him even to the stars shining in the sky?

It is good that Tom doesn't have a brother. At least, the period of fratricidal fights and slavery will be delayed, and meanwhile we may die and won't need to worry about it.

And the girls ... It seems to me that the girls were created to be subjects. Quite probably they won't even understand their raw deal. They will be happy when their brother, husband and master will sometimes be kind to them ... I am sure about it as far as Lili and Rose are concerned. Ada is too young yet, three earth years old, to guess her future relationship with her stepbrother. However, I see that she doesn't love him as much as her older sisters. Tom is also more indifferent towards her.

Being involved in the care for the growth and spiritual development of these four children has recently been my nicest, though sad pastime. Physically, they adapted perfectly to the conditions of the lunar world, much better than we did despite so many years spent here. For example, regulating our sleep time is difficult. During a long day, we need almost as much sleep as at night. It makes it very inconvenient for us as we sleep one third of the daylight and don't get a good rest because it is irregular. Then, we stay up two thirds of the night tormented by cold, darkness and boredom so much worse for us than them. The children born here don't sleep more than an hour or two a day with twenty-hour intervals, but then they sleep almost the whole night with only short breaks. A dozen or so hours after sunset, they are overcome by insurmountable drowsiness. If they wake up at night, it is for two to four hours at most, and then they go back to sleep like gophers. They sleep until the first light glow on the sky announces the approaching day.

They also tolerate the local climate much better. Heat waves don't affect them as much as us, meaning they don't become weakened or irritated nor does it make them sleepy. What puzzles me the most is that these children are much more resistant to cold than we are. In the morning, when the intensity of the cold increases the most, the kids awake from their long sleep often run outside and even far away, while we dare to go out only for ultimate necessity.

Tom is always the initiator of those expeditions. Both older girls run outside after him together with old Zagraj, all led by some blind attachment. This dog and these girls are Tom's inseparable courtiers.

I originally thought that the children were running out to play in the snow before it would melt soon after sunrise. However, I soon discovered that the small team led by Tom was going – hunting! It's strange that we hadn't come up with that idea. All the animals here go to sleep at night burrowing in the ground for protection from the frost.

Tom discovered it by himself and with the help of Zagraj's excellent sense of smell, he was searching for the little monsters' hideouts under the snow and killed them before they woke up. As I mentioned before, the meat of the local land animals is useless, but their hides provide us with beautiful and lasting furs or horn material like tortoiseshell. Hunting during the day is difficult because the animals have already learned to distrust both us and the haunting dogs. That's why I was very surprised, when one morning, Tom brought me more than a dozen hides. Some of them were fresh, and others were already thoroughly cured since they came from earlier hunts. The boy saw how we skinned the killed animals, cleaned them with sharp shells and dabbed with salt available in abundance on the seashore, and he did it all on his own, and not any worse than if done by us!

He is very cunning, no doubt about it! At the age of eight, he knew our factories and understood the purpose, meaning and usefulness of all the equipment and material. I took his education upon myself, but he has no interest in books. He is curious about all things which have a practical use and he doesn't care about other things. I wanted to teach him Earth geography, history of its people, and gently introduce him to the works of its writers in a comprehensible way for his age. However, I soon realized that it wasn't interesting for the boy at all as his curiosity went in other directions. At first, I continued teaching him everything, hoping that I would manage to awaken his aesthetic and historical senses, but I gave up those attempts, when during one of such talk he asked me:

"Uncle, why are you telling me all this?"

I didn't know how to answer him as I didn't know why myself … And he asked again:

"Everything that you are telling me is supposedly about the Earth I remember seeing on one trip I took with you. It looked like a big shining cupola, and Uncle, you told me that you supposedly came from there, didn't you?"

"Yes, this is the Earth, the place I came from and where all people came from."

The boy looked at me as if he was hesitant to say what he was thinking, and he finally said with a frown on his face:

"But I don't know if it is all true ..."

I felt hurt by his comment, although it was so natural, coming from a child listening to stories about things happening on a remote planet he'd only seen once.

"Have you ever heard me telling lies?"

"No, no, never!" He denied vividly, but then he added quietly: "But at present I cannot be sure that you are telling me the truth ..."

I pulled a watch out of my pocket.

"Do you know what it is? A watch ... Do you think that Peter, your mother or I can make such a device? You also see the books we don't print, astronomical tools we haven't made. How would they have gotten here if we hadn't brought them with us from Earth? And if we came here from Earth, then we must know how things are there and how they were before."

The boy was pondering over my argument.

"So, I believe you Uncle, but ... why have you come to the Moon if you are telling me that you were happy on Earth?"

"Why have we come here? Well ... You see, we wanted to find out how things are on the Moon."

"Is it true that I will never get to Earth? Yes?"

"No, you will never get there."

"You know, Uncle, perhaps you'd better teach me how to make such watches and magnifying glasses. And don't tell me how to get from a place called Europe to America, or what Alexander the Great did or that other one, Napoleon ..."

I had to silently admit that Tom was right. Since he had never been to Earth and would never go there, why should I be telling him about the things I care about because I have come from Earth. He will have no use for this knowledge. If he or his offspring ever get to the edge of that deadly desert, and they see that shining Earth in the sky, they will have the books we have brought with us to learn about it. Perhaps by that time, they will have heard stories about that distant planet being the mother of all humans, and our books will be more magical for the future inhabitants of the Moon than the Arabian Nights were for us.

After that I decided to teach Tom only what would have a real value for his future life on the Moon. For this he showed an unusual willingness, and he absorbed all such knowledge eagerly if he understood that it could be useful to him. So, for example, at first astronomy did not interest him at all, but after I showed him the practical use of measuring stars, he took to it with enthusiasm.

I am convinced, that if we hadn't brought the books that will remain here after we are gone, the whole summary of this little bit of man's spiritual achievements I wanted to share, would be lost to the next generations. Though undoubtedly gifted enough to understand it, nothing would be preserved through a strangely hard-headed Tom. I still think about the future generations. I wish they would not become wild people. I want to let them know that the human spirit is powerful and that it creates great and beautiful things. They should know that our spirit searches for God in the golden dust of stars and for itself among the tendons and veins of the body. They need to understand that humans are able to ardently desire truth for truth and beauty for beauty, and that desire, is the most effective weapon in the human life struggle with the nature of all that surrounds humanity. They need to learn to value of this spirit and take advantage of its strength ...

I cannot wait to tell Tom about all of it, though he doesn't always want to listen. I felt forced to do it, as if I was afraid there wouldn't be enough time. If I die, if all of us here from Earth die, he will be the only teacher and prophet of the lunar nation, aided by those old books, brought here from the old world by the first people.

When I told him once that he had to be diligent and learn everything, not only what he liked, because he would be a future educator of the new generation, he looked at me with astonished eyes and asked:

"What about you, Uncle, what will you be doing then? You know everything ..."

"I won't be alive then."

"Who will kill you?"

Tom didn't understand that natural death exists. He saw killed animals and killed them himself, but he hasn't seen a dying human yet. Then, I started to explain the necessity for death. He was listening carefully, but he suddenly interrupted me crying out:

"Will Peter die as well?"

"He will die, son, as well as your Mom and I, and you in the end ..."

"Tom shook his head. "I won't die, because ... what would I accomplish by that?"

I laughed involuntarily at his childish comment and told him again that death did not depend on free will, but the boy was absent-minded and apparently thinking about something else. Finally, he spoke in a low and hesitant voice:

"Uncle, if Peter dies, let him die first, the first of us all, let him die soon. We certainly don't need him at all. Then you would stay with us and Mom, and we would be happy ..."

I rebuked the boy for those words telling him that he shouldn't wish death on anyone, especially Peter, the father of his sisters Lili and Rose. Tom was looking gloomy sighed, and then spoke reproachfully:

"Why aren't you the father of my sisters, Uncle? I prefer you and so does Mom ... we don't need Peter."

I felt some of the most secret, deepest yearnings shivering in me, and at the same time I was overcome with fear. Because it was a thought that recently came to my mind more and more often. I can't blame myself: I upheld my decision once made and also persevered at a voluntarily chosen but so ironic position as a teacher of someone else's children. Still I cannot even express my struggles and my sufferings!

Surely, the woman, the only one in this world so dear to me, was still near me. I saw she was unhappy, and I sometimes deluded myself that she could be happier with me. There were days when looking at Peter, I was grabbing the gun handle in my pocket, and others, when I put the barrel in my mouth and my finger on the trigger, when I thought I couldn't bear it anymore ...

But I bore it and endured. I endured it, although blood sometimes obscured my eyes, and spasms gripped my chest. I endured it, though you can't imagine the temptation which would haunt and disturb me in my sleep or awake.

On that memorable day, when we were about to draw lots for Martha, I thought that by renouncing her as a possession, I would calm down and forget over time, but I didn't. Years passed by for nothing, and I wandered away from her for nothing. I was devoting myself to raising Tom and thoughts about the future generations in vain as nothing has changed. She is still as dear to me as she was there in the Polar Land when, after my lucky recovery from that long illness thanks to her, I was walking with her along fragrant dark meadows, talking about trivial but so meaningful things.

My muscles and tendons are still robust and strong, but I am getting old in my spirit, I can feel it. My longing for Earth is deranging my thoughts and the growing sadness engulfs me. I not only look at everything through my tears, but even think about everything through them. Only my love does not want to grow old and weaken in me. On the contrary, it seems to grow with age, along with my increasing and crushing longing. I know I am laughable, but I cannot even laugh at myself.

I sometimes try to sneer. I brutally repeat to myself that I love Martha because she is the only woman on the Moon, and she isn't mine. I try to convince myself that this kind of sublime feeling is nothing more than a primal animalistic drive distorted by the lens of the human spirit or other similar things. Having said it to myself for the hundredth time, my eyes still search for Martha. I feel I could agree to be crucified for her, if only it would bring one happy smile to her lips.

In the desert, or even on another globe, besides animal instincts, man also has a sense of rightness or law. I do not know, if it is the result of upbringing or some kind of inherited spiritual organization. It is certain that it exists and comes alive even there where there is no one else who could point out his silence.

Martha belonged to Peter and I agreed to it. The thought of it, however, kept me from doing anything more than I might have done otherwise. I tried to remove myself from her sight in such a way as to even dismiss a suspicion that I wanted to please her. Besides, she did not look for my company. I even noticed that my presence always made her uncomfortable. All that changed after the birth of the youngest girl when a complete break up between Martha and Peter occurred.

Two lunar days after the birth of the third child, a little bit before the sunset, though it didn't often happen, we were all sitting together and looking at the wide sea. The setting sun gilded its waters, slightly moved by the wind and already starting to phosphoresce in the shadow of the rocks. The snow on the top of O'Tamor was completely bloody from the sun. Dark red reflections were flashing across the smoke cloud hanging above the crater.

The silence was broken by Martha. Without changing her position, without taking her eyes off the distant view of the sea, she began to speak to us, seemingly calm, as always, though I noticed that her voice was trembling at first.

"I committed a great crime," she started, "as I didn't stay faithful to my dead husband and I am willing to repent for it in various incarnations … But you know that I only did it for my son as he lives in him for me. I don't care what you thought or what intentions you had as I only wanted Tom to have sisters and a brother … Although he doesn't have a brother, he has three sisters, and I believe I have fulfilled my duty. You know, Peter, that it was a difficult duty. I pity you Peter because you deluded yourself that you could be somebody else … Not my fault … Now everything is over. I am regaining my freedom. Peter I am not asking if you … would you, want to give it to me. I am taking it for myself. I am not your wife any longer …"

She took a deep breath and went silent. We were so surprised with the words and the unbelievable tone of what she said that we sat in silence for some time, unable to find an answer. Anyway, what answer could we give her if she didn't even wait for one?

"I am taking my freedom. I am not your wife any longer ..."

These words made a strange impression on me. For a moment they rang in my ears like the slogan of a new life, like a promise of something that I didn't even dare to expect, like ... no! I can't say what happened to me then! It seemed to me that this one sentence blurred and destroyed all of the sad things that had passed. I felt a fullness in my chest and the blood flowing more vividly in my veins...

I looked at Martha.

She was sitting still and quiet, staring at the sea, and only under her frozen, very sad smile, her lips quivered as if she was about to start crying.

"I am taking my freedom ..."

That's what her lips were saying a moment ago, but her eyes and smile didn't say that she was taking it like wings to fly, but more like a shroud that would avail her, finally, of peace. Her freedom wouldn't be a dawn announcing new day, but a twilight bringing rest...

Tears glittered on her eyelids, and through those tears she was stubbornly staring at the lunar sea gilded by the sun. My heart tightened with a painful cramp because I understood that you can turn away from the past, but it is impossible to erase it.

Meanwhile Peter spoke dryly: "I don't care." But soon he added:

"What are you going to do now?"

Martha shuddered: "Nothing ... live a little longer for Tom ... for the children ... And then ..."

"For the children," Peter echoed.

Just then both girls ran from the shoreline, laughing, beaming, with aprons full of collected pebbles, shells, and amber. They were calling out to Tom who was just building some water mills on the stream. Peter followed them slowly with his eyes.

"For the children ...," he repeated once more and rested his head on his palm.

I remember that moment like today. The sun was already touching the horizon, and the gold world was starting to turn purple. A slight wind from the sea brought us the bitter smell of seaweed, the murmur of the waves breaking on the gravel and the children's vibrant silvery voices.

Suddenly Martha stood up and turned to Peter.

"Peter, forgive me," she spoke in low, warm voice I hadn't heard for a long time, "forgive me, perhaps ... I was unfair ... forgive me, but I... you see I couldn't, I can't... I regret that you had such a life ... because of me ..." She extended her hand to him. Peter stood up as well, looked at her and then at her extended hand, and then at her face again, and he suddenly burst into a spasmatic laughter.

"Cha, cha, cha! It is very good, in brief, after so many years! Cha! Cha! cha! You want freedom? A good idea! Maybe a new choice? Cha! Cha! Cha! "Peter, forgive me. I am not your wife anymore!"

He laughed like a crazy man and shouted various incomprehensible words. Then he suddenly stopped, turned, and walked home. Martha stood there for a moment, abashed, with her face showing disgust and humiliation, and finally her nerves failed her. She burst into a loud and unceasing crying, for the first time since that storm after which she became Peter's wife.

I walked away in silence, even more depressed than usual.

We spent the long fourteen-day long night almost not speaking to each other. On the second day, everything seemed to have returned to its former mode. We took to the ordinary daily activities in the morning We even talked in the old way, not mentioning "the divorce", which since that evening has become a truly done deal. Martha and Peter's previous relationship was such that, we all felt their break-up was a relief. Especially Martha's disposition changed for the better. I cannot say that she was happier, but at least you couldn't see the earlier heaviness in her demeanor. She talked more freely and was even nicer to Peter, despite his brutal rejection of the heartfelt words she had directed at him.

What was happening to him? This will always remain a puzzle for me. He seemingly accepted it all with indifference. That unexpected explosion, on that day when Martha broke up with him, was the only symptom of his hidden feelings. And yet how much regret, humiliation, pain must have accumulated in this man's passionate soul. What willpower he must have had to exert in order to suppress it all and contain it! Because he loved her in spite of everything, and I had absolutely no doubt that he continued to love her, even then.

The first day after that breakup, he came to me around noon, when I had just returned from a sea trip and tied the boat to a pole on the shore. He was restless for a moment, as if he wanted to tell me something, but he didn't know how to start. Then, as if he had made a sudden decision, he grabbed my arm and said, looking me in the eye:

"Do you remember your promise given to me when I was taking Martha?"

I looked at him in surprise not knowing where he was heading, but he continued:

"You promised me then you would never try to win Martha for yourself, never! Do you remember?"

I nodded in silence, and Peter smiled bitterly.

"Anyhow, do as you please. It is funny. Do as you please, but first ... shoot me in the head." He uttered his last words in a dull voice with so painful passion that made me shiver. I wanted to answer him, calm him down, but he turned without away without waiting and left.

Since then, the most terrible struggles and torments began for me. Martha didn't belong to anyone, but I felt that reaching for her would be a double crime. The first one would be against her as she only desired peace and after dropping her despicable shackles wanted to live the memory of her dead lover and care for her son. The second one would be against Peter. He was so depressed and unhappy that any harm done to him became more than a crime, it would be ignominy. And still there were times and circumstances when I hesitated. I had to implore my entire being not to follow his recommendation and shoot him in the head to start a new life with Martha. Those temptations surfaced whenever I felt Martha's kindness towards me. She often smiled at me and like before and called me her good friend. It inspired my thinking that if it weren't for Peter, we could be happy together. Fortunately, I always managed to get a grip on it.

Then I thought, "Yes, Martha is kind to me because I never stood between her and her memory of the only man she loved. I have never defiled the sanctity of her affection, never touched her body, nor demanded the soul she gave for eternity to that man   who now lies under the sands of Mare Frigoris. But if I desired something else ..." An awfully vicious circle!

However, I came close to committing a crazy act once ... The three of us went on a trip to the top of O'Tamor crater. We left the girls in Tom's care as he could be fully trusted with such a task. We broke through the vines from the side of the sea and passed the overgrown forests of huge, woody foliage. Then, we got to the sloping plain, similar to a large hall, and overgrown with a large-leaved moss flat on the ground. We'd been there many times, but that time we wanted to get higher, to the very top. We wanted to enjoy the wonderful view that we expected to find from the top of the highest cone in the whole area. The further road was not easy, because you had to climb briskly through a deep gully cut into the rocks of frozen and weathered lava and snowed in almost to the edges. Here on the Moon, with our weight decreased six times, it was easier to overcome such an obstacle, but it still required a lot of effort.

After a dozen or so hours of struggling upward, we almost got to the very edge of the crater. However further climbing turned out to be pure impossibility. Above us, the snow was thawing from the hot steam rising steadily from a huge funnel. Its edges looked like a separate wide range of mountains now protruding above us. The dripping water froze in the wind and covered the rocks with a glassy ice coating which was impossible to hold on to.

Seeing that further climbing wasn't possible, we sat on the snow to rest and look around before going back down. It was a fascinating view. Right in front of us, apart from the mass of blackening forests at our feet, the sea stretched forever filled with all the colors of the rainbow and dotted with islands which looked to us like small, black spots among the glowing plane. Some of the bigger ones formed spots hemmed with a colored band like peacock eye feathers. To the left towards west, we saw blackened peaks and rings of smaller craters peeking from behind the protruding ridge. The blue ribbon of the bay, cutting deep in the land, was glittering here and there among them. On the right, behind geysers whose presence was signaled only by small clouds of whitish fog, there was a vast plain. It was cut by a winding river, and in the distance, small lakes leaning against a range of green hills, shone like pearls on a string.

We were sitting there for a while enchanted by that magical view when we were suddenly alarmed by a muffled underground thunder. The steam suspended over the crater blackened and clustered into a huge billow. Soon small and suffocating ash began to fall on us, so it was necessary to go back as soon as possible because it was apparent that the volcano eruption was approaching. However, we didn't leave early enough. We were just in the middle of that gully ending at the meadows near the forest when suddenly with an increased ground noise, the rocks shook. Avalanches began to fall from all sides, and the cloud of previously black smoke was infused with a bloody glow now.

There was no time to think. We quickly found cover in a nearby crevice, shivering and waiting for the moment when we would be able to go down again. The sky above us, covered with thick clouds of smoke, looked like a fiery hell pit. The deafening thunder wasn't stopping at all and the air, saturated with fumes of sulfur and fine ash, choked us and burned our lungs. Larger, hot slag was starting to fall from above covering the snow around us with a multitude of black spots. We had to escape from the gully filled now by the fast-flowing melted snow mixed with the ash and mud.

The eruption was quite powerful and the shaking of the ground we felt must have also stretched far from the foot of that mountain. When the wind scattered the suffocating vapors and clouds of ashes for a moment, we saw the stormy and foaming sea.

Unsure of our health and life, covered somewhat from the top with protruding boulders, we sat for over a dozen of hours attached to a sharp protruding crag in a place where the top of the gully was separated downwards in two directions. Martha was dead worried about the children. Tom was familiar with earthquakes, quite frequent and not too dangerous in these areas, and one could rely on his prudence and reasonableness. However, both Martha and I were worried that in the event of our death the children would be doomed. Peter looked indifferent and calm, or so he pretended.

Finally, everything got calmer. The strong wind from the sea cleared the air and scattered the slowly thinning clouds of smoke. The rain of ash and slag stopped. We breathed more freely and were about to get back on the road home, when we were disturbed by some strange and powerful vibration and hissing above us. Peter jumped out from our shelter to check it out, but he had barely stepped upon a protruding boulder, when he cried out in terror as a roaring lava stream was rushing from above! I saw Peter trying to return to us, but at the same time a hurricane howled in front of that fluid fire. It swept him out from before our eyes, and we didn't know what happened to him.

The unbearable and suffocating heat was blowing towards us. Both gullies were filled with a liquid, red glowing mass, roaring down with monstrous cascades of fire and stone together. There was not a moment to lose. If the spill increased, the lava could cut off our return, filling the lateral cavities between the gullies. It could even crumble and carry away our rock hold like fast currents of raised streams carry small clay islands. So not thinking about Peter, who could have been killed, I grabbed a terrified Martha and started carrying her down on my shoulders trying to hold onto the rugged edges of the ridge.

Even today, I shiver with terror when I remember that descent! The rocks pounded by the lava waves were trembling under my feet while a horrible swelter could roast us alive any moment. Martha fainted and was hanging limply from my shoulder which seriously restrained my movements. I had to be extremely careful not to slip as each misstep meant death.

I cannot tell today what miracle helped me overcome my being half suffocated from heat and blind from hot smoke and lava glow. Stunned with the agonizing rumbling noise and hammered with falling rocks, I somehow managed to get us to the plain where we had started from several scores of hours earlier.

We were saved as the lava flowed somewhere through the woods, turning them into cinder and smoke in an instant. It left a huge free triangle inside, the top of which was a meadow and a ridge protruding above it, and the base was the seacoast, stretching over a thousand meters below us.

I started reviving Martha. When she opened her eyes and saw that we weren't in danger anymore, she started asking about Tom. I calmed her down telling her that Tom would definitely be home and that we would see him in good health when we would get there around noon. Then she stretched her arms to me and like that time when I found her after the flood in the Polar Land, she started repeating:

"My friend, my friend …"

There was something so soft and sweet in her voice that a shiver shook my whole body, and a spasm squeezed my throat. I lowered my face over her so that my eyes would not betray me, and then she took my head in her hands and held her to her chest, saying:

"I owe you not only my life but Tom's life as well, as he still needs us. You are good …"

Her chest was exposed as I had torn her dress neckline when reviving her. I touched that breast with my forehead and felt her tears on my head. A sudden fire started inside me. I had this woman, so beautiful and so desirable and above all, loved, right in front of me. It was enough to reach out, embrace her, cover her with kisses, squeeze her in hugs. Blood shaded my eyes, and my veins pulsed in my ears. I felt the warmth and softness of her body. Her scent intoxicated me, made me dizzy and mad. A thought flashed through my mind, that we were the only people on that globe, as Peter was probably lying dead somewhere among those boulders. After all, why should I care about Peter or about anything else in the world, when she … A calm wave of an unspeakable bliss and ineffable happiness flowed over my whole being.

"No!"

I jerked myself back with all my strength. Perhaps bloodied, half dead, Peter is lying somewhere on the rocks waiting for help, and I …

Martha looked at me and understood.

"You are right," she said as if answering although I didn't say a word, "you are right, go and look for Peter …" Then she stood up and shook my hand.

"Thank you," she whispered.

I found Peter not far from the spot the wind knocked him off. He was lying hooked over a boulder that saved him from rolling down into an abyss of fire. He was unconscious but still alive. I carried him home and Martha and I managed to bring him back to health.

Quite a lot of time has already passed since this accident. Remembering my weakness at that moment, I try even harder to make sure that my will might always dominate over the essence of everything that I am and what creates the human soul.

And Peter? … He often sits silent and gloomy on the doorstep, and I don't know, but perhaps he regrets that he didn't perish on the slopes of O'Tamor.

As for me, everything is finished. Soon even these children won't need me any longer. I started building my grave on the Cemetery Island.

VI

Six days later.

I am looking at my last words written a few lunar days earlier and my eyes fog, not with tears as those dried long ago, but with a burning film of terror and despair. The grave I built on the Cemetery Island wasn't for me.

"Why … why?!"

An eternal, stupid question without an answer! I am left alone. Alone with four children born here but not mine. I am the last man left of those who came to the Moon from Earth. The other two, Martha and Peter, followed O'Tamor, the Remongers, and Woodbell, yet I am alive. This is the fate I was the most afraid of and expected the least.

Imagine, that it all happened so fast! Six lunar days, half of Earth year! Who could have expected it then! And yet for the third time this lazy sun rose above the sea since I buried them. I am alone, so terribly, so awfully alone that I begin to wake up in the dark at night, and during the day, afraid of rustling and shadows that those freaky plants swaying in the wind throw at my feet. Yes, I am alone, as these children aren't my fellow human beings. They are true creatures from another planet.

What would I give to have Martha or even Peter here with me, even a short moment! When Martha fell ill, I didn't have a clue that it all would end so badly. I had seen for a long time that her body was exhausted by everything she had gone through and weakened by her sadness, but that realization was far from me, so far!

Martha wasn't well on the last day. Quieter and more pensive than usual, she was spending time with the children at the seaside. She was playing with Tom and caressing the girls quite surprised by her rarely experienced by them maternal love. Around noon, I went to remind them that it was time to come back to our house on the ponds because a storm was coming. Martha smiled then and repeated several times:

"Time to go back, time to go back …".

All these small details are so vivid in my memory now. They are so insistent that when I write, I have her in front of my eyes, I can see her every move, I hear her voice - and I don't want to believe that I really don't, and that I will never see her again …

Walking home, she picked up the youngest Ada in her arms and asked her if she loved Tom. The child shook her head in denial.

"No. I don't love him."

Martha got sad. "Why don't you love him? Why Adie?"

"Because Tom is not good. Tom wants me to listen to him."

"That's bad," said her mother, "you need to listen to Tom and love him because you are his …"

"No. I am not his. Lili and Rose are Tom's. I am mine."

"I burst into laughter at the child's answer, but tears filled Martha's eyes.

"You cannot be yours, you cannot," she was whispering more to herself, but she still kissed the girl warmly.

In the afternoon, she talked with Tom for a while. She called him to her and was telling him about his father again. For the thousandth time, she was repeating a lot of details that composed a strange fairy tale. It was like a song of praise for the deceased lover. Thomas was a brave and decent man, but in Martha's memory, he became almost a god, an embodiment of everything great, good, and beautiful. Then she admonished Tom to be good to his sisters. It made me wonder as he rarely heard such teachings from her.

Before evening, Martha started to complain about feeling weak, dizziness and aching bones. She usually bore all ailments in silence, so we could only guess from her face that she was missing something. She never said a word to us and never sought compassion or help from us. Even when we asked, sometimes knowing that she looked bad, she would just shake her head and say with a smile:

"There is nothing wrong with me …" or: "It will go away. I won't die yet because Tom still needs me."

That was why her complaint that evening worried me. I looked closer at her and noticed a feverish flush on her cheeks and dark circles under her sunken eyes. They hadn't lost their perpetual shine as the shed tears and the bitter sadness didn't manage to dim them. Still now they were burning with an unhealthy glow quite different from their starry light.

After the sunset, Martha, who had lied down earlier feeling tired, started feeling anxious and dropped onto her bed delirious. You could tell her fever had increased. She was either calling the already sleeping children or was excusing herself in a hardly audible whisper, either to herself or to Thomas's ghost that she must've seen in front of her. She was explaining her life and giving birth to those poor girls and apologizing for loving them when all her love should be his. She believed any sign of love showed to her daughters was harmful to her son and to the memory of his father.

After a while, she calmed down a little. Both Peter and I were sitting at her bed, gloomy and extremely worried. Her illness without any medications made us feel helpless. Martha was looking at us for some time with her eyes wide open, and then she suddenly asked:

"Has the sun set?"

I answered her that yes, the long lunar night had begun.

"Oh, yes!," she said more consciously. "It is dark outside, and here the lights are on… I didn't notice it right away. What is there now on Mare Frigoris, what is there now?"

"There is day there now. It just after sunrise."

"Yes, the sun has risen… and it is shining over Thomas's grave, isn't it? And the same sun from above that grave will come to us in the morning?"

I nodded my head in silence.

"The same sun …" Martha was speaking again. "And just think, that every day, for so many lunar days, the same sun was first looking at the grave and then at me, me alive here, and then it was going back to tell him what it saw here." She covered her eyes with her hands and began to tremble all over her body.

"This is terrible!," she repeated.

Peter grew sullen and dropped his head. It seemed to me that a sudden bloody blush spilled on his yellow and withered face all the way to his furrowed forehead. She must have noticed it as she turned to him:

"Peter, I didn't mean to upset you … now. After all it is not your fault. You wouldn't have forced me to become your wife if I myself hadn't wanted it … for Tom …"

She got silent, taking deep breaths. After a moment she spoke again:

"I would like to live till the morning. It is so terrible to wander in the darkness and look for the road to the desert. When the day comes here, Earth will be shining over Mare Frigoris. I prefer to stand over his grave in its light as I don't know if I could look in the full sunlight …"

"Martha, what are you saying!" I shouted involuntarily. She looked at me and answered briefly:

"I will die."

Around midnight, I really began to worry that she would die. She was tormented by a disease we couldn't even name. We saw only the unusual drop in her strength, which combined with the recurring fever, did not forecast well.

Anyway, it doesn't matter what medical names mean! I know what illness it is. I know it too well. It is called life! It wakes a man of unconsciousness, caresses him, plays, and among the frolics tugs and jerks him, murders, presses, until finally he is overcome and destroyed. We are all born with this disease and there is no medicine for it besides death.

Peter wasn't leaving Martha's bed for a moment. Looking at his gloomy and frozen face, despite my worry about Martha, I was involuntarily wondering over the kind of emotions that could be hiding under that mask. Unfortunately, I didn't have to wait long to find out.

Before sunrise, Martha was very restless, and only the first glimpse of dawn brought her some relief. "I will see the sun again!," she said and tried to smile with her paled lips. Now, I was sitting by her bed alone as Peter, tired after long sleep deprivation, finally listened to my persuasions and went to sleep in the adjacent room. The dawn was pushing through the windows made of thick glass manufactured on the Moon, and the light of the lamp was getting more and more yellow.

The snow lay in the fields as usual, and when the wind blew off some steam, still rising from the hot ponds, a large and shiny surface was visible through the windows. In this sharp and cold glow of the coming day, as the reflection in the snow contrasted with the dying yellow light of the lamp, looking at Martha, I had no doubt that she would leave us forever. She had changed a lot during this two-week long night. Her face lengthened and paled and her lips, once so full, purple and alluring, were already taking on the ashen color of death. Her already dying and extremely sad eyes were looking from under the lowered, almost transparent eyelids coated with a net of small veins. Resting my forehead on the edge of her bed, I was biting my fingers to stop myself from bursting into unmanly tears which were trying to explode in my chest.

Meanwhile it was getting lighter and lighter. The recently gray fog was now passing outside of the windows moved by the wind like light, snow-white spectra. Sometimes its cloud swelled and obscured the world. Sometimes it stretched out into long, airy figures that appeared suddenly, bowed before the window, and moved away again. Then among their strands you could see the white fields and the pearly geysers wrapped in a white cloud. Above them all, against the background of light blue sky, O'Tamor peak was blushing in the first sun rays.

Martha asked about the children, but when I told her that they were still sleeping, she wouldn't let me wake them up.

"Let them sleep," she whispered "I will see them … before the sun rises. Meanwhile, it's good that it is so quiet."

Then she turned to me:

"You will always be their guardian, won't you?"

"Yes, I will.", I answered in a voice choked by tears.

"And you will never leave them?"

"No, I won't."

"Do you swear?"

"Yes, I do." She stretched her hand to me:

"You are good, my friend," she whispered. "I can die in peace knowing that you won't forget them."

I took her hand and pressed it passionately to my lips. Her fingers twitched slightly, as if they wanted to shake my hand. They were so cold that even my hot lips could not warm them.

"I also wanted to tell you before my death," she started after a moment "that I … cared for you. I was reproaching myself for that, maybe even more than for becoming Peter's wife … Perhaps … if I had been yours not his, our life on the Moon would have gone in a totally different direction, I would perhaps live today …"

She was saying all this in a low, expiring voice, but it evoked a storm in me. I roared weeping like a little kid. Uncontrollably covering her hand with kisses, through tears, I shouted chaotic words of love, so long hidden and unleashed only now for her dying in front of me.

She leaned a bit and put her other hand on my head:

"Stop," she said, "stop … I know … Don't cry … It was better this way … I always loved you for your fairness, for your love for Tom, and I don't even know why … I might have not been good for you if you had stood between me and the dead one, the only one who had the right to me. Quiet, don't cry. Now you know. I think Thomas will forgive me that I told you what I had felt in the hour of my death … I was so unhappy …"

Exhausted, she went silent, but after a moment she started again.

"Let it be … I will confess everything. It is the last time we will be talking … That noon…" She stopped for a moment as if a sudden shame, too strong even in face of death, blocked her voice, but I knew which noon she was talking about! She was silent for a while, only slightly moving her lips until moving her hands towards her temples, she suddenly cried out:

"Why didn't you kill Peter then?"

At that moment I heard a muffled moan behind me. There was something so terrible in it that I involuntarily jumped up and turned towards it. Peter was standing in the doorway with his hand resting at its cornice. He was white like a corpse and was looking at us with wide open eyes. He must have stood there long enough and heard everything that Martha was saying to me. When he noticed that I saw him, he staggered a few steps forward and mumbled something incomprehensible.

Martha turned away with a muffled cry of disgust.

"I am sorry," moaned Peter, "I am sorry, I didn't mean to … "

At that moment pattering and voices could be heard in the other room.

"Children!," Martha cried out and stretched her arms to them, but the intimidated girls stopped in the doorway, and only Tom ran to her, so she took his head in her hands and pressed it to her chest.

Peter looked at them and stepped towards me:

"You've promised her," he pointed at Martha with his head, "remember about all the children… all of them!"

Before I had time to answer that strange comment, he was gone from the room. The sunbeam had already reached through the mist that was vaporizing in front of the window. It turned the upper windows into pieces of shining gold and ran a luminous sheaf through the stuffy atmosphere of the room. Martha ways lying there motionless staring with her fading eyes into the piece of sunlight that was sliding lower and lower on the wall and was floating towards her pillows like a descending angel. The girls started to tip toe towards the bed looking in surprise at their mother's pale and still face.

I had difficulty breathing and felt bitterness in my mouth. This new day was coming to me like a ruthless, painful mockery, because I knew it would bring emptiness and a gloomy look at the past. Minutes were passing in silence.

Suddenly Tom called:

"Uncle, uncle! I am scared! Mom is looking so terrible!"

I turned around. A sunbeam hitting the pillow was illuminating Martha's frozen and dead face still staring at the sun with glassy eyes.

"Your mother has died ..." I whispered in a choked stranger's voice to the scared and surprised children now gathered around the bed. Then I bent to close her eyelids.

At that moment I heard a gun bang. I ran to the door. Peter was lying on the floor of the adjacent room with a crushed temple and a smoking gun in his hand. I staggered as if drunk.

Today, they are both lying in a grave. I gave them the last service myself. I wrapped their bodies in big shrouds woven from plant fibers saturated with resin. Then, I carried them to the boat that would take them to the Cemetery Island. The four children accompanied me and the corpses. The older three gathered around their mother's body. Tom, astounded and scared by the sight of death, was sitting at the corpse's feet. Lili and Rose were grabbing at the shroud and calling their mother as if demanding the caresses, she had skimped from them when she was alive.

Peter's body was lying in the boat by itself. The youngest girl crawled to him, and stroking the thick fabric covering it, she was whispering quietly:

"Poor daddy, poor ..."

Our sad trip was accompanied by a wonderful weather. The sun, not too high above the horizon, lit up a huge and calm sea surface plowed into small furrows by a slight breeze. Distant islands loomed before us sunken in a transparent blue fog. I had never felt that awful irony present in the beauty of nature so indifferent to human pain before. I was carrying the two last humans who came with me to this globe in that boat. They were the only people who knew Earth like I do, and I was carrying them to put in the grave that I had built for myself. From that moment on, I would be a lonely man forever, but it didn't make any difference to the sun which was shining calmly, as beautiful as it was when I was a child playing in its light, on that now so distant planet.

I carried both of them on my back from the boat to the grave I had built on the upland in the most beautiful part of the island. Their corpses weren't heavy being six times lighter than they would be on Earth, but I was bending under that burden. No wonder! I was carrying the rest of my bitter happiness to the grave!

I buried Martha in the grave I had intended for myself and dug another one for Peter a little below that one. But I will continue living ... On several occasions, in the moments when the burden of unspoken longing crushes and breaks me, I am tempted to leave this globe in the only available way to me. I would like to follow those six: O'Tamor, the two Remongers, Woodbell, Varadol and Martha, but then I remember that I promised her not to leave her children. I have to live for them now. I am sentenced to life as much as I was sentenced to love when she was alive. Those two best things in the world became my most severe pain and my most terrible suffering ...

My days belong to those children. I try hard to think about them all the time, take care of them, teach them, hold them close, protect and develop them. Indeed, I, a childless man, am burdened with the spiritual fatherhood of the lunar generation. But at night I return to Earth and talk to the deceased.

Something in my brain broke and tore off, or the pain originating from my heart overshadowed it because waking seems like a dream, and the night dreams are real life for me ... I miss my dreams in which I walk on Earth and kiss its flowers, trees and even rocks with affection. It seems to me now that crazy prideful need to learn the secrets of the starry skies tore me away from it.

On other occasions, I am visited by my deceased companions. O'Tamor, all goodness, comes first and blames himself for his irresponsibility in leading us to this empty globe hanging like a lamp among the skies. Then I see the Remonger brothers. They are complaining that they followed us and found death. Pale Woodbell comes and asks what we did to Martha, if she was happy with us. Peter tells me about his wild passion for Martha which I could see burning like fire in his eyes. Fate granted him not a single moment of happiness but instead made him see all the repulsion, disgust and contempt in the eyes of the woman he desired and forcibly possessed. He had to remain silent and suppress all love and all pain and his offended male pride. He tells me about the hell he felt on that last night, when he saw me with my face on her chest, and when he was putting the gun to his forehead ...

Martha comes at the end of that parade of sad ghosts. She stands sad with a painful smile in front of me. She thanks me for being human, but it sometimes feels to me that her eyes reproach me for not being human.

There is such an abyss of sadness and regret in me ...

This is how those ghosts talk to me, and although what they say is sad, I feel comfortable with them because they are my fellow men.

The new lunar generation growing beside me is somehow different. They are still children, but I feel that they are creating a separate world for themselves. That world will always be as foreign for me, who came here from Earth, as my world is inaccessible to them, and those yet to be born on the Moon.

And still I, the brother of those six graves scattered on the Moon, have to live who knows for how long with those for whom this globe is home …

PART IV - AMONG THE NEW GENERATION

I

Polar Land

The new generation is growing up, and they need me less and less, so I am getting sadder and sadder ... That is why I came to the *Polar Land* to look at Earth and be by myself. Two hundred nineteen lunar days have passed since our EXODUS from the Lost Earth, and sixty-seven since Martha and Peter's death.[3]

It is strange that I am still alive ...

***

I am living on the *Pole* again. The limitless longing for my homeland Earth torments me more and more, and because of it, I even forget the generation Martha gave to me at her death. They are living here at the seaside, and they are happy. When I was leaving, they were discovering the spring feeling of love. It was too sweet and too ... painful to look at that spring ...

There is silence and loneliness, and memories ...

***

There was another solar eclipse, Earth black like a corpse staining golden rainbows, and outpour and a flood ... Two hundred twenty-six lunar days have passed since our EXODUS ... I am getting to feel anxious about Martha's children. I should go again to the seacoast and see if they do not need me. I had a sad dream, and I saw Martha.

***

I was in the Land of the Warm Ponds after seven lunar days absence ... I went there led by anxiety about Martha's children. Tom is now husband to his sisters Lili and Rose. I am wondering why people on the Moon do not grow as tall as they would grow on Earth! Tom is an adult, but his head does not even reach my shoulder. It seems that Ada will be even smaller ...

---

[3]The Lunar day is averages 29 days, 12 hrs, 44 mins, 3 sec which means it was 17.4 years since they left earth.

During my stay at the seaside, there was a horrible *O'Tamor* explosion, the worst of all to date. The southern side of the crater slid into the sea … It was the two hundred thirty eighth day since our EXODUS. The eruption started fourteen hours past noon.

When I was leaving, Rose was expecting a baby. I took Ada with me as she was neglected there … Now, she needs my care more than ever. It is awful that I am not allowed to die yet!

I returned to the *Polar Land* two hundred fifty-one days since our EXODUS. Tom was trying to persuade me to stay with them, but I saw that he was glad I was leaving. He is despotic and did not like my authority   with his wives. He was happy that Ada was leaving as she did not want to give in to him even if she was still a child.

Pale and cold hours pass like the light of the invisible sun at the pole. A long, long, infinite number of long hours! … It is hard for me to keep track of time. I do not talk a lot, and Ada is silent with me. She sits for hours on the green moss and stares with her sad, pale eyes at the pink dappled mountains …

And I? I do not really know anymore … For a long time now, I have not cared about the present and even less about future. I look behind me, continually looking back at my memories. Sad company! I am sad at the seaside, and I am sad here where I see Earth on the horizon.

***

A long time has passed since my last note. Ada is growing up, and she misses her siblings. I see it in her though she does not want to admit it. So I think that it is time for me to return to the seaside. I am growing old, and if I died in this emptiness, Ada would perish. I will return for her sake although God knows that I would prefer to die here, looking at Earth.

I am already afraid that this child has lived too long with me, as she is becoming a silent and sad loner. She is a strange child, and it is also strange that in this loneliness, instead of getting closer, we become more and more strangers to each other. She looks at me with wide eyes, and I am convinced that she thinks about many things she does not share with me.

After all, I can admit to myself. I have been here with this girl for so long, and yet, I have not become attached to her. On the contrary, I am still uncomfortable with her presence, I would like to be alone and think about the past without any obstacles … about the Earth …

Still, we need to go back … to Tom, to Tom's children, to a family who will look in bewilderment and horror at the old, gray-haired man who came from the Earth and for so long now has lived alone …

I have to go back … We need to go back, Ada …
I cannot die yet.

II

At the seaside at the Warm Ponds

Four hundred ninety-two lunar days or close to thirty-eight earth years since EXODUS. I have not written anything on these pages, and I am getting back to them now to note Rose's death. Her death was caused by her brother and husband, who was once my beloved pupil, and now in anger, hit her on the head with a rock!

His second wife and his older children accepted his act in silence. They probably think that he has the right to kill anybody who does not obey him. Only Ada, always keeping her distance from Tom's family now, stood against the killer. Without an explosion, without screaming, only with a menacing face and raised hands, the girl walked towards him. He backed away fearfully although he could knock her down with one stroke of the hand because he is bigger and stronger. She stopped two steps in front of him, and pointing with one hand behind her to the fresh corpse of the woman, she shook the other over his head and shouted:

"On behalf of the Old Man (I am called the Old Man here) I curse you for the blood of your wife".

Tom got scared, but after a while he looked with gloomy eyes at me, still silent, and then said to Ada, trying to make his voice sound arrogant:

"Rose was mine, and I could do whatever I wanted with her … feed her or kill her. Why was she disobedient?"

I think that it was an awful accident and involuntary murder as I could not believe Tom hit his wife with the intent of killing her, but it still made me aware of three things that I had not thought about before. First, I see Tom's despotism and feel that it was my fault as I was bringing him up, and I did not know how to make him better. I should not have left the children to their fate while I am spending lonely years in the Polar Land.

Second, I was surprised by Ada. Her reproof of Tom, and many things that I am recalling now that I had not noticed so far, reminded me of her special attitude, her aloofness towards her brother and his family. It seems to me now that they hate each other, and that all of them fear this girl, the youngest of the first generation of these people. She keeps her distance from them and is like a priestess among them, although I do not know if that word is the right term for this situation.

I feel sorry for Ada. She is lonely and like me, and she will always be alone in this world. I feel even more sorry for her because I cannot be now, what I should have been for her, a good father, or a at least a friend. Her behavior towards me is more like superstitious worship than love. Apparently, that too is my own doing...

And the third thing which scares me the most because it concerns only me is that they believe I ... but no! Perhaps, it is my illusion! So, what does it mean that Ada cursed Tom in my name? I am the oldest among them, so this must be the reason ... still ... if what I am thinking is true, would I be responsible for this ... idolatry?

How strange is the way they pronounce the name they have given me: *Old Man* ...?

***

Last night I had that dream again, the one that has constantly worried me and made me feel even more of a stranger in this world ... I was dreaming that I was on Earth, but it was a strange dream ...

I was surrounded by people who I was seriously talking to about matters of other countries, nations, and progress ... I was told that since my departure from Earth, borders of some countries had changed, and that there were new laws, and that many earlier beliefs had fallen. I became curious about it all and wanted to see Earth with my very own eyes, to check it all out after such a long period of absence.

So, I went on a journey and walked through neighborhoods and cities I once knew. Indeed, a lot has changed. Flying like a bird over lands, I was surprised to see old capitals in ruins and once blooming patches turned into deserts and ashes. In place of deserts, I saw waters, farmland and meadows surrounding new capitals full of life and movement. I sometimes stopped to visit people's homes and asked them about things from my time, but nobody could answer my questions. They shook their heads and said: "We know nothing about it." Or "We have forgotten."

It filled me with fear and an unspoken regret as I saw that Earth had changed and was quite different from the one that I knew.

"It is apparent," I thought in my dream "ages not years, must have passed since my departure from here. It is exceedingly difficult to relate days past on Earth as being similar to days passed on the Moon. I must have lost many of them in my memory ... I am coming to the Earth I no longer know, and it doesn't know me".

I suddenly felt terribly unhappy! I am a stranger on the Moon and not able to get adjusted here, and a stranger on Earth where I miraculously returned, yet it happened too late! Where will I find a place

166

for me?

So, with a tremendous emptiness in my heart, I continued to glide in the air when the night followed the short day. The first stars had already appeared in the sky when some inner force carried me over the boundless ocean surface. Waves writhed below me, like the monstrous undulating twists of an animal with slippery and shiny scales, and a cloud of golden blue light reflected on the waves. I looked around and saw that, only here, nothing had changed! The water was as infinite and as fizzy as before.

As I was thinking about it, I noticed that the sea was swelling up strangely and raising its waves towards me. Now, I saw the full moon directly above me, and a huge tidal wall of water coming towards it. I became afraid of the specter of that lunar world up there, and I wanted to run somewhere where its light did not reach, but I suddenly ran out of strength. I felt I had fallen on those churning waves, and they kept growing and tossing me higher and higher towards the Moon. They twisted into monstrously long necks with foamy manes, roared with muffled laughter, and tossed me higher and higher. In utter fear, I looked at the Moon that was growing and getting closer in my eyes. It puffed up and was taking over the whole horizon, covering the whole sky with its grayish silver glow. On its edges, I seemed to see the heads of Martha's dwarfed children leaning out, and I heard wicked laughter and shouting:

"Come back to us! Come back to us Old Man! You don't belong on Earth anymore!"

Despair, fear, disgust, and a tremendous yearning for staying on Earth, even if it did not want me there, went through my chest like a storm. A terrible scream tore out of my throat, I strained to resist the waves throwing me into space, I gripped the water with my hands, beat the air with my feet ...

In vain! I felt suddenly that the Earth, instead of being under my feet, was already above my head, and I was falling on the Moon again ... That was an awful nightmare, but the reality is even worse ...

**

Five hundred and one days since our EXODUS.

Tom took the ship and his two oldest sons on a discovery trip South. He told me they had almost reached the equator but could not continue further because they were stopped by fierce tropical sea storms. So, they came back with nothing.

After their return, Tom and I had a long talk. He was talking a lot about his mother, and Rose, and regretted her death. Then talking about their journey, he told me what hardships they had experienced. Then he grew silent and after a while, he said he was afraid it was his last trip.

Indeed, I am looking at him, and I cannot understand it … This man, having lived half of my life is an old man. On Earth, he would only be full age… People here mature faster and age faster. It is even stranger that I am still alive …

I said as much to him. He looked at me, and after a moment of hesitation he said:

"Yes, Ada and my children say that you are the Old Man" … Those words sounded strange in his mouth.

"And you" I answered, "you have known me since your childhood, what do you say about me?"

Tom did not say anything.

Tom died fourteen lunar days after Rose's death. He left behind twelve children: five from deceased Rose and seven from Lili. I buried him myself on the Cemetery Island next to the graves of Martha, Peter and his youngest child who had died soon after birth.

Lili is terribly despondent after her husband's death. I think she will follow him soon. Only Ada is calm…

Ian, the oldest of Rose and Tom's sons and married to Lili's daughter, is the patriarch of the lunar people.

And I … I no longer matter, for a long time.

***

Ada told me with strong conviction, that I would not die … I do not know if she, and this lunar generation who listens to and believes her, are crazy, or if I am truly an exception among people … Indeed, why am I still alive?

***

Lili has died. Five hundred and seventeen days since our EXODUS. Ada is the only one left from the first lunar generation.

***

I am overwhelmed by fear because something really strange is happening around me that I cannot, and I don't want to! Understand…

During a storm, more severe today than usual and accompanied by a dangerous eruption from O'Tamor, the tribe came to my house with offerings. They were led by their priestess, Ada, who must have lost her mind due to long and lonely stay in the Polar Land. Since Rose's death shook Ada terribly, I saw that something bad was happening in her head. Now, I know for sure that she is insane. I am the only one who can see it, as they worship her and believe her to be enlightened! Today under her leadership, oh, no, I can hardly say it! They were praying to me! Praying that I would stop the winds and calm the ground swaying under their feet! So, they honestly believe me to be …

Oh! How terribly lonely I feel in the company of that mad woman and those dwarfs, whom I can hardly call people!

***

I am sometimes overwhelmed by a terrible animosity … I started cleaning up my long now dusty library and papers, and suddenly I felt like burning all of it and this diary too … I have not burned them. Still the books and papers have been scattered on the ground. They are lying in a mess in front of my eyes, and I do not even want to feel like reaching for them.

Let them stay like that. When I die, nobody will move them.

III

So many days, so many infinitely long days and nights …

I seem to have lost track of time. It is so hard to count days that are so much alike, days that my earth clock cannot keep up with, and stops before the sun reaches noon … Only my heart marks every bit of the day with its beats, and when I ask it, what time it is, it always replies that it is the hour of unbearable longing, and when I ask it how many hours have passed, it answers only:" Too many! Too many!".

You are right my lonely, inconsolable heart! Too many days, too much longing, already too much life … My hair has been gray for a long time, how long? I do not know. Several scores of years must have passed there on Earth since I buried the first corpses on the *Cemetery Island*. More graves were added to those. I dug graves for Tom, Lili and Rose who were still like children, when I was already stooped. The great grandchildren of those who came to this world with me from Earth are growing up, and I am still alive.

It is so wondrous that I sometimes do not understand my own being. I am even ready to admit that the legend spread about me among the lunar generation was true, that I would never die …

I recall that while still on my beloved and lost forever Earth, I was once reading in a book by a famous biologist, that death is an inconceivable and incidental phenomenon not related to our living conditions. I am filled with fear when I think that death could forget about me and not come …

***

If my math is right, over fifty years have passed since I left Earth together with my deceased companions. It is possible that not many people I knew there are still alive. Those, who in their childhood heard of those madmen traveling to the Moon, are gray now and forgot the names of those travelers believed to be lost ...

Fifty years! How many things must have changed during that time on Earth. Perhaps I would not recognize the neighborhoods I once knew. And my memory is already weakening ... Though there are still many details in it which I caress with pleasure in long hours of reflection. Still, I believe that with each passing day, they are becoming more like unconnected images, rather like a mosaic of precious stones glistening with my longing yet already falling apart and breaking ...

I put this mosaic back in my mind all over again. I supplement the pebbles lost many years ago with some sad daydreaming and change images again, playing in my old age with these treasures of memories like a child playing with a kaleidoscope. My memories resemble pearls when I look at them through tears!

Oh! If only I could spend one day, one hour there, on Earth! If only I could see people, those real people looking like me! Oh! If I could hear the murmur of forests: spruces, lindens, and oaks. If only I could see the birch braids flowing in the wind, grass in the meadows, and smell the earth herbs and flowers. If only I could hear the birds' songs, watch the fields turn green in the spring with winter crops or wave with golden stalks in summer!

A lot of things might have changed on Earth, but people are still there, and so are birds and plants! I sometimes recall someone saying that a human soul freed from the body can freely wander through worlds, stars, and suns. Once, when I was living on Earth as a boy, I was dreaming about traveling through the starry space, but now I would prefer to be on Earth forever, only on Earth! When I sometimes fear that the Earth of today is different from the one I knew fifty years ago, then I remind myself that people are still there, and that there are forests and birds singing in them, there are fields and flowers blooming in them ... It will be enough for my soul if I am free to go there ...

I have not heard birds singing for so long, but I still remember such mornings full of birds singing ... The world gets gray at dawn, and the sky gets pale, then it blushes lightly from the east. The silence is enormous, you hear only the rustle of large pearls of dew falling from the leaves of trees. Then, for the first time, you hear a short, broken twitter, then the second on the other side and the third, fourth ...

A moment of silence, and then as if all the trees and bushes became alive, a twitter starts around followed by clapping, whistling, beating, and buzzing. At first you can still distinguish individual voices: here a blackbird spoke, there you hear the scream of a jay from the forest, and closer to you sparrows, a titmouse, wagtail, and a lark above. Later you can only hear only one huge, joyful choir that makes the air, leaves, flowers, and grasses tremble. Meanwhile, the whole world becomes lighter, and the sky redder, and finally the sun floats on the horizon.

Here the sun rises lazily and quietly ... You could say, it does not hurry because no voices are calling it. Birds songs do not cheer up the gray dawn lasting several hours when this area is always frozen and covered with snow ... Here, on the Moon, the sun always rises above the dead world and in a bottomless silence. Only sometimes, the man, who came here from a remote planet, will shout, or an awaken child will cry quietly. Or the wild dog ossified from the frost will moan in a hole from which before evening, it chased out a lunar creature...

The silence also prevails during the infinitely long day unless a wind has broken and wakes up the sea, and whistles on the rocks, or the wide volcano throat roars answering with a booming thunder ...

***

All I went through has stood in front of my eyes very vividly today. I am flipping through the yellowed pages of my diary, and when I close my eyes for a moment, I think I can hear the rattling of our vehicle carrying us through those awful lunar deserts. I seem to see that black sky with the illuminated Earth, those huge mountains looking like coal in the shade and glittering with all the colors of the rainbow in the sun which, ray less and monstrous, floats among the stars of different colors toward the Earth as it morphs into a narrower and narrower crescent. Then, I remember the first years spent here at the seaside. Through closed eyelids, I see sad and pale Martha, Peter, and the lovely children, who are also dead today.

Only Ada is still alive, but I think she does not remember her parents, even though she tells the new generation about what she heard from me, plus her own fantastic additions. She was so young when they died. Today she is the oldest in this world, and these dwarfs worship her almost as much as me. The only difference is that they are afraid of me although I do not know why as I never hurt them in any way.

It is true that I do not know how to treat them as being the same as humans. I sometimes perceive them as strangely smart animals. Even the first generation born here was different from those of us who came from Earth. Tom and his sisters, even as adults looked like children compared to me. Their height and strength adapted to the conditions of this environment, its smaller mass and smaller weight of objects. I am a true giant among the tribe living around me. Martha's adult grandchildren (people mature here much faster) reach my waist with their heads and bend under weights I can easily throw with one arm. Despite their small forms, they are extremely healthy and extremely resistant to heat and frost. They sleep through the greater part of those long nights, but when necessary they can work in the terrible frost with such zeal that I cannot help but admire.

However, the spirit of these dwarfs is strangely wilted. What happened to those crumbs of civilization we have brought here from Earth? I look around, and I am under the impression that I have found myself among only half human creatures. They know how to read and write. They can: smelt metals, set snares, and weave cloth, use fire. They even know the usefulness of various measuring tools. They can talk to me in good Polish and understand books written in English and French, but when talking to each other, they use a strange, limited dialect consisting of Polish, Malabar, English, and Portuguese words. Thoughts float lazily and heavily in their tight skulls, and it seems that putting them into words is exceedingly difficult for them. They also have to use facial scowls and hand movements like the primitive people somewhere in the depths of Africa or at the southern border of the USA.

Then great sadness fills me when I look at this third generation, born of people who arrived here from the Earth! My sadness is even greater because, in the conviction of my own superiority, I cannot resist the feeling of contempt for these poor pseudo-people. At the same time, I feel that I am complicit in the crime that has happened. We've really perverted the majesty of the human race, by bringing it here in ourselves and allowing it to reproduce on this globe, never intended for such a purpose ... Nature is inexorable, both when it walks forward in a triumphal ascent and fulfills its beloved developmental path for centuries, creates forms that are constantly new and ever evolved, or when offended, retreats and cancels what it created. My struggle to maintain the human spirit in the lunar generation at some level similar to ours which to such heights on Earth is futile. The only and unexpected result of my attempt is the fearful admiration they have for me. I am not only a giant for them, but also a mysterious being who knows what they do not know and understands what they cannot comprehend ...

In addition, Ada often tells them that there is a land in the north where the sun never sets, and that behind it, there is an infinite and deadly desert. She tells them there is a huge gold star shining above that desert, and that I arrived from that star. Isn't it enough to confuse those poor dwarfs' brains? They have never been there and have not seen the shining Earth, but Ada was in the Polar Land with me and now tells them such fantastic stories. They listen to her with bated breath and look with fear at my gigantic and gray form … And I am so lonely among them!

It is night. I am not able to sleep three hundred hours straight like the lunar people do, so I am sitting and thinking.

I live alone in the old house that I built long ago with Peter and Martha. During the day, the dwarfs are hanging around the pond here and looking at me curiously, although they have known me for ages, but I do not know why none of them dare to come in. Only Ada comes to me at a set time of the day, brings food, cleans, and organizes what is needed. If I am home, she asks a few ordinary, common questions, and then sits down on the threshold for a few hours in silence. Then she walks away leaving me alone again. It seems to me that she understands these visits as a kind of duty towards me and fulfills them as if it were a rite of worship due to the Old Man.

This woman suffers a strange kind of insanity. Seemingly calm and conscious, she has a fanatical notion, and I have no idea where she came by it … She thinks I am a supernatural being in charge of this lunar world, and that she is my priestess, and the prophetess of this tribe who fully believes in her.

Some kind of a myth, a new and fantastic religion emerged in her poor head. It consists of sentences from the Bible and my stories about our arrival here from Earth. She spreads it among Tom's children, who believe her more than they believe me. In the beginning, I tried for a long time to counteract the spread of this myth, by every means at my disposal. It is a myth in which my person occupied such an uncommon place, but I finally I figured out that I am completely powerless in this respect. I often explained to Ada that her parents, whom she does not remember, and I are the same kind of people like the lunar folk. The reason for my being bigger and stronger was because of my being born on another, bigger planet called Earth. She listened carefully and in silence, and when I finally got impatient, she whispered, looking at me with a sly smile:

"How did you, Old Man, manage to get here from the Earth and bring my parents with you, which is something nobody else could do? How do you know all those things nobody else knows? But the main thing is, why you don't die like others do?"

I rebuked her and forbade her to spread fairy tales about me, but it did not help. A few hours later I heard her speaking to Ian, the lunar patriarch who was coming to me on some business:

"The Old Man is angry. The old Man doesn't want us to know that he is ... the Old Man."

"It is bad, it's very bad, as I was just going to ask him to bring to my house a rock my sons and I cannot even move."

"We have to appease him," said Ada. "Bring a lot of snails, lettuce and amber, and I will give it all to him. But do not tell him about it," here she put a finger to her mouth. "And don't talk about it in his presence because he doesn't want it! Hush! "

Having stepped from behind the corner where I was listening to their conversation, I rebuked Ada again, and went towards Ian's house to do what he wanted. Leaving, I heard Ada whispering to the worried "patriarch":

"See! He hears and knows everything!"

I do not know where this woman's madness has come from, but it is certain that it is the content of her essence and a secret of her esteem by the lunar people. During the lifetime of the first lunar generation, Rose and Lili were afraid of her. Even Tom, who did not always obey me, trembled before her. Today his children would not dare to disobey her orders.

I am indignant about the confusion she instills in Martha's poor grandchildren, but at the same time, I feel a great pity for her ... Especially that, in this quiet madness of hers, I see bright moments, flashes of consciousness, of which one is, that she realizes she lives in delusions and probably suffers.

I remember once such an incident. It was already after midnight when Ada came to me. I was surprised by her visit at that unusual time, as it is not customary or pleasant to leave one's house in that terrible frost. She found me bent over a book, and not wanting to interrupt me, sat quietly in a corner on the bench. I saw that she wanted to talk to me, but I intentionally ignored her. She sat quiet for a while, but noticing that I was not paying attention to her, she approached me, and touching my shoulder very lightly, she said:

"Sir ..."

I turned around quickly, as she had never spoken to me like that. She always addressed me by "Old Man". Strange thing! Hearing this word: "Sir," I experienced a strange feeling. There was some joy that someone was speaking humanly to me, and indignation that somebody dared to address me like that.

"Sir ...," Ada repeated again.

"What do you want, child?," I asked as gently as possible. I had to repeat this question several times before she answered.

"I wanted to ask … I would like to know …"

"What?"

"Sir! I don't know anything", she suddenly burst out with such tragedy in her voice and such despair in her eyes so intently set on me. When I saw the misery in her face, the sarcastic remark I was going to make about the things she said to the lunar people, froze on my lips.

And she continued: "I know nothing … I wanted to ask you to finally tell me what it all means. Who are you indeed? Then who are we? I see that you are lonely and old, strong and big, but I seem to remember my parents, and that they were different than we are today, that they were like you …"

She stopped talking but after a moment, looking me in the eye, she repeated again:

"Tell me, who you are, and who we are."

Something strange happened to me. It seemed to me that I had already answered her question many times a long time ago, but nevertheless I felt a sudden urge to speak. I wanted to speak in a human way to this woman who finally spoke to me like a human. I was overcome by tenderness, and I felt my heart soften and tears welling up in my eyes. For a moment, I could not get my voice out of my chest.

After a while, I only repeated after her like an echo:

"Who am I?"

It seemed to me that I did not know that myself … And Ada was speaking again:

Yes, who are you, sir? …" We all call you Old Man, but today I was thinking … I have just come to ask you … tell me the truth if you are really the Old Man."

Now, she reverted to using my lunar name, that she popularized once upon a time with a superstitious fear.

Pausing and lowering her voice, "I want to know", she continued "if you really came here from there, from that Earth I saw, and if you can do everything you want. Will you really never die? Are we right in thinking that we would be doomed if you left us and returned to Earth?"

She said it all in almost one breath and stared at me with glistening and restless eyes. What was I supposed to answer? A moment ago, I wanted to talk to her, to repeat everything from the heart, everything that I had spoken of so many times about Earth, about our coming here, and about my dead comrades. However, when I listened to her words, I was suddenly aware that it would all be in vain. She only wanted me to confirm for her, to convince her in my own words, that I was really the Old Man, which in their thinking meant the same thing as being a supernatural being. I was overcome by sadness again and did not know what to say ...

"Why are you asking?," I finally said. "I've told you everything, several times."

"Yes, ... but I would like you to tell me the truth!"

I recalled then that many, many years earlier, my little Tom spoke to me like that as I was showing him Earth and told him that I had come from there. "Uncle tell me the truth now!," he said.

"Tell me!," Ada insisted again, "tell me if it is true that you came here with my parents from that huge star you call Earth?"

She grabbed my hand and was looking at me with ardent eyes. I have never seen her like that.

"Tell me!," she cried," because I keep telling the people that, and they believe in you! She pronounced her last words with such a heartfelt scream that frightened me. I never thought, that in this secretive, insane, aging girl, there could be such emotional struggles burning within her. The statement: "They believe in you," seemed to reveal at last, the whole strange tragedy of her life. She had created a new idolatrous and fantastic faith for the lunar people. Now, when she herself started doubting what she was preaching, she came to me to hear a confirmation because they believe in me! There was something in her request that sounded more like a grievance entwined with a plea, that those the people were so poor and miserable compared to me, and that I would not take their faith away from them.

I was looking at her for a long time, and I think I had tears in my eyes.

"Ada, will you believe what I will tell you now?"

"I will, I will!"

I hesitated for a moment: should I deny my Earthly origin? If they thought that I had been born on the Moon like they were, would they stop considering me a higher being? At that moment, the thought of denying my being from Earth seemed so outrageous that my forehead broke out in perspiration. So, come what may, I decided to explain to Ada that I am really an old man, but not the Old Man of their understanding, and that they should accept it even if they lost faith in their superstition.

"Indeed, I came here from Earth", I started, but Ada did not let me finish.

"So, it is true," she asked, "isn't it?"

I nodded my head in silence. At that moment I felt that Ada was grabbing my legs.

"Thank you, Old Man, and please forgive me that I dared … Now, I know, you are the Old Man!"

I looked at her in amazement. In her eyes, just a moment ago, conscious, and rational, the mysterious fire was burning again, devouring her, her hands trembling, and feverish blushes appeared on her face.

"Thank you, Old Man," she was repeating, "I will go and tell the people …"

Before I recovered from the stupefaction Ada's surprising words put me in, she had already gone. She had sneaked out so quickly that I had no time to stop her or call her. Ada is insane, but it is strange for me that Tom's children believe her words so unconditionally. I am surprised that all those fairy tales found such a receptive audience …

On many occasions, I pondered over how it had all happened. Perhaps, I am guilty of separating myself too much from the lunar tribe. When I paid attention to the realization that they were spinning a legend around me, I considered it to be childishness at first, so I did nothing to try to suppress it or nip it in the bud. As I finally became concerned, and tried to remedy the situation, it was already too late.

While Tom was alive, I noticed that fantastic stories about me were beginning to circulate among his children. From the sentences I overheard by chance, I learned that they believed my knowledge and my unusual strength to be a supernatural compared to theirs. They took me for some kind of a powerful magician. Tom did not propagate such beliefs, but as far as I know, he did not contradict them either. In the beginning I found it entertaining.

However, after Tom's death things took a turn for the worse. It seems to me that I am something more than a magician for this tribe. They think that I know and can do everything, and if I do not always do what they ask, it is just because I do not want to. After all, I was asked to stop the southern storms as they saw that Ada had failed to do it, although she would invocate on my behalf. She sent them to me because I could do everything! Once Ian secretly asked me when I was planning to leave them and return to Earth. Ada predicts that it will definitely happen soon, and they are afraid of my departure!

It is for sure that I look with a painful sadness at what is happening in the heads of this generation, but I cannot do anything about it. I do not care about fighting these people's naïve ignorance … Everything makes me feel tired or depressed. I am happy when I manage to forget where I am and what is happening around me, and closing my eyes, daydream about Earth. There are real people there, and such forests, such birds, and flowers in meadows with such beautiful scent. Oh, it is there.

I feel more and more urge to leave this place forever! Oh, if I only could, as they think I can, return to Earth! Thinking about Earth makes me crazy. Whatever I try to occupy myself with, this thought keeps returning to me all the time, and it does not give me peace at night. When I fall asleep, I see fantastic images, but they are all variations of one motif: Earth! Earth! Earth!

Once, when I was still living there, I was aware of various lands and various countries, nations, and societies, but now they all melted into one thought, one love and longing. Over the passing of years and distance of space I can no longer distinguish the states or peoples of a different language and faith. Humankind blends in my soul as an inseparable unit with animals, plants, and the whole earthly lump, and all this sparkles and shines in my mind, as it does here in the black sky over the deserts.

Earth! Earth! Earth!

***

Today, I remembered Tom from those happy times when he was still a child and my inseparable companion and friend. I was thinking about him for a long time, and now during this long, frosty lunar night, images of his boyish years are moving in front of this recluse's eyes … After all, he was the only person among the lunar generation I absolutely loved, and I was extremely interested in everything about him.

He was developing amazingly fast, probably due to the conditions of this world. He was an adult male when he was only fourteen. His two older sisters were also maturing quickly … I was looking at them as if they were blooming flowers. They were still unaware of their charm, but already fragrant and sensing somehow, perhaps instinctively, that they were alluring. Perhaps they instinctively knew that a secret mystery was completing in them and increasing some inconceivable power through which they become precious, desirable, and sacred.

Their behavior towards Tom changed a lot. Earlier in youth, they were his two servants, two tiny butterflies circling around his fair head always looking for an opportunity to please him or be useful to him. He was aware of his own advantage over his sisters and considered it to be quite natural. He sometimes slighted them. Sometimes, in a moment of rare tenderness, he stroked one of them on her luxuriant and soft hair or even kissed. Still, he always did so with the face of a benevolent ruler who deigns to reward his subjects for their attachment. At the same time, he made sure that he did not spoil them with too frequent signs of his royal satisfaction. From the beginning Tom's behaviors upset me a lot. On many occasions I reprimanded the boy that he was ruthlessly taking advantage of his sisters by allowing them to love him in exchange. I had no inkling that it was about to change.

Quite soon, the girls became very restrained in showing their love to their stepbrother, and it even seemed to me that they started to avoid him. Sometimes, only when he did not see it, they would throw fearful, furtive glances after him, blushing every time he approached them. The more they distanced themselves from Tom, the more affectionate they were becoming towards each other.

This change took place quickly, but so subtly that when I finally noticed it, I could not understand when it all happened. I just knew by looking at the three of them … still children from the earthly perspective, that I had before my eyes a complete upheaval of nature, which wants to create, even if it meant taking revenge on the tools and accomplishments of its great will. So, the children were not siblings anymore.

They changed into two women and one man almost overnight. They themselves did not understand it yet. Tom tried to treat his sisters like before, but it was not easy. He was losing his confidence and looked confused in their presence. It was obvious that now the girls had an advantage over this future ruler of the lunar world. Instead of being served by them, he became their servant. He brought them food, took care of their clothing and comfort, and entertainment. He collected colorful shells for them which they plated in their hair or when the weather was nice, he took them for boat rides on the sea. I always accompanied them on those trips because though the girls grew up with him and were used to spending so much time with him, now they were uncomfortable with him alone. More than once, being stronger and more experienced, I wanted to row for Tom, but he would not allow it. I noticed that it was not so much about protecting me, but rather about showing off in front of his sisters with his strength and dexterity.

The eternal comedy was unfolding before my eyes, but I looked at it with joy. It seemed to me that I had three birds in front of me, and I had my hand on their beating hearts. I knew how those hearts beat, and I understood even what they did not yet understand. It was probably the only time since Martha's death that I almost felt happy … Sort of a fresh spring breeze came to me from those children in which the great mystery of life and love was taking place.

And these are old memories today! I recall them with affection, because I had so few days on this globe that I could remember with pleasure and without pain. Still an unpleasant irony of life accompanied that period of time as well! Tom's love for both Lili and Rose, the love that gilded my heart with bliss, brought to this world the dwarfed generation that gradually populated this area. Whenever I think about it, I shiver as if I had found a basket of disgusting vermin.

Perhaps I am very unfair to these dwarfs. First of all, they are very poor, so poor that when I look at them, my human pride hurts me so horribly ... Tom was much taller than they are. I remember his small but noble form. He was energetic and intelligent, and you could see his soul in his eyes whereas you cannot find it in his children. It is all too emotionally painful for me to write about. Why has it all happened this way?

It is a funny question probably without an answer! Why did we come here? Why did Thomas die and leave Martha among the two of us? Why did I relinquish Martha if she preferred me? Why did she die, and I did not? Was it all caused by some fatal and inexorable necessity, which starts and extinguishes stars, and cares as much for man's will and happiness, as does the wind for a grain of sea sand that it carries ...?

***

I am reading what I wrote on these pages last night, and I am involuntarily asking myself who I am writing it for?

Once, while recording events during our travel through the dead desert, I thought I would leave my journal for the lunar people. I wanted the future generations to know how we had got here and what we had to go through before finding these tolerable living conditions. Today ..., such thoughts sound ridiculous! The lunar people, as I see them today, will never read it. As a matter of fact, I do not even want them to ever read it. It is none of their business. Why should they care about my hardships, feelings, and pains? Could they understand them? Could they see on these pages something more than a fantastic and somewhat vague story for them? Anyway, why should they find out, even if they could comprehend the fact, that they are the degenerate remnants of that magnificent race who reigns on that distant and beautiful star? From the day they understood that they would only suffer longing, shame, and hurt, just like I do when I look at them.

Let these humans here forget what once was on another planet and let them not experience "metaphysical longings." I am writing this journal for myself. If I could dream of some miraculous way of sending it to Earth, I would be writing it as a letter for my soul brothers that I had left behind. I would be sending greetings and blessings on every page to the earth's wide fields, grains, flowers and fruit, forests and orchards, birds and people, everything that is so dear to me today in my memories!

Unfortunately, I know that it will never happen. I cannot send even one word to the Earth. I soar to it in my thoughts and with my eyes each time I visit the *Polar Land*. I sometimes travel there pushed with an overpowering longing to see my country over those deserts.

I am writing for myself. Like all elderly people, I talk to myself. But sometimes when I manage to convince myself that I am writing it all for the people who remained on the Earth, my heart starts to beat faster. My temples start pulsing as I imagine then that I am spinning a thread, connecting me and my native planet though separated from me by hundreds of thousands of kilometers! Then, I would be happy to describe the smallest details of my life here, confess my thoughts, complain about my pains, and list my infrequent and short-lived joys … Only … there were so few of those joys!

***

So, I was writing about the only spring I ever experienced on this sad globe, watching the budding love between Tom and the girls. I should have perhaps stayed with them … Then, I thought it would be better if I left them alone telling them not to take any important steps while I was gone. I thought I could prolong that freshness and that spring, and then I would return in summer just in time for the harvest. I am an old madman! Trying to stop a falling stone by turning away from it would be no lesser kind of a miracle. Life had taken its ordinary course!

When I returned to the seaside after several lunar days spent in the Polar Land, Tom greeted me with a strange seriousness and led me to the old house where we all used to live.

"This is your house," he said, "it is exactly how you left it. We have not touched anything. Only Ada was living here during your absence with the old dogs you had left behind."

"And you"" I asked, "What about the older girls? Where did you stay?"

Tom looked back. I followed his gaze and noticed that nearby, among the thickets on the banks of a higher warm pond, was an almost finished new house.

"I've built myself a new house." Answered Tom.

"Why?" I asked with an involuntary surprise.

Tom hesitated for a moment, finally pointed at the approaching two girls, and looked me in the eye:

"These are my wives!"

"Which one?," I asked almost unconsciously.

A silence fell. Tom hang his head, and the girls were looking at me with some fear.

"Which of them?" I repeated consciously now.

"I love both of them," he said "and both of them are mine."

Saying that, he took both of them by the hands and brought them to me:

"Bless us, Old Man!"

It was then, when he called me by this name, that it clung to me for good it seems.

After that, our life gradually changed, insignificantly at first, but it was an important change. Our small group got divided. Tom and his wives constituted a separate closed in family whose ties got tighter with the births of their offspring. Ada and I were left on the outside. With each passing day, I felt that I was less needed in this world. With each of those days, my longing for my world, so distant and so different, grew, and life went by with an unstoppable rush.

I reluctantly think about Tom's relationship with his wives. He was not good for them even though they invariably loved him. He demanded too much from them and was too despotic. Even I lost my earlier influence on him. Our sour relationship was a partial reason for my second return to the Polar Land and taking Ada with me.

Later, after my second return, the last act of my lunar tragedy started and is still being played: Rose's terrible death, Ada's madness, Tom's and Lili's death, my insoluble, constantly increasing longing for Earth, and a terrible loneliness growing every day in spite of this area of the Moon becoming more and more populated.

Two wives gave Tom a lot of offspring: six sons and seven daughters. The youngest of his daughters died a few days after birth. While Rose was still alive her oldest son, fifteen-year-old Ian, married Lili's daughter. Later, after maturing, the others got married as well. Today with Tom, Rose, and Lili dead, twelve of Tom's children still live here besides me and Ada. There are also twenty grandchildren and two great-grandchildren from Ian's oldest son who has been married for two years. So, the total lunar population count is forty-two people now who continue to settle further towards the west along the seacoast. They move their "civilization" with them. They build houses, workshops, dog pens …

I am still living in the house on the *Warm Ponds*, and I will be here till my death which I hoped would come as soon as possible. I am the exception in this strange world, where people transplanted from Earth mature so early and die so early, too …

IV

I think I could be happy if I could somehow signal to people on Earth that I am living here, and that I am thinking about them. It is such a small thing, but I would very much like to be able to do it!

After all, it is terrible when I think that so many hundreds of thousands of kilometers, such an interplanetary distance never traveled before, separates me from the lump of stone and clay on which I was born! Aren't these dwarfs much happier because they do not share such thoughts with me? They only worry themselves about whether their catch of the fish was plentiful, or how well their lettuce will grow, and if the feral dogs would destroy the eggs of egg laying lizards in their yards …

***

I have spent a few hours on the *Cemetery Island* today. Many years ago, I used to sit there and think about the past of this solidified globe. Now, I visit it quite often again. Sitting on that hill covered with graves, I think about Martha, Peter, and Tom, and about myself. I wonder when it will finally happen that I will rest beside them. Today, as I sat there and looked at the silent sea surface, I was suddenly overwhelmed by a boundless regret. I felt such incessant sadness, that I began to cry like a baby and stretch my hands to the graves asking them to open up, to speak to me or take me in their embrace.

I feel like I cannot live any longer. What exactly keeps me in this world? Pain, regret, longing, the worst loneliness, I have experienced it all. For the longest time, nobody has needed me, so it is time to leave. Yes, indeed, it is time. I want to see Earth one more time and look at its light ball suspended from the sky. I want to see the shapes of the lands orbiting with it and the white clouds moving and shifting above them. One more time, I would try to see if I could locate the country where I was born, and then …

While rowing my boat back home, I understood that this was what I should do. I should go back to the Polar Land and look at Earth from there one more time. With this resolution I approached the house, arranging the whole trip in my mind and thinking about the preparations I would need to make.

On the threshold of the summer house I met Ada. She came at the usual time and was waiting patiently for my return. My heart was so full of the hope of seeing Earth again even from a distance, that I could not stop myself from sharing my plan with Ada.

"Listen!," I shouted as she was greeting me, "I will leave you soon!"

She looked at me with that mysterious, manic seriousness that she always had towards me, and she said after a moment:

"Old Man, I know that you will leave us when you want ... but..."

This peculiar way of treating me by the local people, which I should have finally gotten used to, may never have caused me such unpleasantness as at that time. At first, my heart filled with a feeling of unspeakable loneliness and painful bitterness, and then it changed into sudden anger.

"Enough of this foolishness!," I shouted, kicking the threshold, "I will leave when I feel like it, and I will go wherever I want to, and there is nothing unusual or mysterious about it! Go to Ian and tell him that I want to have the dogs for the cart for tomorrow! I am going to the Polar Land.

Ada left without a word to take care of my order.

About two hours later, I noticed an unusual commotion near my house. Ian, his brothers, their children, and the women had gathered and were standing there with uncovered heads fearfully looking at my door. Ada stepped forward from behind them and stood on the threshold. She was wearing ceremonial clothes and a wreath on her head. Strings of blood red amber beads and bluish pearls, hanging from her neck, were touching her waist. She was holding a cane made of a dog's spinal vertebrae strung tightly on a long copper wire.

"Old Man! We want to speak with you!"

I was overcome with unspeakable anger. At first, I wanted to grab a leather whip hanging on the wall and chase away this scum, coming at me with such clatter, but later I felt sorry for them. What do they know? ... It is not their fault. So, I controlled myself and came out, resolved to speak again to their purpose.

A confused buzz of nodding, which arose after Ada's announcement, got silent as soon as I stood on the threshold. The silence was only broken by the cry of Ian's youngest grandson and his mother's desperate whisper:

"Quiet, quiet because Old Man will get angry ... I was overwhelmed by a feeling of boundless mercy.

Pushing Ada aside, I asked: "What do you want from me?"

Now, Ian stepped forward. The fearful dwarf looked me briefly me in the eye and looked behind, as if trying to draw courage from his companions faces, he spoke:

"Old Man. We'd like to ask you not to leave us yet."

"Yes, yes! Don't leave us yet!" More than thirty voices repeated after him. There was such fear in them and such begging that I felt the emotion stirring in me again.

"Why do you care about it so much?"I responded asking myself more than them.

Ian thought about it for a moment, and then he started slowly collecting his thoughts and feelings and changing them into sentences with visible difficulty.

"We would be alone ... A long night and the cold will come. Oh! And bad frost that bites like a dog, and we would be alone ... Then the sun would rise, and you would not be here. Old Man, Ada has said that you have connections with the Sun and another star even bigger and more mysterious than the Sun. It is sometimes dark and sometimes light, and Ada saw it when she was with you up north ... She said that you came from that star, and that you talk to that star in the same holly language you want us to speak ... We fear your return to that star because we would be left alone ... So, we are asking you ..."

"Yes, yes! We are asking you to remain with us!" Male and female dwarfs were shouting finishing Ian's sentence.

I was standing silent for some time, not knowing how to answer. The men and women now made a tight circle around me and, stretching out their arms, were pleading in a fearful, swollen voice: "Stay with us! Stay!"

I felt that it would be futile to repeat to them now what I had said so many times that I am an ordinary man, without any mysterious powers and just like all of them, subject to death. I didn't know what to do, my ears were filled with a constant chant, like a long litany, "Remain with us! Remain ...!"

I looked at Ada. She was standing away from the people, tremendously dignified in her priestess outfit, but I seemed to notice a half-sad and half-derisive smile on her lips ...

"Why have you brought them here?," I asked.

She smiled again and looked up from the ground:

"Old Man, can't you hear what they want from you?"

The voices around me were constantly chanting:

"Remain with us!" ... It was too much.

"No! I will not stay! I yelled harshly. "I won't stay because ..."

And again, I did not know what to say. How could I explain to them that I was going to see Earth, the huge and light star that I missed so much? How could I do that without leaving them with some conviction that I was a supernatural being?

Silence fell around me. I looked at them, and I could not believe it. I saw that the dwarfs were crying at the idea that I could leave them! They were not chanting or asking me anymore, but all of their teary eyes, looking at me, were filled with dog like humbleness and begging that was even louder than shouts.

I felt sorry for them.

"I will leave you," I said much softer, "but not right away ... You may sleep in peace!"

A sigh of relief could be heard from those forty chests.

"And when I go on that journey north to where the most beautiful star shines, I will take you with me. You will see it and will be telling your children and your grandchildren about the star Ada and I were telling you about."

"You are great, Old Man! Great and magnanimous!" Multiple and cheerful voices replied. "But don't leave us for that star you are talking about!"

"If only I could!" I involuntarily sighed, "but unfortunately, I am only a man, like you are."

Animation spread in the group of dwarfs. They were looking at each other and I thought I saw something like a smile of sly agreement that might mean ..." Yes, we know. Ada has told us that Old Man, for some reason, doesn't want us to know that he is ... the Old Man."

I was overcome by disappointment again, so I turned away and went inside. There was a buzz in front of the house. I could see through the window how everyone drew closer to Ada who was saying something vividly, probably about me and my supernaturalness.

It is now almost sunset, and the lunar folk have long since returned to their houses on the stone banks of the warm ponds, stretching in a long row toward the southwest. In a dozen or so hours, they will get ready for the long sleep and will probably dream about the journey the Old Man promised them and about Earth, the huge, strange, and changing star they know only from stories.

***

In a score of hours, I will be the only awake person on the Moon, but now, there is movement everywhere. Through the window, I see Ian's older sons are bustling in front of their house. Nearby, the women are hastily finishing gathering their food before the nightfall. I do not know if I am doing the right thing, remaining among these people ... Anyway, there is nothing to think about: I promised them that I would stay for a while.

Cheer up, my heart. I will not stay here much longer! In a several days or a score of long lunar days at the most, I will set off north to the Polar Land to die there looking at Earth. I know that these people, remembering my promise, will want to go there with me. I will take some of them with me on this journey. Let them see Earth, and then they will return here to their brothers without me.

My longing presses me too hard. I regret now that I succumbed and agreed to remain here for some time. I am afraid that I may not have enough strength and life to leave for the land where I will have Earth in front of my eyes. But no! My strength should last, it should last for a while! I sometimes wonder about the inexhaustibleness of my body. Well, I am a few years away from a hundred, and yet it seems that every day, instead of depleting my strength and weakening my health, life here only hardens me more and more ...

Again, I think about this peculiar, and even scary, legend spread among these people that I will never die ... A frightening terrible thought! ... because unfortunately, only the physical nature of man can get used to what goes against it, the soul will never do it! Not only my pain and my longing do not diminish with years, but yes, they continue to grow constantly, excessively ...

I push this thought away and think with pleasure and relief that I will see Earth in a score of lunar days. My heart trembles in my chest as much as if I were a twenty-year-old guy and was about to go out with Beatrice, whom I had only dared to talk with in my dreams ...

I know that my lover will be cold, mute, and distant, and only I will stretch my longing eyes to her. Only I will be calling her through the impenetrable abysses in the sky, and she will neither hear my voice nor will she devote one thought or one memory to me.

Having the object of your longing in the sky is both strange and terrible ... It seems to me that I am attached to my invisible native star by a long thread pulled through my heart. It can be stretched to infinity but will never break. Still hanging from the world, which is inaccessible to me, I feel that the land under my feet is foreign and will always be foreign ...

It is awful to love stars. Earth is to me a star that I love above everything. If there are spirits like myself which fall on dark planets, from better and more enlightened worlds or flamed suns and still have a memory of them, so like I do, they must suffer the most severe tortures ...

Many times, during the lunar day, I repeat to myself that this despised by me lunar nation of dwarfs, crawling in the dust before me … the Old Man, is much happier than I am. Now, having finished their work, these little men are wandering around their houses and smiling at each other with serenity and satisfaction. Ian, who by natural right of seniority is their ruler here, will summon them before the evening to read together several passages from the books I selected as I once and for all ordered years ago. In the past, when Tom was still alive and Ian was a little boy, I chaired their evening assemblies and explained the Bible or other books to them. Then, I used to tell them other long stories about people, but now I do not even show up there under the cross, the meaning of which they hardly understand. Why should I speak to them, if they have their own interpretation of each of my words, or if they add fantastic and naive legends to each truth?

Then I repeat to myself: "How are they at fault? Why should I blame them that they try to relate to themselves everything they hear, and that they are incapable of raising their thoughts above the piece of land they inhabit? Why are they to blame, that because of listening to the book of Genesis they think about their grandfather Peter whose grave they saw on Cemetery Island, and that they address me with heathen fear? As it is necessary to believe, because I said so, they think that people can inhabit another world, a star similar to those that shine at night above them, but they find it impossible to imagine.

I did everything in my power to awaken the souls in these people and gave up only when I was convinced of the total futility of my endeavors. I should not, therefore, reproach myself and still feel a terrible responsibility for this failing of the human tribe that depended on me.

The irony of life again: they consider themselves happy, and I despair over them and helplessly caring for them, I increase my pain and my longing ...

V

Years have passed on Earth since my last entry in this journal. Today, I am opening it again, to record the date of my departure from the land on the seashore. I am finally leaving for the *Polar Land*; I believe it will be forever.

Six hundred and ninety-one lunar days have passed since our EXODUS from Earth.

***

Everything is ready. Our old vehicle repaired and reduced to half its size, is stuffed with enough food and fuel to last for a long stay in the *Polar Land*, perhaps even longer than I would need it ... After all I am old ...

I was to leave this morning, but my departure will be delayed for at least one lunar day due to the following circumstance.

Since my last trip south towards the equator with Tom, which almost cost us lives, I forbade such projects. I believed they had no practical use and were too risky for travelers. Up till now, my order has been obeyed, and I was sure it would always be so, as the local generation was absorbed only in practical and everyday matters.

However, I was wrong. A latent bit of this fire, similar to that which pushed Earth people to create progress and to discover new lands among the oceans, was brought here with us and is still smoldering in these dwarfs' chests. I have noticed for some time that some of the men look with a wistful eye to the south, over the distant sea. They used to ask me what was there behind this sea. I answered I did not know, but I saw in their faces they did not believe me. They suspected I did not want to tell them ...

Ian and I spent last night at the nearby lakes preparing supplies for the trip to the Polar Land. In the morning, when I returned to the seashore to say my good-byes to the lunar folk before leaving them for good, I was surprised by the news. Taking advantage of my absence, three men, the strongest and bravest of all the population, left, as their wives told us, for the south. They had built a sleigh and placed a second electric motor in it. In addition to food, they took two dogs and furs and set out at night on the frozen sea to reach the opposite shore in the southern hemisphere before morning.

A crazy enterprise! I am sure they will never come back, but I have to accede to Ian and Ada's begging me to wait one more day to bless them if they return ... before I leave.

I asked Casper's wife, the oldest of those adventurers, why they went south. She answered they wanted to see what it was like there. She could not give me any more explanations. I feel sorry for these brave people, as they will most certainly perish.

***

So, the day of my departure has come! The sun has been up for a few hours, and the ice is melting. I will soon get into my vehicle and set out north. I am leaving this land without regret although I know I will never come back here. I am ... only looking behind at Marta's grave on the remote Island and feel strange at heart.

Yesterday evening, I spent a few hours by her grave. It was hard for me to part with it. This is the only thing I love in this world. I took a clod of soil from it. I will press it to my mouth when I am dying in a distant land.

Time to leave … The lunar people are gathering to say farewell to me. They are not complaining or resisting. They know it is to be. Ada, Ian and his two brothers will accompany me to the Polar Land. I could not refuse them that …

Those three men have not returned yet and will probably never return, but I will not wait any longer. Anyway, everyone is so depressed at my departure that they do not even think about them anymore. This morning Ian mentioned their names and said:

"They met with misfortune because they left without asking the Old Man for advice."

Those gathered around him responded with a sudden explosion of crying.

"From now on, we will have nobody to ask!" They were saying among sobs as they gathered closer to me … I guess these people love me. It is a strange discovery at the last moment … It does not matter! Time to leave!

On the way through the Plain of Lakes.

I am breathing with relief as I think that my lunar life is already behind me, and only a short stay in the Polar Land is ahead of me. It was our first harbor on the Moon, and it will be my last as I will die there looking at my beloved Earth glowing in the sky, my native country. It all changes into a dream. My past life and those people left on the shore slowly pass into a dream. They all disappear in a sleepy silver fog with only a fiery disc of Earth shining through it. In my heart, I am getting impatient and I cannot wait to see it again. I cannot soothe my longing. It is night, but I cannot sleep so I am writing to kill those long hours.

We stopped for the night where Peter once found those petroleum springs. So many years have passed since then! My thoughts are returning to that life that is so far behind me. My deceased companions and Martha, and her already dead children, are all now appearing before my eyes. Ah! These memories are only upsetting me when I need all my strength to make it to the land where I will see Earth!

I could not wait to begin this journey, but I must admit that those last moments of saying goodbye were hard for me. The human heart is so strange, and our habits are so powerful. One can even get used to prison bars.

On that last morning, as I had just finished writing my previous note, I noticed that all the people of this land were gathered in front of my house. They were standing and waiting in silence, gloomy and sad. I counted them from the window: they were all there except those three. The vehicle was ready ...

Then I looked again at this place where I had lived for more than fifty years. Not wanting that house to be worshiped someday as a shrine, as the place where the Old Man stayed, I set it on fire together with everything else that was left there, everything that I once used, and I stepped out to the gathered people ... A light flame jumped through the door and windows. It was my funeral pyre.

A short-muffled scream greeted me when I stepped outside. They were looking at my burning house and me, but nobody moved to put out the fire. They felt it was my will ... Everybody was silent.

"I am here with you for the last time," I had just started to say as that silence, broken by the crackling of the flames, made me sad and despondent.

"I am leaving you," I continued "for the land where I had been planning to return to long ago. I doubt I will ever come back here, but you can visit me there whenever you want until I die ..."

The dwarfs were still looking at me and at the burning roof beams in silence. Some of them had tears in their eyes. I took a deep breath as some weight was crushing my chest.

"All of you have grown up before my eyes," I started again, struggling for words. "You were with me up till now, but from now on you have to govern yourselves. Remember that you are humans. Remember!"

My voice broke.

"Don't forget the teachings I gave you! I am leaving with you the book, the holy book brought here from Earth. It talks about the creation of the world, redemption, and man's destiny. Read it often and live accordingly."

I stopped again, feeling that what I was saying sounded trivial and useless.

Then a young woman stepped out from the crowd and spoke: "Old Man, before you leave, can you tell me if it is good for a husband to beat his wife?"

Her words were like a signal, as in a moment I was surrounded by a swarm of women and men who started asking in doleful voices: "Old Man, say if it is good for a brother to make his younger brother work only because he is weaker?

"Say, if children have the right to drive their parents out of the hut they once built?"

"Say, is it right for one of the people to say: "These are my fields - and not let the sowers harvest them?"

"Is it right for a man to take another man's wife?"

"To break the tools?"

"To take revenge for the harm done?"

"To lie for one's own advantage?"

"Say, if it is right!"

"Tell us before you leave, because both you and the books have taught, that one is not to do such things, but they happen among us every day!"

My heart ached terribly at these words. Leaving these people, I could clearly see which direction their development would go. A lot of the human spirit was lost on the way to the Moon, but human evil came here with us from Earth!

"That is bad!," I finally spoke "if such things happen here on my watch so what will happen when I leave?"

"So why are you leaving?", they answered.

It was a simple and terrible question. Why am I leaving? I hung my head guiltily, not knowing what to say. In the wilderness there was only the crackle of the burning house and a muffled, distant roar of a volcano. The people were not speaking anymore. They understood what I felt at that moment, that my departure was an absolute necessity of fate and resisting it was pointless.

"Perhaps I will come back here, but before I do, live humanly and in peace.", I mumbled knowing I was lying to them and to myself.

"You won't come back!," Ada spoke now.

And then turning to face the crowd, she added in a raised voice:

"The Old Man is leaving you!"

There was something awful in her shout as a shiver ran through all those gathered there.

"There is no other way!", I said dully.

An hour later I was already in the vehicle heading north with Ada and her three nephews.

***

We have been traveling for four lunar days. This morning after sunrise, the sun no longer went up vertically, but having staggered into the sky, was almost crawling on it, blushed and raised only a few degrees above the blue line of mountains in the southeast. It is the sign that we are approaching our destination. In the north, there is a mountain range ahead of me. I can distinguish with the naked eye the highest sunlit peaks and a ravine among them, which is the gate of the polar basin.

My heart is pounding so strongly …

Today won't have an end because we will reach the pole at the time for sunset, but we will be in the land of eternal dawn where at each hour there is sunrise, sunset, noon and midnight for various parallels meeting in a knot here under our feet.   And then I will see Earth.

***

In the Polar Land

After four lunar days of travel, at the time of sunset back in the area of *the Warm Ponds*, the great moment came as we passed the gorge in the mountain range, which is the border wall of the polar valley. I was entering it with strong emotion, my eyes fixed on the side of the sky where I was about to see it. When I suddenly saw it in a crevice of rocks, I was so deeply moved by the view that I had no awareness at all of what my companions were doing. Only after a while, getting up from kneeling (because I greeted my distant homeland on my knees and with arms stretched out like a child reaching out to its mother), I looked at my team. Ian, his oldest son, and his two brothers who came here with me were standing around me with uncovered heads. Petrified and dazed, they were staring at the half circle of Earth. Ada was standing in the front with her hands stretched towards the Desert Star.

Some time had passed before she finally turned towards her thoughtful companions:

"That's where he came from," she spoke in a muffled voice as if she did not want me to hear her, "and he will return there when the time comes. Fall to your knees."

So they fell to their knees at the view of Earth their ancestors walked on … After rising up, they did not dare to approach me until I finally calmed down and called them. Then I began to emotionally explain to them the phenomenon they had in front of them in a broken voice. They were standing around my knees anxious, filled with terror, as if uncertain that in that moment I would not rise above their heads and glide off in pale airy mist, far, faraway towards that shiny star!

Oh, how I wish I could do that! …

While speaking to them, I had a sudden thought that made me grow silent. In that instant, I stared at Earth and felt that I had nothing more to say to those people around me. They were silent for a while until finally they gathered behind me and started to bump elbows and whisper:

"Look, look that is where he came from!" They spoke over each other pointing at Earth.

"When nobody had been here before ..."

"Yes... *He* brought Peter here, our grandfather and his wife Martha ..."

"And he left our forefather dead on the desert. This is what Ada is teaching."

"That is not in the Scripture. It only speaks about Adam like Peter, and about ..."

"Quiet, The Scripture is different. He also brought it from there..."

"He made all this for the first people. He made the sea, the sun, and the ponds ... I turned around quickly at hearing those last words, and the conversation led in undertone went immediately silent. I wanted to rebuke them, but I realized that would be futile, so I told them to put up a tent as we would stay here for a while.

From that moment the hours are passing, marked by an invisible sun on the blushed peaks of the mountains. It seems they flow slowly for them but too quickly for me!

This *Polar Land* is very dear to me, and a thought of the possibility of my return there to the seashore, to the *Land of Warm Ponds* scares me and fills me with pain. Staying here, I am under the impression that I am already in the last foyer, almost on the threshold of the lunar world. I am only one step away from the interstellar space of Earth, and I am more attracted to the infinite desert starting just over the mountains than that fertile land where I lived for so long. Even Martha's grave on Cemetery Island does not have a pull on me anymore. After all, here I had more of her around me than there ... Here she belonged to me, although we never talked about it. She was standing here, next to my bed, when I was sick. We walked here in the green fluffy meadows or climbed the blushing mountain peaks together, but there ... she was another's wife. There I watched her pained humiliation and suffered it myself.

I feel as happy in this *Polar Land* as any man could who has lost everything, even the ground from under his feet and is suspended from this lifeless silver ball in the blue sky. I am living in the past, in the remoteness, and in my thoughts about everything that is irretrievable.

Quiet, quiet my old, obstinate, and inconsolable heart! You have got the lighted Earth disc in front of you. Here you have the same meadows, where she and I used to wander. What else do you need my old heart with the probability of your grave not far away?

Jerzy Żuławski

***

Oh, my brothers, over there on that lighted hemisphere shining before my eyes now! Oh, my distant brothers! Oh, my brothers I do not even know you and yet you are still very dear to me.

Oh, my Earth, my shiniest star and the joy of my eyes, the light shining over these deserts! Earth, my delightful paradise! You, my most precious gem, a light emerald framed by azure seas, oh, you sheaf of flowers and harp of birds singing voices. Oh, Earth! My homeland! My lost mother!

Sobbing is erupting from my old, yearning chest, and I have no more tears to mourn you, the star shining over the deserts! You, world worthy of love over others! Here I reach out to you: the furthest, the most unhappy of your sons, and the only one granted a view of your golden form, a star among the stars in the sky!

Here, abandoned, and lonely, I am praying to you. I whom you once knew as a child, and who has grown old now away from your womb: Earth! Forgive me that I left you because of my madness and appetite for knowledge that you yourself planted in me. It led me here to this silver faced but dead globe which once upon a time you kicked out to light your nights and sway your seas!

I am asking you, your prodigal son, to whom you gave everything good; a haughty figure and a thinking spirit, flowers to please my eyes and birds to please my ears. You gave me brothers I might love and share pain and joy with. I, your prodigal son, and a slave, have been punished, and I am unable to come back to be the most miserable of all your children on your wide bosom:

Earth! I am absorbing your light with all my being! I am intoxicated and maddened with your light!
Your light is reflected from the azure seas, from the snowy peaks and green fields, from the small, glistening leaves of the trees, from the flower goblets, from the dew that shines in the meadows there, from the village thatched roofs and from the towering church towers, from the faces of people looking thoughtfully towards the sky. Your light passes hundreds of thousands of miles, striving here for me through the eternal void and is now everything to me. It has to substitute for the azure of your seas and greenery of meadows, the brilliance of dew and the colorfulness of flowers, and has to be the only reflection of the human spirit, reflected in people's eyes turned to the sky!

Oh, Earth! Oh, my Earth! Oh! When will my spirit, freed from the flesh, be able to follow these light strings, connecting you and this terrible world? When will I be able to reach your womb, and kiss it and everything I loved and missed with a silent wind? Oh! Earth!

VI

I have a premonition that I will die soon. This thought circles around me and fills the air and the sun rays around me. The sky looks like a quiet, soft shroud, and Earth shines on it like a silver lamp in a grave. I have never felt it so strongly that I would die soon …

I think about it without pain, without regret and anxiety, but strangely, also without the joy that the forthcoming liberation should bring to my chest. It seems to me that something else remains to be done, something extremely simple and extremely important, but I cannot remember what. And so, it worries me and takes away my joy of death, the savior that I feel circling around me. As if dreaming I clearly hear them calling to me from Earth. I am, also in my dream, answering them: "I want to come to you, but I don't know the way … Doesn't the route to Earth lead through the airless desert?"

***

I have recently visited the mountain from which Peter, and I were watching the sun eclipse and then the lake flooded the whole polar valley. I took Ada with me for that trip because she asked me to. Seeing that I would often climb the surrounding mountains to look at the Earth or the desert, when they were already visible from our location, she insisted that I take her with me someday because she wanted to see what I looked at and she missed …

To hike there with me, she dressed in her best priestess outfit and told Ian that she was going to look at the Old Man's homeland. I was amused by her seriousness. Looking at her, one might think that she was ascending this mountain to fulfill some great and sacred sacrifice. I am sure the people we left in the tent in the valley thought so too. They looked at her with reverence and a sense of fear.

We were climbing up in silence. The laughter, which I had to control when looking at the priestess robes while in the valley, has somehow abandoned me. I even forgot that this woman was following me. As I was climbing higher, I was looking at Earth slowly ascending over the horizon and at the Sun, which already visible from here, was standing on the opposite side of the horizon. Under my feet I had a carpet of a plants similar to heather blushed by the sun, and the pale, frozen sky above my head …

I was filled with a strange impression! It seemed to me that by climbing this mountain, I was separating myself from the lunar people and from this whole disgusting world. I felt like I was indeed that mysterious Old Man, who had fulfilled his difficult task and was now returning to his homeland among the stars … The sun was burning behind me and saying goodbye to me in this world which had only given me hardship and pain. The huge, lighted Earth was ascending before me ready to welcome me in its shiny bosom …

I was already standing on the top of the mountain in the abyss of unusually clean air when looking up at the Earth disc, I noticed the wedge of Europe moving on it. It was clearly visible, though some clouds moving over France and England had blurred its contours from this side … The wide Polish plains in the east shone like a silver, smooth mirror, on one side nestled by the dark Baltic Sea strand, on the other the Carpathian chain, shining now with peaks like a string of precious pearls.

The view of my homeland was so unbelievable and so enchanting on that blue sky that I was standing there without breath, all eyes, and suddenly bursting into tears like a child, I fell on my knees on the top of that lunar mountain. When I got up after a moment, a little calmer, I was surprised to see Ada kneeling at my feet with big tears running down her face.

"What's the matter?," I involuntarily asked …

Instead of answering, she only put her arms around my knees and burst into tears. After a while, I was able to recognize the broken words among her sobs:

"Old Man, you are so unhappy!," she said.

"Is this why you are crying?"

She did not respond and having suppressed her sobbing, she was gazing at the Earths golden disc. Some time passed in silence again.

Finally, Ada lifted her head and looked at me with strangely penetrating eyes.

"Here on the Moon, everything is sad and unhappy, even you," she said. "Why did you come here from that star? …

She stopped, but after a moment, she spoke again.

"The others, and my parents died. Why aren't you dying?"

"I don't know."

I told her the truth. I really do not know, why I am not dying. At that moment fear gripped me again as I thought of this awful moon talk that I would never die. Meanwhile, Ada was silent for some time and finally spoke in a deep, muffled voice, answering herself:

"Because, you are the Old Man, and still, you are unhappy."

"That is the reason." I answered without thinking.

When after some time, we were descending from the mountain, and I saw Ian and his companions' tent in the same spot where our tent once stood, I experienced an illusion that made my eyes tear. For a moment, it seemed to me, that Martha was awaiting me in that tent with little Tom at her breast and Peter, too, thoughtful as usual but still young and not as depressed as he became later, there on the seashore. This delightful illusion in my aged thoughts was interrupted by the sight of dwarfs busying themselves around the tent. Having noticed them, I stopped suddenly overwhelmed with internal disgust. Ada noticed it.

"Old Man, don't you want to go to them?," she asked.

How was I supposed to answer her? I involuntarily looked back at the Earth. Since I had already descended into the valley, I could only see its small edge.

Ada, noticing my look, showed terror, and put her hands up pleadingly:

"No! No! Not yet! They still need you!" She was afraid I would return to my homeland just then!

"Do you think I can return to Earth?," I asked.

"You can do everything you put your mind to," she answered "but please don't do that!"

When I came to the tent, tired and out of sorts, I went to sleep, but my sleep was very restless. At first, for a couple of hours, the whispers of my companions behind the canvas wall prevented me from falling asleep. They surrounded Ada, asking her about me, what I had said during the trip and what I had been doing there ... Their voices annoyed me, and when I finally fell asleep, I was dreaming about the past, about Martha, about the lunar desert and Earth! Earth! ... These dreams are so tiresome...

***

I would like to be left alone. I am tired and bothered by the company of those people who came here with me. I have a feeling that they are standing between me and Earth, and that they are somehow throwing a shadow on my soul. Meanwhile, they are not thinking about leaving at all! They have set up a camp on the plain, and they are settling down and stocking up food, as if they were going to live here for ages. Could they be deluding themselves that in time they could persuade me to return home with them?

Who knows if it is not all Ada's doing? I am wondering more and more about her ... Sometimes, I do not really know if I am dealing with an insane person, as now I see her deeds and words in a new light. Is it not puzzling that this crazy one is actually the most intelligent one among all the people born here?

Oh! Do I really care? After all, I am a man from a different world at the verge of departure, and so terribly weary of all I have experienced. Oh! If only these people would finally leave me alone and go away. I want to be left by myself!

Oh! My Earth! Earth! You do not even know how hard it is for me to live without you and how much I would like to die! Even tomorrow, today, soon …

***

What blasphemy I wrote! Yesterday I wanted to die, but today I want to live. I'll have to live for a few more lunar days, and then, whatever happens, happens. My head is buzzing, and my chest is filled with some ineffable and delightful fullness. Yes, yes that is what it is! I have to accomplish that! I must do it!

Thank God that I have the old vehicle with me and enough supplies … It is all so simple! It is strange that I did not think about it before!

Oh Earth! Oh, my beloved brothers! I am not as abandoned and separated from you as I had thought not so long ago. There is a way to send you a message about me, and I will do it even if I have to pay for it with my life, oh, God please help me!

So, I will die in the desert, in the full shine of my star and mother, but before …

***

Will I find it? I am thinking and dreaming of nothing else but it, and I probably never wanted something as much as I want to find it, the cannon we left at O'Tamor's grave fifty years ago! When this thought struck me for the first time, I was overcome by a real frenzy of joy. It felt like a miraculous revelation came upon me to show me how to communicate with my brothers back on Earth! Indeed! Never during the fifty earth years that I have lived here, had I thought about the cannon. It is been standing there on Sinus Aestum, at O'Tamor's grave, in the middle of the rock dessert. That cannon, aimed exactly at the center of Earth's silver disc, is just waiting for a spark to throw into space, the letter I will entrust to it, towards Earth.

Yes, I will go to the lifeless desert to look for this cannon. I will go looking for the corpse of the old man guarding it there for those fifty years … I know I will not return from this expedition. I am too old and too tired, and I have no reason to return here. Death turned its back on me as it did not want to look for me at the seaside. I will go to meet it halfway in that dreadful land where it must have its home. Then, I will lie to rest on the rocks, under the lighted circle of Earth at the horizon, next to O'Tamor and the fired cannon forever ... I just cannot wait!

But before this happens ... My heart starts pounding in my chest at the very thought! I will roll up this journal, this book of pain I once planned to leave for the lunar people. I will press it to my chest, kiss it goodbye and put it in a ball like a letter in a steel envelope. Then, I will send it to you my distant brothers, my beloved brothers!

My temples are throbbing at the thought of someone on Earth finding this steel sphere. Perhaps it will happen after a few weeks, perhaps after many years or ages that someone will pull out a paper scroll ... Then, you, my unknown brothers will be reading what I was writing while always thinking about our mother, Earth. You know it as greenery, splendor of flowers and silvery winter mornings, and I also know it as blue light, pure and calm, burning for centuries over the land of silence and death!

Oh Brothers! You have no idea how beautiful your mother is when one is looking at her through the abyss of the sky! You also do not know how much I miss her and all of you there, and how much I curse the sky which separates us even though it makes my homeland shine so beautifully!

***

This is how it happened: Three lunar days passed since our long and tiresome journey to the *Polar Land* when Ian, finding me deep in thoughts on the hills, suddenly spoke to me:

"Old Man, it's time to go back!"

His words startled me as I was so deeply immersed in my thoughts about Earth that I did not understand. At first, I thought he was saying that I should return there, where I came from!

And Ian continued:

"Our wives and children are waiting ... It's time to go back to the *Land of the Warm Ponds* to our fields and our farms, Old Man ..."

He spoke timidly, as if asking rather than demanding, but I could read his steadfast resolve in his voice and face.

Suddenly a great sorrow came over me: these people came here with me and are now thinking about returning, about their plants, about the country they yearn for and which they will see soon - and I? ... My home, my family and my homeland are there, in the sky! I can neither return there nor live there again. Even my longing for it is probably a hundred times stronger than these people's longing for their piece of the Moon on the shore of the lunar sea! I was filled with envy.

"So, go back!," I answered dryly.

"What about you", Ian shouted in surprise and terror, taking a step back from the sweeping movement of my hand showing him the south, and looking up towards me.

"I'll stay here. After all, I told you, before taking you with me on my journey, that I was leaving and that I would never return ..."

"Yes," whispered Ian, "but I thought that with time ... It isn't good for people here ..."

"So, go back. I am staying."

Now, he did not say anything. His head dropped as if he was struck in his neck and quickly walked away. I guessed he must have gone to Ada for advice!

I was right. The lunar priestess appeared alone soon after. I was prepared for a ridiculous sort of scene with the addition of multiple pleadings, begging or even crying like the antics she performed for me before our departure. Then, it surprised me when there were no questions no pleadings, she just said:

"Old Man, are you staying here to look at Earth?"

I nodded in silence.

"But you won't be going there yet, will you?," saying that she pointed with her head at the Earth and the lunar desert below it.

I looked involuntarily in that direction, and then suddenly it dawned on me that I could go there to the desert, I had crossed with my companions fifty years ago, and even dying of exhaustion at least for a short time I could feel closer to Earth, having it straight above my head. Today, this thought has overwhelmed me completely and accompanies my every move, and I cannot get rid of it. At the time however, it was just the first glimpse and I suppressed it quickly, thinking that it was impossible, as if death were at its limit and it was impossible to buy what had to be paid with life.

"You won't leave to go there, will you?," the priestess repeated, and I hesitated.

"No. Not yet."

"So, ... couldn't you return to the seaside with these poor souls? They want to have you with them so much."

"No," I answered quickly, seeing the beginning of pleadings, "I will stay here."

"Old Man, do as you please. It will make them sad, but ... do what you like. When they return home, the others will ask them. "Where is the Old Man we have known since our childhood?" They will only lower their heads and answer: "He has left us." Still, you can do what you want. They understand that you are a guest among them, and that the time will come when you will have to leave, and then they will have to manage without you.

"You will stay with them and govern them. Even Ian listens to you and respects you"

"No, I won't stay with them."

I looked at her in surprise, but after a short hesitance, she bent before my knees:

"I have a request for you, Old Man ..."

"What request?"

"Don't chase me away!"

"What?"

"Don't chase me away. Let me stay here with you."

"With me here in the *Polar Land*?"

"Yes, with you in the *Polar Land*"

"But why? What will you be doing here? Your people are there, on the seaside!"

"I know that you and I are not the same people because you came here from different stars, I know but let me ..."

I pondered upon that strange request.

"Why do you want to remain here with me?," I asked again. "This place is neither good nor happy..."

Ada lowered her head and in a muffled but strong voice, she answered:

"Because I love you, Old Man."

I was silent, but she continued after a moment.

"I know this is shameful audacity when I say to you that I love you, but I can't name what I feel differently. I almost do not remember my family. I just remember that they were unhappy. I look at you in this world, and I see some greatness in you, some light, some power, something I don't know, but I know that it came here with you from the stars."

She grew silent, and as I was still listening for the echo of her words, I was surprised when she resumed again:

"At the same time, you were always unhappy and very lonely, as lonely all your life as I am. I do not know why you came to the Moon from this shiny star ... That was your wish ... I know you can do what you want, you are self-sufficient, and you do not need me, but I want to serve you and be with you till the end. Don't push me away. You are great, you are good and wise!" Saying that, she bent again to my legs and remained so with her head on my knees.

"When you want to leave and return to your homeland shining in the sky", she was speaking again, "I will escort you to the edge of this immense and dead desert, I will say goodbye to you, Old Man, and I will look behind you for a long, long time until I cannot see you anymore, and then I will return to the people on the seashore, and I will only say to them: "He has already left", and then I will die."

While she was saying all this in a strange and dream like whisper, the lunar people had crept up close enough and were listening to her words with bated breath. Suddenly I heard Ian's muffled voice:

"The Old Man will leave us ... for Earth!"

And then crying, a gray, poignant, soft crying.

It was amazing! Usually, I was annoyed by these anthropomorphous cries, but not this time. I don't know if it was because of the emotion Ada's unexpected words evoked in me, or something else, like an emerging idea that, on my final trip through the desert under the shining Earth, I was overcome with a great sadness and pity.

I turned towards them, and Ian, emboldened by my kind disposition, took a few steps forward and looking me in the eye, asked:

"Old Man, is this really irrevocable? Is anybody awaiting you there? Have you announced your arrival? Do we have to be left alone?"

At the moment, as if someone hit me in the head, a thought flashed in my mind: The cannon! Yes, the cannon! The cannon at O'Tamor's grave, here on the desert! My head started spinning. I pressed my heart with both hands afraid it would explode in my chest.

I fixed my eyes on the hem of that disc of Earth visible above the horizon, and crazy lightnings were flashing through my thoughts: a journey, a desert, a cannon, a shot, my earthly brothers, this diary... and then a gray fog, melting everything: I understood, it was death!

I completely forgot where I was, and what was happening around me. They were looking at me with utter astonishment, but I did not see them. As if in a dream, only Ada's voice reached me:

"Go away, the Old Man is speaking to the Earth! He will leave us soon."

When I recovered from that first mind blowing impression those thoughts made on me, I realized I was alone. I understood that I had just had a revelation, and that I had to return to the desert: to find the cannon, to send the last message and last greeting to Earth and die. After a while, I told Ada and Ian about my decision. They received it with sullenly lowered heads but without a word of resistance, as if they were prepared for it. Now them going back home was out of the question. They wanted to stay with me until my departure.

Now, as I stand facing Earth, I have the Sun on my right. Before it makes a half-circle to stand on the left, carrying daylight into the desert hemisphere, I will set off.

***

My lunar tragedy has ended. I am back in the place, where for the first time on the Moon, I saw greenery and life. Then, I came here after a deadly journey through the desert. I am going to cross it again and for the last time. My heart is gloomy but peaceful. I am looking at my past life and I think it is time to examine my conscience. Like people on Earth when preparing for death make a confession, I would also like to confess my sins. However, the list of my mischiefs not my sins comes to my mind, and I do not know if either of them are the same?

So Lord, you who can hear both the tiniest insect's voice and the rumble of worlds rushing through space, you who see me here on the Moon like you used to see me there on Earth, please receive this confession in which I will admit that I was both sinful and unhappy!

Well, when I was a child, the Earth you built for me was too small for me, and I kept flying away on the wings of my constant longing to those remote worlds glimmering on the horizon. I was running away from my mother's caresses to dream about the wonders you had created but not for me. I was an unhappy sinner.

When I was growing up and devouring the crumbs of the knowledge you let people have, my soul still shouted at me: not enough! Then I was dreaming of breaking seven seals and raising the veils closed with your hand. I was an unhappy sinner.

As soon as I became a man, I was possessed by the desire to soar in space, as if being on Earth was not the same as being also in the vastness of the universe and hovering over the abyss. Then I took the first opportunity and with a light heart abandoned my nurturing mother for the Moon's silver face, so seductive for lunatics. Lord, I was sinful, and I am unhappy…

I looked at the deaths of my companions and friends, struggling in my conscience, but I was ready to fight them for a little bit of air needed to maintain my life, or for a woman who did not belong to any of those who reached out for her … When I was a witness to her misfortune whose indifferent tormentor I had become, I did nothing to save her … I was sinful and unhappy.

I was left alone in this terrible world to which my own will had taken me. Having a young human generation entrusted to me, I could not arouse their spirit or turn them to heaven … Yes, instead of loving them, I despised those unfortunate creatures and let them worship me while you are the only one deserving such honor ... I was sinful and unhappy.

Now, broken with pain, tired of longing, I am leaving those entrusted by fate to my care and guidance and going for that last sad bliss, for death in the face of Earth.

Oh, Lord, I am sinful and unhappy.

My life has broken into two great parts, one of which was the desire for the unknown and the other yearning for what I lost ... And both were sad and extremely painful ... I did not achieve what I wanted because I barely took a step in the universe, and I do not even know the secrets of the place where I am. I sacrificed everything for nothing. My travel through blue spaces and a desert more horrible than any of earth deserts were all for nothing. I have lived on this silver globe for nothing as the puzzles from fifty years before are still not solved ...

I will never get what I yearn for as I cannot turn the clock back, and this was my life! Oh! And it is time, time to finish it all! With love and longing, I am looking towards the desert, where I will soon hurl the vehicle to be lonely, until my death.

The last people I see will stay here ... They'll probably go up the hill and look for a long time behind me, behind the black vehicle speeding into the sun filled dawn, and then they will return to their people and tell them: "Old Man has already left." Those words will be the beginning of a future legend, like the one about our arrival here. I am sinful.

The time of my departure is approaching.

VII

On Mare Frigoris.

I am alone, and the infinite loneliness and silence fills me with such an awful fear. It seems to me that I have already died, and that I am floating in my car like in Charon's boat towards some unknown land ... And yet, I know this wilderness and I have already seen these mountains, appearing on the horizon. I traveled this way years ago, long ago! Then, we were striving towards life, but now ...

God! Please give me enough strength to reach O'Tamor's grave! I am not asking you for anything else.

I promised the lunar people that if I have enough strength to return from the desert, I will live among them till the end of my life, but I know I will not return from the desert ... Although now, more than ever I am needed at the *Warm Ponds*. If it is all true ...

At the moment of my departure, I heard a strange and awful news. Listen to me, earth people: I was about to sit in the car and bid farewell to the group gathered around me, when suddenly I noticed two people at the entrance to the valley. At first, I thought it was an illusion, but soon it was impossible to doubt: two dwarfs were approaching us quickly. Ian noticed them and shouted:

"They are sending for us! Something terrible must have happened back there!"

His hunch was correct. The messengers were coming with strange and terrible news. Soon after my departure from the *Land of the Warm Ponds,* the adventurers, we believed to have perished, returned from their expedition to the southern hemisphere. However, only two of them returned, as the third one had perished. The news, the two of them brought was such that they decided to send for me and persuade me to return to the seaside. Two selected messengers went upstream on the river and following Ada's stories they had once heard, they reached the upland above the Lakes Plain, and from there successfully and quickly got here through gorges.

I was listening impatiently to their story to find out what made them undertake such an unusual journey.

Finally, beset by Ada and me, interrupting one another, they started telling us the story of that expedition. The only thing I learned from their chaotic words and sentences was that, thanks to a favorable and very strong wind, during a long night, traveling on a sleigh with sails through the frozen sea, they reached the opposite shore of the southern hemisphere at sunrise. It was clear, but later it was still difficult to understand what they were saying ... Anyway, it was so extraordinary ...

Some creatures supposedly live among the mountains on the vast plains. Half human and half-animal, hiding from the frost in deep pits dug around the rubble of falling apart cities abandoned for centuries. Our travelers had to fight with those extremely predatory creatures. Thanks to possession of firearms, having lost only one companion, they came out victorious. They had to run back in a headlong rush as they were being relentlessly chased through the ice by those creatures.

"Those are bad monsters!," the one telling the story said trembling at the memory," They are small, but awfully bad! They had to run as there were so many of them, and they are so bad! They have such long arms and long beaks instead of a mouth. They caught Casper on a long rope, tore him apart and dragged the corpse to a deep pit where they lived. The land is beautiful there, but those monsters are bad! Poor

Casper's companions told us about it. Those monsters were chasing them, but they had a motor sleigh and dogs, so they managed to escape but not without difficulty. Oh! There is a strange country behind the sea in the south! Very strange! There are huge towers, but they are broken. There are some huge machines or factories, but broken, overgrown. These monsters watch over it and bow to the towers, but they seem not to know what to do with them. They live in pits and are bad."

I tried to learn more details about those creatures living behind the lunar sea, but in vain as they could not tell me more than that. They only told us the scary story of the travelers' return home! On the way back the wind was not favorable to them, so one night was not enough to cross the sea. The ice was already softening in the morning, and still scared, they arrived happily to a small and almost empty island. There, sheltering themselves in the pits from the terrible equatorial heat, they waited all day in the expectation of night and frost, to continue their trip back on ice. On the second night, the wind threw them far west, and to make matters worse, their motor broke down at the end of the journey, so fighting with inexpressible hardships, they had to walk along the sea coast pulling the sleigh on the sand with the dogs.

And then, when they finally reached the *Warm Ponds Land*, they learned that the Old Man was gone.

"So, what do you want from me?," I asked, after hearing that strange story.

"Defend us, Old Man, defend us!," the messengers shouted almost at the same time. "We are not doing well! Calamities fall upon us! No doubt that since those predatory monsters know about our existence, they will cross the sea to fight us, oppress and bother us. There is a bigger number of them than us."

They fell to my knees. I felt Ian and his brothers' looks fixed on me. Only Ada was still standing there, seemingly indifferent.

I was standing there, deeply shocked, hesitating, uncertain what to say, what to do, struck not so much by the possibility of these creatures invading this lunar colony, but more by the news itself that some supposedly intelligent creatures were living here. For a moment, I thought about giving up on my last glimpse of happiness, the beautiful plan of sending a message to you, my earth brothers. I was tempted by the thought of staying with the lunar generation and getting to know those monstrous tribes living on the other side of the sea. I could defend my deceased friends' descendants from the tribes I knew nothing about until now.

My hesitation did not last long. An overwhelming sadness took it over. Why should I care about the lunar people arriving from Earth and those remnants of earlier lunar people who are living like moles in holes around ruins of cities ruled once proudly by their ancestors? Let them fight, let them exterminate each other ... What do I care? I am old, and I do not know if I will be able to survive a long, deadly journey into the airless desert. Should I waste what's left of my life now for stupid pity or even more stupid curiosity? Who will convince me that the two madmen's story is true? Aren't those cities standing there just piled up rocks? Aren't those supposed lunar tribes simply animals? I am already old, and I do not have time to check it out as I am in a hurry to die there by O'Tamor's grave in a full shine of Earth.

"I cannot help you anymore," I finally whispered "you have to think for yourselves. My journey is irrevocable, and it is in different direction than yours ..."

"I knew you would answer like that," said Ada when I was already putting my foot on the first step of my vehicle, but Ian grabbed my knees one more time:

"Just promise us one thing, " he called "if that is the way it has to be, promise us that you will return from the desert where you are heading right now! We will be waiting for you and thoughts about you will encourage us in the fights which are ahead of us!"

I hesitated: "I will return if I have enough strength!"

Ada turned towards the group: "He will return but there!" Saying that she pointed her hand at the edge of Earth shining over the horizon.

I was already inside the vehicle and holding onto its helm, when her last words reached me:

"And he will come here again after centuries, after centuries ... when it is completed ...

***

On Mare Imbrium under the Three Heads

Oh, my brothers, I have traveled an awful journey heading for you! I freeze in terror when I think of this bottomless loneliness and crossing over mountains, chasms, vast and dead deserts. I sailed through the seas of darkness alone, and I still have fiery hells ahead, blinding heat and unforgiving frosts. And emptiness ... emptiness ...

I traveled here through a road different than that first one, but not less scary. Remembering that awful crevice in the *Traverse Valley*, which could trap me for a long time, I decided to circle the *Plato Ring* from the west of *Mare Frigoris*. This is how I got to this great plain which will lead me to the feet of *Eratosthenes* ...

Why should I tell you the horrors of my current crossing? When worse things are still waiting for me. I have also reached the place from which we saw the *City of the Dead,* but the desert is smooth there, so I did not see anything, not even a rock, not even a trace …

Did our senses delude us then, or did I make a mistake in measurements and passed this damned place from far away? Or maybe the caravan of corpses rolled up the stone tents and went further into the desert, to the boundless death plain? …

Fear is following me, and fear is in front of me - and I am here with my terrible final loneliness … The sun rises bright, and colorful stars glisten in the black velvet sky. It is terrible…terrible … Why should I look for the *City of the Dead*? I will find it soon, very soon. I am surrounded by the Country of Death, am I not?

***

Under Eratosthenes.

One last, short effort … Last mountain, last peak. I will circle it from west and south, and that is how I will get to Sinus Aestum, and from there, to O'Tamor's rocky grave …

Wild, torn crags are in front of me, and Earth is already in its zenith, full like a blooming flower, and the Sun soon under it …

I will have enough food and air, but I am not sure about my strength! Every day I am getting weaker and weaker. I cannot sleep any more even at night or the noon heat. When I fell asleep for the last time in the middle of Sea of Rains after sunset, different voices and revelations haunted me in my dream … First, I thought that I could hear the cry of the people I left behind. They were begging me to come back and defend them against those lunar monsters, who having crossed the polar sea, are burning their huts, and killing their wives and children … I had just fallen asleep, awakened by this nightmare, when the figures of my dead friends and comrades showed up again. They welcomed me and called for me to get closer to them, the shadow among shadows, to wander in the emptiness of eternity … And finally, I dreamed that I was called from Earth - and it was the only voice to which all my being answered.

My brothers, oh my earth brothers, I woke up, and I am following that voice. I know that I will not fall asleep again before the time when I will be allowed to close my eyes in the final and eternal sleep.

It will be soon, won't it? It will be soon.

***

At O'Tamor's grave – in my last hour.

Thanks to Supreme God, I have found the road, and this cursed

209

site where our feet first stepped on the Lunar ground and blessed at the same time as I can send from here the news about me, to Earth.

I am standing over O'Tamor's corpse, and I am surprised that he looks younger than I do. Years passed over him without touching him, just as a light wind would pass over granite rocks. There is no rotting in this airless void: the old man O'Tamor, looks exactly the same as he looked when we were leaving him. He is always looking at the shining Earth with his wide open, dead eyes. And I, who left his grave as a young man, now I am standing over him with a gray beard and the remainder of any gray hair on my bald skull, and with horror in my dying eyes ...

I have lived too long, O'Tamor! I have lived too long! ...

I have found the cannon. It is ready and not broken. It is been waiting for me for over fifty years ... so now I am writing my last words before I lock these papers in the ball which will carry it towards earth.

I have run out of my food supply. I have enough air for two or three hours. I have to hurry up ...

Seven hundred and seven lunar days have passed since our Exodus. O Earth! O my lost Earth!

THIS IS WHERE THE MANUSCRIPT FOUND IN THE BALL FALLEN FROM THE MOON STOPS.

Jerzy Żuławski

Book Two
The Conqueror

PART ONE

I

Malahuda jolted and spun around in the armchair. The rustling was so light, lighter than the falling page in the yellowed book he was reading, but the old man's ear caught it immediately in the endless silence of the holy place.

He shielded his eyes with his hand from the light of the half-lit spider-like chandelier that was hanging from the vaulted ceiling and looked toward the door. It was open, and a young girl was standing there, descending just from the last step, with one leg still suspended in the air. Like all unmarried women, she was walking around the house naked at night. Only fluffy white fur dangled from her shoulders, covered with equally soft hair from inside and outside.

It was open at the front, but only had wide openings at the arms in place of sleeves, and flowed softly over her young body, up to her small ankles dressed in shallow white fur-lined silks. Her golden-red hair was tied over her ears into two huge knots, from which loose ends of her braids were falling on her shoulders, scattering golden sparks on the snowy white fur. A necklace made of priceless red ambers ornamented her neck. According to a legend they belonged to the saint priestess Ada, and from generation to generation they were kept as the most expensive gem in high priest Malahuda's family.

"Ihezal!"

"Yes, it's me, grandpa."

She was still standing in the doorway, white against the dark abyss of stairs leading to somewhere, with her hand on the forged door handle, staring with her huge black eyes at the old man.

Malahuda stood up. With trembling hands, he was scooping up the books in front of him on the marble table, as if to hide them, displeased and confused ... He was muttering something to himself, moving his lips quickly, taking heavy volumes and placing them aimlessly at the other side, until he turned toward the girl:

"Don't you know that nobody can enter here except me?" He said almost angrily.

"Yes ... but ... "she paused, as if searching for words.

Her large eyes, like two fast and curious birds, flew around the mysterious chamber, brushing the huge, richly carved and gold stamped chests in which the holy books were stored. They stopped for a moment on strange ornaments or secret signs made of bones and

212

gold on the benches lined with planed lava and returned to the old man's face again.

"But it is allowed now," she said emphatically.

Malahuda turned silently and went towards the large clock that occupied the entire height of the wall. He counted the fallen balls in the copper bowl and looked at the clock hands.

"There are still three hundred and thirty-nine hours until sunrise," he said firmly, "go and sleep if you have nothing to do ..."

Ihezal didn't move. She was looking at her grandfather, like her, dressed in a homemade outfit, his fur was shiny black and under it, he was wearing a caftan and pants made of soft, red dyed dog skin. Over his gray hair he had a gold band, without which even high priests were not allowed to enter the holy place.

"Grandpa ..."

"Go to sleep!" He repeated firmly.

But she suddenly fell to his knees. "He came," she shouted with an explosive and previously suppressed joy, "grandfather, he came!"

Malahuda withdrew his hand and sat slowly in the armchair, dropping his lush gray beard on his chest.

The girl was looking at him now with inexpressible amazement. "Grandfather, why aren't you answering me? Since my childhood, as soon as I barely started speaking, you were teaching me, as the first word, this eternal greeting that distinguishes us, from animals and worse than them Shern or Mortzes. I always greeted you as we should, with the words: 'He will come!,' and you always answered, as it should be: 'He will surely come!' Why now, when this great, happy day has come to us, and I can call to you: 'He came', you don't answer me 'He surely came!'"?

She was speaking quickly, eagerly, with a strange feverish glint in her eyes, catching her breath with her white breast, over which the holy priestess Ada's priceless purple ambers sparkled in the lights reflected in the copper mirrors ...

"Grandfather, Tuheja, the prophet, whom your ancestors supposedly knew, once wrote: 'He will come on the day of greatest trouble and save his people. As he left us as an old man because he had never been young, so he will return after completing his time as a bright and radiant young man, for he will never be old again!' Grandpa! He's there! He is coming! He returned from the land he had gone to ages ago to fulfill what he promised through the mouth of his first prophetess Ada. He is coming in glory and majesty, young, victorious, and beautiful! Oh! When will the dawn come when I am able to see him and throw my hair under his blessed feet!"

Having said that, with a quick, almost unconscious movement, still bent at the old man's legs, she pulled at the braided knots above her ears, unraveling them apart and pouring the soft, gold, scented flood on the malachite floor.

Malahuda was still silent. It seemed that he did not even see the girl kneeling before him or hear the stream of her words. Maybe by habit, he turned his dim and thoughtful eyes deeper into the chamber where the golden holy sign shone on the wall with candlestick reflections. It depicted the Earth leaning out from behind the horizon with the Sun standing above it, as it is seen every midnight by the Waiting Brothers in the Polar Country

Ihezal's eyes almost involuntarily followed his gaze and saw the two joined golden shields on the black marble emerging from the darkness. They expressed in such a simple way all the great secrets, passed down from age to age and from generation to generation. One of them was the people's coming to the Moon from Earth, the huge star, shining over the airless desert. The second was that He, the Old Man (who took this name and did not let them call him anything else) went back there, and from there he will return as a victorious young man and savior. As pious fear filled her, she stood up and quickly drew a circle on her forehead with the index finger of her right hand. Then she also drew a larger semicircle from one shoulder through her mouth to the other, and a horizontal line through her chest, while whispering the usual spell words: "He will save us and destroy our enemy, and it will really happen."

Malahuda echoed after her: "It will really happen ..." Some spasm of bitter pain or irony choked his last word in his throat.

Ihezal looked into his face. She was silent for a moment, and then suddenly, struck with something unusual, and only now noticed in the face of the old man, she jumped back, folding her arms on her naked, breast peeking out from the open fur. "Grandpa! ..."

"Quiet, baby, quiet." He stood up and wanted to take her hand, but she moved away.

Then she screamed: "Grandpa! You ... you don't believe that it's ... Him?!"

She was standing a few steps before him, her neck stretched forward, her eyes wide open and her mouth parted, waiting for his answer, as if her life depended on the words she would hear.

The high priest looked at his granddaughter and hesitated. "All prophecies agree on that, and if the Conqueror was ever to come ..."

He paused and fell silent. How could he tell this so deeply believing girl about what, after a long struggle, he barely dared to admit himself, and what he was still pushing away from his old heart?

He was the high priest, guardian of Truth and Mystery, the last of the centuries old and already dying family of priests. He was the leader of all people living on the northern shore of the Great Sea, far east of the snowy peak of the fire-breathing O'Tamor, at the Warm Ponds, the oldest lunar settlement, and further beyond the Isthmus to the west and north, up to Old Springs , where the route takes you to the Polar Country and where centuries ago the blessed kerosene had been discovered for the first time. How could he tell this girl that he who all his life had respected and commanded others to believe in the coming of the Conqueror: that now, when it was reported to him that he had truly come, he stopped believing that he would come at all?

He himself could not understand what had happened in him, or perhaps surfaced from some unconscious depth in the face of this shocking news.

Before the sunset, he had been still praying with the people and was preaching, quoting the words of the last prophet Tuheja, and now being rebuked by this girl ... He had been doing it every day since he became a priest. He had believed in what his father, the high priest Bormita had taught him, that the Old Man used to live with his people and went to Earth centuries ago, but he would return as a young man to save his people. That faith was so clear to him and so simple. He didn't even think about it more deeply, nor paid attention to the arguments of "scholars" who maintained that the story of the earthly origin of the Moon people was an ordinary legend created over the centuries and that no "Old Man" ever existed, or no "Conqueror" would ever descend from interstellar spaces ... He did not even fight against such teachings, departing in this respect from the old custom which his father, the high priest Bormita, practiced having such apostates stoned on the seashore. When his subordinate priests or the Awaiting Brothers demanded this kind of punishment for blasphemers, he just shrugged his shoulders with calm and great contempt in his soul. He had no patience for those who wanted to strengthen their faith with stones, and for those unworthy madmen who tried to understand the incomprehensible truths with their weak minds, instead of blissfully believing in their starry descent and the Promise that would one day come true ...

Monk Elem, the superior of the order of Waiting Brothers could not understand the reasons for his gentleness, and he often dared to rebuke him by his messengers for this lack of zeal in holy things. Still, Malahuda, was the lord, reigning in the eternal high priesthood capital at the Warm Ponds over all the lunar people. He was to judge, not be judged. He could condemn Elem and all the Waiting Brothers with him for their apparent heresy. Every day they promised the arrival of the Conqueror regardless of the fact that all the prophets had announced it for the future ... He was also uneasy about the respect and influence the brothers managed to gain among the people. The truth is that they never left their headquarters in the Polar Country as the law of their order forbade them to do so. However, every year on its twelfth day numerous pilgrimages marched to the Polar Country. It was a holy and memorable day of the Old Man's Departure, and it gave the Waiting Brothers enough opportunities to influence people.

Malahuda did not have enough authority to forbid these pilgrimages sanctified by ages of tradition. He still looked reluctantly at them, seeing how the Brothers demoralized and distracted people from their real-life tasks, promising them an imminent coming of the Conqueror ...

Malahuda, himself, passionately believed in the coming of the Conqueror, but it always seemed to him as something very distant. He understood it as something only promised, not something definite. If anyone asked him if he believed it would happen during his lifetime, he would surely feel such a question to be a violation of the dogma, declaring that Arrival will happen in the future ... After all, the prophet Ramido said clearly: "Not our eyes and not the eyes of our sons will see the Conqueror, but those who will come after us would see him face to face. " Prophet Ramido died a hundred and several decades ago.

That was so until yesterday evening. He had just finished praying with the people of the group Religion, Salvation, and Priest, and was still standing on the wide terrace in front of the temple. With his back turned away from the setting sun and the sea and his hands raised for last evening blessings, he was saying the eternal greeting: "He will come!," when some movement and unrest began among the gathered people. The nearer ones answered him with the usual words: "He will surely come ..." but those who stood further turned their backs, pointing with their hands at a strange group that was quickly approaching the temple.

Malahuda looked and was very surprised. He saw two Waiting Brothers amongst a small handful of apparently accidentally gathered passers-by. They were walking or rather running. He recognized them from far away by their bare shaved heads and their long gray robes. Nearby, there was a cart with dogs harnessed to it, so this is how they apparently had come here. The very appearance of the monks who never left their monastery during their lives was unheard of. Still the old priest's amazement was topped off by their incomprehensible behavior. He was watching them and thought they were crazy, because according to their order vows they would never take a drink. They were running with bounding steps, waving their arms screaming something he could not hear. The people below heard them and apparently understood, because all of them began to crowd there, all at once bustling, mad and screaming, and soon Malahuda would remain alone on the steps of the temple above the empty square. At that moment, however, a returning wave of crowds hit him. Before he realized what was going on, he saw faces around him, crazy with insane joy, raised hands and hundreds of open and screaming mouths, All of the crowd was now pushing themselves to the steps of the temple, and almost carrying both brothers who were crying and laughing at the same time:

"He has come! He has come!"

He did not understand and could not comprehend for a long time, although the brothers were saying that the prophets' great promise and time had been fulfilled. On the previous day, when in the Polar Land the sun stands over the darkened Earth, the Old Man returned to his people, rejuvenated and radiant, Conqueror and Savior! ...

"The Waiting Brothers" have ceased to exist, and they are now "The Joyful Brothers" They were sent in twos with good news, to all lunar tribes, on the edge of the Great Sea and inland near streams. They were announcing the coming of the Conqueror, the end of all evil and the deliverance from the hands of the Shern and Harassers!

The Conqueror himself is following them together with Elem and a few other brothers for company, and when the new dawn rises, he will appear to the people here on the shores of the Great Sea... That is what the once awaiting and now just joyful Brothers were saying. All the people gathered before the high priest were laughing and crying, and praising the Highest, who fulfilled the promises once given to the prophets.

***

Malahuda raised his hands. A joyful frenzy went through him like a wave. His old chest swelled with the feeling of ineffable, grateful gratitude and a frenzied joyful like a wave enveloped him at first. His old chest groaned with feeling of unbridled gratitude that the Conqueror came now at the time of severe oppression and on the day of bitter misery. His eyes filled with tears, and his throat tightened with a intense spasm, choking a joyful cry in him that was emerging from the bottom of his soul ... He covered his eyes with his hands and burst into tears before the people on the steps of the temple.

The people looked respectfully at the high priest's tears, and Malahuda was standing still with his face covered and his head bent down to his chest ... He thought of his whole life, all his longings, elations, and everything he had seen during his long life. He recalled the calamities and misfortune of the people, and the confusion that he soothed, always repeating the holy Promise which has now been fulfilled ... A strange longing now has taken the place of previous joy in his heart.

"My brothers! Brothers" ... he began, stretching out his hands trembling with age and emotion above the waving crowd ... Suddenly he saw that he did not know what to say. Dizziness very similar to fear, filled his head and chest. He sighed deeply, gasping for breath, and covered his eyes again. A swirling, obsessed thought roared under his skull: "From now on everything will be different!" He felt that it would be different from now on, that all faith, based on the promise and expectation, simply would cease to exist at that moment, and something unknown, something new was coming in its place ...

The people were dancing around and raising bemused joyful cries, and in this great and joyful moment, a sour, painful regret entered the High Priest's heart for all that he knew. He had already missed those prayers at sunset, which he presided over, this faith, the expectation that such a day would finally come, that he would finally come.

Not knowing why, he suddenly thought that the Waiting Brothers were lying. This thought scared him at first as he realized that it was almost the hope that it would be so. He pressed his chest with his hands and bowed his head in a spirit of repentance. Still the first thought kept coming back, whispering in his ear that he, the high priest, was the guardian of faith and must not accept such words shaking the basis of their faith as being true.

The awareness of his duty suddenly struck Malahuda and, having controlled his other feelings, restored his inner balance. He frowned and looked sharply at the envoys. However, those simple, humble and unlearned men, were now sitting on the steps at his feet, exhausted by their travel and joyful screaming. With fanatically burning eyes, they were still murmuring in a hoarse voice, an old song about the prophecies fulfilled today ... Their hearts were pure and bright, burning with great joy, they did not even feel the dilemma that was going on in the soul of the people's superior.

"People came from the stars! So said the Old Man! " Abelar was singing, stooped with age and hardships of the monastic vigil.

"They will go back to the stars one day! So said the Old Man! "Renod's young, cheerful voice answered him.

"For the Conqueror will come and save his people!

He will definitely come! Let's rejoice! "

Meanwhile, the people were already on the steps of the temple and calling the high priest by name, dissatisfied with his long silence. Confused, disorderly voices challenged him to some unspecified deeds, or demanded from him the confirmation of the joyful news. Others called for him to open the door of the temple and distribute the treasure collected there for centuries among the people as a sign that the Promise was fulfilled and from now on, joy should reign on the whole Moon.

An old peasant came up to him and tugged at the wide sleeve of his red priestly robe. Several women and teenagers passed him, moving towards the temple threshold, inaccessible at the moment, and the disorder and the crowds were getting bigger and bigger.

Malahuda raised his head. The crowd was too close and too familiar to him ... After a moment of confusion and weakness, he felt the master and leader again. He signaled with his hand as a sign that he wanted to speak. He said briefly and calmly that the news had come that the Promise had already been fulfilled, but he, the high priest, must examine everything first, before he and the people would dress in cheerful garments. Thereafter he told them to leave him and the messengers in peace.

The crowd, usually obedient at his first gesture, this time seemed not to hear the words of their superior. They continued to talk lively and even yell. There were some who shouted that Malahuda had already lost his power and should not order them since the Conqueror had come, the long awaited and the only lord of the Moon. Others refused to go home, claiming the sun would not set that day, fulfilling the prophet Rocha's rather vague words who said: "And when he comes, the day will become eternal" ...

However, the sun was setting, slowly, but firmly, like every day, bleeding the sky and the water of the Warm Ponds with a wide glow. The vast sea was also turning crimson, and so were the wide roofs of the settlement scattered on the coast. In the distance, above it, the three gables of the stone tower gleamed in the sun where Avij of the Shern himself and his soldiers and Mortzes lived to the torment of the people. They were sent here from across the Great Sea to collect a tribute from all the people's settlements as a sign of submission.

It was hard to tell who first turned eyes this evening to the castle, but before Malahuda noticed what was going on, all faces, menacing, were already looking in that direction. People were raising their hands, quickly armed with sticks and stones. Jeret, the high priest's distant young cousin, was already standing on a road-side boulder before the crowd, and was shouting in the glow of the setting sun,

"Is it not our duty to clean the house for the Conqueror's reception? Would he not despise us and reject us as unworthy to be facing him if we only sought to win with his hands!"

The crowd roared after him: "Let's hang Avij! Death to the Shern! Death to the Mortzes!," and were already marching towards the distant black tower.

Malahuda turned pale. He knew that the staff in the castle were not very numerous, and that a crazed crowd could destroy and flatten the whole fortress, but he also knew that the whole terrible power of the Shern was behind Avij and his handful of followers there. Even one broken tendon in the wing of the abominable governor would mean an implacable war for the whole human tribe. It would bring terrible defeats and unspeakable slaughters, as it happened in the old days of his great-grandfathers.

He began to shout that they should stop, but now no one would listen to his voice even though both of the Waiting Brothers stood in front of the crowd to block it. They were crying that it was forbidden to do anything before the Conqueror's arrival as he was the one who had the right to lead and command. Jeret pushed the eldest of the monks in the chest until he fell backwards on the stones and then pounded forward with the whole crowd through a narrow isthmus between the ponds.

Then Malahuda clapped his hands and at this sign the high priest's guard emerged from the two lower wings of the building. Archers and slingers briskly marched to the right in close line and blocked the passage with weapons ready to strike.

Jeret turned to the high priest. "Have them strike, you old dog!," he roared. "Have them strike! Let the Conqueror find our corpses here instead of the carcasses of the evil enemies! Let him know that besides the Shern, we are oppressed by our own tyrants who also need to be dealt with!"

It was a scary moment. The crowd was shouting insults and was beginning to throw stones at the guard, who so far had stood still under the hail of insults and rocks. However, their quivering faces and clenched fists showed that at a command they would break and crush them. They would not care about the reason for such a command and would be more then happy to be allowed to strike this hated crowd that had always been hostile to them.

The mob was shouting more and more resentment against the high priest. They cursed him and called him names. He was called the Sherns' servant and friend. He was accused of having signed the shameful peace treaty with them even though he was once praised as a savior for that treaty that saved so many people from destruction.

Malahuda turned to the armed men. He was raising his hand to give a sign, when he suddenly felt someone grab him by the wrist and stop him. He turned indignantly: it was the golden-haired Ihezal.

"You! ..."

"He came!" She said firmly, almost imperatively, with blazing eyes, not letting go of the old man's hand.

Malahuda hesitated. Her eyes suddenly filled with tears, and she sank to her knees and, pressing her lips to his hand, which she stopped from giving a bloody order, she repeated quietly and pleadingly:

"Grandpa! He came ..."

The high priest, always firm and although kind, was inexorable when he decided something, but at this moment for the first time in his life felt, that he had to give in ... At the same time, he was overwhelmed with discouragement, an almost spiritual apathy. After all, tomorrow the one who will rule over him will come here, so let him ...

An agreement was made with the crowd despite Jeret's passionate opposition. The falling night made communication easier. The crowd was willing to give in, provided that the armed men surrounded the tower and its fortified garden. They would need to spend all night alternately sleeping in their tents and keeping watch, so none of those already condemned to death would find out about the coming of the Conqueror before morning and escape.

Only now, Malahuda would take the messengers inside the temple and get the exact report from them. The newcomers were tired and sleepy when the high priest nodded at them and led them through the winding cloisters of the temple that led to his private apartment. Religion, the Temple, the passages, and the rooms were already in shadow. Here and there, only the golden sign of the Arrival could be seen glowing in the darkness just past the red light of the oil torch: two joined semicircles of the Earth and the Sun ...

The old high priest was becoming more and more depressed. He looked at the holy signs on the walls, at the tables, altars, and pulpits in the darkness, where he and the chosen ones used to pray for the Conqueror's arrival. Here they were promising his inevitable Coming and now that he has come, an evil, bitter emptiness filled his heart. The austerity of the temple this evening seemed like something relentlessly terrible and unchanging from now on. For the second time today, he felt that the longed-for Coming would be the destruction of what was. It was the annihilation of the religion of awaiting already inherent in his soul ...

He felt as if somebody tied a hard rope around his chest and squeezed it so tightly that he could not catch his breath. Now every attempt of his muscles to take a breath was filling him with a biting pain. He felt a helpless and inescapable terror. Although he had always said that he would accept the Coming as liberation of the future, now that it came so unexpectedly, despite the prophecy and his faith, it made him feel overwhelmed and dreadful.

At all costs, he didn't want to, that's right, he didn't want, to believe what happened. Now, walking through the empty cloisters with the messengers who had brought the news, he did not even try to deceive himself that he truly wanted the news to be false.

When he finally shut himself in with the envoys, they gave him such irrefutable evidence and said it in such a convincing tone that it was no longer possible to doubt the truth of their words. Their sleepiness drifted away when they began, perhaps for the hundredth time, talking about what they had seen with their own eyes. They were telling him, interrupting each other, a real but unconceivable story. They were saying how that day, when everyone together with their superior Elem were busy with ordinary prayers in the face of the Earth, a huge shiny ball flashed above their heads and fell in the very center of the polar plain. Then a fair-haired man came out of it. He looked like the lunar people but was twice their height and strangely bright, smiling and powerful.

Now both of them were incoherently speaking at the same time about Elem, who having noticed that phenomenon, stopped the supplicatory prayers and substituted them with a thanksgiving and triumphal hymn. Turning away from the Earth, he went towards the Conqueror accompanied by still stunned and half dazed Brothers. They were telling him what they had seen and heard and how the Conqueror had greeted them, and what Elem had said to him. They were heatedly recalling all of it in simple spontaneous words with almost childish joy in their eyes.

Malahuda was listening. He propped his gray head on his hand and remained silent. As the Brothers were telling him more and more new details about the strange newcomer, he thought about the old prophecies and the proclamations made in the old books. He was searching in his memories, richly trained over the years, for the words and sentences of the Scriptures and comparing them all with that he heard. He saw that everything fit according to the writings, and instead of joy, greater and unexplained gloom fell on his soul.

He finally dismissed the brothers, when drowsiness began to tangle their weary tongues, but he did not go to sleep for a long time. He walked through the hall with great strides and several times dropped into the deserted cloisters of the temple, as if to find in them, something ... he did not know what to call it: faith? calm? certainty? But he only found more inconceivable fear.

The night snow had already covered the lunar fields and fell in large patches on the freezing sea bays, when Malahuda, weary and torn by his inner dilemma, finally went to his bedroom. However, he could not fall asleep that night. He woke every few hours before the time of the usual night meal, and he was not sleeping long after. After midnight Ihezal came to him, but he dismissed her under the pretext of having important tasks that required solitude and went again to the temple.

He did not even know why he was going there, and what he wanted until he stood in the great hall at the door made of the forged gilded copper. It was outside the lofty pulpit and lead to the holy place where the prophetic books were stored. He understood at once that unconscious thought that had been nagging him since the evening, but which out of some fear he did not dare to follow. He wanted to go there and review once again all these antique and holy books wrapped in expensive fabrics. They were only taken out from there at times of great ceremonies and carried behind him to the pulpit, so he could read the Word to the people.

Yes! Go there to those books, which he had always obeyed, and finally ask if they were not lying. He needed to scan their content one more time with his dimming eyes, but not as he used to with reverence and devotion, but with the vigorous sort of investigative inquisitiveness that was undoubtedly a sin ... He felt that he was committing sacrilege, entering here with such thought today, but he could not resist ... With his old habit, he reached for the golden rim hanging by the door and putting it on his head, pressed the secret lock ...

There was darkness behind the open door to the stairs leading downstairs. He descended them with an oil lamp, taken from the pulpit's feet, mindlessly reading the gold inscriptions on the walls, which heralded sudden death and defeat for all those who would venture there without godly thought. And then, when he was in the ground hall with an ornamental ceiling, without even closing the door behind him, he began to hurriedly open the carved and richly decorated chests. He pulled out yellowed parchments and cards with the prophecies of the first priestess Ada, almost worn out by centuries. They were preserved by the Waiting Brothers for two hundred years before. She had supposedly written them down in the Polar Country before she died. There were other books, containing prophecies and history of his people. There were thick volumes written down by the last god's man, Tuheja, whom his great-grandparents knew.

He threw all this, the whole burden of centuries, on a marble table and having lit the candlestick, began to read quickly, hurriedly, not even making the usual sign on his forehead before opening the book.

Hours were passing, and every twelve of them was announced by a ball falling from the clock into a copper bowl. The old man, weary, fell asleep at times in a high armchair and woke up again and read the books so well known to him, but standing before his eyes in a terrifying new form today. In the past, he saw the truth in them, but today he found only the longing. Now, he saw that it started on the pages of the priestess Ada and the rare first prophets as indefinite and hazy, evoked by the dreamed (or maybe even real?) specter of the Old Man. It grew and crystallized as time progressed and more misfortunes fell on the people. First, there was only talk of the Old Man, who had brought the people to the Moon from Earth and having gone to Earth, was to come back from it someday. Only later the promise of the savior appeared, who, being that Old Man, would at the same time be his rejuvenated form and would come victorious to liberate the oppressed people. Malahuda now noticed that the first time that Ada proclaimed the return of the Old Man, while living at the *Polar Land.* It happened when she was told about the *Warm Ponds* settlement being invaded by the Shern whose existence on the other side of the sea had apparently not even been known before. Over the centuries, every misfortune and every defeat had its prophet. They all promised the earlier coming of the Conqueror, the harder misfortune fell on the people, the sooner the Coming.

A bitter, ironic smile settled on his lips. With ever greater zeal, he was feverishly flipping through the respected and revered writings, rummaging through them with trembling hands and a burning eye, and was finding contradictions and errors. Without knowing what he was doing (and so doing an irrevocable thing), he crushed the edifice of the faith of his whole life.

His hands fell heavily on the last page of the last book. Now he knew for sure that no Conqueror had ever been truly promised by anyone, and that all the prophecies were only an expression of the longing of the people, oppressed by the monstrous and malicious indigenous lunar natives ...

"And yet, he came!"

It was an unsolvable puzzle for him, some ironic and perplexing paradox! Then there was another thing: a vicious circle of feelings emerging from the depths of his most secret gut. Here, just a moment ago, he himself had destroyed all his faith in his soul. Why then does everything in him make him indignant at the thought that this stranger, though not really predicted by the prophets, by simply appearing, will overturn the whole religion of expectation based on these prophecies?!

It occurred to him now, that he may have never really believed that the words he used to speak to himself and the people had a different meaning other than the one he apparently attached to them. It was all a dream which through a strange and perverse accident became the reality, not quite called for ... and he felt regret for the faith.

He tried to put it all into a formula and to understand for himself what he really wanted, but his thoughts were getting scattered every time, leaving only a painful emptiness in his head and heart. Just as he was pondering upon all that, fair Ihezal came in and was standing before him with this terrible question on her lips and burning in her eyes:

"Grandpa! You don't believe it's ... him?"

He took a few steps towards the girl and took her softly by the head with both hands. "Let's get out of here, Ihezal ...

Just a moment ago, when he was reaching his hand to her, she was reluctant. Now dazed, apparently by what she saw in the old man's eyes, she let him guide her outside calmly and without a word. So, he took her by her waist and led her up the stairs, leaving those holy and venerable books scattered behind, books of which he alone was the guardian ... The golden sign of the Arrival glinted behind them in the waning light of the candlestick. When they came back into the temple, the gray glow of the incoming day was already pouring in through the windows, which several dozen hours before sunrise, promises its appearance on the Moon.

Malahuda, still holding his granddaughter, walked with her towards the huge window facing east. Through the vapors rising from the Warm Ponds, they could see in the dim gray glow the frozen sea and the snow-covered mountains on the coast. The silence was enormous in all lunar settlements, except for Shern Avij's three-peaked sleepless castle where a torchlight was glowing red, and some cries could be heard. The high priest's armed men, following his order, were keeping watch around it in tents covered with snow.

They were both silent for a long time, staring at the dawn of the new day, until at last Ihezal, stepped back a few steps and threw her fur on the temple floor. Then, standing naked according to the custom for swearing, turned her hands to the east, and then to the north, towards where Earth was and said: "If I ceased to believe in Him, if I did not give him all my strength, my youth and my whole life and the pulse of all my blood, if I ever thought of any other man except Him, let me die miserably and perish, or let me become a mother a Mortz! You who are, hear me!"

Malahuda trembled and covered his eyes with his hand at this terrible incantation but did not say a word. The dawn was getting more and more silver casting a pearly light on the naked girl covered only with a coat of her golden hair.

II

Elem was standing on top of a hill separating the *Polar Land*, in which the sun never rises or sets, from the great airless desert illuminated by the glow of the holy star Earth. The pink sun, skimming on the horizon, was burning on his smoothly shaved skull, and trembling with metallic shines on his long, black, fuzzy beard. The Earth was in its first quarter, and far away, it was already morning in the land inhabited by people at the Great Sea. The monk, his back turned away from the silver sickle of the Earth, was looking down into the dark green valley. Most of the brothers had already disbursed throughout the lunar world to spread the news about the arrival of the Conqueror over human settlements. A few handfuls of those who remained were bustling with their travel preparations.

Elem could see them from above with shaved skulls, in long, dark habits, maundering diligently around the tents where they used to live while "waiting". They were taking out equipment and supplies needed for the road or preparing carts and dogs for sledding. The Conqueror was probably still sleeping in his shiny vehicle looking like an elongated sphere, in which he had traveled the interstellar spaces, because there was only silence, and no one was moving nearby.

In over a dozen or so hours people were to leave the *Polar Land* forever. These roofs serving countless generations of monks and this cool and green meadow where you can see the bright Earth. Elem was thinking about it without regret. Instead, pride was filling his chest with joy that during his lifetime and his being in charge there, the prophecy had been fulfilled, and the one whose coming was foretold and awaited for centuries, finally came. From now on, a new era would begin. He already saw it in his thoughts, as bright and triumphant.

He could see defeated and humiliated hateful Shern who, as the first ones, dared to claim the only right to the Moon, even though it had been given to people by the Old Man. He was imagining with delight the extermination of the damned Mortz. He was also thinking about the great triumph of his order of the Brothers who were once called Waiting, and now would be called the Joyful. They were the first who, according to the promise, saw and welcomed the Conqueror. Now, as his faithful and ever-present retinue, they will go to bring a new kingdom to the lunar countries ...

He could not wait to go south; into the people's lands which he had not seen since entering the Order as a boy. All his life had been devoted to staring into the desert at the distant Earth. Still they all knew him as a master at least an equal to the high priest in the capital at the *Warm Ponds*, and even higher than him, because he ruled their spirits from far away and was independent from the conquering power of the Shern.

In the meantime, before he could finally lead the living Brothers of the Order from their perpetual quarters where they were rewarded for all their waiting, it was necessary to deal with the dead.
He looked around. At the top of the hill, where he was standing, and further, on other descending ridges to the Desert, all the Waiting Brothers who had died before the Conqueror came were sitting supported by boulders, and their dead, dry faces were thoughtlessly looking towards the silver Earth on the black horizon.

So, centuries ago, facing the Earth, Ada, the first priestess and saint of the Brotherhood, ordered to be laid down like that facing the Earth. After the departure of the Old Man, she lived in the Polar Country until she died, looking at the Great Star over the Deserts, and so following her example, all brothers who died were placed there like her.

Anyone who entered the Order once, renounced everything and did not leave the Polar Country during his lifetime or after death. The brothers lost their families, they did not know property, drink or cooked food. They were supposed to be pure, temperate and truthful and obey their superiors. Their first duty was to wait in the ready ... Since in this evil land, time did not have day or night, they spent the night on handwork and prayers that were celebrated on the mountain, facing Earth. Those who died freed themselves from work but would accompany the living ones in prayers. They were not burned or buried, but they were carried to the hill and placed there with their backs leaning against a boulder to look at Earth and wait there with the living ones for the Coming. There were those who, feeling the approaching death, asked their comrades to take them there so they would end their lives in the face of the Earth.

The dead bodies did not decompose in the cool and diffused air. Over the years, this dead Order became more numerous than the living Order. The sun revolved around dead corpses, and they lasted there unchanging, calm and "expectant." When the Earth was new, and the fiery sun stood above it, the blackened faces glowed red and glowed so until the sunlight moved away from them, giving way to the ever-increasing, deadly blue light of the Earth. At the time of the full Earth, the Waiting Brothers came to pray up the hill, and when they sat on the boulders among the corpses, with the sun behind them, it was difficult to tell who were alive and who were dead.

This is how they were sitting the day before, the dead and the living ones together, when this great thing happened. When Elem called out, "He came!," he was surprised that only the living stood up to greet the Conqueror with him, that these corpses did not rise at the same time and did not join in the joyful hymn, as they did, that the prophecy was fulfilled, and it meant the end of the troubles for the lunar inhabitants ...

Now he was looking almost indignantly at this dead mass, still thoughtlessly and aimlessly waiting, with their dead faces turned to Earth, though the long awaited one was already among them. It still seemed to him that all the corpses, old, dry and falling apart, should be moving, and other, apparently still alive, recent ones, should rise and walk in crowds down there into the valley and welcome the one whom they were expecting while still alive and then again after their death.

But there was only the immeasurable, eternal, and solemn silence among the dead. Elem was walking slowly. He had passed a few recently laid down brothers, ascending to the top of the hill, where priestess Ada's tomb was. A huge boulder on the bare top of the hill was visible from afar and always lit by the sun. Beneath it, on the side facing the Earth, the small dead corpse of the holy prophetess, who knew the Old Man, was sitting on the throne of black stones: a handful of bones, wrapped in dried, blackened skin still in stiff priestly robes, with densely sewn in gold decorations. The graves of the Orders' superiors and exemplary holy men were arranged at her feet as a reward for their devotion.

Elem rested his hand on the foot of the grave throne and was looking towards Earth ... It was standing there in the quarter, bright and distant as always, with the outlines of seas and lands clearly visible on its silver disc known to the lunar people only from the ancient and dull stories.

Jerzy Żuławski

Fear overwhelmed him at this moment.

"Mother Ada," he whispered, raising his hand to touch the dried feet, "Mother Ada, Saint Foundress!" Here, somehow, as you had promised, the Old Man returned a young man to his people and is among us! Mother Ada, go and greet him ..." He embraced the body cautiously and wanted to move it from the age-old siesta when he suddenly heard the voice behind him: "Don't touch!"

He turned around. Choma, the eldest of the Order's Brothers and doting from age, was sitting among the corpses. He was looking angrily at his superior and kept repeating, shaking his gray beard: "Don't touch! Don't touch! Not allowed! ..."

"What are you doing here?," Elem asked.

"I am waiting as the Order says. It is the waiting hour. Saying this, he reached out with a trembling, dry hand, pointing to Earth, standing exactly in the first quarter.

"The waiting is over," said Elem. "Go to the valley, the Conqueror is there."

Choma shook his old head: "The Prophet Samielo said: 'Those who have died will rise up to greet the longing of their living eyes!" The dead are still waiting, so I am waiting with them. The Conqueror has not arrived yet!"

Elem got suddenly angry: "You are stupid, and so are the corpses! How dare you to doubt when I am telling you that the Conqueror is among us? The corpses aren't rising, because they are dead, and it is not their fault, but we will drag them all to the feet of the Conqueror.

Saying this, he stepped on a pedestal and wrapped his coat around Ada's body, took it in his arms and began to go down with that burden. Choma groaned deafly and covered his eyes so as not to look at such sacrilege of his superior who was now walking towards the valley, firm and calm, with the body of the first priestess in his arms. Having met several brothers who had come out to look for him, he ordered them to collect other corpses and to put a great pile of them on the plain ...

"The time of their waiting is over," he said. "Let them rest ..."

In the meantime, the one, whom they called the Conqueror, woke up and came out of his shiny steel car.

Elem, seeing him from far away, quickly placed Ada's body on the moss and ran with a greeting. "Lord, Lord!," he said bending, be greeted ..."

All his fervor and self-confidence left him at the sight of this giant newcomer, twice exceeding the height of the Moon people. It was written down the first people brought to the Moon by the Old Man were that tall. It was also difficult to communicate with him, because he spoke in a strange language similar to that preserved only in the oldest books. The lunar people who had been illiterate for quite some time did not understand that language anymore.

Seeing the monk's perplexity, the newcomer smiled. "They call me Marek on Earth," he said.

Elem bowed his head again. "You are allowed to bear the name you want on Earth, but here you have only one for centuries: The Conqueror"!

"I have actually won more than you might think," Marek said, "coming here from Earth." They had companions, I am alone," he added to himself, looking towards the distant Earth in the sky.

Then he turned to Elem again: "Are you not surprised that I came?"

"We knew you would come." Elem looked at him with astonished eyes. "How's that? Did you not give Ada a promise when, you were leaving as ...the Old Man? And then all our prophets ..."

He broke off with fear, because the "Conqueror" burst out in such crazy and uncontrollable laughter that had not been heard in the quiet Polar Land for centuries. His mouth and eyes were laughing, and his whole young face was laughing, too. He sat down on the ground and began to strike his thighs with his hands with amusement.

"So, you, so you ...," he said, choking with laughter "think that I am your 'Old Man', from six or seven hundred years ago? This is so extraordinary! Here, as I guess, the whole legend has grown! And I have to be like a Chinese god ... Oh! Ye, my earthly comrades! If you knew what kind of welcome these lovely midgets have prepared for me! Come, my Pope, let me embrace you!"

Saying this, he grabbed the speechless Elem and lifted him like a feather from the ground and began to dance with him across the plain.

"Oh, beloved, noble descendant of madmen like me!" He cried, 'how glad I am that you were waiting for me here! We will live happily here, you will show me everything I want to see and then, then I must take you with me when I return to Earth!"

He put the monk back on the ground and continued speaking: "Do you know that I can go back any time I want! Not like those madmen seven hundred years ago because of whom, you now roam the Moon."

He grabbed his hand like a child and pulled him toward the vehicle. "Look, first of all I fell here, not on some airless dessert which they had to struggle through. Was not the shot well aimed? Didn't I fall right in the middle of the polar valley among your houses when I did not know that you were expecting me here?... Look, the missile is standing still wrapped in its steel shell, hollowed out as if in a cannon! Yes, venerable shaman! I arrived here in my own culverin, which filled itself with compressed air, falling down. Do you see how it is standing perfectly situated, at the same angle, as it fell ... There are special legs underneath, which sank into the ground, a beautiful carriage! It is enough to shut the door and press the button there and - I'm going back to Earth. The same way, do you understand? I am going back to Earth mathematically the same way I came!"

He was speaking quickly and cheerfully, not aware that the monk did not even understand all his words. In this chaos Elem managed to catch only one sentence: 'I'm going back to Earth!', and a sudden, monstrous terror filled his throat.

"Lord, Lord!" He managed to choke, clinging to his sleeve with his raised hands.

Marek looked at him, and the joke died on his lips. The monk looked terrible. His small, ardent hands were shaking, and a dreadful request and despair and fear howled in his raised eyes...

"What? ... What are you?', he whispered involuntarily, stepping back.

Elem exploded: "Lord! Don't go back to Earth! We were waiting for you! Lord, do you understand what this means: we've been waiting for you for seven hundred years! You have come here, and you say things that neither I understand nor anyone on the moon will! We only know one thing: if it weren't for our faith in you, if it weren't for the belief that you would really come, our life - in oppression and in such misery would be impossible here! And now you are saying that you will leave, and you want to show me..."

He turned and suddenly stretched out his hand to the silent, small corpse of Ada, brought in the monk's coat from above, from where both the Sun and the Earth can be seen. "Look! Here is Ada your priestess who knew you when you were an Old Man here, and to whom you made a promise to return! She waited for you until the end of her days, and when she died, she still waited with her blind eyes turned at the Earth, as we waited every day, as those with her and with us waited!" Saying this, he pointed to the hill with his hand, where the Waiting Brothers were busy, moving the corpses from their eternal places to bring them down under the feet of the Conqueror.

"Those don't need you anymore! You came, and their tedious posthumous vigil has already ended! They will burn for eternal rest here in this valley, where fire has never burned, because we have been waiting for you in these tents for seven centuries without fire, as if we had left home for a short time. But we need you, everyone here needs you, all of us scattered over the Moon's globe, on the distant sea, on the equators, on the mountains and on streams! ... And you, when you have finally come, you are playing with me, and then, you want to go back!" He said all this hotly, almost solemnly, without a trace of fear that choked his first sentences in his throat. At the last words, his voice twitched, as if with some bitter painful irony.

Marek wasn't laughing any longer. He was looking at the monk with wide open eyes, as if he had just realized that his crazy arrival to the Moon had been accidentally linked to something great, that he had taken, without knowing it, a burden on his shoulders ... He had just laughed at the legend, in which he accidentally got involved, but now fear filled him. He rubbed his forehead with his hand and looked at the monks, who were carrying the corpses down from the mountains and silently laying them on the moss, all facing him.

"What do you want from me?," he said in spite of himself.

"Save us, Lord!" Elem shouted.

"Save us, save us, Lord! "The Waiting Brothers repeated in a chorus, like the echo.

"What's going on with you? Please tell me ..." He paused and took a deep breath. "What's wrong with you?"

Elem looked at the brothers behind him, then stepped forward. "Lord," he began, "we are troubled by evil. The Shern oppress us. When you were leaving us as the Old man…"

Marek interrupted him impatiently. He sat on the ground and beckoned the monk to himself. "I'm sorry, brother," he said, placing his hand on his small shoulder, "I'm sorry for my behavior, but ... Listen to me right now and try to understand what I am saying. I will do for you everything that is in my power, although ... I am not, do you understand me? I am not your Old Man. He died seven hundred years ago, here on the Moon, in the airless desert, and I know about him and you only because before he died, he had sent his diary to Earth in a sphere ... I came to the Moon quite accidentally, not knowing that you were waiting for me."

Elem smiled lightly. Ada recorded in her writings that the Old man didn't want anybody to know that he was the Old man. The same is true for the Conqueror. However, he bowed his head in silence as if accepting what he heard.

Marek, meanwhile, continued: "But I came. Finally, knowing that you need me, I'm ready ... I don't know if I can do what you are expecting from me. Who are these Shern? They are the indigenous natives, aren't they?"

"Yes. They are very scary. Since you have left us ... since the Old Man departed, our whole life is one constant struggle against their evil violence. There, by the Warm Ponds where the first settlement was, there are books stored in the underground treasury ... We don't need books here; word of mouth was spreading about you, but there are books. Some of them proclaimed your coming. Others always begin with the words: 'That the Old Man might live and know the misery of his people when he returns as a Conqueror ...' And indeed, there are few cards in them that would speak of anything other than the misery of your people, Lord. Our history is written there. When you arrive at the Warm Ponds, Lord, and read these books, you will learn that the Shern have bothered us for seven hundred years. Immediately after The Old Man's .... departure, they crossed the Great Sea and began destroying our houses. There were times when no one could breathe. They burned our homes, murdered our young people and abducted our women. Today, today as you have returned, Lord, it's worse than ever! The Shern rule over all human settlements, north of the Great Sea to the ends of the Desert! At the Warm Ponds, where we have our capital and a high priest, they have their governor, who rules from a fortified tower and extorts a tribute from us. A peace was signed with them, Lord, but death would be better than such a peace. Here, in the Polar Land, where we, the Waiting ones, have lived, this is the only place where their power seem not to reach! They are afraid of seeing the blessed Earth, which they call the evil and the cursed star, as if in their animal darkness they sensed that you would come, our savior, and their slayer. Save us, sir!"

"Save us, save us! The monks shouted again and began to surround the Conqueror and embrace his legs with theirs hands. They, who renounced their families and property to wait for him, now remembered that they had relatives and acquaintances there in the occupied country. So they began, interrupting each other, to tell him haphazardly all of the wrongs done by the Shern, all the murders, fires and oppression.

Marek was sitting on the ground with pursed lips and eyebrows. He was weighing something in his mind for a long time, though the begging voices had already ceased and changed into full of expectant silence ... There was a moment that he involuntarily looked at his shiny vehicle, ready to leave at any moment, as if he wanted to sit in it and escape back through the planetary spaces there to Earth, but he quickly rejected this thought. A hard resolution cut the features of his young face.

"What do the Shern look like? Are they similar to people?" He asked.

"No, no! They look very scary!"

"Terrible, terrible!" Shouted the monks.

Marek turned his questioning eyes at Elem. The monk's face was full of disgust, bordering on pain. He bowed his head and then said: "They are scary. You'll see them yourself, sir."

"I want to know now. Do they have anything human in them?"

"Nothing besides their brain. And theirs is different, because it does not distinguish between bad and good."

"What do they look like?"

"They're smaller than us. Yes, much smaller. They have wings, but they have difficulty using them. They know how to speak and they can understand human speech, but among themselves they communicate by light flashes on their foreheads ... Ah! They are scary! And hideous! Hideous! And bad ..."

Marek rose. All the Brothers were gathered around him now, and nearby lay a huge pile of flesh and bones, carried here from the sunny hill. Old tents were also brought there, and piles and canvases lined up to feed the flames better. Elem, noticing that the Conqueror was looking at the pile, interrupted his story and looked into his face with a questioning look.

"Are we to we burn them?" He said after a moment.

Marek did not answer. So, the monk stepped closer to him and said again: "Lord, should I set fire to the pile? Are they allowed to rest now, and can we return to people, to our homes and to once abandoned families?"

Slowly and hesitantly, Marek bowed his head. "Yes," he finally said, "I accept my fate ..."

When, a dozen or so hours later, they set off along the eternal path through the gorges connecting the Polar Country to the inhabited world of the Moon, a huge fire made of the now useless tents of the dissolved Order and its members' dead bodies were burning high. Marek looked behind him at the sun red from the roaring smoke that obscured the gray-silver slice of the Earth, still looking from behind the horizon.

At the stream, they met people from closer settlements, who, having heard of the arrival of the Conqueror, were already hurrying to greet him. Marek was looking at those dwarfs with curiosity, among them a few women, small and quite pretty. They all fell on their faces, touched his garments with signs of worship, and greeted him in a strange language, in which he could barely grasp Polish, English and Portuguese words twisted beyond recognition.

At the first meeting, he was too interested in seeing these little people to pay attention to how they greeted him. However, later, as more and more crowds arrived, he tried to protest against the idolatrous signs of worship, but he soon realized that he was powerless in this respect. When he rebuked them, either they did not understand what he was talking about, or they considered his anger a punishment for some wrongdoing and began to explain themselves with even greater signs of subservience. When he tried to gently convince them that he was a man like them, although he came from Earth, they were only smiling slyly, just like Elem, when he told him that the Old Man had long since died, and that he had nothing to do with him.

He stopped defending himself in vain and postponed the clarification of this strange misunderstanding until a more appropriate time. He was proceeding towards the Great Sea in a procession of his unsolicited followers, like a young and fair god, twice as tall as the faithful crowd.

The men we cutting in front of him with small steps and apparently complaining about something (he did not understand them well and often resorted to Elem's help who, as a literate, knew the "holy", Polish, which the Old Man used to speak). Everyone talked about their wrongs, quarrels and troubles, and everybody asked him again to avenge or reward him, before everyone else, because they deserved it. That led to quarrels and even fights which often made Marek laugh in spite of his restraint.

The women were more temperate. They were walking at the side and looking at him only with large, delighted eyes, and when he spoke to any of them, they fled without answering, like frightened deer. He once mentioned half-jokingly about the Shern ...

"Lord! Do what you want, but it's better not to talk about the Shern in the presence of women." Said Elem.

"Why?"

The monk bowed his head "There are terrible things ..."

However, before he could finish his sentences, he was interrupted by a commotion that suddenly began in the pilgrim's group. The first day of the journey was coming to an end, and they were just descending to the plain, hurrying for the night towards the settlements of the Old Springs, where centuries ago kerosene was first discovered on the Moon. Suddenly the pilgrims and monks in the Conqueror's procession began to crowd together and shout, pointing towards nearby thickets. Marek looked in that direction and saw a man, slightly larger than others, who, leaping out of the thicket, stood on a rocky promontory above the road and began throwing insults and curses.

He was answered with a hail of insults. Some of them threw stones, which, however, did not reach him. Women hid behind the backs of men weeping, and the monks spat alternately and drew the holy sign of the Coming on their forehead, mouth and chest.

"Mortz! Mortz!" Some of them yelled. The man on the rock laughed derisively, pulled the bow in his hand and released an arrow. It whispered into the crowd, accurately striking the neck of a young, small woman, who looked for shelter at Marek's feet.

The cry of horror was answered by the ambusher's triumphant laughter again. He was flexing his bow with inconceivable speed, sending arrows into the frightened and dense cluster. One of the arrows scratched Marek's forehead, marking a wide bloody gash on it. Instinctively, he pulled a weapon from his sleeve and fired towards the assailant.

The shot was well aimed. The man on the rock released the bow, fluttered his arms in the air and without a shout fell head down, landing right next to the road. Several men leapt toward him and began to tear apart the leather tunic on his chest. Marek thought that they were looking for a wound from an unknown firearm, but when they saw two red moles on his chest looking like six-fingered hands, they began to shout again: "Mortz! Mortz!," and began to beat him with rocks, as he was still panting and rolling his eyes, and bloody foam was coming from his mouth.

Marek threw himself at them, horrified. "Stop you dogs!', he shouted, "this man is still alive and cannot defend himself anymore!"

Elem stopped him: "Lord, don't worry. This is not a human. It's a Mortz ..."

Seeing Marek's questioning eyes, he added bending his head:" I'll tell you later, sir. Leave it. It's good that he died.

Only a bloody mass was left of the stranger's body and stones were still thrown at it. Marek turned his head in disgust at this sight, while the monks dancing around him sang a triumphant hymn:

"The Conqueror has come to us!

He struck the Shern, he struck a Mortz with a lightning!

The Moon is for people, death to our enemies!

Glory to the Conqueror, wherever his blessed feet step! ... "

Marek silently slipped out of the circle of singers and moved on. From the last bend of the road, just near the settlements, apparently frequently visited, one could see the whole wide plain, dotted with small annular hills. It was the same one at which the Old Man as young as he was now, seven hundred years ago, looked upon for the first time. He sat on a roadside stone and pondered over it all. ... And he was troubled that he couldn't formulate his thoughts properly.

He was looking at the boundless plain, already gilded with the sun already bending toward the west and full of the black round lakes. He thought that having spent some time so far in Polar Land with eternal half-dawn, he would now see the first sunset on the Moon, and that he was indescribably sad at this time of the sunset ... He realized that his shallow gaiety had disappeared after only a few hundred hours.

Marek understood that he was pursuing with a pang in his heart toward the distant sea, where his fate would be decided, so incomprehensible in the light of people's affairs on the Moon ... Now he felt longing for the Earth, which he, the bold and hungry for new things playboy, had left so recently, laughing ... There was a moment that he wanted to get up and run away, return to the Polar Country, and sit in his shiny vehicle, which was standing there ready for the return trip. Then a sudden inertia enveloped him, he rested his elbows on his knees and hid his face in his hands ...

"I promised to accept my fate," he whispered.

A light touch woke him from his reflection. He raised his eyes. A young and emaciated woman was kneeling in front of him and raising at him her face full of boundless, blind, and dead fear. Her hands and lips were trembling like in a fever. She could barely get the choked voice out of her jammed teeth...

"Lord, lord," she moaned "you know everything, yes ... you looked at me ... I know you know,.... but I am innocent, lord! I was abducted by wide violence ..."

Then suddenly, in insane fear, she shouted, clutching at his legs: "Lord! Conqueror! Have mercy on me! Do not hand me over to them, because they will bury me in the ground! I know that the law says so, but I am innocent!"

She fell on her face, shaken by desperate sobbing. She couldn't speak anymore, she just mumbled and muttered words that were incomprehensible and imploring with her teeth chattering.

Marek jumped up. A terrible and unbelievable thought struck him. He grabbed the crying woman by the shoulders and set her on the ground in front of him. She stopped suddenly and looked at him with dumb eyes, apparently waiting for death. "What is your name?" He said in a strangely unbelieving voice.

"Nechem ..."

"And this ... Mortz, the one who was killed? ..."

"Yes, sir, yes, that's my son, but I'm innocent!"

She tried to touch his hand with her mouth. But he jerked her and shouted: "Your son and ... whose?"

The woman began to shake again. "Lord! I am not guilty! I was violently abducted by Shern! Nobody knows about it but you ... They believed that I was with a sacrifice at the Waiting Brothers ... I hid ... Lord! I know I should have strangled him as soon as he was born, but I couldn't, forgive me, I couldn't! After all, he was my son!

Marek reflexively, in an attack of boundless revulsion, pushed her away and covered his eyes with his hands. There was something so monstrous and terrifying about it, and at the same time, turning physiological laws upside down, that he squeezed his head with his hands, feeling that insanity was gripping him ...

He came to his senses only when he heard the call of his procession. He turned quickly to the woman still lying motionless:

"Nechem, get up, and don't worry."

She wanted to thank him, but he withdrew his hand in disgust. He couldn't force himself to look at her.

He walked the rest of the way in silence. It was already evening when they found themselves on the plain among the settlements at Old Springs. From low, stone houses, usually dug into the ground for better protection against night frosts, the people came out to meet the arriving Conqueror and greeted him with noisy cheers, but he could hardly hear them. He walked among the joyful crowd with a scowling face, avoiding especially the eyes of women, each of whom could be as tainted as the one who had recently wandered at his feet. The people looked at his menacing face and heralded a swift and firm destruction of all the Shern. Some of them looked on with delight at his haughty height and powerful muscles, only by timid worship, not daring to touch them, and spoke loudly how these strong hands would defeat the Shern.

He was placed in the best house for the winter night. Like all of the other settlements on the Moon, there was a separate and uninhabited house here, kept by the Waiting Brothers from the old order and called the "House of the Conqueror," where the newcomer could find refuge when he would arrive. Since for generations the Conqueror had not arrived, it now turned out that the neglected house was adapted into the communal granary and so ruined that it was impossible to stay in it. This problem was solved by giving him the hut of the village head who was also a local priest.

When Marek was alone in the evening, he ordered Elem to come to him immediately. The monk stepped in for the first time wearing the red robe as a sign of joy and a silver diadem on his forehead, as he had in a small village temple where he had announced the arrival of the Conqueror, whom he was just bringing with him ... He stood respectfully at the door and waited.

Marek, in a small room, too small for his height was lying on a bunch of skins with an oil lamp near his head. When Elem entered, he rose on his elbow and stared at him with glistening eyes.

"Who are Mortzes? He asked suddenly.

Elem paled, and something like a shadow of bitter shame mixed with hatred flashed across his dry face. "Lord ..."

"Who are Mortzes?," repeated Marek zealously - is that ...?

He did not finish, but the monk understood him "Yes, my lord," he whispered, "yes ... They are Shern."

"So, your women ... give themselves to these monsters?"

"No sir. They don't give themselves up to them."

"And then how? How?"

He jumped up suddenly and sat down on the bed:" Listen, so you are the dogs! I know this story! And once upon a time they were talking on Earth about devil offspring! Listen! You all should be stoned instead of the unfortunate ones!"

His anger almost choked him. "Come here! And tell me immediately, where did the fairy tale about the Shern's children originate, which even women themselves believed in their madness!

"No, sir, it's not a fairy tale."

Marek looked at him with wide eyes.

"Lord, let me speak ... The Shern have strange powers. Under their wide wings of the membrane stretched on the bones, they have something like flexible six-fingered hands. Their whole body is covered with black, short hair, soft, dense and shiny, except for the forehead, but those hands are naked and white... And these hands ..."

He took a deep breath and wiped sweat from his forehead. It was visible that it was difficult for him to talk about this terrible thing. "Their power is in their hands," he began again after a moment. "If both of them touch a human body at the same time, it is shaken by a painful and often deadly shiver, similar to some poisonous sea fish ... and if it is a woman ..."

"Ah!" Marcus shouted.

"If this is a woman ... or a bitch or any female, she conceives and gives birth. She gives birth to a fetus, according to her species, similar to her only on the outside but angry and perverse as all Shern ...

"Are you sure this is the case?"

"Yes, sir ..."

A whirlpool of screaming thoughts whirled in Marek's head. It was so inconceivable ... and yet, he remembered the studies of some terrestrial biologists, who, acting mechanically on unfertilized eggs or using the help of chemical agents, forced them to divide and received the alive fetus from them ... Apparently in the hands of these lunar monsters there was some ability to release electricity or other emanation, which, shaking the whole body, played the role of a spermatozoid...

"No, no, no! It is impossible! He repeated loudly, pressing the raging pulse in his temples with his hands ..."

"And yet, sir, it is so. You killed a Mortz today."

"How do you know it was a Mortz?"

"A Mortz has the red-blue stigma where his mother was touched by those cursed hands. You saw it yourself ...We kill them and exterminate them like wild animals, because they are even worse than Shern. Their perverse anger is combined with a human appearance."

There was a deep silence.

After a long moment, Marek raised his head and asked without sound: "Are these ... common cases?"

"No. Not now. A woman who met with a Shern is buried without a judgment in the ground up to her neck and left there until she dies of hunger and thirst, but in the past..."

It was hard for him to speak. It was obvious that his human pride, brought by distant ancestors from Earth, suffered inexpressibly from these confessions. He bowed his head before Marek's blazing gaze and finished quietly: "There used to be a lot of Mortzes. Fortunately, they are infertile. We exterminated them. There was no mercy on one side or the other ... Now it is rare ... Unless the Shern kidnap a woman."

"In the past? Did the women themselves? ..."

Elem shook his head. "No. Never. This is supposedly a terrible pain. Cramps wring muscles and break bones ...But ..."

"What?"

"There was a time that, being defeated, we had to as a tribute.".

Marek threw himself on the bed." ... Give them your women?"

"Yes. Ten every year. The Shern need Mortzes, who are hated by us, yet serve them like faithful dogs ... and Shern don't like to work themselves ..."

Marek covered his eyes again. A shiver shook his body despite the heat that spread from the fire around the room. "And these women ... have they always stayed with the Shern?" He asked without looking at the monk.

"No. The Shern killed them or sent them back when they got old ..."

"And then you? ..."

"Then we killed them. They were, after all, mothers of Mortzes.," he added in a tone of justification.

In the silence that followed his last words, one could hear only the sound of the wind that was agitating the falling snow, covering the lunar globe on a long, dark, night lasting fourteen Earth days.

Marek sat silently for a long time with his face covered. Finally, he took his hands away from his eyes and, frowning, said to himself loudly and hard: "We have to win!"

III

Avij despised those earthly intruders on the Moon, called people, too much to send messengers and ask why wasn't the usual tribute paid to him at the sunset, or what was meant by the hostile movement he saw in the evening around his three-peak castle. Instead, he decided to burn the entire settlement at the *Warm Ponds* and slaughter the people. However, he did not give the order that the Mortzes around him were longing for. He knew that his crew was not very numerous, and he saw the gathering of armed men. In the event of resistance, it could have come to a heavy fight with a dubious result, so he preferred to wait for the arrival of reinforcements. It was the night when the Shern came from overseas to pick up the submitted tribute and change the crew in the castle.

The fortified tower, where Avij lived, was standing among the walled garden that connected the small, secured marina at the sea. The Shern, making up Avij's entourage, and above all, his few Mortzes never dared to go beyond the gates of these walls. They knew very well, that despite all the pacts, there would have been death awaiting them at the hands of the hated and hating human population, but within the stronghold they felt completely safe. They trusted the breadth of those walls, and even more the terror inculcated by their terrible name, which kept every human away from them. In the event of killing a Shern, or even an assault, they avenged mercilessly. They cared less about Mortzes, even if one of them curious about their neighbors was killed. Even though they used them, in their hearts they despised them almost as much as the people.

At the same time, in the event of a serious danger, the retreat from the castle was always open, in the daytime by boats, at night on sail sledges across the frozen sea. Avij's monstrous countrymen came for that tribute every fourth night, and he was waiting for their arrival now.

However, the Shern's congenital proclivity for laziness, more than the lack of these reinforcements, prevented him from giving a bloody order. One would have to decide and speak to the Mortzes and issue the appropriate orders ... He was thinking about all this and imagined with pleasure the flames and moans of slaughtered victims in the night, but in the meantime, he did not even want to move or nod.

He was resting on a wide sofa, with soft red fabric wrapped around his shiny hairy body. His legs with sharp claws were pulled under him while his grotesque six-fingered hands were hidden in the folds of the sagging membrane of broad bat wings ... Next to him in the copper tripods, special herbs were burning, whose pungent and intoxicating odor gave Avij a peculiar pleasure. His four round bloody eyes looked with a misty and sleepy gaze toward the door where six Mortzes were keeping guard huddled from the cold.

It occurred to him that it was midnight and that the Shern emissary should have arrived. He wanted to say something, to give an order, but he did not feel like it. The Mortzes hardly and inaccurately understood the speech of the colored flashes on his white, phosphorescent forehead, and he was reluctant to use voice. So, he only stretched his numb wings and flicked them off. Then, he yawned loudly, opening his toothless mouth, framed by a horn-shaped growth in the shape of a wide and short beak, with one hook in its center.

The Mortzes jumped up like a pack of well-behaved dogs, and one of them, a man, huge for the height of the lunar people, with a bloody six-finger mark on his cheek, jumped towards his lord and sat down on the floor, looking questioningly in his bloody eyes.

"Has the message arrived?" Avij flashed towards him.

The Mortz called Nuzar looked at him in desperate confusion and groaned: "Lord ..."

Avij grunted: "You beast! We have to use a voice to talk to you like you do to dogs or people! Have the emissaries arrived? - I have asked."

"Not yet, my lord, but they will come soon ..."

"Stupid."

He turned to the other side and ordered more herbs to be sprinkled on the tripods. Mortzes, who had human lungs, were suffocating from that thick, unbearable smoke, but neither of them dared to admit it. It would be a disgrace not to enjoy what the Shern, a higher being, enjoyed.

Meanwhile, Avij closed his two lower eyes used for looking closely, and left the upper ones, far-sighted, open and was looking into the darkness ahead and dreaming of the intended slaughter that he will soon be watching from the top of his seaside tower ...

"When the emissaries arrive with reinforcements," he grunted again after a while, "you will set fire to the village ..."

"Maybe sooner ..." Nuzar shouted, his eyes sparkling.

"Hush, dog, and listen ... Kill everyone. You are allowed. They did not pay tribute ... and I like it that way. Malahuda ... You can give him to the dogs. He's too old for me, and he must have tough meat, it would not get tender in half a day... But he has a daughter." He grunted loudly, tapping his tongue against the horned beak.

"Her name is Ihezal ...!" One of the Mortzes, a young boy, barely adolescent, snapped out.

"Shut up, dog. Maybe her children would be smarter than you ... As soon as I receive the message..."

But the emissaries didn't come. A long night passed, and it wasn't until the dawn when one of the two Shern standing on watch, and being Avij's personal companions, reported they could see the sails of an approaching sleigh at the sea ...

Sudden energy filled the governor then. He jumped up and flapped his heavy wings, making a grinding noise that meant what people called laughter. "In a few hours there will be a sea of flames here!" Then he frowned for a moment. "It is a pity that the night is over, it would have been better at night ..."

Nuzar, who was standing by the window, turned his wild hideously stigmatized face towards Avij: "Can we go to help them?" He held his hand out in front of him. "The castle is completely surrounded. I see snow-covered tents. They stayed awake all night ... They posted guards even at sea."

Avij rushed towards the window, straining a pair of his far-sighted eyes into the weak, sharp dawn of the coming day. Indeed, an unbroken double ring of snow mounds covering the tents of armed men stretched around the castle. Here and there the rising smoke proved that the people were on the alert. It was towards these mounds that the Shern' winged sleighs were quickly approaching from the side of the frozen sea.

The governor stared for a moment, and suddenly his monstrous face lit up. "Cowards! Look: no help is needed!"

Indeed, as the sled approached, the people's guards parted themselves, letting them slowly into their dense ring. What appeared to Avij to be the result of fear, however, was Jeret's wisely devised plan. He and his men had taken over the most important post on the sea ice which was neglected by the armed Mortzes. He did not want to let these arriving enemies sneak out, and at the same time he was afraid that in the event of resistance and battle, the Shern might let their compatriots know too early and prematurely bring overwhelming help. However, the ring closed again immediately behind the sleigh.

Meanwhile, the dawn was drawing near, and before the delayed Shern had rested from the hardships of their night journey, great events had occurred in the settlement at the Warm Ponds, the capital of the lunar country. The almost rising sun, slipping down the snowy slopes of O'Tamor's Crater, peeked over the seashore. Now, Jeret's guards were moving hastily from the ice that might be starting to crack soon as the messengers from the north announced that the Conqueror had set out from his last night's stop and would soon be among the people waiting for him.

The joyful news spread all over the village in an instant. The inhabitants, who could not wait for the morning throughout the long night, at dawn, despite the frost, started to emerge from their houses. Now, they were standing on the slope of the hill, from where a wide, snow-whitened plain could be seen. The sun was rising lazily from the sea, and now the hill on which the city was built, cast the shadows of those who were waiting far, far away onto the white plain, making them as if emissaries of the people's longing, spreading them under the feet of the coming ...

Marek was walking towards the rising sun on the melting snows, and on the lush, vivid, lunar greenery shooting from beneath them. He himself was as bright and radiant as the sun. He was happy to see the light again after the long night and anxious to hear the roar of the sea on the rocky shore. Young, robust and daring, he was enjoying his life and his fiery adventures, forgetting the despondency and doubts that plagued him the previous day and through the long night.

The role that he had involuntarily taken upon himself yesterday (ah! It was "yesterday" two earthly weeks away!) threatening him with such a heavy and unbearable burden seemed to him amusingly light today. With almost a childish joy in his twenty-year-old heart, Marek was thinking that he had come here like a young, victorious god, sent from a distant star, and that he would liberate and make the lunar people happy. Then he would fly away again through the abyss of space to his distant homeland, leaving behind a good memory of himself for centuries. He thought that after his return to Earth, he would be telling people, pointing to the bright rising moon, that he had been there, and in those heavenly precipices they would be blessing his name for the good he would do now. It seemed to Marek that by his extraordinary act of going through the interplanetary space, he had gained the right to accept upon himself the legend of the savior that had grown up over the centuries. However, such right also carried the duty to perform according to his ability what they expected from him here. Besides, wasn't this a twist of some inconceivable Fate or Providence that it was he who got to the Moon while the people here were awaiting the arrival of the Conqueror coming from the stars?

Marek was thinking about it all as he was walking along the bank of the stream unleashed from ice, over strange flowers and herbs bursting from beneath his feet to life after a night's sleep. Great joyful pride filled his heart, and self-assured potency rumbled in ripples through his veins. He smiled at the "dwarfs" running alongside and enjoyed the rising sun of the "new day" with them. He was filled with a profound, kindness typical of merry people. He was graciously talking with the crowding dwarfs, smiled at women and even at poor Nechem. She had not stepped away from him since the moment of her memorable confession, running like a dog at his leg. Today he was looking at her with a different attitude. He felt sorry for her, and he was happy and confident in his strength. He believed that with his coming the Shern's omnipotence would end, along with their oppression of the lunar people. As he thought about it, he smiled at the woman who was still staring into his eyes and stroked her head with his hand.

"How good you are, my lord!" She exclaimed, with an expression of indescribable doggish gratitude in her large, pale eyes.

"Why are you calling me good? After all, I killed your ..."

"Ah, yes, yes, my lord!," you killed him, but he was a Mortz, and he even dared to hurt you," she said, looking at the wide bloody gash on Marek's forehead. "But you wanted to defend him when he was being stoned, and you showed pity on the poor man! If they knew..." She trembled and shrunk under a wave of indescribable fear.

Marek wanted to answer, but was interrupted by a sudden buzz, mixed with distant screams. They were already spotted in the settlement at the Warm Ponds and people, waiting on the ramparts, began to run down to the plain, and joined the Conqueror's entourage with shouts. Soon, the city gates were opened, and the elders were coming out to greet them.

Now, Elem surrounded by the Brothers of his Order, stepped forward, serious and solemn, in his red-lined priestly robes, and led the whole procession towards the gates, among the crowd pressing in from everywhere.

Malahuda was not in the welcoming delegation. The elders of the people came for him, but he sent them away, saying that he would wait for the Conqueror on the steps of the temple to receive him there, where the Old Man had once lived ... After the elders' departure, he summoned Ihezal, and without calling his servants, he began to dress with her help. He ordered the most expensive garments to be pulled out of wooden trunks encrusted with gold and copper. There were old tunics that had been laboriously made by pious women, coats of the finest furs with pure gold fasteners, and belts so densely set with gems that leather rollers had to be placed under them not to hurt hips with their weight.

"For the last time, for the last time ...," he said, looking at Ihezal bustling about.

Finally, he selected a red tunic, reaching to his ankles and embroidered with all the strange flowers that had never been woven on the moon (some say that such flowers were supposed to grow on Earth). He fastened it above his hips with a wide belt made of yellowed bone, gold, and gems, which was once owned by the great priest and prophet Ramida. He covered it all with a priceless black coat made of fur stripped from an alive Shern. This coat, a reminder of the great victory won centuries ago (unfortunately rare in the history of the lunar people!), was valued as much as the greatest holiness and hidden within the underground treasury. Ihezal had now carried it out from there on her grandfather's orders, together with an ancient looking cap having strings of amber and enormous pearls hanging down to the waist. A bright precious stone that was supposedly worn by the Old Man was set in its golden, butted browband, and surrounded by fabulous emeralds.

Malahuda put on a cap over his hair tied with a ritual, golden ring, and put on white sandals, ornamented with rubies. Then he put an expensive chain around his neck and reached out with his hand heavy with rings for an intricately chiseled bone staff...

Now, Ihezal supported the old man bent under the weight of his robes and chains and was leading him to the temple ... and he was pausing on each step and looking behind, mumbling indistinctly to himself. In the great hall, he went to the main pulpit and, leaning his arm on the golden sign of the Coming, shining on its front and wiped the sweat that copiously appeared on his forehead.

"For the last time, for the last time", he whispered and nodded his head covered with the high priest's cap...

Ihezal stepped a little forward. She had been silent and obedient so far, but at that moment, she felt that breathlessness was descending on her in this deserted temple. She stood at the wide-open front door, leaning on one of the two enormous alabaster pillars, supporting the portal and was looking ahead, beyond the city, to the distant plain where the Conqueror was walking. There was a moment when it seemed to her that she heard her grandpa's crying behind her. In one blink of an eye her features contracted with a kind of cramp like pain and dislike, but she did not even look back ...

Without knowing, with an almost sleepy motion, Ihezal reached beyond her ears with her hands and, taking a lot of her golden and long hair, pulled it over her mouth, on the white neck and her breast peeking out from under the parted amethyst robe, ... A flame hit her temple, her scarlet lips began to tremble, and she covered her huge black eyes with her eyelids, listening to the soft and bright singing of her soul:

"Oh, come...Oh! Come...

I will come out from the dark temple to meet you, I will kneel before you on the golden sand and I will look into your eyes, which must be bright, as the stars from where you come to me! You will come to me, because I am the longing of the people's, for generations preserving the memory of the distant native star. I am the love that nurtured the phantom of your appearance, I am the last beauty of the sad exiles.

Oh come! - oh, come! Radiant, victorious, divine! ..."

A hot wave fluttered in her chest and choked her breath with a delightful hug.... The dark temple began to disappear in her eyes, before which only a sea of light, glow and green rippled ...

Ihezal reveled in this long sweet, half-sleepy numbness until she was suddenly roused from her reverie by the sudden thud of footsteps and the screams of people pouring in from everywhere. They were calling for the high priest. The Conqueror had already entered the city gates and was on his way to the temple.

With a sudden toss, she lunged backwards. Her heart pounded in her chest with some unexpectedly filling her fear, and she wanted to hide, to run away, but at that moment a great impotence of emotion overwhelmed her ... Pressing at her roaring heart with her hands, with incomprehensible tears in her eyes, she fell silently to the foot of the alabaster column.

Like in a dream, Ihezal saw her grandfather, who, in his priestly robes, suddenly changed and calm, with a strange boldly raised head, led by the hands by the younger priests, walked past her to the open door with a long procession hurriedly crowding behind him. She heard, as if in her sleep, the noise of many footsteps on the stone floor, and the shouts and the distant hum of the people rippling in front of the temple. Then a sudden darkness enveloped her, some tones roared in her ears, and it seemed to her that she was flying in a swirling, accelerated motion into an endless and bottomless abyss.

Meanwhile Malahuda was already standing on the steps of the temple on the same spot where he first heard about the Conqueror's arrival. Now, the news had become reality: this strange and incomprehensible newcomer was walking towards him, almost carried by the hands of the people maddened with joy, visible from afar, enormous, bright, radiant ...

The high priest frowned ... Tough, hateful, and stubborn obstinacy was frozen in his face. He leaned on a bone staff with both hands and waited on the procession of the city and temple dignitaries, to the great amazement and umbrage of the people who were expecting that the high priest would descend down the steps to humbly greet the Conqueror at the bottom of the stairs.

"Malahuda! Malahuda!" Shouts were heard from everywhere.

But he didn't even flinch. He was staring calmly from under his gray, bushy eyebrows, and only as the screams grew more insistent, merging with the insults thrown at him, an ironic smile twitched on his pursed lips.

"Malahuda! Step down and bow to the Conqueror whom I am bringing to the people!"

Elem stood before him, in the purple robe he had worn since the day before, and with an almost commanding movement of his hand, he was pointing to the swarming square.

"I am called His Majesty," replied the old man, "I am the high priest who rules over all the people of the Moon!"

The monk's black eyes suddenly flashed with impetuous anger. "You're nothing! He exclaimed, "Now only the Conqueror, and those who serve him are the rulers!"

"Until I relinquish my authority, I am what I was ...", said Malahuda calmly, "and before your Conqueror enters the steps of the temple, I can have you shackled and throw you into the dungeon together with the Brothers who broke their law, leaving the Polar Country without my permission."

Elem's face reddened and blue veins appeared at his temples. "I don't need anyone's permission," he said, choking with rage, "and I listen to no one, especially you, the Shern's servant and henchman!"

The Conqueror was climbing the steps of the temple, so Malahuda, no longer responding even to the monk's terrible insult, only waved him away with his hand and faced the strange newcomer.

Marek, standing a few steps beneath him, looked at the old man with a good bright smile and extended his hand in greeting. He, however, did not respond with a smile, did not extend his hand, did not even bow his head, although everyone around him bowed down in welcome.

He looked the newcomer straight in the eyes for a few moments, and then said: "Welcome sir, whoever you are, because the universal will of the people has brought you here ..."

"I came myself, of my own free will only", Marek answered becoming serious.

Malahuda slightly bowed his head. "For me, you were brought by the will of the people who have been waiting for the Conqueror for seven hundred years and are appointing you to be him today."

"I am not yet a "Conqueror", but I would like to become one, seeing what is going on here ..."

"You are him, my lord!," said Elem, "you have been him since your foot was set on the Moon!"

Malahuda slightly frowned, and not minding his competitor's words, continued: "You must be a Conqueror, Lord, when you come here and overturn everything that has been ..."

Marek wanted to answer, but the old high priest raised his hand as if ordering silence.

"I don't know where you came from, or how, or why," he said, "but I see that you are bigger than us and perhaps more powerful, and if you wish, perhaps you can remedy that which we have not been able to cope with ... if you really came from Earth, and if it is true that centuries ago a man like you had relocated people here, from that great star, where life was supposed to be better, then you know that it is your duty to redeem today this terrible guilt of those who came before you and to save us from the misery, to which we have been condemned for centuries ... So far, the hope that the Conqueror would come has sustained us. In this temple, in front of which I am greeting you, I nurtured the people with this word. Remember that from today, since you have come, there is no more hope, there must only be results!"

Not everyone in the crowd could hear Malahuda's speech, but those who heard it began to murmur aloud at the incomprehensible and simply stupid words that the holy high priest uttered, but he did not care. He now pronounced clearly and emphatically the sentences that would have seemed so terrible and monstrous to him yesterday. They would have been hard to think of to say in front of the people, to whom he always said that they should bless the Old Man who had brought people to the Moon, Therefore, he had always preached to them that when the Conqueror came in glory, they should fall to their knees to greet him and rejoice in their hearts.

"I do not know if you were promised", he said, and his voice now grew stronger and thundered against his small chest "I do not know if you were the promised one, although all the Books are full of Promise. I see that you have come, and therefore I tell you again once: you must fulfill what our bloody longing has dreamed of for ages. If you do not fulfill it, verily, it would be better for us and for you that you had never set foot on the Moon, for you will be accursed among us.

Suddenly, shouts of terror, indignation and even fear burst out in the crowd who thought that the powerful Conqueror might take revenge on the people for the blasphemy of the high priest. They called out that Malahuda deserved death for these words if he was not struck by sudden madness. They called to Elem to take the high priestly cap from him and lead the Conqueror to the doorstep of the temple. The old man waited unmoved by this storm, and when it was somewhat quiet for a moment, he said again, turning to the Conqueror:

"I am the forty-fourth and perhaps the last high priest ruling people of the Moon." I led them, strengthened them, and disciplined them in their need, as my fathers and ancestors did, while they were longing and waiting. Today these people say, naming you, the stranger, the expected Conqueror, that my role and hard work are finished. I am glad for this, because I do not have enough strength anymore, and I do not know what else I could do here

... So, I place my position and power on the threshold of the temple and with the last high priestly act I proclaim the dissolution of the old religion, which has so far strengthened and sustained us. Now, it is your turn to build a new one with your deeds. God knows I can't do otherwise." Saying this, he reached with his hands for the heavy priestly cap to remove it from his gray head ...

Marek stepped forward quickly and took his hand. "No! He cried, "Remain what you were and rule as before! From what you said, I believe we can be friends and even brothers ..."

Malahuda freed his hand from Marek's grip. "No! We cannot be friends or brothers. We are from different stars, and it would be too much to talk about. As a matter of fact, you could either be my subject or I would be your servant. The first is impossible, the second I do not want until I find out from your deeds who you are. Starting today, what was is gone, and I am not needed anymore.

He took the cap off his head and threw it on the stone pavement, threw down the staff, the belt, and the expensive chain. Finally, he removed from his shoulders the Shern skin coat that had been sewn in the year of victory and bowing for the first time, spread it under the stranger's feet.

"Your entry to the temple must be through this cloak made of our enemies' skin and worn for ages by our high priests," he said. "Remember, you must trample on it to enter. You destroyed our religion, so you must destroy our enemies, if you want us to bless you someday."

Having said this, freed of all the signs of his authority, and in only one robe and with his gray head uncovered, he began to descend from the steps by himself, straight into the crowd, which now, oblivious to their earlier hateful cries, parted before him with involuntary reverence.

Marek was silent, standing motionless, although after Malahuda had left, more and more voices of the people urged him to enter the temple. Elem, who picked up the abandoned high priest's cap and, as a sign of his new authority, covered his bald skull with it, was also calling him to enter.

He was standing there for some time, silent and pensive, apparently weighing what he had heard, until finally the people were silenced by his disturbing behavior. Then Marek suddenly raised his head and stepped confidently onto the black leather coat embroidered with corals and pearls spread out by the last high priest between him and the golden gates of the temple.

When the crowd saw it, they cried out with joy and excitement. They began to press against his feet again, his power was glorified, and his name was blessed ahead of his future victories.

Marek raised his hands and signaled that he wanted to speak, but it was a long time before the people, quieting down a bit, allowed him to say a word. But as soon as he opened his mouth, something unexpected happened. Behold, on the north side, where the three-peak Shern castle was rising, a wave of thick black fumes burst forth. It obscured the sun in the blink of an eye, and a terrible cry of fear and fury rose with it. There were also clinks and calls from the suddenly rising fight. The crowd spun and moved, and some pushed to the Conqueror, calling for his help, while others ran, shouting, towards their homes in danger.

The Shern led by Avij fell out of the citadel, and with a sudden attack breaking through the chain of the high priest's guards, burst into the settlement spreading fear, murder and fire. Marek, raising his head, saw in the distance their black figures, rising heavily on their wide wings above the crowd, hurling missiles and flaming torches at them from above ...

IV

Ihezal, pressed against the feet of the alabaster column, could not understand the words with which Malahuda greeted the Conqueror, but from the sound of his voice she understood that he was saying important and solemn things. From her hiding place, she was looking all the time at her grandfather, at his black coat and high priestly cap, which blocked her view of the stranger from a distant star standing below. She silently cursed that broad coat and the endlessly stretching greeting, trembling with impatience to see the face of the long awaited one sooner. However, she did not dare, frozen by some strange fear, to leave her hiding place or even to move. She was straining her eyes as if she wanted to pierce the figure of the high priest standing between her and the Conqueror, but when he made a movement that might have revealed his sight, she closed her eyes involuntarily, pressing her hands against her that was beating so fast...

"Now I'll see him!," she thought, as Malahuda stepped to one side, and closed her eyes tightly again. Some inner weariness seized her, and she turned her face towards the inside of the temple and began to stare blankly at the golden sign of the Coming in the front of the pulpit. It seemed to her that there everything was still the same, like it used to be...

... Here is the high priest, Malahuda, standing on the pulpit and preaching, and she, a young girl, hidden in a colorful crowd of people, is listening to this strange novel or fairy tale ...

"From a distant star, shining over the deserts, people came here long ago ...

And when the time is finished, the Conqueror will come from there, bright, and radiant ...

Then there will be eternal happiness on the Moon ... "

The sun was rushing into the temple through the colored windows and trembling on the dark, painted walls, quivering on the heads of the listening people, golden like this dreamy fairy tale:

"From a distant star shining above the deserts ..."

What will He look like? Will his eyes be blue? Is his hair golden and long? And when he opens his mouth, young and purple, what voice will fall out of it? What will be his call? What blessing will he say? He will go through the lunar mountains and valleys, to the last edge of all countries, from the desert to the blue sea, bright as the sun, smiling as the dawn ...

She flinched. After all, He is here! A step away, nearby. She turned abruptly towards the door and saw her grandfather taking the golden cap off his head and throwing it on the stone floor. Then she saw how Elem bent down eagerly for it. She wasn't aware why she was following the urgent movements of his white hands, chasing the cap rolling down the stairs ... And then ...

She heard a scream and became frightened when she realized she screamed. He stepped on the skin of a Shern spread on the highest step and filled her gaze with his superhuman visage.

"It's him. It's him!,"... she whispered, unable to take her eyes off the enormous, bright form, towering above the lunar crowd like the lofty O'Tamor crater towers over the surrounding hills. The fear, that was paralyzing her a moment ago disappeared suddenly. Now, she was only feeling a combination of unbearable and delightful annihilation and peace, a calm sudden quiet wave flowing from somewhere ...

"Yes. It was him," something was speaking in her with a deep and certain conviction.

"He came."

Therefore, everything else seemed unimportant and meaningless to her. She looked with an indifferent smile at Malahuda, stepping down the steps with his head uncovered, at Elem, dressed in a high priest's cap, at the crowd pressing in around the Conqueror's legs.

"Around His legs ..."

She smiled even though the sudden storm of the rising battle at the gates of the city blew the crowd away from the steps of the temple in the blink of an eye. She was still smiling as she watched the Conqueror run, like a young bright god, towards the smokes and fires that shot out of them, calling men and armed men, retreating in the first moment under the attack. When he disappeared from her sight, she was still looking after him with enchanted eyes with the same calm smile on her lips.

Women began to rush into the temple, according to the custom seeking refuge from danger here. They were running, screaming, and complaining, some of them with paralyzing fear, maddened out of terror. The pungent smell of burning smoke was drifting behind them through the open door.

Ihezal, motionless, looked at them in amazement, as if not understanding what they were screaming, and what they were afraid of when He was among the people ...

"He!" ...

One woman, seeing the granddaughter of the old priest standing in the doorway, tugged at her wide sleeve, saying something quick and urgent that she did not understand at all. Others called her too, dragging her into the dark depths of the temple, but she freed herself from their hands and went out to the gate. The square was completely empty. The tramped coat of Shern skin was lying on the steps with crushed pearls and coral beads...

Ihezal picked it up and, throwing it on her shoulders, went back into the temple. The women hid themselves in further cloisters, and some in the underground vault, still opened since earlier today. There was no one in the great hall. The girl stepped through it, and past the pulpit, turned to the left, where a winding staircase wrapped in a serpentine spiral around the pillar led to the top of the lofty roof.

She was climbing it slowly, closer, and closer to the painted ceiling. Without thinking about anything else, she was smiling softly, getting closer and closer to the flowers and figures at the top. Every time she found herself at the height of one of the windows, a mixed wave of noise from the ongoing fight hit her, but she did not pay attention to it, instead only rejoicing at her getting higher and higher ...

She finally came to her senses, when having reached the roof, she felt the fresh wind from the sea blowing into her eyes. At first, she hardly knew how she had gotten here on this elevated terrace overlooking the city and its surroundings. It was only now that she noticed consciously that she had that trampled coat on her shoulders, and she threw it away with a sudden disgust. An involuntary and violent spasm squeezed her by the throat. She forcibly restrained herself from crying, although she did not know what she wanted to cry about and why she was stopping herself from crying ...

The sea was wildly roaring, golden, and mobile in the sunlight. As the waves approached the shore, they acquired their white manes and threw themselves against the sand with a dull thud, spilling silver rings over it. A whirlwind rushed them, arose somewhere far in the middle of the waters, under the lazily rising sun, far away and beyond the *Cemetary Island* visible from afar. It was named so, because according to legend, the remains of the first people, who came from Earth with the Old Man, were buried there. Ihezal, leaning back against the stone railing of the roof, was gazing at the sun and the island, visible from here like a dark blemish on a silver mirror.

The wind and the incessant roar of the sea were very strange with the serene sky and the bright sun, which, already high enough, poured heat on her face, buffeted by the salty breeze. She drew in a fresh breath of the sea into her chest, parting her scorched purple lips. Everything began to blur and ripple under her closed eyelids, in her eyes blinded by the glare. The rough and golden sea, the sky and intense sun, and that black island which seemed to fly towards her with an accelerated movement on the crests of the waves... "From the distant star shining above the deserts, people descended at that time ...," a memory rang in her ears.

Suddenly she turned away. After all, He is there, and He is fighting! As if only now realizing why she had come up there, she sprang up abruptly and ran across the platform to the other end, from where she could see the city and the broad plains beyond it. The clang of battle had already died down, and the fumes were slowly falling over the dimming rubble.

Despite being victorious in the first wave of the attack, the Shern were forced to flee shamefully. It was mainly caused by the panic that broke out in the ranks of their loyal Mortzes at the sight of a giant fighting on the people's side. In panic, they threw their weapons and ran to hide behind the fortified wall, abandoning their masters to their fate, oblivious to the terrible and cruel punishment for such a betrayal. A handful of Shern, left to their own strength, were fighting fiercely, but could not stand up to such an advantage. Hovering in heavy and ineffective flight over the humans ranks, they were striking them from above with fire and arrows, but every now and then one of them fell, struck by the Conqueror's terrible bullets or well-aimed slingers' stones. Despite their losses, however, they did not retreat until the last moment as their wings began to swoon, delivering them to the fury of the enraged crowd.

Ihezal, was watching from the above, as those closer to the fortified castle suddenly began their crooked, sluggish flight towards its towers, falling just outside the fence because of their wounds and weariness. However, those who had ventured too far into the human settlement no longer managed to reach a safe place and fell among the fighters on the roofs of houses or on the pavements to find their immediate and terrible death at the hands of the formidable victors. Their wings were broken, and their limbs smashed with stones, or they were tied and thrown into the burning houses. However, none of the tortured asked for grace or mercy, either because they knew that the request would be in vain or because of their infinite contempt for the human-kind.

Ihezal looked indifferently at these final battle scenes and scanned the crowd for the Conqueror. He was standing nearby, done with fighting but still holding his fearsome weapon in his hand, alert and attentive. He was looking around and giving orders with his voice and hand. The girl could not hear the words, but she easily guessed that it was about cutting off the retreat of two or three Shern, lost in the turmoil of the battle over the village, and now wanting to get to the stronghold. One of them, unable to fly from weariness, hid on the rooftops, using his wings only to jump from one place to another when he was scared away. Another sat down on the wall and waited calmly for death at the hand of the Conqueror, who, having just noticed him, aimed his deadly weapon at him. The third one was chased with screams and shouts.

The Shern, knowing that his retreat was cut off and unable to rise high enough on his weary wings to be protected from the people, rushed to an area free of warriors, towards the temple and the sea, and disappeared among houses. People, having noticed his escape and fearing that he would sneak around the settlement and get to the castle above the sea, began to search for him hastily and passionately.

The Conqueror, having killed the second Shern, was also chasing this one and ran towards the temple, looking all around with keen eyes.

Ihezal was just looking at him, willing him with an involuntary desire to look in her direction, when suddenly she was struck by a thud as if a body had fallen right behind her. She turned quickly, and her blood froze in terror. The hunted Shern lay a few steps behind her on the flat stone roof of the temple. He lay apparently limp, one wing wounded and lacerated in several places, bleeding yellowish-green blood. He also had wide arrow wounds on his chest and legs, however, she could see that he was alive, because he was breathing heavily, and his four glistening red eyes were staring insistently at her.

She couldn't even scream, bewitched by that terrible gaze. She recognized the governor Avij by the gold rings on his shoulders and the joints of his feet, and was looking at him with a deadly horror, combined with a growing curiosity. The monstrous and wounded Shern, seen up close for the first time in her life, nevertheless seemed to her strangely and menacingly beautiful.

There was some evil power and perversity in him that filled her with fear, but also with awe. He was lying on one side, on a broken wing. The other, black and shiny, with a navy-blue sheen, was spread wide on the tiled floor. His head was slightly raised, and four horrible, bloody eyes glittered under his faintly phosphorescent forehead ...

"Hide me! He growled in a human language, still looking at the girl. There was no pleading in his words, but rather an irresistible command. Ihezal unconsciously took a step towards him.

"Hide me, bitch! Quickly!"

The Shern hissed again, and she was still approaching with automatic, passive movements, unable to tear her eyes away from his burning pupils. Suddenly, just when she was just a step away, the wounded Shern lunged violently with the last of his strength, and his repulsive white hands swung out from under his wings.

With a sudden scream of horror, she leapt backward, avoiding the fatal embrace. At that moment, her awareness returned. She grabbed the high priest's torn coat and with an unexpected movement, threw it over the enemy's head. Then, having nothing else at hand, she began to tear off her clothes and use them to bind the Shern better.

Meanwhile, the running warriors, led by the Conqueror, were already at the gate of the temple. She heard their footsteps pounding on the stairs and loud shouting. Regardless of the fact that she was almost naked, she rushed to the railing and, leaning with her loose hair, began to scream: "Here! Come here!"

She soon ran out of breath, so she could no longer say that she had captured the fleeing governor.
However, from her voice, they understood that the Shern was there, and they hastened to catch him.

"Alive, alive!" Cried Jeret, who got up there first. "The Conqueror ordered to take him alive!"

In the blink of an eye, Avij was covered with a pile of wrestling, mobile bodies. Weakened by his wounds and tangled up in the torn women clothes, he could not even resist, but those taking him did not trust his inactivity. They knew of the terrible weapons the Shern had in their soft white hands, which, when joined together, strike the enemy with a lightning like deadly current and destroy the man's muscles. So, they threw him on his chest, trying to hold each hand separately.

They quickly tied the left one from under the wounded wing, but the right one, which he fell on, was difficult to reach without releasing him. After a short discussion, Jeret ordered four of the heaviest peasants to kneel on the fallen's back, and with the help of two more braves, he began to break out his healthy right wing to dig out a hand hidden under him and under his chest.

The Shern, until then contemptuously silent, barked in pain and threw himself violently to his side, knocking over the people crushing him, but he fell immediately, stunned by the mighty blow of a club on his neck. Now the other hand was pulled out and tied.

Jeret kicked him as he was lying still with his face on the floor. "Stand up, you snake!" He yelled.

Avij looked up with a glare in his bloody eyes but didn't move. Then three people took each rope, firmly tied them to his wrists, and, making sure that he did not join his hands, pulled him to the edge of the roof, from where the square below could be seen filled with crowds of people. Here, Jeret put a pitchfork under Avij's armpits and lifting his arms, tossed him over the stone railing so that he hung by the ropes over the temple abutment.

A great cry of triumph rose from below when they recognized the governor. The teenagers were throwing stones, which, however, did not reach the prisoner hanging too high above. Then, they spat in his direction and hurled hateful insults and mockery at him. The Shern did not even groan. Crucified in the air at the front of the temple, with his limp drooping wings and his arms bent back, he only stared with his four small eyes at the crowd with unfathomable hatred and contempt.

The Conqueror stepped out on the roof with ever-present Elem.

"Here he is, here he is, lord! The new high priest called, leading him to the front of the platform.

Marek leaned out, and seeing the Shern there, he backed away with sudden disgust, at this both monstrous and hideous sight.

"Bring him back!," He exclaimed.

The people, holding Avij, dragged him up, reluctantly, but did not dare to resist the order, and led him on the ropes, with his arms still spread, before the Conqueror.

Elem's eyes lit up. "What kind of death do you want for him? He asked insistently, moving around Marek's knees. "He could be roasted on a spit or, better, given to the fish to eat ... You do not know how to do it, sir? The flesh is torn into shreds on the legs to attract the fish, then we would immerse him waist-deep in the water ..."

"Go away!" Marek hissed through his teeth, then looked around.

"Who caught him?" He asked.

There was a hollow silence. People were looking at one another. Those who came later pointed to the earlier arrivals until all eyes turned to the girl nestled in the corner of the platform.

"Who caught him?" Marek repeated.

"I did."

She stepped out of the crowd and stood in front of him. Just as she was when she had ripped off her clothes to tie the Shern, she was now standing naked to the waist with a purple skirt covering her from her white hips down to her feet ... Marek looked at her, and she blushed all over. In an involuntary movement, she pulled her hair scattered over her shoulders onto her chest, as if to hide in it, wanting ...

"You?" He whispered in amazement "You?!"

"Malahuda's granddaughter!," the crowd murmured, recognizing her. "The old high priest's last descendant!"

Meanwhile, she was standing, looking into the Conqueror's eyes, with the tied up Shern almost at her feet, and she felt that under his gaze all her strength was leaving her. The blood from the whitened lips leaked to her chest and twitched in goose bumps in her arteries. Suddenly her weakened legs were bending ...and she had to exercise all her will not to fall ...Suddenly she felt someone put an arm around her.

"She's my fiancé," said Jeret, supporting her stagger.

She pouted and snapped out of his embrace with sudden energy. "Not true!" She shouted, "Not true!"

And folding her hands on her breast, she called out quickly, as if of the gravest objection, wanting to clear herself: "You do not listen to this, my lord, because it is not true! Maybe ... once ... indeed ... but now ... ". Suddenly she fell silent.

"Now?" Marek asked, amazed at the whole scene.

"Now," she finished, her voice trembling involuntarily, "now you are the Conqueror, you are my only lord, since you came from a distant star, and whose name be blessed forever and ever!"

As she spoke, she dropped to her knees and fell with her forehead to his feet, tilting her head down over them and covering them with the liquid and glowing gold of her hair.

Meanwhile, near them, murmurs were rising and suddenly erupted in a storm of noisy voices. Marek, who was about to answer the girl kneeling in front of him, raised his head and looked around with inquiring eyes, unable to understand what was going on from the confused words and exclamations.

"Lord!", Elem spoke "The people demand the death of Ihezal, Malahuda's granddaughter."

Marek felt the girl clinging to his feet in sudden terror.

"What?," he asked "What? What did she do?"

Nobody replied. Sudden silence fell, and all the gloomy and silent faces looked at the golden-haired girl with merciless judgment in their eyes. Marek looked at Jeret, who, a former high priest's relative himself, had claimed to be her fiancé a moment ago. The young warrior's brow furrowed, and he bit his mouth, but he did not utter a word of protest.

"She must die." Elem said at last.

"She must die! They shouted at once from all sides.

"What do you want from her? What was wrong?" Marek repeated, putting his hand defensively on her hair.

"She's not at fault," said Elem, "but she must die. She was alone with the Shern, here he pointed to Avij who was wheezing in the ropes, she was with him by herself, so she must die.

"But she captured him! "Marek shouted.

"Yes, but in doing so, she was alone with him here and therefore must die buried in the sand."
That's the law. That's the law! She must die! The cry came from everywhere."

The Conqueror flared with sudden anger: "I spit on your law! I am making the law here, since you made me your lord! She will live because I want it!"

Elem bowed humbly. "You can do everything Conqueror, but you will not want what we do not want. You will not want children of our blood to be bred to Shern, so that the blood of our world will spring to death!

Ihezal sprang up abruptly. "I am pure!" She shouted, her eyes blazing, facing the crowd, "you hear, pure! Who dares ...?" A sob choked the next words in her throat. She covered her eyes and, falling again to Marek's knees, repeated in a low and pleading voice: "I am pure…Conqueror, send me to death, but believe me that I am pure…"

Marek bent down and took the crying woman in his arms. "She's in my care! Do you hear?" He said. "Nobody can touch her. I myself take responsibility for her."

A murmur passed through the crowd, but no one dared to object. Marek added, turning to Elem:

"And you are responsible to me for her! If a hair falls from her head, I'll have you buried alive in the sand!"

He spoke in a hard-commanding tone he had quickly acquired in the short lunar time since his arrival.

Elem bowed silently. "What would you have us do with the Shern, sir?" He asked after a moment.

"Let him stay alive for now. Put him in a safe and good hide out. Now, all of you go and leave me alone.

The platform was emptying quickly. Avij was dragged on ropes down the winding staircase. At Elem's command, he was chained with his arms outstretched, the cords replaced with chains, in the underground treasury of the temple, which was to be the Conqueror's home, as the only building in the whole settlement fitting his height.

Only Jeret, too reluctant to leave, and Ihezal remained with Marek on the roof. The Conqueror looked at him questioningly.

"Lord, said the young man, she was to be my wife ..."

"And you wanted her dead!"

"No. I didn't want it, but that is the law."

"It was."

"All the better for her that it was. However, no man will take a woman who is tainted by a Shern's touch."

"Don't you believe she's pure?

"I want to believe, and I believe, when you say it, Conqueror, sent from the stars to the joy of our eyes! But if so, I am begging you, I, who is your dog, will serve you as you please. Don't take her from me my lord! I love her."

Marek laughed his free, earthly laugh. "Even as a boy, I did not play with dolls! What would I do with her?"

Ihezal, who had been indifferent to the conversation so far, raised her eyes at him. A painful question twitched in them, but she said nothing; she just pursed her lips and stared at the distant sea ... Marek looked at her and for the first time it occurred to him that she was almost naked. It made him vaguely upset that Jeret was looking at her like that. He took off the wide red bandanna that he wore around his neck and draped it over the little girl's shoulders. She didn't move at all, didn't thank him even with her eyes.

"What are you thinking about?" Said the Conqueror, a bit harshly, turning to Jeret, who was looking at the girl.

He smiled. "I think, sir, if it weren't for you, I would have lost all the happiness of my life." For I would neither dare, nor would I be able to resist the law, and Ihezal's body would be eaten by the sand right now ..." He looked at the girl with blazing eyes, not daring, however, to approach her, either because of the Conqueror's presence or because of her immobile and pensive attitude.

"And you," Marek asked, "what are you thinking now?"

She looked up at him with sad but clear and calm eyes. "I dream of an old novel, written in books hidden in the treasury of the temple ... I dream of Ada, the blessed prophetess, who, unmarried, once served the Old Man. When he decided to return to Earth, she escorted him to the ends of the Great Desert, and there she lived till the end of her life looking at that distant star ..."

The Conqueror laughed a little forcefully. "I am the Young Man," he said, "and when I return to Earth, I'll take you with me ... I'll take you both," he corrected himself, pointing to Jeret, "you'll be happy there ..."

Ihezal, smiled slightly, not taking her eyes away from the great bluish sea.

V

The sun was just beginning to tilt towards the west when, after the destruction of the Shern's castle, the people triumphantly led the Conqueror to the temple, proclaiming him the sole lord of the lunar globe ...

The battle had been hard and long. They attacked at noon, the time when the storms rage over the great lunar sea and broke the defensive walls in the blink of an eye. The people, who formerly were paralyzed by fear at the thought of Shern, now with the promised Conqueror at the head of the ranks, were throwing themselves into battle with passion and incredible courage. However, at the gates of the three-peaked tower, they met with resistance, which almost crashed their valiant attack. This time they were not the Shern, but the Mortzes, who, having fled miserably in the first fight, now were defending themselves desperately until their last breath, knowing what awaited them in the event of a defeat. Each door, each corridor and turn of stairs, almost each step had to be separately conquered.

The Mortzes, pushed from one position by a greater number, retreated to the higher one, still defending themselves fiercely. In the deafening thunder of the raging storm, the people proceeded slowly towards the top of the tower. They were slipping on the blood and getting lost in the darkness of the narrow passages, intensified by clouds still thick in the sky and heavy rain.

The Conqueror was not personally involved in the fight inside as he was too big to be able to move freely in the narrow cloisters. He remained outside and was leading the whole battle from there, also watching that none of the besieged could escape, taking advantage of the confusion of the fight. That was really the intention of the Shern locked in the tower. Realizing that the earlier fear of even their name being spoken, had disappeared without a trace, and doubting their victory, they left the defense of access to the higher floors to the Mortzes. They began to gather on a narrow platform between the three peaks, waiting only for right moment to escape. Marek saw them there and understood from their movements that they wanted to take advantage of their frail wings and fly to the sea over the heads of their attackers. Then, having captured the ships left under a weak guard, they would escape without fear of pursuit to their native countries. So, Marek shouted at Jeret, whom he had as his adjutant at his side, to guard the flotilla in the bay. He himself gathered the best archers next to him and with their help began to strike the Shern who appeared on the roof. Arrows from the bows, drawn with weak hands, rarely reached them and did little harm, but the Conqueror's fire, wreaked an awful havoc among the Shern. After a while, the survivors ceased to even appear on the roof, and having doubted the possibility of escaping by using their wings, they sought salvation inside the walls.

It was, however, the moment when the thinned ranks of the Mortzes threw themselves in a panic towards the top, wanting to take the last defensive position at the gate that closed the entrance to the roof. The two waves met on the dark stairs, and the Shern, enraged by the slaughter, rushed down from the roof into the Mortzes to re-engage them in a mortal combat. The Mortzes, now attacked from both sides, became consumed with rage. The suppressed fear and reverence hatred towards their lords who had pushed them around, suddenly exploded with irrepressible force. Ignoring the fact that the people behind them threatened to kill them, they turned upward and charged violently at their fathers and oppressors.

The fight was short. The Shern, unable to withstand the pressure of the larger crowd, rushed back to the roof, opening the way for the Mortzes chasing them. Here, however, they were greeted once again by the Conqueror's deadly fire. So, they went mad, having lost all hope, and they all flew, like a swarm of gigantic and terrible vultures, right at Marek, wishing to at least avenge their sure death on this dangerous giant.

There were only a few of them, but the Conqueror, suddenly attacked, would have undoubtedly succumbed to them, had it not been for the archers gathered around his knees, who skillfully pierced the attackers with their arrows. Nevertheless, he received several terrible strikes of electricity from the attackers. One had even thrown himself on his chest and was strangled by the giant's mighty hand, but was still hanging on to him, clinging with his beak and his feet claws.

Marek, weakened and exhausted from the long struggle, slumped to the ground when a shout of triumph sounded from the top of the tower. After slaughtering all the Mortzes, the people captured the castle completely.

The only one left was Nuzar, Avij's assistant, with a bloody stigma on his face. He climbed one of the three sharp peaks of the tower and from there, breaking the tiles, was striking the attackers who were trying to reach him in vain. The people, fighting inside the tower, had no bows or slings with them, and they called out to the others below to bring weapons when a sudden unexpected fire in the lower floors forced them to retreat.

Nuzar was alone. Seeing the conquerors retreat, he slipped from the sharp cone and sat down on the cornice of the platform, waiting calmly for death. The Conqueror saw him from below and cried out to save himself from the fire, promising him life and health. The Mortz hesitated for a moment, apparently not trusting the promise, but when Marek repeated the promise, he pulled a bundle of ropes out of his hiding place and, tying them at the railing, descended from the blazing tower into the middle of the crowd. Seeing him suspended in the air, several archers drew their bow strings, targeting him with sure shots, but Marek stopped them early enough, commanding respect for his promise.

'This Mortz is my property," he cried, "whoever touches him violates my property!"

Meanwhile, Nuzar had already reached the ground, but did not yet believe in his salvation, because he did not stray from the blazing tower, only glancing with the distrustful eye at the surrounding people.

Elem approached him. "Come to the Conqueror, you filthy dog" he said.

The Mortz muttered something, but obediently followed the high priest among the loose ranks that parted with an expression of disgust and hatred.

Marek, still sitting on the ground, motioned for him to come closer.

"Lord, he's unbound, have your gun ready," Elem warned.

Jeret, who had just returned from the ships, laughed. "Better to tie him up right now," he said, throwing the noose to catch his neck in it.

But it was too late. Nuzar, having deflected the rope with his left hand, with the right one, pulled out the knife hidden in his sleeve, and with a quick movement rushed at the Conqueror, striking his naked neck.

The Conqueror dodged the blow and grabbed the Mortz's arm, lifting him high above his head. The Mortz tried to defend himself with his teeth, but only reached the Conqueror's hanging sleeve and began to bite fiercely.

"Death! Death!" Outraged, hateful voices cried from everywhere.

"He'll be left alive," said Marek, "I need him for my menagerie ... Only give me a rope."

The Mortz curled up in Marek's mighty grip, but he didn't groan or defend himself anymore while he was tightly restraining his clasped hands behind his back. He tossed the end of the rope to Jeret.

"Take him to the treasury, where the other bastard is strapped down. And keep an eye on him. When I go back to Earth one day ..." He didn't finish the sentence. He just laughed loud out ironically to himself at the thought of what extra-ordinary specimens he would bring with him.

Meanwhile, the fight was irrevocably and successfully over. Apart from the captured Mortz, not one of the inhabitants of the tower was alive.

The storm, raging almost the whole time, has now stopped. On the northern side of the sky, around the high cone of the O'Tamor Crater, black clouds were still swirling and rolling over. The thunder from there was still muffled, distant, but the bright sun was already shining over the city and the sea in the moon pale blue sky...

Marek was returning to the temple in a triumphant procession. He was looking at the sun and felt as if it had scarcely had time to crawl from the horizon to its zenith in the time in which so many things had happened ... At dawn, he was looking at the city walls far away, and he was greeted on the steps of the temple in the morning. Now, the people are bringing him here, making it his home and are praising him as the Conqueror in two bloody battles and the self-proclaimed lord of all the lunar land.

It was so inconceivable and so sudden, and it just so happened that he smiled involuntarily, as if at his own dream, thinking about it all. It is true that from the dawn to this moment, a week has hardly elapsed in earthly terms. Here it is only half a day, and it would seem like a dream if it weren't for the people shouting around him and spreading greenery under his feet and the heavy smoke still roaming around the rubble and ruins under black clouds in the northern part ...

From the steps of the temple, he sent the crowd home. Despite his clear wish, they did not want to leave. For a long time they praised him there, calling him a savior, a Conqueror, a beloved and the centuries-long-awaited blessing of the lunar globe, until he finally had to escape inside before these endless adulations ... He didn't even want Elem or any of the people added to his entourage.

He felt an irresistible need for solitude. Apart from the bustle of crowded events, he wanted to reflect a little, understand them and ponder upon them. It seemed to him that his mind was out of sorts, and he had to take a breath now if he was to catch up with the events happening without his participation.

At the same time, he was weary and sleepy. In the hundred and a few dozen hours since dawn, he had slept very little, and he wasn't like those lunar dwarfs who could go through a three hundred fifty-hour day almost without sleep ... He was overwhelmed by the noon heat and the steady rumble of the sea still undulating after the storm.

He stepped inside the temple and closed the bronze wrought doors behind him. He was enveloped by a sudden darkness interwoven with rainbow colors from the stained windows and a chill emanating from the underground parts of the building.

The empty temple seemed like something great and mysterious to him. It was like a living creature whose heart and the content of being had suddenly been torn out. It almost felt like a gigantic machine that had been in motion for ages and whose motion was suddenly stopped by his arrival. He looked at the golden signs and inscriptions, made from strangely tangled letters, and thought they once had mattered, but they became mute and deaf the moment he came in. He involuntarily turned into the great prophecy which they had preached. Almost superstitious fear seized him now. In the morning he still thought that he was, without knowing it, that promised lunar savior. At this moment, he was almost ready to believe that he had entered a place that really belonged to someone else, and that he had recklessly usurped some enigmatic and great rights. Here, all those mysterious and golden inscriptions on these walls are looking at him ominously and menacingly, as if looking at an impostor ...

He instinctively wanted to run and call the people and scream ... He smiled to himself. "I am weary and sleepy," he said aloud.

Then he remembered the words that had been uttered by the great philosopher ages earlier on Earth: "The law of man reaches as far as does his power ...".

"I am exhausted and sleepy," he repeated, and so weak now, and therefore I do not believe in my right to save these people ...

"The law - salvation! ..."

A bed was prepared for him among two pillars a little further on, but he could not yet dare to fall asleep here, in this holy place. He still felt a need for both air and space. He climbed up the winding stairs, almost too small for his size, to the roof and threw himself in the full sun on the stone slab of the platform.

For a little while he tried to think about everything that was going on here, and to understand why he should even care about it, and why he was taking such an active part in events, but his dispersed thoughts would not listen to him. Heavy drowsiness was slowly closing his eyelids. The hot air, quivering from the sun, was burning his chest with each breath. The heat enveloped his head with fire, but he no longer felt the strength to move back into the shade ...

"I'll do it in a moment," he thought, falling asleep, embraced by a lazy weariness ...

The sea had calmed down after the storm, and when he looked at it for a moment, it shone in his eyes with a huge surface full of light and space, merging in a dream of his dimmed thoughts with the dreamy images of the Earth.

He was falling asleep, when it suddenly seemed to him that a sweet and fragrant chill blew into his face as if someone had called him softly by his name. Some golden hair loomed over him, spilled on a small, amusingly small, and white girl's chest, twitching, red lips. ... So, he wanted a name, just to remember a name ... and he fell asleep.

When at last he woke up after a long and heavy sleep, it still seemed to him that he was asleep. A few steps ahead of him, Ihezal was sitting on the spread white leather. She only had a blue, open robe over her naked body. Her hair was tied in two enormous knots above her ears with its ends slowly falling onto her breast, forming a broad golden embroidery around the edges of the split tunic. She was looking at him with a soft smile ...

For some time, he did not dare to move, so as not to frighten off this phenomenon, it seemed so beautiful and sweet to him. He felt that he was no longer lying on the stones, but had soft and fluffy skins beneath him, and a tent-shaped curtain above his head to protect him from the scorching sun.

"Ihezal!" ... He whispered involuntarily.

She smiled again. "Have you had enough sleep, my lord?"

He didn't answer. For a moment it seemed to him that he was falling back to sleep again, quite sweet, and delightful ...

Suddenly he jumped up: Did I sleep ...?"

"Yes, my lord. You slept more than twenty hours."

He looked at the sun. It was standing in the same place it had been when he fell asleep. "Ah, right! - he thought. "I'm on the Moon ... "

He slowly turned his eyes to the girl. She lowered her head. "I watched over you almost the entire time you were asleep, Conqueror."

"How did you get in here?," he asked. "I closed the door behind me ..."

"I live here ... - I stayed in the building connecting with the temple, which my grandfather, high priest Malahuda, left. I wanted to be around to serve you, my Lord. But if you wish, I'll leave these chambers."

"Stay. Where is your grandfather?"

"He's not here. He has gone to the broad plains which you can see from here, my Lord, or perhaps to those mountains over there in the north beyond the snowy O'Tamor, or to the blue sea ... He is gone, like everything that was yesterday, is gone today: only you are ...

She spoke it singingly, with an eerie intoxication in her voice that seemed to rise and tremble, as if she wanted to say more than these simple words expressed. Marek reached out his hand slowly and laid it lightly, carefully on the little girl's arm. He was looking at her for a moment with some involuntary awe, until suddenly he asked:

"Listen! do you believe that I am the Conqueror announced by your prophets? Do you really believe it?"

Ihezal looked at him with wide eyes. "I know that," she replied.

"How ... how do you know? ..."

She folded her hands on her breast and began to speak lively: "You have only just come, and all the lips and hands are blessing you! You are as strong as a god, and you can be harsh and terrible to the enemy in a battle, but I have also been told that you have already performed acts of mercy which we, here on the Moon, only know from the old name ... And you are beautiful, my Lord, beautiful with your exuberant power and more beautiful than anything my eyes have ever seen! Probably only Earth, a bright and holy star, which I looked at once while in Polar Country, is as beautiful as you are... But that is where you came to us from, down to this valley of misery, pain and tears! Oh, how bright you are, how beautiful and divine, my only Lord!"

"Stay with me," whispered Marek, "stay with me ... I am not what you think I am, and Earth is not as bright as it looks from here when you look at it through the stars and the sky; but you, stay with me, and then ... I would like to leave only good behind me, so that you all could remember and bless me ..."

Ihezal was looking at him with delighted eyes, unknowingly cuddling at his knees. He smiled and hid her tiny hands in his hand.

"I would like you to remember me too and bless me. You are like a flower ..."

Suddenly, changing his tone, he pushed the girl away from him and said almost sternly: "Why are you naked?"

A blush suddenly covered her entire body, making the almost opal fingernails of her hand pink. With a quick, nervous movement, she picked up the folds of the open tunic, completely covering herself in it.

"Lord," she said, "don't be angry ... Here, the girls always walk around the house like this ... On my way to you, I forgot that I am no longer at home ... It is not due to disrespect ..."

She was still gathering up the folds of her dress, although she was already tightly covered with them, looking fearfully into the face of the Conqueror ...

He moved his lips as if he wanted to say something, but only after a while he spoke in a seemingly indifferent tone, which, however, sounded false in his own ear: "Does ... does everybody see you ... like that?"

Ihezal suddenly understood. A delightful, overwhelming shudder ran down her tiny body, her hands clenched around the folds gathered on her chest, slackened along her hips. She looked him straight in the eye. "No one will see me from now on, " she said.

Marek shrugged. "It doesn't matter to me," he said, almost harshly, looking away. "If this is a custom ... But, but! What did I want to say? Oh yes. Where is your grandpa? I'd like to see him ..."

The high priest's granddaughter suddenly grew serious. "He's gone, my lord. I've already told you. Now Elem ... But when you tell him, they'll look for him everywhere ..."

"Yes. Yes. Give the command. I would like to talk to him about many things ..."

She was standing there looking him in the eyes boldly and calmly, as if already feeling as his exclusive property, holy and untouchable.

"Give the command," he repeated.

She extended her hand to him: "Lord, give me a sign, that I have the right to give orders on your behalf, and I will send people to search."

Marek hesitated, not knowing what to do, when suddenly he remembered the old earthly custom of transferring of power, found only in novels. Smiling, he pulled the ring off his finger and handed it to the waiting girl.

She took it and, without a word, turned towards the stairs leading from the flat roof into the temple. She crossed the nave and through the side door entered the abandoned high priest's palace ...

When she left it after some time, she was wearing a sumptuous outfit: a light golden fur coat over her purple tunic tightly fastened and a string of bloody ambers one worn by the prophetess Ada around her neck. She now approached the brass doors of the temple, bolted on the outside, and, shifting the spindles aside, opened them wide.

The people were waiting in courtyard. The older and more dignified were gathered with Elem on the steps, waiting patiently for the Conqueror's awakening. They hoped to return the customs disturbed by Malahuda's abdication and set out a new order of things. Nearby, Jeret and other young men were standing and making war plans in their fiery heads. They couldn't wait to be led by the Conqueror to the other mysterious side of the Great Sea, to choke the monstrous Shern in their nests before they even noticed them...

And then there were the people. There were those who fought, and those who watched the fight from a distance. There were others who wished to bring their grievances before the Conqueror, and those who had come with pleas. Still others who were brought there by pure curiosity to see the great visitor from Earth. Women were also standing there, shy in the presence of their husbands and rulers, but mostly with glowing eyes and a blessing on their lips for the one who came to change what was. They knew that whatever would be new, it would only be better for them, since they had been carrying up to now the hard and harsh yoke of their husbands' law.

This swarm of people stretched as far as the eye could see, and it rippled, humming, almost like a sea on the other side of the temple. When the doors of the temple opened, it was thought at first that the Conqueror would emerge, and a great tide like wave of motion passed through the crowd, hurling it against the steps of stone as if against a rocky shore.

Elem and the elders came closer as well. Seeing the emerging girl, he fumed with anger.

"How dare you wander this way," he shouted, "while we are waiting for the Conqueror?

Ihezal didn't say a word. She walked slowly and confidently to the lofty place on the right side of the stairs, from where the mighty high priests would usually announce their will to the people.

Elem grabbed her by her dress. "Where are you going? Better be careful that you get out of the high priest's building as soon as possible, for it's time to move me there ..."

She did not answer now. Having freed herself from the monk with a firm move, she climbed on the platform and raised her hand with the ring above her head.

"People! She exclaimed in a loud voice, "Through me, the Conqueror is sending you peace and greetings!"

"Down with this crazy one!" Elem shouted, "Don't let the one accused of intercourse with Shern Avij speak from the high priesthood stool!"

At the sound of the hateful name, the people moved: murmurs and menacing shouts were heard.

Jeret sprang to the podium: "Ihezal, come down! Come down if you value your life! You are really crazy!"

She seemed not to see him. Her eyes, calm and clear, as if enchanted by a dream, wandered over the wavy sea of people's heads.

"Away, away from the platform!" They were shouting. "The Conqueror is the only one who has the right to speak, or Elem, his faithful servant!"

Ihezal raised her hand again, as the bright stone in the ring shone in the sunlight.

"Here is a sign: It is the Conqueror's ring, and I am speaking in his name. I, the high priest's granddaughter, the captor of Shern Avij, and like the prophetess Ada, unmarried, servant of the one whose name let be blessed forever! He saved me from your hands when you threatened to put the innocent me to death, and he has sent me here now that I may be his blessing mouth."

"She's lying!" Elem shouted. "She has stolen the ring! Hey, people! Pull her off there!"

The crowd, however, no longer listened to his words. A broad cry in honor of the Conqueror hit the walls of the temple. They all began to press towards the girl to greet her message of joyful words. So. Elem stepped forward, lifted the high priest cap with both hands and cried out:

"Look! A stone from the Old Man's hand shines above my head, and I alone have the right to speak on behalf of the Conqueror, I, who greeted him first, greeted and brought him here!"

Two camps began to form below. Some, seeing the high priest's cap with a sacred stone on the head of the former superior of the Waiting Brothers, stood by his side and called for Ihezal to step down, but the great majority of the congregation stood by her.

"Who gave Elem the cap?," people asked. After all, Malahuda laid it at the Conqueror's feet, and he gave it to no one, then Elem appropriated it himself!"

Even those, who had themselves begged Elem in the morning to take Malahuda's cap, were now shouting loudly that he was self-proclaimed and that Ihezal alone, with the Conqueror's ring, had the right to speak to the people on his behalf. The insults that had recently hurled in the face of the old high priest for his strange speech had been forgotten, and people were almost sorry that he had resigned and disappeared. So, when Ihezal said that the Conqueror wanted to find the old man and have him by his side, the people shouted with joy and were ready to run through the entire lunar globe to find him.

Hearing this, Elem, turned pale. For a moment he looked at the crowd and at the armed men, whom he now actually had under his authority as the high priest, but he was apparently afraid to try his command away from the Conqueror's side, so he only beckoned to the elders and they hastily entered the temple. Not finding Marek there, he turned with his followers, always shadowing him, to the stairs leading up.

Marek, having sent Ihezal away, still lazy after a long sleep, was sitting on the stone railing facing the sea and looking at the distant islands scattered over it, and did not hear any of the quarrel on the other side of the building. He was a little excited by the short conversation and the strange behavior of the golden-haired girl, so he was glad that no one interrupted his solitude up to this moment. He frowned reluctantly when he saw Elem coming in and the elders accompanying him.

"Didn't Ihezal tell you," he began, anticipating his greeting, "that I wanted to be alone?"

Elem trembled. "Lord, " he said," we thought you said it in order to free yourself from the intrusive girl who was probably bothering you with requests to forgive her grandfather, who insulted you this morning ..."

Marek shrugged. "You are wearing me down by coming here unnecessarily."

"The matters of the people are waiting, Lord ..."

"We are waiting for your orders! The elders said in chorus, making a low bow.

"Who has ruled so far?"

There was silence until one of the elders said: "Malahuda, the high priest, but he ..."

"He got lost. I know. I ordered for people to look for Malahuda, and when I see him, I'll find out about everything from him and decide ... From what he said when he greeted me, I think he is the smartest man among you."

"I am your high priest," Elem said.

Marek was getting impatient. "So be him, my friend, and I will have you summoned when I need you."

"You ordered to look for Malahuda, Lord ..."

"Yes, I did."

Elem took a step closer. His voice quivered with a secret indignation, barely a threat, as he said: "Lord, I greeted you first, I brought you here, I declared you the promised Conqueror on our globe, and now..."

"Now get out of here while you stay in one piece!" Marek shouted, hitting the floor with his foot that made the walls of the temple shake. "I am the Lord here today, not because of you, but because I wanted it so! Do you understand?!"

Frightened Elem bowed humbly, but there was venomous anger in his lowered eyes. "Blessed be thy will, my Lord", he said, "we are only thy servants ... And if we dare to remind you not in time, it is only because the people are awaiting your command, as their shepherd and ruler ...

Marek smiled. "Do not be angry, high priest," he said, emphasizing the title, "but now really it is not the right time." I'd rather see a cook to feed me, because I'm damn hungry ... I'll talk to you later ..."

Elem turned away silently gloomy and walked down the steps, apparently weighing some plans or intentions in his mind ...

PART TWO

I

The news of the Conqueror's arrival and the terrible slaughter of the Sherns spread widely throughout the country. On that day when the time for the evening prayer came, the large square in front of the temple could not fit the large crowds arriving from everywhere. First there were the inhabitants of the Warm Ponds and those who accompanied Marek. They were followed by groups of fishermen from the seashore and hunters who lived in the deep thickets on the slopes of the sprawling O'Tamor. They were joined by the seekers of amber and pearls and the farmers who cultivated those fleshy and edible moon plants. There were also the half-savage inhabitants of Oewantju settlements between the seas, seasoned by constant battles with Mortzes, and others from flowering villages who were accustomed to luxury and comfort.

Local merchants set up stalls on the steps of the temple, advertising their merchandise to the visitors. The simple people who came from afar often looked upon those goods in amazement, not knowing what use such things would be for. The traffic around the stalls was constant.

The sides of the square were equally crowded as a few Waiting Brothers were standing under the arcades protecting them from the noon sun. For a thousand times they were telling people about the miraculous coming of the Conqueror, who revealed himself to them first, as it had been foretold for centuries and who now was bringing peace and blessing to the lunar world. Others crowded around high-priest's and Jeret's armed men, listening with interest and joy about the course of the battle that ended with the slaughter of the Sherns. They raised their hands up in praise of the Conqueror's greatness and power. They were willingly buying the skins of the killed Sherns paying for them with amber grains. The victorious soldiers offered them to the most generous buyers to afford the intoxicating sap of the noja plant, or to throw the bounty as a stake in a game with their comrades.

Some were also going to the sea where a merchant of women set up his stall on the steps of the great building, selling them, according to their age and beauty, for two to six handfuls of amber grains. Some were grumbling about such high prices on the account of the coming, but it didn't stop them from buying because the crowd of newcomers was great, and there were enough of those willing to buy fair-haired slave women for their distant households.

Different dialects crossed in the warm evening air and so did curses, laughter and calls. Merry singing of strong noja juice drinkers could be heard from the open doors of the taverns. All that was mingling with the sound of the hymns of the brotherhoods devoutly awaiting the Conqueror's appearance.

He finally showed up so tall and stood in front of the temple at the same evening hour where for centuries the high priest had received the people with the greeting, "He will come!"

As soon as he was noticed, all the bargaining, chants and noises stopped. They praised his name with a thousand voices. They first blessed the day and hour of his arrival to the Moon and they separately blessed the time when he entered the temple, and the time of his victory over the Sherns, the eternal enemies of the people.

So he was standing there amidst increasing shouting in a place where the usually richly dressed high priests stood. He was standing there in the common clothes with his head uncovered and only in a leather shirt unbuttoned on his chest. Still such brightness and power emanated from his tall, young form so that not only those who saw him for the first time, but also the inhabitants of the Warm Ponds, who had known him since the morning, turned their eyes to him in delight, forgetting about Elem pressing around his legs.

Marek held up his hands to signal that he wanted to speak. It was a long time before the noise ceased enough for him to speak without fear that his voice would be lost in the confused chatter of the crowd. Some people were still rowdy and singing in the more distant corners of the square, but a crowd of listeners gathered closer to the temple, awaiting with devout concentration and curiosity the Conqueror's first words to the people.

He looked around and tossed back his lush bangs from above his temples. "Brothers," he began, "I came here from a distant star, Earth, but I call you brothers, because you too, through your forgotten fathers, originated from there. I did not know why I was coming, but I found here the task that I am undertaking ... It so happened that I had to act first before I could speak to you. And it is good. If I had spoken to you at the beginning of this long day, which has long passed to the west, I would have denied many things, and probably dispelled many of your dreams ... but the day left us in the common bloody struggle. I have fought with your enemies, and I have learned how terrible they are. I learned about your wrongs and your hardships, which you are partly guilty of, but this does not diminish your suffering. Your complaints and these books which you call holy have told me about it ... I have read them all, while resting after the fight which cost you a lot of blood and life. But the fight is not over, and you know it. Your enemies are evil and strong, and they must be crushed completely in their own nests ...

I have also learned from your old books, which I have already heard about, that you were awaiting an arrival from your star, the Earth, a Conqueror who will liberate you. I came here from Earth, and I want to free you. I will teach you everything that I can do myself. We will make the firearms that you have seen in my hand. I, with the help of selected leaders, will train the ranks with which we will go across the Great Sea to break the Sherns' hostile power forever ...

Sudden outbursts of joyful shouts interrupted Marek, so he waited a little until it was quiet, then resumed: "But this is only the first part of the task that I have undertaken. Then I want to eradicate the evil that has taken root among you. I see masters and slaves among you, I see the rich and bullies, the victims, and the wrongdoers ... I see cruel laws, errors and superstition, strictness on one hand, and indulgence on the other hand for those who know how to buy impunity. Your women are oppressed, and their husbands are satisfied that they have fulfilled their duty when their wives are not hungry. It used to be like that on Earth, and we went through it, so I believe that you can live differently with my help."

Again, cheers answered him, but this time not as numerous and common as before. Indeed, some of the dignitaries and richer merchants started to murmur among themselves frightened by the alien's innovative plans. But they did not dare to oppose him, so it was only quietly said that the order of things on the Moon was fixed, and that no one was being harmed, let alone the poor, who lost nothing, having nothing anyway. The fate of the powerful and the wealthy is worse, because in addition to their struggles associated with acquiring that wealth, they must also endure the fear that they may lose their property or power.

The Conqueror did not hear those comments, so, taking a little breath, he continued: "And when everything is as it should be, when you are free from the enemy who oppressed you, and free from the evil that lives in you, I will leave you alone to rule yourselves, returning to my homeland, which is now in heaven, my bright native star ... Maybe I will take some of you with me, so that you can see the expanse of the universe and the stars above and below your feet, and the Earth from which the Moon began and that gave the beginning to the people living here.

Before this happens, before I leave you alone here (because I can't take all of you with me!), I am your master. You have to obey me in everything, if you want me to really become the promised Conqueror that you are already proclaiming me to be.

I ordered you to look for a man who had greeted me on these stairs this morning and spoke wise words. Together with him I wanted to make new laws for you, but he has not yet been found. Therefore, in the meantime, I am leaving the government in the hands of Elem. He will execute my will over you until you learn to govern by yourselves and your own rational will, as the peoples of the Earth have ruled for ages. The brave Jeret will oversee the armed men, and he will also help me with forming the ranks I mentioned. And so that you may know that I value women as much as men, I will have Ihezal, the granddaughter of your lost high priest, as the bearer of my personal will ... "

The shouts and calls resounded again. Marek's words were repeated and interpreted in various ways. They were talking about the lost high priest Malahuda, and about the Elem's new power but above all, they were talking about the intended trip to the country of the Sherns. That undertaking was admired as something unheard of, which had not yet been even thought of as no one would have even dreamed about something like that ...

"He will arm their ranks with firearms," they repeated, "with the terrible weapons which he himself used before our eyes against the fleeing Sherns! And he will distribute the thunderbolts among the warriors!" We will acquire the Sherns' wealth and bring them to their feet!"

"Yes. Yes! The Moon belongs to the people. The Old Man handed it over to us to have!"

"Long live the Conqueror! Long live! Long live!

He was praised again and adored endlessly.

Nodding to the crowd with a dignified movement he was about to step back with a gracious smile on his lips, when suddenly he felt that someone touched his elbow with a raised hand ...

There was a small man standing next to him, with a large, lush hair on his head, staring at him penetratingly, almost menacingly, with small grey eyes.

"If you have a complaint or a request, go to Ihezal with it," Marek said. The little man shook his head in denial. "I want to speak to you," he said, "and I want to ask you why you are deceiving the people?"

"Oh! What? What?"

Marek was so surprised by this unexplained question or objection that at first, he was unable to find the right answer. The little man explained to himself the giant's confusion in his favor, for he frowned and repeated sternly: "Why are you deceiving the people? Why these fairy tales about the Earth? I will not argue in front of the crowd here, but if you want, come with me to the temple and explain yourself..."

Now the whole thing seemed immensely funny to Marek. He was interested in this self-confident man. "But yes, yes ... I will be glad to hear"...

As he spoke, he grabbed the serious little boy under the armpit and walked inside with him. "And now," he said, when they were alone, "tell me, my friend, how am I a fool?"

The little man cleared his throat and tried to look as serious as possible. "I'm Roda," he said with dignity.

"I am incredibly pleased. "

"I am Roda," repeated the other, seeing that his name did not impress Marek at all.

"I hear you! So what?"

"The high priest Malahuda should have had me stoned ... "

"Fortunately, he didn't. I would have no pleasure now ... "

Roda frowned: "Let's leave the jokes alone. That's not why I wanted to talk to you ... "

"Very good. So what?"

"All my life I have fought against stupefying the poor crowd with these priestly fairy tales about our earthly descent. "

"And so?"

"You know as well as I do that the Earth is completely uninhabited, and at least there are certainly no creatures like us. "

Marek was listening with a real and ever-growing curiosity. "How's that? And I?"

"You have never been to Earth, Lord," said Roda with deep conviction ...

"This is a new thing for me!," Marek called.

A shadow of reluctance flashed across Roda's broad face. "Let's not play hide-and-seek. It is unnecessary for me. I know. "

"So, people, you say, sir, have always lived on the Moon?," here. They have always lived here. "

"No. They didn't live here. He brought them here, I do not know for what purpose, the man in the legend called the Old Man. "

"He brought them from where?"

"Where you are coming from now," replied Roda, staring sharply into the Conqueror's eyes. "

"And where do I come from, if you please?"

Roda did not reply immediately. Sitting on the table next to which Marek had taken his seat, he rested his hands on his knees and leaned forward a little, still looking Marek in the eye, as if he wanted to examine in advance the impression that his words would make. After a while he said slowly and emphatically: "You're coming ... from the other side. "

"I don't understand," Marek said quite sincerely.

Roda grimaced again in disgust. "I know you don't want to be honest with me," he said, "but never mind. "As a proof of how well I know the truth, I will tell you all that you know best, and then perhaps we can communicate when you see these fairy tales miss the point for me. "

"So where am I coming from?" Marek repeated with a little impatience.

Roda smiled with a tinge of self-assured superiority. "Let's start at the beginning," he said. "The legend, upheld by the priests, says that people came to the Moon from Earth. Well, I maintain, first, that Earth cannot be inhabited. Secondly, even if it were inhabited, the beings living there would not be like people. Thirdly, that even though they were like people, they could never get to the Moon. And I will prove to you ... "

Marek smiled. "My dear Mr. Roda, a few thousand years ago there was a sage on Earth who argued first that nothing exists, then that even if something existed, man would not know about it, and finally that even if he did, he could not share it with anybody. He was a paid teacher of knowledge about all things ... "

"What's the connection? ... "

"Small. In any case, it is funny for me, who came here from Earth, when you, whose fathers also came from Earth here say something like that.'

"Even if you really came from Earth, I would be right anyway. But it is out of the question. Just listen to me. The Earth, much larger than the Moon, is also heavier than the Moon, and therefore objects weigh more there ... "

"Where did you get this kind of information?", Marek interrupted in amazement.

"Unfortunately, I must confess it: from you. "

"How's that?"

"Simple thing. Your countryman, known in the legend as the Old Man who centuries ago brought people from 'the other side' to this one, had books with him ... He was jealous of his knowledge, like all of you (I see it in you, too), then returning to the 'other side', he burnt his house with the books in it. Fortunately, some of them were saved ... But those are not the ones kept by the high priests, no! They were only hiding books with futile fairy tales! This treasure, snatched from your envy, has been guarded by my family for ages, and that's why I know many things. "

"Yes, I understand. From the books written on Earth you get evidence that the Earth is not inhabited. Very rightly so."

"Never mind where I get it from. But it's certain that I have it, and it is true. Are you saying that people on Earth are of your height and shape? My dear man! A giant like you, weighing six times as much, despite the strongest muscles, could not even move there! The very pressure of the dense air on the chest there would crush him. Cha, Cha, Cha! I would like to know what you would look like on Earth!"

Having said this, he rubbed his hands contentedly and laughed slyly as he met Marek's eyes. "And," he said after a moment, "those short days and nights there cannot be favorable to the development of life; the vegetation, before it had time to develop in the sun, would have to perish in the night shadow... Anyway, do you know what these white spots covering some parts of the Earth for several days mean? Do you know?"

"I would like to hear your opinion," Marek said.

"It's snow! Exclaimed Roda triumphantly, "It is snow, testifying that it is winter there, and also during the day, and for such a long time that no living creature could bear it!"

"I am almost beginning to believe that the Earth is uninhabited ... but I don't know where I really came from!"

Roda looked carefully at Marek. "So, you still don't want to confess? ... Well. I could add a lot of evidence that people neither live nor can live on Earth, but I see, it does not take us anywhere. So, I will tell you directly where the "Old Man" came from and where you came from ... "

"I am waiting. "

From the large portfolio he had with him, Roda pulled out a map and unfolded it in front of Marek's eyes. "Look!"

"A map of the airless hemisphere of the Moon," Marek said, glancing at the card, "a map drawn from the photographs we take on Earth ... "

Roda laughed. "I do not know what "photos" you take on Earth, but it is certain that such maps cannot be drawn from a distance! The one who crossed it was right there. Such maps are only made from afar!" Saying this, he threw a fragment of the destroyed page of Europe in front of Marek which was once saved from the Old Man's burnt house.

Now Marek laughed in turn. "But dear Mr. Roda! Isn't this map much more accurate and detailed?'

"Exactly. To draw such a "precise" map, one must have many... fantasies and a pattern far, far in the sky! See, how many beautiful colors here, what limitations of land, in fact non-existent! And those circles! What do they mean? Each of them even has its own special and witty name. "

Marek shrugged. "I am beginning to assume for real that I have never been to Earth.'

"If you believed you were there, then you are crazy," said Roda. "However, I do not suppose it," he added after a moment. "You are too rational ... We were the only ones supposed to believe you!"

He jumped off the table and walking with great strides, began to speak quickly and fluently, as if repeating a speech, he had already made repeatedly. "In the airless hemisphere of the Moon there was once a lush and abundant land ... People lived there in the glow of the star of the Earth, in green meadows, under the peaks whitened with white snow, on the shores of blue, undulating seas ... And here where you cannot see the Earth, and the shadow is impenetrable at night, only the Sherns lived. They didn't dare to venture into the vicinity of that hemisphere as it was the country inhabited by people ... The people there were powerful, terrible, and happy. With time, however, the benevolent star Earth, for an inexplicable reason, stopped heating that country at night, the air escaped, the seas dried up ... And then its people..." He paused and stared sharply at Marek.

"Then?" Marek picked up.

"I know your secret," said Roda after a pause. "Just look at the map, it has betrayed you! That side of the Moon, facing the Earth, is full of gaps, cracks, and abyss. These are the entrances to your land, to your country, which you have made for yourselves under the surface of that empty land! There, in artificially lit caves, you live up to the day happy, in prosperity and luxury ... You have underground cities, meadows, and underground seas. You are jealously guarding the secret of your existence before the Sherns and perhaps before us whom you banished."

His face twisted in a wanton hatred and his teeth glowed from under his tightly pursed lips. "Let the Old Man or whoever brought us to this awful poverty be cursed! But we will return there sooner or later. It is true that we are weak, but we are greater in numbers, that's for sure. There cannot be many of you living in those caves"...

Marek put his hand on Roda's shoulder "Sir, calm down", he said. Please believe me that all you said is a creation of your imagination... The other side of the Moon is uninhabited. People live on Earth. It is another question if it wasn't a crime to transplant people here, but it happened. "

"Yes, it did happen! And to prevent us from correcting it and to stop us from returning to you, you, sir come here and tell us this ancient fairy tale about Earth! Yes! We should only stare at the blue color of that distant star, so we would not look at the Moon, at what rightfully belongs to us! Perhaps," he continued, "perhaps the Sherns became a nuisance to you as well. Perhaps, they discovered your secret passages, and they also ... bother you and torment. Isn't it true that you were sent here when you remembered us, the poor descendants of the banished ones or a criminal whom our priests tell us to worship? So now, we will go to the Sherns country under your heroic leadership, and we will fight and defeat them in their own country for your profit! You are announcing that expedition!"

He was almost suffocating with his words, throwing them out with passionate hatred and a sneer in his eyes. All Marek's attempts to interrupt him were futile. The resolute sage wasn't listening to him at all. He was waving his hands at all arguments certain that he knew the substantial and undoubtedly truth that now was being torn away from his entire understanding of existence.

Finally, Marek lost his patience: "So, what do you want from me?," he exclaimed.

"I don't want you to deceive the people, stupefied enough by the priests. "Roda answered firmly. "I don't want you to wake in them any confusing and unfulfilled longings! Our life here is hard enough that you would make fun of us and turn our eyes towards the blue star and talk to us about our supposed homeland which we will never see. This is what I demand from you. If you want me to believe in your good will, I will request you to show us the way to the country where you live ..."

"But if I don't fulfill your wishes?"

"Then I will be your deadliest enemy. "

"Even if I helped you defeat the Sherns?"

"Yes. Even if you helped us with defeating the Sherns because you harm us more with your fairy tales than the Sherns could do. "

Marek stood up and with his enormous height suddenly towered over his opponent's small frame. Roda instinctively took a step back but not to show the involuntary fear that grabbed him, he frowned and said firmly: "I am awaiting your response. "

"My Mr. Roda," said Marek "now, I can solemnly promise you that I will not tell the people fairy tales, but I nevertheless firmly declare to you that I will not cease to remind them that their ancestors came here from Earth and there, in the sky, is their righteous homeland. It can only raise you and ennoble you ..."

Roda turned to leave without saying a word.

"Wait another minute," Marek called after him. "You also demanded that I show you the way to the country where I come from and lead you there. When I return, I cannot take you all with me, but in my vehicle, there is a place for six people of your weight ... Would you like to travel with me to Earth and see for yourself that it is inhabited?"

Roda paused, listening carefully to Marek's words. A cunning smile played around his lips. "Oh! Rightly. You want to take me with you, so that here, after your departure, no one will weaken the faith in the earthly fairy tale, so the spark of disbelief will fade out here ..." He paused and looked thoughtful. "So how did you get here?" He asked abruptly after a moment.

Marek made a wide movement with his hand. "In the missile ... You can see it in the Polar Country. It is there in its own shell ... "

"And you can come back ... in the same way?"

"Yes, that's right. I can come back. It's enough to go inside and, having screwed the hatch tightly, press the button, breaking the glass that covers it ... "

"A button behind the glass?" Roda asked greedily.

"Yes. Then the missile pushed out by the air, which has densified itself in its shell, will return exactly to the place from which it was ejected, i.e. to Earth ... "

The usual sly smile reappeared on Roda's broad lips. "Suppose not to Earth, but to one of the openings that are the entrance to your underground cities on the other side ... But never mind ... I wanted to ... Never mind. Perfectly conceived communication, perfect! Especially since in this way, the envoy who returns cannot disclose the way to us ... However, ..." he abruptly broke off and left the temple hastily.

The Conqueror looked after him and waved his hand contemptuously. After a while, however, an unexpected cloud crossed his brow. He made a move as if he wanted to follow the guest. It occurred to him that a guard should be posted at his vehicle the Polar Country, but soon he laughed at himself, at his fears.

"The guard has to be posted after all," he whispered, "I'll be safer. "

It seemed to him that the golden-haired Ihezal's amethyst tunic glittered in the dark depths between the pillars, and he shouted out to her, but only the echo answered him. So, he smiled to himself again, but no longer as freely as before, and turned inward toward the great black marble pulpit and the wrought-iron doorway behind it. He opened it in a manner already known to him and, lighting the lamp, began to go down the stairs.

The formerly hidden treasury of the temple was deserted. After the Conqueror ordered that the former high priest's palace be left to Malahuda's granddaughter, the new high priest then directed that all the lofty and rich chests, full of costly garments and all the precious equipment, be moved to his apartment on the other side of the square. In the now emptied vault, there were only books, once sacred, now stacked randomly in a pile next to the malachite table moved against the wall. And in the back, above a slab of polished lava, a mysterious golden Sign of the Coming shone. Now, there, beneath the golden inscription, whose strange, eternal letters intertwined into the words of the great Promise: HE WILL COME, the once mighty governor, Shern Avij was standing with his hands crossed in chains. Today he was a weak prisoner and the proof that the promise had been fulfilled and the Conqueror has really come on the Moon ... His drooped wings, pressed against the wall, were still bleeding despite the dressing. There was also a wide wound on his neck, from which the blood dripping down his chest formed a puddle at the feet of the defeated ...

Marek lifted the lamp up and lit the Shern's monstrous face. The Shern glared back at his victorious opponent with bloody hate filled eyes. At one point, the muscles in his chained snake like arms twitched and his crushed wings twitched, but he apparently remembered his powerlessness immediately. Then without further trying, he closed his eyes and hung heavily on his iron fetters. Marek stepped back a few steps ...

He already knew that the Sherns who encountered people understood human speech, but he had not yet been able to bring himself to say a word to this so inhuman creature ... When he opened his mouth, his voice died down, and he was overcome with disgust, almost bordering fear. Once, in his presence, Elem spoke to Avij. He told him then that on the Conqueror's orders he should not be afraid of tortures or death as he would be transported alive to Earth in the Conqueror's shiny vehicle. Then Avij sputtered a curse. Even today Marek could hear the sound of that hideous and improbable human voice because it emerged from the monster's snout having no resemblance to a man.

He sat down on a low malachite table and put a burning lamp beside him. The flickering light lit the golden shields of the sacred sign and covered them again with a huge, moving shadow of the Shern, which wandered like a ghost along the smoothed wall with every flicker of the flame. The monster, seemingly dead, stood limp with drooping wings and bowed head, and the shadow leaped from behind him with a sudden lurch, swayed, fell, and rose again, suddenly extinguishing the gleaming letters and golden shields of the Coming. Involuntary fear began to fill Marek. He moved as if he wanted to stand up and run away, when he noticed that the Shern opened his eyes again and was staring keenly at him …

Marek forced himself to stand up. "Are they treating you all right here?," he asked in a strangely modulated voice, as if weren't his own.

The Shern lazily closed his eyes, and only after some time responded: "Go away, you dog. You are boring me. "

Marek felt a sudden anger. "Shut up, animal! I am your master, and I will have you whipped!"

"Go ahead!"

"I caught you. "

"Not true. The girl accidentally captured me, not you, boor. "

"I will take you to Earth with me…"

"You yourself won't return to Earth. You will die here. "

"I will go back, but first I will kill all the Sherns. I'll wipe you out in your own country in the same way as I have done it here. You are the only living Shern here. "

Avij opened both pairs of his eyes and looked closer at Marek. "Unchain me and let me free," he said after a moment "and I will allow you to return to Earth in one piece. "

Now Marek laughed "Certainly I will unchain you under one condition that you will serve as my guide to your country I want to conquer. "

The Shern didn't bother to answer. He turned his head away and started to look keenly at the light of the lamp. Then Marek, overcoming the feeling of disgust, came closer to him and touched his hairy chest with his palm. "So, what? Will you be my guide?," he repeated.

Avij slowly moved his eyes to the Conqueror's face, looked at him calmly and long, and then barked: "You've made a mistake not killing me. In the end I will be the Conqueror because you are stupid like all these other people. "

"So, you won't be my guide?"

"I will be your guide," an unexpected voice reached him from a corner of the room.

Marek turned around quickly. He had forgotten about Nuzar's presence, who was lying down on a pallet chained by his leg.

"You? You? Do you know the Sherns country? He asked.

"Yes. "The Mortz answered getting up. "I was born there from a human captive who was later strangled. And I will guide you, sir as I see that you are stronger than the Sherns, and because I know you will win.

"Avij turned his head towards his former servant and with immeasurable contempt barked just one word: "Stupid!"

II

"Haven't they found Malahuda yet?"

Sevin bowed his head. "No, Your Majesty, he hasn't been found yet ..."

He paused and looked into the eyes of the new high priest, as if to read from them the essential point of this question. Elem also stared briefly at his confidant. Then, with his eyes lowered, he began to move the piles of scriptures lying on the marble table with a hand full of precious rings. Without looking up, he asked casually: "Maybe ... they aren't looking for him diligently enough? The Conqueror wants ..."

A sly smile played on Sevin's lips. "The messengers would like to fulfill the Conqueror's wishes and Your Majesty's, but there are insurmountable difficulties. Everyone has seen the former high priest, but it is surprising how few people know him well enough! Among the messengers there isn't even one who could recognize him, especially if he is hiding in disguise ... "

Elem sighed with relief.

"Should we keep looking for him?" Sevin asked after a moment, not sure how to take the high priest's silence.

"Yes. Yes. Let them look for him ... "

"The same people as before?"

"If you can't find others who know him better ... "

"We will do as Your Majesty wishes".

"But I would like to know where he is," said Elem after a moment.

Sevin looked into his eyes and bowed his head to show that he understood.

The high priest stood up and walked towards the wide window that opened onto the square in front of the temple. Here, in the vast open space, the soldiers under Jeret's lead were practicing using a new firearm, made by trusted workers, to whom the Conqueror entrusted the secret of making this terrible tool. Elem listened for a while to the rumble of shots hitting targets and the screaming voice of the command, then turned again to Sevin humbly waiting there.

"Who are those men listening to?" He suddenly asked.

"Your Majesty is the ruling high priest ... "

Elem interrupted him with an impatient movement of his hand. "Sevin, who are these men listening to? The Conqueror or Jeret?"

Sevin shrugged his shoulders. "I don't know. "

"You should know!"

"As Your Majesty orders, but ..."

"What did you want to say? Speak!"

"I don't know how to say it to Your Majesty ... Perhaps it would be better if they were listening to the Conqueror not Jeret ..."

Master and his confidante looked each other in the eye.

"You think that Jeret?"

"Yes, Your Majesty. Today he is completely devoted to the Conqueror, but he is grieving over this girl and maybe someday, with time... "

Elem took his time to answer. He was weighing something in his mind for a long time, watching the thick wall crumble under the impact of bullets shot at it by the practicing soldiers until he said slowly:

"You are wrong, Sevin. Jeret is devoted with all his soul to the blessed Conqueror, as well as to me, the high priest, so we can easily instruct the warriors that they should obey him first. They will understand it even more easily as the Conqueror himself put him in charge.

Then the high priest has stepped away from the window, and after crossing the great hall several times at a slow pace, he sat down again in front of the table strewn with various papers and plunged into reading.

Sevin did not leave. Then Elem, noticing his expectant attitude, raised his questioning eyes at him.

"Do you want anything else?," he asked.

"I would like to ask if Your Majesty would have our former brother, Choma imprisoned?"

Elem moved quickly. "Ah, yes! Choma ... So what?"

"We have always known that he had gone loony with age, although there were people who often believed his words ... but now I am afraid that his madness might have exceeded the measure permitted by law ..."

"Are people listening to him?" Elem asked, impatiently dismissing all the discussions that he usually used even in conversation with his confidante.

"Not much so far, but they might start listening to him one day..."

Elem thought about it. "It won't happen soon!" He said after a moment, as if to himself.

"I do not know. I have just been informed that Choma has turned up among fishermen around the Isthmus where people are dumb, wild, and rough ..."

"Many of these fishermen have joined Jeret's ranks," the high priest said.

"Yes, but not all of them. Those who remained in their homes are now listening to the blasphemy of the bitter old man. Your Majesty knows what he is saying ..."

Elem nodded his head in silence.

"He says, " continued Sevin, keeping his eyes fixed on his superior, "that the Conqueror is not the Conqueror, and given that the dead had not risen for his welcome as it had been foretold in Scripture, so all of us, the Waiting Brothers, who have come out of the *Polar Lands*, are faithless and even he dares Your Majesty ..."

"All right," Elem interrupted, "it's okay. It does not matter. I will not order him imprisoned. He is senile, and no intelligent person will pay attention to him, but make sure that he stays among the fishermen. Don't let him venture any further."

"As Your Majesty ..."

"But this reminds me of that wise guy Roda. What's up with him?"

Sevin tossed his head contemptuously. "This one is not dangerous! Too many attempts at proving and trying to instruct everybody. People laugh at him, as always, as in the days of Malahuda ... "

"Doesn't he have followers?"

"A handful not even worth mentioning! And if Your Majesty is willing to listen to my advice ... ".

"Speak!"

"Better leave him alone. If he is not persecuted, only lazy scholars and, in a way, enlightened scholars can believe him ... and such a move can be easily disregarded. The people ... the people are greedy for the fertile countries where the Sherns live beyond the sea, but they do not believe that there is anything desirable in the Great Desert. Only if Your Majesty issued severe orders against Roda or, worse, condemned him to death, the crowds would begin to wonder and suppose that there must have been some truth in the words of the condemned man ... The old Choma is different. He, as a member of the order, reports directly to us ... and that would not offend anyone ..."

The high priest motioned for him to be silent.

"Yes. Yes. It's okay. I will think about what to do ..."

Sevin bowed, and seeing that Elem, staring at the spread papers, was no longer asking him anything, quietly slipped out of the room. As soon as the door closed behind him, the former superior of the Waiting Brothers sprang up from the table and started walking briskly around the room. His hair was already thick on his once shaved skull and a long black beard stood out sharply from the shiny yellow robe, he was wearing. His firm and proud lips pressed tightly together, and his eyes darted uneasily beneath his narrowed eyebrows constantly turning to the window overlooking the square where the Conqueror was training his warriors.

He stopped and looked. He was watching each turn of the efficient group with a greedy eye. He was catching the quick movements of their hands that raised the weapon towards their faces. After each flash of the shot he looked towards the wall crumbling under the impact of bullets.

"It's already night," he whispered to himself.

He looked at the sun, still very high, and was seized with sudden impatience. He, who had lived in the Polar Country for years without knowing time, days, sunrise, or sunset, was now trembling at the thought that the end of the day was still far away. He couldn't wait for the water to freeze in the evening chill and build a bridge for the Conqueror's winged sleighs which would let him travel across the wide sea towards the mysterious land of the Sherns. He felt a great urgency for the expedition to set off, and he was telling himself aloud that he wanted the quickest possible destruction of his people's eternal enemies. Still, in his heart he felt that he would also be glad when the Conqueror left to fight, leaving the undivided and undisturbed power to him, the high priest.

And when the Conqueror returns ...

He didn't think, didn't want to think anything wrong. He firmly believed that the one who came was the one foretold by the holy books and prophets and waited for hundreds of years by the Waiting Brothers as a Savior. He believed that in him there was a fulfillment of the prophecy and a complement to an old era. He believed a new lunar world order was beginning, but he involuntarily imagined this new order as the period of his rule and reign ...

And when the Conqueror returns ... from across the Great Sea...

He hasn't thought of anything bad yet. In his imagination, however, he saw the Conqueror's miraculous, shining vehicle taking him back into space, towards Earth! He also saw himself, the high priest, blessing, and mourning that departure and giving thanks to the Conqueror leaving in glory for destroying the Sherns, that the people might live carefree under the unshakable governance of Elem, the first of the new family of high priests.

But what if ... If? ...

He did not want to suppose that the Conqueror would want to remain on the Moon and rule arbitrarily, leaving only a fraction of power to him ... No prophet ever said that the Conqueror would remain on the Moon, so it was not a dogma to be believed ...

Elem couldn't think clearly anymore. He was using his will to hold back his foreseeing imagination, which in spite of him loomed before his eyes with the indistinct figures of Choma, Roda, and even old Malahuda, who had dared to greet the joy of people's eyes, bright and blessed stranger arriving from Earth with blasphemous words ...

He quickly shook off these delusions and wiped his forehead as if he wanted to chase away the last trace of involuntary thoughts. Then, he anxiously looked out the window at Jeret, who was just talking to the Conqueror, and smiled contentedly, seeing the young warrior's formal but sullen demeanor.

Indeed, from that first day, when on the roof of the temple he asked the Conqueror not to take his beloved's girl from him, he didn't say a word to him except the necessary exchanges about the army and the expedition. That reluctance pained Marek, who liked the eager and passionate young man. He tried to break it, sometimes trying to start a livelier conversation with him but all in vain. Jeret answered his questions briefly and respectfully. He obeyed his orders promptly but never smiled, nor did he ever allow himself to be drawn into a chat about things not related to the war with the Sherns.

In the end, Marek gave up. For several long lunar days, more than half a year according to the Earth's count, they have lived next to each other, almost touching each other, setting up firearms workshops, selecting workers and training, and then training soldiers again together. The Conqueror had to admit that it would be difficult for him to imagine a better, more intelligent, and more devoted assistant than this man, more and more distant to him in his soul and more of a stranger ..

Today there was the last exercise before the expedition. Marek, sitting on the steps of the temple, was watching with contentment the astonishing skill of the shooters who were hitting the clay vessels with their bullets, almost never missing, when Jeret unexpectedly stood before him.

"Everything is ready, Conqueror" he said, "and if you like, we can leave today as soon as the sea freezes after the sunset ..."

"Yes!" Marek replied, involuntarily taking on the curt tone Jeret had brought to their conversations.

The commander of the lunar youth turned without a word towards the seashore, where the tall sail sleds prepared for the night ice were already waiting, but having just taken a few steps, he suddenly stopped ..."

"Jeret?"

"I thought you called me, lord."

"No, I didn't call you ..."

Then he turned and resumed on his way, but now Marek really called him.

"Jeret, come, I would like to talk to you ..."

He stood up and walked towards the youth who obediently stopped in place, waiting carefully for an order or question. But the Conqueror did not order or ask, and after approaching him, sat down on a stone, as he was his custom to do when he spoke to the lunar men so much shorter than himself. Taking his hand, looked into his eyes for a long time, with a bright but sad look. The young man withstood that gaze calmly, not taking his pupils down, his eyebrows just frowned and hardened into two shrunken arches, separated by a deep furrow ...

"Jeret" Marek began after a while, "since I am here on the Moon, I have met only three people, whom I would like to have as friends ... One of them, the old man Malahuda, disappeared at the hour I met him, and you are the second ..." He paused as if searching for a word...

Jeret raised his eyes quickly and moved his lips slightly, and though he said nothing, Marek felt and understood the movement of his lips that was telling him: "You have got Ihezal, sir ..."

"It was Ihezal I wanted to talk about", he said, as if answering something spoken aloud.

The young warrior snorted involuntarily. "There is no reason, my lord, for us to speak of what is in complete order."

"Or is it so?"

"Yes, Conqueror. Ihezal serves you as I serve you, and as everyone on the Moon should serve you ..."

"And yet you hold a grudge against me for that. You think I took her from you."

"What are you asking of me, my lord?"

He asked the question so simply and suddenly that Marek found no answer to it. Indeed: what did he expect, what did he want from this young man, from whom he had taken his only love, although despite his will and faith? He felt that he was being ridiculous in his willingness to establish friendly relations with a disadvantaged man, and he was overcome with anger at the thought that he was humiliating himself in Jeret's eyes. He frowned and was about to make some bossy command, short and irrevocable, that would cut through this false mood and designate the proper position for them both. Meanwhile Jeret spoke in a strange voice that he, the Conqueror, had never heard from him: "And disappointment ...? I could only blame the fate and order of things that one cannot serve two masters and that whoever gives his soul to holiness is lost to life."

He fell silent and only after a while added: "If you were a man like me ..."

"But what am I?" Marek replied involuntarily, seeing that Jeret is not finishing his sentence.

The young man looked up at him with bright and calm eyes: "You are a god, Conqueror."

Before Marek, stunned with the weight of this word, managed to answer and deny it, he was already far away, like a black moving stain, visible on the yellow sand of the coast. Soon he disappeared near the sledge among the hustle and bustle of the last preparations for the journey into the depths of the Sherns' terrible and unknown land.

Marek rose and turned lazily toward the gardens steeply sloping from the rear of the temple to the seashore. Nuzar lived here hidden from the inborn hatred of the Moon people since the day when he offered himself to the Conqueror as a guide of his ranks conquering the Sherns' country. The garden was poorly guarded as the guard, posted at the gates, was to defend the interior from possible fanatical attackers rather than to guard the prisoner, who had complete freedom of movement. Indeed, the Mortz could escape at any moment. He could follow the seashore, which stretched from here to the north, a steep and rocky gulf and disappear in the dense forests at the foot of O'Tamor, where no one could find him anymore. However, he did not even try to escape. He twice witnessed the terrible destruction of the Sherns and the torment of the once all-powerful Avij. He saw the Conqueror carry a lightning weapon in his hand, and when he pounced on him, he had the opportunity to see how powerful those hands were. From then on, in the Mortz's mind, always filled with dark bloody images of struggle and murder, a significant transformation took place. The Conqueror appeared to him as the most powerful being, and therefore worthy of the most honor and love on the Moon. Had he been able to believe for a moment that his new ruler might die or be defeated at all, he would undoubtedly have attacked him again with a knife. He would simply do that because he would have the glory to himself at the time of death that he, the Mortz Nuzar, had overcome what was the most powerful, but at this time nothing was as far from his thoughts as a similar supposition ...

So, he thought with delight that he was serving the immortal and all-powerful lord and rejoiced in advance in the soul of the final destruction of the Sherns, which he didn't doubt would be terrible. At the same time, he was dreaming that after destroying the winged natives the people's turn will come. He did not dare to make plans as it was his master's role. Still, he was sure that it would be a bloody hunt, where, like a faithful dog at the Conqueror's feet, he would hunt every living thing, so that it would perish at his hand.

As he thought this, an indomitable, idolatrous love towards the new lord filled his heart, and he trembled with impatience to rush to the south in a winged sled ... He wasn't given a gun but asked for a bow, and he himself made a bowstring to it from a dog's intestine and made volatile reed arrows to slay the Sherns with them at the side of the victorious slayer.

Now when the Conqueror entered the garden and informed him that the expedition would start in the evening, he trembled with joy and began to howl and jump like a hound before the hunt.
Marek had to tell him to calm down, just like a dog called to his feet. "Listen!" He said," I let you serve as a guide, although I could do without you, but if you betray me, I will have you skinned!"

Nuzar didn't understand what the word "betray" meant. He considered moving, if possible, to the enemy in the event of a defeat, as a natural thing, which only hatred could prevent, but betraying the cause of the Conqueror was totally incomprehensible to him. So, he stared with a dull astonishment at Marek, trying to understand the secret meaning of his words and the threat attached to them. At last a smile twisted his broad, hideous stigma: "I'll betray you if you tell me to do so!" He said with confidence, believing that the Conqueror wished to command him to obey himself, even if he knew that instead of a reward death awaited him at his hands.

Marek laughed involuntarily ...

He crossed the garden and walked through the back entrance to the temple. He met Ihezal in a vaulted corridor. He summoned her, and together they went down to the cellar where the Shern Avij was chained to the wall. On several occasions, Marek tried to give him relative freedom, at least by loosening the chains on his hands. Each time the Shern used his freedom of movement to attack the caretaker who fed him, or to pounce on the Conqueror in uncontrolled rage. These attacks were all the more dangerous as they came unexpectedly, and suddenly, as for most of the day, the Shern lay numb, not even bothering to move away as the caretaker kicked him to clean up the prison. So, he was tightly chained again, but to put an end to the tormenting of the powerless prisoner, no one was allowed to enter there except in Marek's or Ihezal's company, who had the keys to the dungeon.

Nothing has changed in the former treasury since it was turned into a prison cell. However, now only a thick dust settled down on the pile of holy books scattered on the floor, and it darkened the golden signs and inscriptions on the walls ... There was a miserable emptiness of what had already been done and belonged to the past. You could almost hear some violation and disgrace weeping in the corners at the hasty conversion of all that had still been holy until yesterday ...

In the light of the torch, Marek noticed that Ihezal had suddenly turned pale ... Standing on the last step, and as that night, when she surprised her grandfather over the books, she hesitated for a moment, as if unsure whether to enter ... her shoulder against the door frame. Her white arm slipped out of its wide sleeve; her chest tightened under the light shining fabric. For a moment, it seemed as if she would fall ...

He picked her up with a quick movement, but at that moment he noticed the monster's round red eyes, shining in the shadows and turned directly at him. He withdrew his hand in embarrassment and walked towards the prisoner.

The Shern's bloody eyes faded suddenly. He cuddled his head between his round arms, from under which his wings protruded like two black sheets, hung in loose folds on the horn skeleton. Only his white hands, clasped in iron, glistened against this background. Those white tormented hands were terrifying in their inert immobility.

Marek looked at him for a long time in silence. He couldn't understand what he came here for, why he had come here at all when he felt a painful disgust at the sight of this prisoner and his inevitable torment. Yet, he was drawn here by some irresistible attraction, like an evil charm, thrown at him by this weird monster. He would tell himself a hundred times while leaving the dungeon with disgust that he would not return here again. Then, he came there again, making up appearances or pretending that he wanted to get some information out of the Shern that he could use on his intended expedition ...

The Shern rarely answered his questions, and never again uttered a word that would have any meaning for the Conqueror. Sometimes he didn't speak at all. And now that Marek had spoken to him, he didn't even move, as if he hadn't heard the indifferent question thrown at him. After some time, only his white, phosphorescent forehead became a cloudy color, through which quick successive flashes began to shine through with the whole ranges of colors, at times dissolving into a general, purple tone ...

"He is speaking." Ihezal whispered staring at the Shern with wide open eyes.

Meanwhile, the colors played stronger and stronger on the monster's forehead. They were sometimes changing like the bustling northern lights and so bright that the whole cellar shimmered with a rainbow-like light, and sometimes again they dimmed, lazily and sweetly pouring into each other ... Marek, looking at it, had an impression that some weird kind of hymn of light and color was sung in front of him, capable of expressing things which would never fit in a human voice.

Suddenly, a bloody glow flared on the Shern's forehead, like a loud scream interrupted by several cold flashes of blue, and it went out in one moment, like a suddenly stifled fire...

Avij now opened his eyes, which had been closed so far, and looked at Marek.

"Why did you come here?" He said with his voice, "why did people come to the Moon at all and bother higher beings? You are a dog, but listen to what the wise one says, before you die miserably for the punishment that you dared to raise your hand at a Shern. All evil comes from the Earth which is a rebellious and cursed star not fit for our eyes to look at. The Moon was once a wonderful orchard, and it was inhabited by the Sherns, living in rich cities by the rustling seas! Long, long time ago ...

And the days were short then, and the Earth rose and set in the firmament of heaven, circling the whole Moon all around and serving the Sherns with its light in the night!

But the time came that the ominous star suddenly halted in the sky, having rebelled, and the land it stopped over became cursed! The insatiable Earth had stolen water and air from it, and the desert is now impassable there, where delightful gardens once grew! Piles of mountains, and the corpses of crumbling cities are standing over dried out rivers. Cursed is the Earth, and cursed is all it does, and cursed are all creations that come from there."

He was saying it in the usual rattling voice of the Sherns, but something in the manner of his speaking and his intonation made his words resemble a hymn or a repeated ancient curse or a prayer ... When he fell silent and fell into the previous, motionless indifference, Marek lunged vigorously towards him:

"Talk, talk! So once upon a time, on the other side ...? Has the legend been kept among you until now?"

He trembled with excitement to hear some more of these words, a tradition, perhaps passed from a generation to a generation, which in a different way revealed to him a piece of the ancient secret of the Moon, when the desserts were seas and the rich cities stood by the rustling rivers ... But he insisted in vain, trying by promises, pleas or threats to get more out of the silent Shern. Avij once more raised his shining eyes at the Conqueror and grunted hatefully:

"Go back to Earth! Go back to Earth while there is time! We made only one mistake, letting a human generation live and multiply here! But now we will destroy you all if you don't want to be our dogs!"

Then he nestled his head against his shoulders again and hung heavy and unfeeling on the chains which chained his hands.

Marek thought that now he was going to wipe out all the Sherns, but he did not say it ... He even hesitated for a while whether not to liberate the Shern and persuade him in a friendly manner to tell him the rest of the story. He soon abandoned that thought knowing from experience that it was going to lead to nothing, and that it would endanger everyone at the hand of this unpredictable monster.

A soft sigh broke him out of his reverie, so he quickly turned: Ihezal was standing motionless leaning against the door with her back. She was as pale as a corpse with her eyes wide open, insanely fixed on the Shern's eyes, which, facing her directly, glowed again bloody and ominously, like four red rubies, shining against the black, velvety background of the curled up monstrous body ...

"Ihezal! Ihezal!" Marek called.

"I'm scared ..." she whispered through her worried lips. A sudden shiver ran through her, but despite the apparent efforts of her will, she couldn't take her eyes away from the Shern's bloody pupils.

Marek caught her in his arms and ran quickly into the daylight. In the passage, the girl unconsciously, with the movement of a frightened child, embraced him by the neck with her hands. While she was hugging him tightly with her whole body, he, carrying her in such a way, could feel the rippling of her small, warm, and firm breasts and the violent pounding of her heart through his loose shirt. There was one moment that a delusion struck his temples and embracing her more strongly with his mighty hands, he bent his lips over her fragrant, so like a golden flower head. He could feel the warmth of her forehead and the sweet tickling of loose hair on his thirsty lips when the full daylight hit them with a golden wave... Marek snapped out of it and set the girl on the steps. She opened her eyes as if still sleepy and a slight shiver ran through her body and flushed cheeks ...

The sunset was near. Marek, walking with the girl along the seashore, was stubbornly silent. They had passed the settlement and the last warm ponds, steadily fuming with silver vapor, slowly ascending to the deserted highlands where not so long ago Avij's menacing tower used to rise. There were only debris left there now and some partially burnt beams among the broken wall. Lush weeds loomed around the dry bushes broken in the victorious fight in the vast and once delightful garden. There was now an empty wasteland, but so cursed that no one dared to build a hut on the wreckage.

Marek sat down on the bald part of a hill, not far above the rubble, and was looking at the city gilded by the setting sun. Ihezal was sitting silently at his knees and turning her pensive eyes to the radiant fiery sun, slowly bending towards the horizon.

Suddenly Marek shuddered and looked at the girl. "Don't you want to marry Jeret before he goes on that expedition tonight?" He asked abruptly, brutally breaking the strange silence of the place and the time.

Ihezal slowly raised her large, black pupils at him, still full of sunlight, still smoldering at their bottom with a hot, golden glow ...

"Jeret?" She repeated, as if not understanding the question, but she smiled and shook her head. "Ah, no! Neither him nor anyone, now nor ever!" Her long-lashed eyelids fell halfway over her eyes, in which the sunlight had faded, and her purple lips twitched.

Marek leaned back and lay on his back, resting his head on his clasped fists. He looked at the serene sky, painted with the evening aurora wide to the zenith.

"It is actually strange," he began after a while, "I came here, and I am going today to destroy the Sherns, in their own country, on their own globe. "Because people want to live here ... because they are weaker and because they did not come to Earth thousands of years ago and did not make us their cattle ... And what right do I have? And what right do you have at all? ..." He paused and laughed widely, somewhat wryly.

Ihezal looked at him in amazement: "Lord ...?"

"Yes, yes, I know! You told me! The blessing comes from the Earth, and holy is everything that comes from it. Holy is murder, holy is harm and looting ... and even these shackles ..." He felt that he was saying things that would not affect his actions at all, so he fell silent without finishing his sentence.

"You are so beautiful, my lord!" Ihezal breathed softly, looking at him with loving eyes.

Dogs barked somewhere below, and a long, choral singing started... You couldn't hear it clearly from a distance. It seemed that the air itself, rippling and resonant, was casting some intuitions and memories of the melody, that the song smelled only instead of sounding...

The sun was huge and red, hanging low over the distant, blackened plain ... The pre-afternoon chill was already coming from the sea.

Marek sprang up suddenly and sat down. "Let's go." He said. "As you wish, lord..."

Ihezal raised her hands to gather her untied hair, but loose gold slipped from her trembling fingers and glistened in the sun on her shoulders and on her face ... She lowered her hands helplessly. Her head tilted back a bit, almost touching Marek's chest. Suddenly she turned pale and her eyes closed, her lips slightly parting. "Are you a god, my lord?" She whispered sleepily.

Marek felt her held back temple brush against his lips ...

Down below, somewhere at the coast, far away, a trumpet sounded hard. Marek stood up in one jump. The girl fell face down to his feet with a soft groan, but he was already looking towards the city, towards the sea. The muster call sounded again heard clearly in the silence.

"This is my time," said Marek. "They're calling my soldiers."

He bent down and picked up the lying girl.

"Ihezal, listen, if I don't come back ..."

She was looking into his eyes. "You are fair and so you will circle the lunar globe like a flame! The sea will carry you away, and winds, thunder and lightning will follow you. The fear will be your messenger, it will be announcing your great holy name! And those who will fall will be blessed to fall at your side, and those who will survive will cry out: 'Praise to you Conqueror!' ... and I ..."

Her voice trailed off in her chest, her mouth moved soundlessly, and she suddenly burst out into spasmodic sobbing.

The trumpet sounded a third time: The Conqueror was now summoned to get his warriors on their way.

III

Every morning there was a time of great silence at the sea that preceded the arrival of a raging thunderstorm as soon as the sun reached the top of the sky. In the east, somewhere beyond the Cemetery Island, the black clouds were already gathering, and a menacing murmur was coming from them. A distant white lightning, announced it as if the fangs of a monstrous beast which had fallen on the sky and was creeping slowly, chasing the fleeing sun across the sea. In a few dozen or so hours, its mighty roar would shake the air. Its heavy paws would fall on the water and trample it with a furious foam splashing up to the sky, where the gray fur will spread in the sky. But for now the beast was still lurking in the distance cuddled up between the sky and the clear circle of the sea, and the silence was immense.

The surface of the waters looked like an enormous perfectly carved fine-steel shield. You could almost feel its scratch free hardness suddenly changed from liquid to metal. Around the shores of the distant islands, only the color of the sea changed: there were some peacock eye rainbows trembling like rings, framing precious gems. Over the shimmering surface of the sea a gushing motionless heat hung in the air, almost heavy and dejected, pierced through by the sparkling glare of the sun ...

Ihezal, running along the coast, had already passed the last houses of the settlement. All the doors were tightly shut, and the windows shuttered. The previous evening the youth had followed the Conqueror on the expedition. Those who remained hid in the dark interiors from the midday heat which seemed more oppressive than usual.

The girl overcome with heat and running, stopped in the shade of a rock headland. Her eyes were getting dim from the excessive glare, and at times the sea seemed to her like a black stain, spilled over the vastness. For a moment then she seemed to see the red light of torches, and countless sleighs with sails unfurled in the night wind, and almost heard the sharp whistle of shackled skids and the loud scream passing like the wind.

She glanced up involuntarily to see if those fading flames looking like a handful of stars scattered on a slippery sheet of ice were still there, but the sunlight struck her open pupils again, and the lightning melting in it reached just above the horizon. She looked quickly at the lurking clouds: the imminent storm was coming, but so lazy that you could barely see its sluggish pace across the pale blue sky.

"I'll make it in time," she whispered almost aloud, and after making sure that no one was following her, she ran swiftly towards the bay stopping among the rocks. With steady hands she untied a small, hidden boat under a boulder and, jumping into it, headed for the high sea, towards the visible Cemetery Island. The oars bent in her tiny hands, and the boat continued, cutting the dark steel of the water like a diamond blade ... The sun sparkled in its trail with shimmering pearls.

A few steps from the shore Ihezal lowered the oars. Her strength left her in that overwhelming heat, and her clothes though light choked her body. So, she quickly peeled them off to move more freely, but as soon as the sun touched her white skin, a sudden, delightful faintness penetrated all her limbs with dreaminess. She threw herself at the bottom of the boat, closing her eyes.

Through her tight closed eyelids, the red glow, painted with her own blood, was pulsing in her pupils. On her breasts and hips, she felt the fiery sunshine, as if some mighty, unsatisfied lips engulfed her with kisses ... The fair, victorious figure loomed in her memory, and an almost icy shiver ran through her body, embraced by the heat of the sun ...

She was awakened by a stronger thunder booming in the distance. Suddenly she jumped up: the surface of the sea was already creasing with the first, low moving wind. She picked up the oars again and began to work hurriedly with more effort. Now, she had to struggle with every now and then blowing counter-breeze, and smooth and round waves which were swaying the boat in rhythm and splashing into the white combs against its sharp edge.

The impatient wind was already rising, its wings flying restlessly into the water, when golden-haired Ihezal, falling from weariness, finally landed in a tiny harbor hidden under the trees on the low bank of the Cemetery Island. She had hardly had the time to attach the boat bow to a stump and grab her clothes from its bottom when the storm fell with its full weight on the foaming water under the darkened sky. The whirlwind grabbed the girl's golden hair and tugged it, throwing it at the glare of lightnings. It jerked the clothes she was carrying in her hand and wrapped it in a mad whirl around her white body. She jumped under a flat stone, protruding from beneath the green lawn, and struggling with the wind, she began to dress hastily. The first warm drops of rain fell on her bare shoulders.

She was blindly running in the downpour, tramping through the familiar wilderness between the clumps of trees, suddenly rising before her in the flashes of lightning. She was jumping over boulders hidden in the grass and sliding down the slippery slopes of the hills. Then having passed the graves of those legendary first people on the Moon, she turned again towards the seashore and ran to the top of a low hill, between the piled-up boulders.

Under one of them, there was an entrance to a large cavern. Ihezal entered it and stopped here, taking her breath with her tightly rising breast. Water dripped from her hair and from her thin clothes wrapped around her slender limbs.

An old man stepped out of the side chamber and looked into the grey twilight of the cave. "Here you are!" He cried, "I was worried about you ..."

"I am a little late, Grandpa," she said, "but I couldn't leave sooner; I was afraid of being noticed.

Malahuda took her hand and pulled her behind him. He had a true hermit dwelling in one of the forks of a large cavern. The former high priest slept on a bundle of skins, as did fishermen near the Isthmus and large stones served him as chairs and table. In the corner, there was a stone stove hastily erected, which apparently heated the cave during the night frosts.

Ihezal, forgetting her weariness and drenched clothes, stared at her grandfather in the dark light coming from somewhere through cracks in the ceiling. He seemed older and sadder but at the same time more dignified, even though he was standing before her now without the charm of holiness and the cap he had abandoned that day, welcoming the Conqueror ... Her heart squeezed at the sight, and she involuntarily compared him to his replacement Elem. Her grandfather, even in his voluntary abandonment, maintained his dignity, while the sly and greedy Elem awoke an unsurmountable disgust in her. Perhaps unconsciously she was sensing his hypocrisy towards Marek under the guise of submissiveness and humility. It occurred to her that Malahuda, left on the high priest's stool, would now follow the Conqueror's holy will and with generous hands throw the blessing of a new age on the lunar world. The unrepentant grief swelled in her and instead of greeting the long-missed one, she exclaimed reproachfully: "Grandpa! Why did you go away and why don't you want to come back!"

But the old man did not listen to her words. He was already bustling around the cave like a good host, pulling out a simple leather outfit from a closet. "Take off your clothes," he said, "you have to put on something dry."

At the same time, with his hands, once white and now muddy from work he began to unravel the knots tied in haste under her neck

The girl grabbed his hands: "No, no ..."

He looked at her in amazement: "You have to change."

A sudden blush painted her all over. "I will change, Grandpa, but there, behind that stone.

She knew that the old man, accustomed to the innocent shamelessness of the Moon women, did not understand her flinching at all, so she added in a tone of explanation, blushing even more: "I swore to the Conqueror, whom I serve, that no one will see me naked, not even a woman ..."

"What a ridiculous vow this is!" Malahuda muttered, far from guessing an erotic innuendo in such a strange oath. He did not argue, however, and while Ihezal was changing in her private nook, he kindled the embers smoldering in the oven to cook a meal. In a short while, Ihezal was standing by him wearing a hard leather shirt on her white skin and helping him.

Meanwhile, a noon storm was raging around the world. A dull sound of thunder fell into the cavern, and it seemed that the wind was opening the stone door with a thud. You could already feel its cool breath, and imagine that in a moment it would fall inside and then stand there dressed in a bright lightning ... The powerful, steady, and grand rumbling of the sea could be heard in the short intervals of silence patiently hitting the rocky base of the island. It had that certainty that in one or two wretched thousand years, it would consume the rest of the old land as it had already consumed hundreds of miles, before it in its turn runs dry and perishes ...

After a short meal, the old man and his granddaughter sat on a boulder covered with fur, and with his hands on his knees, Malahuda started to speak slowly: "Only after the army had left for that expedition, I could let you know where I was. My only sworn confidant, a fisherman and a voluntary guardian of ancient graves on this island, informed me that you had sworn to the Conqueror to find my hiding place and inform him of it. I don't want to ... "

The girl wanted to say something, but the high priest ordered her to be silent.

"Don't interrupt me now," he said. "I have a lot to tell you, and I want you to listen to me carefully. "You don't understand why I left. I know some people suppose that the old man, they had gotten accustomed to didn't want to share his power with the visitor from space and preferred a voluntary exile ... It was not like that. I will not explain to you all the reasons that made me hide, because I would have to tell too much about the buildings that collapsed in one night, and I'm sure you wouldn't understand me well.

You have already welcomed this Conqueror, but I am still waiting for one. I am not like Choma who as I hear does not want to acknowledge this one and preaches the arrival of another righteous Conqueror. No, I am waiting for this one to become the Conqueror. Nevertheless, I am waiting.

When I see that he is the true blessing for the Moon, I will die in peace, and if he needs me for something, I will appear before him, but now is not the time.

Last night I came out of the cave and saw the winged sleighs full of armed, young, and self-righteous men dashing south. I will wait for them to come back the same way. I will accept the Conqueror if they return in the same way, not scattered and fleeing from the enemy pursuing them.

My old age has taught me one great thing: every endeavor is blessed when its result is successful and blissful. I have seen too many defeats and failures in my life to rejoice in good intentions, or to show gratitude and praise in advance on deeds yet to be accomplished.

But I missed you, because you were always my flower, the only child of my dead children, and that is why I called you, sending the keeper of the local graves with the news. Please tell me now how you are and tell me what your eyes have seen."

Ihezal stared in the dim depth of the cave in silence before she started speaking: "Grandpa, my eyes can only see one thing now … My eyes pierce the storms over the swaying sea and look in a distant and awful country. I see a bloody battle, and I hear the thunder of shots and the moans of those falling, and my heart beats in me with the song of victory. It rejoices because the bodies of the dead Sherns cover the line up the battle fields and because the unrighteous Mortzes are moaning as they are struck in the chest with thunder and the word of the Bright One. Grandpa! I see him victorious, laughing and like a young god, but my heart cries in me that he is not a human being like me!"

She fell with her face to her grandfather's knees and suppressing her voice with his robe, she began to complain with her hot words: "Grandpa, my blood is raging in me! I did not know what fire is, but it devours and consumes me, that I will wither like a flower in the southern heat. Oh! Let the rainstorm come! Oh, let the destroying wind or a killer thunderbolt come!"

Malahuda did not answer. He only took her head in his thin hands and stayed immersed in deep silence.

Meanwhile she was crying without tears, only with a jerking spasm, tearing her tiny chest, until after a while she calmed down a little and began to speak: "Why don't you answer me, Grandfather? I fear your silence! I would prefer you to scold me, to punish me by dragging me by hair to your feet! The Conqueror, the blessed lord, said that he wanted to give new laws to the people and regulations similar to those existing on Earth, and that he wanted all men and women to be equal, so that a woman would not continue to be a slave! Grandpa! Why won't the wise Conqueror, transform the men of the Moon to become, like him so serving them would be sweet and worthy? My woman's heart does not want freedom, nor equality, but yes, it wants to serve the most powerful who has come down from the Earth to the Moon! Why does he not burn the flower of my body with his mighty mouth? After all, I am a beautiful and fragrant flower, the most fragrant on the lunar globe which is shiny and quite like a great star … Is it because he decided to be a god, so I must perish from the longing of my own blood?

I am sworn to him, and he isn't taking me! I am afraid, Grandfather, that I will hate him out of love and reach out for his heart, to see if his blood is red like ours... "

Saying that, she threw her head back and flashed her white teeth like a golden panther, already gathering momentum to jump.

The old man rose slowly. "It's bad, it's bad," he said to himself, not looking at his granddaughter," who knows, perhaps I should have stayed there, and watch" ...

He looked at the girl staring in his face and smiled sadly. "No, not you, no! Here, vigilance would be useless. I already knew that you were sold when you entered the treasury and found me over the books. I am afraid that I should have watched over the one you have already named the Conqueror and worship over any measure. I am convinced that if he is victorious and like a lord tries to change the things that have grown crooked on the Moon, everybody will turn against him, and even you, even you! But now is not the time. I acted according to my conscience, and I will not take back what I once let go."

They were sitting for a long time in silence or talking to each other in silent broken sentences, until a ray of sunlight, coming in from somewhere through a crevasse, informed them that the storm was over and that the world, refreshed with streams of rain, was enjoying life again.

Then Malahuda took the golden-haired girl's hand and they both went out in the sun. They both ran on the freshly washed grass, still slippery from the rain. It stroked their bare feet with a cool caress, on their way along a small meadow towards the top of the hill for centuries called Martha's Tomb. The boulder here was large, sloping, with traces of letters, perhaps forged centuries ago, which no one could read anymore ...

Malahuda rested his trembling hand on this boulder and said: "Today, I don't know what is true, but there is a record in the books that the mother of the Moon people lies in this tomb. She was the blessed mother of the first man husband and his sisters, and the inspired prophetess Ada, who as a virgin served the Old Man. But the legend says that the Old Man was not the father of the lunar people, but a guardian ... Yes, some people maintain, on the basis of some cards, apparently found in his burnt house centuries ago (I do not know, is it true?), that love for this human woman brought him, a god, to the Moon and that he suffered until he departed for Earth ... Why shouldn't you suffer?"

He was saying it like he did when he was a priest who had been accustomed for years to interpret the words of the Scriptures and to draw a lesson or console. Soon, he came to his senses as he realized that he was saying things that could not be applied here and were not convincing at all. Besides, he himself did not believe what he was saying ...

He fell silent then, especially seeing that Ihezal was not listening to him. Her pale face was facing south, and she was looking at the swirling white clouds on the horizon that looked like troops, fighting in the air above the sea amidst the pearly dust. Malahuda also noticed a resemblance, for he suddenly said, thinking of the actual battle which was perhaps taking place at that moment: "What if the Conqueror died?"

At first, hearing these words, Ihezal turned even paler, so that it seemed that there was not a drop of blood in her body, but then she shook her head with a smile, "No! He cannot die!"

She said it with such profound conviction that the old man said nothing but bent his gray chin over his chest and pondered, looking with red eyes at the broad and bright sea.

About that time Marek was resting in the first conquered city on the Sherns' land. The maddening rush of the wind blowing in the shattered sails carried him all night. Guided by the compass, he was passing black shapes of islands looming in the starlight. Sometimes Nuzar warned him about hot whirlpools, where the water did not freeze even at night ... The sleighs, scattered in a wide chain on the vast surface, kept in touch with each other with the glow of red torches placed on the front, and they continued without stopping for eleven earth days ...

In the morning, forty hours before the sun was about to appear and a gray glow was creeping across the ice from the east, Nuzar signaled to the Conqueror that they were approaching the coast. In fact, Marek noticed a distant white line of snow on the horizon torn here and there with protruding shapes resembling towers.

The Mortz was standing next to him and pointing with his hand: "This is their largest city, where almost nobody lives anymore. Half of it has fallen into the sea along with the ground, and when it is quiet, you can see the towers above which the fish swim. The Sherns withdrew inland and further east from there. Here is their settlement where they have a harbor" ... He pointed to a hardly visible group of houses on the coast, around a deeply cut bay.

The sleigh Jeret was riding approached the Conqueror's. The young warrior was pale, and his lips were tightened, but his face was calm. "Conqueror," he said, "the wind is rushing us straight to the village, we will be there in a few hours."

Marek gave the order, and the sleigh rudders, cutting sharply into the ice, grinded as they were twisted with robust hands, and the whole train began to tack back in a huge semicircle along the shores of the bay. The sleighs, on which the field cannons had been placed, came out closest to the land, and at a certain moment they burst into fire on the Sherns' sleeping village. The dust, suddenly rising from the collapsing houses, was visible now and the people were already loading up the cannons that had been fired for the second time, and again an accurate and terrible volley sounded up close.

Before the villagers, frightened in their sleep, could realize what had happened, the morning wind had swept the attackers away and carried them on, towards the empty place, where, according to Nuzar's words, they could land safely. The sun had risen when the train of sleighs, now pulled onto the land, was turned into a fortified camp.

The Sherns also began to appear from a distance, stunned with the completely unimaginable attack. From time to time, they flew on their heavy wings towards the camp and died from the sure shots of its crew. Then they suddenly withdrew, leaving their attackers alone for a moment.

Marek knew he needed to hurry and not give the Sherns time to think, but he was forced to wait out the morning thaw before he could begin his terrible hunt. Meanwhile, he kept the camp in a defensive position and looked around curiously at the surrounding land.

It was flat and wide. As far as Nuzar's stories could tell, relatively few Sherns had still lived on the Moon. Most of their cities were rubble, deserted, and wide fields lay fallow, unless they had Mortzes' hands to cultivate them. Lazy Sherns were reluctant to work, almost considering work a detriment. Even more reason, Marek marveled at their terrible power, by which they were able to subdue an industrious and a more numerous human tribe.

The marshy ground was still wet from the melting snow when Jeret drew Marek's attention to the approaching crowds. A huge group of Mortzes was marching towards them pushed by the Sherns into the field of fire, but it did not even come to a regular battle. Dispatching several volleys of firearms into the packed mass dispersed it in a flash. The young grass unfolding from under the snow turned black with numerous corpses. People went to finish off the wounded.

It was a disgusting sight for Marek, who, seeing animal creatures in the monstrous Sherns, did not reproach himself for murdering them, but shuddered at the thought of slaughtering helpless Mortzes, who looked like people. Since he could not hesitate; he just gave the merciful order that the wounded be killed quickly.

Nuzar chose two or three slightly injured Mortzes, and with the promise of life, persuaded them to join him in his service as the guides to the victors. The corpses were fed to the dogs brought as a part of the harnessed teams. Soon, the hunt after Nuzar's bloody heart began.

The wheels were put on the sleighs and the rolling train advanced slowly. They stopped in places, and then fighters emerged from them. Marek walked on with three Mortzes and a few ferocious dogs with a good sense of smell, followed by the armed men, with hand on trigger, keen and watchful eye, checking out every corner of the ground around them. When a Mortz or a Shern appeared, they were killed, and the march continued towards the walls of the settlement bombed at night.

In the meantime, the sun was bright in the sky, and the sea swayed sweetly, with ringing against the sand of the flat coast. The smell from the unfolded lunar plants was intoxicating, and at times the silence was such that Marek wanted to lie back among the greenery and gaze at the enormous blue sky, stretched over this sad and dreamy country. But here a dog growled, or a Mortz hooted near his leg, and Marek swiftly raised the weapon to his eye to kill a fleeing Shern, or to order a group shot at the Mortzes, quietly working in the field and unaware of the attack. The houses encountered along the way were burned in haste, and if made of stone, they were demolished conscientiously, so that they would not serve as a hiding place for the Sherns. They worked like this with numerous pauses, slowly but tirelessly. The Sherns had not put up any serious resistance so far, so it seemed that the land would be conquered without much sacrifice and without much effort, and the race of the Moon natives would be destroyed.

Meanwhile, the noon of the long lunar day was approaching. During the greatest heat, Marek and his troops approached the city walls. The new settlement, which he had passed before it was crushed by cannon balls and now completely empty. Apparently, all the inhabitants had taken refuge in the old hillfort, the defensive walls of which, neglected and half-scattered, shone blindingly in the midday sun.

The Conqueror felt that he would meet desperate resistance here. He stared at the mighty, jagged towers, at the arches, and at the enormous gates with vaults, often crumbling with the sinking of the ground. Behind them the city was flowing in a wave of stone houses to the sea to finally drown in its depths. This view made him think of the message sent by the Old Man of the Earth hundreds of years earlier that there were ruins of similar cities in the Great Desert.

Who knows what treasures and secrets this disintegrating city hides within itself? And what could it tell him if he had not been forced to turn it into a shapeless pile of rubble, torn with cannon balls? ...

It briefly occurred to him to send parliamentarians like Nuzar for example, and to try to save this ancient city from destruction, but he laughed himself at it. What kind of agreement could there be? The dilemma was clear: either people would forever serve the Sherns on the Moon, or else the Sherns must be exterminated to the last one. The experience of the ages has already taught these people that no pacts, no agreements would work with the unfaithful Sherns, as the moment they have a chance of breaking them, they do so without hesitation. Was he then going to propose to them that they all go out and drown themselves voluntarily in the sea, leaving their own globe to the stellar visitors, or should he take all the people back to Earth? After all, there was no other option!

As he was thinking about all this, his able warriors were already hastily turning the gleaming maws of their cannons towards the quiet looking lifeless walls of the city. The ruffled air trembled from the terrible heat of the sun, turning the stones into some unreal dream, shimmering in the eyes and divergent. There were moments when it seemed to Marek that the whole city was only a reflection of a dream in a busy and glowing water, and it would soon dissolve like a dream on that empty seacoast.

He didn't even know when he nodded his head as a sign to Jeret to begin. The terrible thud of gunfire had sobered him up. He looked at the weathered walls that crumbled under the impact of cannonballs, and the towers, apparently strong, swaying suddenly at their foundations. The cannon roared again at close range, and a cloud of dust burst up from the collapsing houses.

At the same time, Nuzar's sharp scream rang out at his feet. He looked in the direction the Mortz were pointing to, and it seemed to him that a heavy, low-slung black cloud was flowing at him with incomprehensible speed.

"Sherns! Sherns!," There was a shout in the ranks.

In an instant, with a trained movement, the warriors scattered so as not be a target of the Sherns' missiles thrown from above. Small arms grated, and there was a rattling of shots, irregular but incessant. Every now and then heavy bodies began to fall to the ground and bleed... Not much time passed, and the deadly chase after the monsters scattered in the escape began.

Most of them, however, took refuge within the city walls, and the thunder rumbled again. The still standing houses, half-broken towers and shops erected many centuries ago were hit, changed into rubble, and finally into a chaotic mass of piled up boulders and stone.

Meanwhile, the storm broke out in the world and thundered downward, helping the people in spreading destruction.

Sometimes a Shern broke out from a heap, desperately trying to escape, but soon fell struck with a bullet, not even able to reach the ring of the besieging destroyers. Some, mad with the fear of death, flew over the raging sea and died quickly, falling into the waves.

The victory was complete without the loss of a single man.

However, when Marek, after some time, wanted to lead his people to the smoking ruins in order to search them, Nuzar grabbed him by the edge of his tunic and shook his head in negation.

"These soldiers do not need to be sacrificed," he said, pointing to the winning ranks, "they will still be of use to you, master. "

Marek looked at him with a question.

"The Sherns are still hidden in the pits. Deep caverns stretch out all over the city. Whoever enters there will perish."

"And the entrances to the caverns?" Marek asked.

"There are plenty of them. Some of them were walled up by Mortzes under the whip because the sea was rushing through them."

"Where are they?"

"The captured Mortzes will show you them without fail. They know these places all too well, because the walls break down constantly under the impact of waves and they always need to be reinforced and repaired" ...

Marek didn't even wait for the storm to calm down. The sea, still swaying and furious, beat against the rubble, blurring it with blows when at the Conqueror's command as mines were hurriedly put in to remove the stone barrier from the waves.

Soon a mighty roar sounded, and columns of water and stone sprayed upwards. Then, the sea receded for a moment, thrown backward with a burst, but at that moment it boiled with a violent vortex and tumbled across the torn barriers into the mysterious caverns.

Threatened by the flood, the Sherns began to flee from their hiding places through side exits and were mercilessly killed at the people's hands so that the words of the Scriptures that the Conqueror would come to the Moon would be fulfilled.

He himself sat over the rubble, and in the new, fresh sun, peeking out from behind the clouds, watched as the sea, calmed down after the storm, having filled the caves, was slowly smoothing out. Now there was a wide rainbow mirror through which you could see the city sunk in the depths, the only trace left that once, here this rubble was once inhabited by intelligent beings.

The warriors were finally resting ...

A bird with golden wings sprang up from the nearby bushes and, shining in the sun, began to circle over the Conqueror's head, making wider and wider circles.

IV

The news came out of nowhere and was spreading among the people passed on from mouth to mouth. They were telling each other about Marek's amazing advantages, and even though the sacred "Conqueror" won them, they were scorned at, hardly believed, especially as no one could give a reliable source of this information ... Someone pointed to the half-wild fishermen from the area of the Isthmus, who had once come in the company of an old madman near the Warm Ponds. It was said that one of their countrymen, having left the Conqueror's ranks, returned home for some unknown reason, and brought the good news. Since the rumors came from a second and uncertain hand, they were received with caution. Still people listened to it greedily and looked in the old way to the Great Sea, beyond which the country of the Sherns lay.

This expedition seemed totally improbable to people for generations accustomed to the Sherns' yoke that so far, they could not get used to the thought that it had actually gone overseas. Despite the good news, they expected defeat and the arrival of the terrible first natives. There were already some, who explained the lack of confirmed information as a proof of the utter loss of the insolent madmen and were cursing the Conqueror, until recently praised by them over the measure ...

When, at last, one day, at the gray dawn of a rising morning, two winged sleighs appeared on the shore of the frozen sea, the people frighteningly approached the newcomers. They didn't even dare question them if they were not the last to survive the slaughter. They came out of the sleigh, weary, but happy, and laughing, proceeding towards the city, giving signs of joy from afar ... So, people shouted with joy and began to run towards them, surrounding them with a tumultuous and curious circle ... The warriors were saying unheard-of things that the Conqueror was proceeding in glory through the land of the Sherns and destroying all of them without mercy. He had already conquered all the cities by the sea and the plains, sweeping the land with fear and death. Now, he had gone up the mountains south of the pole, where the Sherns who were still alive had hidden. He had sent them here to bring back a new supply of ammunition, which was already running out.

The crowd, maddened with unbridled joy, took the newcomers in their arms, and carried them in triumph towards the temple, shouting.

The morning was still freezing cold, and the snow had not melted in the fields when it happened. Many of the inhabitants of the settlement at the *Warm Ponds* were still sleeping or waiting inside for the warm rays of the sun. The still growing noise woke them up, so they came outside, often half asleep. Having heard what was going on, they joined the crowd, which at such an early hour had already filled the entire square in front of the temple.

Elem, having heard the noise in his palace, at first thought that the Conqueror was returning, and hastily ordered the high priestly robes to be put on him, until Sevin informed him that it was only the messengers coming with joyful news. So, without waiting for his ceremonial robes, he went out as he stood, in his house clothes covered only with a fur thrown on his shoulders. He shouted from the threshold that the envoys should bow down to him first and report the message. They, however, according to Conqueror's apparent order, went first to look for the golden-haired girl. Having found her in the passage from the former palace to the temple, fell on their faces in an unprecedented way, handing her expensive gifts.

There were pink pearls, torn away from the eternal ceremonial robes of the noble Shern elders, bones carved in a mysterious country perhaps hundreds of years ago, and ornaments made of stretched gold, resembling uncanny flowers.

Ihezal accepted those gifts in silence with only an eerie smile on her lips. When her hands were already full of all precious things, it seemed to the deputies that an evil light suddenly shone in her eyes, like the flash of a short dagger, suddenly striking in the chest. But soon she lowered her eyelids and, smiling lovingly and temptingly, spoke to the amazed envoys: "Haven't you brought me the most valuable thing, which is much more expensive than these pink pearls, rolling, out from my too full hands? Hasn't anyone brought with you the reddest thing for me which booms like a bell in the Sherns' country? Why haven't you brought me the most precious gift that I ask to have?"

This is how she was speaking, as if unconscious from a secret joy, and when the envoys began to ask: "What is there that you would like? And say that they will eagerly report this to the Conqueror, she added these, quite incomprehensible words: "His heart, I would like his bloody red heart!"

There was a young boy among them, who had been asking Marek to let him return, allegedly longing for the family. From the beginning, as if in delight, he was looking at Ihezal's face, and when she finished speaking, he suddenly took a short dagger from behind his belt and with an unrestrained motion plunged it in his throat. Blood gushed from the open wound, and he fell to the floor, kicking it with his legs.

There was a commotion. In astonishment, they jumped to his rescue, but he waved everyone away, looking only at the golden-haired girls with a fading smile ... Only when Ihezal, whose curiosity prevailed over her feeling of revulsion at the sight of dying, bowed her head over the wounded, while he, gasping with his pierced throat, whispered with difficulty: "I had to die, for I understood your words, and if I had lived, I would have fulfilled what you demanded!"

He could not speak more, and Ihezal didn't ask anymore, either. She turned away from the dying man in disgust and, shrugging her shoulders slightly, walked away with an expression of disgust and pity on her purple lips. Her own words and the death that immediately followed seemed abhorrent to her. Now, she was under the impression that it was not she, but some evil spirit speaking through her. Her eyes filled with tears, and her heart suddenly surged with unbridled love for this distant and bright god ... She pressed a handful of cool pink pearls to her hot womb and face whispering in elation: "No, no, no! Let your mighty heartbeat and thunder, let me perish in vain longing! I would be the first to deliver your murderer to severe torment, my beloved! ... and it is good that this boy immediately punished himself for having dared to think what I had said!" ...

At the same time, however, the shadow of the imprisoned Avij loomed in her eyes: his four bloody eyes and black wings, spread wide on the stony wall below the golden Sign of the Coming. She felt an irrepressible, unconscious desire to look into those terrible and captivating eyes, to see their despondency at the sight of the gift of the loot sent to her ... Mechanically, hardly thinking of what she was doing, she descended the stairs and opened the door of the cell.

Avij raised his head. And Ihezal, slowly lit up all the lights on the ceiling and on the walls. Then, slowly and without haste, began to play silently with pink pearls, pouring them from hand to hand to make them gleam with colors of a rainbow, and was glad that her fingernails had the same gloss and color. She suddenly threw some pearls in the monster's face with a loud, silvery laughter. Avij cuddled his head in his arms and followed her movements with his burning eyes. Ihezal came even closer towards him.

"Can you recognize them?" She said, showing him gold ornaments and pieces of weaved cloth from across the sea, sent to her by the

Conqueror. An innocent, almost flirtatious smile played on her lips.

He recognized the jewels being poured out before his eyes, and for one moment his forehead turned a dark steel, cloudy color and his bloody pupils died out covered with his active eyelids. But soon he opened his eyes again and looked sharply at the girl.

"Can you recognize them?" She repeated. "For fun, the almighty Conqueror sent me gifts and trinkets as a sign that he had walked with his mighty foot through the Sherns' land and struck them with a lightning weapon! He conquered the cities and wiped out their inhabitants! He broke down the walls, and the trenches, and made the towers bow their heads to his feet. Blessed be the Conqueror, the slayer of the Sherns, and blessed is the Earth that sent him!"

Something like a smile twitched around the monster's horned lips. "Yes," he said after a moment, "a fat man whom you prematurely called the Conqueror passed through our country, plundered our cities and killed their inhabitants. I see these bright jewels in your hands which are a part of the inexhaustible treasures that we had gathered for centuries even before people appeared on the Earth which used to shine bright for us like a fiery and moving sun ... So, your Conqueror walked through the coast and the plains, but then something happened that you are not telling me, but that I know. He reached the lofty mountains and stopped helpless before them! The lightning weapons and iron poles flashing with fire will not help. The famous Conqueror stopped before the lofty mountains where the Shern cities are on the headlands of the rocks and inside them! He is looking up, like a dog whose bird has escaped into a tall tree branch. This is the strength of your Conqueror; this is his strength! The Sherns' broad wings will carry them, as centuries ago, to the tops of rocks, to inaccessible houses, from which they can sneer at the attackers and their untamed pride!"

The Shern, chained with irons to the wall, screeched with his malicious laughter and stared with his bloody eyes at the girl, whose hands slowly fell along her hips, spilling pink pearls on the stone floor of the prison.

"What are you, vain and imperfect creatures?," he began again after a while "what are you to us? You boast of your reason, and you have grown little more than dogs that can reproduce on the Moon in a similar way as you do! A man from Earth has come to you, and he tells you about the devices, arts, and inventions that they have there ...

We had them a long time ago, and we Sherns have already forgotten, having come to this mature wisdom that we only need to live and make others work for us! Go! Tell your Conqueror to go to the Great Desert and search the ruins of those cities changing into dust. He will learn there what we knew centuries ago, when there was no life on Earth yet! Let him fasten some wings to his shoulders and conquer our greatest city over the sea on those high rocks. Let him learn how to read a book hidden there, written only with colors and see how we knew the Earth, when it did not even dream of us, and what weight of the knowledge we had rejected long ago as unnecessary! It was all that you are trying to defeat us with, what you boast about today on Earth, what you have as the most precious thing and the thing unique only to you!"

The girl was listening to this stream of hoarse words in a strange bewilderment, not even daring to take her eyes away from the figure of this Shern who suddenly seemed to her not only a terrible, but also a superior being ... He apparently noticed it, because his eyes flashed with unrestrained pride, unfit for a captive, and began to speak again mockingly: "And what about your Conqueror's temporary advantage? If he does not return to Earth, he will die here, and you, despite the lightning guns, will serve us like you did before!"

He suddenly stopped and fixed his captivating eyes on the girl's flushing face. "The tribe of men will be serving us," he said, "except for the one who wishes to become the queen and will voluntarily follow the Shern into a wonderful city, built on the mountains to reign with him there. They will have Mortzes more obedient than dogs and captive people for servants. They will also have inexhaustible treasures, shinier than the stars sparkling in the dark night! A woman will reign, a woman chosen by a Shern. She will reign from the moment she knows and understands that there is no evil or good invented by the weak, there is no righteousness, no harm, no merit, no reward, no punishment, no sin, but there is only one power which is contained in the highest creation of the world, in the knowing-it-all Shern!"

Stunned, terrified, Ihezal was backing out by the effort of her weakening will, trembling all over her body in a strange, incomprehensible feeling ...

"Come to me!" Avij called.

She screamed loudly and threw herself towards the door. She fell on the stairs, exhausted, bursting out into spasmodic tears. When she finally came to herself, she heard voices of many people filling the temple. She was relieved that she was not alone, and, rising, she ran almost joyfully to join the crowd.

The high priest Elem was standing at the pulpit, empty for so long, and telling the crowds the message brought by the victorious warriors from overseas. He glorified the power and courage of the human tribe and praised their superiority above all the creatures of the

314

world, and at the same time spoke of the animal ignorance and ferocity of the doomed Sherns... His voice, not too loud, but penetrating, sounded sharply among the pillars of the temple, sometimes causing a stronger word to evoke the echo sleeping under the dome.

He preached until he finished with a hymn awaiting for the Age of the Conqueror, who came from Earth, and when he fulfills his life, he will return to Earth again. When he stopped speaking, there was a momentary silence, and then a voice suddenly sounded from the entrance of the temple: "Not true! Not true! The Conqueror has not arrived!"

All faces turned that way. An old man in the old monastic habit of the Waiting Brothers with shaved head and blazing eyes was standing there on the broad base of a pillar, with his back to it. He raised his dry hand over the heads of the people and, shaking it in the air, shouted in frenzy:

"Not true! Elem, the Order's traitor, and dishonor is lying! The Conqueror hasn't come to the Moon! I am the last and only Waiting Brother! That one is an impostor! The dead hasn't risen! The dead hasn't risen!"

Commotion and confusion started. Many listened with horror to the words of the old man, as if the voice of a prophet came alive, but others rushed to him with hateful shouts, to draw him and throw him out of the temple door. However, he was rescued by half-wild fishermen from the area of the Isthmus who were seasoned to all kinds of hardships.

They were waving their strong fists, shouting: "The prophet Choma is telling the truth! Down with Elem! Away with the false Conqueror!"

A fight started at the door, in which a few fishermen, despite their desperate defense, had succumbed and had to be thrown out with old Choma over the threshold. In the square, however, they surrounded the monk with a tight circle, and he, lifted on their shoulders, began to speak again:

"A curse to the Moon for falsehood and hypocrisy! Behold, the Order of the holy virgin Ada is trampled, and her body is burned to dust! The temple was plundered and defiled by a Shern locked in the place where the Word was kept! Woe, woe to the Moon because of sin and scandal! The enemy sent a false Conqueror, who seduced the people, so that they would not wait anymore! Despite the battles you hear about, he will not deliver our redemption, and a worse woe will come upon us! Worse evil and disgrace!"

The people were listening to him with horror, but at that moment the steady step of the armed forces sent by the high priest hammered on the pavement. Walking in a tight column, trained by the Conqueror, they split the crowd in the blink of an eye, surrounding Choma and separating him from his defenders with an iron ring. They wanted to take him back, but he himself signaled to his supporters that they would not prevent his martyrdom. Then the armed men put his thin hands in chains, and, watchful against an attack, led the prisoner to the vestibules of the new high priest's palace.

The high priest Elem himself, having moved there from the temple through a recently erected covered porch, was already inside and talking to Sevin. His confidante stood before him, humble and seemingly intimidated by the anger of his superior, but his sly eyes turned often knowingly at the agitated high priest, seeming to speak more than his mouth.

"Why weren't my orders followed? Elem shouted, "Why was Choma allowed to come here? ... "

Sevin bowed his head low. "Your Majesty is undoubtedly right and always giving wise orders, but it was difficult to fulfill them in this case, especially since Your Majesty did not allow Choma to be arrested... "

"There were a thousand other ways to stop him!"

"Probably. Therefore, it is my fault, as the chief of Your Majesty's police, that I could not find a single effective one among the thousand ... Anyway, the longer stay of this madman among the fishermen, in one place, was a danger. His followers grew stronger and joined into an ulcer that could form on the body of our state system. So, we allowed him to go from place to place and throw seed everywhere, rather than expecting a harvest in one place. Now, it all depends on Your Majesty's will. We can suppress the rare germinating seed or, if appropriate, let it grow as Your Majesty sees fit ... Choma has done his job and is captured. I even admit that I allowed him to enter the temple on purpose today, just today, when we have a counterweight to the blasphemy of the madman in the news that we have received from the Shern country... "

Elem looked thoughtful. He was sitting motionless for a moment, his white hands stroking his long black beard, and he stared at Sevin without anger, but even with some admiration. The chief of police had his eyes lowered, but a vague smile was playing around his mouth.

"Let them bring him here," said Elem suddenly. "I want to talk to him alone."

Sevin bowed and left, and after a while two soldiers brought the old man with shackled hands into the hall. The high priest signaled them to step back, leaving him alone with the prisoner.

Choma stood with his brow furrowed and his head held high, expecting with some satisfaction the martyrdom he had foretold of since long ago. So, he was greatly astonished when he saw that the high priest was approaching him in a friendly manner, and with a completely harmless, yes, intimate movement, putting his hand on his shoulder. A shadow of unpleasant disappointment flashed across his scuffed face, but then he thought to himself that his words must have touched the hard heart of the high priest, and that it was a good time for him to soften it with his eloquence. Then, he raised his shackled hands with an inspired movement and began to prophesy: "Misfortunes will fall to the Moon, worse than before! The Sherns will taint all our women, and then the great sea will dry up and the fields will cease to give crops. All people will die one by one, because they did not wait for the righteous Conqueror, the resurrector of the dead, but they were seduced by the self-proclaimed one! The hungry desert will come out of its borders and devour the people's land, so that there will not be even a trace of the sinners!"

He was speaking for a long time, inventing new and more terrible curses and threats, until he fell silent at last, tired, when he thought that he had touched the high priest's heart sufficiently. The only thing he didn't care about was that Elem did not fall to his knees and bow to him. After all, his fishermen, after hearing the fourth part of such threatening words, had long ago hit the ground with their faces, swearing not only to the sins committed, but even those that they had not dreamed of so far.

Elem listened to the prophet's words calmly and attentively, though with a smile on his lips as if he seemed to value their meaning and importance in his mind. At each happier and more thunderous turn, he nodded his head appreciatively, but made a reluctant movement when the prophet repeated himself or became boring. Finally, he smiled with satisfaction. "Not bad, not bad!" He said, patting Choma on the shoulder. "I did not even think there in the Polar Country that you were such a speaker, or I should rather say: a prophet!"

The high priest's behavior seemed a little unfitting to Choma, but not wishing to discourage the soul leaning towards him at the outset, he did not say a word and only weighed in his mind which path to follow to accomplish the conversion.

Meanwhile, Elem sat down and told him to come closer to him. The Prophet involuntarily, instilled with years of obedience to his superior, approached him eagerly and was almost ready to worship him, if he had not remembered early enough about his changed role now. However, he did not have time for further considerations, as the high priest suddenly asked: "But tell me what proof you have that the Conqueror from Earth is not the real Conqueror? Just don't prophesy right now but speak clearly and right."

Choma stretched out his hands as far as the shackles would allow him and began counting on his fingers. "First of all, the dead did not rise to greet him, as it was written. Secondly: the day did not become eternal, but the night falls in the old way, contrary to the words of the former prophets. Third: the sea did not open a way for him to reach the country of the Sherns. Fourth: He does not overcome the Sherns by himself but commands the people to fight them. Fifth ... the dead did not rise" ...

"You said it before!" Elem exclaimed, "Come up with something new!"

Choma got angry and fell back into the prophetic fervor, especially since it was easier than tedious enumeration. But now the high priest did not want to listen to him as patiently as before. Yes, he rather brutally interrupted him with a flood of shocking words and summoned the soldiers to escort him to prison.

"And come up with something better, just in case!" He even called after him.

Then the soldiers dragged the prophet out of the room because he began to resist them, not because he wanted to stay here longer, but for the sake of principle, sensing that his martyrdom was beginning. He was again quite astonished when he was led into a dry and light cell and given all the modest comforts which his health and age needed. Glancing around at his new apartment, he shook his head gallingly and asked, somewhat intimidated by the guard through the door window: "When will I be stoned?" The guard just smiled broadly and advised him to eat the piece of bread he had on the table, as he must be hungry. Choma then, out of habit, began to convert him, persuading him to swear off the false Conqueror, but the guard was sleepy and therefore little prone to his words. Indeed, he soon yawned and fell asleep just now when the old man was in the middle of his predictions about the inevitable and terrible destruction of the lunar world.

Meanwhile, Sevin was standing in the square in front of the palace, talking to the people who were agitated both with Choma's performance and his imprisonment ...

The high priest's henchman was greeted with screams and a barrage of insults, but he waited out the outburst calmly with a frozen smile on his thin face, and when there was a moment of silence, he used it immediately to exclaim: "His Highness the high priest Elem is sending me to find out about your wish for the captured old man!" ...

These words made an impression. The people were used to always learning the will of the high priests, and then they never hesitated what to do. If they were in a good mood, they would listen, if they weren't, they would object loudly. But Sevin's question completely confused the crowd. They were ready to defy Elem today, but they didn't know what his intentions were. Even from the attitude of his soldiers it was impossible to deduce anything as they were seated quietly with their weapons laid on the steps of the palace and were talking to each other, stretching in the sun ...

The screams stopped, but quarrels began in smaller circles among the crowd. Sevin and those people near him quietly waited for them to stop as well, and he finally spoke up, although the crowd had not revealed their will at all: "His Majesty will be glad that his will is in agreement with yours. In fact, he has decided what you demand: to question Choma, who now has a comfortable room in the palace, and then give him to you, that you may act with him according to your judgment ..."

The crowd dispersed praising Elem.

At the end of that long day, Ihezal visited Malahuda again. When she told him everything that had happened, the old man pondered gloomily. "I shouldn't have allowed Elem," he said after a while, "to take the priestly cap. It was a mistake."

But at the girl's remark that it could still be fixed, that he had enough to show himself in the crowd to be greeted back as a master, he shook his head in negation. "I told you once," he said, "and now I repeat too late! At present, I would only add to the confusion. I have to wait here, in hiding."

Ihezal did not insist. She was very strange that day: her eyes looked out into the world as if through some fog, her lips were pale and trembling ... When she was returning across the cool sea before the evening fell, facing the golden sunset, her cheeks had an unhealthy blush. Her black eyes, bluish-rimmed, seemed deeper than usual.

Having arrived at the shore, she heard the noise of the crowd, still gathered in the squares and in front of the houses. She heard curses, calls, singing, quarrels, and fairs, all the busy and full of tumult littleness of today, and her lips suddenly pressed together with unrestrained disgust. She closed her eyes, trying to make the Conqueror's figure appear in front of them, but against her will, only a wide-winged black shadow of Shern Avij appeared under her closed eyelids, staring at her with four bloody pupils.

V

It really happened as Shern Avij had foretold. The Conqueror completely conquered the lowland country, skirting the shores of the Great Sea, and the mountains rising near the South Pole. He demolished thirty towns and wiped out the Sherns without a trace. Fourteen long lunar days have passed since the conquerors landed on the mysterious shore, and up till now the lucky streak has followed them without end and change. But on the fourteenth day, after over an earthly year of hardships and continuous struggle, they found themselves far from the sea, in a mountainous and inaccessible country.

The sun was moving low here in the daytime and made an arch behind their backs across the sky. The evening aurora burned long into the night, testifying that the star of the day wasn't crawling deep hidden under the horizon. They had already passed the southern storm zone, so the days were cooler, and at night the frost did not bother them so much.

Huge ring mountains rose in front of them like fortresses. Steep green meadows laced with deep gullies glistened in the sun above the foothills covered with the impassable belt of forests and thickets. And higher, there was only a solid rock, jagged in crags and cliffs and covered with a gleaming crown of ice from above ... Beside those enormous rings, others low and vast rose and formed a round, forest covered embankment ...

There was no living soul to be found in the narrow green valleys between the rings. Here and there, they only found abandoned and deliberately demolished houses. The ruins, however, looked inconspicuous. Apparently, those were only shepherds' huts, hurriedly abandoned and destroyed without regret, while running away from the approaching enemy.

But where did the Sherns hide? Marek involuntarily turned his eyes to those mighty and natural stone strongholds stretching to the south with which the whole country was covered. Mountains piled up behind the mountains, enormous ramparts, dangerous and unattainable. The Conqueror realized that here his devastating expedition must end. From now on his only task could be to harass the Sherns so much in their inaccessible strongholds, that they would finally demand peace themselves ...

He frowned and sat down on a boulder and looked at the strange country in front of him ... 'Peace with the Shern! – Peace with the Sherns!' He knew it would equal a defeat, for it would bring no benefit to the people, nor would it guarantee anything to them ... When he leaves, the Sherns will rise in power and begin to disturb the people again, not caring about the promises and assurances he would force out of them. For a time, they would still be held back by the memory of the terrible defeat on the plains and the horror of the Conqueror's name, but what will happen later? Will they not be willing to take even a more awful revenge to make up for the unexpected defeat?

Giving firearms to the people, Marek kept the secret of making explosives to himself. He thought that returning to Earth after the destruction of the Sherns, he would take it with him, so as not to give the people the opportunity to use this terrible weapon for domestic disputes ...

Now, he sees that he will not be able to completely extinguish them. So what? People must be given an effective defense in their hands for the future. He must teach them how to produce explosives and, having left from here, to think what disastrous consequences this knowledge may have on the silver globe ...

Worried, he looked behind him, over the vast plains they had crossed, stretching as far as the distant sea, over which the sun lingered low over the horizon. To leave this conquered country was the same as giving the Sherns the opportunity to recapture it and to grow in strength again in these fertile fields which had been their granary for centuries ... The whole expedition was then undertaken in vain, and it would have been better for it not to be started at all ... And bring people from across the sea here and spread them out on these fields? Help them build houses and settlements?

It is easy to predict that when he goes back to Earth, they will be the first victims of the vengeful Sherns! Forever and ever, these settlers would have to be condemned to a life of war, with their hands attached to their weapons, with vigilant eyes that would have to keep watching if the flood of enemies were not approaching them from the inaccessible mountains. Who knows if they still would be able to resist all this, being cut off from their distant brothers by the sea, relying only on their own strength in the closest neighborhood? Who knows, would the men settled here not become slaves of the Sherns in time? Wouldn't their women be forced to give birth to Mortzes for the new and perpetual disgrace of the human family? The people still living in the old cities, beyond the sea, instead of supporting their brothers, would despise them in time, as unclean creatures. Then, they would become hostile to those who were to be the first defense from the Sherns for the lunar people.

And that would be the blessing that the expected Conqueror has brought to the lunar world! That would be a deed for which future generations should sanctify his name!

Marek jumped up and looked at the looming mountains in front of him. No! You cannot stop here! Once started, the game must be brought to the end: win it completely or fall. There is no other choice! He summoned Jeret and Nuzar. When they came for his orders, he first asked the Mortz: "Where are the Sherns?"

Nuzar looked up at him, not sure whether the Conqueror was asking him if he really wanted to know, or just to test him. Reluctantly he pointed towards the mountains: "Over there …"

"Where?"

"There. Inside."

"Inside? Beyond these ring chains of rock?"

"Yes."

"Have you been there?"

Nuzar shook his head in negation. "No. They don't allow Mortzes there. Whatever …"

"What?"

"To get there you must have wings like them, the Sherns. Those rocks are inaccessible. "

The Conqueror pondered. Then the Mortz, having made sure that Jeret, turned away and was not listening, climbed the boulder and whispered to Marek:

"Is it not time, Master, to betray?" The Sherns have already taken refuge so could we start hunting the people now?"

Marek waved him away without even answering. Then he looked at Jeret. "Well?"

Jeret shrugged, uncertain. "You must have wings ... "Saying that he looked at Marek's face."

Marek was silent for some time, but his eyebrows were slowly drawn together above his eyes in one hard bow, until he finally said firmly: "So, we'll have wings. Our determination will be our wings."

Jeret's face lit up. With a quick movement, he bowed to Marek's feet. "You are the real Conqueror sent to this world!"

Soon they were folding their tents and preparing for the further expedition. Marek understood that, first of all, he had to show the Sherns his irresistible power by accosting and defeating them there where they felt safe. Their cities were no doubt hidden in these ring mountains; but which of these countless rock walls was worth checking out? Do the Sherns live everywhere? What if, after unheard-of hardships, he and his warriors will get on an icy ridge where you only to see get an empty valley in front of them?

When they asked the Mortzes whom Nuzar had once saved, they could not give a certain explanation. They were not from here, so they were giving contradictory and chaotic directions ... Making inferences didn't lead them anywhere. If the Sherns in this country had been disturbed in the past, they would have built their cities among the most inaccessible mountain rings, but if they always had peace here and did not need to hide from any enemy, what would force them to choose defensive and difficult places? Would not they rather settle among these sloping embankments covered with a forest? On the other hand, they could now, having left their former nests, just escape from the invasion to the mountains, which gave them a safe and secure shelter.

Marek felt that he was facing a problem that thinking alone could not solve. You must try, search, and win. With this unhappy thought, they set off towards the South Pole, leaving the choice of the future path to a coincidence.

During the day, they walked around the vast, wooded embankment of one of the lower mountain rings, and before the sunset they stopped where the gap in the upper embankment created something like a wide gate that was dropping down to a level opening a convenient path to its inside. The valley was enormous and slightly recessed in relation to the surrounding land. There were some scattered mounds and several silent and dead ponds.

There, at that entrance, they spent a long, but not a very frosty night, keeping guard against the Sherns 'attack. But they didn't show up. So, with the first light of day, just when dawn began to draw the gray outlines of the mountains on the still starry sky, the Conqueror pushed his ranks into the interior part of the valley.

They walked across it, examining every ground elevation and every curve of the few hills. However, they only found some abandoned settlements like those on the plains, and the fields that were still cultivated, and traces of a hasty escape ... Not a single Shern was found.

There was no doubt now that the inhabitants had taken refuge in inaccessible areas and prepared to defend themselves there. Marek's gaze shifted involuntarily to the enormous, twisted ring, rising straight in front of that open gate to the south. A few tens of kilometers separated the conquerors from that unconquered fortress, which glowed before them in the bright morning sun with its icy peaks.

The Conqueror raised his hand and pointed to Jeret a ridge suspended under the sky. "I'll take you there."

The young man bowed his head in obedience. "We'll follow you everywhere," he said.

Then their arduous journey began. From the north side, the walls, visible above the forests, seemed so inaccessible to Marek, that he decided rather than waste time and circle the ring, looking for a pass that would make getting inside easier. But the farther they went, the more strongly Marek felt, that he and his men were walking along the wall surrounding an impenetrable fortress. At the same time, he was afraid of an ambush, and he did not dare to go deeper into the forests to look for a better route.

It was already the second week on Earth since they began to circle that enormous "crater", and it was close to the lunar noon when they came upon a slope free of forest and less steep, it seemed. This was the way the Conqueror led his warriors.

Having reached a certain height, at first, they walked over lush meadows, and then it was less and less green, and the stone ground often came out to the top with hard bald spots. Then, they ploughed up through huge fields, covered with thick scree, jumping from stone to stone in a continuous and arduous hardship ... The streams, flowing down from the snows crowning the top of the peaks, disappeared here without a trace among the boulders, so that the thirst tormented the ascending people more and more. They were almost collapsing with weariness, but neither of them dared to demand a rest. All eyes were glued to the Conqueror, marching at the head of the crowd. As long as he was walking, no one wanted to stop.

Marek ordered frequent but short stops, wanting to get above the scree as soon as possible, so that he could find the water dripping on the rock. But the fields, strewn with shards of rock, seemed to stretch endlessly ... Then there was a mound of boulders as huge as houses, between which there were gaps so great that only thanks to a small weight of bodies on the Moon the warriors were able to jump over. Those were followed by the screes even more burdensome, petite, and mobile that moved from under your feet with each step, dragging people behind them. So, they walked a little to the side towards a protruding stone perch.

It was cracked and insecure because of a multitude of loose, moving boulders, deceptively pressed all the way in. Legs were no longer enough here, and they had to resort to using hands.

At one point it seemed to those walking at the head that they saw a Shern nearby, but it soon turned out that it was only an illusion. A mountain animal flashed through the rocks and vanished from sight ... People exhausted by thirst and toil were beginning to see things.

Their strength was declining.

In one place, when it was necessary to switch to the other side of the perch to avoid the smooth cliffs, one of the soldiers stumbled and fell into the abyss. Those following him stopped suddenly. Their legs began to tremble, and their fingers, pressed tightly into the cracks of the stone, closed more and more tightly, losing feeling. People began to look back and sit down as much as possible. There was a moment of depressing silence. Suddenly someone groaned, and a spasmodic sigh responded on the other side ... He heard the rumble of another falling body. This time a soldier jumped into the abyss by himself, head down, hands extended ...

One moment more ...

Then at the front, among the handful of a few more courageous and skillful people who had not noticed the fall of the two companions, climbing with all their effort, there was a salutary cry: "Water! Water!"

Everything was forgotten, and they madly rushed forward. The people, overwhelmed a moment ago, were climbing with incomprehensible dexterity along the toothed and steep ridge and drawing their lost strength from somewhere. They began to shout joyfully and race towards it.

The ridge bluntly ended here, propped up against a wide and spacious ledge, overgrown mostly with grass and cut with a small deep gully, at the bottom of which a stream gurgled, dying in the screes below.

Marek watched as the soldiers pressed together, seizing the water with their hands, mouth, caps, and tin foils, as anyone could and managed. The Sherns' attack at this moment could simply be fatal, but fortunately no living soul was around ... Even so, the Conqueror understood that he could not go any further in this way if he did not want to waste these people and himself. So, when the first thirst had been quenched, he ordered the warriors to rest. Having chosen some of the most daring warriors and Nuzar to accompany him, he went up to find the best passage to the ridge. He hoped that standing there, he would see whether it was worthy for the soldiers to be summoned from their rest, that is to say, whether there is a Shern settlement inside the ring ...

Jeret wanted to go with him, but he ordered him to stay with the army and watch out that they were not suddenly attacked.

The climbing up was indeed very arduous. Marek, still thinking that he would need to bring forward the whole crowd of armed and laden people, was seeking to choose the easiest passages, all of which led to a considerable waste of time ... Long hours were passing, and the sun, hidden earlier behind a sharp rock when they were walking along the northern slope, tilted now to the west and looking from the left in the wanderers' faces, began to burn them with its golden rays ... The difficulties of the passage increased with almost every step. They had to switch to steep ledges, hanging among the cliffs above the chasms, and often pierced with chimneys full of obstructed boulders, which made the march much more difficult ... They marked the path behind them with small mounds of stones in visible places, on protruding rocky or meager lawns.

They had not yet reached the line of eternal snow. The nature of the rock forced them to make a significant traverse eastward, with only a slight upward climb. They were circling this way under the edge of the snow, only crossing the gullies strewn with it, which, however, were too sharp and cut off from above to serve as a straight path upwards.

At last they found a gully, although not wider than the others, but much less steep and steadily climbing up to a wide snow pass. Moreover, Marek wondered over some traces in the snow. They looked like the Sherns' footprints and furrows, torn apparently by heavy objects that were pulled through there. He did not doubt that he had found the right way, and that he would indeed meet the Sherns within the mountain ring.

There was no point in making the journey alone and wasting time unnecessarily. So, keeping only Nuzar with him, he sent the rest of the people back, so that they could bring the rest of his army through the passage they had discovered.

Long hours of waiting followed, somehow more tiring than the climb up. Nuzar curled up under a boulder, as if he were an animal, and was sleeping in the snow. In solitude, Marek began to be tormented by various thoughts and fears. He already regretted that he had not gone to fetch his companions as the envoys might have overlooked the mounds, which were quite rarely erected, and would not find the right place ... He was also afraid that without his help and his company, the people wouldn't be able to overcome the difficulties of the passage, or that some inevitable accident would cause panic to break out again. He also trembled thinking that the terrible mountain sickness could overwhelm them at the sight of inaccessible crags and chasms peering out from everywhere.

He also thought of the danger from the Sherns, which he had forgotten completely in the constant struggle of ascending. After all, at any moment they could fall out of from their stake-out and completely wipe out their slim ranks with stones simply thrown from above! On that thought panic choked his breath. Only now did he understand how madly and recklessly he had ventured into those crags with a handful of devoted and steadfastly believing in him people.

He looked at the sleeping Nuzar and thought about waking him up ... but he soon abandoned this intention as ridiculous and unnecessary. How could this Mortz with a half-animal brain help him now? But he felt more and more anxious and couldn't sit still. He stood up and walked alone back to the perch that bordered the gully from the west. As he stood on it, coming out of the shadows, he got immediately blinded by the sun. He narrowed his eyes against the glare and began to diligently look around. He examined every head of rock, every bend and fissure through his binoculars and saw nothing but boulder and stone.

Apparently the Sherns, trusting the inaccessibility of the rocks, had not even thought of the need for an ambush ... They probably did not believe that the Conqueror would dare to make this crazy passage, or what's more that he could perhaps find a way to the top that would be accessible to people. He breathed more freely. At least for the time being he was not in danger from this side.

He was about to go back down the path to meet his troops, but suddenly he was overcome by uncontrollable laziness. He stretched out on the rock in the sun with the thought that he would only rest for a short while, but as soon as he put his head on his folded hands, the sweet and deep sleep engulfed him ...

After a while, a light touch awakened him. He opened his sleepy eyes. Nuzar was sitting beside him, pointing down. "They are coming, my lord," he said.

Marek sprang to his feet. "The Sherns?"

"No. Your people are coming."

But Marek looked in vain in the indicated direction. The Mortz's keen eyes saw what he could not even spy through the glasses. He already started suspecting that Nuzar was wrong when he heard the barely audible buzz of voices. He was seen from below, standing on a lofty perch against the white snows, and he was joyfully greeted. Indeed, he finally noticed a small, moving swarm among the boulders. His people were really approaching.

In a few hours they started up together. The stronger ones led the way, chopping the wide steps in the snow into which those who followed them were walking, slowly moving towards the pass along the gully, steeper in some places than it initially seemed to the viewers below. The road was arduous and dizzying. Those weaker and more prone to mountain sickness were tied with long ropes, thus preventing them from falling. Moreover, Marek strictly forbade the armed men to look beyond their immediate path. So, gazing at the blue sky above the white snow of the pass, they were walking forward in silence, fearing a shout or a song would warn the Sherns prematurely

More than once it seemed to those who were walking only a few steps from the summit, that only a little effort was still needed to achieve the desired goal, and they chopped the snow harder and harder with impatient haste, but soon hope turned out to be deceptive. The saddle, which they already saw as their highest ridge, was only a threshold, beyond which again a sloping, shiny plane stretched upwards ... So, their weary hands fainted, and the snow suddenly turned black and seemed to wave like the sea in their eyes blinded with the light...

Marek then would stand alone in the passage and, loudly repeating the order: "Don't look! Don't look down!," Led them falling from their weariness, hypnotized by his will, still higher and higher.

The proper gully was now converging and spilling from overhead into a vast slightly concave snowfield. Chopping the steps on a plane that was not too sloped was no longer necessary, so the chain of walking people soon scattered into a wide semicircle. Everyone looked for their own way here, as they were able to and knew how.

Suddenly something weird happened. Before the soldiers' eyes, thus so often disappointed in their hope that they had already reached the summit, suddenly in the least expected moment, a view opened inside this enormous cauldron in the middle of the mountain ring. Those who followed them, did not yet realize that their companions had already reached the highest elevation in the pass... They ran to them in small groups and stood in their turn to take in the sight, extraordinary, even to their Moon eyes. From the immense plateau they looked at the enormous circular valley, surrounded by a mighty mountain wall with ice peaks. The valley gleamed with all the delicious green from which numerous ponds stood out like the darker eyes of a peacock tail. Low heights, as if green mounds, were scattered sparsely along the bottom of the valley, which climbed gently towards the wooded slopes of the mountains. Small white settlements were visible, surrounded by extensive orchards on these terraces and on hills, as well as at the banks of some ponds. But in the middle of the valley they saw a mighty, blunt-cut cone protruding about halfway up the surrounding mound. It was bearing at its peak a fortified and large city, bristling with hundreds of towers and other strange soaring structures.

The shadow of the south-west ridge of the ring already covered most of the valley, hiding the dead ponds in a sapphire band, and hugged the foot of the cone, crawling slowly up to the gates of the city, which shining all gold and purple in the light of the descending sun ...

Marek was standing there for a long time and was looking speechless at this wonderfully beautiful and quiet country, which, before the sun goes out, he was to turn into an arena of a battle, perhaps the bloodiest that has ever been fought on the Moon. Suddenly he was roused from his reverie by the broken voices of the soldiers and exhaling with some kind of holy fear.

He looked around. His people were standing facing away from the mysterious land of the Sherns, and eagerly indulged themselves in some unusual thing on the distant southern horizon. Above the land, as if a sea with waves, like an infinite tangle walking along the mountains, a dim and whitish cloud bit into the sharp saw blade of the farthest peaks, circularly vaulted over the top, and quite different ...

For a long time, Marek could not recognize this phenomenon, until suddenly, his lips twitched ... Yes! For it is already near the South Pole and at this height! ... Yes, Yes! This insignificant scrap, this narrow white sickle, with a jagged horizon at the bottom, toothed from the mountains! ...

"Earth! Earth!" Meanwhile, the soldiers started shouting.

Some fell face down in the snow, others raised their hands and were standing there, delighted, unable to understand how a star, visible to them from another end of the lunar globe, appears again before their eyes!

"The Earth is following the Conqueror!" Someone whispered with pale lips.

"The Earth has come to look at the final pogrom of the Sherns."

Jeret spread his hands wide: The Earth is everywhere! He exclaimed. "People see it as standing in one place, but it orbits the Moon" and guards the boundaries of the Great Desert!"

"The Earth is everywhere!" The choir shouted.

Soon they began to fall on their faces before the Conqueror, praising him, a messenger from Earth. And he was standing there motionless, for a moment forgetting the Sherns and the people at his feet. For the first time he was looking at the white apparition of his homeland across the sky with wet eyes ...

VI

The noise in the small and cramped room was intense. They were waiting for Master Roda, who was later today than ever. They were killing the time with heated disputes, which every now and then turned into heated arguments. Young excitable people with glittering eyes, jumped at each other, screaming, and waving their hands as far out of the crowd of bodies and the thinness of the space allowed.

A youth with flaming eyes and disheveled hair argued furiously: "The deeds of the so-called Conqueror are without any significance! It does not matter what he accomplishes, even if it is to our relative advantage, compared to the sum of our harms from the people of the Great Desert ... We must get there, live there!"

A man, completely bald although not old, was sitting at the edge of the table. He had a smooth face without stubble and was smiling incessantly with a grimace glued to his mouth. He turned his faded fisheyes to the speaker and spoke, swaying his upper body slightly: "And I repeat: there is no place for us anymore" ...

"Must be!," the other shouted furiously.

The bald man spoke in a calm and monotonous voice: "There is no place for us. The caves and caverns in which they live, I believe, their heavenly lifestyle, are small in relation to the population ..."

"Then let them yield it to us! Let them come here and fight the Sherns!"

"Yes, yes!," they shouted from all sides.

The bald man smiled constantly. "How can we make them do it? How? Do you know?"

Some hot head with a thin, blackened face leapt at him with fists: "Mataret! Be silent! You are bribed ..."

The noise started to get louder again. The room rumbled like the inside of a hive in a swarm; shouts, arguments, and calls crisscrossed the air. At times, when the buzz faded for a moment, you could hear Mataret's measured, stubbornly repeated words: "And I am telling you there is no place there anymore"...

The rest of the sentence, however, was invariably lost in the breakout of a passionate scream.

At one point someone standing by the door shouted: "Roda is coming!"

The master was greeted eagerly. He did indeed enter, or rather ran, throwing himself immediately and breathlessly onto the nearest chair. He was without a cap, his sweatshirt was torn, his matted hair and numerous bruises on his face and exposed chest testified to the fight in which he had been involved.

"What happened? Master!," Was shouted at him from all sides.

Roda gestured with his hand for silence. He was sitting with his head limply resting on the arm of the chair and panting. His eyes were closed, a hole made by knocking out his two front teeth was visible between his bloody lips.

Mataret for one did not move. He was still sitting on the table and with his usual smirk was staring at the master with narrowed eyes. "I told you so!" IIe said after a moment. "You must have preached to the people again!"

Roda jumped up. His eyes sparkled and he raised his fist sticking out of his torn sleeve. Shaking it menacingly, began to shout with his mouth swollen from the blows he had suffered: "Unworthy! Unworthy slaves! Mean dark crowd! Cattle!"

"That's right," said Mataret calmly, "but you should have known about it for a long time" ...

Roda shot him a furious glare from his side. "Yes! You don't care about anything; you don't really believe anything! If you could sit on the table, nod, and smile, you wouldn't care that the priests are deluding the people? You are not concerned that the so-called Conqueror uses them shamefully for his purposes, and that the only moment of salvation may pass irretrievably and for nothing! It doesn't matter to you that the people live in a shameful and deplorable blindness. They just don't understand what is good for them. They constantly turn their eyes to the barren Earth, not wanting to seek their due paradise here, where it is, here - on the Moon! You don't care, but I, I want to ..."

"... collect bruises!," finished Mataret.

"Even if only that! In any case, I have this conviction"...

They started screaming again so much that the master's words were lost in the tumult of excited voices. Some cried that the high priest Elem and his messengers were guilty of everything because they turn the people against the apostles of the truth. Some yelled that the fight must be started against the superiority of the high priest. Others, more reasonable, however, spoke of the impossibility of dealing with the forces of the authority, at least for now, until ...

"The people are hostile to us," they said, "we will not persuade them or drag the masses to our side! All efforts turned out to be in vain! We have to act on our own!"

After some time, everyone agreed upon it, but no one was able to clearly understand what this action on their own was to be about.

When Mataret came forward with the opinion that it is best to leave it all alone, as the people are apparently too stupid and unhappy, he was shouted at immediately and almost stoned to death. Fortunately, there were no items in the empty room that could be used for this traditional and temporary administration of so-called justice.

Finally, Master Roda spoke. The attendees calmed down a bit, and he began to speak at length, repeating for the hundredth time what everyone in the congregations had known and passionately believed.

So, he talked about the uninhabited Earth and the age-old citizenship of people on the Moon, about priestly fables, and about the unmistakable paradise that lies on that supposedly empty side of the Moon.

He was listened to with due respect, but not very attentively, for everyone present already knew these things by heart. On the other hand, they got more excited when he began to enumerate the wrongs that they, the members of the Brotherhood of Truth, had to suffer from the society and the authorities. They were laughed at and persecuted at every turn. Meetings had to be held in secret for the fear of the high priest's servants, and the public appearances of the members of the Brotherhood trying to spread the truth brought only bruises, bumps, and wounds as their only accomplishment. Here the audience nodded vigorously, especially since there were few of them who had not painfully experienced the truthfulness of the master's words on themselves.

"And yet," continued Roda, "we must not neglect the issue! At present, the man visiting this side of the Moon has come from the secret interior of the Great Desert. He has come here, and we must seize the only opportunity to discover the way to our happy homeland! We used all means to arouse the crowd and open its eyes to the essential goals of the alleged Conqueror. If we had succeeded, the game would have been easy! After returning from the land of the Sherns, the Conqueror, who apparently claims extraordinary victories while taking advantage of the blood of our countrymen, would be caught, and forced to reveal his secret anyway. You all know, however, that all our attempts have failed in the face of the people's overwhelming stupidity, who believe more in the old, naive, and absurd fairy tale about human descent from Earth than in the most obvious and fruitful truth! There is only one way for us, which the Brotherhood of Truth can choose by itself and achieve the desired goal without anyone's help!"

He paused for a moment, and the disciples and followers began to crowd around him and beg him to share his thoughts, which he had promised to reveal for a long time. Even Mataret stopped smiling and leaned slightly towards the speaker to hear his words better.

Roda uncrossed his arms, placing them on the shoulders of the two closest companions. Now his face, cut and bruised, lit up with the light of some evil smile. "We must take control of his vehicle," he said, "there in the *Polar Land...*"

"The Conqueror's vehicle," they shouted.

"Yes, that's it. The Conqueror can defeat the Sherns and woo the people as he pleases, but he will not leave without our permission"!

Mataret grimaced reluctantly and waved his hand. "Nonsense! If they want to take the vehicle from us by force, our strength is not enough! ..."

Roda laughed and began to whisper something vigorously in a lowered voice. He told his plan extensively and in detail. As he spoke, even the most distrustful began to nod their heads contentedly at his words. When he had finished, a unanimous cry of delight erupted from among the audience.

The young people sprang up as if they wanted to run to the Polar Country, certain of their destiny and victory. This and that made fantastic plans aloud about conquering and dividing mysterious countries on the "other side". In the eyes of those enthusiasts, the entire airless desert seemed at once an unheard-of magical paradise, a collection of the most wonderful caves, full of crystal cities, meadows, flowers, artificial suns, and riches for all! They were talking of bright nights, when one looks upward through the crevices of deep ravines to the radiant Earth overhead, and of delightful days whose heat is softened by the sweet and moist shadow of the stone vaults.

Someone took a map of the Moon from the wall and threw it on the table. It had been redrawn from the precious remains of the Old Man's cards. A dozen or so heads bent over it and dragged their fingers across the vast plains of the Moon, facing the light of the Earth at night. They were pointing to nicks, crevices, and mountains. They argued about the location of the largest cities and the way of communication between them ...

Mataret, dissatisfied that he had been thrown off the table, moved to the corner of the room and was sitting silently on the pile of books scattered in the dust. Roda approached him. "How do you like my plan?" He asked casually, not wanting his tone of voice to betray that he cared about weirdo's opinion.

Contrary to his habit Mataret stopped smiling. He just raised his eyebrows and shrugged his shoulders slightly: "His vehicle is supposedly guarded," he said.

"The guard is small; we can easily overtake them ..."

"Yes ..."

He put his hands on his knees and was lost in thought for some time. Suddenly he raised his head: "Roda, when are we going to the Polar Country?"

"Do you want to accompany me?"

"Of course. It will be interesting ..."

"I'd rather leave you here at the head of the Brotherhood of Truth ... Because we can't all leave. It would raise suspicions."

"I will go," said Mataret firmly, and repeated: "When are we leaving?"

Roda looked at the large calendar clock placed in the opposite corner of the room: "It is close to noon, then it's better to postpone the trip until tomorrow, so we'll have the whole day before us ..."

"And what if, meanwhile, the Conqueror returns tonight?"

"I don't think so. And it is even better for us. In the confusion that will undoubtedly follow his return, we may disappear unnoticed..."

Mataret shook his head. "Many things may happen. Perhaps our Conqueror may come here, fleeing the victorious Sherns, and then he will surely rush to the Polar Country, to disappear quickly in his vehicle..."

"Do you think the Sherns could actually win?," asked Roda anxiously.

"I don't think anything else except that it is better to leave today..."

"Yes, we can do it so ..."

He paused, then laughed out loud. "Oh! It's going to be something extraordinary! When he wants to escape and finds out that he cannot leave, because parts of his car have been unscrewed and hidden! Oh! It will be fun! Then he must make deals with us, and we will dictate ..."

Mataret, lost in thought, seemed not to listen to the master's words. Suddenly he interrupted: "Are you absolutely sure he did not come ... from Earth?"

Roda looked indignant. "Do you still doubt? Why, then, do you not go to mingle with the crowd that keeps staring at the Earth forever? Why did you join the Brotherhood of Truth?"

"Because I want to find the truth at any cost," answered Mataret shortly, and rose from his place, ending the conversation.

Meanwhile, an argument broke out at the table over the map. It was about the meaning of a line copied on the map, exactly as shown on the original pages from the Old Man, on which it was drawn separately ... This wavy line, stretched out in red, began with a cross, in the place marked with the other name of the Sinus Aestuum. Then, it ran in slight twists by Mare Imbruim, all the way to Plato's mountain, breaking then suddenly to the east, to continue rolling again among the mountains towards the North Pole of the Moon ...

The members of the Brotherhood of Truth have long tried to explain to themselves the meaning of this twisted serpent that cuts through a quarter of the lunar sphere. Some speculated that it was a trace of the path the Old Man had once traveled, but Master Roda was against this notion. Yes, he even considered it heresy to the truth.

334

"Why," he said," should the Old Man walk with difficulty and danger on the dead surface of the Moon, when there must be convenient communication canal beneath the surface between hidden sediments?"

The red line, then, remained a troubling mystery to the members of the Brotherhood, a cause of frequent and endless disputes among the more ardent believers of the Truth.

One of them, the disheveled young man who was speaking earlier when Roda arrived at the meeting, now came forward with a new theory. He maintained that it was a "line of danger," as he put it ... He claimed it was not a road traveled by the Old Man, but a possible surface to travel, which the inhabitants of the Great Desert probably guard in constant fear of the return of the "outcast" ...

He cast the thought as a supposition, but as he was argued against, he challenged the Truth more and more and insisted, until he began to consider his guess as unquestionable and proven truth at last. He even demanded that the Brotherhood should draw a practical conclusion from it to get to the mysterious country beneath the Great Desert without the Conqueror's help. Roda was summoned to settle the dispute.

Mataret, standing in the doorway, watched for a moment as the master was speaking his opinion with immeasurable seriousness, running his finger across the unfolded map ... He even made a move as if he were to come closer and listen, but only smiled and put his hand on the doorknob ...

Through a long, narrow, and dark corridor, he walked out onto the street unnoticed. It was the most deplorable part of the city, the habitat of poor laborers half-sold into slavery to merchants and manufacturers who lived in beautiful houses in the middle of the settlement, near the temple and the high-priest's palace. Poor and crooked mud huts were pressed on either side of the narrow street that sloped down in bends towards the seashore. Heaps of junk were scattered in front of the doorsteps, rotting in the midday sun. Wilting stalks of lush weeds protruded from behind the broken hedges. Several dogs lounged in the shade, lazed by the heat.

Mataret ran swiftly along the alley, trying to avoid being seen. It was assumed that he was a member of the secret Brotherhood of Truth, especially hated in this section where the Conqueror had the hottest supporters and followers. These people, living in hard work and bitter hardship, saw a better future in this bright Earth stranger. All of them were eagerly waiting for the moment when, having overcome the Sherns, he would return from across the sea to introduce a new order on the Moon.

But today no one looked out of the window or cursed through their teeth, passing the "desert fanatic," as the Brotherhood members were contemptuously called here. This quarter, which was usually swarming with people even during the strongest noon heat, forced by poverty to work hard, looked as if it had died out. Only on the wider square, from where the beautifully paved roads towards the city center started, did Mataret meet a group of several workers. They were standing in the shadow of an empty stall talking lively, gazing out to the sea with apparent anxiety

From a few words overheard in passing, Mataret understood that something important had happened that had to do with the Conqueror's expedition to the south. So, he quickened his pace, turning towards the city, where he hoped to get some true information.

The square in front of the temple was crowded with people. They were talking of the arrival of envoys who, due to the unfavorable wind at night, got lost, and having landed far east beyond the summit of O'Tamor in the morning, had to spend half a day before they could reach the city on foot. Mataret was listening intently to the fragments of sentences. From the chaotic snippets of talks he could learn little of the details, but he got the impression that this time the envoys were bringing less optimistic news. The people were restless. Instead of joyful shouts there were disputes and complaints. Concerned faces looked towards the sea as if they feared a storm of enemies coming from that direction.

He started doubting that he would be able to learn anything definite when, unexpectedly, on the steps of the temple, he saw Jeret among the crowd. He was greatly amazed, for he did not think that he, the Conqueror's right hand, was sent as an envoy ... If that happened, it must have been a particularly important thing with which the young warrior came.

He knew Jeret long and well. They were even friends once, before their differences of beliefs and views on the Conqueror's case separated them. However, counting on the old familiarity, he pushed his way through the crowd, and pulled Jeret by the sleeve, signaling that he wanted to speak to him. The young soldier recognized him and greeted him. "Oh! Mataret! ... Later! In a moment!," he added, hearing the growing buzz around him. "Come to the temple in two hours!"

He was saying his last words as he was ascending the high priest's stone pulpit by the stairs.

The people moved and rippled when they saw him elevated above them. Louder complaints and shouts were heard again. Some of them have already blasphemed the Conqueror.

Jeret took a deep breath and said:" I am ashamed when I look at you, when I listen to your women like voices, not those of men! The victory will be ours, but we still need effort and help! I have come here not to listen to your complaints, but to gather a new team that would support the fighting ones! There are more weapons still in stock. Let the young people report and join the ranks, because when the sun goes down, we will set off south again on the frozen sea!

He spoke for a while longer, casting short, rock-hard sentences over the heads of the crowd. Meanwhile, Mataret stepped slightly aside. He noticed Ihezal in the temple doors. She was leaning against the jamb, staring ahead with sleepy, strange eyes that did not even seem to see what they were looking at. Her face was pale and emaciated, and her white hands were folded over her chest, on the costly chains hanging from her neck.

Mataret was born to one of the city's most distinguished and richest families and was once close to the house of High Priest Malahuda. Seeing the girl now, he approached her and bowed. "How are you, golden-haired?" He said with a smile.

Ihezal looked at him distractedly and, turning away, entered the temple without an answer. So, he shrugged and sat down on the threshold to wait for Jeret. He was no longer at the pulpit. He finished speaking and joined the people in the crowd. Looking down from above, Mataret noticed him talking to some of the elders, eagerly answering some questions. Then Sevin approached him. The high priest's henchman spoke to him for a long time with a polite and sly smile on his lips, pointing several times with his hand to a group of fishermen standing apart, who had come here before with the now imprisoned Choma.

Mataret saw as Jeret snorted and pushed the high priest's servant away from him with his hand. Then, he grew weary of looking at everything and raised his eyes to the sky, exceptionally peaceful at this time of day.

The noon storm was delayed. The sun had already tilted from its zenith to the west and it was pouring a fine ember on the facade of the temple. Mataret closed his eyes as drowsiness was overtaking him in the heat of the day. He was just dreaming about some strange entrances to crystal caverns on the far side of the Moon when a light touch on his arm woke him from his half-asleep. Jeret was standing in front of him. "You wanted to talk to me …"

"You are tired," said Mataret, looking at his blackened and emaciated face with suddenly wide eyes.

"It's nothing, it's nothing, I'll rest ..."

They went deeper into the temple and sat in one of the darkened cloisters. Jeret folded his hands on the boulder and rested his forehead on them. "I'm really tired," he whispered after a moment without looking up.

Mataret looked at him silently, blinking nervously. It seemed to him that he was reading, on that weather-beaten and lined face, above the folded hands, the whole story of the trip: the story of unheard-of hardships and efforts, battles, doubts, and despair ...

"Why did the Conqueror send you?" He asked suddenly.

Jeret twitched and looked into his eyes. Absent at the time when the Brotherhood of Truth was finally established, he had no idea of its existence, but he knew from earlier times that Mataret, a born skeptic, looked at the Conqueror with great distrust ... This was even the reason that their relations, once very cordial, cooled down with time. Nevertheless, he could never resist the feeling of a certain awe and almost submissiveness towards this strange man who smiled constantly, and who constantly denied and thought. He never seemed to get excited for things, as if he were standing above the events and not in their strongest currents like the others. He, Jeret, knew only how to act, explode, rejoice, or gloomily close himself up and withdraw ...

So now, when asked, he hesitated for a moment, but was overwhelmed by the desire to open himself up to someone for whom he would not need to play the role of a leader, messenger, or teacher...

"I'm needed here," he whispered, speaking more with a sullen frown than with these indifferent words.

"Aren't you doing well?" Mataret said, not taking his eyes off him.

Jeret shrugged. "No ... you can't say: badly ... but ..."

He paused and fell silent, as if searching for an expression. Mataret was also silent for a time, then, standing up said: "If you don't want to talk, I'll leave. Why should I make you lie to me?"

Jeret grabbed his hand vigorously. "Stay. Yes. I just want to talk ..." He was shaking. "You see, I don't know what to call it. So far, we have not done badly, even though it is difficult now ... We have done everything that humans could do ..." He raised his head and looked Mataret in the eye.

"Everything that humans could do," he repeated emphatically, "but nothing more than that."

He blushed at once, as if involuntarily a word of great importance had slipped out of his mouth ...

Mataret was not smiling. His bulging and usually mocking eyes stared into the distance, almost sadly. He reached out and placed it on the clasped hands of the warrior. "Speak," he said.

Jeret began to speak. He was telling a long and bloody story, as if unfolding it in his mind. He spoke of the battles in the lowlands, of the conquered and destroyed cities, of hundreds and thousands of Sherns killed without mercy, struck with fiery weapons, drowned in rivers or in the sea, or burned in fires. He was speaking about it all calmly and evenly, like a laborer who in the evening repeats in his mind the hard work of the past day ...

Then he told Mataret how they had come to the inaccessible mountains and began to emerge on the back of the enormous ring of rocks. He spoke of the hardships of the passage, of the Sherns' strange city in the valley, and how the Earth, visible from everywhere there appeared before their eyes.

"We took it as a good omen and a sign that the Conqueror was there with us. But in the meantime, from the moment we looked at the Earth from that plateau, the most terrible effort began for us, because it was fruitless. I thought we would fall like a whirlwind and sweep that city down. I almost felt sorry for its doomed beauty, but here the Conqueror hesitated. He acted like a human being: rationally. He did what each of us would do in this case ..."

Then he continued how the Conqueror, having counted the ranks, did not dare to lead all of them into the valley, lest he had a cut off path to retreat.

"He ordered a part of the army," he said, "to go back and watch the road (oh! If it can be called a road), which had led us to the pass, lest the Sherns from other cities get behind us ... He was made their leader. The rest of the soldiers, under his own leadership, descended towards the interior of the valley, almost halfway up the mountain embankment and set up a fortified camp there. Only small teams descend to the plain below, harass the Sherns, and return to the camp again, often with losses. We stopped winning, we are fighting now."

"Is it still like that, no change?" Mataret asked after a moment of silence. Jeret shook his head.

"No change. We can do nothing more with the number of troops left that is for sure. The Sherns saw our helplessness and became insolent. They're accosting us now. There was hardly an hour that my team and I would not have to fight with them. It seemed earlier that the whole country was empty, but in the meantime, they appeared from somewhere and charged us with whole troops. The rocks turn black and swarm with them like with evil birds. We shoot them all the time and we stay and fight, but we have to conserve our cartridges for fear that we will run out of them. Then we would be lost ..."

"So what will happen next?" Mataret asked.

"I do not know. One morning, the Conqueror himself walked over the mountain pass dividing us and talked with me for a long time. He had not spoken of a retreat yet, but you could read that thought in his troubled face. He told me to come here and get reinforcements, weapons, and cartridges as quickly as possible. Getting to the sea and the sledge guarded by a small handful left behind was exceedingly difficult. I had to sneak around with a companion like a reptile, but I know that it will be even harder to come back with reinforcements because the Sherns want at all costs to annihilate the Conqueror and us with him ..."

There was silence. They were both staring ahead, wandering in thought, far away from where they were.

"Yes. They must be notified," Mataret said suddenly after some time.

"Who?"

He did not answer. He just smiled his usual smile and held out his hand to Jeret. "I don't care about the Conqueror. He doesn't matter. Perhaps the people don't matter so much either. I don't know what matters any more. Collect reinforcements and hold on while you can. I'll do my part."

He turned to leave and gave a slight shout. Ihezal stood in the shadow under a carved corner. Noticing that she had been spotted, she stepped quickly forward. She passed Mataret and was walking straight towards Jeret.

"Jeret!" She cried, folding her hands pleadingly, "Jeret! Take me with you!"

"Have you heard everything?!"

She confirmed with a silent nod of her head.

Jeret frowned and moved his hand restively. He looked at Mataret as if his presence was preventing him from responding.

"Take me!," she repeated. "I want to go to the Conqueror!"

Her eyes blazed almost joyfully; the gleam of some hope illuminated her white, fever-consumed face.

Jeret turned. "Watch over the Shern you have been in charge of! One in chains is enough for you!" Ihezal turned pale and stepped back. "Jeret!" She screamed.

But he had already stepped out of the temple without even looking beyond himself.

The girl dropped her head and was standing motionless for some time. A whirlpool of strange thoughts dancing in the crazy circle, overwhelmed her. Some joyful hymns roared in her chest that he was ... that he could be, like her, human, and at the same time she felt pain, as if someone had created a sudden and incomprehensible emptiness in her soul ...

She looked around fearfully. Her inner emptiness made her feel the desolation of the place where she was even stronger. The vast, abandoned temple chilled her to the bone. Instinctively, she fell to the foot of a pillar, cuddling between the bases of the great stone censers.

They were empty and cold. For long days no one had thrown fragrant sap into the inside of the copper bowls, where the remains of coals, once holy, were piled in the dust. There were still black traces of smoke on the column, where it used to rise from.

She stared at the emptiness surrounding her with her eyes wide open in fear, as if today she had just noticed it for the first time.

"How was it?" She repeated in a whisper unconsciously. "How was it? ..."

Her childhood dreams came back to her, then an apparition of the fair terrestrial visitor ...

"Where is he now? ..."

The once-screeching words rang in her ears: "The Conqueror passed the sea and the lowlands, and behold, he came to the lofty mountains and stood helpless before them ..."

And again: "The tribe of men will serve us, except for the one who would like to become a mistress and follow the Shern ..."

"No! No! No!" Something shouted in her in desperate rebellion.

She held out her white arms, extended from the wide purple sleeves. "Jeret!" She cried aloud, although he had been gone for a long time. "Jeret! Have mercy! Take me with you! I want to go to the Conqueror! Don't leave me in here under the Shern's spell! There are no chains on his eyes! I want to go to the Conqueror! I want to know, to feel that he is stronger, that he ..." She dropped face down on the stone floor until the expensive chains dangling around her neck rang.

The sun, silvered in the foggy mist, was still streaming through the window into the temple, but the thunder of the approaching storm had already roared, loud and menacing. Ihezal didn't move.

"Here, the vault of the temple is bursting above me," she thought, "here the columns are collapsing, and the stone frameworks will open ..."

"Let it be! Let it be! Let the whole world collapse and bury me under the rubble!"

Another roaring thunderclap that was already close, shook the walls, and the sunlight, engulfed in a cloud, suddenly went out. Ihezal was crying softly.

Meanwhile, Mataret, having said goodbye to Jeret, who had been summoned to the high priest, went forward, thoughtfully, without even thinking where he was going. At the corner of a street he unexpectedly ran into Roda. The Master's eyes were sparkling and there was brightness in his scarred face. Seeing his companion, he stopped and called aloud to him: "Mataret, do you already know?"

Instead of answering, he approached him and took him firmly by the elbow. "Call the people, who are to accompany us," he said," we will leave at once."

"Are you crazy?", Roda shouted, "Look!"

He pointed at the sky darkening with clouds, under which the wind was already banging and whistling into the deserted streets, tearing clothes on them, the only two persons who had not yet sheltered from the storm.

"We leave immediately," repeated Mataret calmly.

A firm, almost commanding tone that he had never taken before shocked Roda. He looked at his companion in amazement, hardly knowing how to behave ...

Mataret, noticing his embarrassment, smiled: "Master, you are great, and I will never stop worshiping you, but believe me, we must not waste our time now. I have my own ideas ..."

The rain was still pouring down, as if the sky had melted into water as eleven men wrapped in their coats crept out of the city gates with a small team of dogs, following the eternal trail to the north.

VII

"But if I do not allow you to gather new reinforcements?"

Jeret slowly raised his head and looked at the high priest's face. "Then I will gather them without Your Majesty's permission," he said calmly but firmly.

Elem laughed. "I like you, boy," he said, "it was just a test. Reinforcements will leave at night ..."

"I know."

"The Conqueror really needs servants like you. Without them, we would probably not do anything ..."

"Will Your Majesty let me go?"

"Wait. I'd be glad to find out a bit more."

"I have already told you everything, Your Majesty! ..."

"The high priest approached him and turned his steady black eyes on him. "Then you are fighting, and you winning," he said slowly.

"Yes."

"Thanks to the Conqueror? True?"

Jeret nodded.

"And if the Conqueror had not been with you," Elem continued, not taking his eyes off him," the whole expedition would not have been successful, huh?"

"Without a doubt. Without the Conqueror, nothing would happen."

"Even if you had firearms?"

Jeret shook his head involuntarily and looked at the high priest. He did not answer at first. It flashed through his mind that ... in this case ... "We have a firearm from the Conqueror," he said aloud, with some haste.

"Yes, you already have it ... from the Conqueror ..." Elem repeated slowly, as if absentmindedly.

"Your Highness ..." Jeret looked at the door again.

"Have you seen Malahuda's granddaughter?" The high priest asked, changing his tone suddenly.

Jeret's face grew gloomy. He frowned and didn't say a word. Meanwhile, Elem continued with a friendly smile: "I left her the old palace. Not so much because for the Conqueror, who wouldn't care about these matters, but because of the memory of her dignified ancestry ... Does she still care for nothing besides the Conqueror?" He added, addressing Jeret directly, "even now that he's not here?"

Jeret moved his shoulders reluctantly. "I didn't ask her about it. My business is the war on the Sherns. I don't care about the rest."

"Yes," said Elem, stepping back a bit, "yes, they rightly consider you here as the greatest hero of all who have ever lived on the Moon ..." The previous envoys said that you were actually preparing the ranks and you are actually winning."

"Your Highness!" Jeret shouted impetuously "Please let me go!"

"Go now," said Elem, smiling. "and bow down to the Conqueror's feet on my behalf, whose servant and dog we both are."

This time the youth did not eagerly join the ranks, and with the greatest difficulty Jeret managed to gather only three hundred volunteers with knowledge of firearms, who agreed to enlarge the Conqueror's slim army. They were mostly poor people, laborers, and artisans, used to hard life, for whom the Conqueror's blessed name had not yet faded. People, who lived in the villages and more distant settlements, were not so eager to respond to Jeret's emissaries, telling them about the imprisoned old man Choma, supposedly enlightened by a prophetic spirit. The wealthier and, as a rule, devoted to every ruling high priest, mocked Choma, and instead repeated the words that Jeret had heard from Sevin, that the Conqueror, if he is the real one, should do without help and strike the Sherns with his own hand ...

The Brotherhood of Truth also had its impact. Although there were relatively few members, they were all the young and enthusiastic people, on whom the Conqueror might otherwise have counted the most..."

In the evening, a fairly large crowd led the volunteers to the prepared sledges, but among them there was more crying and farewells than the cheers of encouragement that had once rang out as the Conqueror himself led the sleigh south.

Ihezal watched their departure from the upper terrace of the temple. Wrapped tightly against the frost in her white fluffy fur, she was looking with thoughtful eyes as the lights of the sleighs quietly faded into the distance. Even long after they had already gone out, she was looking for a long time in the direction where they had disappeared. Then she entered the inside of the temple and, with a slow, sleepy step, turned towards the entrance to its underground part where Shern Avij was locked.

Meanwhile, Roda with Mataret and their nine companions set up camp for a night on a broad plain in the north.

As the destination of the expedition approached, the master made plans that were more and more fantastic. He was talking in detail how he was going to take over the car and make it unusable. Then he listed the conditions under which he would be ready to make peace with the arriving Conqueror. So, first, the revealing of the path to the mysterious land on the 'other side' ...

Once he demanded that the stranger announce this path to all the people. Now, after some reflection, he came to the conclusion that it would be better for the members of the Brotherhood of Truth to know the secret, and then to explain it to the people only when needed and at their discretion ... not all associates need to know right away. They are all quite different. For now, if only eleven, hear it ... Finally, if the Conqueror resisted it, let him say it to him and Mataret, or at least to him. But he will not depart from that anymore. He, Roda, must know everything, the whole truth he knows today, but not yet as clearly as he needs to. In general, as soon as the Conqueror returns ...

"What if he doesn't come back? Mataret interrupted him."

"How's that?"

"If he dies in the Sherns' country, he and his people?"

"It would be terrible!" Roda said, perplexed, "really bad! We would no longer have the means to find out ..."

"And nothing else?" Mataret asked.

"I do not understand you. "

"It's clear. What will happen to us if the Shern finally prevail? Have you thought about it?"

"Why supposes such things!"

"Perhaps, but I just wonder if it would not be right to support the Conqueror first, and then make demands on him ..."

"Since when do these things come to your mind?"

"Recently. But never mind! ..."

Roda thought about it. "But you said Jeret was supposed to gather reinforcements," he said after a moment.

"Yes, reinforcements. Probably. Let's not talk about it anymore."

Roda returned to this topic several times, but Mataret did not respond. He only smiled as usual and stared with his bulging fisheyes at the mountains blackening in the distance against the westerly glow, where their path would take them in the morning ...

They spent the night in one place in peace, not moving forward, not so much for the fear of the frosts to which they were accustomed, but rather because of the abundant snow that covered everything around them. In the impenetrable darkness of the "lunar" night it was impossible to orient themselves on this fluffy shroud obstructing their progress.

The next day had no more evening for them, as by the time the sun tilted towards where it usually set, they were already making their way through the winding ravine into the valley of the eternal dawn at the North Pole of the Moon.

They held a war council before entering the open country. They were all carrying weapons, firearms, the secret of which the Conqueror had brought to the Moon, and ready to act. They did not doubt even for a moment that they would have to fight once they reached their destination. They did not know how numerous the guards were at the vehicle but assumed that at least there would be more of them than their slim handful. This guard had to be disarmed or defeated.

Master Roda had for a time intended to speak to the watchful soldiers with a fiery and strict speech in which he would convince them of the truth of the position of the Brotherhood of Truth and make them submit to his plans, but Mataret resisted this firmly.

"It doesn't lead to anything," he said to the master," they will only laugh at you and beat you in the end, and you have tried this so many times that it is not worth trying one more time to show off your orator skills in vain ..."

Roda resented it at first, but finally relented, not too sure of the outcome of his sermon himself. "This is only because," he said, "I am not sure if the soldiers on guard are rational enough to understand my words, otherwise! ..."

Ultimately, it was decided to use force. Approach the guards in a friendly way and if possible, take their weapons, or if it fails, kill them at the sign given by Mataret. Roda basically condemned this last resort and declared emphatically that he himself would not kill anybody but admitted that in such a case there might be no other way out. Anyway, the goal of the Brotherhood of Truth is so important, he said that you can even sacrifice some blood for it.

The first thing to do was find the vehicle on the vast plain. From the accounts of witnesses, they knew that it had fallen near the old tents of the Waiting Brothers that were once situated at the foot of the hills separating the polar basin from the Great Desert. They had come from the other side, and to get there they would have to pass through the center of a wide and smooth plane, risking waking the vigilant guards prematurely. To avoid this error, it was decided to take a circular path, along the chain of hills, which, because of the unevenness of the ground, presented an incredibly good cover for their small handful.

The road was arduous. People were moving slowly among mossy boulders, on slippery, wet slopes, never illuminated by the sun. Every crevice was breathing chill, making the weary travelers' shudder. The plane in front of them was still smooth and their eyes could see nothing indicating the place where the Conqueror's vehicle could be.

After several dozen hours of the extremely unpleasant traversing in the wilderness, through the boulders and thickets of some huge horsetails, the weary travelers saw the rounded and bald hills where once the graves of the Waiting Brothers were.

On the ridge, visible from below, there were still huge stones that had once served as support for the corpses. On Mataret's advice, the strenuous climb along the slopes was abandoned here, and they decided to boldly climb the ridge hoping that the old tombstones would be enough to mask them.

On the plateau, the red sun struck their eyes, already moving over the Great Desert towards the Earth shining on the horizon with its narrow crescent, curved towards the sun.

Apart from Mataret and Roda, only one of the participants of the expedition had once seen the holy Earth. When he was a boy, his parents took him on a pious pilgrimage to the Pole Country where the Waiting Brothers used to wait for the promised Conqueror. So, the whole group stopped silently in awe, staring at the sharp silvery sickle that cut into the sky almost black from this side.

Some sudden fearful intimidation overwhelmed these people. By contradicting all the 'fairy tales' about the Earth, they slowly and unconsciously began to consider it also as a fairy tale, so now they stood in unexplained and involuntary amazement, seeing it shining and enormous in the sky. The young man, who was once a believer, instinctively raised his hand to his forehead to draw the Sign of the Coming ...

He stopped his hand in time and looked around with a shameful fear that someone had not noticed the suspicious movement, but no one was paying attention to him. They were all looking at the Earth in silence. Suddenly, Roda broke that silence: "Yes, yes, it is completely natural that this fairy tale was created, that it even had to arise..."

At first his voice sounded uncertain, like an excuse or rather a justification. Soon with the sound of his own words, awakened from that heavy spell, he began to speak with his usual eloquence and conviction: "A man, in order to add meaning to himself in his own eyes and to rise above the worthlessness he feels, is happy to seek for himself a higher beginning than what surrounds him. I would not even be surprised if the fairy tale of people's earthly origin were older than our expulsion from the paradise to which we are trying to find our way back. Maybe already there, in the delightful cities hidden beneath the Desert that people dreamed, in the long nights brightened by the silver light of the Earth, that they had descended to the Moon from that empty and sterile star which so easily enchants their eyes with its true beauty ..."

He spoke in this way for a long time, and the disciples and companions listened to him with devout concentration, trying to boldly look at the Earth, the seducer.

Roda held out his hand: "Look at these boulders around us and think about man's strange madness! The drive for self-preservation and the desire only for rational, lunar happiness, sometimes give way to false thoughts, yet capable of determining man's actions against nature. Generations spent their lives in this valley, praying to the dead silver star, and whole generations looked from beneath these boulders with their dead eyes to its variable disc, waiting with the living for the messenger from Earth, the Conqueror ..."

"Has he not actually arrived?" Mataret muttered in an undertone, lost in thought.

Roda heard it and turned eagerly towards the speaker: "From
Earth?"

There was silence. After a while, Mataret shook his head and
smiled: "No! After all, I find it impossible."

Roda wanted to say something but was interrupted by the
slight cry of one of his companions.

"The vehicle!," he called, pointing towards the shaded valley.

The discovery shocked everyone. Those who were seated
sprang up and ran towards the speaker. People crowded and strained
their eyes to see the longed-for destination of their journey.

Indeed, they all saw it. It was standing at the foot of a hill in
a meadow, looking from far away like a shining pebble half hidden
in the green. The guards were not in sight. There was only a small,
clumsily put together tent nearby, like a shepherd's hut, and it was
overgrown with lush greenery to the middle of its low walls.

It was impossible to suppose that all the guards were housed in
this miserable mud hut. They had apparently hidden, reasoned Roda,
in dug out holes hidden from above near the wagon, and kept watch
there constantly as ordered by the Conqueror. If they fail to surprise
them, you must be prepared for a hard fight.

After a brief council, they started downhill without wasting
any time. Each of the eleven participants of the expedition, with ready
weapons hidden under their clothes, walked a different path. They
were taking advantage of each corner of the ground, each boulder
and crevice, to hide from the vigilant eyes of the guards who were
undoubtedly watching the area. They were crawling on their stomachs
and pausing with bated breath when a stone that had been accidentally bumped, in turn rolled down the grade, which could disturb the
guard's vigilance.

According to Master Roda's plan, everyone was to approach
the wagon as close as they could without drawing attention to themselves, and then rush into the fight at the sign given with the whistle...
The sign was to be given by Mataret. He was the only one who did not
hide. He was supposed to go straight towards the hut seen from above
and engage the guards by himself.

After an hour, Roda crawled so close that he was only a few
dozen paces away from the vehicle. He hid in a tuft of lush weed that
had grown from the ruins of the pile where the bodies of the deceased
members of the Order had once burned, and trembling all over his

body, waited for the agreed signal. The fact that he did not see his opponents depressed and disheartened him. From time to time he peeked carefully out of the fleshy and lush stalks, watching with a wary eye the space separating him from the vehicle. But he saw no one as there was a total void all around, and there was no indication that there was any living creature here. Weeds never stepped on were swinging freely on all sides of the decaying shack. Except for the decaying shack on the other side of the vehicle, there was no other place for a man to hide.

Suddenly he saw Mataret. He was walking knee-deep in the weeds to the mud hut and looking around him in surprise. Roda saw him pausing, sometimes bending down, and examining the ground under his feet. He finally reached the hut and knocked on the locked door with his fist. It was opened quickly. Roda could not see from his hideout the person standing on the threshold, but he saw Mataret, talking lively with someone who was behind the door. After a while, Mataret stepped back and sat quietly on the rock against the wall. A woman came out of the house and was telling him something, pointing to the vehicle with her hands.

Roda could not hold out any longer. Although he could spoil the whole plan by a premature appearance, he jumped out of a clump of weeds and ran quickly towards the mud hut. Mataret saw him and began to signal him, shouting aloud for him to come closer. "Come on, everyone!" He exclaimed, "there is no danger."

Seeing the people suddenly popping out of the bushes, the woman tried to run away in horror, but Mataret grabbed her by the sleeve ... "Don't be afraid, Precious!," he laughed. "They will not hurt you!"

Roda was already standing with them. "What is this? What is this?" He cried.

With a pathetic movement of his hand, Mataret pointed out to the woman who was still trembling with fear. "It is my honor, Master, to present to you the guard of the Conqueror's vehicle" he said.

But Roda wasn't laughing. Rage filled him, and he felt that he had been" deceived again, not realizing that he should rather enjoy this disappointment, that instead of the armed guard, they met only one scared woman there. "Who are you?" He shouted, turning to her.

"Nechem, mister ..."

"Damn your name! But what are you doing here?"

"I watch the vehicle..."

A choral burst of laughter answered her.

"Alone?" Roda said, biting his lips in fury.

"Yes, my lord. The others left."

"Who? Where? How?"

The woman fell to her knees in fear. "Do not be angry, my lord! I'll tell you everything. I am not to blame ..."

"Speak!"

"Lord! The Conqueror showed pity on me. Once upon a time, that day, when he set off south to the sea from here ... I always wanted to serve him, but he did not need me. So, when I heard, over there at the *Warm Ponds*, that he was sending the guard to the *Polar Land* to guard his vehicle, I asked his people to take me with them, that I would cook for them for them and patch their clothes if necessary ... I thought I would be useful to the Conqueror in this way ..."

"To the point, to the point! Where is the guard?"

"They are gone, my lord. At first, there were twenty of them here, but here the country is boring and only the Waiting Brothers could endure it here. The guards missed their homes and had nothing to do here. First, two or three left, for a short period of time, leaving the care of the vehicle to those who remained. But neither of them came back after they left. In the end, I was left with the two youngest only until they got tired of it. They couldn't stand it. They also went when the sun was setting in the south, just over these mountains. They told me to watch over the vehicle, so I watch ..."

"Isn't it fantastic?" Mataret laughed. "Venerable Nechem as the only steadfast guardian of the holy chariot!"

Roda snorted. "This is a villainy! Such an escape, such a disregard for the imposed duty!"

"What are you angry about?" Mataret asked in an undertone, looking at him with surprised eyes. "We probably came out best on this carelessness of the guards. "

"But we could have gone the worst!" The master was indignant. "Just think if there was someone who came before us and broke the vehicle ..."

"I wouldn't let them!" Nechem shouted, and flashed her teeth, ready like an animal to pounce on anyone who would dare to infringe upon the Conqueror's property. "I wouldn't allow it, gentlemen, even though I'm alone!" Tell the Conqueror who sent you that everything is alright ..."

Roda wanted to say something, but Mataret quickly grabbed his hand, signaling his silence.

"Yes, the Conqueror sent us here," he said, addressing the woman. "He orders us to check the condition of the vehicle and report to him if everything is all right ..."

"Sure!," cried Nechem with joyful pride. "Check it! After the guards left, I looked after it and even cleaned it. It shines like gold..."

"The Conqueror told us to take some parts of the vehicle to him," said Roda.

Nechem looked at him suspiciously. "Take some parts, you say?"

"No, no, calm down! Only by chance, if we did not find everything all right", said Mataret quickly, then, drawing Roda aside so that Nechem could not hear them, turned to him reproachfully:

"Why are you scaring this woman? She is ready to interfere ..."

Roda shook his head contemptuously: "I'll have her tied up right now!"

"You don't need to. "

"Yes. Especially since I am afraid of betrayal, attitude, and the lack of trust. The guards may return. Maybe they are somewhere nearby ..."

"That is why we must act immediately ..."

As he spoke, he looked at the mountains. Their tops were illuminated from the north as the sun seemed to be approaching the Earth.

"Look! There is already day on the other side..."

"So what?"

"Nothing. We must hurry ..."

"Without a doubt," said Roda. "But Nechem will interfere if we try to dismantle the vehicle, if I don't order her to be bound ..."

Mataret grabbed his hand again. "Wait. First, the vehicle must be inspected. And inside too. After all, the Conqueror explained his device to you?"

"Yes. "

"So, let's go ..."

He approached the vehicle surrounded by their nine companions, admiring in a silent praise the extraordinary machine. They were staring at the enormous steel cylinder buried deep into the ground with the conical top of the missile protruding from it with a half-rotten rope ladder hanging down.

"This is how the Conqueror got inside," said Roda, pointing to it.

"Let's go in," said Mataret.

His lips twitched nervously, and there was an unusual glow in his eyes. He was already grasping the rope with his hand, hastily, greedily. He looked as if for the first time in his life he was anxious to do something, and he was changed beyond recognition.

Master Roda was not looking at him now. Surrounded by his disciples, he began to lecture to them again that the Earth was uninhabited, and then pointing to the missile, he said how absurd it was to suppose that such a block of steel could reach Earth, no doubt very distant from the Moon. Mataret finally interrupted him impatiently: "Are you waiting for the guard to return?"

Roda looked at the vehicle. "I don't know how to get down to business," he whispered. "We'll see. First, everything must be examined ... "

Having said this, he started climbing the ladder again. But the ropes, faded in the humid air, loosened in his hand before he could put his leg in the loop. So, they started to discuss what to build a new ladder from. There was no material at hand until one of those present noticed the hut where Nechem lived. It was decided to dismantle the roof and the walls supported with poor poles and build a scaffolding from it, over which it would be possible to get to the top of the missile, where the entrance hatch was.

The woman raised a wail, but she was ignored now. Strong young hands hurriedly tore down the pitiful building, piled the poles and tied them with shreds of garments instead of ropes. Roda watched the work idly, only giving orders.

Finally, everything was ready. They constructed something like stairs that made it possible, with some effort, to reach the opening of the iron cylinder and the missile tucked inside it.

Mataret went first, and Roda followed. After long unsuccessful attempts, they finally managed to open the hatch leading inside. A metal ladder led from the hatch to the bottom of the missile. Roda, looking down, hesitated: "We have no reason to go in there, it's dark..."

"Come in," said Mataret, pushing him lightly.

As Roda plunged into the abyss, Mataret, still standing on the steps, slammed the hatch behind him. At the same time, electric light flashed on, mechanically ignited by closing the door.

"What are you doing?" Roda called.

"Nothing," said Mataret calmly, and went deeper.

Roda was uneasily concerned to find himself alone with his companion inside the mysterious missile but was ashamed to let it show. So, he began to look around and, in a teacher's tone, began to explain to Mataret the mechanism and device that he had heard about from the Conqueror.

Mataret was listening distractedly, examining the walls of the missile.

"It's the button, isn't it?" He said suddenly, showing a bone knob in a metal frame, stuck in the wall behind a pane of thin glass.

"What button?" Roda asked.

"You have to press this button to ... go on a journey?"

"Yes. I think ... Be careful! Do not touch!" He added eagerly, noticing Mataret's hand reaching out to the button. "We could unintentionally fly out ..."

"Why accidentally?" Mataret said with a strange smile.

Roda shrugged. "Let's go out now. We've been here for quite a long time. "

Mataret stopped him. "Wait. What if the two of us really went 'to the other side'?"

"Are you mad?!"

"No. After all, the Conqueror fights in our cause, and he needs help, otherwise he will fall in the war with the Sherns ... He could get this help from the other side" ... They will probably support him when they find out ..."

Roda stood between Mataret and that ominous knob in the wall. "Let's get out of here immediately!" He said. "Go ahead and open the hatch!"

Mataret laughed. "Did I scare you? Do not be afraid! I'm not going to ... It was just a joke ..."

At that moment, however, with a quick movement, he reached over the master's shoulder and thrust the knob into the metal ring, crushing the glass. A slight shudder shook the floor of the missile.

"What are you doing!" Roda shouted.

Mataret was pale. "I don't know if didn't make a mistake..." he said. "It seems to me that we are standing still ..."

"Have you pressed the button?!"

"Yes."

Roda lunged for the steps, but Mataret stopped him.

"However, if we are already in space, the hatch cannot be opened. There must be a window down here ..."

After a long search they found a metal plate in the floor covering a thick glass block.

Mataret knelt and looked for a long time. When he rose, he was pale as a corpse, with the utmost astonishment in his eyes. "I believe we're going to Earth," he whispered.

Roda rushed to the window and looked. There, under their feet, the Moon was running away with terrifying speed. They could already see a large part of the Great Desert, from which they were moving further and further, bursting into space.

Roda fell to the floor without strength. "To Earth, to Earth ..." he whispered through dead lips.

"Yes," said Mataret softly. "The Conqueror was telling the truth. I did not think ..."

Then Roda jumped up suddenly and shouted, jumping with his fists at Mataret:" But the Earth is uninhabited!" Do you understand? Uninhabited!! I'll prove it to you right away…"

PART THREE

I

After escaping from the hands of the members of the Brotherhood of Truth, terrified Nechem was running across the plain when she suddenly heard a monstrous boom behind her and felt the air current throwing her violently to the ground. After some time, she regained consciousness and got up. When she looked back, it seemed at first that nothing had changed around her. The vehicle was sticking out among the green bushes as before, and there was complete silence. So, she began to go back to the site, timidly checking for where the people clinging to the walls of the vehicle could have disappeared.

As she came closer, she was disturbed by the change she saw. The outer shell of the vehicle was practically in the same place as it had been. When she looked closer, she saw that the cone of the missile itself, which had been previously protruding from the mouth of the shell, was missing. She also noticed that the scaffolding, built from the remains of her shabby little house, had disappeared without a trace. She remembered that while escaping, she had turned around once and saw the members of the Brotherhood of Truth, ridiculously clinging to the mouth of the machine, just around the shiny top of the missile itself. Now, they were nowhere to be seen. She had a bad feeling, and she walked towards the vehicle, with fear in her frozen heart, cautious and ready to run again at any moment.

A few dozen steps before reaching it, she stumbled, and looking at the object on which she had stubbed her foot, she cried out of terror. It was a head detached from the body and hideously mauled. Her legs refused to obey her, and she could not even run away from the terror. So, she glanced around wildly, and everywhere she looked, she saw the remains of bodies, horribly torn, together with swept away pieces of scaffolding.

Nechem stared in silent shock for some time though she did not understand why, until suddenly she screamed again, and started running away. She ran without knowing where she was going or what for. She fell over on the stones, rose again and raced forward breathless. She was losing her strength but was pushed by only one urge: to be as far away as possible from this place where that terrible and incomprehensible thing had happened.

After a few hours, she reached the end of the plain and fell exhausted on the moss. After a short rest, she began to wonder and gather up her scattered thoughts, trying to organize them into a logical whole, but it was so astonishing that she could not comprehend it. The vehicle, or at least its most important part, the middle part, was gone and that was certain. It disappeared in the blink of an eye as if it had vanished into oblivion. At the same time, she heard a terrible boom and felt a terrible jolt of air which threw her on the ground. She was quite sure that the same shock had caused the horrible death of the intruders clinging to the top of the vehicle, but she couldn't think any further. What does it all mean? Why did this happen? For what purpose or for what reason?

She felt that she would never solve this mystery, and fear seized her again. At least, something happened that shouldn't have happened, and who knows if she's not responsible for what happened. She did not think of the escaped guards at all, or the fact that if they had stayed at their post, they would probably have been able to overcome this raid which she could not resist. She only knew that these intruders had deceived her, and they had caused willingly or unintentionally, some terrible accident that could no longer be reversed ...

And the Conqueror? A hunch told her it happened without his knowledge or his intention. And if he gets angry now? He will, of course, get angry with her first because she was present there and did not prevent it. Should she go and confess? Or rather, hide and not tell anyone?

This last thought dominated her brain supported by the involuntary reasoning: "If the Conqueror is omniscient, he already knows about the accident, so she needs to hide from his wrath. And if he is not omniscient, it is better that, having found out on some occasion, he should not know that she, Nechem, took any part in it. Anyway, she had to hide.

With this decision, after a short rest, she set off along the winding ravine to the south. From there she would head west, towards the settlements scattered among the mountains, to be as far away as possible from the city by the *Warm Ponds*, where the Conqueror is undoubtedly staying ...

Nechem did not even know that at that moment the sea was between them, and that he was still fighting with the Shern near the other pole of the Moon ...

At that moment Marek, who was standing on the mountain wall and staring at the Earth on the horizon, did not have any idea that his vehicle was heading towards his home star, with two people locked in it.

It was late afternoon, and he was expecting the reinforcements lead by Jeret. The fighting was getting harder and harder, and they were already running out of strength because of the lack of sleep and constant toil. Now instead of being the attackers, they became the attacked. Nobody thought about defeating the Shern in their nests anymore. Now, it was just a matter of holding their positions and waiting for the reinforcements to arrive. No one spoke of retreat, but most of the warriors had already thought of it as inevitable. It had only been delayed because of the weakness of their number, which might perish in a harsh march through a country recently triumphed over. They were waiting and looking longingly and anxiously for Jeret to arrive with the new troops, with whom, it would be easier to retreat towards the Great Sea ...

The Conqueror's star was fading. He himself said nothing and didn't share his intentions with anyone. He only ordered them, after discovering a more convenient "path" through the snow-covered gully, to pull up on the ropes hoisting the cannons that had been left below. He had them set in position, turning their mouths towards the Sherns' lovely city and waited. The cannons remained idle, as there was little ammunition left, and no offensive steps were taken. They only limited themselves to fight back the Shern suddenly descending upon them and their corpses already littered all the rocks around them.

One more infinitely long lunar day had passed. Toward the evening, the Conqueror, not worried before, began to look visibly uneasy. He and a handful of auxiliary troops were standing on the highest saddle of the pass. He was scanning the countryside through his field glass, keeping his eyes fixed on where the reinforcements were coming from. His face stretched and he frowned, unable to see any sign of Jeret's troops walking among the gorges that were visible from here ... Not more than five dozen hours remained until the sunset...

He was about to signal his people to return to the inner side of the mountain ring where his main forces camped, when he saw a sudden movement below where the Shern would be circling around his army like flocks of inseparable ravens. He had a feeling that it was Jeret with the reinforcements, and the Shern wanted to interfere with their reunion. So, instead of returning to his camp, he and his men set off down the road towards the troops left there to guard the path and ordered the fire to begin immediately with the rest of the ammunition.

Small arms rattled and arrows drove into the cloud of Shern suspended in the snow below ... Suddenly, as if divine music, the answer rang in the Conqueror's ears from below as shots rang there, too.

It was undoubtedly Jeret.

Two hours later, the troops were already visible, climbing up the steep gully amid the constant battle. The people were walking slowly, because they had to shoot often, and they were burdened with crates of ammunition and weapons. Marek sent them a number of his ranks to help.

When at last the troops came together on the steep snowy slope, and the Shern disappeared into the crevices, leaving numerous corpses behind, Jeret, dripping with blood and sweat, approached the Conqueror to report on his mission ... but Marek did not listen.

"Later, later," he interrupted. "Are these all who would come?"

"I left Anash beyond the Sea. Perhaps tomorrow, he will bring a some more ... if he can manage to reach us ..."

"Well. There is no time to rest now. Take command of them all and follow me to the other side, to my troops."

"Wouldn't it be better to summon the others here?," said one of Marek's subordinates, the current commander of the army on this side of the pass who was thinking about the retreat to the country.

Marek started up without answering. They crossed a snowy pass and descended on an alp suspended among crags, where the main part of the army was resting. The new arrivals began to greet the old warriors loudly, who for their part welcomed them, confident that their arrival signaled their pending return to their homeland. The presence of the recently deified Conqueror was almost forgotten, and the only concern was that a long night would come, which still had to be spent here.

Meanwhile, the Conqueror quickly interrupted those greetings and, to the great amazement of the army, immediately ordered the ammunition to be distributed and ranks to be formed. The soldiers obeyed out of habit, but with a murmur of dissatisfaction. Some were already complaining aloud that they were too weak, and they gasped that the whole expedition was a vain and blood costly madness.

Marek heard it and, as if in reply, ordered Jeret to set up the people at the long-prepared cannons. Then, looking at the leaning sun, he turned to the army: "We have forty hours until the sunset. That should do. We'll spend the night in the Sherns' city."

These short but unexplained words fell on the soldiers like a thunderbolt. They were all stunned for a moment, until suddenly there was a loud shout of enthusiasm. People, already shaky and ready for a disgraceful retreat, or escape, felt that there was a righteous Conqueror above them again, with whom they would follow through life and death.

Marek did not let their fervor cool down and did not leave them time to think. The cannons roared, and under the cover of their fire, the army began to hurry down the valley.

Apparently, the Shern were not prepared for this mad attack, especially now, when the day was about to end. They did not even put up a token resistance. They only ran together in loose groups, circled helplessly over the heads of the advancing army, and died terribly in masses, failing to stop the march. The victory, which seemed to have fallen behind in the wide plains, was again ahead of the men, as in the good recent days ...

In a few hours, without stopping the march, Marek swept over most of the valley, filling the silent sapphire ponds among green meadows with blood and corpses. Homes encountered along the way were hastily demolished with destructive bombs while they were still marching forward towards the city built on the central, rocky mountain cone. Meanwhile, the cannons that were dragged down the slope, came behind them and over their heads shot more and more horribly against the already wobbling walls ...

Jeret looked at the Conqueror with passion in his eyes. He did not say a word, but it was obvious that he again saw in him the fair god of light, sent to the Moon for the destruction of the enemies of humanity. Now, he adored him with even stronger fervor that he had dared to doubt him recently.

And meanwhile, the Conqueror, had led the troop to the foot of the hill to the base of the gates and towers of the city, but he did not stop there. Then, he pointed with his hand to seemingly inaccessible crags: "Forward! Forward! Before the sun goes down!"

It was easier to order than to do. The soldiers were literally falling from exhaustion. Their throats went dry, their hands shook, and their eyes, blinded by the flash of constant shots, could barely make out the road ahead.

"Let us rest, my lord!" Jeret interjected timidly.

But Marek shook his head negatively. "Not even for an hour," he said, "the sun is escaping us, and the Shern may come to their senses!"

"Half of the soldiers will die ..."

"Yes, but the other half will follow me there!" Saying this, he pointed to the towers, glistening with the last rays of the sun already hiding behind the surrounding crags.

So, the cannons roared again, and they started climbing the steep slope, under a barrage of missiles and stones poured by the Shern from above.

It is hard to tell what the outcome of this maddening assault would have been had it not been for the fortunate of chance. The soldiers were already starting to get confused and to withdraw involuntarily, and a disastrous panic could break out among them at any moment. Just then, Nuzar, walking along the ravine. Next to the Conqueror, thanks to his keen eye, spotted under the bend of the rock an entrance to a cavern with steps leading upwards. It was apparently the way to the city for the inhabitants who wanted to use their legs instead of their wings during strong winds or their weariness.

Marek immediately led his warriors into that dark neck, which provided protection against stones thrown from above. They used a mine to blow up the wrought-iron gates, blocking the passage to certain heights and climbed up, shooting blindly ahead to clear the path of enemies.

At last the corridor cut in the rock ended, and the warriors suddenly emerged into a vast meadow on the gentle slope of a hill above the rocks. It was not visible from below, nor could they see their companions left behind at the cannons from there. They could still hear the rumble of shots against the walls of the city, which rose a few hundred steps ahead of them. Marek ordered a three-time salvo to be given as a pre-arranged sign to stop the fire from below, and they headed straight for the city through the breach in the walls.

Panic engulfed the Shern. Apparently, this was quite unexpected to them, for without even trying to defend themselves, they sprang up like a scared cloud of birds of prey and began to flee down, leaving the city to the victors.

The sun had just set when Marek, having ordered the cannons to be pulled up on the ropes from below, was fortifying himself for a long night in the abandoned city. The fires were kindled everywhere, and the guards were put on alert for fear of a night-time attack. A part of the army was standing on alert, hand on weapon, watching for the Shern to faintly flash above their heads, and ready to strike immediately with a sure shot.

Meanwhile, in the ensuing darkness, Marek locked himself with Jeret in a huge and vaulted building, falling into rubble from old age and the recent cannon pummeling. He was sitting on a rock resembling an old altar, with his elbows on his knees and with his chin hidden in his hands, and staring with his wide open, motionless eyes at the blazing fire. Jeret was lying on a leather spread nearby. He was wounded in the leg by a stone thrown from above. His eyes shone with a feverish glow on his thin face, blackened from the recent hardships. He raised himself up a little on his elbow and was telling the Conqueror, gesturing with his other hand, about the passing day.

He told him how they had walked from the sea to the mountains in a deserted land, finding only the cooled rubble left behind at the first crossing. He said that at the beginning of the mountains they were met by a host of Shern, trying to stop his march with a battle. He talked about the immense hardships and efforts, and about the never-ending fight, where each mile of the road had to be purchased with blood. In the end, he spoke about their inevitable defeat at the foot of the mountain, from which Marek's troops had saved them ...

The Conqueror was listening in silence, gloomy and motionless. Only when Jeret, having mentioned his mission, was describing the confusion and resentment there in the land of the people, his eyebrows curled for a moment, and he tossed his head with a movement of disapproval ...

The young warrior finally fell silent and looked into Marek's face inquiringly. It was visible that his lips were quivering with the question which he held back with reverence: what next? After Marek's last deed and simply inconceivable victory, he lost all doubts, if any, about the mission and divine power of the fair stranger from Earth, but his concern for the future dimmed his joyful thoughts. He knew that even if the Conqueror wanted to continue the fight, the soldiers would die from the effort and exhaustion.

Marek felt it, too. Now, in the conquered city of the Shern, in the mountainous, defensive, yet conquered country, he saw clearer than ever that the final, complete conquest of the lunar natives was out of question. It would take years and effort incomparably greater than what the people here could ever have at their disposal ...

His gloomy reflections were interrupted by the entry of several soldiers from the guard. They brought a Shern, gray in old age and captured in a nearby building. Since he made no effort to defend himself or to flee, he was not killed. He was not harmed, following the Conqueror's order, who wanted the captives to be taken alive for the sake of possible information.

The Shern was wearing a strange cape heavy with densely sewn in priceless gems and had gold hoops on his arms and legs. Brought before Marek, he looked at him curiously but calmly.

Marek spoke to him, but he only shifted his head to indicate that he didn't understand and began flashing dim lights on his forehead. Among those present, no one understood this so they went searching for Nuzar and the two men captured in the past who were under him, who had been brought up in this country and could possibly serve as translators.

So, they waited for them, and meanwhile Marek began to question the soldiers about the circumstances in which they had captured this Shern. They told him something strange. When looking for a place to sleep, they went to a building next to this one topped with a round tower. There, just below its very top, they discovered a fortified door ...

As the whole city was empty and abandoned without any Shern in it, they did not expect to find one there either. The door, however, was locked. They thought that the Shern fleeing from the invaders through the window, had left the door blocked. So, they went to work to hack the door, just like that, without thinking, because they could find another place to sleep. ...

"We were very tired," said one of the soldiers "it is true, but when you get excited in fighting, even though you fall off your feet, you enjoy hitting whatever else you find ... And at the same time this tower was interesting, so it inspired us. There were various signs on the walls along the stairs. Looking at the tower from outside you could see some incomprehensible instruments on its flat roof ... After applying a lot of effort, we managed to split the strong and thick door. My companion and I were first to run into the room where I saw this Shern. I do not know what to say about it, but when I saw him, I thought immediately that he was crazy. He was sitting calmly with his back to us and painting pebbles."

"What was he doing?" Marek asked, not understanding.

'I said: he was painting pebbles. He didn't even move when we entered. That room is full of round pebbles, not bigger than a fist and completely covered with splashes of various paints. There are many of them on the shelves. Here is one for a specimen.

Saying this, he handed the Conqueror a large sphere of turned stone, which was covered from one pole to the other with a densely coiled spiral line, composed of small spots of various colors. Marek took the ball in his hand and looked at it for a long time, then turned his eyes to the Shern. The prisoner was trembling now, looking with the utmost anxiety at Marek's hands. The Conqueror began tossing the sphere as if playing with it, and the Shern's eyes darted after it, still following its every move through the air.

At this time, it was reported that Nuzar and his companions were arriving. The Mortzes came in and, seeing the Shern, they were so moved by the sight of him that they forgot to even bow down to the Conqueror. They stared at the old monster for a while, speechless and almost apprehensive, staring in apparent astonishment at the tangle of raw leather straps twisted around his wrists, next to the gleaming gold hoops. Suddenly Nuzar, glancing at the sphere rocking in Marek's hand, raised his hands up and, turned and fell before the Conqueror, with his face on the floor.

"You are the Lord", he cried, "you are the mightiest man! You captured the great Shern, of whom our ears only heard, for we were not allowed to see him! And here we are looking at him standing before you, my lord, and in chains!

His two Mortz companions also fell on their faces, mumbling some incomprehensible words. After a long time, Marek managed to get some explanations from them ...

They had heard from Sherns long ago that in one inaccessible city there was an omniscient old man, called the Great Shern, the keeper of all secrets, written down for centuries in colors on round stones. The Shern considered him as holiness and the only untouchable being, though he did not rule or command. They themselves did not want to know anything, considering it an unnecessary burden and valuing oblivion over all other good. He is the only one who knows everything, and when he feels the approach of death, he chooses a successor whom he lets in on everything, so the knowledge wouldn't be lost ...

The Great Shern also writes down and oversees everything that happens. The Mortzes recognized him by his cape and golden hoops, and moreover by the round stone, which in the country of the Shern, except for this dignitary, must not be written on under penalty of death.

Marek was listening to the story with amazement, looking at the old man curiously. Then he asked the Mortzes if they would be able to communicate with the Shern.

Nuzar got abashed: "If he wants to speak with flashes, perhaps we will understand something' he said, "but he will not understand a voice if he has never been among the people. Sherns use their voices only in the way of loosely moving their hands or heads, to express the simplest things when they cannot look at each other's shining foreheads. And what will we tell him then?

Even so, the Conqueror demanded that they try to ask the Shern why he didn't run away with the others? Nuzar stepped back, not feeling up to the task. Then the other two Mortzes began to make small and scratchy voices, helping each other with certain movements. The Shern looked at them contemptuously, then flashed his forehead. Mortzes, silent, stared with intense attention at the passing lights ...

"What did he say?" Marek asked impatiently.

"He says that's what he wanted," replied Nuzar, with some hesitance in his voice.

"How's that? And nothing more?"

"Nothing, my lord. He says that's what he wanted."

Marek got up and approached the standing Shern. The monstrous face of the native was quiet and a little contemptuous as he looked at the giant twice his height. There was no sign of fear or confusion in him except a hint of curiosity could be seen in his four bloody, dim eyes ...

"Tell him," said Marek, addressing the Mortzes," tell him that he will be alive and free, if he wants to answer my questions ..."

The Mortzes began to howl and bark again, gesturing vigorously, and when after a while the Shern flashed something, they turned to the Conqueror with an embarrassed expression on their dumb faces.

"He says that if he cared about life, he would have fled with the others ... He just wanted to see ..." The Mortz stopped short.

"The Conqueror!" Nuzar prompted quickly.

"Did he say that? Did he really say it?"

"He said something else, but I don't dare ..."

"Speak!"

"He wanted to see the fat and stupid dog," the Mortz finished with a troubled smile.

Any further attempt to get something out of the Shern failed. He seemed so indifferent to whatever awaited him or what they would do to him, that neither a threat nor the promise of reward could force him to answer. Only once, when the Conqueror asked about the contents of the stone books in his possession, he smiled haughtily and replied:

"Go and read", and then fell into an unshakable silence, in the form of a shadow on his forehead.

Marek ordered him to be brought back to the vaulted chamber in the tower and to station a strong guard with him. After dismissing the Mortzes and Jeret, he went outside to breathe some fresh, frosty air...

The sky was clear, and the stars were sparkling. Snow had not yet fallen, and the streets and flat roofs of houses were covered only with a brittle coating. Marek, walking with a lantern, discovered the half-ruined stairs leading to the top of the dome of the building and began to slowly climb up. The narrow passage built with boulders still emanated warmth sucked in during the hot day. In the uncertain light of the lantern, he could see the remains of some sculptures and paintings on those boulders apparently faded centuries earlier and vanishing out of neglect. In one place, a corridor rising upwards expanded into a multitude of low circular chambers. The Conqueror was surprised by a strange painting representing a bunch of connected spheres. He raised the lantern and gazed at the pale remains ...

"I wasn't mistaken," he whispered to himself, "but that's strange, very strange!" ...

These circles were nothing than maps of the Earth drawn from different directions. The obliterated drawing did not make it possible to distinguish too many details, but he could see that the maps must have been exactly accurate once. The outlines of lands, seas and mountain ranges were marked without error or with thick lines ... and above all this stretched a wavy black band with brick-yellow tongues against it. "Could this mean a curse on the hated star in the Sherns' colored language?" Marek thought, ascending higher.

After a dozen or so steps, he found a wider niche again and found similar drawings in it, only obviously older, so that the shapes were almost lost in the gray of the stone. There was Earth again, but different from what people know. Inside one of the circles you could see something looking like Europe, but the Mediterranean Sea was just a narrow, closed lake, and a deep-sea bay cut from the north to the Carpathian Mountains ...

A strange feeling overwhelmed Marek. He had no doubts that it was a map of his globe from those prehistoric epochs before him, when perhaps even the people had not existed yet, and the Shern had already been looking at that star, hanging in the black sky above the desert ... A terror gripped him, so he quickened his pace to get out of those stuffy corridors to the top of the dome ...

As he stood on a small platform at the top, the night on the Moon was impenetrable. A thick shadow lay under the stars in the city, in the whole valley and in the mountains, so even the whiteness of snow covering them couldn't be seen. Only on the south side there was a slight silvery ripple above the blackened peaks which the Conqueror recognized as the glow of the distant Earth, hidden under the horizon...

He stretched out his hands with great longing, and he was consoled to think that a few more long lunar days, and he would fly home in his gleaming chariot across the blue skies, leaving behind this terrible world without regret.

II

The sun was still hidden behind a circular mountain rampart, and only the snowy peaks in the west turned pink with the first golden rays when Marek, accompanied by Jeret and some of the elders, went out to see the captured city.

He was glad that the long, hard night had passed, during which thoughts, gloomy as ominous birds, sat at his head. They were waiting for him to wake up from his short tiring dreams to invade him in a whole swarm. In this vigilance, by the light of the fire that burned on the stone, his deed and all his "victory" stood before him in a gloomy shape. He understood that he had undertaken to do something crazy and unfortunately, fruitless. He had this city in his possession, and he already felt that he would be a prisoner there in spite of his will ... When he fell asleep for a short while, he had nightmares of night attacks, so he jumped up from his bed in fear and ran outside to see if the guards were awake. Then he would look up to see if he wouldn't see the pale lights of the oncoming Shern cloud shining up there, under the dim stars. However only the silence and peace greeted him there. The Shern apparently did not want to risk an uncertain struggle in the night shadow or were afraid of the cold. The recent defeat of their forces probably scared them, and they had not gathered new forces, so for now, nothing disturbed the peaceful sleep of the conquerors ... Then Marek returned to the room and stared at the burning fire and tried to make some plans, to scatter the hopeless darkness surrounding him. But whatever directions his thoughts went, they always mired in some fundamental impossibility, in the inability of drawing a conclusion which could make sense ...

Eventually he grew weary of pointless thinking. In the morning he had a dream, which lasted nearly a day, from which he woke up stronger and refreshed. However, no inspiration reached him, and he had no plan for further action. Due to the reaction of his wholesome physical nature he had fallen into a certain careless indifference to anything that might come. He thought only about the present moment, about the fact that he was in an astonishing city, where every boulder and every building could tell him unspeakable and extraordinary secrets.

So, he hurriedly dressed, and without waiting for sunrise, he summoned the group of soldiers to accompany him on the trip. At the outset, however, he received unpleasant news: The Great Shern, captured in the evening, disappeared during the night without a trace. The soldiers who watched over him swore that it must have become some kind of unholy force, because despite the fact that the prisoner had no shackles, the cell door was closed tightly and constantly guarded. Moreover, the painted stones that filled the room disappeared with him.

The news made Marek very pensive. Even supposing that the Shern had escaped, taking advantage of the guards' momentary carelessness, then how this "library" of boulders, weighing too much to be lifted by more than one, but even a hundred Shern, might have gone anywhere? The guards would undoubtedly have noticed ... such a crowd, coming for stones, the guards would undoubtedly have noticed...

Suddenly a thought flashed through him, like a ray of unexpected light. He realized that the Great Shern had only remained to save his "books", which he could no longer hide during a sudden and apparently unexpected incursion by people. Now he has done his job and is gone. He fulfilled the task, that is, he threw those precious stones into some secret hiding place invisible to the eye, maybe carved inside the wall, and covered with a smooth boulder. Having done this, he also got through a secret passage to the roof and, taking advantage of the night, floated down on wide wings unseen into the valley.

At the first impulse, the Conqueror wanted to order his people to search the cell and, if necessary, to break down the walls to find the hidden stones. Soon this intention immediately dissolved into an awkward and unpleasant, but intricate feeling.

He bowed his head and stared silently at the people around him... For one moment he felt as if he were an ally of these defeated Sherns and would defend the treasure of their knowledge from the destructive hand of the human barbarians. He shook himself from it, but at the same time it occurred to him that if he found those stones, they would be of no use to him as he would never be able to read their colorful writings. They would have to spend a lot of time and effort to knock down the wall, and it could also be fruitless ... So, he did not say a word to the soldiers who brought him that news and walked slowly through the city ...

All the houses were built of stone and rarely had doors at the street level. Most of them had circular windows and narrow balconies or stone beams sticking out, apparently serving their inhabitants for flying off. All these buildings were old and, apparently, unrepaired for centuries. Stones poured down from the upper floors, the pits were covered with moss in the damp shade, giving the buildings the appearance of spontaneous rocks.

Marek entered one of such houses and, passing a gloomy and narrow hall, he found himself unexpectedly in a round room, with unheard-of splendor. The stonework was covered with sheared and patterned furs, resembling woven carpets at first glance. Some kind of weapons, tapestries, and sculptures of ineffable work hung on the walls. Purple and soft fabrics lay on the low square sofa and gave off a pungent, intoxicating scent ... There were chests made of interlocked pieces of carved out bone. They contained all precious dishes, pearls, and gems. Copper basins on forged tripods with extinguished embers stood among appliances and mirrors made of unknown black metal.

The open door above the high stone threshold indicated the way the inhabitants had escaped ... Marek, bending down in an opening that was too short for his height, went out onto the balcony, suspended in the air by the gray wall.

The sun has just risen, half a disc from behind the toothed saw of the peaks lazily leaning out. Its rays were already gilding the city without heating it too much. A whitish fog resembling a sea surrounded by a mountain ring drifted in the valley, at the foot of the hill in the middle of which stood the lonely steep rock bearing the city upon itself.

A feeling of hopeless loneliness seized the Conqueror. He looked at his companions and from their faces he understood that they must feel the same. Here they are, a handful of brave people cut off from their homes and families by this valley and the mountains and the wide country and the sea. They are the supposed conquerors occupying the enemy city, and do not even know what is happening around them under this shroud of fog that covers the entire valley.

The Conqueror mused like that, when anxious voices wafted on the streets of the city – a few at first, and then more and more crowded. The soldiers ran in confusion and asked for their leader. Jeret saw it first from the high balcony and turned to Marek.

"Conqueror," he said, "something is wrong;" they are looking for you.

Marek turned his head down the street, trying in vain to understand something of the noise. But Jeret's hearing was obviously sharper, or he understood the dialect of his fellow men better, as after listening a little, he said in a low voice: "The Shern are pushing ..."

There was no time to waste. Marek went back to the square in front of the building, where he had spent the night. When he was passing that rich room, it occurred to him that it was peculiar, however, that there were so many treasures in the city left by the fleeing Shern, and so little food that the soldiers only hardly managed to collect. At first, he didn't think much of it, but then the thought came back to him with terrifying clarity. After all, this is certainly not a coincidence! The Shern carried their supplies with them, or destroyed them, if time allowed them in a hurried escape, handing over treasures and other possessions to their enemies! And now ... now?

In the square, the army waited impatiently. A handful of soldiers, left at the foot of the hill for the night, had just returned, tensed by the Sherns' attack. Those who remained alive said that the valley is full of terrible natives who are surrounding the city with a dense ring with the apparent intention of imprisoning and starving the bold conquerors ...

When Marek got the news, he looked Jeret in the face. This one stood with his head bowed and brow furrowed.

"What shall we do?" The Conqueror asked.

The young commander shrugged. "Are you asking me, my lord? You have done a divine deed, conquering the Sherns' inaccessible city, and now ..." He paused and fell silent.

Marek didn't ask any more. Gloomy, but firm, he ordered the army to prepare to leave this bloodily conquered fortress. As the ranks hurried down the rocky slope, the mists had already cleared below, revealing an entire wide green valley. It was now black with the Shern filling it everywhere. The Conqueror raised his hand, pointing the distant mountain rampart to his companions...

What began to happen now could only be like the confusion that arises in a full hive when a destroyer beetle wants to pass through it. The defending people's hands fainted, and pain broke their necks, numb from raising their heads towards the enemy falling from above.

Every inch of space had to be conquered, every step had to be bought with blood. They walked like lumberjacks in a virgin forest. The only difference was that they did not have to cut dead logs and creepers but were making a passage with iron among living bodies, and the valley in front of them seemed to grow forever ...

At last they leaned on the circular pond, and here, standing under the coastal rocks, they began to make their way to the mountains with their thick shots. When the Sherns' attack weakened for a moment, and their hordes, unable to withstand the fire, began to scatter, the people leapt forward without waiting for the enemy to come to their senses. On their way, they were hacking the loose groups of the Shern not fast enough to escape.

So, they were moving slowly towards the mountains, blinded by the smoke and the flash of shots but staring at this soaring rock wall, as if it were to be their refuge and protection ...

Marek didn't share this hope, but to the contrary, he was convinced that the moment he ascended the mountain slope, the battle would only get worse. He expected the Shern would take advantage of the troops' inconvenient position while pushing up. He often looked towards the snowy ridge, trying to spot the Sherns waiting at their ambush site, ready to roll down rubble and stones ... Fortunately, however, his fears turned out to be exaggerated. Was it that the Sherns, in spite of their overwhelming numbers, were weary of the fights so costly for them? Or was it that they simply did not think that the people would be able to break through the valley alive? Whatever was their reason, they did not think about guarding the mountain pass. They even stepped back from it when Marek started to climb up the slope, giving his exhausted people a moment to breathe ...

The soldiers rested a little, and after a small meal, started up again without delay. Marek was walking at the lead, keeping an eye on all sides, but he did not dare to look back, or to count the ranks, of which half was left. His only advantage were the firearms, so now he trembled at the thought that the Shern, having looted the fallen, might take their weapons and cartridges and turn them against these remaining handful. So, he rushed all the more, feeling that his only salvation was in running away.

People would sometimes address him, "Conqueror!," and every time he heard that name, he clenched his teeth, as if he heard a sneer. Anyway, the arduous march was happening in silence, interrupted only at times by the hustle and bustle of less and less frequent fights with the Shern catching up with them. Then, they stopped for a short while and hit the attackers with bullets and advanced again, but only higher and higher.

Marek scheduled a longer rest at the past. The soldiers, weary, not minding anything, oblivious to the still looming dangers, threw themselves into the snow and fell asleep in a flash as if dead. Soon only the Conqueror was standing and staring against the sun at the deserted valley.

He wiped his forehead and his eyes with his hand as if he wanted to wipe a nightmare off his eyes. Yes. It all seemed to him a terrible dream now: the battle and the conquered city, and then this bloodiest retreat ... He was surrounded by the silent, snowy mountains, and down there was a silent valley, green and rainbow-colored ponds, sleeping in the sunlight. Now, his thoughts were hitting some strange void.

"Why, what's all this for?" He asked himself and could not find an answer to this simple question ...

He slowly turned his eyes to the south, to the Pole. A light, white, spherical cloud above the mountains. Earth. It had already emerged from the first quarter and was slowly approaching its fullness, with its the upper edge visible to the Conqueror. The immense silence was everywhere as if the entire lunar world froze in the glare of the sun moving in a low arc across the sky.

Marek pondered. He was staring at the Earth now and thinking about the hard struggle still awaiting him before he could return to his native planet after his job was done. He also thought about what he would leave to the lunar people.

He had not accomplished and knows now that he would not accomplish the task he had undertaken. It was impossible to exterminate the Shern from the Moon, but he had passed through their whole country with fire and sword and taught them to fear man and his weapons. His army though decimated knew now how to face the Shern in an open battle and defeat them, should they ever try to conquer the people's country ...

He consoled himself with these thoughts, and also with the fact that when he returned happily to people's settlements, before departing to Earth, he would initiate a change in relations there, give rights to the disinherited and the oppressed, teach the strong justice and mercy...

Anything to go back and go back sooner!

He stood up and began to wake the sleeping soldiers. They got up reluctantly still half-conscious from heavy sleep. Marek, however, did not allow any more delay. They were barely on their feet when he made them descend toward the plains, toward the sea. Noon found them already at the foot of the ring mountains, so they hoped to reach the plain valley before night.

Indeed, they were progressing briskly. The Shern hardly bothered them in their retreat. There were small victorious skirmishes with the randomly encountered groups, which quickly dispersed after one or two volleys. The natives evidently, taught by bloody experience, did not trust their own forces in an empty and exposed country. A cheerful spirit entered the soldiers. They were glad, feeling (as Marek did not say so) that they were going home, and that they would be able to rest after their unprecedented hardships. Only Jeret was just staring grimly ahead and avoided the Conqueror more and more.

In the afternoon, as they had already entered the vast plains, Marek approached him at a stop. They hadn't spoken to each other for a long time, so Jeret was startled when he unexpectedly heard the Conqueror's voice.

"Jeret," he said, "I wanted to council with you ...

"I am here, my lord, to obey your orders."

Marek nodded at him, and the two of them walked out of the camp onto a small elevation above the lazy river. From there you could see the few tents (the rest of them were lost in the fights irretrievably) and the soldiers bustling around them. They were tanned and sunburned with the traces of their recent hardships clearly visible on their thin faces. However, they moved lively when carrying water in buckets to cook the food. The guards with weapons on their shoulders walked around the camp with a measured step. Marek looked for a time in silence at this half-diminished host of his faithful companions, until suddenly he turned to Jeret with a question:

"What do you think about those people?"

"Conqueror, we were all faithful to you and did what was in our power..."

"Why do you keep calling me 'Conqueror'"? Marek asked.

Jeret didn't say a word. So, Marek asked again after a while:" And what do you think about me?"

Now the young commander looked up at him and replied frankly: "I do not know."

Marek smiled. "It doesn't matter now. I did not want to talk about it .... I got to the Moon, and I am carrying out all the task that I voluntarily took upon myself. The Sherns once lived in the countries that stretch from here to the sea. We haven't managed to destroy them in the mountains, but the fertile fields in front of us are vacant. I will give them to the people to possess."

"Before the people come here", said Jeret after a while, "the Sherns will return to their ruined cities in the lowlands, and a new battle will be fought."

"No. People are already here, and they shouldn't let the Sherns come back."

Jeret stared at him in amazement. "You wish, my lord? ..."

"Listen to me," Marek said, interrupting him. "I thought a long time about what to do, and even hesitated ... Having the Sherns in the mountains as neighbors is neither safe nor comfortable. However, we should not leave the conquered country behind as it would make our entire enterprise completely fruitless. There, on the other side of the sea, it is beginning to get tight for you, and the lands here are lush and rich ... and you will be able to defend yourselves from the Shern ... We mustn't leave these countries anymore."

Jeret's eyes flashed suddenly. "Conqueror! So, we're not going home?"

"You said it with joy! ..."

"Yes, my lord. With joy. Because I ... have nothing there ...".

He stopped and suddenly looked glum. Marek realized Jeret was thinking of the girl. He reached out and touched his arm lightly ... "Jeret," he said, "believe me you have no reason ..."

"Let's not talk about it, my lord. I am glad that our blood was not spilled in vain. I was already afraid that you would dissuade us from here ..."

"But will you all want to stay?"

"People are tired, and they want to go home, but I think they will stay when you, the Conqueror, command them to do so. At first it will be difficult here, because the Shern will probably not leave us in peace, but we will stay until others come to settle down here and a permanent defense is formed.

"Do you want to stay here too?"

"Yes. Forever".

"As you wish! I was thinking of taking you with me."

"No, sir. You go back, alone to the Warm Ponds and teach people the law ..."

"I'll wait for Anash. According to what he said, he should have brought reinforcements today ..."

"I think that tomorrow we will meet him at the seaside or on our old route inland ..."

He was silent for a moment. Only after some time Marek said again, looking from the side at the pensive young man:

"The settlers will want to build houses and start families here ... What about you? ..."

"I?"

"Yes. You were once going to marry ... Malahuda's granddaughter. Shall I send her to you here after returning overseas?"

Jeret looked him straight in the eye. "Lord, do you think that Malahuda's granddaughter can be sent to anyone?"

"I think she will listen to me when I tell her that this is my will..."

"If she listened to you, sir, do you think that I would like to take her from your hands?"

They didn't talk about it again.

The tents were quickly folded, and they headed north again, out to sea. The crews would be left only on the larger rivers and near the coast.

Before the evening fell, they met Anash leading a small but well-armed handful of people. He said that his arrival with reinforcements was delayed by the difficulties he had suffered from the ruling high priest Elem, and by the unexpected raid of the Shern from the side of the Isthmus, which, however, was easily repelled by Malahuda's help.

"Whose? Whose help?" The Conqueror asked.

"Malahuda's," Anash repeated clearly, "the former high priest. The missing old man appeared unexpectedly at the hottest moment, just when everyone had lost their heads, and took command of the armed men whom Elem could not lead. The attackers were surrounded and killed to the last one."

When they set up camp for the night, before the frost began to envelop the land, Marek summoned the combined troops and revealed to them his intention to leave the crews in the conquered lands. The news was received without enthusiasm, but also without murmuring. Everyone understood that it was necessary to keep what had been bought so bloody and that there was only one way to do so: by populating these lands previously inaccessible to the people. Then Marek gave the floor to Jeret, who summoned volunteers to stay with him at the post until the arrival of the new settlers from overseas.

There was no shortage of such volunteers especially among those who arrived with Anash, but there were also some veterans who were ready to provide a buffer for future cities and villages of men.

In the end, there was quite a large crowd, which could already be divided into several, quite strong ones. The Conqueror left these people the freedom to divide the land at will, with the condition that certain areas should always be owned by a community and never by themselves.

This order seemed strange to soldiers, but they accepted it without protest and promised to keep their oaths, especially when they heard that it was an introduction to new and beneficial laws that the Conqueror wanted to make the people of the new country happy with.

It was decided to set up the first settlement on the spot where they had just spent the night. Here, on an original trail leading from the mountains to the lowlands, Jeret was to stay with a handful of the best men as a watchman and headman.

In the morning, when the rest of the camp, apart from the post, was moving on, the Conqueror said goodbye to him, touched by the thought that he was squeezing the warrior's small but stout hand for the last time ... When he was about to leave, he was tempted to ask what to say to the golden-haired woman if she asked about him, but looking into Jeret's gloomy eyes, he only shook his hand once more, vividly and warmly, and left without a word ...

And so, they were moving towards the sea, leaving crews on their way, in places suitable for settlements but defenses as well. Finally, in the late afternoon when only a handful remained with the Conqueror, they saw the undulating blue expanse of water from afar. At the seaside there was a troop guarding the sleighs waiting for them there. Anash was to remain there as the head, but for the time being he would go to the old country with the Conqueror and return with the settlers.

The sun was setting when the sleigh, ready for the journey, was waiting on the sand for the night frost to cut the sea in a glassy pier.

Marek, stretched out on the coast, was looking at the western glow. It burned broader, redder and bloodier than usual, as if the last and farewell symbol of those long days full of toil, murder and fire ... as if thanking God without words that his greatest effort was already finished and that he was returning to the country, from where he would soon fly away from the Moon forever ...

The glow, meanwhile, did not go out, but it seemed to burn more and more widely and bloody almost embracing half of the sky. Suddenly an eerie fear filled Marek, as if this sky fire and this blood after sunset meant not only the past days, but was also supposed to be an omen of some terrible fate for him ...

III

This time the news of the Sherns' attack on the people's settlements came from the west and caused an enormous panic. The escapees from the fishing countries on the seashore near the Isthmus reported that the natives were approaching. They appeared from nowhere and were burning and murdering everything along the way ... Nobody thought to resist. They could only run away to the east, towards the town near the Warm Ponds with groans and curses. They were shouting that the Conqueror and his companions had probably died, and that now the inevitable and terrible revenge of the Shern would begin. The people raised their hands in helpless fear and crowded around the high priest's palace, calling in vain for Elem to appear and save his people.

Elem did not come out. Locked in his residence, he lost his head completely and did not know what to do. He did not believe that the Conqueror was already lost, but hearing the curses outside the windows, thrown on his head by these people who until just recently consider him an idol, and at the same time the voices calling him, as high priest, to help and protect them in this misfortune, he felt the utter helplessness of his own authority and position.

He could not prepare ranks or lead the armed men to resist the terrible enemy. He also felt that even in the event of the reversal of the ruin threatening the people, the high priest's throne was wobbling under him. He knew he had to do something and plan if he wanted to keep his position in the event of a miraculous rescue.

Meanwhile, the people were agitated in fear and despair. There were voices saying that they should humble themselves before the Shern and beg them for mercy, especially Avij, who could be a mediator. There were those who, no longer considering and waiting for the order of the high priest, began to rush to the temple and demand that they would be allowed before the former governor ...

When Sevin informed Elem of this movement, he thought deeply for a moment. An idea began to dawn in his head. He did not believe that Avij, imprisoned for a long time and tormented, would be a gracious mediator between the people and his fellow-countrymen after his release. It would be a far too optimistic supposition, but he thought that a prisoner could become a means of salvation as a hostage. He might even want to persuade the attackers to make peace agreements through some writings for the safety of his own life. So, he decided to talk to the Shern himself.

Sevin announced this high priest's will to the people from the window, while Elem had himself dressed in the ceremonial garments. There was an abundance of previous high priests' clothes in the treasury, but Elem chose from there only the brightest jewels. He ordered himself to be dressed in new garments, brighter and more colorful than the old robes. He wanted to dazzle the Shern with the splendor of his figure. He hoped that in this way, having shown his power outwardly, he would make him more inclined to submit.

Ihezal reported what happened to Avij. She entered the underground room with no intention of talking to the prisoner about anything, rather a habit that had become her inner need. People moved away from her more and more. As the charm of Conqueror, now lost in distant countries faded, people began to look at her differently, with a worse and more suspicious eye. It was even forgotten that she was Malahuda's granddaughter and the last offspring of the eternal family of high priests. Now, they only saw her as the guardian of the Shern, and therefore she began to be considered an impure creature. The youth still hailed her seductive beauty as in the old days, but even so, they felt fear and even hate.

People looked at her from a distance and strange things were said quietly. Some attributed supernatural and dreadful powers to her. It was said that she could travel from place to place without being seen or that she could send sickness with her eyes. It came to the point that when passing her people drew the saving Sign of the Coming on their lips. Although that sign had lost its former meaning by the fulfillment of times, but nevertheless remained among the people as a means of rebuffing all evil spells.

Ihezal did not look for anyone's company either. She had even stopped visiting her grandfather for a long time. She had the very feeling that anger, and venom were building up in her, like in a shining reptile locked in place which could not bite anyone. Disgraced and pushed aside, she began to despise everybody with redoubled strength, especially since she felt her power over them. She knew that when she appeared on the steps of the temple, those who fled so as not to touch her clothes looked sideways into her black eyes, and at her one call they would sell themselves to evil, just to feel her hands on their forehead in the face of death. It was strange that the more she was feared and the more she was avoided, the more her power grew.

She sometimes liked to experience this strength. She stood on the threshold of the temple and locked her gaze on a passerby, luring him for a moment with an irresistible smile, and to turn away from him in that instant, as if from a dead and quite indifferent object ... On other occasions boundless contempt was rising in her when she walked among the loathing crowd, her face frozen and pursed, not even bothering to glance around her or to answer the rare greeting ... On such occasions, she hid in the depth of the abandoned temple or arrogantly challenging the voices condemning her, she went to the cellar to spend time in Avij's company.

She rarely spoke but listened more and more willingly to the Shern's strange stories. He was telling her about his country and the dead cities in the desert, and about the living cities among the mountains, which might fall, defeated, at the Conqueror's feet, but they would never reveal their secrets ... After such talks she often went on the roof of the temple and looked out over the wide sea. She gazed towards a dark outline of the Cemetery Island on a shining surface at the waves that went far away, mobile, and continuous, to the distant horizon in the blue mists, drenched with the sun ... and then she remembered the Conqueror. Sometimes, his memory came like the light and fog of the day before yesterday. At other times, it felt like a wave of hot girly blood, storming suddenly with a delightful wave on her lips and on her breasts, burning them more strongly than the sun under her light clothes as if they ached to break out of the clothes and cool down in the fresh air, or to faint under kisses ...

However, most often she thought of him with a wild, passionate sorrow. Why did he show his strength to her and walk away from her as if he had never noticed her? Why were the battles and people's good and his mission more important to him than she, the flower, and the pearl? Her lips swelled with bloody mockery, and then she went back to the monster's cave to listen to his insults and blasphemies, tossed against the fair one ... She sometimes hid in a dark corner under an alabaster column and trembled with inner sobs, unable to spill tears through her eyes.

That day the news of the Sherns' invasion reached Ihezal when she was returning from the sea in the morning. She couldn't even tell who brought it to her and when ... She saw a bunch of running people, but she didn't care why they were running and what they were shouting about. She hardly heard the sound of their fearful voices ... She passed one group, the other, and the tenth, and without asking, not listening to anything, she noticed, as she was climbing the steps of the temple, that she already knew about everything.

Several of her maids were waiting for her in the hallway as they wanted to tell her something, but she dismissed them without a word with a wave of her hand and went straight to the old treasury ... That day Avij was gloomy and gruff. He did not answer her questions, he did not tell ordinary, long, strange, and terrible novels ... He only repeated several times, as if in a tone of command: "Let me go, untie me!"

And now these were the first words with which he greeted the golden-haired girl entering the chamber. His long-dead wings spread, as far as the chains allowed him, and he began to send those bloody lights.

"Let me go!" He finally shouted, "let me go! I feel the wind over the sea waves and the sun. Let me go, I want to be free!"

"By my grace?"

"You cannot grant me any grace. I stand far beyond what you call grace or pity or harm. I want to be free by my will, of which you are the tool."

"I'm not."

"You will be."

"You will die if I release you."

"I won't die. If you untie me, I'll be king over you, I'll be the king of this mob of dogs no matter for how long."

"The Conqueror is exterminating your brothers."

"A stone, falling from above, crushes the bushes along the way, and yet it will fall low and lie forever, and the bushes will grow back. We have the power."

"Meanwhile, you are in chains and I can beat you if I choose to."

"You talk to me so that you can hear your own words, because you feel that you are no more than Words, but I have the Power..."

Ihezal approached the monster slowly and, grabbing a piece of an abandoned staff, she aimed to strike him in the face. The Shern didn't even flinch. He just opened his four bloody eyes wide, to the four still fires alike now.

Ihezal dropped her hand limply.

"Avij! Avij!" She cried involuntarily.

She stepped back, crossing her arms over her chest.

"Your compatriots have attacked our country, "she said after a moment, quite unexpectedly.

The Shern showed neither anger nor joy. He was silent for some time. "Too early," he said after some time.

His further words were interrupted by the entry of messengers from the high priest.

Six of them entered the cell, tall and dumb peasants, who, having passed Ihezal, as if they didn't see her, approached the prisoner directly, throwing loops on his hands freed from the shackles. Two held ropes on each side; the other two began to break open the iron and to open the padlocks that stuck to the stone wall.

"What are you doing!" Ihezal shouted.

They ignored her question and dragged the freed prisoner upwards on ropes behind them. Ihezal followed them slowly.

They came to the center of the temple where on the throne of the high priest, Elem sat in all his ritual splendor in his priestly robes glittering with jewels. He was surrounded by dignitaries of the capital city. They were all gathered, as if for a celebration, but their eyes, despite the external seriousness, ran restlessly to the temple gates every now and then, and it was obvious that the slightest rustle frightened them. When the Shern was brought, they looked at him as if they were the convicts, and he was the judge holding their fate in his hand. Only Elem kept an appearance of power and dignity.

"You should know" he said to the former governor, "that your brothers in the overseas land are defeated and destroyed forever. We, however, want to show mercy on them, especially on you ..."

He paused for a moment to take the breath he was short of in his chest.

Then the Shern suddenly asked:

"Are the victorious Shern far from the ramparts of your city? I see that you are scared and that your colorful clothes cannot hide your wicked fears."

A hollow silence filled the room.

Elem was the first to come that awareness, and, rising a little in the seat, spoke as if he had not noticed the haughty mockery in the tied Shern's voice:

"Indeed, the remnants of your tribe, scared away by the defeat, fell here to our country, but I am even ready to spare their lives ..."

"Ha, ha!" The Shern laughed.

"Yes, spare their lives if ..."

"What?"

"If they want to yield."

"Ha, ha, ha!"

Elem's face grew gloomy." Otherwise you will die before they reach the city walls."

"What do you want from me?

"Warn them, write them, hold them back ... You are our hostage here. We will send a messenger to them ..."

"Which of you will go with my message?"

There was a silence. No one gave an answer, and no one even thought there would be a daredevil who would dare to go, knowing that a certain death and torment awaited him. Avij got it.

"Free me," he said.

Elem hesitated. "Who will promise us that when you are freed, you will want to protect us and not take revenge?"

"I guarantee you," said the governor, "that when freed, I will avenge you, and not protect you, but if you don't free me, our revenge will be even more terrible!"

The high priest wanted to answer, but at that moment he was interrupted by a sudden commotion at the door of the temple. Screaming and lamenting people ran in with the news that the Shern were already burning the settlements near the city. The smoke could be seen from the embankments ... The panic erupted at once. The dignitaries rose from their seats, some of them huddled around the throne of Elem in fear, as if expecting help or refuge from him.

Helpless Elem was standing there, unable to control this disastrous confusion ...

Then the Shern, stroking on the ropes, stepped up to the elevation of the throne and grunted: "To my feet, dogs! On your faces, on your faces! Beg me here for a life that I will not grant you!"

It is hard to imagine what would have happened, because instinctively, in unconscious fear, some of the elders and the people had already staggered as if they were about to fall at the monster's feet, when suddenly a powerful, familiar voice sounded at the temple gates: "People! Stop!"

Everyone turned. They saw Malahuda standing on a low square stone pulpit by the entrance. He was wearing a gray robe, with no signs or ornaments, and only his long, gray beard stood out, but his whole posture radiated the old and compelling dignity. It was obvious that he had come to take over the rule at this difficult moment.

"Malahuda! Malahuda! The high priest appearing miraculously!" They began to shout from all sides and press towards him.

And he, having looked over the temple, restrained the pressure and quieted down the confused shouts with a single movement of his hand.

"Take the Shern back to the dungeon," he said, "and the people to the square in front of the temple. I'll give my orders there."

Avij was pushed to the ground in a flash and led away to be tied to the stone wall again. Meanwhile, the crowd started to pour out of the temple through the wide gates to the square.

Malahuda waited until the whole wave had passed below him, then as the last one left the deserted hall without even glancing at Elem, sitting there still and alone. From the stairs he went directly to the high priestly platform overlooking the square. He was greeted with a passionate cry of joy. The wind blew his long white hair not covered by a priestly cap or clasped by a golden ring. His hand raised over the crowd was without golden rings and his high priest staff, but all of them bowed at this sign ready to obey his commands.

The former high priest spoke briefly. He ordered women, children, and old men to go home, and to gather in the square all those who were capable of fighting. Apart from that, he ordered Anash to gather and prepare the men who were familiar with the use of firearms.

"The Conqueror" he said (he pronounced the name for the first time before the people, applying it to Marck) the Conqueror did not die or fall. Be convinced. If it were, otherwise, not only the small handful I hear about, but a whole host of Sherns would come down on us here. This attack is apparently their last attempt to rescue themselves. They tried to cause panic here. Let them find men instead and let them find their final destruction. I have led you into battle more than once, and today I will succeed in the absence of the younger ones.

In a few hours, the assembled ranks, led by Malahuda and Anash, spilled out of the city walls, heading west towards the smoke that stretched across the horizon.

The people in town were impatiently waiting for the news. It came earlier than expected. Soon after the noon storm had barely subsided, the first messengers came running to report the victory. A handful of impudent Shern were suddenly surrounded and killed so none of them survived.

There was an indescribable joy. The people ran out to the gates to greet the victorious old man, just in time to arrive. It was already shouted that he must re-sit the high priest's stool to replace the unworthy Elem. But the joyful messengers met only Anash, returning at the head of the victorious ranks. Malahuda was gone. He did not hide now that he was staying on the Cemetery Island, but at the same time he ordered no one to dare to interrupt his solitude.

Anash announced this to the people and said that Malahuda had ordered him not to deviate from his original intention of leading reinforcements overseas to the Conqueror at night. Only an emergency service was to be created in the city to defend against any accident.

The people were touched and outraged by Malahuda's leaving them. They felt it as contempt on the part of the proud old man. Some even forgot in anger that by his appearance he had saved the city from disgrace and destruction by a few Shern. Elem quickly took advantage of this mood, sending Sevin among the people. He spread rumors that it was the high priest himself who had summoned the old man to defend them, knowing his greater experience in the trade of war.

Anyway, it happened so quickly, and apparently so easily, that the people soon stopped believing in the danger of which they had been so scared recently. Now they talked about it with laughter, and even more with a certain unpleasant shame, and only reluctantly recalled the past panic. That day, the Shern simply ceased to be scary, so they no longer blessed Malahuda for having defeated them. They even began to speak lightly of the Conqueror and his expedition, which they had once considered a miracle of insane courage.

Now they almost blamed Marek for having taken, so long with wiping out the hateful tribe. Some were convinced that he shouldn't actually be sent any more reinforcements. Anash would have probably never gone overseas despite Malahuda's express command, if volunteers were not attracted to a possible loot like the jewels sent by the Conqueror to the high priest's golden-haired granddaughter.

For Ihezal, all that had happened seemed like a strange dream, which had left her with an awfully bad taste. She saw the Shern pulled out of the dungeon and the people's terrible humiliation who were almost ready to fall on their faces in vile fear before the bound monster ... She felt that was the moment that the angry and inhuman animal was the only higher and proud being in the crowded temple. Sudden and hot shame overwhelmed her. It was a shame for the wretched people, for that hour of shame and disgrace she had to witness, and even for the Conqueror who had imprisoned a helpless monster ... Avij, was the witness and the indirect cause of it all ...

At the first impulse she wanted to go and kill him, but fear overwhelmed her at the thought that she would first have to look into his bloody and mocking eyes. So, she hid herself in her rooms and did not come out for long hours ... Malahuda sent for her to come to the Cemetery Island on important matters, but she did not answer the messenger or even let him in her presence ... In the evening, when Anash was departing with reinforcement overseas and the entire population showed up onto the frozen shore, she did not bother to even look towards the window ...

She spent the whole night alone but didn't sleep well. She sank into a deeper and fiercer reflection in long breaks between one dream and another... Several times she jumped up, as if intending to go to the cellar, where the Shern was locked up, but each time she didn't have enough courage and retreated again into her hidden rooms, not allowing even the servants to check on her.

This is how she spent the morning of the next day. She spent hours as if frozen in an eerie numbness, lying with her eyes wide open ... Only around noon, when the air, heavy with the approaching thunderstorm, overwhelmed other people, she suddenly felt some feverish energy filling her.

She was still in her rooms but sprang up from the wide sofa and told her maids to summon her men servants. Four of them came: stout farmhands looking like torturers. Ihezal motioned for them to wait.

Then Ihezal and her two maids went to the small rear room where she used to get dressed in front of a metal mirror above the semicircular pool in the floor. She stood in front of the mirror and ordered them to undress her.

They both rushed to untie the ribbons of her outer garment over her shoulders and over her breast, always covered since the Conqueror's arrival the Moon. Then one of them bent down to her feet to take off her sandals. The other, with quick, caressing movements of her fingers, removed the clasps from her hair, which soon ran in a golden wave down her already naked back. Her under garment cloth in the color of the changing sea water, hung loosely on her hips, tied at the womb with a thin gold chain, hanging down to the feet. She tugged on it herself with both hands, and when she opened them, this last piece of clothing also slid softly on the white fur, thrown to the edge of the pool.

She has now blossomed like a magical flower in her eyes fixed in the mirror. Her lips curled lovingly, and heavy eyelids drooped over her pupils as she was looking at the reflection of her body ... Her tiny white arms coupled with two pale pink roses of her breasts gleamed under the cascade of her loose gold hair ... Her slender hips, with a light pink stream of luminous blood, flowed sweetly with pearly lines down to her round knees and small feet resembling two lilies ...

She bent over her reflection in the pool and undulated in a snake like movement, raising her arms above her head:

"I'm beautiful ..."

'You are beautiful, lady!" The two handmaids answered in unison.

She stood like that for a moment: slim, flexible, naked, and perfect, until suddenly, as if a memory struck her, she cupped her hands in front of her eyes, bending her head against her chest. The servants seemed to hear a groan, or some spasm of suppressed sobbing.

When she took her hands off her face again, her lips were pursed, and her eyes were hard and commanding.

"Dress me," she said shortly.

They both jumped to wash her and rub her skin with fragrant oils, but their work went sluggishly, because their hands trembled from the lustful trance, sliding on the white body of the lady. Ihezal nodded silently to the chests where her most expensive outfits were kept.

After a few minutes it would be hard to even imagine the naked and dreamlike miracle of her body under the stiff outfit and under the purple cape ornamented with jewels and gold, They wrapped her hair in a high crown around her temples and added pearls and a veil sewn with coral. Her legs were shod in green booties, with long golden chains that trailed on the ground at each step. Huge roses of precious stones shone on the backs of her hands, pinned with golden strings to four rings on the fingers and a wide rim around the wrist.

When Ihezal came out to the waiting servants, they bowed their heads involuntarily, backing respectfully to the wall. Ihezal motioned for them to follow her.

They passed the corridors connecting her chambers with the temple in silence and turned directly towards the descent to the former treasury. At the door she ordered her men to light torches. Suddenly her pursed lips twitched with some terrible, cold cruelty in the glow of the flaring tar torch...

Ihezal pushed the door to the cellar and told the men to come forward. They lined up on either side, lighting the room with tar torches. She entered with a frozen white face, stiff in her rich and heavy robes and the sound of chains at her feet, flashes of precious stones

The Shern looked at her in amazement. Since that momentary release, during the panic, he was not chained, only ropes were hurriedly tied at his wrists and pulled through rings on the iron wall and his legs were tied with a rope to the eye in a stone mess ...

"Ihezal!" He snarled after a moment. She approached him without a word, her face still motionless and as if frozen. She slowly took out a sharp dagger with a flexible blade from the folds of her dress and began to flash it in the light of the torch as if playing.

"Ihezal!"

Sharp pain choked off that scream in his throat. The girl with a sudden and seemingly innocent movement put the blade of the dagger to his forehead, marking a wide scar on it. Then she stepped back a little and signaled to the two of her servants to come closer with the torches. For some time, she was looking at the monster in the bloody glow of the tar candles, until finally she slowly took them out of her hands and pushed them under his outstretched black wings.

The Sherns crumpled in pain and the cellar smelled of burning.

"People are the masters here," said Ihezal, pulling her torches back a little, "they own the Moon and all the creatures living on it. We rule from the sea to the ends of the desert over which the Earth shines, the blessed star: at sea and over the sea, in countries as yet unknown..."

Her voice cracked and broke. She violently struck him in the chest with the flaming torch, which fell from her hand and smoldered, spilling on the tiles with a stain of tar in a wide red fire.

The shadow of the Shern tilted away from the wall moved up and loomed like a big black nightmare under the gold letters of the once sacred inscription ... and four terrible, bloody eyes glittered from the curled monstrous body ... Ihezal suddenly felt that her strength was leaving her. She looked around involuntarily reaching with her hand for support, but her servants were gone. They fled in some superstitious fear, and she was alone.

For one moment, she wanted to run away, too, but she felt that her legs were not serving her. Some sort of breathlessness overwhelmed her, and her stiff, precious clothes were suffocating her. A soft moan escaped her bluish, half-open mouth.

The Shern has not said a word yet. As he curled up in agony, his horny lips were pressed together, and now he looked only silently with terrible eyes at the staggering girl who could not take her eyes off his eyes. Never before had she felt so helpless as now, when she had come to show her power and splendor to the proud monster. She stared at him motionlessly with wide, blunt pupils, unable to even take a step. There was a wound in his chest burned out by the torch that was now becoming extinguished in red leaping flames at his feet, and his eyes, eyes ...

A terrible, mad scream wrenched from her chest and froze halfway on the highest pit, like a fountain suddenly cut down by frost.

Then the Shern began to speak: "The Shern, who do not know bad or well, are the true masters, even when they are in bonds, or wounded. Every creature that came to the Moon must serve them, and even if it breaks away from their power, it will fall.

They were the masters from the beginning, when the servile Earth shone their nights, and they will be the masters until the end of time, when the Great Desert drinks the sea and swallows up the Moon..."

... Ihezal moved her lips soundlessly.

"Come closer," said the Shern again after a moment, his eyes never leaving her. She staggered, but obediently took a few steps.

"Closer."

She walked closer and was only half a step away from him.

"Have mercy!"

"Cut the ropes," Avij said.

With a mechanical, passive movement, she picked up the dagger, and bending down to the monster's legs, began to cut the bonds binding them.

"Hands ..."

She straightened herself up, and slowly, as if drowsily, she pushed the edge of the dagger between his hand and the iron ring on the wall. Avij had one hand free. He did not, however, reach for the dagger to free the other himself, but repeated in the same soft, commanding voice: "Go on to the second ..."
Ihezal cut the rope.

And suddenly she felt that some terrible black mass fell on her. She wanted to defend herself, she wanted to repel the weight with her hands, to push at him with a dagger, but it flew out from her hand like a withered leaf. At that moment somewhere up above her head two wide, up-stretched wings, fluttered and fell on her, softly enveloping ... She felt the horrible hands, sliding along her sides and searching through the rigid folds of robes for her flesh, and then the touch of cold, slippery hands on her bare hips. Sudden night enveloped her head and heat burned her mouth and throat. It was immediately followed by some monstrous, inhuman, and terrible pain that twisted her muscles and her inside, pain so hideous that it resembled blissful pleasure. She fell unconscious.

IV

The gray dawn rose over the frozen sea. Malahuda, dressed in a warm fur, emerged from his cave on Cemetery Island. He was accompanied by two faithful dogs that had been sharing his solitude for some time. After running outside after the master, they began to bark and jump merrily, burying the white snow with their feet and sniffing around for the hiding places of the Moon animals sleeping for the night.

The old man looked for a moment at the dogs' jumps, glad to be free after a long night confinement and then turned slowly towards the hill hanging over sea. The dogs, noticing that he was going to leave, stopped their frolics and ran after him. His legs were sinking in the powdery, frozen snow, and he leaned on his long stick as he walked.

Having reached the top of the hill, he sat down and was resting for a long moment, staring down at the wide ice plane stretching at his feet with the unblemished mirror. It was still a long way to sunrise. The snow just turned blue with the first lights, drizzling from the pale sky, in which the whole world was melting evenly, with no transitions, no shadows, no sharp outlines ... Only a broad, pearly and silvery ripple under the stars in the east announced that these lights heralded the coming sun, which, having run a long way over the Great Desert, is now moving above the seas, to finally emerge from under the ice in this country.

Malahuda focused his eyes on the boundless seas in the south. His face looked old and weary in the morning light. Looking at him now, it would be hard to believe that he was the same man who, two days earlier, managed to galvanize a crowd into action and, in a moment of danger, equally with the young, lead the ranks to destroy the terrible enemies of the people. Now, in solitude, his eyes lost that commanding gleam, his lower lip hung motionless above his long, gray beard at times tugged at by the morning wind ... The dogs, seeking warmth, came closer to his knees and were watching the wide sea with him.

They spent some time like that, when suddenly he heard a strange barely audible whiz. It was as if the ice cut with sharp iron had begun whimper softly, or as if the wind was blowing and whistling, when rushing through the cracks in the ice. Malahuda stirred, and rising, walked quickly to the very edge of the hill hanging over the sea. He stood over the suspension itself and stared intently for a moment. There, far away, on the glistening surface of the ice, he spotted something like a few black points, seemingly still, but still growing in the eyes and constantly moving away from each other ...

Now the old man turned to the highest spot of the hill on his right. There was a large pile covered with snow-shrouded branches. With a quick movement, he ripped off that protective roof. Using his stick, he straightened the bundles of torches stacked underneath. In a moment, a fire flared up, soaring up with blowing wide fumes.

Meanwhile, the black points had come much closer and one could already distinguish several sleds, rushing on the ice with sails blown by the wind. Malahuda, standing beside the burning pile, counted them from far away ... He frowned and his lips twitched with concern.

He walked down the hill by a circular road and came ashore, where the sea was cutting into the land with a shallow bay.

The fire and its meaning at such an early hour were noticed and understood on the sleighs, as soon they began to make the wide arch, and slowing down, rode into the bay sheltered from the wind. At the shore, the sails were hurriedly lowered, while the sleigh braked with chains thrown under the skids.

Anash jumped out from under the leather roof on the first sleigh, which had reached the landing much earlier than the others. Malahuda ran towards him. "The Conqueror?"

"He's with us on that sleigh in the center ..."

"What about the rest? The first ones and Jeret?"

"They stayed."

"Alive?"

"Yes. Although many have died. The living ones were left as the crews on the plains of the conquered country... and I will be returning there soon."

At that moment, Marek's sleigh had stopped in place, plowing a wide furrow in the coastal snow with the front of the metal wrapped skids. Soldiers began to pop out from under the leather covers and shout cheerfully. Finally, Marek appeared as well. Seeing Malahuda, he lunged quickly towards him. "Old man, I gave orders to look for you everywhere ..."

The former high priest made a sign with his hand. "We'll talk now. It wasn't possible. Before. Sir order these people to go straight to the city while the ice still holds before sunrise. I will send you back later in a boat."

Marek gave Anash the appropriate order, and he was standing beside Malahuda, as the stationary sleighs began to unfurl their sails again and spread out in a wide semicircle for the road ahead. At one point, it occurred to him that these fellows would see the golden-haired Ihezal before he would. She would probably come out on the steps of the temple and would be looking for his lofty form among the visitors ... Meanwhile, the sleighs were already racing beyond the cape bordering the bay.

"It's cold," said Malahuda. "Let's go."

Without waiting for a reply, he went ahead with the dogs that were always accompanying him. Marek followed him. They walked in silence for quite a long time, circling the shallow valley, passing two hills, until at last they were at the foot of the elevation with the entrance to the cave where the old man lived.

Marek was astonished to see this extremely primitive shelter of this high priest once ruling over all the lunar people and accustomed to luxury and splendor, but he did not say a word, following him inside through a low rock neck.

Here Malahuda took his hand, signaling him to sit down.

"I want to speak to you, son," he said. "It was not the time when you came to the Moon, but now I must. Perhaps you will understand many things when I tell you ... Do not be angry that I call you a son, you who are huge and named a conqueror here. I am old and I wish you well ..."

Marek bowed his head. "Old man, from the moment I heard your words for the first time, I wanted to be with you and to speak candidly!"

"It was premature then, premature! Only now ... But you go ahead, tell me where you have been, and what have you accomplished, that I might hear it all from your own mouth ..."

So, Marek started his long story while sitting on a boulder covered with leather, in the darkness of the cave, where the light of the oil lamp turned yellow more and more in the bluish dawn, penetrating through the cracks in the ceiling. He spoke extensively about his whole journey, about fights, skirmishes, victories, and failures. He did not conceal anything, not even his fears that the incomplete destruction of the Shern would not be fruitful and would not ensure a lasting peace. He also did not hide the fact that, in his opinion, further war with the natives in their mountainous country was almost impossible ... He also related how he had left the troops in the conquered country with a great fear about their uncertain fate, if not in the near future, then later on, when the proximity of the Shern would weigh over new settlements, like a hail storm threatening them with destruction at any moment.

Malahuda became lost in thoughts as he listened to these stories. He wiped his high and furrowed forehead several times, but he didn't interrupt Marek until he finished speaking. Only after some time of silence, when Marek, pensive in his turn, stared with a dull, weary gaze at the shadows that lingered on the bends of the boulders, the old man stood up and said: "You did everything you could do, son. Now I should give you some explanations so that you can understand me better ..."

He broke off suddenly, as if changing his mind, and said shortly: "It doesn't matter. This is just my advice to you: get back to Earth as soon as possible, if you can."

Marek looked at him in surprise: "I want to go back, and I will go back, but I don't understand ..."

The old man smiled faintly. "It seems, I need to say everything, otherwise you might not trust me. Listen then. I was a high priest, and I believed with all the people, together with my fathers, in the coming of the promised Conqueror. The day you came to the Moon, I stopped believing. It so happened that I could not cope with all this, because it was the faith of my whole life, and I am already old, so old. Still, I knew that if you wanted, you could do a lot more than we could, and that is why I left the field open to you. As for myself, I came back here to meditate on everything in solitude and in hiding."

He stopped talking for a moment, then, taking a breath, continued: "Having lost my faith that the supernatural Conqueror, the reincarnation of the Old Man foretold by our books would ever be sent, I decided to wait here. I was hoping that you, a random stranger from Earth, would become for us the Conqueror that the longing people had appointed you to be at first seeing you. However, if you had not fulfilled our hopes assigned to you without your will, I was ready to curse you with others... Perhaps only because of the fact that you crossed the interstellar space that had existed from the beginning as a wall between the worlds .... Those first ones, whose graves lie near here, had also broken this law of distance, and because of that, misfortune came to them and to all their descendants until today ... Escape, before it is not too late."

"That's a strange talk, old man ..."

"Yes. Yes. This is not what I wanted to talk about. My thoughts get muddled and keep coming back to what hurts me. Well, in solitude, I have learned to look at things more calmly and not to expect anything over a man's ability, even if he came from Earth.

You may not have done anything for us, but you went and fought with us and for us. For what is it to you, after all, anything that is happening on the Moon? One day you will depart from here and only the legend will remain: may it be bright and holy! Your victory, my son, is not complete, and you are right to fear for the fate of those who remain there as troops and those who will go after them to live in the fertile lands that have been taken. But you can't do otherwise ... You've finished your assignment and I bless you."

"I'm not finished" said Marek. "It is urgent for me to get back to Earth, and yet I want to stay here for some time, to repair your laws and change the existing relationships. Things are not right here."

"Things are not right here, and they will stay that way. You can't help it," the old man replied glumly.

"I want to help."

Malahuda shook his head. "You won't help it, and it could mean your doom. I stopped your sleigh with the burning fire because I wanted to speak to you and warn you. Go back to Earth. There, at the Warm Ponds and in the whole lunar country, people have already changed since the time of your arrival and your departure for the conquest of the Shern country."

"They are hungry for power," Malahuda continued, "and now they think that they could have done all that you had done without you. They will start reproaching you for not having accomplished the impossible, you will see! If you touch what is evil, but sanctified by centuries, the most powerful ones will rise against you. You will not be able to overcome them, although you are earthly, and even if the oppressed ones stand by you. Leave, I'm telling you."

"No. I have undertaken this task voluntarily, and I consider it my duty to fulfill it. Perhaps the more so that my desire pushes me to do something else than, to listen to your words, old man. I will only leave when I do what I intended."

Malahuda was silent for some time. Finally, he raised his head and said: "May it not be too late then! ... But if you absolutely want to, take at least one piece of advice from me. I have been a high priest and have ruled longer than you have lived in the world. When you come to the city at the Warm Ponds, become the master right away. Before you begin to do anything, teach people to worship you and fear you. Destroy your enemies, open and hidden, and even those who might become such in the future. Destroy even those who may be in favor of you but could turn the crowd against you. Make me a prisoner, who may not leave this island. Order immediate beheading of Elem, or bury him in the sand, without delay and without looking for a pretext. Kill the most powerful and let there be no man who does not fear death looking at you. Then surround yourself with guards and give orders without asking anyone's will. Only then will you be able to save them."

"I don't believe it." Marek said after a while. "These are old methods used centuries ago on Earth as well ... We abandoned them a long time ago because they are not effective: they lead nowhere. I do not deny that I want my will to be followed at first, but not through fear. People must understand that it is beneficial for them ..."

"And if they don't understand?"

Marek shrugged. "I will return to Earth."

"You will return sooner than you think at this moment."

The conversation broke off, especially since the Conqueror's eyes, tired after the long night journey, were already closing.

Malahuda showed him a pile of soft furs in the corner and placing a piece of cold meat and a jug of water by the bed, he slipped quietly out of the cave.

The sun, slowly following the dawn, had just risen, and was reddening the vast snow that quickly softened in the morning light. The first lights of the day burned, sparkling in tiny lumps of ice at the top of the mounds, which were called Martha's Tomb and Peter's Tomb. On the horizon, across the sea, the enormous cone of O'Tamor was rising before the eyes of the old man. It looked like it was lazily waking up from its sleep because it was still covered with a cloud from above as if with a curtain shielding the sleepy eyes from the sun. From the east a narrow strip of golden light ran like a stream of lava to the foot of the lofty mountain, into the frozen sea, but its west side was drowned in a dense blue shade. The shade was also beyond the mountain on the vast coast, but there, straight to the west, the city glittered with sun-lit windows, wrapped here and there in vapor clouds, constantly floating over the *Warm Ponds.*

Here we have a new sun, thought Malahuda, and we don't know what it will bring us. But whatever happens, it won't change the usual order of sunrise and sunset in any way, not even the waves going across the sea when the ice is gone. The wind will be able to tear the stone from the top of O'Tamor and throw it into the valley, but the greatest people's happiness or misfortune will not move a grain of sand on the water's edge ..."

Far, far to the east, where the day was already bigger, the ice in the sea was breaking and a dull, muffled rumble went around the world, with its vague echoes bouncing off the walls of the far mountain. On the other side, he heard the barely audible sounds of heavy hammers from the city flooded by the sun. They were hammering huge bronze shields hung as a sign of joy. Malahuda seemed to recognize even the sound of the trumpets blown by the west wind. The victorious visitors were apparently greeted there ...

The day was already at its fullest, and the ice had long since flowed away when the old man, looking again from the cave at the top of the hill, saw a fleet of boats sailing from the city to the island. He guessed it was a welcome retinue for the Conqueror and went to inform him about it.

Having slept and rested well, Marek was just sitting in front of the entrance to the cave and watching the plants around him, which were quickly opening to the sun, when Malahuda advised him to get ready to leave.

"Go to meet them by the sea," he said "because I don't want the greenery trampled around my house. They are coming for you, but I have nothing in common with these people as I've been alone for too long.

Then he began to say goodbye to him with tender fatherly tenderness. "We spent only a few dozen hours together," he said, "and I genuinely love you. I have thought more than once, and now I think again that I made a mistake leaving the people when you came, but then I could not do otherwise. Now, you have my blessing, and I wish you the best of luck in everything. I can't do anything more for you. Don't disagree, don't smile! You think that you are strong, but I tell you that I would say goodbye to you with the words: 'Come back here to me, when you have nothing to do there anymore', if it were not for the fact that you have another plan to return to the star shining above the deserts, from which people had once descended to the Moon. You are trying to repair our forefathers' guilt and bring us power and light: may you be happier than them and not find a grave here like them ..." Saying this, he was pointing to the mounds, hidden in the spring green.

Marek wanted to answer him, but Malahuda just nodded and, without looking back, entered his house. So, he wandered slowly to the seashore, thinking only of the old man's strange words.

The boats were getting close. It was possible to distinguish the black hulls under the dazzlingly white sails and the people on the deck. Suddenly, it occurred to Marek that Ihezal could be between these people ... A delightful wave hit his chest. Yes. Yes! She is surely there, and in a moment, she will jump out onto the green grass of the coast and walk towards him like a flower, with her lips parted in a smile. He was already smiling that she was coming here to welcome him and ran down the hill to the spot where the boats were about to land.

But only Sevin, Elem's henchman, and some of the city's elders stepped out of the pier thrown ashore. Marek glanced anxiously at the other ships: they were full of strangers, mostly irrelevant, and commoners who greeted him with a shrill scream and wreaths of green branches.

"Conqueror" Sevin began, bending so that his forehead almost touched his shins.

"Where is Elem?" Marek interrupted him hard.

"His Majesty, the ruling high priest could not come ..."

"Why? He should be here. He is my servant."

"His Highness is busy with other matters..."

Marek pushed the monk away with a quick flick of his hand and, and not listening any further, jumped into the boat.

"Sails up! To the sea! He commanded the steersman. The steersman looked at Sevin, who was still on the shore.

"To the sea! I say!" Marek repeated.

The stretched ropes creaked, and the rudder chain clanged ...

Sevin, seeing the departing Conqueror, got into another boat with his companions, and the whole flotilla, with unfurled sails, followed him towards the city.

Straight from the bay, buried inland near the former Shern castle, Marek went to the temple, not even responding to the greetings of the large crowd gathered on the shore. Once there, he immediately sent people to summon Elem to him. The high priest appeared quickly but with a face quite different from the old submissive and humble one from before. He skillfully prostrated before the Conqueror, calling him lord and ruler, but in his eyes, there was a proud gleam, lying to his servile words.

Marek remembered Malahuda's council. Looking at the former monk, he thought that it would actually be a good and smart thing to shorten his short body by the head because he would undoubtedly stand in the way of all his plans, but he rejected this involuntary thought, feeling that after such a beginning, he would not be able to stray from a bloody roads ...

So, he only asked him menacingly, not returning his greeting why he was so late.

"Conqueror," said Elem, "I rule the people and have little time." I thought you would like to come to my high priest's palace yourself and report on the expedition ..."

Blood rushed to Marek's head. However, he restrained himself and only grabbed the dwarf by his garments at the nape of his neck as if a dog taken by the skin and raised him with one hand up to his face.

"Listen," he said in a muffled voice, "Why don't you tell me, what you were doing here while I was gone? Is it true that you wanted to bargain with the Shern?"

Elem turned pale with fear and rage in this awkward and ridiculous position, but as soon as Marek, shaking him a little, set him back on the floor, he arrogantly replied: "Conqueror, I figured, that you have withdrawn from the Shern, although I only know about it for sure now, so I wanted to get some time ..."

Marek bit his mouth "Go back home," he said, "and wait for my orders. I'll call you again soon. Now I have other things ..."

Saying this, he looked around, but only after the high priest's departure he asked: "Where is Ihezal that she had not come out to greet him so far?" No one could answer him, but he was informed of imprisoned Avij's escape. At this news, Marek jumped anxiously.

"How? What?" He called people and asked, but here too, no one was able to give him a precise explanation. People were told that Malahuda's granddaughter tortured the Shern, but what happened after she had left the cellar? The people who went there later to bring food to the Shern, found empty hoops on the wall, and cut ropes hanging in them. The dagger that had been seen in Ihezal's hand was found on the table next to the burned torch. It was evident that after the girl's departure, who had accidentally left the weapon behind, the monster somehow managed to free one hand and cut the ties binding him. He took advantage of the open door and looking for him now would be futile.

Although, there was little hope for catching the fugitive, Marek immediately ordered a chase. A group of people and dogs set out, to search the entire rocky seacoast and the dense thickets on the slopes of O'Tamor. Nuzar also joined the hunters.

Meanwhile, the Conqueror went alone to look for the golden-haired Ihezal. The servants told him that she was in her rooms, but that she was sick, and that she could not see anyone. He didn't care. He pushed her maids aside and pushed the door open.

He walked through a long series of empty and cool rooms, until at last he found Ihezal in the last, small room. She was lying on the low sofa, naked and with her hair loose wearing only a wide scarf wrapped in a strange manner around her hips. She didn't even move when Marek entered, and only looked at his face with wide open eyes as if in some dull stupor.

"Ihezal! My golden bird!" The Conqueror exclaimed happily, holding out his hands to her.

She moved her pale lips soundlessly, opening her dry, dumbfounded eyes still wider.

"What is wrong with you, child?" He said meanwhile, kneeling next to her sofa and involuntarily tilting his face over her small, lilac, almost child's breast.

She slightly pushed him away with her arm. "Why only today? Why?"

She rose slowly and went to the second room, bolting the door behind her.

Marek rose from his knees in amazement. A foreboding clenched his throat, and the blood hit his temples. He stood motionless for a moment, then suddenly lunged at the door where Ihezal had disappeared and began pounding on it with his mighty fist.

"Ihezal! Ihezal! Open up!"

Nobody answered him. He grasped the ferrule and tugged at it with all his strength, but the iron did not give way. He turned, his eyes searching for some heavy object to smash the doors with and backed away in amazement.

Calm and pale Ihezal in a flowing robe was standing on the threshold of the second door, just beyond him. "What will you order me, my lord?" She asked in a strange voice, in which something quivered as if mockery combined with sadness ...

Marek did not reply at first. This girl seemed so different and strange to him at that moment that he could hardly connect the thread of his memories to the impression he had now.

"What's up with you?," he finally stuttered ...

"What will you order?" She repeated again, this time with an unexplained flirtatious smile, during which the corners of her mouth twitched a little. Marek approached her and sat down.

"I put the Shern under your guard. What has become of him?"

"I do not know."

She was standing right in front of him, her small thighs under the light robe of his knees, almost touching him. With a slow motion of her fingers, she untied the ribbon around her neck and opened the colorful, fragrant fabric.

She was naked, as before, but the scarf was always around her hips with a wide twisted curl. Suddenly Marek felt that she was taking his face in her hands and pressing it against her breast. An intoxicating scent overwhelmed him, he closed his eyes and, hungry, touched her body, feeling her sharp nails dig into the skin beyond his ears. He was about to put an arm around her when he suddenly staggered backward, pushed by her. Ihezal slipped from his hand, and he heard only a silvery mocking laugh and the slam of a closing door. He was alone again.

V

Marek was making slow progress with enacting new laws, as the old high priest had predicted. Invariably, they all stood against him. To his amazement, he noticed that enemies were springing up from everywhere, even where he least expected it.

It started right on that first day when he returned from an overseas trip. He then called for the afternoon a great assembly of the people to the temple, where he wanted to introduce to them his plan of reforms. A big crowd had gathered there, but there was some unease in it from the beginning, quite different from that godly expectation which had preceded every instance of the Conqueror's public appearance before. Indeed, people were impatient and shouted as if he had been summoned before the people and would appear to account for his actions. When he entered the pulpit of the high priests, he was greeted by a mixed cry, among which, however, only a few voices praised him.

Marek didn't care. It was urgent for him to tell the people how he wanted to arrange their life on the Moon before leaving for Earth. So, after ordering silence with his voice, when the hand movement did not work, he began to speak, outlining the existing evil that must be erased. He spoke about the unfair inequality of rights that allow one too much, binding others at every step. He talked about the open slavery and the hidden one, which makes the majority of the poor population work hard to increase the wealth of the rich. He spoke about the oppressed women, about lack of education and the governing system that needed to be changed. He told them that the government should be taken from the hands of lawless priests, and given to the people, so they may decide their own fate.

They were listening him quite calmly, occasionally only interrupting with a murmur. When he wanted to move on to the positive part of the speech and develop a plan to improve the existing relations, someone would unexpectedly ask about the fate of the overseas expedition. At such moments, there was a terrible noise, as if prepared in advance. They were calling and constantly shouting that despite all efforts, Marek could not get his words out. What was strange, that all that noise would stop as soon as Elem rose, silently sitting opposite Marek on the lofty throne under the pillars.

He was speaking in Marek's defense. At the outset, he asked the people to listen to the Conqueror's words with due reverence, for undoubtedly there would be many beneficial and useful ideas among them. Although Elem himself was the ruling high priest by the will of the people (so he said), he would not dare to speak today if he were not sure that when he spoke, he was in agreement with the Conqueror, who from the beginning unquestionably recognized his position and sanctified it.

"The Conqueror," he continued, "has done a lot for us, and we need to be thankful for it. It is true that the military expedition to the south, despite the extraordinary zeal of the army under his command and the generous sacrifice of the people who gave their blood and property, didn't accomplish everything that we expected. Nevertheless, a piece of land was conquered and, if only the Shern will be quiet in the future, new settlements can be established there.

Now the Conqueror comes out with some projects that are worth listening to. Admittedly, people who are knowledgeable about lunar relations find them too daring and extraordinary. Still, the Conqueror is the Lord, so if he chooses, he may experiment with the happiness and welfare of the people regardless how dangerous it can be."

Then he finished: "However, I believe that today you are not focused enough to listen to the advice and commands of the Blessed Conqueror, therefore I am ordering you to go home now, and we will pick the time when you will appear here again ..."

The people started pouring out of the temple with screams.

Marek was so astounded with the content and tone of Elem's speech that he even didn't try to interrupt him. He only sat on the pulpit and was looking with interest at the high priest. He noticed that when Elem was speaking, he was often looking at Sevin who standing nearby in a humble posture sometimes nodded at his words with a slight movement of his head. But when the people, after shouting praises of the high priest, were quickly leaving the temple, showing no desire to listen to Marek's teachings, he jumped to Elem and stopped him with a movement of his hand, as he was about to leave too.

"What's that supposed to mean?" He asked menacingly.

"They are leaving." Elem answered innocently.

"It is your villainy and your intrigue! I will have you whipped before the people so that they may know how you behave towards me, you dog!"

The high priest turned pale. "Do it, Conqueror," he said, "but don't expect the people to obey you afterwards ..."

Suddenly, seeing that there was almost no one left in the temple, he humbly bowed down to Marek's knees.

"Lord! You unjustly admonish and condemn your lowest servant and your faithful dog! After all, you saw the people were restless and distracted today. I did not want your words to fall on an unprepared ground. I was afraid that if they did not listen to you once, your sacred and non-lunar authority would suffer severely. It would be even more regrettable as it would mean committing a sin by the people. That is why I acted correctly making them go away today. Then you will summon them when you see fit."

Marek did not deceive himself for a moment about Elem's true intentions, but he had to agree with him that the first assembly was not at all tuned to listen to his plans with willing ear. Since he really and deeply wanted to carry out the intended reforms, he decided to choose another path that seemed to him the most appropriate for the time being. He established a committee composed of the various members of the local elders. They were expected to consider in silence, under his personal direction, all the deficiencies of their system and draw new laws. In this way they would be recommended for the people and not imposed by anyone, even by the visitor from Earth.

Elem backed out from participation in this committee, arguing that it was impossible to reconcile it with his position and duties. He sent Sevin instead to be present at all the deliberations and report them to his master. But the Conqueror was most affected by the impossibility of winning Malahuda over. The old man's resistance was so firm that all attempts to persuade him failed. He would not leave the Cemetery Island, and to all requests, he had only one answer:

"I am too tired with my long life and I am not happy to meddle where I am not needed. Leave me in peace..."

When Marek himself visited him with that request, he said: "Son, you may need me later. Let it be debated without me. If in case of need, I will back you up (I think I will do so because I think your intentions are good), nobody will say that I am supporting my case."

The deliberations didn't proceed energetically at all. From the very beginning there were many almost insurmountable difficulties. Marek sometimes felt as if there was a jinx that took the sole task of destroying everything that he did or even intended, but he decided to persevere, at least for a while. He only grumbled and became indignant more and more often, not even noticing that his anger made less and less impression on people.

At the same time, strange things began to appear in the lunar world. An unknown source started to spread exaggerated and monstrous news about the work of the committee. It made the people hostile in advance to whatever was decided there. It was said, for example, that property would be divided evenly to all citizens, but in such a way that those for whom there wouldn't be enough of land would simply be killed. In the future, the growth of families will also be regulated with drowning of surplus infants ... High priests' power will be abolished. Women will be given the most extensive freedom, so that in the future they will not need to be subject to or be faithful to their husbands. And the Mortzes will probably be equated with people ...

These and similar stories circulated among the people, stirring them up more and more, and all Marek's attempts to put an end to them failed completely.

At the same time, there was a talk of the prophet Choma's reappearance, who somehow managed to escape from the high priest's prison. Now he was jeering at the high priest's supposedly vigorous pursuit circling among people and proclaiming that the Conqueror was not the true Conqueror, but a sinful self-proclaimed man who must be disobeyed. He called the faithful to repentance and gathered a crowd that followed him from a settlement to a settlement.

The Brotherhood of Truth was not idle either. It had inexplicably lost its most eminent members, and assumed it to be Marek's doing, who had his spies and thugs everywhere, so they tried to incite the population against him. It had already been said aloud in certain circles that he was an impostor who pushed people to death in the Sherns' country to distract them from the inaccessible paradise on the other side of the Moon. Moreover, after the loss of Roda, Mataret and their companions there were no more scholars in the Brotherhood, they started to invent and spread the most fantastic assumptions. They no longer believed in the unlimited extent of the Great Desert, stating that it only encircled with its broad band the most wonderful, delicious, and fertile country.

Marek, discouraged by the failure of the plan, which he hadn't dropped only through stubbornness, was longing for a person with whom he could speak honestly and openly ... He had numerous and hidden enemies and a small handful of friends who followed him only because they still considered him a supernatural and somewhat divine being. He felt he was in a very peculiar position being forced to lie. To tell these few believers that he was really and undoubtedly just like them meant to lose the last of his allies. For even those for whom, he wanted the change: the poorest, disinherited, and poor, were the ones who more and more willingly obeyed evil promptings. Whether it was a fear of losing favor with the powerful, in whose overthrow they did not believe, or simply not understanding their best interests, they didn't want to help Marek in any way.

Then only at certain times, he was gathering a small crowd of his friends, and, thinking of the seed for sowing that would remain here after he left, he preached to them for a long time about all good things, elevated them, and taught them.

Ihezal was not involved in these meetings. Changed beyond recognition, she was now apparently avoiding Marek, or again, in some crazy fits she teased his senses, only to suddenly slip away from him with a mocking laugh on her lips. Marek began to really want her company, but the stranger and wilder she became, the more he longed for the girl that he had met at the beginning.

He did not want to admit aloud to himself that she was one of the reasons, perhaps the most important, for which he was still on the

Moon, taking his time not to depart ...

One day, after a violent quarrel with Elem, who, feeling almost all the people behind him, began to reject even apparent submission, he went out to the roof of the temple to rest a bit and to watch the wide sea. Unexpectedly he found Ihezal there. She was standing there pensively leaning against the railing. The sea hummed loudly below and drowned out his footsteps, or she was so lost in her thoughts that she couldn't hear him ...

Only when he came close enough to her that he could touch her shoulder with his outstretched hand did she suddenly turn and scream out loud in terror, seeing him close behind her. She was standing in the corner and could not get out, without passing by Marek, then she pressed herself only deeper and was looking at him with fearful eyes. Marek took a step back, opening a free passage for her.

"Ihezal, do you want to leave?"

"I have to," she whispered dropping her head but didn't budge. Her face showed pain, but it was quiet as before when she used to spend long hours with the Conqueror listening to his strange words about Earth and stars.

"What is wrong with you?" Marek asked after a while in a soft voice, as if being afraid of frightening her with a louder word.

She said nothing, except her shoulders suddenly trembled, and two large tears hanging from her eyelashes, fell slowly onto her pale cheeks.

Marek took her hand and pulled her lightly toward him. She did not resist him and sat down on the indicated stone bench. He now threw himself on the floor like before, and resting his chin in his hands, looked at her for a long time. She withstood his gaze for some time, only her pupils were cloudy and dim. Finally, she lowered her eyelids.

"Ihezal," The Conqueror began, "why are you avoiding me now? I need you so much ..."

She shrugged her shoulders slightly.

So he continued: "You were once for me, like a golden and heavenly but tame bird that sits on one's shoulder. I had you close, and it was enough for me to reach out ..."

She looked up at him with sad eyes. "Why didn't you reach out for me then, Conqueror?"

"I do not know; I do not know! Maybe I wasn't feeling that bad yet, maybe I wasn't so lonely ... Today I have to pretend to be strong in front of those opposing me, and to deny my humanity in front of my friends. Still, although I was born on the distant Earth, and although I am bigger than you all in my height and thinking, I am the same person as you are, and I am alone, alone! Ihezal, be with me!"

"Too late," she said soundlessly, "too late. You could have had me then and forever, and now I am so terribly far away from you ... Escape, escape while there is time. Go back to Earth!"

He stretched out his hands to her, but she pushed them away slightly.

"Oh! Why have you hurt me so much!" She said again after a while, with an eerie ferocity in her voice, "why did you abuse me so much? Why did you not look at me when I was in front of your eyes, or why did you not drive me away immediately but let me ..."

She broke off suddenly and looked into his eyes with crazy pupils. Malicious laughter was making her lips twitch.

"There is nothing between us, Conqueror ..." she said. "Or maybe I am just the Soul of the Moon people and you needed to have me in your hand? ... You missed the right moment, and now you reaching for a bird that has already flown away, ho! Ho! It flew away ... And now you – the Conqueror ..." She laughed dryly and hideously.

"Ihezal!"

"Go away! I don't want to look at you, I can't! I cannot!" She repeated, falling to her knees.

A terrible fear showed in her eyes, and she stretched out her trembling hands to him. "Have mercy on me! Go away! Go away! Don't let me see you again! Let me forget ..."

Marek got up slowly. Endless sorrow filled his soul and almost paralyzed his movements.

For a brief moment, he was standing in front of the girl with some pitying, good intention to reach out to her ... but a great weariness fell on him. He turned and walked slowly towards the stairs leading down from the platform. She could still hear his footsteps on the stone steps, getting more and more hollow ...

After he had left, she suddenly threw herself on the stone floor with a terrible, unrestrained sobbing. She was trembling like a leaf in the wind, and she hit her light head against the ground, tugging on her hair and her clothes with her hands.

She slowly calmed down. She lay motionless and lifeless for a while longer, and only a rare fleeting shudder, violently tugging at her arms, showed that she was alive. At last, she stood up as if still asleep, with a deathly pale face and blue lips. Her sunken eyes, with dark circles under them, were open wide, and a vertical line cramped on her smooth forehead. She began to automatically pull herself together, rearranging her clothes and smoothing her tattered hair ...

Finally, she went down to the temple. Here she found the Conqueror talking to several people, including the commander of the high-priest palace guard. Marek did not look at her, he was busy talking, so she stood aside to listen.

There was a talk of terrible events which had been happening in the city and the surrounding area for some time. People died unexpectedly, especially when they walked away from the houses by themselves, but it also happened that a whole family was murdered at home. All of them had blue marks from being touched by the Shern's killer hands. There was no doubt that this was the runaway Avij's doing, who was apparently hiding nearby and only coming out at a good time to hunt. Guards were set up and manhunts were organized. They searched all the area, every group of brushes, and every bend of coastal rocks, and always in vain.

Apparently, the monster seemed to be hiding somewhere close, as evidenced by the main area of its operations which extended into the city. The people were completely helpless in the face of this mysterious disaster always hanging over them. Now, they were angry at the Conqueror who didn't allow Avij to be killed but imprisoned him instead.

Marek felt that this one hidden Shern was more dangerous than the entire squads of Shern in the country overseas, where it was possible at least to fight them openly, but he could not find a solution.

Nobody thought that the animal would be able to gain voluntary help among the people, but it was feared that they might have been forced by threat, and people had already begun to suspect each other. They looked at one another with distrust and fear. Finally, all resentment turned against Nuzar, whom the Conqueror still had with him. The damned Mortz, was probably protecting and serving Avij! They wanted to kill him, having first forced him to confess where the Shern was hiding.

This is what they came to Marek with now and demanded that he would hand Nuzar over to them. Ihezal heard the Conqueror resist this firmly, allowing only to lock the Mortz up for a while under the strictest guard to try and see if the Shern was in any communication with him, and if he would then risk being captured without his help. .. He, the Conqueror, would not allow torment, especially since he was deeply convinced of the Mortz's innocence who, like a dog, was constantly at his leg.

The deputies did not accept that as a sufficient response, and they were just starting to quarrel with Marek when Ihezal, smiling slightly, left the temple, heading towards her rooms.

When she found herself in the corridor, she suddenly turned to the right and, checking if no one was watching her, pushed with her full strength on one of the stone slabs in the wall. It gave way slowly, opening a dark passage in the wall, and closed right after the girl disappearing into it.

Ihezal was running in the dark, every few steps counting boulders protruding from the wall with her outstretched hand. When she counted seven, she turned to her right again and began to search for something on the damp floor with her hands. At last she felt the edge of the opening and the first step of the steeply descending stairway. She slipped down on them, and after a short journey through the winding passages, she found herself in spacious natural caves, dimly lit by daylight. They stretched just below the gardens, connecting the temple with a rocky seashore. Daylight slipped in here through several covered cracks in the vertical wall of the inaccessible rock hanging above the sea.

The existence of these caves was a secret, carefully guarded in the high priesthood, and no one knew about them now, except Malahuda's granddaughter ... Standing in a huge cave, full of fantastic stalactites, she struck her hands three times. At this sign, Avij appeared in one of the side galleries. He had a purple cloak on his shoulders, the ends of his wings on his chest, and an old golden sacred hoop of the high priest's head, crossing his forehead low, just above the pair of upper eyes.

Ihezal began to tremble all over her body, and he, like the strange royal Satan, approached her and stretched out his terrible white hands. The girl stood limp, hands down, as Avij began to take off her clothes. He tossed her luxurious cape and an expensive-embroidered bottom robe to the ground, and when, at last, tearing off the last white tunic, he untied the shawl wrapped around her hips, two hideous marks appeared on the girl's snow white and sheen sides made by the grip of the Shern's burning hands...

Then she fell on her face before him, and he, spreading his black wings wide on both sides, stepped up with one foot on her fair head, spreading his claws into the scattered gold of her hair.

VI

The news of Malahuda's death shocked the Conqueror like a thunderbolt. Everything was going as badly as possible, and Marek decided he would just make one last attempt, before leaving the Moon: to summon Malahuda to come out of his solitude at last and to support him with his old authority. Just then a fisherman, usually serving as a messenger to the old high priest, informed him that he was already dead. He had reportedly been killed, the fisherman said, trembling all over his body.

At first Marek assumed that the crime had been committed on Elem's orders because he was still somehow threatened by his former rival. So, he stormed into the palace of the high priest and dragging the trembling monk out of the middle of the meeting that was just taking place, began to curse him and threaten him with immediate death. The former monk, not knowing anything, was dumbfounded with terror. When after some time he understood what it was about, he showed such astonishment and swore so sincerely that Marek began to believe in his innocence ... He let him go, threatening that he would investigate the whole thing. He said that if there was even a shadow of Elem's guilt, he will be in spite of his guard and in spite of all the people, punished so terribly that, as long as the Moon exists, people will remember the Conqueror's revenge with horror and fear. In the meantime, he had a boat ready to go to the Cemetery Island and see what he could do.

On a glorious morning, the Conqueror with a fisherman and a single oarsman approached the small green harbor where Ihezal had landed visiting her grandfather for the first time. Weird bushes and trees, with long branches descending to the water, stood by the shore, full of reflection and sadness in the extremely quiet air. Below them, one boulder protruded from the green turf, sloping like a falling wall or a gigantic gravestone ... Their boat had just landed on the shore next to this rock. Marek was the first to jump ashore, and while the others were busy tying the chain to the stump sticking out over the water, he was already running up.

Something flashed in the trampled grass beneath the rock. He paused and picked up a gold-colored dress clasp with a piece of ribbon from the ground, still hanging by it. It was small and flat, decoratively shaped with a large stone in the center. He recognized the jewel that he had sent once to the golden-haired Ihezal from the first spoils taken from the Shern ...

Meanwhile, the other two having secured the boat, approached him. So, he quickly put the clasp in his jacket and the three of them set off along the road past the hills to Malahuda's cave. When they got close, the hungry and wild dogs cut off their way, and they rushed furiously, especially at Marek, although they had shown a friendly disposition towards him in the past. Marek, when the soothing words did not work anymore, he aimed his stick at one of them, and at that moment the other threw himself under his raised arm and grasped his shirt with his teeth. Marek sneered at it, leaving rags of torn cloth in the mouth of the furious animal. Suddenly both dogs, leaving Marek alone, rushed fiercely to tear the cloth. A buckle with a piece of purple ribbon shone among the scraps ...

The Conqueror didn't sense the dog's behavior as being glad to get rid of some intrusive attackers. On edge he ran towards the entrance of the cavern. Malahuda's corpse was lying here at its entrance, as it had fallen, on its back over a boulder. His eyes were glassy, half-open, and his mouth parted in the final scream. It was clear that he was attacked and killed before he had time to try to defend himself.

There was no blood anywhere, nor was there any trace of the blow on the head. So, Marek ordered taking his clothes off to find a wound. As soon as they unbuttoned his brown leather overcoat, both helpers stepped back in fear. The old man's body showed the hideous blue stains, like the other people killed by the Shern. Marek bit his lips in silence.

Soon they began to dig a grave among the mounds that marked the resting place of the first people on the Moon. They wrapped the body in fabrics found in the cave and covered it with soil, pressing it down with large boulders so that, his starved dogs would not get into the corpse.

The Conqueror silently completed these last rites, and he was still silent as the boat made its way back through the tranquil waves towards the city.

He met some people in the marina, who informed him that while he was away some news had come from overseas. Indeed, he soon saw the messengers sent by Jeret. They had already arrived on the ice at dawn, as they said, but they were stopped by the high priest's guards, not allowing them to appear immediately before the Conqueror. The letters Jeret had written were taken from them, as well, so that now that they have finally been released, they don't even know what to say. They can tell only as much as they have seen with their own eyes, but it will not be much or nothing very good.

So, Marek took them to the temple with him to speak freely. On the way from the marina, he was suddenly puzzled by an unusual commotion. People were hurriedly running and throwing some distrustful and fearful glances at him. There were larger clusters of them in the squares, which, however, parted quickly as soon as he approached them. Still, Marek was too busy thinking about Jeret and what the messengers would report to him to pay more attention to it.

The main door to the temple was closed, but he entered through a side entrance, not closed tight enough to block his strong arms. Anyway, he did not pay attention to that either. Apparently, it was not known yet that he had returned, so his apartment was closed to unauthorized visitors.

When alone with the envoys in a spacious room outside the main hall, he began to immediately question them about the fate of the crews left behind the sea and the newly arrived settlers. The messengers did not really have much good to say. The fight there was fierce: the people, plagued by the constant attacks of the Shern, who, not daring to appear in an open fight, harassed them with guerrilla warfare, had to withdraw from the farthest posts to save the rest of the conquered country. Jeret's idea was to form a light chain of troops stationed in defensive settlements that would be in constant contact with each other. To accomplish that he needed more people, which he was still short of despite the strong influx from the old countries. Meanwhile, they defended themselves as much as possible, setting up expeditions to fight the Shern from time to time, to keep them in constant terror. But all this tired the people so much that they almost had enough. There were many who spoke loudly that they should leave this ungrateful country and return to the old towns overseas as soon as possible. This is what Jeret supposedly wrote about in the missing letters. By word of mouth, he only ordered them to inform the Conqueror, that he might still be at peace about the fruit of his labor, for as long as he, Jeret, was alive, the country would be maintained. He also bid the Conqueror to continue the good work in the old settlements and make the promised laws there, before his departure from the Moon to Earth.

Marek was pensive after hearing this message. The messengers were to return with a new party of settlers, and he promised to give them letters for Jeret, only begging them not to lose them. So, he immediately began to write.

He mentioned the difficulties with which he had to struggle here, and that the people opposed to a new order would block his every attempt. Sometimes he was losing hope that he would accomplish anything without the use of force, but so far, he didn't want to use force.

"I still counted on Malahuda's help and authority," he wrote at last, "but the old man is no longer alive ... He died mysteriously, apparently from the hands of the fugitive Shern Avij. I am now alone, and I have only two paths to choose from. ... Give up everything and go back to Earth or call you with a handful of my faithful comrades from the battles in that country and make order here, removing all those who are in the way. I still hesitate and can't choose. I'm sad. Despite all the grudge which you felt for me, or maybe you still do, I believe you because I know that you are devoted with all your soul, not to me, but to the cause. And I trust that if I give you a sign: "Come!" - you will come, and you will stand by my side, but I don't know if this is what I should do ... "

He continued in this manner, finally outlining a detailed plan for Jeret regarding the orders he intended to introduce.

"If by chance" he concluded "I am forced to leave the Moon without accomplishing anything, let this at least be left after me, all that I am telling my few friends here, and what I am writing to you now. When the time is right, come yourself and gather my remaining friends and continue what I have started. Maybe you really need to do everything yourselves, and I, a stranger from a distant star, should not try to do it for you. I don't know what else to say at the moment and the lunar days are long. Before this one ends, many things may still change, and a lot may be decided ..."

He gave the letters to the messengers who bade farewell to him in a hurry, because at sunset they were to go to the seaside settlements on that side, and only at night go south from there on the ice.

After their departure, Marek closed the door to the temple and walked alone in long strides around the hall, pondering. He understood this more and more clearly that it was the last chance to try a different path on his own than the one he had taken so far if he did not want to admit defeat and give way. After all, he thought, there would be many among the people who would have understood their best interests and followed him, were it not for the deceptive Elem's plots. Indeed, Malahuda was right. It was necessary not to wait, and not to look for pretext, but return victorious from overseas, to order Elem to be executed immediately or imprisoned at least, and perhaps then everything would have been different.

He gritted his teeth and furrowed his brows. "Yes, he or I! He said aloud to himself, "there is no alternative!"

He almost wished now that he had written to Jeret at once to come without delay with a handful of armed men, but at last he thought that he would be able to handle things himself in the meantime. He threw back the hair falling on his forehead and, with his head held high, turned towards the temple door.

There was the buzz of a large crowd in the square. The Conqueror, too lost in his thoughts, did not notice it at all, although for some time he could hear them well and inside the building, especially since sometimes noisy and prolonged shouts erupted from it. Only when Marek opened the door, locked from inside with the iron bolts, he heard these voices clearly. He did not wonder at first where they came from and what they meant but was glad that the people were congregated, and he would not need to summon them to speak to them.

So, he went out to the raised porch in front of the temple with a sure step and called right away to the crowd to be quiet, because he wanted to speak. Indeed, the deep silence followed but only for one blink, because before he could even open his mouth, mixed voices burst out from everywhere, like the roar of a rough sea.

It was almost impossible to understand something from the muddle of shouts. Marek only caught some loose, louder shouted words, all attacking him. Some were screaming about the murder of Malahuda, about the Shern sent against the people, about the army left to perish, and even here and there were insults, especially from the followers of the Prophet Choma and members of the Brotherhood of Truth.

Marek was looking calmly at the crowd, wondering what impression it would make on the people if he called Elem now and crushed him before their eyes ... He already knew that at this moment he could not count on any help or obedience from anyone, and he himself would have to perform that disgusting act. He was ready now. He looked to the side, towards the steps of the new high-priestly palace and saw Elem, surrounded by his retinue of servants and associates. He took a deep breath, to yell at him in the same way as a master calling his dog to his feet ready, and if he did not obey, to make his way through this crowd and just squeeze Elem ...

Instead, his agitation was soon replaced by sadness and powerlessness. The futility of the intended act, the futility of all his endeavors, stood before his eyes vividly all at once - and only a great, unfathomable longing burst forth, screaming in his soul, and like a little child stretching out his hands to his mother: "To Earth! To Earth!" ...

He sat down on the boulder formerly used by the high priests for the podium, and with a dull weary gaze, he looked around the crowd. People were silenced for a moment, and he asked his thoughts rather than the people, saying: "What do you want from me? ..."

Apparently, the program of these people's assembly was pre-arranged by some wise organizers, for the tumult was slowly coming to an end, and some activists were hushing the crowd and forming it into smaller groups ... After a while, delegations began to appear in front of the Conqueror. There were merchants and those who owned the land, the priests who were in the villages, and the owners of various shops, bakers, and butchers. They were followed by craftsmen of all kinds and peasants who worked hard all day, town laborers, fishermen, pearl hunters, and even the half-wild hunters from the forested slopes of O'Tamor. There were also women who, gathered in a separate group, moved towards the Conqueror's feet, a bit fearfully, pushing each other with their elbows.

Marek was staring motionlessly at this colorful procession. For some time he had the strange impression that he wasn't witnessing the facts unfolding before his eyes, but the memories of some long-lived and experienced things flowing through his soul. He felt as if he had already returned to Earth and his thoughts were still wandering over this lunar country ...

He almost frowned when he heard a voice directed at him. The leaders of the merchants and landowners were standing before him and, stretching out their hands, shouted:

"Conqueror! Leave us the peace we used to have! Leave our property in our hands as it was gained through generations! Don't destroy our prosperity!" ...

The priests were coming right behind them shouting with raised voices accustomed to initiating a song before the people: "Conqueror! Mighty terrestrial stranger! Do not touch the laws that we have worked out for centuries! Do not put power in the hands of the dumb and inexperienced!"

"They all walked in front of his knees and asked him to leave everything as it was. So, the owners of the shops did not want to change their wages, saying that it would ruin them and destroy all craftsmanship. Fishermen and hunters refused to donate, even the smallest amounts for the general benefit. The farm and town laborers pleaded not to let the mighty, who had their lives in their hands and gave them an opportunity to earn a living, get angry with them. Finally, women fell at his feet, begging for permission to keep the previous female reverence, that is, to be subordinate to their husbands at home and to sin secretly ..."

He was listening to all these speeches sad and bitter. His eyes looked far beyond the groups bent at his feet and went looking in the crowd for people who would think otherwise and were ready to object to the speeches of self-proclaimed leaders. He felt that if he now saw such people in the crowd, despite his weariness and suffocating sadness, he would get up and smash those bent with his foot, and gather friends who would go forward with him ...

Instead he saw only crude and agitated faces, impatiently awaiting his answer. He saw fierce and possessed people, who if he didn't listen to the pleading words, were ready to break out in open rebellion against him. He felt that was what they wanted, eager, like every mob for shouting, insults, fights, and confusion.

He laughed bitterly in his soul and with an infinite gaze full of contempt and ... pity at the same time looked at the speakers begging him. He saw blunt or cunning faces, dim eyes, in which the reflection of fanaticism had already started burning. He saw, fleshy lips and protruding cheekbones of those held back in spiritual development.

Suddenly he was filled with a deep disgust and a terrible, ineffable, caustic longing: "To Earth! To Earth!". With a dead gesture of his hand, he pushed aside these leaders who were pressed to the knees, wanting to kiss his robes in the hypocritical humility.

"Go away! Do as you like. I am going back to Earth ..."

A shout of joy was his answer. He no longer listened to them, stepping quickly back into the temple ...

Here, however, he wasn't left alone. The high priest Elem's envoys followed him, apologizing that he himself was not showing up, but that he was busy at the moment. He had ordered them to come here, so in his highest high priestly name they would express a true sorrow, even despair, that the blessed Conqueror intended to leave the Moon so soon. He told them to ask at the same time what his orders were, which the high priest was ready to fulfill immediately with his ordinary obedience and submission towards him, the divine man.

Hearing these insincere words, Marek didn't even laugh anymore. He didn't care, and he just wanted to get rid of the pesky intruders as quickly as possible. So he told them that His High Priestly Highness had nothing to command, and that he only wanted to be given a few people today, who would go to the Polar Country inform the guard of his car that he would be arriving there tomorrow. For he had sent a few trusted people from across the sea, but they have not yet returned, and he does not know whether the guards are keeping everything in order, as he had commanded them before.

After the deputies had left, he began to get ready for the travel. He organized his notes and arranged photos, packing it all slowly and systematically. He had more than enough time as it was a long day, and the night was still ahead of him. He thought he had once promised himself to take the gaged and bound Shern and a few lunar people with him to Earth. He smiled now at that thought. The Shern had escaped, and he was fed up with the lunar people!

He would only take Jeret, but he was the most needed here and too good to be stared at on Earth like an oddity ... He laughed silently: maybe he should take Elem and present him in a cage later, but this sinister and malicious thought quickly faded in him. He sat up and propped his head on his hand.

He remembered the same Elem as he had first seen him: in a gray, monk robe, with a shaved head, with the fiery eyes of a fanatic who waited, with the living and the dead, together in steadfast faith that the Conqueror would come ... Is he the same man? What about the others, and all those who waited? Were they calm, meek, believers?... After all, Malahuda, welcoming him, said: "You have destroyed all that was - build now ...". What happened!?

He sprang up and grabbed his head in a sudden fear with his hands. He saw clearly what he had at times only sensed, that his coming to the Moon, instead of being a blessing, had become a terrible and irretrievable defeat. It became a violent intrusion into the natural, slow development of this world, or, at least, the people already at home here. This is what turned everything upside down, unleashed passions, and revealed the hidden meanness more bluntly ...

He shrugged his arms: "Ha, tough! It probably had to happen this way."

But he felt that this fatalistic sentence uttered by his words served only to drown out the thought that was saying something else ...and this thought ...Ihezal ...

Yes, that name had been crying in him for a long time, from the moment he thought about returning, already irrevocable ...

"Oh, bird, my golden bird!" A terrible sorrow so potently disturbed his insides, that he bit his hand with his teeth so as not to scream ..."Forgive me, forgive me ..." he began to whisper to himself after a while, as if she was standing in front of him. He was not able to clearly realize what he was apologizing for, or to define his actual or imaginary guilt. Still, he felt that he was guilty of the destruction of a dream more beautiful than all rainbows and a defilement of pure things by simply not taking them in his hands and pressing to his heart. And so, he was also guilty for a lost life, maybe even for the lost ... love ...

A selfish thought kept telling him that he had done nothing wrong, and he did not even know where this strange change had come from in the girl, and what it was about. He felt, contrary to this thought, that it had been up to him to make her the most fragrant flower, and that now she changed into something so incomprehensible and terrible...

He wanted to drown out all these internal dilemmas with his work and the preparation for the trip and his thought of the Earth was joyful, but his work was slow, and the memory of the Earth was covered with some dead gray fog before his eyes.

In solitude, he passed the time until the late evening, when the sun began to bend to the west and blush in the sky. He was staring at the sun through the reddened panes of the windows when he was disturbed by the knocking of the door, first slight, then more and more insistent. He got up and opened.

He saw Elem before him. He was in the solemn high priesthood robes, in an ancient high cap with two censers in his hand. Behind Elem he saw, on the porch and on the wide stairs, a colorful retinue of elders and dignitaries, who were joined by the enormous crowd in the back, filling the entire square. As soon as Marek appeared at the threshold, the high priest fell on both knees before him and began to wave the censors, surrounding him with a thick, fragrant smoke. Other members of the retinue followed His Majesty's example, and the people who could no longer kneel in the because of the crowd, bowed their heads, greeting the Conqueror with a long shout.

Then high priest sang, bowing continuously:" Blessed be you, my lord, who arrived from Earth to be the joy to our eyes, who are leaving us! O-ha!"

"O-ha!" The crowd echoed behind him with a mournful groan.

"Blessed be you, the Conqueror, who has smitten the Shern and put power into the hands of man! Our hearts are crying that you will be gone! O-ha!"

"O-ha! O-ha!" The crowd groaned.

"You have given us peace, and wisdom has flowed from your mouth, that we might be enlightened! Why are you leaving us now, poor orphans, returning too soon to the radiant Earth? O-ha! O-ha!"

"O-ha!"

"We bring our thanks to you ..."

Marek turned and entered the temple, slamming the heavy door behind him.

His eyes, blinded by the sun on the porch, directly on his face, were wandering at first in the darkness that covered the enormous hall ... He did not know whether it was illusion or reality: there in the background stood Ihezal against a black pulpit with a golden inscription ... He had not seen her for a long time, almost from that fateful day on the roof platform. He approached her now slowly.

"Ihezal! I am returning to Earth ..."

"I know you intend to return ..."

In the twilight, he noticed that her eyes were frightened and as if crazed, and there was a frozen smile similar to a twist.

"Ihezal!"

She looked around quickly. Some barely audible rustle from the pulpit ...

With the frozen mask on her face as if under the force of a some-one's will, she opened the robe on her chest with her trembling hands.

"Come to me ..."

Suddenly she stretched her arms out in front of her." No! No! Run away from me! She began to call in a muffled voice, "call the peo-ple here and go away!" Have mercy on me and over yourself! Run away! Go back to Earth!"

He grabbed her by the outstretched hand. "Girl! What's with you?!"

He heard a rustle again, and Ihezal turned pale, an expression of terrible dread reflected in her eyes.

"Come," she said soundlessly, "hide your face here, on my breast, bend down ... My body smells and is beautiful - like death ..."

At that moment, the side door opened; a few people slipped shyly into the temple. Ihezal noticed them and gave a half-scream of terror and joy and ran away quickly. Marek turned reluctantly towards the newcomers. They humbly approached him and bowed their heads to greet him: "Greetings, master!"

They were his few students who came to bid him farewell, and who were really sad. So, he sat down with them on the floor at the foot of the pulpit and began talking. At one point it seemed to him that a black shape flashed in the darkness beyond him, disappearing quickly in the passages leading to the former high priest's palace, but it was appar-ently only an illusion ...

The students were crying. So, he consoled them, explaining that he had to go away, because his longer stay here would do noth-ing good, and he believed that they were the grain he had left here for sowing. He believed that he would yield a harvest after centuries ... the resentment of the mighty against him will pass when he slips from their sight. At the same time, he is already terribly tired and longing for his home, which is on the shining star above the Great Desert ...

They began to ask him about many things, and ask his advice as what they were to do when he was no longer here, and demand that he promised them that he would return one day ...

They were talking in low voices in the falling dusk, when sud-denly knocks and terrified voices calling for the Conqueror were heard again at the door. Marek stood up reluctantly to open up.

At the threshold, the envoys, recently sent to the Polar Country, were standing with fearful faces.

"Lord, your missile is gone!"

At first Marek did not understand this terrible news.

"What? What?!"

"Your missile is gone, my lord!" They replied.

Apparently, this news had spread out before the people, for there was trouble and confusion throughout the city. Groups formed in squares and streets and shocked people were loudly discussing the disappearance of the Conqueror's vehicle.

Marek was standing unable to speak as if crushed by a thunderbolt.

PART FOUR

There are three accounts of the death of a man once called the Conqueror, who came out of nowhere during the times of Malahuda the high priest, and was publicly executed during the reign of his successor Elem. The oldest of these accounts comes from the time when Sevin, having ordered the strangling of his predecessor Elem, succeeded him on the high priest's chair. At that time, the memory of the Conqueror was not yet holy, because only at the end of his reign Sevin ordered him to be worshiped as a prophet and martyr.

The second, much later account, was written by the historian Omilka, an excellent scholar who for a long time was the chairman of the Brotherhood of Truth.

Regarding the third account, opinions are divided. Some attribute it to be very old, claiming that it is the work of one of the friends and disciples of the executed Conqueror. Others, on the other hand, believe that it was created in more recent times, from legends and oral traditions passed down through the generations.

All of these three accounts agree more or less in the description of the events accompanying the death of the man called the Conqueror, but their views on the person himself differ so greatly that we consider it appropriate to quote all three here, without giving priority to any of them.

The story from the first half of the reign of high priest Sevin comes out as the first in chronological order:

I

A true story about the ignominious execution of the infamous felon who pretended to be the one announced by prophets as the Conqueror and was severely but justly punished for his fraud.

Be cautious reader, that you learn from these writings! The high priest Elem was rightly strangled by the command of his Ruling Highness, the holy Sevin, for he had done a lot of evil not limited to the summoning of the self-proclaimed Conqueror and the dissolution of the holy order of the Waiting Brothers. The High Priest Sevin, with the advice of Choma, the blessed old man and the prophet, reinstated the brotherhood and subjected it to the immediate authority of the ruling high priests, thus securing it for centuries against unwise attempts. During this Elem's (may his name be forgotten!) rule the man called the

416

Conqueror was executed, but not because of the advice of an unworthy high priest, but by the will of a people outraged by his evil deeds. That man caused a lot of confusion in the whole country and entangled the people in a difficult war with the Shern, which only thanks to the extraordinary courage and bravery of the ranks commanded by him did not end with defeat. He pretended that he wanted to return to Earth, from where he claimed to have arrived, although it was much more likely that he was a Mortz of an enormous height. He wanted to buy control over the Shern, his fathers, with the people's blood, and only when he failed to do so, did he try to control men. His association with the Mortzes is also a proof of his impure background. He was even close to one named Nuzar, who remained faithful to him until his last breath and died with him. In addition, even though fighting the Shern, he protected them as much as he could because of his ingrained inclination.

Well, this man, having failed to acquire power over the Shern, pretended that he wanted to return to Earth. He thought that the people would stop him by force as their benefactor and protector and make him their king. However, those calculations failed, as besides the unworthy high priest Elem, who was apparently in a secret partnership with the Conqueror, no one even tried to persuade him to stay. People saw how much evil his perverse and unwise innovations could cause.

He made a spectacle of a solemn farewell, and in the meantime he sent some men to the Polar Country, where he himself had set up a huge and useless iron pipe, persuading the gullible that it was the vehicle in which he had come from Earth, and with which he could leave. He told those men that they should check what was inside the pipe, and that they should let him know at once, if they found nothing. He himself marked the day for his farewell so that the messengers could return to him at that time.

So, they came back and told him that there was nothing in the pipe, of which the alleged Conqueror, already knew. However, when he heard the news, he feigned a great commotion and began to shout that his vehicle had been stolen, and that he could not return to Earth. All of this was arranged and done to make people believe that he was reluctantly staying on the Moon forced to do so only by necessity. To make this more convincing, for a time he showed severe depression and even tried to build a new vehicle, but nothing came of it.

Then, his secret intentions surfaced not much later. When after some time, he noticed that he had lost his former authority among the people, he put aside all scruples and pretenses, and stood in all the shamelessness of his true being before the eyes of the people from whom he had only experienced good.

He summoned a great assembly, and when the people, more curious than obedient, appeared, and made his famous speech. He then declared that since he was forced to stay on the Moon, he did not want to sit on his hands, but would do the thing, he was destined to by fate, from which he almost departed, discouraged by the difficulties. Since, he had no other choice, and therefore he would not hesitate, but carry out what he had intended, and if he couldn't do it with their cooperation, he would do it by force. Everyone would have to listen to him because he wanted it so.

From then on, he just began to show who he really was, and what he could do. He picked some henchmen to work with him, and when his perverse and foolish laws were not accepted, he began to oppress the people and forced them to obey him with fear.

In the former temple, which he had defiled, turning it into his home, he established his adjutant court. It was comprised of rogues like himself, with whose help he planned to take over the whole lunar land that was inhabited by people. However, he faced unexpected resistance, and that slowly drove him mad. Stern and immoral, he marked his self-proclaimed reign with his blood. Nobody was safe from him; he wanted to change everything and did not grant anybody the benefit of natural rights. He took away from the venerable men their various fields, supposedly planning to give them to a community of farmers to work on. In fact, he did it in order to weaken the powerful who could effectively resist him. He also caused a similar confusion in all the factories and ordered the mob not to pay the rent for their housing because, he said, everyone had the right to have a roof over their heads. The mob, however, was wiser than he was, and did not act against the beneficent owners of those houses. They knew that they would stand longer than the Conqueror, who claimed to be the protector of the miserable, but he himself profited from all kinds of pillage.

For this indomitable man did not hold back on anything, let alone pleasures with women. At that time, there lived a girl named Ihezal who was the granddaughter of the former high priest Malahuda who was also said to have been strangled in his hermitage at the Conqueror's behest. This girl, whose memory is rightly venerated today for her great purity of morals, had the misfortune to catch the eye of the pretender and was often harassed by him. She resisted him with a brave heart to the end, and neither force nor promises could force her to succumb to him.

The resoluteness of that virgin made him so mad and frenzied that, wanting to make up for her resistance, he began to bring various women to himself, mostly the loose ones although he did not let the honest ones pass him either. Supposedly converting them, he celebrated sexually debauched orgies with them, the details of which are not even suitable to be discussed here. Through his secret spies he also learned which women had once fallen into the hands of the Shern and had given birth to Mortzes, and he invited them to himself, enjoying their impure company.

It must also be said that apart from a few Mortzes, including his most favorite already mentioned Nuzar, he also had a Shern, a former governor Avij at his place. This malicious Shern, whom he had hidden on the temple grounds so that no one knew about his existence for a long time, was brought up at night at his command to kill people and caused all sorts of filth. All this became clear only after the death of this alleged Conqueror.

Finally, the people's patience ran out. That bane and menace finally had to be removed. All the more worthy citizens of the lunar community had long spoken about it, and the prophet Choma, an inspired old man, echoed them, calling for a holy war against that fraud. However, since there was no desire to shed blood in vain, for it was expected that the Conqueror would defend himself, it was decided to catch him by deception, preferably in his sleep, and to put him before a judge.

The criminal apparently sensed what was going on, because just before the night, when the plan was to be completed, he left the temple with his entire court and prepared to leave the city, saying that he was going to a deserted area to establish a new state according to his wishes.

He was not allowed to do so, though, as it was rightly feared that his country would be a worse evil and a greater danger to order and peace than the Shern's immediate neighborhood.

Thus, the fate of the criminal would be fulfilled in the place where he had committed so many atrocities. The city gates were closed, so as not to let him out of it, and when he wanted to break them by force (he had very strong hands), when the previously instructed messengers ran to him, as if from the high priest. The priest supposedly wanted him to return quickly to the temple, because the elders and the high priest himself wanted to have an important talk with him. The Conqueror did not trust them much, because he felt his belt to check if he had his firearm with him. He was probably ashamed to show fear or take his guards with him because he was overconfident in his extraordinary strength. Not wanting to refuse the summons, lest it be said that he was rejecting the chance for an agreement which he himself had been calling for, he told his followers to wait at the gates for him. Then he turned towards the city center, having only Nuzar at his side as faithful as a dog.

However, he did not get far when, from behind the corners of the narrow street, ropes were suddenly thrown on him, and he was soon thrown onto the pavement. He tried to defend himself and called Nuzar to get his followers standing at the gates, not knowing that at the moment they were already surrounded and captured by the army. The Mortz, like a mad dog, threw himself at the people, and when his hands were tied behind his back, he bit whomever he caught with his teeth.

Meanwhile, the alleged Conqueror was lying on the ground, tied with ropes and unable to move, but the people were afraid to come closer to him, still scared by his enormous form. Finally, when they saw that he was tied well so that he could not free himself or move, and would do no harm to anyone, they began to approach him more boldly. Some kicked him with their feet or pulled at the hair of the huge head lying limply on the stones. It was decided to hold the trial on the same day to end the menace before the night came.

The high priest, Elem, excused himself from judging, as he was probably ashamed that he himself had brought this criminal and sacrilegious heretic to power and wanted Sevin, who was not yet a high priest, to act in his place. Sevin, an incredibly wise and virtuous but modest man, refused for a long time, until finally, almost forced, he gathered a court of the elders and more worthy citizens in the square in front of the shamed temple and ordered that the prisoner be brought him.

Covered in bruises and spattered on, the Conqueror was placed on a cart, for no one dared to untie his feet to let him walk on his own fearing that he might slip away or do something unexpected. So, then he, who had proudly proclaimed himself the Conqueror, was now delivered in shame like a stack of brushwood.

When Sevin saw him, he rose quickly from his higher seat among the other nobles and said aloud that he did not want to judge the man himself but would prefer to hear the people's will regarding him.

A great number of people gathered in the square. The holy old man Choma was among them, who was already almost blind but could still hear. This prophet, having heard that the false Conqueror had been brought to judgment, began to scream at once, inspired by God's spirit, that such a criminal should not even be judged, but must be stoned at once by the will of the people. At his call, screams came from all sides to hand the prisoner over to the people who already had a reward prepared for him for all his misdeeds.

The venerable and dignified Sevin listened to these cries for a long time in silence, pondering in his soul what he should do. Finally, when there was no indication, they could remain silent, and indeed demanded louder and louder for the criminal to be turned over to them, he signaled with his hand to be allowed to speak. Then he spoke these words more or less:

"Dear highly respectable citizens and my fellowmen! We are gathered here as judges on the order of the ruling high priest, His Majesty Elem, to consider the matter of this subdued man, who you are now demanding to be given to you!

We were going to carefully examine everything, and after quietly listening to the testimonies and judgments and even the defense of this unfortunate man, to pass a just sentence of which, at this moment, it would be hard to foresee the outcome. Still we are all only servants of the people, and your will is the highest law for us. You, with fierce indignation, do not want a court and you do not want to allow us to conduct the trial in an ordinary manner. I dare not judge if your will is right and just as I am only your servant.

What should I do then? I cannot do otherwise, and I know that all the other judges agree with me but listen humbly to your voices and act accordingly. Thus, I entrust the defendant into your hands. Deal with him according to your understanding and conscience, and I am asking you only to be merciful to him.

Therefore, let the owners forget that he wished to deprive them of their property, nor the dignitaries not remember that he violated their eternal rights. Let husbands not remember his instigation of the rebellion of their wives, and fathers the disgrace of their daughters. Don't forget the venom that was dripped into the hearts of the young men. Let the faithful forgive him for defiling the holy religion. Let the wretched forgive him his deception and the failure of his mad promises, and let soldiers forgive him the blood of their companions, shed in vain on the distant overseas meadows! Remember that he might have had good intentions, and that the court might even acquit him if you wished to leave it to the normal course of justice ... especially if His Majesty the High Priest Elem had his way. He would like to protect his former friend and protector, thanks to whom he took the cap from your father, Malahuda, first exiled and then miserably murdered.

If you wish otherwise, however, let your will be done. Just never forget that, at this moment, we of the court are not judging the man called the Conqueror … you are! Do what you please with him, and I wash my hands of the matter. I will not be responsible for spilling his blood, so let it fall on you and on the heads of your children if you so wish!"

Saying this, the noble Sevin covered his face with a part of his robe and sat for a long time in silence. When he opened his eyes again, the Conqueror wasn't on the cart anymore. The people seized him, and after tying ropes around his feet, dragged him head over the cobblestones to the seashore, where there is a place called the Landing of Good Waiting. Here a huge pole was dug into the sand. Having undressed the false Conqueror (his clothes had to be cut to tear them of him, for fear of loosening the ropes), they tied him naked to the pole so that he could not move.

His favorite Mortz, Nuzar was brought there with him. He was promised that he would be let free (no obligation to keep your promises to slaves) if he ripped his former master's belly with a wooden knife. He refused to do so, in a foolish belief that his master, whenever he wished, would pull the pole out of the sand, and kill them all. They did not play with him any longer but turning him on his face buried his head in the sand, so that, when dying, he was kicking with his upturned legs making some laugh.

Now, they started discussing what type of death they should apply to the famous Conqueror who hung on the pole as if dead, for he had closed his eyes, not wanting to see his Mortz's death.

There was no agreement as people suggested all kinds of torments, so that it was impossible to communicate. Meanwhile the mob, impatient with the long wait, began throwing stones at him, at first for amusement only, and then more and more passionately to kill him. At first, he opened his eyes and jerked on the ropes as if to break free but having apparently found out that it was futile, he hung limply and waited for death, mumbling something to himself.

It was taking a long time, because this Conqueror had a hard skull and a skin much thicker than ordinary people, so the stones did not do much harm to him. It is hard to tell how it would have ended if a good spirit had not sent the already mentioned virgin Ihezal to the place.

She, having come there, stood right in front of the stoned man, so that when he opened his eyes, he saw her right in the crowd. Because of his strong impure passion for this girl despite his imminent death, he began calling her name.

Then Ihezal stepped out of the crowd and came close to him. Stones stopped for a while so as not to offend her. The virgin then asked, "Conqueror, what do you want from me?" Having said this, she pulled out a knife. Since she was short, she rose on her toes, and began to jab her blade at his chest where the heart was. She had a hard job, because, as it was said, his skin was hard, but in the end she succeeded. When he was taking his last breath, the Shern, he had secretly been hiding, was spotted on the roof of the desecrated temple. He flapped his wings in the air, and feeling that his mighty protector was dying, flew towards the forests on the slopes of O'Tamor and disappeared there without a trace.

On that day, in the evening, the virgin Ihezal disappeared forever. There was a probability that, as a reward of her virtuous life, she was taken alive to Earth, where the Old Man and good spirits lived , who look after the humble generations on the Moon, and from where the true Conqueror will come in time, be it as soon as possible!

Thus was a miserable end of the man who had caused as much havoc on the Moon as no one before him had, and surely no one will do after him. Hence the great and beneficial lesson that the rulers must be obeyed in everything and you should not believe the innovators who incite and lead people to evil and misfortune ...

II

From the work of a historian, Professor Omilka, some observations regarding the history of the so-called "Conqueror".

One of the most mysterious figures in the lands of the lunar people was undoubtedly Marek, called the "Conqueror". However, a lot of stories about him, circulating until the present day among the commoners, must be put down among legends that have absolutely nothing to do with the truth ... They say, for example, that he was enormously tall with the height more than twice the height of the strongest people on the Moon. They believe that he had an extraordinary strength, and that he himself could lift what six male peasants could barely manage. There are more such fairy tales, showing how people are prone to exaggeration, and how their passions inflate to impossible limits the much more modest reality, as far as it concerns people who have occupied their imagination. In any case, he must have been a handsome man of a good height and strength, when his physical qualities stuck in the minds of the people so much that he was then made into a giant.

It is extremely interesting: when the fairy tale about his earthly origin was created. Was it still during his lifetime, or only sometime after his tragic death? Much data suggests that they were already circulating during the time of his activity in the capital of the lunar country. Based on the misleading, priestly legends about the people's arrival from Earth centuries earlier, the mob began to whisper to themselves that such an extraordinary man must have come from that star being the most interesting celestial phenomenon on the Moon. I personally do not believe, however, that Marek could spread this nonsense about himself as he was too wise to risk being ridiculed. At most, I am inclined to suppose that by passive behavior towards the emerging legend, if it had reached his ears, he could in a way allow it to grow and develop, benefiting himself in such a statement among a crowd of lunar origins. Such passive consent did not compromise him in the face of rational people, and in the eyes of the crowd gave him an elevated status.

In any case, the origin of that odd man has not been completely clarified yet. He suddenly appeared one day in the Polar Country, if you want to believe all such stories, beginning far from the regular human settlements. He then takes the Waiting Brothers with him and heads for the capital at the Warm Ponds. Having chased away the ruling high priest Malahuda, he immediately takes the helm of all matters into his own hands.

Nobody knew him as a child, so nobody knows where he had grown up, and from where he got the vast knowledge which helped him so much in his further life. His Mortz like origin does not seem quite probable to me. Mortzes are usually dumb, and it is hard to believe that one of them could come up with such inventions like firearms by himself. Those had even been unknown among Shern, as they generally attribute them to Marek, the so-called Conqueror.

It is certain that he did not hide in a country inhabited by the people because every rational man must reject the fairy tale about his miraculous arrival from Earth. Since it is an extremely distant star from the Moon and devoid of all life on its shining surface, he couldn't have come from there. That's why there is nothing else left but to acknowledge as a fact, the allegation originated in the bosom of the Brotherhood of Truth, that Marek the Conqueror's homeland, was the other side of the lunar globe inaccessible to us.

There is no doubt that, in that once fertile and wealthy country, there is an ancient nest of humanity. This truth was first noticed by the prematurely lost sage Roda. Around that time he proved conclusively in his writings that the Earth was not the cradle of the people now living on the Moon, and that there were no living creatures on it at all, so there can be no life there. However, my views differ significantly with the venerable founder of the Brotherhood of Truth as to the reasons that prompted people to move to this side of the globe, inhabited by the Shern centuries ago. Roda, the father of our knowledge believed that the legendary Old Man was an exile who had been expelled for some crimes from the flourishing homeland on the other side. As for his contemporary, Marek the Conqueror, he supposed that he was simply an envoy who was meant to push the local people to fight with the Shern, already disturbing those delightful areas hidden under the surface of the wild desert.

I treasure Roda's authority immensely, and I do not doubt for a moment that the great scholar must have had good reasons for his convictions. Nevertheless, I must state for the sake of truth that what he said is utter folly. The old people's realm in the Great Desert is by no means a flourishing country today. Things are starting to look bad there, because it is getting tight for them, as the desert absorbs more and more of those scarce, fertile areas, where one can live. The so-called Old Man did not come from the desert by himself but brought a few people with him. It was undoubtedly a trial expedition to investigate the possibility of being worthwhile to move to this side.

I cannot say yet why that intention did not come to fruition, nor why the first expedition in the course of the ages did not beget yet another one. Perhaps the empty country and the harsh living conditions in the new world scared away the inhabitants of the old towns, accustomed to comfort, in the desert. A handful however, who had come with the Old Man, stayed where they were and having procreated, formed the second human settlement on the Moon with no connection to the first one.

Apparently, centuries later the former expedition was remembered in the old settlements, and Marek the Conqueror was sent to see how things had evolved, and whether it was worth moving here in view of the increasingly difficult living conditions in the Desert. However, from the start, Marek saw that the Shern had conquered the country here. He concluded that they had to be put in their place first, before moving the rest of the population from their current homes only to be harassed and captured by the Shern here. Hence, he organized that military expedition to the south, which in the end was not entirely fruitless. A great deal of land was conquered, and settlements were established there. Although they fell into dependence on the Shern, they nevertheless constitute a buffer for this country by ransoming them-selves and us with a certain, though very unpleasant, not too heavy tribute.

It seems that after the end of the war, Marek the Conqueror re-ally wanted to return to his homeland. I do not consider stories about his vehicle as a fairy tale. Marek clearly had some kind of a vehicle, able to rise up by a strange power, in which he had flown from the desert, and that vehicle had been broken or stolen from him, so that he could not go away.

From then on, his tragedy began. In another chapter of this work, in connection with people's battles on the Moon, I also write about Marek's trip to the south. Here, I will only briefly recount the events immediately preceding the fall and death of the once-glorified Conqueror.

Everything Marek the Conqueror did was aimed at this one purpose to prepare this new location where the ground was suitable, for the desert people who would follow him. With this thought, as it was said, he started a war with the Shern. At the same time, he drove out the energetic high priest Malahuda and tried to take over the rule of the country. The high priest Elem, a cunning man who had been elevated to power by the Marek the Conqueror, at first obeyed him in everything, apparently having a plan perhaps after the Conqueror's departure to fully profit from the accomplishments of his reign.

Meanwhile, the resentment against the newcomer began to in-crease. This was mainly because he had subjectively, as he saw fit, set about changing the eternal and sacred laws governing the order of life on the Moon. No one had foreseen that he had a cunning goal in that. He aimed at loosening all laws and weakening the wealthy to facilitate the conquest of the country by his countrymen. In any case the general outrage was increasing from day to day.

Since I don't want to be unfair to Marek the Conqueror, already ill-treated by so many, I have to make an exception here. Most scholars believe the above-mentioned objectives validated the reasoning for his innovative endeavors. However, there are others who stand up for him claiming he had no ill-will in this regard. Perhaps the man, without any malicious intention of weakening and betraying the local society, tried to introduce the societal order here that in his opinion was good and indeed worked in his own homeland. He obviously didn't understand that relations here were different, and what could be good in the Desert would become disastrous here.

I leave this matter unresolved for the time being. It is certain that he was preparing the ground either for the conquest of the local society or for the consolidation of the separate human societies on the Moon, and in that, he failed.

He was allegedly requested to leave the area and to leave promptly to go back to where he had come from. He was ready to do it, maybe even with the thought that he would return soon with his compatriots, but in the meantime his artificial car had broken down. They say that after receiving this news, he fell into despair. At first, he did not want to believe it, and immediately set off by himself to the Polar Country, where his vehicle had been hidden in a huge iron pipe. (The pipe is said to be standing in that place until this day, and it is already half rusted away.)

Having confirmed this most unpleasant truth for himself, he returned to the capital, and thus began his downfall. The man was ambitious, restless, and greedy. If he had settled in a remote place or had moved to new settlements in the former Shern country beyond the sea, he might have lived to a relatively quiet old age. Yet his temperament would not allow it. He wanted to reign at all costs, and if he could not count on his countrymen's help, he would do it himself. He attempted, in his own way, to make the people happy though they did not want it at all.

So, he lived in the former temple, and he began to give orders from there. At first, he was mostly ignored, so he surrounded himself with a small and ready for everything group of supporters. He gathered a number of his comrades-in-arms from the time of the expedition to the South, and with their help began to force other's obedience to his will.

It is hard to tell whether it is true what was said about the orgies he was supposed to have set up in his household. In any case, his way of life could not please the inhabitants of this country, who would prefer that the stranger, though forced to stay among them, would show more restraint and humility.

The high priest Elem, later strangled by his successor Sevin, didn't like it at all, but as a wise and cautious man he was afraid to openly act against the self-proclaimed ruler. So, he retreated into the shadows, all the while inciting the people more and more against the Conqueror. His then trusted servant Sevin, as well as the equally devoted old man Choma, later recognized by some as a prophet, helped him in that.

Finally, things reached such an intensity that at any moment there was the threat of an outbreak of open chaos. Apparently, Marek the Conqueror had felt it, because he gathered the strength he could muster, and even wrote letters to a certain Jeret, then the chief ruler of the conquered countries, to come to his aid. This Jeret, a very brave, though not very wise man, did not like Marek, having some personal disputes with him, allegedly arisen during the war expedition. However, he was so devoted to his reforms that he was ready to come with valiant people to Marek's summons and murder Marek's opponents.

Marek, the Conqueror, was waiting for his arrival, when suddenly he received the news that Jeret had died on his way at the hands of an unknown assassin. Some claimed that he had been attacked by a Shern, but there were also some who suspected that the high priest Elem had been behind it, rightly afraid of the arrival of reinforcements and the outbreak of civil war.

So, those calculations by the crazy stranger also failed, and he saw at last that he was left to himself. Although he had named himself the "Conqueror", he could not count on a victory here with only a small handful of supporters. That's why he decided to leave the area of the *Warm Ponds*, but this was not allowed. He was captured by a ruse and brought to trial.

There have been long disputes over who should pass the verdict on this matter. High Priest Elem excused himself from this court and wanted to put everything on Sevin's shoulder as he did not like to speak out openly. Perhaps he was fearing an accusation that the suspect was the man whom he himself had brought here and named the Conqueror. It was very sly and wise as people are changeable, and Elem apparently foresaw that the executed one would one day be celebrated, so he wanted to prepare a retreat by acting through his henchman. Anyway, Sevin was already becoming inconvenient and dangerous for Elem. That's why I believe the high priest also had a plan to exploit the sentence against the Conqueror in the future, a sentence, which would not come out any other way than according to the will of the people, that is say, death.

However, Sevin was no less cunning than Elem. He read into Elem's intentions and so influenced the matter in a way that it was not he who declared the prescription for justice, but the people themselves. He went even further and took advantage of the still fresh indignation against Marek the Conqueror for his own plan. When Elem expected it the least, Sevin prepared a plot to have the ruling high priest judged as the accomplice of the alleged Conqueror. Then he had him captured and strangled, while proclaiming the high priest's position for himself. This, however, did not prevent him at the end of his life and his reign to declare Marek a martyr, who should be remembered with gratitude for his benefaction.

The martyrdom stories about Marek the Conqueror are very exaggerated. It is true that, according to the ancient custom on the Moon, he was stoned to death at the seashore. It wasn't done more cruelly or more fiercely than for many others who had in ancient times turned against the established and recognized order of affairs on the Moon. It is said that the granddaughter of the old high priest Malahuda delivered the last knife blow to his heart. She did it to avenge the death of her grandfather, who had supposedly been killed on the Conqueror's orders.

If we take a look at the whole thing now, strange, and yet logically evolving and attempt to summarize it into a number of clear and unmistakable judgments, then we should formulate them more or less this way:

1. Marek the Conqueror deserved death, due to the following:
    a) according to the real order of things,
    b) because of the perfect order of things on the Moon.
2. His death became a misfortune, namely:
    a) due to the real order of things,
    b) due to the ideal order of things.

As for paragraph 1, it must be noted that everybody who receives the death sentence, deserves it. This is clear and needs no further evidence. The only question that may arise here is: was this sentence in accordance with a reason of a certain order? In other words: can we, from the general point of view, give it the fairness in a given place and in a given period of time? This is what I'm going to discuss.

On the subject of paragraph 1. a) – According to the real order of things, I understand the sum of existing relations comprised of social, economic, and state existence of a given society. If certain relations have evolved, it means that they were needed and hence necessary. Whoever tries to break this existing state of affairs, even with the best of intentions, acts against what is vital and necessary, and thus becomes guilty of the crime of social upheaval and earns the punishment.

I, Professor Omilka, do not hesitate to say aloud, that although I am a member and presently the chairman of the Brotherhood of Truth, which is suspected by many as having subversive aspirations. Perhaps in the past, when our Brotherhood was still a secret society, similar thoughts appeared in the minds of some of its members. Since then we have had a lot of time, and today we proudly admit that we only want to slowly improve and brighten the existing relationships and not overturn them carelessly.

Marek the Conqueror's activity was just careless. This is the most appropriate representation. By his innovations, he was destroying the existing order, wanting to replace it with a new one that no one wanted, thus it was neither needed nor necessary. Then, as a destroyer of things that had been built over the centuries and a violator of naturally developed relationships, he deserved death.

It is different with a perfect order. Her, I call it the order, which does not yet exist, towards which society is striving as a result of the development of given relations. For example, the Brotherhood of Truth aims at this ideal order, trying to speed up its realization by means (as it should be) allowed and legal.

Well, to secure the successful future of the people on the Moon, it is necessity to understand this undoubtedly and not yet widely recognized truth that man was born on the Moon and is to live here. All the stories about his stellar origin are a harmful fairy tale because it distracts him from the only real tasks of life. Unhealthy dreamers chose the largest and rarely seen star as their supposed homeland, calling it Earth. It's time to change this ridiculous name. Here on the Moon, we use this name for the dirt or soil under our feet, describing it as fertile or barren, and so on. Well, since the time it was assumed that this star was the breeding ground for man, it was also called "Earth". This is the real origin of this misleading naming, the removal of which could put an end to many errors.

As for the matter of Marek the Conqueror, it should be noted that his appearance delayed the realization of this ideal order of this future and truth. Many of his followers became set in the ridiculous belief that the so-called Earth is inhabited and that the people originated from there. The fact that Marek himself never claimed that he had come from Earth does not diminish his guilt, because he did not contradict such claims, which was his first duty. He was rightly condemned to death for being a hindrance to the spread of truth on the Moon.

This is one aspect of the whole thing, but there is a different one as well. I said that his death became a misfortune. Each death is actually a misfortune, and above all for the person who suffers it, especially involuntarily and in full health. As a member of the Brotherhood of Truth, I always have a real and perfect order of things on the Moon on my mind. Marek the Conqueror, introducing various innovations into social devices, only succeeded in causing a lot of confusion, and prematurely executed, he could not bring anything to an end. If he had been alive and active, it would have been revealed in the end either that his intentions were good and that their realization might have benefited the society's relations on the Moon, or that they were undoubtedly evil and could not be fully realized at all.

Either way, it would be a good thing. First, although I consider it unbelievable, his death obstructed the improvement of the current order of things on the Moon. Second, it stopped demonstrating the undoubted perfection of the foundations of the present order. Then there would be no disputes today about the value of his theory, and there would be none of the confusion that often arises.

Also, in view of the perfect order, his death was by no means a happy ending. As we know, his body was torn off the pole from under the pile of stones with which he was killed, then burnt or hidden, so that the body was never again seen by anybody. This led his dumb followers to suppose that after his death by some extraordinary force, Marek the Conqueror himself came out from under the stones and returned peacefully to Earth, like in the legend of the so-called Old Man. This again, only strengthened a large part of the people in the old error about our earthly descent. If he had lived to the end and died later, as every decent man on the Moon dies, such a fairy tale about him could not arise.

Moreover, by living longer, he might have eventually been persuaded to reveal the Truth that we members of the Brotherhood serve. He could have admitted that he had come from the other side of the Moon and that people originated there. I believe that this would have finally put an end to any errors once and for all and speed up the realization of the ideal and so desired order. Nowadays, with the exception of the members of the Brotherhood of Truth, everyone stares at the Earth. The supporters of the slain pseudo-Conqueror, stare there, convinced that his spirit is looking at them and their opponents from there - waiting for a new, this time righteous Conqueror, to come from that empty start. It's not good by any means.

III

Postscript for the Brethren, wherever they may be, with good news about the Conqueror who lived among us.

Chapter Fifty-Seven

So that evening the Conqueror gathered his disciples by the city walls in the place where the castle of the Shern had once been destroyed, and seeing that they were all seated around it, he spoke to them, saying: "I am telling you the time has come for me to leave you and return to the bright star Earth, from where I came to you, and where the eternal house of the Old Man, the father of your spirits dwells. I have counted the days I've spent with you and weighed all my labor here, and I see upon looking back, that I can add nothing more to what I have done. I am weary and my soul longs for rest, and my heart looks to the star far away over the deserts.

You will remain on your own here, so that you may cultivate the seed sown by my hands, and if they persecute you for my memory, rejoice in your thoughts, and draw strength in that your grandsons will harvest plenty … For me it is time to go the Polar Country, where my winged car awaits, ready to carry me across the broad sky to my bright house."

When he had said this, crying broke out among his disciples. Some covered their faces and fell on stones, sobbing; others grabbed his hands, begging him to stay with them on the Moon for a little longer.

Especially the women who had once fallen into the power of the Shern, and now, by the grace of the Conqueror, were returned to the people community, fell at his feet and covered his shoes with their hair, begged him not to leave them, but to always remain on the Moon.

The Conqueror listened to their cries and pleas for a long time, not answering at all, until finally he stood up and, stretching his hands above the heads of the bowed, said: "My longing is calling for my family star, but perhaps I would stay with you if I knew it would benefit you. After all, it is not good for you to always have a shepherd above you when I am teaching you that a man should govern himself and decide about himself. If you become my children and my subjects, how will you later become good masters of yourselves? It is better for me to go now … "

Having said that, he went down the hill to the city, and his disciples followed him, sad and distressed. The evening was near, and the sun was about to go down, hanging low over the plains along which is the way to the Polar Country.

When the Conqueror and his disciples entered the city walls, they were met by some of the ones whom he had once sent to the Polar Country. They began to cry from afar, that the miraculous vehicle that had once brought him here from Earth was there no more. Then the Conqueror was greatly terrified and asked them to tell the truth about whatever they knew.

They began to tell him how, not having found the wagon on the spot where it was expected, they were returning in severe confusion. Then, in the first of people's settlements, they encountered a woman named Nechem, whom the Conqueror had appointed as the guardian of his holy chariot. She told them with weeping and great lamentation that at a certain time some spirits had come, and having encircled the vehicle with bright lightning, and thus covering it before her eyes, they carried it up into the sky.

This was a sign that those on Earth wanted the Conqueror to stay on the Moon forever and die here for the good of people who would believe in him.

Chapter Fifty-Eighth

And for the nine days and nights the Conqueror was building a new vehicle, until the tenth day, having found that the spirits did not want him to depart from the Moon, he summoned his disciples and spoke to them thus: "My fate is complete now, and I am fated to stay with you until my death. So far, I have been throwing seeds. I will not reap the harvest, but I want to plow the land so that the seed will not be lost in it.

You are the shovel and the plowshare and the plow, which I drive over hard beds, tearing away the furrows and destroying the lush green weeds on them. They will rise up against you, because you are destroyers, but have trust in me and in my words that I have spoken to you.

I have not come to teach you humility, nor submission, nor idle patience, nor renunciation that bears no fruit. I am just telling you: think more about tomorrow than about the present, more about the next generation than about what lives around you. Here we will set up a forge of the fire to light the ages to come, and a house of a storm to refresh the rotten air at noon. "

This is how the Conqueror spoke to his disciples, who listened to him in silence, ingraining his words in their memory. From that day on, the Conqueror settled in the temple in the middle of the city, near the *Warm Ponds,* and he shut himself up in it with his friends, in case the enemies, who had already planned to kill him, might attack him.

Then those who wanted to hear his teachings came day and night, and he went up to the roof with them, and here, in the face of heaven and sea, he told them all that was already mentioned in these books. If he saw evil or heard of any high priestly wickedness, he sent armed people and punished.

He was waiting for his friend and servant Jeret, who was over the sea as he had written letters for him to come with what forces he could gather to help him bring order to the lunar world. Unfortunately, after three days and three nights, it was learned that Jeret was attacked on his path by the Shern, whom the high priest Elem had hidden for himself to destroy the people with its help, and he killed him. Hearing about this, the Conqueror wept bitterly and did not eat or a long time, mourning his friend and servant.

Later when noon was in the sky, he called his disciples and said to them: "We are cornered here, and we cannot do anything good, because the enemies bind our hands, threatening our lives at every turn. Gather here, all of you, and we will leave this city and go to the Polar Country, where the Earth is visible in the sky. There I will teach you and say the last words, which need to be said, before my fate is complete".

Then they all got ready and gathering together put on their weapons and went with the Conqueror to the gates of the city, to go out into the plain, but the gates were closed. The high priest Elem had already heard that the Conqueror wanted to leave with his disciples and had planned to kill him before he departed.

They began to hammer at the gates to break them down, but at that moment the messengers from the high priest came and, pretending humility, begged him not to go away just yet, but to meet with His Majesty. He supposedly had called a great crowd of the people, and there in the face of all the lunar people wanted to make peace with him.

The Conqueror knew that the high priest had planned evil in his heart, but he felt that this was his fate, which he would never escape. That's why having commanded the disciples to wait quietly at the walls of the city, he went alone, with Elem's envoys on both his sides.

When they entered a side street, where his disciples standing by the gates could not see what was going on, the high priests' servants jumped out from behind the corners and threw long ropes on the Conqueror's head and hands, and suddenly threw him to the ground.

The disciples, hearing his cry, wanted to run to his aid, but the army, hidden in the neighboring houses, suddenly rushed out and surrounding a handful of his people with an overwhelming force, began to bind the disciples confused by the loss of their master and leader.

Chapter Fifty-Nine

The Conqueror, captured by a ruse, was to be brought before the high priest's judgment. But first, for the sake of greater ridicule, he was dragged by his bindings to the underground cellar in the temple and chained to the wall where the Shern Avij, a former great-governor, had once been held, after being captured by the Conqueror in the first battle.

The Shern had escaped with Elem's help and was living in hiding under his protection, as has already been said. Now, when the henchmen had left, leaving the Conqueror alone, the Shern appeared before him and sitting on the pile of discarded holy books in which the Promise was written, began to insult him.

"Free yourself," he said, "if you are the real Conqueror! Behold, I was chained here by you, and now I am free to look at you who will perish. I could kill you myself, and you would not even be able to defend yourself against my hands, but I prefer to leave killing you to the people to whom you have done good!

I have been waiting a long time for your death and when I see it, I will return to my brethren overseas and will tell them how he who dared to call himself a Conqueror over us perished!"

That was what the Shern was saying, and he laughed. However, the Conqueror did not answer him, being deep in his thoughts about the Earth to which he was about to return soon in spirit.

The Shern approached him and set out to tempt him saying: "You promised to take me to Earth with you and show me to the people who live on it. You yourself will not return to Earth, but many of my countrymen overseas have not yet seen you. Bow down to me and swear that you will serve me faithfully like a dog, and I will tear you out of the hands of your people. I will take you to the Shern, so that you may live there peacefully and train Mortzes in making firearms, with which we will send them later to conquer your brothers ... "

Then the Conqueror opened his eyes and looking at the Shern, replied: "Your tempting me is futile, beast. Though I will die, your reign is over for I have shattered it with my hands, and never again will even the weakest man serve you! "

At the same time, while the Conqueror was being harassed, the elders of the people gathered in the palace of the high priest and counseled with Elem what to do with him. Soon everyone agreed that there was no other way, and it was necessary to kill him to extinguish the light which he bursts with and offends their eyes, so accustomed to the darkness and the shadow of the soul.

Thus, his death was proclaimed, and as soon as possible so that his friends, gathering together, might not release him from prison. Yet, they were afraid to pass judgment by themselves in case the people, having seen through it in time, turn against the tormentors of their benefactor, savior, and teacher. Therefore, they decided to impose the events in such a way that the mob would demand the death of the Conqueror, as if against the will of the high priest and the elders.

Slyly, Elem sent his spies and instigators among the people to teach them how to cry when the court would assemble, and he sent his confidante Sevin to join the elders in the square to judge the Conqueror. Sevin was very devoted to the high priest, and he intended to do whatever he wished. But on that day, the grace of the Earth descended upon his soul, and he saw the light, and it was terrible for him that he was to judge and convict; he, who was the light of the Moon.

Meanwhile the Conqueror, bound like a criminal, was brought before the court and some bribed individuals appeared to testify against him. There was no crime or guilt which was not thrown on his fair head. He was accused of plunder, rape, rebellion, and treason, even in alliance with the Shern, whose slayer and destroyer he had been.

The Conqueror did not open his mouth but listened in silence to everything of which he was being accused. He was already thinking about the bright star of the Earth, from where these people had their beginning and where their saved souls resided.

Finally, when the slanderers and false witnesses stopped speaking, he seemed to wake up and, rising on the cart as far as his bonds allowed, he cried out with a strong voice to the people:

"Coming here from Earth, oh! People of the Moon, I didn't even know I was so generous! I have given you my life, and I am giving you my death! I have truly become the Conqueror expected by you, and today is truly the crown of my triumph! After death, no one in your souls will be able to fight me! My disciples and friends, who may be here, will remember the crimes they accuse me of, for soon the time will come when they will be called virtues! ..." He wanted to continue, but a cry rose among the elders, and then also among the crowd, that he was committing blasphemy.

Then one of the hired henchmen jumped toward him, and fearing to come any closer, struck him on the head with the long stick he was holding in his hand, saying: "Shut up, dog!"

Sevin rose from among the judges, and with pale lips exclaimed: "I will not judge this man! My heart is full of pity as I see his fall, and I ask you for mercy on him, but do with him as you please."

When he had said it, he turned and covering his face went away. Other judges rose and followed him, giving the Conqueror to the mob.

Chapter Sixty.

Ropes were tied at his feet, and as he was lying on the platform of the cart with his hands bound, they pulled him from it. Then they tied six people to each rope and dragged him along the streets of the city until his fair curls were stained with blood from the wounds caused by the hard cobblestones.

A great crowd followed the procession, shouting, and inciting those dragging him to run faster and faster. When the mob had passed,

436

the Conqueror's disciples went secretly (as they were afraid of the crowd) and collected his precious blood with cloths, weeping.

Among the crowd, there was also a loose and possessed woman named Ihezal. She was the granddaughter of the high priest Malahuda who had been slain by the Shern, hidden by Elem for the destruction of people's souls.

The Conqueror had once chosen this woman, thinking to bring her to Earth with him for good, as he felt sorry for her lost soul, for she was beautiful in the body and quite like the rising sun. She, however, was obsessed with a wicked frenzy and wanted to make the Conqueror her husband. When she realized that he was a completely divine being, she hated him and swore revenge upon him.

Then she was running after the procession and taunted the dragged man and cursing him loudly, shouting, until at last she stopped from great weariness for she was as fragile as a flower. His disciples collecting his blood found her lying face down sobbing on the cobblestones with her hair full of his blood. They were terrified, therefore, that she would report them, but she, rising up with a new madness, cried out, pretending to be very sorry, that they should run and save the Conqueror from the hand of the executioners.

When they were standing in confusion, not knowing what those unexpected words should mean, her face changed, and she suddenly burst out laughing and began to use foul lewd language, hurling severe curses on the Conqueror's fair head, crying and laughing alternately. Then she went to her house to put on wedding robes and to fix her matted hair.

It was then that the henchmen dragged the Conqueror to the seashore. After reviving him, because he had passed out, they lifted him on ropes tied under his armpits and tied him to a tall pole that had stood there from ancient times, serving as a sign to the boats flowing into the harbor.

They also brought the Mortz who having sworn off the Shern, had faithfully served Conqueror like a dog and was captured with him. He was promised a great reward to kill the Conqueror, for they wanted him to perish by an unclean hand for the greater shame. The Mortz, full of good spirit, however, refused to commit this crime and then he was buried upside down in the sand, right at the Conqueror's feet, so that, kicking his feet before he died, he kicked the Conqueror's bare and bloodied knees.

The mob began to shout and stone the Conqueror so that the prophet's words could be fulfilled: "I have given you grace, but you have become a stone for me. My blood is a seal."

Then the spirits of the Earth, sent from above, surrounded him with an invisible cloud, which weakened the momentum of the thrown stones, so that they fell softly on his body, doing him no harm. Suddenly, turbulent wind blew up, unusual at this time (for it was already before evening), and roaring, it smashed the sea waves on the sand of the coast.

The crowd started to feel a great fear, and there were voices to take the Conqueror from the pole and let him go, or to take him back, leaving him to his own fate and the frost of the coming night. While they were saying this, Ihezal, dressed in bright robes and with her hair nicely fixed, came to this side of the city. She was walking with a laugh, as if she were going to a wedding, though madness was visible in her eyes as her gaze darted anxiously around.

The Conqueror saw her, and since he had done her good all his life, he thought she was now running to help him. He lifted himself a little and raised his bloodied head and called to her "Ihezal!" He cried out, not to ask for help from her, for he knew that he had to finish his work with death, and that no one's hand would save him. He hoped for a change of heart and believed that at the last moment a good spirit would come upon her at the sight of his severe torment.

Her heart, however, was extremely hardened, and so as she ran towards him, instead of showing him pity, she took a sharp knife and standing on her toes, stabbed his heart until he died. Once she had done it, the evil spirits attacked her instantly. She began to dance and groan and sob, and totally possessed she rushed to the gardens on the slopes by the temple, and there she was lost forever, apparently carried away by the unclean spirits.

At the very moment, when the Conqueror died, the Shern, with his black wings spread, appeared on the roof of the temple. Then, he flew crookedly with incredible audacity in the midst of the people and sat down on the top of the pole where the body was.

Chapter Sixty-One

The crowd, frightened by the Shern's appearance and a suddenly rising storm, ran away swiftly, leaving the still and bloody body tied to the pole.

Only in the evening did the servants of the high priests come, and having cut the ropes, removed the body, and covered it with a great pile of sand and stone. In the middle of the night however, an immeasurable brightness befell the scene and with a roar like a thousand thunderbolts, the Conqueror's bright chariot came in the fire and stood over the grave built on the seashore.

This light was seen by many people who at the sound of thunder ran out from their houses, wondering in fear about that unusual phenomenon. The Conqueror came out from under the boulders with which he was covered, young and bright, with no sign of any wound on his fair body. Standing at the top of the grave, he motioned to the chariot, and like an obedient dog trained to his master's hand, it turned a great circle, and lay down at his feet. The Conqueror went into the chariot and flew over the city in fires, soaring to the star of the Earth, where his homeland and ours was.

Therefore, do not worry my brethren. Do not worry that you are forsaken, for indeed, you should rejoice that he sealed the truth with his severe death. Thus, he gave his last evidence to the good cause of his life and left an example for us to go through life towards your goal without fear for your own life. He also gave us hope that a revival comes out of death.

He is looking at our affairs here from the high Earth and blesses your daring deeds. When the times are finished, he will return here in his brightness, not to lead and teach, but rather to punish the enemies of his teachings with his fierce right hand. That is what will happen.

The Old Earth

PART ONE

I

They did not know how to determine the passing of those long hours, as time was not marked by a clock. Their vehicle, rushing through the interstellar space, would fall out from the abyss of sunlight onto the vastness of the Earth's shadow, and the travelers locked in the steel shell would be enveloped by night and frost … Then, suddenly without any warning, in the time shorter than a blink of an eye, when they were getting crazy from almost freezing to death, they would return to the light. It was blinding them and heating the walls of their vehicle to redness.

They did not feel the movement at all. The Moon was becoming smaller and smaller and shining stronger until it was beginning to resemble the star illuminating the Earth nights. The shadows slowly covered it on one side and then cut into the jagged semicircle of the Great Desert, which they now saw for the first time … Meanwhile, Earth was growing bigger and swelling to a monstrous size. Its strong silvery glow faded, as if thinning, as it covered half of the blue abyss with a giant sickle It seemed as if it were made of opal, whose milky color was changed by various colors of seas, fields, sands. Only here and there, some snow glittered with its silver light blinding you against the velvety blackness of the sky.

This is how, seemingly motionless, they were rushing through space between two bright sickles: Earth and the Moon. The first of them, concave, was continually growing underneath them, the other one convex, was getting smaller and smaller above them.

Roda, the scientist was silent during this whole inconceivable journey. Pressed into the corner of the vehicle, he was sitting pale, as if dead. His cheeks yellowed even more than usual. His terrified eyes, wide open, sank deeper into the sockets under his raised eyebrows. On the other hand, Mataret, was bustling and playing host in this so regrettably possessed Conqueror's vehicle. He found water and many stored supplies of various extracts he could eat, forcing his companion to take a bite as well.

Roda was eating reluctantly, looking at the still growing Earth with fear and hatred. A vortex of thoughts whirled in his head, which he tried in vain to organize. Now, everything seemed strange, incomprehensible, and crazy to him. He was thinking over and over about what had happened. He was still getting lost in some chaos of contradictions and going against everything that he had believed to be the obvious and undeniable truth.

Indeed, there was a strange and even funny improbability in all of that ... He was born on the Moon and that is where he grew up among people cultivating that strange legend. It told that ages earlier, the first pair of parents came to the Moon from Earth, led there by the legendary Old Man, and that they gave a beginning to the new generations. The legend also said that when those people, bothered and tormented by the indigenous Shern, black raptor beaked monstrous creatures, would find themselves at the end of their rope, a Conqueror coming from Earth will reappear on the Moon to save them from their oppressors. He was fed with these fairy tales since his childhood, but as soon as he reached the age of reason, he stopped believing in them. Instead, he believed that the Moon was the eternal cradle of all people, and Earth was a huge, glowing star shining above the airless, desert hemisphere of the Moon. He thought that Earth was also dead and empty without any form of life on its glossy surface.

He believed that he had discovered the truth covered up by the priests for their own selfish goals who were feeding people with fairy tales about humans' earth origin. He believed it so strongly, that he even became the founder of a brotherhood aimed at spreading and developing this belief. It was when the Brotherhood of Truth which he formed began to grow in power and significance, gaining more and more followers, a mysterious man arrived on the Moon from Earth, and was soon named the awaited Conqueror.

Then Roda remembered all his battles and bloody efforts in defense of the Truth with the strange newcomer's increasing advantage ...

He never believed that huge man in his flying vehicle fell from Earth, but he was sure he came from the other side of the Moon. It was generally believed that, the other side was most likely a desert with deep and defensive canyons, but that certainly was a deception used to cover up a delightful and fertile country. It was the original homeland of the first people, now jealously hidden from the exiles by the lucky tribe living there.

They decided to take over the Conqueror's vehicle while he was occupied fighting the Shern overseas and thus force him to disclose the route to the secret interior of the first people's original homeland. They succeeded in taking over the vehicle, but he and Roda would have definitely accomplished his goal of returning the lost paradise to his people if it were not for that damn bald Mataret. Now, locked in that metal shell with him, he is rushing through the abyss of the star space and looking at him mockingly with those bulging eyes.

Mataret knew well that the vehicle was ready to roll because Roda shared with him earlier what she had managed to extract from the Conqueror. Still, when they entered its interior, sure of their triumph over the hated newcomer, Mataret, either carelessly or on purpose, pressed that fatal button. It made their beloved Moon disappear so strangely from under their feet, as if it had fallen into an abyss, and now they are both flying into space, helpless, imprisoned, neither knowing their fate nor even if the next moment would come.

Maddening rage, shame and despair overwhelmed him all at the same time. So much so, that he wanted to howl in helpless anger and bite his hands. Mataret's calm and seemingly derisive eyes were hindering his outburst. Now, the scientist Roda, admired by his supporters on the Moon, was hiding in the darkest corner of this vehicle like a captured animal. There, he was endlessly pondering upon his shame and those thoughts bothering him so much, unable to reach any reasonable conclusion.

Then, when maybe for the thousandth time he was thinking upon his hopeless situation, Mataret approached him and pointed to the window in the floor. Behind it, Roda saw the Earth rapidly growing under their feet.

"We are falling to Earth!," he said.

It seemed to Roda that he heard mockery in his voice. There must have been mockery in the content of these simple and short words. They were mocking his learning, his knowledge and authority, all his teachings and theories according to which there was no connection between that alleged Conqueror and Earth. Blood rushed to his head now. At that moment, he did not care what would happen to him in an hour or two. He would even gladly give his life in that twinkling, if only he could shame and humiliate his suddenly hated comrade.

"Of course, you fool!," he shouted. "We are certainly falling on Earth."

This time Mataret really smiled. "You are saying, of course, Master, so ..."

"So, you are a nitwit," Roda roared, unable to control himself any longer. "Nitwit, if you don't understand that it is all that damn newcomer's ruse!"

"A ruse!?"

"Yes, that's what it is! And only a man as limited and dense as you could fall into it ... If only you had listened to me ..."

"You didn't say anything, Master!"

Mataret pronounced that last word with a certain perhaps involuntary emphasis.

"Yes, I told you not to touch that button. Do you think the Conqueror was that stupid to leave his vehicle ready to travel at the slightest push of the damned button and carry any fool into the country he had come from, to the happy cities on the other side of the Moon? That is ridiculous, don't you think? With resolution he set up his vehicle for this very purpose to kick the unwelcome trespassers to Earth."

"Do you think so?," Mataret whispered seeing a certain probability in this assumption.

"I believe it, I think so and I know! He got rid of his most dangerous opponent, he got rid of me because of your stupidity. He will get to his homeland in any other way, and we are lost without help. After all, we are speeding like two worms in a nut thrown by hand without our will, without sense, without purpose, and we will fall sooner or later on that damn, empty uninhabited star Earth. We will die there quickly even if we do not die during the awful fall. Oh, I can imagine him laughing at us and ridiculing us!"

This memory brought a frenzy of fury upon him. He extended his fists towards the Moon that was running away above them and started to curse that victorious stranger swearing with the thick, folk expressions, threatening him as if he would see him yet again and harass him.

Mataret no longer listened to these screams. He thought about it and then said:

"Are you still certain that Earth is uninhabited and impossible to live for any creature?"

Roda looked in his companion's face not believing his own ears that such blasphemous doubt could even emerge from his lips, and then he laughed bitterly.

"Am I certain? Look!" Saying it he pointed at the window at their feet.

Thrown into space by the strength of the explosion of the compressed gases and in view of the slow speed of Earth's rotation compared to the progressive movement of the Moon, they were approaching Earth circling a huge parabola. More and more approaching a straight line, they were falling to Earth, which swirled from west to east in front of their eyes, showing them more and more new seas and lands. They were still far away in space, and that movement, slight at first, still seemed slow.

However, the lands visible moments ago have already disappeared behind the slice of the horizon. They were just flying over the

Indian Ocean which was filling almost all their view up till the arch line of shadow in the west where the escaping night was cutting into the light sickle of the day on Earth.

Following his master's hand with his eyes, Mataret stared at that hopelessly empty silver surface. His usual smile died on his fleshy lips, and a net of tiny, vertical wrinkles covered his high forehead. He looked for a long time, and finally he turned his sullen but calm eyes at Roda.

"Indeed, we will perish." He said shortly.

Something strange happened to Master Roda. He completely forgot that the word, "perish", meant death for both of them, but felt a joyful triumph that he was right after all calling the Earth inhospitable and empty.

His eyes smiled, and he started shaking the twisted hair on his big head, throwing loud sentences out of his mouth, as when still self-confident, he was ruthlessly teaching a crowd of followers on the Moon.

"Yes, yes," he said," we will die! I was right, and one must be a fool like you are to even for a moment assume that this shiny round star swelling in front of us now could be a habitat of any life! I am glad you and everybody else will finally find, that what I was always ...

"Everybody else won't find out," interrupted Mataret shrugging his shoulders. "We will die ..."

He stopped and looked at his companion in whom, under the influence of those repeated words, the awful awareness of the hopeless situation suddenly arose. He stood up and flushed with anger jumped toward Mataret with clenched fists mumbling insults.

"You fool, see what you have done!"

He was repeating it over and over, and finally grabbed his head in both his hands and throwing himself to the floor, he began to moan, and curse the day and the hour, in which he accepted this half-wit to the venerable Brotherhood which was now orphaned without a master and was left alone on the Moon.

For a moment Mataret stared at the teacher, who was wriggling in a spasmodic unmanly cry, but not finding any words to calm him down, he twisted his lips and turned away contemptuously.

The time was passing in slow motion. He had nothing to do because there was nothing to do at all. They were rushing towards Earth, or rather falling on it with a speed Mataret could not even comprehend. He felt like looking through the window, but some kind of fear was stopping him from doing it. He put his hand behind his back and started staring thoughtlessly and without any feeling at the walls of the vehicle. He had that cool, persistent awareness that soon, perhaps in a few moments something horrible would happen and nobody could prevent it from happening.

The nearness of Earth could be felt by the increase of gravity expressing itself in the increase of the weight of all objects. Mataret, with his midget height and strength, felt that his limbs were heavier and heavier every minute. He would not be able to move objects he could easily move on the Moon. It seemed to him that some invisible wires bound everything together in one inseparable mass the weight was pushing it towards that horrible Earth. A moment later he started bending under his own weight. His arms sagged limply, and knees were trembling under the pressure of his body.

He slumped down on the floor next to the circular window and looked down ...

What he saw was so terrible that only the excessive heaviness stopped him from throwing himself back from that first look. The Earth was now expanding before his eyes with inconceivable, incredible speed. At the same time, he experienced the presence of a vortex that made him dizzy and nauseous ...

The terrestrial view was growing nearer, and the surface was spinning now in front of the vehicle, pushed with the relative movement of the Moon on a west to east trajectory with the speed of four hundred and several dozen meters per second. With every blink of the eye, as the falling vehicle was approaching, this monstrous momentum apparently increased. After a few moments, Mataret saw nothing totally fixed in place, everything looking more like a storm of shapes flying away.

Because of the increased viewing angle from a closer distance, the shiny sickle, not so long ago under their feet had, changed into this mad disc that began filling the whole horizon. The ocean was already pressing behind the suddenly limited horizon view. Some lands were flashing below, impossible to differentiate any more, and disappearing at once as if a space hurricane had kidnapped them. Suddenly, they fell into the spinning Earths' atmosphere, and their vehicle, stable up until now, swayed, and folded. Under the influence of air pressure, some protective wings automatically unfolded from its sides and broke at that moment ... Mataret could only feel the heat from the walls of the vehicle being immediately intensified by friction and an inhumane fear. He wanted to scream ... A sudden darkness came over him.

II

"Unheard of, incredible inventions and discoveries of the passing century make us face problems that must fill man with pride, but also fear. We are moving so fast that we have lost all measure of speed in this drive forward. Nothing seems improbable or outlandish to us anymore. Those, who know so much and have learned such secrets of being, understand everything that emerges as a natural and necessary result of what is. They accept everything new as only one of the applications of the eternal and unchanging forces of nature that are realized successively in a human brain ...

And for others, there is nothing strange because they simply know nothing and do not want to know anything anymore. They are just used to encountering a new wonderful thing that they do not understand but consider it as simple. Nobody, except for the wisest of men, ever thinks of the greatest miracle still not discovered by our brains, such puzzles as the development of organisms, the formation of stars, and the very fact of being, in general ...

Nobody knows how far we will get, but it is certain that we will get remarkably high. We will get as far as the limit of human ability if such a thing exists. There are people who claim that understanding the forces of nature and their multiple applications for human need is nothing other than creating them in a new form in the human spirit, and creation has no end and will never end as long as there are elements that can be joined together.

In any case however, there is no doubt that in a few scores of years or a few hundred, people will be able to acquire such a perfect control over nature that what we can do today will seem like nothing to future generations.

Thinking about such a development fills me with pride but also with fear as I said earlier. There are strange contradictions in man's mental existence. They are necessary, unavoidable but have fatal consequences. Who in a few hundred years, let alone a few thousand, will be able to embrace with the human brain the whole of knowledge acquired by mankind? Will this increasing power of the human spirit not have to go through some solstice in some unexpected but terrible way?

Once, centuries ago, progress developed more evenly. There was not even a slight similarity in the difference between the spiritual level of the most educated man and a half-wild peasant like the one existing today between the leaders and the seemingly cultural mob carelessly taking advantage of their inventions and discoveries.

Roman Caesars who lived in marble palaces, in luxury and pro-miscuity, did not differ much in their knowledge, even if they were thinking about Plato, from a dirty farm hand biting a piece of onion while standing in the shadow of the pillars of an amphitheater to pro-tect himself from the midday heat. Today, a shoemaker lives in the same way as I do. Perhaps he even has more money than I do and uses all the appliances and improvements like I do. He has the same protec-tion of the law and follows the same laws giving him his social value, and yet he does not know anything, and I know everything …

It is getting harder to know everything or at least a lot, so only a handful of selected ones consider it to be possible. We are bringing education to everybody; we are teaching people everything, but how does this "everything" compare to the vastness of knowledge already impossible for human brains and memory to grasp? Besides those who truly know, as they are the only creators of knowledge, art and be-ing, there are two kinds of conceited people who consider themselves smarter than everyone else, but it is hard to tell which of them is worse.

The first kind includes the group of those who consider them-selves smart because they know titles of books and names of inven-tions and can comfortably talk about everything. The second kind is the group of those "smart" people who concentrate on studying one field of knowledge and reject everything else with narrow minded con-tempt. They also believe themselves to be smart, but they also truly know nothing.

At present they create a lot and will probably continue doing so, but not always. The time is coming when they will feel crowded, in those narrow wells they have drilled for themselves, and find it diffi-cult to breathe.

They are approaching the core of being where all veins con-nect, and those who do not know all of them get lost in their incom-prehensible network, unable to go any further or be blind. So, they are climbing to the surface, but they get lost there.

Now the constantly shrinking team of know-it-all leaders is carrying the progress and the fate of humans on their shoulders and caving in under that burden, but what will happen if they are no more? If their superhuman powers won't be enough to carry such enormous burden?"

Jacek threw the book away.

He rubbed his high forehead with a narrow white hand and gave a faint smile with bloodless lips. His flaming black eyes were fogged with thoughts ...

This is how they were writing at the end of the 20th century, but how many centuries have passed since then! Yes, there was a period of incredible, unbelievable inventions when one discovery led to ten new ones. Then it seemed that man was on the path of some fabulous endless development terrifying in its magnitude. However, a sudden standstill followed as if the secret forces of nature used by man, became totally depleted. Since all of them had already been harnessed to a triumphal chariot of human prosperity, they had nothing more to reveal. The time has come for more and more comprehensive exploitation and use of achievements of human thought which had supposedly reached the deepest knowledge.

In the meantime, with each passing day, those scarcer and scarcer truly knowledgeable individuals were discovering that they really knew nothing. They felt like those first people when the human spirit was just beginning to fly.

At the same time, when a series of inventions seemed to grow at a dizzying speed and ever-increasing steps, before suddenly halting, knowledge, a true knowledge about what was true, began to move slower and slower.

It was as if the sum of the information already acquired, century after century added only half of that available to be acquired. It showed that although humans could see a limit of possibilities in the distance, they would never reach it. One could approach it, but there will always be about half of what you do not know yet always remaining with the shadow's secrets. Finally, one becomes struck in the head by the same unsolvable riddles the Greek wise men faced.

What is in the deepest principal and why is it at all?

What is an essence of a human thought and what is the cognizant spirit itself?

What kind of threads connect a human brain with the world? Where and how does the human being turn into awareness? And finally, what happens at the moment of death?

A slight grin appeared on Jacek's beautiful, almost feminine like lips.

Oh so!

At the time this discarded book was written, people could not deal with these kinds of questions. At that time, when man, becoming stunned by the progress of knowledge, seemed to think that only issues with proven answers to problems or those portending such answers in the future could have some meaning ... Everything else that could be called "metaphysics", was shrugged upon ...

But in the meantime, this "metaphysics" comes back and stands in front of man always with a covered face, and it torments him because if you do not know it, you truly know nothing!

And just as centuries ago, prophets appear one day and bring Revelation, to people willing and able to believe. Its role is to simplify all thinking and calm down hearts and give a final answer to all questions. Religions always existed and regardless how many times their end was predicted, they are stronger today than ever before although their range and meaning have changed.

Crowds stop believing and searching for gods in the sky because they are dazzled by knowledge too incomprehensible for them. Blinded by the glow of treasures acquired by superior spirits, they take advantage of them without any mental participation in their accumulation.

But the smartest ones, while peering down from the top of their successes, were the first to reject religion naming it a "superstition". At one time, they were trying to disperse it as something redundant and dubious. Now, one after another, are hiding under its wings with some fear in their eyes from looking too closely at unbreakable secrets. They are hoping for consolation for hearts strained by their sagacity.

What is more, from the sky-high mountains, from the depths of forests, still hidden in Asia, strange people keep emerging. They do not study the details of the secrets of nature, but they have a great power over it. They do not take advantage of it as they do not need anything. Imbued with great peace of mind and with a mysterious smile, they look with pity on those "knowing-all" who have discovered the nothingness of their knowledge ...

With an ivory knife in his white hand, he unconsciously began to turn the pages of the book in front of him ... In the silence of the room, there was only the rustle of the yellow paper and the ticking of an electric clock.

He, Jacek, is one of those "know it all's". He does not even know when and how he has managed to embrace this enormity of spiritual wealth gathered through centuries. He sometimes asks:

"What's the purpose of all this inhuman effort?"

Nature has supposedly opened all its secrets to him and obeys him like a master. Still he knows all too well that it is only an illusion, not so much his own, but those that look at him with awe for his wisdom and power.

He himself knows that his giving orders to the world is as ridiculous a behavior, as that long lost and forgotten Iroquois chieftain who before each dawn, would stand on a hill and pointing his hand to the east, order the sun to rise there and then drawing an arc on the sky with his finger show its daily route. And the sun obeyed him.

Indeed, it is true that knowing things means having power over them because then one knows how to manage them. And yet all of his power, that led to so many blessed and miraculous inventions and his personal power, means nothing compared to that of the Asian he'd met a week before. Jacek saw him using only his eyes and his will power to upset a bowl full of water. He did not even understand how he did it nor did he care if his funny deed would benefit anybody.

Whatever, he himself doesn't know much more than that miracle worker. He manages to harness some forces with an even smaller effort of his will because he actually learned how they work. Three years ago, without leaving this room, he drafted a design of a vehicle that his friend Marek could use to get to the Moon. He also mapped a route that could take him there through space as perfect as that of stars. Then, without getting up from this very table, he threw that vehicle into space with the traveler locked inside. He accomplished it by pressing a button, and it took him only a fraction of a second. He is absolutely sure that this vehicle fell on the surface of the Moon without any harm, in the exactly calculated moment and location. However, he does not know much about the movement he so precisely prepared and used.

In this aspect, he is more or less in the same place Zeno of Elea was centuries ago. Using naive examples, he tried to show the contradiction that struck him in the concept of movement.

Zeno claimed that Achilles would not catch up with the turtle, because in the time he would use to travel through the distance separating them, the turtle would always move a bit forward ... After a few dozen centuries, he also knows that what is moving is also standing at the same time, and that, what is standing is moving. All kinds of movement and rest are relative. What is more, the movement, this unique and elusive reality, is a change of position in space, which itself is quite unreal ...

To stop that flow of thoughts tormenting him, he stood up and went towards the window. With a light touch of a button on the wall, he opened the curtains and made the shiny glass panes open. The silvery moonlight poured into the room illuminated without lamps by streaks of brightness running below the ceiling. With a slight movement of his palm, Jacek turned off the artificial light and gazed at the Moon approaching its fullness.

He was thinking of Marek somebody from a different century. He was brave, exuberant, cheerful, and eager for action ... They were

distant cousins who grew up together, but they picked such different life paths. While Jacek feverishly accumulated knowledge without
even understanding his drive to do so, Marek also ran wild and acted.
Seeking incredible adventures, he threw himself out of romance and
into public life, took part in great social gatherings and defended various issues, all of which were quite indifferent to Jacek. Then he suddenly disappeared for some time, simply to fulfill his fantasy of scaling
an inaccessible Himalayan peak or to spend a few weeks in some daze
of love.

And then, that beloved madman, who saw everything through
rosy lenses, came to Jacek one day and told him that he wanted nothing less than to take a trip to the Moon.

"Jacek, I know that you can do everything," he was begging
him like a child, "build me a vehicle that could take me to the Moon
and back!"

Jacek laughed: "Oh, everything ..." No doubt, he could make
such a trifle. He was grateful to Marek that he only wanted to get to the
Moon instead of another planet in the solar system, as that would be a
much more difficult task.

They both laughed and joked.

"And, why would you go there?" He asked Marek. "Aren't you
happy here on Earth?"

"No, but I am curious about the fate of O'Tamor's expedition
several ages ago. I think that he and two other men and one woman
had themselves thrown to the Moon in a missile in order to start a new
society there.

"O'Tamor was accompanied by three men and one woman."

"Oh! It doesn't matter ... Besides, I have another reason. I have
gotten tired of Aza."

"Aza? "Who is she?"

"How is it you don't know Aza?"

"Your new hunting dog or horse?"

"Ha, ha, ha!"

"Aza!"

"A wonderful woman! A singer, a dancer raved about on both
hemispheres ... Look after her, Jacek, when I leave!"

That is what Marek said at the time, laughing, cheerful, boiling
with lush and young life ... Jacek frowned and rubbed his forehead
with his hand impatiently, as if he wanted to chase away some unpleasant memories.

"Aza ... Yes, Aza, raved about on both hemispheres ..."
He slowly lifted his eyes to the Moon.

"And where are you now?" He whispered, and "when will you come back?"

"What will you tell us? What did you find there? What happened to you?"

"You are happy everywhere," he added in an undertone.

Yes, he feels good everywhere, he thought, because he still has this original, unstoppable, creative rush for life, which can create the desired relations around him, and finds good sides in the worst scenarios ...

After all, Marek felt good here ... happy and comfortable here. He never complained although it was difficult not to in the situation around them ... But he is so different from all those others who are happy.

He closed the window and without turning on the lights returned to his desk in the middle of a round room. He moved quietly across the soft carpet and feeling with his hand in the dark, sank into a highchair. The memories were coming to his mind of all the changes that happened over the centuries, which were supposed to lift and liberate people and make them happy ...

Would the author of this book from the twentieth century, the book that had been banned, be ridiculed, if in that ancient time period, they could look today at the map of the United States of Europe! What was once perceived to be a distant and unachievable idea, came considerably easily and inevitably.

First, all those shocking coups, we learn about from history, had to happen. So, there was that terrible, incredible, unparalleled defeat of the German State by the Eastern Empire, formed from Austria after its invasion of the Polish parts of Russia and its merger with South Slavic countries ... It was followed by this unexpected three-year war with a powerful England, the master of the half of the world, with the Union of Latin Countries. After that, the British Empire, invincible but also not victorious, actually fell apart into several independent countries, with all those storms, battles, and confusion that followed!

The day finally came when people understood that there was really noting to fight about and began to wonder about the reason for such frenzied bloodshed. After several centuries of historical development, the peoples of Europe matured enough to unite. They united on the principle of intrinsic national units enjoying complete freedom.

The economic and social development came soon after. Once there was a fear of sudden upheavals in this area, and everything seemed to indicate the necessity of some inevitable disaster, but in fact everything went very smoothly and without excitement. An extraordinary growth of companies and corporations made such transformation almost unnoticeable. Taking advantage of new inventions called for joining all efforts, but it incredibly quickly led to the increase of general prosperity ... Soon, having personal assets was no longer something worth worrying about.

However, it did not result in the Utopian equality expected by some. Human rights were equated, and human dignity was raised, and prosperity and education were given to all, but human spirits were not considered, nor were the values and scope of the individual. Oh! How far is all of this different from that once dreamed about paradise!

Like in the past, there were rich and relatively poor people. The people, who held "useful" and important positions for society, often received huge pensions after a relatively short time of service. They were set for life and could spend the rest of their days entertaining themselves. They rarely chose to do even voluntary work.

Governments owned everything but cared more about their own pockets than private people did earlier. Huge cities were full of elegant hotels, theaters, circuses, and ballrooms dripping with gold, while singers and actors of all kinds were paid incredible sums of money ... In this way the money was returning from officials' and retirees' pockets to state coffers.

Many "unproductive" people did not know hunger because work was compulsory for them. If they could not manage what they were paid for their reluctant work, they were taken under the state protection ... Sometimes young people fell into that category. Some of them became inventors and discoverers later in life. Writers and artists were forced to work manually, and often deteriorated to become famous only after their death but in their lifetime were pushed in the shadow by the happy and fashionable colleagues, mob flatterers.

Jacek was thinking about all that again, weighing the book he had read earlier in his hand ... That banned writer from twentieth century got it all wrong in his pessimism. People did not divide into two parts but three. There is a mob at its center as the majority. It is full of, overfed, often resting and if possible, the least thinking creatures. They have rights, prosperity, and education. Schools teach them about what was done for them. They have a sense of duty and are usually virtuous. They are divided into nations, and they are proud that they belong to their nation, but they would be equally proud if they had been born to another nation. In the past, there were nations united by the sanctity of blood relations, but they slowly degenerated into something like different national costumes without a significant difference. The difference in spirit has blurred. The mob everywhere has become very much alike in the content of its small souls in spite of different languages, incomes, and governments.

There is an impenetrable gap of spiritual development separating those "knowledgeable" individuals at the top, still aware of differences between races and nations from that glittery European mob. But they rarely talk about their nationality as they are connected by the brotherhood of knowledge and fate.

At the very bottom, under the full and happy mob, there is an international mass also separated by a layer of differences. That fact is always loudly denied, but it is true. The most beautiful and sincere words about equality and about a comprehensive right to life and prosperity, about the absence of an oppressed class will not help. Besides, they are not oppressed at all.

Millions of workers are needed to operate those millions of machines serving people. They need to be watchful, skillful, and completely devoted to those metal, ruthless monsters. They are not thinking about anything more than that at a given moment they need to push a button or a lever. They work relatively short hours, and are paid well, but their mind, focused at one activity, loses its acuity for everything else, slowly making them indifferent to what is happening outside their factory, workshop, and their nearest family.

It is noteworthy that they do not protest, or rebel as did workers in the past. They are wisely given everything, and they get everything they want, but in the end, they stop wanting, even things which could be easily attainable. They do not have a homeland as they have to follow their jobs from place to place. They have even developed a separate, international language, in a strange way made of scraps of different languages.

So basically, everything is as it was! Only the blurred international borders, the abolition of which was once so important to those on the top and so objected to by those at the bottom, have become more visible now. They have grown wider and harder to cross now when their existence is negated. The bilateral pressure outside ceased, but somehow naturally the layers started to condense and seal, involuntarily and unconsciously retreating and growing more and more apart.

So everything is as it was despite the prosperity, despite the knowledge, despite the freedom and almost perfect laws. As in centuries ago, it is shallow, dark and more and more stuffy on Earth today, in this life ending with death, with its always hidden and incomprehensible face.

And happiness? Man's personal happiness?

Oh, you, the human soul, never satisfied and still incorrigible! Neither science, nor knowledge or wisdom will eradicate from its depths those unreasonable, sometimes ridiculous desires devouring it like fire.

The clouds which covered the moon darkened the room. With an almost involuntary motion of his palm, Jacek reached out and touched the button hidden in the carvings of the desk. A colorful image flickered on the oval surface of milky glass in a brown frame, and he saw a small, seemingly light face under the lush wave of light hair and dark blue eyes, huge, wide open ...

"Aza, Aza," he whispered in the silence gazing at this dim reflection.

III

Having regained consciousness, Mataret could not fully comprehend what had happened to him nor where he was for a long time. He rubbed his eyes several times, not sure if he was surrounded by the impenetrable darkness or whether his eyelids were still closed. When he remembered that he was in the vehicle that rushed from the Moon to Earth, he tried to turn on the light. First, he could not find the button, as everything in the vehicle was strangely upset, and when he finally found it, pressing it was futile. Something must have broken in the wires as he was still surrounded by darkness.

He started calling Roda. There was no answer for a while, but finally he heard a grunt that let him know that his companion was alive. Groping at his surroundings, he moved in the direction of the sound. It was difficult for him to orientate himself. During its travel the vehicle, affected first by the gravity of the Moon and then of Earth, was always turning in such a way that they always had the floor under their feet ... Now, Mataret noticed that he was crawling on its concave surface.

He found the master and shook his shoulder.

"Are you alive?

"Yes, I am still alive."

"Are you wounded?"

"I don't know. I am dizzy. My whole body hurts. And it is so awfully heavy ..."

Mataret felt the same, being able to move only with great effort.

"What happened?," he asked after a while.

"I don't know.

"We were already close to Earth. I saw it spinning ... Where are we now?"

"I don't know. Perhaps we were flying over it! Obviously, we have passed Earth and we are probably speeding through space in its shadow."

"Don't you think the vehicle has taken a strange position? We are walking on its wall."

"I don't care. It doesn't matter. Either way our death is inevitable whether we are on the wall or on the ceiling."

Mataret became silent admitting in his soul that the master was right. He stretched out on his back and closed his eyes, surrendering to the drowsiness that was slowly overwhelming him, which he suspected to be an announcement of impending death.

Still he did not fall asleep. In some semi-conscious dream, he saw wide lunar plains and a city situated by the *Warm Ponds* on the seashore ... He saw the people returning from some kind of ceremony at the steps of the temple. The arrogantly named Conqueror was standing there and was looking at him sneeringly ... He even called him by his name. Two times.

He opened his eyes. Someone was really calling him

"Roda ...?," ventured Mataret.

"Are you sleeping?"

"No, I am not. The Conqueror ..."

"To hell with the Conqueror. I've been calling you for half an hour. "Look!"

"Brightness!"

"Yes. It is getting brighter. What is this?"

Mataret sat up and looked up. Indeed, the side circular window, now on the top, was slowly changing into a shiny spot against a dark background.

"Dawn is coming," he whispered.

"I don't understand," said Roda. Until now, we have been moving from light to darkness and vice versa directly, in one moment...

At that moment, with a suddenly increasing brightness, they heard some rustling, the first sound they have heard from outside since their take off from the Moon.

"We are on Earth!" Mataret exclaimed.

"What are you so happy about?"

But he was not listening anymore. Struggling with the unbearable weight of his body, he climbed closer to the window. Something like clouds of sand were moving above it, thickening sometimes so that darkness covered the inside of the vehicle again. Mataret was looking but not understanding what he saw. Then he closed his eyes blinded by brightness. The sand has disappeared, and the blinding sun hit the round glass pane. He clearly heard a whistle of the blowing wind.

When he opened his eyes again, it was bright everywhere. Through the window, he saw a dark blue sky, not black as before when they were flying through space.

"We are on Earth," repeated Mataret with conviction and started undoing the screws locking the exit from their long imprisonment.

It was taking time. Everything seemed to him to be excessively heavy, and his limbs felt numb and tired so quickly, that he had to rest every now and then. When the last bolts dropped down with a noise, and a fresh breeze came through the opened window and hit him in the face, at once he staggered. He was so drunk with the air and tired from the effort that he was unable to get out into the world at all.

After a long rest, he regained his balance and grabbing the frames of the window with both hands, lifted first his head and then his body to the outside. Roda was already pushing behind him and sticking his large, disheveled skull out of the vehicle.

For a while they were both looking in silence.

"Didn't I say that Earth is not inhabited!" Roda finally spoke.

Around them, as far as they could see, a yellow vastness of sand burned by the sun stretched everywhere broken only by humps or waves. Their vehicle, falling to Earth, fell into a giant dune. The just now ceasing wind has unearthed it.

Mataret did not respond to Roda's words. He was looking around with his eyes wide open and organizing the impressions in his soul ... Everything around him was quiet, dead, and motionless. It was hard for him to believe that this is the same Earth he saw, only a moment ago in a crazy whirlwind under his feet ... He was wiping his eyes and collecting his thoughts, uncertain whether he was dreaming now or awakened from an inconceivable sleep.

At times, he felt overwhelmed by a fear which he did not understand. Then his whole body was trembling feverishly with a terrible, crazy desire in his heart that everything which happened, this journey and this Earth would only be a nightmare ... He tried to control himself and think consciously.

Finally, he felt hungry, so he returned to their vehicle and got out the rest of the water and the already scarce supply of food they had left. He turned to Roda:

"Eat!"

Master shrugged his shoulders.

"Actually, I don't know why I should eat and prolong my life by a few hours." However, he ate greedily and Mataret had to stop him with a remark that they had to save the food.

"Why?" Barked Roda. "I am hungry. "I will eat whatever there is left and will hang myself on the top of this damned vehicle!"

Not listening, Mataret was packing a bag with the rest of the food and was gathering all the small items that could be useful. Then he tied everything together and tried to throw the bundle over his back but saw that he had miscalculated, not remembering the weight on Earth was six times greater. Not happy, he threw out everything that they could do without, and split the rest into two bags.

"Grab this one," he said to Roda, "and let's go!"

"Where to?"

"Anywhere. We will just go forward."

"It doesn't make sense at all. I don't care at which point of this plain I will die."

"When Earth was whirling below us, I saw seas and some lands which looked green. Perhaps, we will get to a place where life is possible"

Mumbling reluctantly, Roda hung his bundle across his shoulder and followed Mataret.

They walked east, bogging down in the sand, overwhelmed by the heat and the air too thick for their lunar lungs, and above all the weight of their own bodies. In spite of their small frame, it seemed to them as if they were made of lead. They often stopped to rest and wipe sweat off their foreheads.

At those stops, using every detail he noticed, Roda continued to prove that the Earth was uninhabited and could not be inhabited by any beings at all.

"Think," he was saying "this great weight! What creature could bear this weight for any long period of time!"

"But if people here were bigger and stronger for example like the Conqueror?"

"Don't talk nonsense! If the people here were bigger, they would weigh more and wouldn't be able to move at all."

"And yet ..."

"Don't interrupt when I am speaking!" Roda got indignant. I am not arguing with you, but I am telling you only what I know. You need to listen and learn.

Mataret shrugged his shoulders, picked up his bundle and started forward in silence. Master was following him and though out of breath, he continued to voice the truth of his opinion.

"We will perish here." He repeated. "There is no living creature here."

"So, we will be the first," interrupted Mataret." We will own the whole Earth."

"How good will it be for us? Sand and water, which we saw from above, if it is water at all, and not some polished stones reflection..."

Meanwhile, Mataret stopped and was looking ahead with interest.

"Look!" He said after a moment pointing with his hand.

"What?"

"I don't know what it is ... Let's get closer."

After several dozen steps, walking on harder, rocky ground, they could clearly distinguish a line, crossing their path and going both ways forever. When they got closer, they saw an iron bar supported by metal stands and cutting the desert from end to end.

"What is this?" Whispered surprised Roda.

"So, there must be some living creatures here." Spoke Mataret. "This strange thing seems to be done by a human hand."

"Not human! Not human! Perhaps ... there is some kind of life here, but there are no people on Earth! It is certain, you will see ... Why would an intelligent person make this thing and waste so much iron for no reason?"

"Then who lives on Earth?"

"I don't know. Some kind of creatures ..."

"Shern," Mataret muttered through his teeth, and they both shivered at the mere memory of those horrible lunar aborigines.

They were examining that mysterious rail with curiosity, which in the meantime had begun to ring lightly; and suddenly ...!

They both jumped backwards in fear. A giant, shining monster with a flattened head, zipped with a bang on the rail with a speed so terribly fast that by the time they recovered, it was already far away. They were looking with fright and wonder not even daring to think about what it was.

After some time, Mataret spoke as he looked distrustfully in the direction where that phenomenon had disappeared,

"An Earth animal ..."

"Oh, right," mumbled Roda. "If such monsters even live here. That thing must have been one hundred or more steps long, and it was racing like wind. Did you notice any legs?"

"No. I only noticed along the whole body up to the tail a number of eyes, which looked like windows ... However, I think that it was moving on wheels. Perhaps it is not a monster but a strange wagon?"

"You are foolish! Where would such a wagon speed to so fast not being pulled by anything?"

"And who was pulling our vehicle into space? ...," interrupted Mataret. "Perhaps this is customary on Earth."

Roda thought about it for a moment.

"No, it isn't possible. A cart could not run on a single rail like this one, it would fall over."

"That's true," admitted Mataret.

They crawled between the stands supporting the rail to the other side, gazing at it distrustfully and then walked again with concern and anxiety in their hearts. They felt strange on this Earth. According to the legends they essentially rejected, Earth was the original cradle for people, but it looked awful and empty to them. Roda, tiring more quickly than his companion, stopped every now and then. He complained of the unbearable heat, which, although not even close to the lunar heat at noon, seemed more painful to them in the dense earthly air. There was no shade around them on that yellow sand plain.

Only there, far ahead of them, they saw some rocks looming with strange shapes almost white in the dazzling sun. Then, among them there was something like giant jagged plumes on high, slightly bent poles.

They were moving toward those rocks, exerting their strength in the hope that they would find a little shade under them. Suddenly they noticed some shadows quickly sweeping across the sand. Roda turned around first and they both looked up. Between them and the sun, he saw something like monstrous birds with wide white wings and flattened tails. Mataret noticed that those closer to them had wheels instead of legs and were moving fast in the air without moving their wings. In front of their heads not clearly distinct from their bodies, there was some kind of hardly visible whirl.

They disappeared in the direction where the first shiny monster had gone.

"Everything is awful on Earth." Whispered Roda.

Mataret did not respond. As he was looking at the birds, he was surprised by the sun's location in the sky. It was already standing low and was beginning to blush and disappeared behind a golden fog.

"How long ago did we leave the vehicle?," he asked after a moment.

"How would I know? Perhaps four, maybe five or six hours ..."

"Was the sun on the horizon then?"

"Yes."

Mataret pointed towards west with his hand.

"Look, it's already going down. It is simply inconceivable. Could it run through the sky so quickly?"

At first, even the master could not understand this strange phenomenon. He got terrified again and was looking with dumb eyes at the sun which went crazy, having run through half the blue sky in six hours, while on the Moon it needs several scores of hours. But soon a smile brightened his lips.

"Mataret!," he said "have you really forgotten what I was teaching in the Brotherhood of Truth?"

The bald student looked questioningly at the Master.

"After all," Roda continued, " the days on Earth are short as they last only twenty-four of our hours, so ..."

"Oh, yes, that's true. Yes, it is true."

Still, they were both gazing with awe at the sun flashing across the sky as they believed ...

"The night should come in an hour," whispered Mataret.

"Bummer! Whispered the Master, forgetting what he had said earlier, bummer! Three hundred fifty hours of darkness and frost. And what will we do now? We shouldn't have left the vehicle ..."

Now Mataret was the first to realize that it was not so,

"Twenty-four or even only twelve hours because it is Earth."

"Oh, yes, that's true. Yes, it is true!" Responded Roda now.

"Still, it is strange," he added after a moment, "very strange. In any case, the frost will make our situation exceedingly difficult before the sun rises. Although I do not know what will happen to the snow. On the Moon, it falls only twenty to thirty hours past the sunset, and here it will be a new day.

"Perhaps snow falls here earlier."

They continued moving forward while talking. The heat of the day eased a bit, and they were becoming used to the increased weight of their bodies, so that they were walking faster.

The rocks were close. Under their feet, here and there, a faint and yellow grass peeked from the sand in the granite crevices.

They both stopped and looked at it for some time trying to guess how lusher plants on Earth would look if there were any.

The two Moon men reached the rocks soon after the sunset. When they were looking for a place to sleep, they noticed in the thickening darkness a huge stone figure, half human, and half animal. The monster's body resembled a dog, but it was it was rounder and more muscular. Its raised neck supported a human head.

"There must be intelligent beings here on Earth, people like us or the Shern," Mataret said after some time, "if they can make such things out of stone."

"If they look like this one!," added Roda pointing at the unmoving monster.

They felt indescribably terrible and sad.

They found a hiding place in the crevice of a rock, as far as possible from the amazing statue. They were preparing to somehow protect themselves from the night frost, when the eastern part of the sky began to slowly gilded and filled with a bright glow. First that glow eclipsed the earlier shining stars and then a huge, luminous, red sphere emerged from it.

It was ominous and inconceivable, like everything that happened to them in this shortest day in their lives. The sphere, meanwhile, as if a pumpkin filled with light, rose up, appearing to be smaller and smaller at the same time. The shadow disappeared, and a soft, silvery red gleam glistening on the sands and rocks, giving the appearance of life to that terrible stone monster.

"Which star can it be?"

Roda was searching his memory for a while, but finally shook his head in contradiction.

"I don't know this star," he said looking at the Moon they had arrived from a few hours earlier.

But Mataret suddenly remembered the view from the window of the vehicle speeding through space. Although that one seen from close looked bigger and less bright, but still there was some similarity.

"The Moon!" He exclaimed.

"The Moon!"

They were both looking on with a terrible, stinging longing in their poor hearts, as their irrevocably lost homeland was moving gracefully across in the sky.

IV

A young blond girl with dark blue eyes got off the Stockholm-Aswan express train. She was followed by a gray but healthy-looking gentleman with slightly protruding eyes who was carrying a few small suitcases. He was uncomfortable in his new fashionable outfit; one he could not get used to. He also felt a little tired of persistently playing the role of a young man, although he tried not to show it.

As soon as the girl got to the station hall, the director of the biggest hotel, the Old-Great-Cataract-Palace, ran up to her and with a dignified bow pointed to the electric car awaiting her.

"Apartments have been ready since yesterday," he said with the slightest reproach in his voice.

The girl smiled.

"Thank you, my dear director, for going out of your way to greet me, but I couldn't come yesterday. I telegraphed after all."

The director bowed again.

"Yesterday's concert was canceled."

Saying that, he pointed again to the waiting car.

"Oh, no! Just take my things ... You have the receipts somewhere," she turned to her companion. "I can walk, can't I, Mr. Benedict? It will be nice. It's so close."

The lively old man muttered something under his breath, looking for receipts in his pockets, and the director stepped back discreetly, trying not to show his indignation. The famous Aza could have such improbable fantasies like walking.

After passing the railway buildings, the singer was walking briskly along the avenue lined with palm trees and enjoying the sweet air of the spring afternoon. In the morning, dressed in a warm fur coat, she got on the train in Stockholm. After several hours, she was flying through a tunnel under the Baltic Sea and across Europe, and then through another tunnel under the Mediterranean Sea, and the eastern part of the Sahara. She got to the bank of the Nile River before the sunset. Now, after so many hours of sitting she enjoyed stretching her slightly numb legs.

Aza was happy moving and walking fast, forgetting her companion who was having difficulty keeping up with her. In no time, she found herself in front of the huge hotel.

They prepared her rooms on the most expensive top floor with the wide view of the Nile lagoon. Once, ages ago, it used to fall from here in a cascade from the rocks, which was gone now because of the water raised by the dam and fertilizing the once desert land.

Getting into the elevator, she asked about her bath and was told that it was ready for her. As she did not want to go to the downstairs restaurant, she ordered dinner in her private dining room in two hours.

Having instructed Mr. Benedict to watch over the servants carrying the packages, Aza locked herself in her bedroom and even sent away her dressing attendant. She opened the door to the bathroom and began to undress by herself. Wearing only her underwear, she sat on the sofa, and put her face in her hands. Her big eyes lost their childish expression and some kind of obstinacy peered out from them as she pursed her little purple lips. She thought for a moment ...

She got up quickly and ran to the phone on the opposite side of the bed. She dialed rapidly.

"Please connect me with the European operator" ...

She listened in silence.

"Yes. OK. Aza speaking. Where is Dr. Jacek now? Please check"

She was answered in a few seconds:

"His Excellency the Chief Inspector of the United States of Europe Telegraph Network is now in his apartment in Warsaw."

"Please connect me and ..."

She dropped the phone and walked back to the sofa, stretching back on soft cushions with her arms tucked under her head.

A strange smile parsed her lips now, and her eyes gazing at the ceiling were shining.

A faint ring called her back to the phone.

"Is that you, Jacek?"

Yes, that's me."

"I am in Aswan."

"Yes, I know. You were supposed to be there yesterday"

"I wasn't. I didn't want the concert to take place yesterday"

"Yes?"

"You don't want to know why?"

"Hm..."

"Your annual Academy meeting was scheduled for yesterday..."

She quickly grabbed a small ivory notebook from the chair next to her and looking at the note there, she continued:

"At eight p.m. In Vienna. You were supposed to speak on ..."

She could not decipher her own scribbling, so she dropped her notebook and finished with a slight reproach in her voice:

"You see, I know!"

"So what?

"You wouldn't be able to attend.

The concert will take place tomorrow."

"I won't be there tomorrow either."

"Yes, you will."

"No, I can't"

"But you will be here in a few hours by plane ..."

"So, I don't want to"

She laughed loudly.

"You want to! Oh, you want to Jacek and you will be here. Bye! No, not yet! ... Are you still there ...? Do you know what I am doing now?"

"It's dinner time.

You will be eating soon."

"No! I am about to take a bath! I am almost naked ..."

She dropped the headphone laughing and taking off her slip, she jumped into the marble tub.

Meanwhile, Benedict, having sent the servants away, began carefully counting the packages in front of him. Everything was in order. He went to his room, but at first glance it really worried him. It looked too big and too fancy. He checked the walls for a price list and when he could not find it, he telephoned.

When a butler showed up, he asked him for the price. The servant looked incredibly surprised as it wasn't customary to ask this kind of questions in the Old- Great-Cataract-Palace, but he still answered respectfully naming a really high amount.

Benedict, with a kind-hearted cunning expression on his face, opened his bulging eyes and made a mysterious and confidential face:

"My dear, don't you have a cheaper room? This one is too expensive for me."

The well-groomed butler tried to keep his cool:

"There are no other rooms on this floor."

"Why haven't you asked?"

"We thought that as Miss Aza's companion ..."

"Yes, yes, my heart, but I have worked hard all my life not to stuff your pockets unnecessarily now."

"Perhaps a floor below..."

"Ha, what am I to do! Have my things moved there, my dear?"

He went downstairs and made himself comfortable in the room pointed out to him by the butler. It was not much cheaper, but dark, almost completely, and full of the odor of gasoline, flowing from a motor in the yard. Benedict sighed heavily and having put his things in order went out for a walk, not forgetting to lock the door tightly behind him.

There was a huge casino across from the hotel. The older gentleman slowly turned in its direction. He would never risk a single gold piece for things as uncertain as roulette, but he liked to watch others lose money. It excited him in a strange way. Comparing himself to those losers lifted his spirits and almost incensed him to pride himself of his own intelligent thriftiness. Benedict was neither greedy nor stingy. He had a passion for singing and willingly roamed the world by expensive trains, just to be in the company of singers who delighted him. He also thought seriously about having some kind of love affair, but because he lacked experience in this respect, he put it off till later.

An elegant looking butler approached him at the entrance and asked looking at him critically:

"No tie and tails, sir?"

Benedict got furious.

"I am not wearing a tie and tail, you fool!," he replied with an utmost dignity and, pushing away the servant blocking his way, went inside.

But this small incident ruined his mood. He was wandering around the room for some time angry that the people he saw there were winning. They got richer without difficulty, causing him mischief, and when finally, some painted coot asked him for a loan of one hundred gold pieces, he turned away without a word and headed back to the hotel.

Aza was already expecting him in the dining room.

After dinner, Benedict passed the cigarette case to the singer. She lightly pushed it away.

"Thank you, but no. I am not going to smoke, and I would like you not to smoke today. I need to take care of my throat for tomorrow."

The old man willingly put the case away although with a sad face.

"Why don't you go to your room for a smoke and come back soon," said Aza. "It's just next door."

"No. I have moved to a lower floor."

"Why?"

"This floor was too expensive for me."

Aza burst into laughter.

"You are so funny, Old man! Don't you have tons of money?"

Benedict felt hurt. He was looking with a fatherly kindness at the laughing girl, and with a slight reproach in his voice said:

"My dear Miss, if you don't respect money, money won't respect you. I have it because I don't spend it foolishly."

"So, what do you need it for?"

"It's my business, and also, to be able to shower you with flowers after each of your performances. I worked hard for half of my life ... If I behaved like you do, Miss ..."

"Like I do?"

"Of course. You telegraphed ahead to cancel your performance yesterday, and now you have to pay a huge penalty to the Society ..."

"That's the way I like it!"

"Oh, it was because you liked it, Miss? Dear Miss, you missed the last train staying too long at that club party. Didn't I tell you so! ..."

The singer jumped off her seat. Her childish eyes burned with anger.

"Sir, not a word more! Do not tell anybody about it! After all it is not true. I didn't come yesterday because I didn't want to"

"But my dear lady, why this anger?," the terrified old man was trying to soothe her. "I didn't mean to hurt you and I didn't think ..."

Aza was already laughing.

"Not a problem. Oh, you look so embarrassed!"

"Mr. Benedict," she unexpectedly added, "Am I pretty?"

She stood in front of him, erect in a light, colorful, wide-sleeved home dress with the hemmed neckline. She tossed back her head crowned with fair hair, put her hands on the back of her neck, sticking out her round white elbows from the falling sleeves. Her pouted lips trembled with an alluring smile ...

"Beautiful, very beautiful!," the man whispered looking at her with awe.

"Very beautiful indeed"

"Very beautiful?"

"Oh yes very"

"Exquisite?"

"Exquisite! Dazzling! The only one!"

"I am tired," she spoke again unexpectedly changing her tone. Go to your room, sir."

She did not go to bed after he left. Propping her white elbows on the table and with her chin pressed in her hands, she was sitting deep in thought with furrowed eyebrows and tightly closed lips. There was an unfinished glass of champagne in front of her displaying a to-paz rainbow in the light of electric candles glowing from everywhere. The glass was Venetian, old, priceless, and as thin as a rose petal but slightly green, as if sprinkled with light opal fog and gold powder. Next to it, on the snow-white tablecloth, there were huge, almost white wine grapes from Algeria and smaller ones from the Greek Mykonos islands, with a color similar to clotted blood. A half-split peach, parted like a woman's lips, fragrant, moist, longing for a kiss and cool lips ...

A butler stood in the doorway

"May I take it away, now, Madam?"

She shivered and stood up,

"Yes, yes. Please send a chambermaid with a bottle of cham-pagne for my bedroom, but don't cool it too much."

She went to the bedroom and taking out a steel travel box, opened it with the secret gold key that hung from the key ring on her belt. She threw a wad of notes and bills on the table. For a while she was counting something, quickly writing some sums on small ivory boards with a pencil, and then took out a pile of separately folded telegrams. She was going through them copying dates and places from some of them. There were mostly requests from cities all over the world, asking her to honor them with a visit to perform a show or two in their biggest theaters. All the messages were truly short and differed only in the amounts quoted at the end which were always very high.

Aza rejected some of them with a contemptuous or reluctant expression or thought about others for a long time before writing down their dates.

A piece of paper, which was accidentally placed among the telegrams fell out. There was only one phrase on it: "I love you!" And a name. The singer smiled. She underlined the name with a red pencil twice and, thinking for a moment, added the date from a few weeks ago. Then she reached into the box, looking inside for the right place for the document.

Letters and cards spilled from her hand, some torn from notebooks with just a few words hastily written. Some had short comments in her handwriting: dates, digits, or symbols. She was looking at them smiling or frowning as if she was struggling to remember something. She held one piece of paper closer to the light trying to decipher the illegible name:

"Oh, that's him ...," she whispered. "He died."

She tore the paper and threw it on the floor. Now, she grabbed a handmade paper card, a little yellowed and as if smoothed by frequent touching of fingers.

The smell of her dress and body was still on it. She must have had it on her for a long time before placing it here in the steel box with other papers.

Her lips twitched as she stared at the few words almost blurred now.

Only three words were still easy to read:

"You are beautiful." And a name: Marek.

Aza was looking at these words for some time, at first thinking about the one who had written them, and about the day and time when they were written. Then going back in her memory more and more, she thought about her whole life: her youth and her childhood.

She remembered her life in poverty with her father, who was always drunk, and her constantly crying mother. Then, she had a recollection of her work in a lace factory and men checking her out, a teenager, in the street.

She shivered with disgust.

Then an image of a circus loomed before her eyes and a dance on a stretched line and applause.

Yes, applause at the moment, during the impudent love pantomime, while holding onto the rope with the toes of one leg, and with the other raised, abruptly bent back and letting the hideous clown standing behind her kiss her lips ...

The theater was shaking with applause, and terror was gripping at her heart, because every time the clown, looking at her with his red eyes, whispered in a choked voice: "I will push you and you will break your neck if you don't agree ..."

Dinners in expensive restaurants and those stares again, and dignified gentleman's lewd smiles which she, though still a teenager, learned to exchange for gold ...

Aza hated the goodly, but hideous man, whose name she almost forgotten. She remembered the singing lessons and her first performance, followed by... flowers - fame - wealth. She reminisced how she learned to lure people and treat them like dirt and walk out on them with indifference when they got boring or ruined.

She looked at the sheet in her hand. He was the only man she avoided because she was afraid of him.

She remembered writing to him in a way people used to write in those funny old days: "If I didn't have all this life behind me, if I could kiss you and say that you were the first one, I kissed ..."

She suddenly stood up, threw all the papers back in the box without any order, and slammed it shut. She strutted around the room for some time with her eyes flashing from underneath her eyebrows. Her beautiful little lips curved into a smile that was supposed to be mocking, but it raised the trembling corners of her lips as if she were about to cry. She reached for a glass and a bottle of champagne that had been waiting there for a while. She poured it to the brim and chugged the slightly frozen sprinkling liquid while the white foam was running down her fingers.

Almost at once Aza wanted fresh air. She jumped in her private elevator and pressed the button for the roof.

There was a garden on the flat roof of this enormous building. It was full of dwarf palms, strange shrubs, unique cactus's and flowers with a strong, suffocating scent. She walked quickly along the paths, lined with reed mats, and stood at the balustrade surrounding the platform.

The refreshing night wind was blowing from the desert. Dwarf palm trees were rustling in it dryly, and the parchment thin leaves of fig trees were trembling. She was standing, inhaling the wind through her bloated nostrils with pleasure. The desert behind her was enormous, impenetrable, undefeated by hard-working people for its vastness. In front of and below her was the huge Nile Lagoon, above which the fiery Moon was rising from the direction of Happy Arabia and the distant Red Sea.

The water began to shine and glisten with silvery streaks. Far away, some blackened spots were protruding from it like boulders and trunks protruding from a flood, and the temple ruins, once dedicated to Isis, became clearer and clearer in the moonlight on an island sunken for centuries.

The girl's gaze stopped at these ruins, and a smile of triumph slowly parted her beautiful lips.

V

Hafid despised this entire civilization and all its inventions. He brought dates to the market in the old way. He carried them on the back of his camels, like his father and forefather, and great-great-grandfather in ancient times. Everybody did it like that, when the Libyan Desert had not yet been crossed by one-rail or two-rail railways, and birds made of canvas and metal did not fly above it, carrying people inside.

Perhaps, he was also the only man in the world who was genuinely happy that despite extraordinary efforts, the planned hydration of Sahara failed. He was happy to live in a family oasis full of date palms and bring his dates to the crowded market in the city on the Nile.

It was an early morning. Sitting on the back of an old dromedary, he and his two farm hands were leading eight camels, bending under the weight of dates. He was happy to think that after unloading his lot in the warehouses, he and his companions would spend the money getting drunk. The drink was the only thing he valued and respected in civilization. Allah, in his old age, became more forgiving and in order not to discourage the rest of his weak followers, he no longer forbade them so strictly from those warming drinks.

So Hafid was incredibly happy in his simple heart that palms bearing dates were growing in his oasis, and that he could deliver them to Aswan where people wanted to buy them. He was grateful that the only and benevolent God allowed those unfaithful dogs to build those taverns and that he closed his eyes when the faithful got drunk in them. He was proud of this true and perfect world order when Azis, his farmhand, bored with a long silence, said as he pointed to the west:

"People are saying that yesterday an enormous rock fell from the sky somewhere behind the railway."

Hafid shrugged his shoulders philosophically.

"Perhaps a star fell, or one of those damn artificial birds broke its wings ..."

He laughed loudly.

"It is nice to see that man is falling from the sky, where he had no business flying, instead of sitting on a camel's back given for man's convenience by God."

But as he was a practical man, so he looked behind him and asked with interest:

"Do you know where it fell?"

"I do not know. They say that it was somewhere behind the rails, but perhaps it is not true."

"It may be true or not. Anyway, we have to check it out on the way back. One who falls from the sky must get killed. Dead people do not need the money they could have with them. It would be a shame if it fell into a bad man's hands."

They were riding for an hour in silence. The sun was already scorching when they reached the rocks separating them from the city on the Nile. Hafid looked at the rocks with pleasure. They were an important link in the chain of the divine harmony of the world. On his way home, although drunk due to some sense of heroic duty, despite his tiredness, he always hurried back. Still, his dromedary, which had no responsible soul, would kneel here in a known place, and threw its master in the shadows on the scant grass under the rock. In this way, Hafid had a clean conscience and could sleep and rest.

He was still thinking about this wisdom of Providence when suddenly the camels began to snort and stretched their long necks toward the cracked rock protruding from the sand. Azis and the other helper, Selma became interested in it and went to check what it was. Soon, they called Hafid. Among the rocks, they found the visitors from the Moon trembling with fear ...

That day after waking up, Roda felt as if he had just gone to sleep. He was surprised to see that the sun had already risen on the horizon, and it was getting quite hot. Only after a moment, he remembered that he was on Earth, and that it was normal here. His companion, who was sleeping vigilantly, jumped to his feet as soon as the master moved.

"What happened?," he asked rubbing his eyes.

"Nothing. The sun is up."

They both stepped out of their hideout, still surprised that the night had passed without snow and frost. After a day, the area still seemed to them no less empty and terrible, than it was in the evening darkness. They also just realized that there is some vegetation on Earth. A few dozen steps ahead of them, there were a few strange trees with tall trunks and a green crown of huge leaves at the top. It offered them some reassurance that they would be able to survive there, and only the memory of the horrible monsters of yesterday was filling their hearts with anxiety.

Looking around at each step, they began to walk carefully towards the trees. On the way, having passed a bend of rock, they stopped surprised by a new, unbelievable view. Before them, there was something like a house for giants, crumbling into rubble. They looked at the columns of incredible thickness and the rocks piled up on them to form a ceiling.

"The creatures who used to live here must have been much bigger than the Conqueror, perhaps six or ten times," said Mataret looking up.

Roda, with his hands behind him was looking at the ruins. "They have been abandoned and crumbled for a long time," he said. "Look, some thorny shrubs are growing in the cracks of these walls"...

"Indeed, master, but it is a proof that Earth isn't as empty as you were always teaching us. There must be people here although noticeably big. Oh, look at those drawings on the walls! They look very much like humans, although some of them have dog or bird heads ..."

Roda reluctantly bit his lips.

"My dear," he spoke after a moment, "I always maintained that there were no people on Earth now but could be earlier. I said nothing about this. Yes, it is quite probable that there was life on it before it became this infertile desert, and that it was inhabited by human like creatures. As you see, their houses are in ruins as all life here expired and ..."

He paused, disturbed by some sound that came from the desert. He saw frightening four-legged creatures approaching. They had two heads, one of which was on the long neck at the front, the other, quite similar to man's, was protruding above the animal's back.

"Let's run!," the wise man shouted and they both rushed towards the hideout where they had spent the night. Here, buried in dry palm leaves, they waited in dread for the bizarre monsters to pass them.

However, that was a futile hope. The camels got wind of them, and soon Hafid's servants dug them out astonished with their discovery and called for their master. Since his helpers were black, it would not look right if Hafid showed too much eagerness in reacting to their calls, so he approached slowly until he saw something really strange.

Next to the broken stone and dried plant thicket, there were two ridiculously small figures with man shapes and looking extremely scared. One of those men was bald and had bulging eyes. The other was shaking his disheveled head, muttering, and mumbling something that no decent man could understand. His helpers waved sticks at them in a pretended threat, laughing their faces off at their mad fear.

"What is that?," asked Hafid.

"Who knows? They may be trained monkeys or people. They are saying something."

"How could people look like that! They do not resemble anything we know."

He slid off the dromedary's back and taking one of the disheveled men by the neck, lifted him up to the level of his face to look at him more closely. The little man began to scream and kick his legs, which made the servants laugh again.

"Should we take this with us to the city or what? Perhaps someone will buy it."

Hafid shook his head. "We can profit more showing it in a cage or on a rope. What were they doing when you found it?"

"They were both lying down hidden," answered Azis. "I could hardly pull them out. They got very scared and looked at me and at the camels mumbling something to each other."

Meanwhile, the bald midget climbed on a rock to make himself taller and started saying something and gesturing with his hands. They were looking at him, and when he finished speaking, they burst into laughter thinking that it was one of the tricks he was trained at in a circus.

"Perhaps it is hungry," Hafid made a comment.

Selma took a handful of dates from a sack and handed them to the dwarfs. They both looked distrustful, not daring to reach out for the fruit. Then the compassionate helper grabbed the hairy one by the neck with his left hand, and with his right tried to push the fruit into his mouth. At that moment, however, he cursed terribly. The little man grabbed his finger with his teeth.

"It bites," said Azis and ripping a piece of fabric from his dirty burnous, he tied it tightly around the head of the dangerous monster. Then they secured them both with a strap on the pack camels and headed for the city with an unexpected prize.

"First, we will have to buy a cage." Hafid said on their way. "We cannot show them like that as they would escape." After more thinking, he added: "It would be better not to let them be seen for free. We need to hide them in sacks for now."

Before reaching the city, he put palm bags on the resisting dwarfs and tied them inside securely. Throughout the day, busy with sales, he almost forgot about them, especially since it was a day unusually full of wonders. Apparently, a famous singer was supposed to give a performance that evening, and a lot of people came from all over the world. Crowds spilled out from every train that stopped at the station. Planes were landing all the time like flocks of swallows flying from Europe in the fall. There were a lot of dressed up ladies and gentlemen who had nothing better to do than changing their clothes several times a day and showing themselves to people in different outfits, as if they were going to play in a masquerade ball.

After unloading the dates from the camels, Hafid was wandering around, looking and marveling. Toward the evening, while in a bar, he remembered the monsters they had found in the morning. He called on the farm hands to bring them to him. Selma ran to the camels for those trophies, and Azis began to tell him how with some effort he had managed to gain enough trust in the creatures to feed them with coconut milk.

"They are not dumb," he said, "and they have names! They kept pointing to each other and repeating Roda and Mataret!"

"Aha! They must have called them by those names in the circus they had escaped from. They are well trained monkeys," remarked Hafid.

Counting in advance on the large amount of money he would collect for showing them, he ordered a full bottle of vodka for himself. He also felt generosity in his dignified heart and called several friends to a separate room to treat them. He wanted to show the dwarfs Selma had just brought, for free at first.

The table was cleared, and the dwarfs were place in the middle. Camel drovers, riders, carriers, and cabbies were watching them with great interest, turning them in their hands in all directions, and touching the skin on their faces with their dirty fingers to see if it was similar to humans. Hafid was showing off their ingenuity.

"Roda, Mataret," he said, pointing at each one with his fingers.

They nodded their heads vigorously and with obvious delight that they were finally understood. So, some asked them various questions but without getting any obvious answers. Attempts were made to communicate with signs and hand movements to find out where they came from. After some time, the dwarfs apparently understood what the people were asking. Then one of them, Roda, leaning towards the window, pointed at the Moon just peeking into the room, and was repeating some incomprehensible words.

"They fell off the Moon," joked Hafid.

A chorus of laughter followed. So, for fun now, the Moon was shown to the dwarfs, and it was indicated by hand movements that they had fallen from it. Every time they nodded their heads in confirmation, unbridled and long laughter broke out among those present. They were all rather drunk.

Finally, someone prompted Mataret to have a sip of vodka. He, apparently thirsty, took a larger sip and began to choke tremendously to the delight of all present. Then the other man got truly angry and shouted, stamping his foot on the table, and swinging his hands. It was so funny that when he finished and cooled down a bit, one of the on-lookers, the carrier, took a turkey feather and teased the dwarf's nose to stimulate him to a new explosion.

Meanwhile, Mataret, poisoned with vodka, was lying on the table, and moaned holding his bald head with both hands.

VI

Gently, slowly, like a bird suspended on its wide wings flowing down to the ground, a white plane was descending from the sky onto the Nile reservoir quiet in the evening. Jacek was flying it himself. He had just stopped the spinning propeller and was now sliding on wings spread out like a giant kite, swaying slightly with a breath of wind. Far ahead of him, on the mountain side where once the holy island of File was, the ruins were glowing with thousands of lights.

At the moment he almost touched the water, he took his hands off the helm and suddenly pulled at the two levers on the sides. A canvas canoe opened up underneath the plane, and its front struck against the wave, splashing drops full of the silver Moon.

Moving two levers, Jacek turned the white wings upwards again, so they formed two cross-folded sails like on the boats sailing on Lake Geneva under the Alps.

A sweet breeze came from the side of Arabia, and a small shiny wave followed him. He let himself be carried by the wave and wind listening to the light rustling of the droplets splashed in front of the boat. Only when the shore loomed in front of him, he woke up from his thoughtfulness, began to catch the breeze, and turned the bow towards the ruins visible in the distance.

For some time, he was rushing alone in the moonlight, but as he approached the former temple of Isis, he encountered more and more numerous boats, and finally got into a crowd where he could hardly see the water. All those boats were heading towards the ruins, racing, and crowding each other. Here and there one could hear the curses of the carriers. Sometimes women would scream afraid of the leaning of the frail boat, accidentally struck by an oar from the side. Numerous fast motorboats pushed with electricity could barely move in this crowd and struggled trying to make their way with their glittering bows.

After successfully gaining a few meters of open space, Jacek spread the wings of the plane again and released the propeller.

Light as a seagull, leaping from the water to fly, he rose up and circled high above the crowds. Underneath, boats thrown on the wide reservoir were shining with various lights, like a handful of sparklers spilled from the hand ... Where there was a little more space, the reflection repeated fires burning on the boats, tearing them with a small wave into vivid, vibrating, golden elongated spots.

The Temple of Isis was glowing with light from inside as if as if someone had hidden the sun in it under the purple curtains suspended from the headless columns.

Guards were standing by the remains of pylons at the entrance, taking tickets from the arriving boats and handing them over to the guides who were directing them to their moors in the flooded shrine. Jacek lowered his ticket wrapped up in a handkerchief and dropped his winged canoe on the water in the first, uncovered vestibule of the temple.

Columns of monstrous sizes were sticking out from the water here to the half of their height. They were already covered with mold at the level of their contact with water. Their tops were still shiny with an indelible beauty of colors, which had survived for centuries impossible even to count. More custodians were guarding the entrance to further aisles now covered with a giant peplum of purple fabric and full of glowing light. They were standing in small balconies attached to two pylons above the water, securing the way from any unlawful entry. Here, Jacek rolled the wings of his boat completely and, taking them off, strapped them to the sides and continued to sail in the inconspicuous boat, into which his plane converted.

The temple was like a marketplace shack, full of civilized and rich barbarians from all parts of the Earth. This crowd was moving in all sorts of boats: barges, motor canoes, and in Venetian black gondolas, drifting along the brazen metal galleries fastened to the walls and columns. They were brushing against old hieroglyphs and images of deities carved in the stone centuries earlier and often sunk in knee-deep with water which flooded their holy island.

Wearing inconspicuous, travel clothes, Jacek was passing those people not catching anyone's attention. He was heading deeper into an even denser forest of carved columns with their chapiters wrapped in artificial electric lights.

There were no lamps in the last room where the ancient granite ceiling was still resting on the huge lotus buds. Only a luminous bluish fog was floating in all directions from the head of the giant statue of the mysterious goddess. The water, shallow here on the tiled floor of the former temple, was also imbued with waves of blue light. It looked like some kind of fairy-tale pond, the pool of an enchanted spring ...

Isis's old statue gloomed in those glares, immobile, huge, with a raised hand, with its mouth half-frozen. It seemed that centuries ago the word of the unspeakable mystery died on those lips and stayed secret forever.

At the foot of the statue, a woman was standing on a large artificially made lotus leaf. Her light hair was covered, like that of an Egyptian goddess, with a big striped scarf and crowned with a tiara with a bird's head and a sun disk on its top. Her small shoulders were wrapped only in silver gauze. Her hips were pressed with a rigid cover and a belt, clasped by a huge and priceless opal at her groin. And her white bare legs with gold ankle hoops peeked from under her veil.

Jacek suddenly bowed his head, seeing how the crowd was looking lustfully at her, and bit his lips.

Aza was singing while accompanying herself with barely perceptible dance movements of her shoulders and hips. She was singing a strange, rhythmic song about gods that no one had worshiped for decades.

It told about the fight of light against darkness, about the highest wisdom, the unfathomed secret, about Life and Death.

She was singing about heroes and blood and love ...

Tuned and hidden music seemed to be emerging from the lighted depths. Obedient and trembling, it followed her voice as if in holy fear that her singing spoke about the secret of Return. It supported her with a storm of sounds when she praised the victorious heroes of light.

Aza was singing in a semi-dilapidated, water-washed temple, before the adoring crowd, which did not believe in heroes or gods, in life or in death or love ... They came here only because it was unheard of to have concerts in an ancient temple. What is more, Aza, famous all over the Earth, was performing there, and the price of the admission would feed a poor man for a year.

Few came for the artist's great art, gloating now in her wonderful and expressive voice, that was recreating through its magical spell all that had been and gone and was now almost forgotten. They were mostly looking at her face and her bare knees and shoulders. Some were guessing the value of the precious but exquisite gems she was wearing. They all could not wait for her to finish the heretical hymns and begin to dance in front of the crowd.

However, a miracle began to slowly take place. The artist's voice found the people's souls hidden in the depths of their bellies and awakened them ... Their awkward eyes opened, amazed with their own existence, and began to follow the rhythm of her singing. Some pressed their hands to their chests and, as if for the first time, with wide open eyes, were swallowing those strange reminders, sleeping for generations in the innermost sectors of their brains. For a short passing moment, overpowered by the artist, they believed that they were devoted to their deity and ready to fight for the light and go where her lips would call them out, royal, pouting, strong ... Then they were listening for all the sounds of her voice. Their passionate eyes were watching every movement of her almost naked body. During short breaks, when she stopped singing, only circling in a holy dance, and swaying to the rhythm of the music thrown at her from deep within, everything around her stopped. In such moments, the silence was so perfectly filling the old temple that the lapping of the barely noticeable wave could be heard. And some say that same wave had for centuries tirelessly washed away powerful columns and bit at the secret signs engraved in granite ...

Jacek slowly lifted his eyes. The lights were now passing subtly from blue through violet to the blood-red glow. The bright streaks, wandering beneath the ceiling were suddenly gone, and only the water was burning, like a sea of cool flame. Some red frozen lightning came from behind the statue of Isis, which blackened even more against that background and seemed to have grown and expanded ... The mysterious smile on the goddess' mouth was no longer visible in the shadow. Only her hand, raised to the level of her face, ordered silence in vain with that subtle, discreet movement, or perhaps it was giving a sign that was inconceivable for centuries, misunderstood.

For a moment, Jacek felt as if he saw divine eyes, alive and looking at him from that dark face... There was no anger or indignation at these people, who organize shows in a place once devoted to the deepest secrets. There was no regret nor sadness for the former place of worship, or that the desecrated temple was inexorably falling apart, enduring, strangely waiting there for thousands of years. Perhaps she was waiting for the coming of a man who would listen to the command of her silencing gesture and accept the supreme riddle from her mouth. Would he come tomorrow, in a century or in a thousand years?

Isis, on her high throne, does not see the destruction spreading around her. She does not see this crowd. She does not hear the bustle, screams, singing, and she apparently never saw the humble pilgrims or priests nor did she hear their prayers, requests, or worship. Was she looking at the distance or into the future and commanding silence with her hand and waiting ...

Is he coming? Is the awaited one coming? Will he ever come?

Suddenly, the bright lights and the returning singing struck Jacek. Aza was singing now about the lost, divine lover Hathor. Her voice and dance movements were rendering the feelings of love, pleasure and intoxication, desire, longing, and despair ...

Jacek shivered and turned his head away, feeling his forehead blush with some incomprehensible shame. He wanted to recall the smile and eyes of the goddess he saw in his thoughts just a moment ago, but instead his imagination got caught by a glimpse of another kind of divinity: the movement of the dancer's breast and her small, childlike, partially open and moist lips. A hot wave filled his head. He raised his eyelids and stared defiantly, passionately, forgetting everything, everything ...

Her white arms trembled, and a shiver went through her from head to foot, when she sang about her divine Hathor and the delight of their embrace, and her destructive, ardent devotion. Her mouth looked swollen and hurting from those passionate kisses ... and the delight of the embrace, and the destructive, ardent devotion ...

Then suddenly the spell that kept the audience in an enchanted circle was gone. All pretense left them. They could not hear her in any other way than with lascivious nerves arousing their cool blood. Their eyes fogged, lecherous smiles curved their lips, and lustful tickling went through their throats ...

Now this crowd was the master, and she was its bought slave. For money, she exposed her arms and womb, and under the guise of art, let their sticky, disgusting thoughts love her as she threw the secrets of her emotions to the public ... Jacek involuntarily lifted his eyes to the goddess's face but: she was undisturbed as always, strangely smiling, waiting ...

Suddenly, after a moment of deep silence, the whole temple shook with thunderous applause, breaking from all sides, like a storm. The water under the shaking boats started to ripple and wave.

Aza finished singing and was leaning exhausted against the knees of Isis's statue. Two servants put a white coat over her, and she was not backing out yet, thanking them with her eyes and mouth for insane, crazy applause, which constantly erupted. People were shouting her name endlessly and throwing flowers under her feet, so that she soon stood as if in a floating garden, powerful and triumphant. Above her, the goddess's hand was still risen, silencing them in vain with a secret gesture ...

After a moment, Aza, as if remembering something, began to look in the crowd with her eyes, and suddenly her eyes fixed on Jacek's. A smile flicked on her lips, and she turned her eyes the other way. Jacek saw that Benedict, whom he knew, approached her. She said something to him and then talked with others who were crowding around her, smiling, flirtatious together and royal. He felt that having ascertained his presence, she now intentionally avoided his eyes ...

He sailed in among those giant columns and was sweeping past them toward the exit. He was troubled by some kind of shame and irritated by the astonished looks directed at him. Those people could not understand that someone was actually leaving the theater right now, when Aza, having finished the first part of the program, was to play Salambo, her most famous role in which she performed a naked dance with snakes, and the second dance with the holy veil of the goddess ...

He felt claustrophobic in the huge hall and wanted to get out into open space faster, see the stars and the water, silvered only by the moon.

The crowd in front of the temple has already thinned. Some of the boats were inside, others, not finding a place, returned to the city. Only a few steamers waited for those who could fit into the balconies in the temple. Jacek passed them and slowly turned to the shore. He did not want to open his wings or start the motor, so he sailed with a light wind blowing from Arabia, swayed by a small, softly flowing wave.

Near the shore, he thought someone called him by name. He looked around in amazement. Far away from the city everything was empty and quiet there. He could see only three lofty palms in the moonlight. He was about to sail away when he heard or rather felt that voice calling again ...

He reached the shore and jumped out of his boat. A half-naked man was sitting beneath the palm trees. Long black hair fell on his shoulders from his bare head. He was motionless, eyes staring, arms folded on his chest.

Jacek leaned forward and looked into his face.

"Nyanatiloka!"

The dark-skinned man turned his head slowly and smiled friendly, showing no surprise.

"Yes. It's me."

"What are you doing here? Where are you coming from?", Jacek almost shouted.

"I am here. And you?"

The young scientist said nothing. Nor did he not want to answer ... After a while he asked again:

"How did you know I was here?"

"I didn't know."

"You called for me. Twice."

"I didn't call. I was just thinking about you right now."

"I heard your voice."

"You heard my thought."

"However, this is ominous," Jacek whispered. The Indian smiled.

"Is it stranger than everything that surrounds us?," he said.

Jacek sat on the cool sand in silence. The Buddhist was not looking at him, but he had a feeling that he saw though him, and that he saw his thoughts as well. It was an extremely uncomfortable feeling. He had recently met this mysterious man in one of his frequent wanderings, and he still could not understand why he felt so intimidated in his presence. What was it that made him, who possessed all the modern knowledge and had power in his hands like hardly anyone in the world, feel so inadequate compared to this hermit? How did this man, with an abyss of a soul but as simple as that of a child, do this to Jacek, who used to look with contempt at people from the lonely tower of his spirit? What attracted Jacek to him so powerfully? ...

Since the first time they met, they had met again, often, and inexplicably in different parts of the world. Now today, this strange meeting here on the Nile ...

Nyanatiloka smiled and not even turning his head, as if sensing his surprise, said:

"You have come here by plane, haven't you?"

"Yes."

"Why have you come?"

"Because I wanted to."

"So why are you so surprised that I am here if I also could want to?"

"Yes, but ..."

"Do you think that I couldn't because I do not have a plane?"

"Yes."

"What is a machine? Is it not only the means by which your will causes changes in the position of your body and in the images visible to your eyes?"

"Probably."

"Don't you think that the will can do the same without artificial and complicated means?"

The scientist bowed his head. "Everything I know would make me say 'no!', and yet since I met you and those like you ..."

"Why don't you want to try the power of your will directly?"

"I don't know what its limits are"

"It has no boundaries."

They were both silent for a while looking at the Moon climbing higher and becoming brighter.

After a moment Jacek spoke again: "I've already seen the cool things you have done. You overturned a bowl of water with the movement of your eyes and walked through a closed door ... If the power of will has no boundaries, say, could you just push the Moon in the sky on another route, or travel without protection into the space that separates us from it?"

"Yes." The Indian answered calmly, with his usual smile.

"So why don't you do it?"

Instead of an answer, Nyanatiloka asked Jacek: "What are you working on?"

The scientist frowned: "I have an amazing and terrible invention in my studio. I have broken the concentration of energy that binds matter. I found a current that, when passed through any body, relaxes its atoms into their original components and simply destroys them ...

"Have you performed any tests?"

"Yes. With extremely fine micron particles. Such fine powder, loosening up, causes an explosion, like a handful of burned dynamite..."

"But with the same ease you could force larger masses to loosen up. Explode and destroy a house, a city, or a land."

"Yes. That is what is strange about it. It would be just with the same ease. It would be enough to pass that current through them ..."

"Why don't you do that?"

Jacek stood up and was walking around under the palms for some time. "You've answered my question with a question, but it is not the same," he said. "I would cause harm and destruction ..."

"And what about me?," answered Nyanatiloka "would I not cause confusion in the universe, which apparently has to be what it is, if I were to throw stars on other paths?"

"I know," he said again after a moment, "you laugh at the liberated ones that they are doing little tricks and fun ... Do not deny it! If you do not laugh, then many other scientists laugh both at this and our exercises in movements and breathing, tedious and long, and seemingly childish ... And yet one has to control oneself, one must learn about one's will. These exercises, these fasting's, denial, and loneliness lead to that. When the will is liberated and is able to concentrate its power, does it matter what it manifests itself in?"

"I don't think so. You could work for the benefit ..."

"Whose? Only a man himself can work for his own benefit. Cleansing his soul would benefit a man. A free will does not see any other benefit or purpose. How would you want me to do things that are meaningless to me and might entangle me back into the primitive forms of life I have just freed myself of?"

"Everything around us is strange," Jacek said after a while, "stranger than people who never look deep could ever dream about. And yet, I get the feeling that the things you do are the most bizarre of everything that I know.

" Why?"

"I don't know how you do them."

"Do you know how you move your arm or what happens when a dropped stone falls to the ground? You are too wise to answer me with a meaningless word that conceals a new ignorance."

The young scientist remained silent, pensive, and the Hindu continued speaking:

"Explain to me how this is happening, that your will raises your eyelid, and I will explain to you how the stars prefer to move. Both are an equal miracle and an equal secret. The will is greater than the knowledge, but it is subjected to the body, and these are its usual limits. So, the will must dare to go beyond the body and be totally independent of it. Only then will it have full control because there will be no difference between its "I" and "not I."

"And are there are no boundaries then?"

"They can't be there. There are boundaries for movements, for desires, and also for knowledge, but not for our will. They cannot be there, for the same reason that it stands above the body, above all form and all existence ... After all, your poet said centuries ago:

> "I feel that if I pressed and strained
>   my will and light together,
>   I could perhaps snuff out
>   a hundred stars and

light up one hundred others!".

"And he was right except for that unnecessary word 'perhaps'. That was the reason of his failure."

Jacek was looking at him in surprise. "How do you know our poets?"

The hermit was silent for a while. "I was not always the 'bhikkhu'[4] I am now", he said with some hesitation.

"Are you not a true Hindu?"

"No."

"And your name?"

"I took it later, Nyanatiloka or Three-worlds, when I learned the secret of the three worlds: matter, form and spirit ..."

He grew silent and Jacek no longer asked about anything, knowing that the hermit was reluctant to answer. He sat down again on the grass under a palm and was watching the water. He saw the faint lights of boats flashing in the distance and the gate of the temple between the huge pylons. From this distance it looked like depths of a burning furnace ...Suddenly, as if waking up from his thoughts, he raised his head and looked sharply into the eyes of Three-worlds.

"Why do you keep looking for me?," he asked suddenly.

The bhikkhu slowly turned his bright wide eyes towards him. "I feel sorry for you," he said. "You are pure, and you cannot free yourself from the quagmire of matter, although you already know that it is an illusion and less than just a word."

"How can you help me ...," whispered Jacek, lowering his head.

"I am waiting for the moment when you want to go with me into the wilderness ..."

Jacek was going to say something but got distracted by the lights on the water and voices that reached him from the distance. Lights swarmed in front of the gate of the old temple and slowly formed a long chain that stretched toward the shore and into the city.

Shouts were ringing in the quiet night air, the calling of drivers and women's laughter, rolling like pearls on the glass like sheet of the artificial lake. The show was obviously over.

Jacek turned sharply to the Buddhist unable to hide his nervous agitation.

"No, I won't go into wilderness: he said, but I would like to invite you to visit me in Warsaw."

Nyanatiloka took a step back and looked at him with a gentle smile.

---

[4]An ordained Buddhist monk

"I'll come."

"I'm just afraid" smiled Jacek "that it will be strange to you, being used to loneliness, to hear the buzz of life ..."

"No. It doesn't matter. Today, I can be alone in a crowd, just like you can't be alone even when you are by yourself."

Saying that, he nodded slightly and disappeared in the shade of the palm trees on the coast.

Aza's triumphal procession was coming closer. Jacek seemed to hear her silver like voice.

VII

The cage, placed on the back of the donkey, was quite spacious for two or more people of this height, but inside there was nothing to sit upon. There were two swings, hung from the top grille, but both Roda and Mataret found it improper to use this ridiculous device.

The donkey's wobbly movement did not allow them to stand, so they sat down on the bottom, which was lined with a palm mat, trying to avoid each other eyes. Shame and despair simply took away their will to live. They didn't know what was happening to them. Malicious, big Earth people imprisoned them in a cage, like some unintelligent animals. The once highly venerable pride and reverence of the Brotherhood of Truth on the Moon are now driven around populated squares for some unknown reason. In addition, a third companion was caged with them, and they could not clearly tell whether it was an animal or a human. He was about their size and had a face resembling human, but its body was overgrown with hair and it had a second pair of arms where people have legs.

This companion seemed completely satisfied with his fate in the cage and even took exclusive control of both swings, jumping constantly from one to the other. Roda tried to communicate with him, at first in speech and then in sign language. He heard the words, was making lewd grimaces, and finally jumped at master's neck and rummaged violently in his disheveled hair. They decided that it was an animal even if there was some similarity to a man. This company, however, humiliated them even more, especially since they were forced to eat from one bowl with this strange monster.

Around noon, after a long silence, Mataret looked into the Master's eyes and asked:"So what? Is the Earth inhabited?"

Roda dropped his head: "Now is not the time for mockery. In any case, we are here because of you, and it is your fault ."

"I don't know ... If you hadn't insisted the Conqueror was not from Earth ..."

"It's not certain yet," the master mumbled to preserve some remnant of his honor.

Mataret laughed bitterly. "Never mind," he said after a moment. "You were wrong, or we were wrong, it doesn't matter now. At times, I am ready to suppose that the Conqueror must have come to the Moon from elsewhere, because he is an intelligent man, and you cannot communicate with these people ... What do they take us for?"

"I don't know"

"I think I can guess. They just think of us as animals or something ... After all, you can see how they look at us."

Roda was pacing in the cage like a small lion shaking his lush mane. Anger, despair, shame, and indignation were choking his throat so much that he could hardly speak, and Mataret was sneering as if he wanted to bully him.

"Try to climb on the swing", he was saying "and make a forward roll like that hairy animal. You will see how you will make them happy! After all, they are waiting for it. If you roar beautifully and stick your tongue out, they may even give you a handful of that fruit which would really be useful because we are hungry. This four-handed animal ate everything that was here."

Roda stopped suddenly. "And you know, I think ..." He paused.

"What?"

"Perhaps they ... are punishing us? Maybe they can guess that we stole the Conqueror's missile?
They could find it there, in the sand ..."

Mataret frowned. "Yes, that would be the worst. Then there would be no hope for us."

"And as usual, it is your fault! Why were you letting them know that we came from the Moon? You could have pretended that...?

"What could we pretend? What?!"

"Oh, Earthly Powers!," moaned Roda, out of the childish habit calling for help from the power perceived as divine by the people on the Moon. "What will we do now?"

Mataret shrugged his shoulders. He really had no idea how to get over this terrible situation. They both were standing thoughtful and worried. The monkey accompanying them in the cage came closer, trying to imitate their posture. But the lack of activity of those in the cage tired off one of the spectators, so he threw a date stone at Roda's nose. When that did not help, he began to tickle him with a piece of cane and poke him in the place where true monkeys usually have tails.

Hafid allowed such familiarity only to those who paid for it separately. This time it was a boy, starring at the residents of the cage for a penny, so he got angry and chased the attacker away with a rope.

In general, the Arab was not in a good mood today. The business went perfectly well and in half a day he had recovered the money spent on buying the cage and renting a donkey, so his pockets were full. Money was not a problem, but something else was the matter.

Hafid had a natural aversion to associating with the authorities and representatives of the public order. A vague premonition told him that sooner or later they would summon him and begin to ask him how he came into possession of these dwarfs and what right he had to show them in the city. He did not think about it beforehand, and now he felt that something bad was going to happen. His friend, a carrier, a very intelligent man, shook his head in the morning when he was going to the market, and the policeman, usually standing on the corner of the square, looked at him too long today.

In the end, Hafid decided to get rid of his trophies and the problem as soon as possible and sell both dwarfs. Unfortunately, no merchants surfaced. The parts of the city where he wandered with the cage were inhabited by poor people, and he did not dare to get too close to the vicinity of large and shiny hotels frequented by rich foreigners.

He was still thinking whether to gift these monkeys to someone or drown them in the Nile in the evening. He did want to take them with the caravan to the oasis. Suddenly, he saw a dignified gentleman with a gray head walking slowly through the square. It was Benedict who was seeking to buy a huge basket of fruit for Aza's departure the next day. He calculated that it would be cheaper if he went to the market himself instead of trusting the hotel servants.

Having noticed him, Hafid started calling to him in all the familiar languages he knew or at least imitate the sounds that according to him were appropriate for addressing worthy and dignified people. When Benedict heard him, he came closer as he thought the Arab was selling bananas.

He was very surprised when he saw the cage with people and a monkey in it.

"What is it," he asked.

Hafid made a mysterious face. "Oh, sir! These are . These are this kind of creatures ..."

"What kind of creatures?"

"Very unique."

"Where did you get them?"

"Oh, sir! If I started to tell you about the efforts, I incurred to acquire these two humanoids, grass would grow around us, and we would not move, with you listening and me speaking!"

"So, be brief: where do they live?"

"Oh, sir! There is an undiscovered oasis in the heart of Sahara where only the sultry wind visits. My faithful dromedary and I were the first to …"

"Don't lie! Where did you find these dwarfs?"

"Sir, buy them from me."

"Are you crazy?"

"They are very amusing. They know a lot of tricks, but they are tired now, so I do not want to show them. The one with big hair performs flips on the swings, and the other one pretends that he knows how to read imitating a man! It makes their friend the monkey laugh…"

Benedict had an idea:

"Do you think they would learn to be house servants?"

"Sure! At my house, they sweep the rooms and clean my grand-mother's shoes. She still walks barefoot, but only because of stubborn-ness, and because I don't deny her anything. She is so old …"

"Don't talk nonsense!"

"Oh, sir! I will be silent like a grave if you want."

"Will they know how to serve at the table?"

"Like the best butler in Old-Great-Cataract-Palace, who is a friend of mine and can testify …"

"How much do you want for these monkey men?"

"Oh, Lord, if I wanted to calculate my effort …"

"Speak quickly."

Hafid named a sum and after a half-hour bargaining, he agreed to sell his trophies for a tenth of the price initially requested. Benedict paid, and the Arab hid the money up his sleeve. Then, having prepared two rope loops, opened the cage, and began to catch the scared Moon men. Finally, he succeeded. He tied the tether to their feet and, setting them on the ground, stuck the ends of the ropes into Benedict's hand.

"God bless you, sir!" He said, getting ready to leave.

"Wait! Wait! I won't lead them like that. You have to carry them to the hotel."

Hafid shook his head. "That was not a part of our agreement, sir! I don't have any more time."

Having said that, he rushed the donkey and disappeared into the crowd, glad that he had disposed of the unsafe merchandise for a good penny.

The bustle of people in the street now surrounded the embarrassed Benedict. He didn't know what to do. The dwarfs were harassed from everywhere. They were again scared by the uncertainty of their fate but laughed when their new owner threatened the attackers. A racket started around them, among which it became impossible to move forward.

After a while, not able to manage the situation, he tried to promise a good tip to those teenagers, if only they carried the monsters to the hotel. But those, amused, pretended to be afraid of them, and ran away screaming whenever he tried to stick the tether in their hands. Not happy, he headed for the hotel, leading the little men himself, accompanied by a crowd of children and street people.

On his way, he went to the children clothing store. He selected velvet pants and sailor blouses with gold braids for his pets and ordered them to change into those outfits. When he showed up again in the street with the members of the Brotherhood of Truth dressed in this way, the joy of the people waiting patiently for him simply had no limits. Mataret with a bald skull, and a wide white frill collar around his neck, was particularly delighting. They were also amused by Roda, casting insane glances everywhere.

And so, they began walking in a triumphant crowd towards the hotel where Aza was staying.

VIII

Grabiec, bald on top with a high forehead and a long blond beard and a faint mustache was sitting in the hotel cafe. With the stub of a cigar clenched in his teeth peering over the top of an open newspaper, Grabiec was looking through the windows, at the crowd in front of the cafe. An unfinished cup of already cold coffee was pushed aside on a marble table in front of him. He was thoughtlessly and carelessly turning an empty cognac glass in his hand.

He had stopped reading the newspaper a while ago, although he kept it in his hand, perhaps to cover himself from curious eyes or separate himself with a paper wall from his companion sitting at the table. He gazed absentmindedly at the people sitting at the small tables in front of the café, or at the other side towards the square decorated with flower beds. The afternoon traffic was already starting in front of the huge and disgustingly decorated casino.

Some low-risk players with small sums in their pockets were scurrying up the wide staircase lined with an ornamented runner. They chose this early time not to be constrained by the presence of nabobs, throwing all their possessions on the green cloth. Addicted gamblers were also squeezing themselves through the crowds of people walking below. They swallowed their breakfast in a hurry, so as not to waste valuable time and the moment that could bring happiness. Several automobiles stopped in front of the gate. Among the men stepping out of them, Grabiec recognized some of the regular and serious players who arrived earlier to secure their favorite places. The bored waitstaff were standing on the stairs and chatting in undertones.

Every now and then someone would get up from the tables in front of the cafe and walk away towards the wide vestibule. Sometimes it was a young, dashing, and sleek young man but more often a dignified pensioner or one of the ladies skilled at watching for those pockets of gold. It was not difficult to tell those gold diggers from those female gamblers rushing to try their luck at the blackjack tables on their own. They were walking slowly, lingering, and they knew and valued their market value well enough to encourage passers-by with propitious look. However, the expressions on their faces and the way they were walking said unmistakably that they were not such shy creatures, especially for those sportsmen who wanted and could spare their gold.

Grabiec's eyes distracted screening passers-by as if only touching people's heads in passing, so indifferently as if they were trees or stones rolling from above. Sometimes, in one blink of an eye, he rested his eyes on some sort of senatorial face, or on a man with a knightly form. Then he would look again with disappointment at the crowd of women all dressed up and laughing loudly or at the confident swarm of people. His lips bent in a barely perceptible, contemptuous smile, which slowly stuck to his lips, so they finally looked as if having a slight curvature.

"What do you think about contemporary literature, sir?"

He was slightly started, as if an unpleasant insect sat on his face. Lost in thought, he almost completely forgot about the uninvited companion sitting on the opposite side of his table. Medium height and chubby, he was holding a daily paper in his fingers covered with freckles and diamonds. Now, he leaned confidentially across the table, looking proudly with his bulging and fish like eyes through his thick glasses, on a ridiculously humped, red nose. His thin greasy hair was combed to the front of his head to hide the pimples covering his forehead. His fleshy, protruding but thin lips moved as if he were repeating quietly and chewing the question he had just asked.

"I do not have an opinion, Mr. Halsband." Grabiec answered forcing himself to sound polite.

The man dropped the daily, and gesturing vividly with his hands, began to speak in a throaty voice with a characteristic Jewish accent that had survived for millennia.

"You always answer strangely, sir! It's like you want to avoid a conversation, and I'm asking you, and if I'm asking ..."

"I know, I hear you," Grabiec smiled, "but that's such a vague question ..."

"How can I say otherwise? I am not concerned about a particular case, but about your general opinion, about the synthesis of your opinion. I am just reading in this 'Review'...", he struck the abandoned weekly with his hand.

Grabiec shrugged his shoulders slightly. "I don't know anything about it," he said, looking with a pretended interest at the crowd of people in front of the cafe.

Halsband got testy. "That's not an answer, it's an excuse! You are a writer yourself, aren't you? So how can you ...?"

"No, sir. The fact that I sometimes write, does not by any means qualify me for making judgments, especially those that could be useful for you. Rather the opposite ... Talking, constant and endless scrutinizing is the job for you: editors of big dailies, critics, and historians of literature and art. I don't even know the titles of the literary works that you can discuss for hours."

"You are too modest," Halsband smiled bitingly. "You are a well-known erudite, but you are mistaken if you think I need your opinion. If I ask, it is only because I am interested in how you focus the synthesis of some facts in the lens of your individuality ... You, sir interest me, he added with a hint of a certain kindness in his voice.

Grabiec was not listening. Something in the square out in front of the café really interested him, because he began to look diligently through the open window toward a strange looking man sitting at a table by himself. He didn't have a hump, but he seemed disabled because of his long arms and huge head, deeply pressed in his shoulders. He was dressed neatly but unskillfully. His hair bristled unruly in all directions from the skull without a hat now. The whole figure would have been funny if it were not for his huge eyes. They were so abysmal and so inconceivably fascinating to muse that when you looked at them, you forgot about the rest of the almost monstrous body.

"Would you perhaps know" asked Grabiec interrupting his companion's flow of words. "Who it is?"

Halsband reluctantly looked in the indicated direction.

"I can't believe that you do not know him. That's Lachec."

"Lachec?!"

"Yes, the same one who made the music for your hymn, which Aza sang yesterday in the temple of Isis. He works for me. I took him in ..."

Grabiec threw the money on the table and began to leave. However, before he managed to squeeze toward the door among the crowds of cafe guests coming in, the strange man sitting at the table disappeared, as if he had fallen underground. He sought him in vain with his eyes. He could not be seen among the pedestrians apparently due to his short height. He could have also entered the casino whose vestibule was getting more and more crowded. Some people were already leaving, crisscrossing with those arriving. Some were returning with the same masks of indifference on their faces as they had entered. However, in others one could read from their movements, from their posture, from their eyes, from the expression their mouth, what happened to their gold there, at the green tables. Will they run away for a few minutes so as not to lose their last penny, or are they just carrying away their coveted prey, which they will come to lose again before evening falls?

For some time, while standing in front of the cafe, Grabiec thought about going to the casino and looking for Lachec in the rooms. He didn't know his music before. Lachec was a young, beginning composer, whose name he had heard a few times. Once Aza, while asking for permission to use his Hymn about Isis for the concert, told him that the strange Lachec, phenomenal Lachec, transformed his words into sounds, but Grabiec did not pay attention to this. He didn't care. He had reluctantly agreed to this whole farce, and only while being under the irresistible influence of the singe. Yes, turning the ruins of an ancient temple into a theater and parodying its old and mystical rites sounded like a farce to him. That is why he did not even want to get involved in anything, and he did not until yesterday.

Only yesterday he gave in to Aza's long and persistent persuasions (he was one of the few she did not command) and yesterday evening he came to the Philae temple. He was sneering and in a bitter mood thinking that he would hear his own words sounding foreign to him in those defiled ruins. They would sound funny, never experienced, unconceivable, and therefore blasphemous. After all, Grabiec sang in his hymn about greatness, heroism, mystery, and the power of passion. Her dignified audience would not understand such content, but if they did, they would hate them and fear them.

He was also thinking about it yesterday while leaning against a column with a moisture eaten hieroglyph. He was waiting with a contemptuous smile on his lips when he suddenly heard Aza's singing.

At first her voice seemed to be almost dying in the powerful, strange, inconceivable waves of the orchestra. He had not heard this singing and those sounds before as he had refused to attend the rehearsals. That is why the impression of a sudden and dazzling revelation took him totally by surprise.

Suddenly he felt as if he was raised high above the Earth, and shown worlds he had only dreamed up ... As if his words became some living beings, as if his own thoughts got wings, lightning, and god's power to kill and resurrect! He saw a vortex of cherubs dancing in the fiery air. He could hardly believe they that they had originated from him, for they seemed so great and ardent. He also saw the angry sea hammering the shores with ruffled and foaming waves!

He involuntarily looked at the audience. It was as if he were looking at the sand on a seashore. Fine, powdery sand that was giving no resistance, no echo to those powerful waves. They were gazing at the singer and looking at her feet and her bare knees. They nodded with appreciation when the orchestra threw some extraordinary lightning bolts. Still, they were not blushing under the whip hitting at the tawdriness, and no hands were stretching towards the greatness shown on the golden clouds, towards the revealing of a secret in front of them ...

He ran out from the old temple yesterday, away from of his own scream, the embodiment of a vain and miserable death, but the thud of these wings pinned by the musician kept roaring in his ears and in his brain ... It roared through the small matters of his whole day, through all the small talk with various intrusive Halsbands.

And at this moment an orchestra of storms, the sea and the sun singing on the woolen clouds, on the spraying foam, danced in his mind with an insane reminder.

"It must, it must, it must be," he said to himself almost aloud, answering his own thought.

Something raged and boiled in him. He took off the wide-brimmed hat and ignoring the admiring looks of the people around him, he began to walk rapidly around the flower bed, sparsely shaded with palms. He forgot that he wanted to look for Lachec in the casino. He felt overwhelmed by disgust at the thought that he could now find himself in a crowd behaving in a similar way like yesterday. He could not stand a crowd mesmerized by a roulette ball in the same way as it was yesterday watching the singer's moves ... Mindlessly, he turned left towards the huge gardens, which occupied the wavy ground, above the casino and gilded hotels and were reaching the yellow shore of the Nile River.

The spring sun was very strong, but under the palms there was the fragrant freshness from dewy lawns and from flowering shrubs scattered in clusters all over the vast space. Artificial brooks carried life-giving moisture to fancy trees imported here from all over the world. A Lush fig tree with shiny leaves draped with a network of roots hanging in the air were sitting over small ponds full of lotus. Cacti of various shapes and origin stuck out from among stacked up boulders on man made hills. Some of them resembled poles, balls, or strangely bent snakes. There were spiky prickly pears, with monstrously thickened stems, and silver-green agaves with giant candlesticks of inflorescences shooting up from among fleshy leaves. Ferns and northern plants were hidden from the excessive sun in the grottoes where the air was cooled by water flowing through artificial ice.

Grabiec passed the main, wide avenues and began to wander alongside paths among various groves over small streams with densely overgrown banks of bamboo and broad-leaved reeds. He encountered fewer and fewer people there. The afternoon heat was rising and hanging heavily in the still air, saturated with hot moisture, and suffocating. Grabiec was still walking forward, with his head down, lost in thought. He didn't even notice how he got into the large enclosure on the elevation above the gardens. Without looking he passed fenced meadows on which antelopes were grazing among artificially stacked stones. Their huge, dumb eyes were looking through the fence towards the distant desert - their home. He walked by small ponds full of crocodiles hidden up to their nostrils in the shallow, water warmed by the sun. He passed huge cages, in which the lions, with dim eyes and their fur shagged and unclean, were dozing off languidly because of their bondage.

At the top of the elevation, there was a tall cage, shaded with several palm trees. Four huge royal vultures were sitting on the branches of a dead tree in its central, narrow part. Their heads, armed with powerful hooked beaks, were pressed among the shoulders of their sagging wings. They raised the feathers at the base of their naked muscular necks and their round eyes turned at the sun. They were standing as still and frozen as some Egyptian goddesses, awaiting terrible and secret sacrifices.

But there was only inappropriate and insolent noise around them. Due to some involuntary, strangely malicious stupidity, a bunch of busy, variegated, constantly screaming parrots and monkeys were placed in both wings of the huge cage. Every now and then a gibbon or maggot with a hideously bare, red butt, stretched its hairy hand through the grille, trying out of mischief to reach the feathers in the tail of the royal birds. The parrots were hanging on the dividing bars and, gaping their beaks so ludicrously similar to eagles, were echoing the loud scream of those grimacing monkeys.

The vultures looked blind and deaf in their stone peace. None of them ever turned their heads, or even flapped their wings. When a disgusting maggot with a long hand reached out and jerked out a handful of sagging feathers from one of them, it moved only a half-step further on the branch, without even looking at the attacker, as if he could have done it in the past somewhere on the rocks removing itself from a branch blown by the wind. At first, Grabiec, deep in thought, was looking at the birds vacantly, but suddenly something caught his attention. He slipped his hand carefully through the rods and tried the strength of the divider.

"Strong," he whispered to himself, "What a pity!"

One monkey, bigger and more malicious than the others, extended its shaggy arm again and with long, flattened fingers tried to grab the feathers on the vulture's breasts. The bird raised its neck and threw its head back, tilting it slightly to the side. His bloody eyes stared at the monkey's busy hand, fingers moving in front of him. He pulled his head back even more, as if to strike, beak parted slightly.

"Attack!" Grabiec hissed, watching the scene.

But the vulture, noticing that despite its effort the monkey could not reach it, did not bother to do anything about it. It closed its eyes, stuck its terrible head between its wings again, paying no more attention.

Grabiec smiled contemptuously. "Stupid!" He said in a low voice. "You think it's greatness."

"Yes, it's greatness," he was answered from behind.

He looked back with a frown, displeased, that someone was spying on him and heard him.

"Master Jacek!" Besides surprise some involuntary respect quivered in his voice though without a trace of humbleness.

The scientist held out his hand to the writer. They shook hands in silence and were standing side by side for a while. Jacek was looking at the cage with apes, with an ordinary, indulgent smile in his sad eyes. Grabiec turned to the side towards the huge, glassy-opaque mirror of the distant Nile lagoon glistening through the jagged crowns of palms planted below. Only the sun floated in its middle on its lonely depth, paled, as if spilled on the surface. Still the banks were full of boats, sleeping in the afternoon heat with sails sagging on arched spars. Shiny motor canoes were hiding somewhere, or they could not be seen from this distance among the black hulls of the barges. Luscious palm leaves hid the new city from their view with its disgustingly rich and common style ... For a moment, Grabiec had a fleeting impression that time had gone back and here he was a witness to a certain century known from ancient past, when kings and gods reigned here.

"I heard your hymn for Isis yesterday ..."

He turned around. Jacek was not looking at him while saying those words. His eyes were fixed at the Nile lagoon towards the ruins drowning in the sun lit water.

"You heard it, sir ..."

"Yes, if I did not know it was yours, I would have recognized ... that shout, that plea ..." He was saying it slowly without looking at Grabiec.

"Sir," he began, "a moment ago, you scolded me for wanting to see a vulture use its beak to crush the paw of the shameless ape attacking it. I admit that I would be glad to open the cage for these birds to enjoy a slaughter. But what would you say if these royal vultures, without fighting, could not keep peace in captivity and give a spectacle of their own in the face of the parrot mob? What if they began to hit the bars with their heads and drag their wings on the ground? If they called winds, called rocks and sea squalls that would not come here? If they did so to make it known that they knew greatness and freedom, and that they sorely missed it ... to enlighten the parrots and monkeys.

"We're getting lost in comparisons," Jacek replied "let's leave these animals and birds alone, even the royal ones. It may sound beautiful, but it is never accurate and may lead to false conclusions. Regardless of your surroundings, you stand like a monarch over the crowd that listens to you ..."

A sharp, snappy laugh interrupted his words. "Ha, ha! I know those beautiful old theories which we hammered out ourselves! I know what you mean, sir: 'All the true art has power over souls.' It imposes one's own feelings, ideas, and thoughts on others! Do you believe that this is the case? "

"Yes, I do."

"No, it was true so long ago that today, it sounds like an improbable legend. These hotels, these houses, so common and so alike hundreds of others all over the world, replaced those mighty temples and ranks of mysterious deities that once stood here. But then, not only art, but wisdom and knowledge were like queens, not paid servants."

Jacek was listening without a word. From the look on his face, it was difficult to guess whether he agreed with Grabiec, or if he only did not want to argue with him. Meanwhile the writer, while leaning back against the trunk of a palm tree, was speaking slowly, as if not caring whether anyone was listening to him and only as if he was giving voice to his old and painful thoughts.

"It was so in Greece, Arabia, Italy and Europe until the middle of 19th century. Then, artists, often dying of hunger, were the self-proclaimed rulers of peoples, and they carried, lifted, and threw them into the dust. They lit a fire or changed wild animals for thoughtful ghosts. They had subjects who obeyed them but lost them when they traded their places with them. Now, they keep us up to provide them with emotions, great words, sounds, colors, and they keep you, the scientists to give them knowledge like they keep the cows for milk."

Jacek threw his head back with an expression of disgust.

"And who is to blame for that?"

"We are. At the moment when art ceased to be a self-governing lady and to influence people's lives, to make them act (after all only deeds matter!), it got abandoned as a worn-out thing. Other appropriate means for governing the spirit had to be searched for, or a new world had to be created in which it would have people who could be its subject. Art was once a means of life and power, but it was changed or rather its form was altered to satisfy the goal of artistry, craft dexterity, and a toy. It is no longer about what will it impose on people's minds, in which direction the wind will sweep the field of grain, or where the sun or the moon are told to rise, but about how the words will sound, how the colors or sounds will be arranged ... What was once magic, now it is more like juggler's acts because it is what people of today are able to see or hear. It is too late to strike the sand with lightning today. A tsunami would need to be released on it to sink, groove, and absorb it! The art of today won' be that tsunami."

"And yet we still have, today like before, great creators who sometimes have suns in their mouths." Jacek said thoughtfully.

Grabiec nodded. "Yes, there are some, but their value in relation to society got reversed. They stopped using words to lead because there is nobody to lead, so they keep talking to themselves just to talk. They even came up with a rag to cover their misery: art for art's sake. Oh, how nice it sounds! I am not talking about the smiths of words, sounds, and colors. I don't care about them as much as I don't about tightrope walkers and swallowers of live frogs. I mean the creators! They treat art (art for the sake of art, sir!) as a safety net, so that the worlds conceived in their souls would not explode their chests since they have no power to release them in truth and in deed. Look sir! The artist and creator always expose the depth of their essence. When Phryne once stood naked on the sunny seashore in front of the people, were not lascivious tongues smacking or eyes gaping? Yes, they were!

But at the same time, all heads bowed as before the revelation, and she expected it to happen because she knew there was the holy power in her beauty. Today, we strip ourselves shamelessly, like girls in a cathouse that imitates a palace, or even a church with so many gildings, marble, and lights! But these are just appearances: it is still a market vendor stall!" He raised his hand and flicked his fingers as if he was showing emptiness in his hand.

Jacek was listening to him, sitting on a stone bench, with his chin in his hands. He fixed his calm and deep eyes on him ... He smiled a barely perceptible, sad smile.

"Sir, have the courage to say," he said "that only our thoughts and our intentions can change every place, where we are, into a true temple ..."

Grabiec pretended not to hear these words or did not actually hear them, still deep in thought. He was silent for a while, turning his eyes down toward the city, then he started speaking in a muffled voice full of boundless hatred and contempt.

"Monkeys, parrots and all mindless vermin have too good of a life because of their numbers and their organization to hold all the power! We only know about rebellions from novels. Once the oppressed, the poorest, and the trampled rebelled. The laborers feeding the world with their hands rebelled and shouted: 'We want bread!' For the sake of decency, the leaders gave them "right" as well. But that was foolish because they only wanted bread. Now they have it, so they stay calm, because what else could they want? There is too much equality in the world, too much bread, universal rights and common happiness!"

Then he turned to Jacek and looked directly into his face. "Sir, don't you think," he said "that the time has now come for the highest spirit, seemingly lacking nothing, to rebel? Is it not time for them to protest against the established equality, which is an insult to them?"

Jacek stood up and his face suddenly sobered.

"Sir, there is no need to protest something which does not exist. We are not equal. You yourself know that we are not equal. We use the society in the same degree as it uses us ..."

"Ha, ha, ha!" Laughed Grabiec. "Well, this is one of the fairy tales imposed on us by the mob. I am just saying that the time has come for those supreme individuals to finally stop believing in the alleged grace of the monkey society, which supposedly enables them to think and be creative by giving them abundant means of living and facilitating their research ... Never mind that not everyone is so fortunate, and that like before, half of those greatest spirits will die of starvation, that does not matter, I say! But for me, for you, for all of us, it is a disgrace to be given as if by grace and by measure, what we ourselves should dispose of and without limits! All goods and all miracle of life belong to us because our spirits created them, but we can gift them to the mob. Today the world resembles a monstrous animal whose bloated belly has grown more than normal at the expense of its legs and head. Instead of making the crowd work for us, we all work for this hideous, stupid, idle mob that has no real purpose besides the posts they hold. Laborers, and scientists work for them, and they digest ..." He stopped in mid-sentence.

"I can hardly stop from saying it coarsely", he said after a moment, "but so be it. Everything that surrounds us is vulgar. You have to get out of it or perish. It must be put in a reverse gear now: a tidal wave of the sea receding for centuries. A new holy war will begin and the conquest, rather the realization of supreme rights, not common at all. We do not need freedom today, but control and slavery! Not equality but differences! No brotherhood but fighting! The world belongs to the superior ones!"

"What powers do you plan to face in this battle?," asked Jacek raising his eyes at him." On one side, the whole society, perfectly organized, satisfied with what they have and ready to defend the existing state by all means, and on the other?"

"Ours."

"Meaning ?"

"Creators, thinkers, believers: the ones alive."

"You're writing a drama."

"No. I want life. I create life. You can elevate a huge mass, the important workers, supporting the world from on Atlas' shoulders: let them shake it up! They will prefer to serve the superior ones over these clerks, those retired, mindless idlers and parasites.

"Illusions."

"Whatever ..."

"What?"

"You yourselves are the power! You have knowledge, you have power!"

Jacek slowly, but firmly shook his head in disagreement and said with some inner pride: "No, sir. Just knowledge. We give the power that it brings because of us our inventions, and their practical applications to people for their common use. This is what you would call our service. We keep the knowledge to ourselves, because no one in the mob would be able to handle it. Nothing more."

Grabiec looked at Jacek with curiosity as if he had reason not to fully believe that he gave away all the magic and tremendous power, resulting from the knowledge, to the mob, but he stopped himself and in an outwardly calm voice asked:

"Is it always supposed to be this way?"

"I don't see any other way. Through the law of gravity, life-giving water flows from the glaciers reaching towards the sky, down into the valleys."

"A good comparison. Do you know that this water also crushes mountains and washes them away from the Earth's surface in order to raise its lowest level by one finger and to slightly lift the sea bottom? It will all be flat at the end. There will be no more mountains and glaciers, and the valleys will never rise to the sky."

"Life-giving stars are extinguished, having exhausted their power to heat the infertile space. This is the law of nature ruling the Earth, the universe and the human society."

"Yes, but it is not the only possible outcome. By the law of nature, extinct suns also collide, so that new, future worlds of the nebulae shine from them. By the same law of nature, the internal fires push new mountain ridges from the depths of the Earth. But destruction must precede every rebirth! We also need an earthquake, which collapses cities and turns entire lands upside down.

"And if a new life does not bloom after it?"

"It must."

Jacek lowered his head in thought. "Power, deed, fight, life ... Don't you overestimate the strength of the people who essentially gave away their whole character of thought? I am not even talking about the fight itself. Let's imagine the unbelievable possibility that those superior ones could rise, and with help, whose help I don't know, but maybe their own knowledge and genius. Perhaps those working masses, calmly slumbering today and always exploited, will help them. Let's assume they will win. And what will happen then? Do you believe they will rule or act? You say that the true and great art is vapid today because it is a pointless outlet for the energy of the spirit, while it could discharge itself better in deeds. Now mind you, it is only an illusion that such a thing is possible. Our thought has detached from our deeds, and yet we believe that it will be possible to return to them. Sir, stay with your art and the dramas played at the theater, and let us remain in this broad world of thought, in which no unauthorized person can break in. It is not worth going down."

"What about lord Tedwen?," asked Grabiec. Silence fell for a moment.

After a while Jacek answered: "Lord Tedwen gave up the power and is only a sage. It is proof that today you cannot connect thought and life. Leave us alone, sir."

"Is this your last word, sir?," said Grabiec with a gloomy frown.

Something in his tone struck Jacek so he looked sharply into his eyes. "Why are you asking?"

Grabiec leaned towards him. "If I told you that the Earth is already trembling, that there, under its solidified shell, the wave of a fiery tide is already swelling, what would you say then?"

Jacek suddenly raised his head. They were looking at each other in silence for some time.

"And what then?," repeated Grabiec.

Jacek didn't answer for a long time. Finally standing up, he said calmly but firmly:

"Yes. Then I won't give another answer either. I don't believe in mass movements. Hear me, sir. It is all disgusting, but when this feeling of disgust takes over all my other feelings, when I finally realize that it is better to destroy such a thing and this is the only way to push away that shallow wave seeking to flood us, I myself will do what is needed." Having said that, he nodded and turned to leave the city.

IX

"I'm going to break the bank now," Lachec said to himself, counting the gold he had left from the fee he had been paid by the International Theaters Society. There was not much left of it, maybe twenty pieces. After separating the silver, which was not accepted on the gaming tables. He smiled. "That's good; I won't lose anymore."

A strange sadness fell over him. He was intimidated by that dense crowd of dressed up and sophisticated men circling in the magnificent vestibule, those women with bare shoulders, laughing, shrouded in the scent of perfect perfumes ... He had the feeling that they were looking at him with derision and scoffing at his not so well-cut clothes and rather awkward built. He tried in vain to pretend an air of ease and confidence. He had forgotten that all of these people were crazy about his music yesterday, and now he just felt small, frightened, ridiculous, and miserable among them.

He wanted to hide in the crowd sooner. He gave his ticket at the door and entered the room. He heard the well-known, ticklish, fine clink of gold, constantly poured. The tables were already crowded. Besides the row of players seated in chairs around them, there were others standing behind them, pressed together, throwing bets over the shoulders of the first row. They a created a gallery of all types, characters, and "naked souls" united by a desire for gold, stripped of all

502

appearances. Before the start of the game, Lachec liked to walk around looking at faces, movements, catching a few words of broken conversations, short, but so eloquent. Today he was pushed by some internal anxiety as he was anxious to get in the game. He passed quickly through the first and second rooms without even glancing at the players. Only in the third, he looked around to see if there was a free spot. Someone stood up and, leaving, began to break through the ranks of those standing behind the arms of the chairs. Lachec used the breach to get closer to the table on the sly.

"Messieurs! Faites vos jeux!" (Gentlemen! Place your bets!)

Stacks of gold and oblong strips of paper marked with the casino stamp lay on the green fabric. Those were issued to the players at a separate cash register as receipts for deposits of larger sums. Handfuls of money were thrown in from different spots. The older dealer, with a deck of cards in hand, was waiting for the last late bets:

"Rien ne va plus!" (No More Bets!)

Someone else wanted to put a few gold pieces on red, but the dealer's helper rejected the stake with a quick push of his rake.

"Trop tard, monsieur, rien ne va plus!" (Too late, sir, no more bets!)

In the utmost silence of anticipation, the cards rustled, thrown individually at the leather pad. With a quick and elegant movement of his white gloved fingers, with the most perfect indifference on his shaved face, the dealer put all bet chips down on the black and red numbers, adding odds.

"Trente neuf!," ("Thirty-nine") he called, breaking the first row.

The eyes of those who bet on red lit up. In all likelihood the second row would not reach this figure, only one slot lower than the maximum.

"Quarante!," sounded unexpectedly: — Rouge perd et couleur!" ("Forty!" Red loses and color.")

Someone hissed softly. A woman nervously twisted in her hand the last banknote lying in front of her. Someone laughed briefly on the side of the table. The dealers' rakes greedily fell upon the gold, scooping everything from the middle of the table in a wave accompanied by that fine, pouring, and clattering sound again. Golden rain began to fall on the other winning stakes. One of the dealers was skillfully throwing money from above, covering the coins and papers lying on the table. The players' hands stretched out from everywhere. Some were withdrawing the sums they had won or moved them to other bets. Others put new handfuls of gold replacing the lost ones.

"Messieurs, faites vos jeux!" (Gentlemen! Place your bets!) The older dealer repeated the sanctified words with the cards ready again.

Lachec had not bet yet. He was standing behind a large woman's chair and his eyes were wandering around the players squeezed around the table. He knew some of them. They came here every day and always played. You would inevitably see them there at any time of the day, if not at this table then at another one. They were sitting there with equally focused faces, with a pile of gold and banknotes in front of them and with white slips of paper, on which they were carefully recording every game.

It didn't seem to make any impression on them whether they were winning or losing. Lachec understood that these people were only playing to play, with no other purpose, no further thought. He was looking at them almost with envy that they were happy and occupied with what was the most unpleasant work for him: the game itself, watching the cards in the dealer's hands, the look of the shuffled gold. Losing was a disaster for them because it could prevent them from continuing their game. Winning pleased them as it increased the capital that could be thrown again on the green cloth.

It was easy to see that they were looking with surprise mixed with a certain amount of contempt at those running to the table to win a few pieces of gold and leave, with the loot in their pockets, as if it could be better used outside the casino than here, thrown on the table again.

There were a lot of such grasping hands. They stood in compact rows outside the chairs, they squeezed into every empty space at the table and they ... enriched the bank. Some of them played single pieces of gold, anxiously watching each card falling from the dealer's hands as if the fate of their stakes depended on them. Others threw all their assets at once, heaps of ore and banknotes, with seemingly indifferent looks, which, however, were thwarted when the cards were beginning to fall on the table.

Unbelievable sums went across the table for every game. Lachec was watching this ebb and flow, flooding the green fabric with a golden wave. He was counting with his fingers all the pennies in his pocket that he was about to cast into this flood. He fell into bitter laughter.

For a long time, he has played here every day. Flawlessly, without enthusiasm, without passion, even without a bit of eagerness, doing these few hours every day, as if an imposed duty. It bored him and even tired him, but he decided to persevere.

He wanted to win. He just wanted to free himself from the suffocating dependence that weighed on him like a nightmare all his life. It did not matter to him how he would achieve the goal, and this way seemed to him the simplest and the final.

As a young boy he thought that he would soon be on the top with his talent, in which he believed steadfastly, and with his compositions that he dreamed of like birds with broad wings, with lightning in the claws flying in sunny glory throughout the world ...

He dreamed of some impending royalty, which the people would bow to, some joyful and sacred ascension, but he was awakened too early from those dreams ...

Because of his malformed body and his bad temper, he was the laughingstock of his classmates at the elementary school. The teachers did not like him because of his forgetfulness, preventing him from focusing on any subject long enough. He was called a "nitwit" who would be of no use for the world.

He was also awaiting leaving school as his the day of his liberation. His parent's financial situation would not allow him to even dream of devoting himself to studying music, which was the only thing in the world that had value and charm for him. But in this perfectly organized society, among its basic acts their was a paragraph which the right to free education and support at the expense of the national treasury to all who could show a specific talent.

After graduating from elementary school, he hoped to be able to get under the protective wings of this benevolent law. However, he did not do well during the exam which was meant to show his musical talent. Professional musicians, with high salaries from the treasury, said bluntly and unanimously that he should rather scrape pots, because he was a freak. There was also another paragraph in the act that required everyone to do their duty. Anyway, if he didn't want to give up, at least for a while, he would have to starve to death.

Lachec was assigned to a small job in the Office of International Communications, where for several years he pretended to be a nitwit eating bread for free. He put a lot of effort into educating himself. He paid a big portion of his small salary to private teachers to open the kingdom of sounds to him while starving and dressed in rags. After completing the necessary years of "social service" in the Office of Communication in an invariably low position, he retired. He went quickly and recklessly into the world, with a pension so ridiculously small that he would eat every third day to make it last and with a portfolio full of orchestral works that no one wanted to play.

He himself, the composer, did not possess the skill of a performer. He was looking at the notes he had put on paper and longingly dreaming about a day when he himself could hear them. He would tremble with anxiety and desire at the very thought of them being resurrected with all their living sounds.

He went from one famous musical authority to another, knocked on the doors of theaters and concert halls, talked to virtuosos, and always to no avail. They shrugged hearing about his self-mastery. He did not have a graduating certificate from a state music school. He had not even been admitted to it, and therefore he did not have talent. They didn't want to talk to him anymore.

Only once had a director, being in a good mood, promised to listen to his concert. Lachec waited a few weeks for admission before the dignitary. The great day finally arrived. He came to an elegant office with notebooks in hand, intimidated, frightened, and even more awkward than usual. The director presumptuously pointed at the piano.

"Play there," he said "I only have fifteen minutes."

Lachec blushed and mumbled something incomprehensible.

"Hurry up, time is money!," insisted the dignitary browsing through some notes.

"I can't"

"What?"

"I do not know how to play," repeated Lachec. I only compose and conduct."

The director rang his bell. "Next!" He said to the butler who showed up at the door, and this was the end of that memorable audition for him.

Finally, he was forced to ask Mr. Benedict, a distant uncle on his mother's side, for help. Mr. Benedict, who liked to be known, at least in his own thoughts, as a benevolent man, did not refuse help. In the past he had loaned him small sums on several occasions, but he was not generous, especially since he did not believe in the talent of this strange musician who wasn't even able to play.

Soon after that, Halsband discovered him and started giving him orders for writing music to various shabby poems on given topics. He paid pennies, but they meant Lachec's survival. Halsband, a middleman, a reporter, a journalist, and an owner of a great weekly, was currently involved in the history of art and literature. At the same time, he headed a huge "Society for the Propagation of Modern and Ancient Masterpieces by Means of Updated Record Players" and Lachec's music served this purpose. Sometimes he even wrote for him "newly discovered" pieces of dead masters. Infuriated by that, he took revenge, as much as he could, on the audience listening to these atrocities, parodying the greatest motives bitterly, but few noticed it.

What's more as an art and literature theoretician, and also a former journalist, Halsband had his aspirations. He was considered as good, and he always praised things he did not understand. He was apparently convinced that this was the surest way to show himself as smart and deep. Since he also intelligently cared for the so-called tastes of the audience, he did not mind certain "concessions". That's why Lachec received from him some most unusual material for "artistic editing". Sometimes it was just chaos in which some really brilliant pieces were accidentally mixed with popular abominations and desperate trash, consisting of nothing besides the sound of senseless and pompous words.

The atmosphere in which he had to live started to suffocate him almost to death when by accident he caught the attention of that famous Aza. She learned from Benedict's joking remarks that Lachec had written music to a famous hymn about Isis written by that haughty Grabiec. She decided to sing it in the ruined temple on the Nile, which had never been a theater before.

Something like this seemed incredible at first, but Aza overcame all obstacles and got what she wanted. The old ruins on the Nile were turned into a concert hall for one night. It attracted people from all over the world to be witnesses of this marvel. They were lured more by the singer's overwhelming fame and her extraordinary idea than by the names of well-known Grabiec and the totally unknown young composer.

Still, Lachec was paid a relatively large sum. He turned over and over and counted the checks in his hands, issued to him for the first time ever. He suddenly felt that there was power in the gold he could get for them. It was a strange, power forged into the ore with heavy hammers in the mint that gives its holder the freedom to do what he pleases, ordering people, using, creating ...

He clenched his hand ... A vengeful fury tightened his face muscles, and his hands curled into fists: for all the humiliation, for hunger, for misery, for those dirty rags he wore, for bowing to Halsband, for serving record players, for slavery, for almost half of his life wasted!

Strange voices of unknown origin sounded in his ears: ineffable songs, thunderstorms of sounds, and winds blowing on the dried herbs of the dying step ... He opened his eyes wide and put his chin in his hands. His features were slowly smoothing out now. He was looking deep into his soul, at the treasures hidden there, which were ready to shine at the world at any moment.

He was sitting in silence for a long time. He jumped up suddenly and started counting his money again. Yes, never in his lifetime, had he acquired such a great sum, and yet it was small, desperately small, if he wanted to use it to buy peace and freedom and the right to create ... It was enough for a year, maybe for two years. Then once again, there would be a return to harassment, to dirt, to humiliation, or at best, to the need for solicitation, trade, and sales. He would have to deal with the burden of thinking about succeeding, about the tastes of ruthless crowds, about seeking favors of virtuosos, buffoons, historians, and about the support of singers...

A wave of blood unexpectedly rushed to his head. At first, he couldn't tell if it was a shame or another new and strange feeling. He understood one thing, that he did not want to, he could not accept the notion that he would owe anything to Aza as his benefactor. At the first impulse, he wanted to take the money and go and throw it at her feet...

He came to his senses. Aza would then burst out in laughter, look at him as some jester and at this insignificant sum for her, which for him, however, was all he owned. She earned it! It was her caprice that he would have it. It was her gift to him.

He closed his eyes and clenched his fists in front of his face. He vividly remembered her as he saw her while conducting his composition during rehearsals: haughty, royal, and beautiful. And sweet, as sweet as life, as insanity, as death...

Oh, how he would love to stand differently before her at least once in his life. How different it would be, to be a master, a ruler, a god despite his awkward figure, despite his hideous disheveled head. Power and greatness would make him beautiful! It is necessary to work and create! It is necessary to keep oneself up. With an involuntary contempt, he crumpled the checks dazzling him a moment ago and slipped them into his pocket. At the nearest state money exchange, he changed the checks into gold and went straight to the casino.

He was playing with persistence, fiercely and yet coldly. He decided to win an incredible sum that would give him a complete independence for his whole life. He was not risking; he was not in a craze. He was simply working hard, winning one piece of gold after another at one of the green tables, or ... losing in the same way.

After long hours he would step out to take a breath, after such ridiculous results that at times he was overcome by despair. He knew that even losing his money would not rid him of the oppressing and illusive hope. There were moments that he wanted to lose everything in order not to feel the obligation to throw himself into this unbearable whirlpool of the game, but such moods passed quickly.

"I must win!," he repeated again and returned to the rooms to "work hard".

He played cautiously; one would say: like a peasant. He started with insignificant bets and increased them only when the win allowed him. Meanwhile, fate played with him like a cat with a mouse. When, after the fight, in which he earned one piece of gold, he moved to a more vigorous attack and threw a larger sum on the table at once, he invariably lost it.

Sometimes, when he saw the gold flowing in waves right in front of him, how people won such fantastic sums in a few minutes, he was overwhelmed by the impulse to risk everything he had with one throw. After all, it is so easy to win: to bet the sum on a lucky color and double it, after the second throw it will be quadrupled, after the third eight times ... Yes, just have this happy moment, just strike home!

He bet one piece for a test and won. His hand trembled, but he threw six pieces. The dealer's predatory rake grabbed them to the cash register. He started again with one piece. It had been like that all the time until now. He was afraid it would be like that again. He began to bet shyly, timidly, moving his hand with a shiny ring of gold, over the shoulder of the lady sitting in front of him, who looked at him every time with evil eyes fearing that he would hit her strange hat. Then Lachec drew back modestly and repeated:

"I'm sorry", barely daring to reach for the win later.

Because the fate began to finally smile at him, he was winning all the time. At first a few pieces, then a handful when he got bolder. After some time, he felt that the pocket into which, while standing, he was pouring the money in, began to weigh on him. He reached out and got frightened. The pocket was full, and among the gold, receipts given for even larger sums, rustled under his fingers.

"My time has come," he thought. In a heroic way, he drew a handful from his pocket and hesitated a moment ... "I will bet on red; I will bet five times in a row! " Not counting, he threw it on the table.

"Trente deux!" (Thirty-two), the dealer's bored voice sounded after a moment ...

Lachec paled slightly. "I will lose," he thought. A second later...

"Trente un!" (Thirty-One).

He won unexpectedly. His ears roared. The dealer quickly converted the money and added an equal amount, as indifferently, as if he were moving a handful of peas for a toy on the green fabric. Lachec's hand shook and he wanted to withdraw the win.

"I told myself I would bet this color five times in a row," he thought and left everything on the table.

Red color won again. This time the dealer, having calculated his stake, removed the gold, and laid a few long strips of paper.

"I told myself I'd bet five times," Lachec repeated persistently in his thought, holding back his hand that wanted to rake the banknotes to his pocket. Red came out again. And once more. Four times. They began to look with jealousy at the lucky player. The sum lying on the table and, undoubtedly, his own, was really huge. He felt the pulse in his neck choking him. He wanted to grab money and run away.

"Until the fifth time, I said!" Droplet of sweat covered his temple. If the sum now doubles ...

The dealer, placing the cards, looked around with his deck in hand, asking if all the stakes were in place. "No, no! It's impossible for red to come out again!" It roared in Lachec's head.

"Rien ne va plus!" (No more bets!)

He grabbed the rakes with a sharp motion and moved a pile of banknotes to an adjacent field in the middle of the table, just at the last moment, when the first card was falling. He waited with bated breath.

"Rouge gagne, couleur perd." (Red wins, color loses.)

Lachec just moved his stake to the couleur. He lost everything.

Somehow it did not move him, and it was surprising, instead, he felt only terrible stubbornness.

"I deserved it," he thought. – I should have left." I will correct it now - improve now."

Whatever he could get in the open hand, he took the rest in his pocket and put it on the Rouge.

Cards began to fall from the dealer's hand with that familiar rustling. The precious seconds seemed extremely long. Lachec looked up indifferently and began to watch the players around the table. The first to catch his attention was the bearded Jew standing behind the chairs, who, although he did not bet anything himself, looked on in extreme irritation at the game in the hands of the dealer, shaking his head nervously and smacking his tongue on an apparently dry palate.

"Rouge perd, couleur gagne." (Red loses, color wins)

"Aha", thought Lachec watching as the money he lost was moved to the register. I should have left it on the rouge last bet and then moved it to couleur." The incredible clarity of this sentence hit him. "It's so simple," he said over and over again, unable to figure out how to make everything right now.

He didn't even notice that several games had passed in the meantime. He tried to remember and thought he heard the black color was still winning, but one game was undecided.

"Then you have to bet on noir (black)." He pulled out a hand full of gold again.

The dealer stopped him with a polite move. The cards were being shuffled again in the center of the table, and during this solemn and ceremonial ritual all bets had to be withdrawn.

"That's good, that's good"! He laughed to himself. I would make a blunder again. After all, reason itself indicates that if black has won several times, it must now change, so I should continue to bet on red.

"Faites vos jeux, messieurs!" (Place your bets, gentlemen)

He bet on red and lost. He bet on red seventeen times and black won seventeen times. He was still looking at the Jew shaking his head. He noticed that he was holding a gold coin in his hand and could not decide where to put it. His eyes popped out, his tongue clicked disgustingly and louder. Lachec was smiling. "This one must feel really tortured!"

He reached into his own pocket to bet again, and his fingers touched canvas as they curled under the last pieces of gold. He sobered up suddenly as if from some dream in which he was not himself. Horror overwhelmed him. "How is that?" He kept repeating, "after all I had so much ... "

It seemed to him that everyone was looking at him and laughing. He backed away from the table as if he were running away. Blood throbbed in his temples and clammy shivers spread all over his body. Only now he was thinking consciously about his game. Every moment he acted carelessly at the table was vivid in his mind. He began to reason. He should have gone to black because apparently there was a run of luck. It would have been enough to put a few pieces on a noir (black) and wait calmly. It would be a fortune. And if he didn't, he should have given up when he noticed that he was unlucky. He had always done that to this day. If he had only left fifteen minutes earlier, he would have ...

He counted in his mind how much he could have had a quarter of an hour earlier. And now? He put his hand in his pocket and walking around the room with his head down, counted the remaining gold. He bumped into people, or gave way to them awkwardly, stepping on others' toes. Someone hissed through their teeth, someone gave him a not very flattering epithet. He didn't care because he just couldn't hear.

He counted the coins in his pocket with his fingers, constantly getting them mixed up and he forgot the numbers and began to count again. Finally, he stopped and no longer embarrassed by the presence of people looking at him, spilled a last handful of gold from his hand, counting. He had more or less the same as before the start of the game, so he lost nothing, but the money won. He said it to himself almost loudly, as a consolation, but still he could not get rid of his depression, which with every moment was more like despair.

He was rich a moment ago. Yes, what he won was undoubtedly his, and it was after all, a fortune capable of giving him that freedom forever, his liberty, and the life he missed. Fate smiled at him and brushed gold through his pockets for such a short moment, not giving him time to enjoy its taste and carried it on like dry leaves. Only to let him experience that feeling of loss. And what now?

He would need to start again with a cautious, arduous, miserable game with leftovers, or renounce it and spend the last pennies fallen to him at the mercy of the singer, return to Halsband to record players, to waiting in the hallways of theater directors, to paid work that destroys everything born in the soul...He felt that he had no more strength for either and wanted to cry like a child. At the same time a strange indifference filled him.

"It doesn't matter," he whispered, smiling with a feeling of unbelievable relief. After all, it does not matter what will happen tomorrow! And today ... I can still drink a bottle of champagne! I have enough. He went into a bar and threw himself onto a round couch in a corner and ordered wine.

"Half a bottle?," the dignified waiter mumbled with a barely discernible shade of impertinence, casting a quick look at Lachec's modest figure.

"Full bottle. Extra dry."

"I am at your service."

Lachec threw his long arms over the back of the couch and folded his legs. He was overcome by the sweet feeling of a divinely carefree man who had virtually nothing to lose. He smiled to himself, thinking about his game and losing, he smiled even at the thought that he was a poor man, and he threw gold and drank champagne here when he liked it.

He poured himself a glass to the brim from the bottle and without raising his head, resting on the back of the couch, brought the glass to his mouth. He felt the taste of the microscopic droplets spattering liquid on his lips, and a refreshing scent struck his nostrils. With the glass to his mouth, he looked through his lowered eyelids at the people circling in front of him. The first sip of wine went straight to his head.

"I am my own master," he thought, "I lost because I liked it. I can do it. I drink good wine here on a velvet coach because I like it. If I want to, tomorrow I will spit in the face of these dressed up scoundrels who look at me like a wolf. And if I want to, I will hang myself and it will be over! I do what I want".

He was extremely pleased with this awareness of absolute, undoubted freedom. He repeated the sentence several times, laughing in his cheerful heart that it was so simple and clear that he had never thought of it before.

A slender figure of a woman talking to someone moved in front of him. Her back was turned toward him, but he recognized her at first sight. He felt it was she before his eyes even saw her movement, or before he saw the color of her hair.

Something in his chest hit like a hammer, and he felt like choking. He stood up, bumping into the table, and sat down quickly, as he wasn't clear why he wanted to stand up. Meanwhile, the woman, having looked behind at that noise, saw him and was standing there smiling graciously at him, expecting his greeting.

"Aza ..."

He stood up again and awkwardly approached her. His hands were trembling and sweat suddenly covered his forehead. When he held her hand, it occurred to him that seeing him there, she would definitely think he was playing with the money she had earned. Shame and biting rage filled him and took away the rest of his consciousness. He hardly noticed that Aza introduced him to her companion as he only heard the word "my musician" which inconceivably stung him.

"I am giving up music, Madam", he spurted out without thinking.

"You don't say!," the singer laughed. "Have you won that much?" As soon as she said it, she felt pity. Lachec's face reddened and he smiled strangely as if he was about to cry. She touched his hand.

"Henry," she spoke to him with a slight hint of a good excuse in her voice. "You should not even joke about it! You are a great composer, sir, and it would be a shame to waste such beautiful talent, which must now stand out."

The musician's reddened even more, and he felt as if blood would spurt from his eyes. Aza, meanwhile, continued with amusement, tilting her head with gracious flirtation. "Why didn't you come to see me after the concert? I was expecting you. I wanted to thank you again for this wonderful music. It was your triumph, not mine and not even Grabiec's!"

"She wants to flatter me with grace," he thought. It seemed to him that Aza's companion, a young, extremely sophisticated man, felt it also and looked at him mockingly as at a beggar.

His pride jerked him, and he threw his head up. He suddenly paled and, ignoring the dressy man who was just opening his mouth to add a little praise to Aza's words, looked straight into her face with his clear, abyssal eyes.

"It's I who need to thank you, madam," he said slowly, drawling out his words. You were an excellent performer of my creation. I couldn't wish for someone better. I am completely satisfied and thank you again."

He bowed quickly, with an unbelievable dexterity for him, and left. At the door he remembered that he had not paid for the wine. He tossed the servant casually a few pieces of gold, almost half of what was left to his soul, and ran out, without looking back, up the stairs. Here, his momentary confidence suddenly left him, and his strained nerves refused to obey.

"I'm an idiot," he thought as he squeezed through the crowds towards the gardens, "an idiot, a clown, a harlot and a bore. What will she think of me now? She is probably talking to that dude and laughing..."

He was overcome with an insane nervous despair. He pressed his fingers into his wide mouth and was biting them, rushing through palm avenues devoid of all pedestrians because of the heat. "As far away as possible. Just move on!"

He felt his sobbing was choking him in his chest, that he would give everything, life and soul, to be able to speak with her differently, like that man, and that she would look at him the way she looked ...

"I will hang myself," he thought. He clenched his teeth with a sudden and steadfast resolution and began looking for a secluded tree with a comfortable branch.

"Yes, I will hang myself," he repeated. "It doesn't make sense anymore. I'm too miserable and too stupid." He saw a dead tree with broad, winding branches. He found a good one and reached out with his hand, to check if it was strong enough. He threw his hat on the ground, ripped off his collar. He was ready.

Suddenly, he remembered that there was nothing to make a loop from. His suspenders were too weak and inevitably would break off. All this hideous and tragic comedy in the whole situation appeared before his eyes. He sat down on the ground and began to laugh spasmodically, although large hot tears were flowing from his eyes.

X

Jacek decided to leave Aswan without meeting with Aza. He was angry at himself that he had succumbed to her persuasion at all or rather obeyed her casually dropped summons. She did not even need to persuade him, and he just came against his better judgment, probably only to experience the captivity of her charm again. Talking with Grabiec made him angry. He now saw that this unique man, genius as a writer, and insane in his thinking about elevating creators, was actually preparing a revolution, and he did not like to think about it not believing in its success. Admittedly, he himself often felt the need to revolt against the autocracy of all those mediocre people who really exploited creators and thinkers for the sake of their prosperity and only seemingly left those geniuses some freedom. He extinguished such feelings quickly with his strong will as the reflex to feeling unworthy of the spirit which is great in itself. Feeling even more elevated, he merely looked at those people around him with indulgence. He had no desire to get mixed up in the confusion of any fighting unless it was absolutely necessary. Those with the most zeal had too much to lose, so it would not be worth throwing it all away on the draw of one card for the not-so-valuable profit of gaining control over the hustle and bustle of life.

Still, he neither wanted, nor could stop Grabiec. First of all, he felt that Grabiec was right in what he was saying, and then knowing that it would do no good. He thought about it in the hotel, closing his small travel bag that he carried with him on the plane. At the moment, someone knocked on the door. He looked back vividly.

"Who's there?" It occurred to him that this might be a messenger from Aza, and though he supposedly decided to fly away without meeting with her, his heart was beating with joyful hope. With some disappointment, he saw the butler assigned to him on the doorstep.

"Excellency, if you wish, the plane is ready."

"Well, I'll be down soon. Has anybody asked about me?"

The butler hesitated. "Your Excellency did not allow to let anyone in."

"Who was that?"

"A Messenger".

"Where from? Who from?" He said it so loudly despite his will that he was ashamed, especially when he noticed a discreet smile on the butler's narrow mouth.

"From the Old Great Cataract Palace. He left a letter." He handed Jacek a long, narrow envelope.

Jacek glanced at the paper. "When was it brought?"

"Just now."

"Yes ... good," he said, scanning through the first lines of the
letter in a large, expressive script." Get the plane back into the hangar.
I'll go later".

Not changing from his travel clothes, he jumped into the elevator, and in a few moments he was already downstairs. Aza's apartment
in the Old-Great-Cataract-Palace, was rather far, not nice to walk there
now in the heat, but he nevertheless dismissed the approaching car and
walked away. Although he had enough walking today, he felt the need
for exercise that always calmed him down.

On the way, he had an impulse to turn back and fly away, just
apologizing to Aza with a card. He laughed at himself. What do these
childish ploys do? It was obvious that he would see her. If she hadn't
even sent for him, he would certainly have invented a pretext at the last
moment and go there.

His attitude towards this woman was strange. He knew that she
did not love him and would never love him. Still, at the same time he
knew that she was holding him with her conscious irresistible charm.
It apparently flattered her to have among so many gilded fools a wise
man at her feet. It might have amused her to bind him to herself and
see him helpless and weak..., and besides, she could have hidden personal reasons for not letting him go. After all, with his status, knowledge, and name, he could often be useful to her in important matters,
and in such circles, where her overwhelming feminine power no longer reached.

He knew all this, and that she consciously chose this hypocritical form of friendship for their relationship, to torment him to keep
even more and more securely attached to her, but he was not upset
or regretful. If he sometimes wanted to break free from her advantage over him, it was only to save himself from nonreciprocal torment
and to free his thoughts from the spell, under which they crumbled
and mixed more often than not. He still lacked the strength for it and
thought then that this torture and this intoxicating look at the miracle
of her body was his only role which he took from life while the rest of
his being floated outside of its circles.

Sometimes, when his blood was rising, and he was overwhelmed by a mad desire to kiss her and hug, he wriggled like a worm
in unspeakable pain. Then, he thought that she squandered her priceless beauty and traffics it, not only on the stage of the theater in the

hundreds glowing lights, but also in the fragrant silence of her room. Everyone thought so, and he could not think differently but usually tried not to remember it at all. When his insanity overwhelmed him, he struggled with it and crushed it inside until it was extinguished in some vast sea of longing tenderness, ready to forgive and to have pity on everything.

"You are mine, you are," his mouth whispered then, "mine, though thousands look at you and hands reach out for you. I may be the only person able to understand the beauty of your body and feel your poor, bright soul, hidden at the bottom of your heart where only an echo of your life reaches." Then he looked at her again with good, though sad indulgence and accepted his weakness towards her and what could be called humiliation. He was like an adult who gives in to the whims of his beloved child telling him to run around on all fours. He had that feeling now, walking to her hotel at her summons, not even sure how she would receive him, or how she would welcome him. He knew that it would depend on her temporary disposition, but he was walking because he wanted to see her alone. His thinking of her was sweet and quiet.

He stopped involuntarily in the place where the turn of the wide palm avenue was almost touching the desert. He almost closed his eyelids leaving the pupils as small as a pinprick. It was enough for the sun falling on his face to cast, apart from the color of his own blood, the gilding of sands even beyond the green fields of scattered and yellow clover.

Slowly everything in his consciousness began to dissolve and disappear. He almost forgot where he was, why he had left the house and where he was going. A feeling of unspeakable and sweet relief, a feeling of unfathomable peace flowed down on him with the rays of the sun. He then remembered: Aza, Grabiec, some higher and hard spirit toil, and Nyanatiloka. All that was melting now like the spring snow there, in his homeland, when the heat radiates from heaven, from the already loosened soil, from the unleashed water.

"The sun! The sun!" There was a moment that he was no longer thinking of anything, but the sun and the wind reflected from the distant, pink rocks. The wind was hot from traveling through the desert somehow from the blue sea, from warm waves slipping on the sand like cats that purr hungrily around the hands stroking them. He was intoxicated by the fragrant, ringing in his ears in the afternoon silence and the caress of the sweet wind, which he felt on his face, in his hair, on his parted lips. A strange, ticklish feeling of almost physical pleasure flowed through his limbs.

"Yes, this is how her lips must kiss, this is how her hands must caress so soft, sweet, fragrant..." He stopped his awareness and sensitivity at some point of feeling like a crystal bullet on the knife edge beyond time and space.

"Her lips must kiss like that ..." Suddenly, he opened his eyes, as if awakened from eternal lethargy. In the hot air, a sudden shiver overwhelmed him. The space around him flooded with light darkened in his pupils. He realized that he had wasted the whole morning, sitting in the hotel, who knows why and cultivating his "manly pride." He could have been by her side, look into her eyes, feel the touch of her hand, and hear her harmonious voice. And now, when she called him, he is still wasting time... With a reckless nervousness, he waved at a passing electric cab and ordered to be taken to the hotel.

Aza was waiting for him in her room. She greeted him vividly and with evident satisfaction that he had arrived, but it did not last long before she reproached him for coming so late and only for her explicit invitation. "Didn't you like me yesterday?," she asked in that recently adopted tone of brotherhood familiarity. "You escaped before the end of the concert, and I could hardly wait for you."

Jacek was still dreaming about her, still there, in the sun, and without answering, he looked at her for a moment with a smile, as if in a revealed dream. Any talk would be disturbing him now, instead he would like to look at her and feel her presence, but Aza urged him to answer. He reached out and touched her dreamed of hands with the tips of his fingers.

"You were a miracle," he whispered, "but I'd almost prefer not to have seen you there yesterday, not to listen to this song with others."

"Why?"

"You're beautiful." He absorbed her with infatuated eyes.

"Well then?," she spoke ... defiantly. "So, because I'm beautiful, you just have to look at me and love me, and not run away ..."

Suddenly, Jacek shook his head. "I can never resist the impression, looking at you in the theater, that you abuse your beauty and throw it at the mercy of the crowd. I feel sorry and hurt that you are beautiful and divine then."

Aza smiled. "But I'm beautiful and divine?"

"You know it all too well. I am sometimes surprised that this awareness is not enough for you, and you are still using your beauty to fetter people who are not even worthy of looking at it. "

"Art is for everybody who wants it." Aza answered melodramatically and histrionically. "I am an artist, and what I have within me must be thrown away with a movement and a voice. When I create, I

518

don't ask at all ..."

He interrupted her, smiling slightly. "No, Aza. This is an illusion. After all, you don't create anything. By being a miracle yourself you only make a miracle of what others created. They want your beauty there! They pay you only for that, for one thing only, and you commit to be beautiful to anyone who throws a penny at the door. You lose the freedom of beauty. You expropriate yourself in the theater for the benefit of all those who, with happily discussing art, only follow every move you make with their lustful eyes ... I saw it yesterday and you must have felt it yourself. You are too good to be in their service."

She laughed loud and haughtily. "I myself know best what I'm good at! I do not serve, but I rule. I am the one who theater's were built for, operas were written for, and musical instruments were invented. The ones who built this temple on the island centuries ago worked for me, and so did those who after centuries flooded it with water, so that I could see my reflection in it, dancing and singing. I am beautiful and mighty ... I can and want to rule so that is why ..."

"You sell the beauty of your body ..."

"Like you do with the power of your spirit," she retorted defiantly in his face.

Jacek remembered his recent conversation with Grabiec. He bent his head and wiped his white forehead with his hand. "Like me, the power of the spirit," he repeated, "it could be, maybe ... We're all in one position." It seems to a man that he rules, orders, carries, takes whatever he wants, but it is only an illusion. In the meantime, since his birth, he is just a paid mercenary serving the crowd for the payment agreed without his complicity. The crowd itself buys leaders, jesters, artists, and farmhands, and when there were kings, it bought them and paid them for being kings, though they seemed to rule by God's grace. Even the conquerors are bought by a crowd together with destroyers and enemies because it needs them too.," he added, thinking about Grabiec.

Aza no longer paid attention to his words. She rose from her chair and, to interrupt this conversation, threw with intentional indifference: "So let's agree with this ..."

"Probably. We always agree to everything, as if what surrounds us was worth something, as if it were really needed ... After all, you could be as beautiful in the wilderness, lonely as a flower ..."

She shrugged contemptuously. "And what would I get from it?"

"Oh yes. One always thinks what will come of it. You, me, them, everyone. We cannot value what is in us, so we are looking for confirmation of our judgments about ourselves in others, we build our own for others. We do not believe sufficiently in our eternity, so we look for other, like us insignificant, apparent immortality (fame, fame!) And in our work, or even in action we want to give to our thoughts the duration we want ..."He said it with his head resting on his hand, as if talking to himself, though he was looking thoughtfully at the woman standing in front of him.

She was listening reluctantly. She was bored with words which were not comprehensible enough to her. At the moment, her ear was detecting only the external sound and the gist of the content, and she did not want to reflect on them. And what's more, she always got irritated with Jacek at the moments when he was spinning his thoughts for himself in her presence like he was doing now. She was afraid then that he was strangely and almost completely removing himself from under her magic. She suddenly put her hands on his shoulders. "I want you to think about me, only me when you're here with me."

He smiled. "I am thinking about you, Aza. If I believed in the immortality of the soul as strongly as I desire it, and in its perpetual progress independent of nothing ..."

"Well then ...?" She interrupted his sentence with this question, thrown slightly and not expecting an answer other than a smile on his lips. Her long eyelashes fell halfway over her big, ginger eyes. She pouted her lips, trembling with a hidden smile or sensing kisses. Her tempting breast, outlined with a clean line under a light dress, rose with a deep breath.

He was looking at her face without lowering his eyelids, with such a clear, calm look, as if he really had a flower not a beautiful and desirable woman in front of him. And he told her his dream: "I would take your hand and say: Come with me, let's try to be lonely even to each other. Bloom like a flower because you don't need people's eyes for your beauty. Embrace the world with your soul as much as you can, like the light of the sun, and don't worry about anything else. The sweetness of your lips won't be wasted, though no other lips will drink from them. No single movement of your body will be lost, not a single smile will get lost, though they will not be perpetuated in strangers' eyes and lust for their mortal existence. "

Now, she looked at him with a true amazement, not sure if he was serious, or if he was making fun of her. Jacek noticed that uncertainty in her eyes and suddenly went silent. Sadness and embarrassment overwhelmed him that he might have sounded funny to her because his incomplete, sentences were emerging detached from the ground of his thoughts from which they had arisen and got scattered around.

He stood up and reached for his gloves on the table next to him. She jumped lively towards him.

"Stay!"

"I don't want to. It's time for me … I need to be high in the air above the Mediterranean Sea before the sunset …"

"Why are you saying this if you know you will stay here?"

Of course, he would stay for a moment or an hour. He felt that he would stay with her for ever if she wanted him to. And at the same time, he understood that she would never want to, because he could not want to. He had somehow gone beyond the boundaries of life and was now telling her about lonely beauty, instead of stretching out his arms and pulling her onto his chest, on his lips, forcibly overcoming her resistance if it appeared.

He saw that she was beautiful, alluring, tempting, the only one. He sensed that she was all pleasure and happiness. Some hot fog filled his brain, and he stared at her with his eyes slowly beginning to burn with the passion of love, as bottomless and sad as death. Waves and shivers were waking up in his blood which only seemingly served his exuberant thought. Then it was buzzing, infused with some ancient reminders, of those times maybe, when some of his ancestors were ready to die or kill for one flash of seductive eyes. Just like the sea, pumping its waves towards the Moon, so was his blood flowing with its huge tide towards this great mystery of life, which is love. That mystery was already somehow lost at the heights, and yet alive and reminiscent in the breath of his mouth, in his heartbeat, in the pulse vibrating within the currents of his veins.

"Aza…!," he whispered.

She came closer to him. "What?" She looked at him from under her eyelids, with a look of gazelle hypnotized by a snake, but her lips twitched vigorously, indicating that she was not a victim here ... She reached out and lightly touched his forehead, like a quiet, filled with the sun, wind moving his hair fallen down hair away from his temples...

Like there on the border of the desert, he felt the sun heating his blood, which was getting hotter by the minute. It expanded his arteries, fogging his eyes and spiriting his thoughts into a swirling dance ... Like there, on the borders of the desert, the unspeakable, overpowering sweetness suddenly flooded his whole being.

He leaned his forehead to her hands, and she raised his head slightly. "Do you love me?" She blew these words in his face so close, with her lips almost touching his raised lips.

"Yes."

She was standing over him with a conscious feeling of irresistible, overwhelming advantage. Here through this man, silent like a child in her hands, the unfathomable knowledge of the world and all the highest wisdom were bending at her feet. Because of her beauty and sex, she could order them now, as she already ordered all these creators, poets, painters, musicians who were supposed to be above her! She ordered them in the same way as she ordered the crowd of the rich, dignitaries, old and young people.

She remembered what Grabiec recently shared with her: "Master Jacek has a mysterious and scary invention. He himself will not take advantage of it, but whomever gains control over him will be the self-proclaimed king of the world."

King of the world! She leaned toward him even more. Small strands of her hair, falling from her temples, brushed the white forehead of the genius. "And do you know that I'm beautiful? More beautiful than life, than happiness, than sleep?"

"Yes."

"And you have never kissed my lips ..."

Her words were like a breath that can hardly be heard.

"Do you want to...?"

"Aza!"

"Tell me your secret, give me your power, and you'll have me..."

Jacek stood up and took a step back with an ashen face. His lips tightened, and he looked for a moment in silence at the girl blown away by his movement.

"Aza...", he finally began, speaking with difficulty. "Aza, I love you or desire you, whatever it is, and regardless of the secret and power I have, but I do not want to ... buy you like others do."

She straightened up proudly. "What others? Who can brag that he saw the miracle of my body? Who had me?"

Jacek threw a quick, astonished look on her face. She caught it on the fly and laughed.

"For one ... less than a smile, less than a glance, people hang at my feet and die when I desire it! Nobody has met the price to buy me yet. Today I am worth giving the world to me!"

He was staring at her with bated breath and felt she was telling the truth right now.

She bowed her head and frowning, as if under the influence of a memory, she said: "I had to bear too much dirt as a child to even get dirty now. I was taken and abused, I was defenseless, but I did not give in to anyone but the one you sent to the Moon!"

"Aza...!"

She heard a strange note in his voice, drawn out of the bloody depth of his heart, and immediately a feminine cruelty rose in her. She understood that she held a tool of torture in her hand, which would tie him to her even more, the more she would tug at it and wound him. She regarded him with her eyes wide open. A half laugh played on her lips similar to the one Roman ladies in antiquity would show while listening to the moans of slaves murdered in the arena.

"He is the only one who knows me," she said, "he, your friend! He, the only one in the whole universe knows what my kisses are like, how my chest smells, how my palms can caress, and he is not here on Earth. To the Moon, to the stars, to the wide and blue sky, he carried the secret of my love which could kill someone else with unspeakable delight ... Don't you believe me? Ask him when he comes back to me ... He will tell you, after all you are his friend and my noble friend, the only one who wants nothing..."

He swayed as if drunk. "Aza!"

Behind the wall, an unexpected laughter broke out at once. You could hear pattering of the feet of the running servants, the hotel boys high-pitched voices and the manager's bass voice trying to silence them in vain.

Jacek did not pay any attention to all this. Staring at the singer, he was chewing on a word in his mouth ... Aza, however, rushed towards the door at the sound of the hubbub. When she seemed to recognize Mr. Benedict's voice in the hustle and bustle, she opened the door wide.

The sight that struck her was totally unique. In the hallway, crowded with servants, Mr. Benedict was standing, defending himself with one hand from a small man with a disheveled hair, who, like a cat clinging to his chest, was pummeling his face with a fist. In his other hand, the noble pensioner, was holding a string tied to the leg of another midget, who was trying in vain to stop his companion's anger. The servants were helpless, because when one of them reached out to capture the enraged dwarf, Mr. Benedict shouted viciously:

"Keep away! Do not harm him, it is for Ms. Aza!"

Thesinger frowned. "What is going on here? Have you gone crazy?!"

At this moment, Mr. Benedict finally managed to free himself from the assailant and ran toward her quite youthfully. "Madam," he began, panting and raising his brows covered with bruises, "I brought you something, my Madam ..." Saying this, he pulled the strings of the dwarfs dressed in sailor's clothing.

"What is this?"

"Dwarfs, Madam, very gentle! They will learn service ..."

Aza, irritated by the conversation with Jacek so brutally and stupidly interrupted, was not in a good mood. On another occasion she would burst into laughter, but now she was angry. "Get out, you, old fossil, while you are still in one piece, and take your monkeys with you!" She screamed out of place, like a real old-fashioned circus staff, stamping her wonderful foot on the tile floor.

The servants, suffocating from suppressed laughter, disappeared quickly, and Mr. Benedict was speechless. He never expected such a welcome. He grabbed her wide sleeve while backing away from Aza and began to apologize. He was swearing that he was sure he would please her, bringing her the rare specimens he had by chance purchased for her.

Lured by the loud conversation, Jacek appeared in the doorway. He had completely cooled down, but his face was paler than usual. The singer saw him and began to complain. "Look," she said, "you can't have peace even for a moment! The old man has lost his marbles, as he is not only bringing me some apes, but they are vicious! "

Jacek looked at the dwarfs and winced. Despite their funny look in these outfits, one could see their intelligence was not common for apes or even people with this kind of handicap. He felt an indeterminate hunch. "Who are you?" He asked intensely and without thinking in his native Polish language.

The effect was unsuspected. The lunar people understood these words in the "holy speech" of their oldest books and began to speak both at once, in a disorderly manner, in joyful hope that their long and fatal misunderstanding would end.

Jacek's ears could hardly catch the meaning of the mixture of twisted words which they were throwing at him. He asked them a few more questions before turning to Aza. His face was serious, his lips were twitching nervously. "They came from the Moon," he said

"From Marek?" Shouted the girl.

"Yes. From Marek."

Mr. Benedict's eyes widened, not understanding properly what it all meant.

"An Arab sold them to me," he said." Apparently, some creatures like these live in the desert in a distant oasis ..."

XI

"Listen to me, at least this time," said Roda to Mataret, "and believe that what I do is good."

"This lie will bite you in the butt, you'll see!" Mataret said reluctantly, turned his back on the master and began climbing from a chair onto the table by the window in the hotel room. When he got there, he tilted his head and looked with curiosity at the traffic, pretending not to hear what was being said to him.

But Roda was not so easily discouraged. He adjusted himself in the corner of the soft armchair and, throwing back the hair falling into his eyes, continued to prove that all the evil that had happened to them was only Mataret's fault. That itself was enough to leave it to him, Roda, and their fate will improve immediately. "You can't admit", he said, "that we were hostile to that Marek, because these people here could take revenge on us for that ..."

Mataret couldn't bear it at last. He turned away from the window and said angrily: "But it does not mean that we are to present ourselves as his best and trusted friends, and you are doing just that."

"My dear, I am not so untruthful in this statement ..."

"What? What are you saying ...?"

"Naturally. He trusted us when he told me everything about himself and his vehicle. And friendship ... What is friendship? When one man wishes good to another. The greatest good of man is the truth of his life. And all our activity was directed at that, so that the Conqueror could be deduced from his error about his supposedly terrestrial origin, so we wished him well, that is ..."

"Are you crazy? Didn't Marek come to us from Earth!," interrupted Mataret, putting a stop to his teacher's rapid flow of words.

"You think hard as always. Well, so what that he came from Earth? Even from the sun! We had no obligation to know this in advance. It is best for you to remain silent and let me speak."

"You will lie again about friendship ..."

"This is not lying, I said. We are in a position where only his most sincere friends can be. We came to Earth in his vehicle and straight from him, so in a way with his message. And hence the conclusion that we had to be his friends. Sometimes effects decide on the causes. Don't grimace, I'm serious. Maybe we didn't know ourselves about this friendship."

Mataret spat and jumped off the table. "I don't want to get involved in it all. Do as you please, I wash my hands off it."

"Well, I just want you not to interfere. I can handle it. Was it not for my energetic speech towards this old man who was leading us on a string, we would be still in that cage? Now, thanks to me, you see, they are starting to respect us! You will see that soon we will be quite respected personas here. I am good, lenient and forgiving, but as soon as I come to some influence, I will have this bastard who locked us in a cage, skinned alive or buried head down in the sand."

Jacek's entry put an end to the lunar master's speech. He jumped up briskly to greet him. Having no time to slide down from the highchair, which he always did with great caution, now he stood on it. Clutching on the armrest with one hand for support to maintain balance on its soft cushion, he used the other to bow to Jacek's arrival.

"Hail to you, dignified lord!"

Jacek smiled warmly. "Gentlemen," he said, "I can't stay here anymore, but we'll have enough time to talk." I think you would like to accompany me and be guests in my home?"

Roda bowed deeply from the height of his armchair, and Mataret said with a slight bow of his head:
"We are grateful to you, sir. Anyway, you ask unnecessarily, after all, we have no choice, we are at your grace."

"No," answered Jacek. "It is my good duty to serve you as my friend's messengers and try to make you forget about the unpleasant-ness you experienced at the beginning of your visit to our globe. I am embarrassed. Forgive our Earth for its barbarity and stupidity." Having said this, he turned to Roda with a somber face:

"Master, no letters were found. I went myself to his vehicle in the desert, but they were none. We searched everything."

Roda pretended to be very embarrassed. "That's terrible! How-ever, I know the content of the letters Marek wrote to you, sir, and I will be able to repeat it from memory ..."

"Then, there is no problem ..."

"Oh no! I'm afraid there is... because it was our only authenti-cation ..."

"No, it is redundant. I take your word for it."

Roda slapped his forehead. "I remember now. Indeed, there were no letters in the vehicle. The blockhead who put us in the cage took them from me ..."

"Sir, don't mention this unpleasant misunderstanding any-more. I have already requested a search for Hafid. If the letters have not been lost, we will retrieve them. However, duties call, and I cannot wait for the result of the search here ... I would even like to fly away now if you do not mind accompanying me."

"We are ready," Roda said, bowing again.

In a moment they were getting on the plane. Jacek, sitting himself at the front, glanced behind to check whether his companions were well secured, and lowered his hand to the lever that connected the propeller to the battery system. Its wings growled in a crazy turn, and the sand from the compressed ground of the courtyard in front of the hotel splattered to the side in a whirlwind of air. The plane soared up almost vertically. Roda screamed involuntarily in terror, and closing his eyes, grabbed the metal bars in front of him so as not to fall back.

Jacek turned back with a smile. "Don't be afraid, gentlemen," he said, "everything is fine."

Mataret was even paler and clung to the bars as well, but he didn't close his eyes, trying hard to overcome his dizziness. He could feel the slight swaying and the whistling of the wind coming down at him from above, straight from under the outstretched wings, on his forehead. The sky was in front of his eyes. When he bent his head and looked down, he saw the hotel amidst a palm garden between his raised knees, receding at an amazing speed. He recalled the departure from the Moon, and a sudden shiver of fear shook his body. He shut his eyelids fast and clenched his teeth so as not to scream. Meanwhile, the plane, taking on a more horizontal position, was still rising upwards in a spiral line, making wider and wider circles under the sky.

When Mataret, after overcoming his fear, opened his eyes again, Aswan was only a small tuft on an immeasurable yellow plane cut by the Nile as if it were a blue ribbon with green edges. The circling motion of the plane made the world seem to spin slowly down below. When the sun hit Mataret's face, he noticed that it was high on the vault again, though it was still there when they left the house. The color, however, was golden, as if exhausted by the light of the day, running through some pink ashes, which slowly settled on the solar circle, darkening it in one's eyes over the falling red sky.

Some words caught Mataret's ear. It was Jacek who turned back again and was talking to him. At first, he couldn't understand what he was asking him. He looked sideways automatically. Roda, entwining a safety net with one hand, with the other was quickly drawing on his forehead, mouth, and chest the Sign of the Arrival, which he used to sign on the Moon, and was also loudly chattering his teeth.

"Calm your companion," Jacek said. "We're safe".

Roda suddenly opened an eye, stopped his signs, and started screaming instead. Mataret understood that he was cursing Jacek in the lunar colloquial speech, threatening him that if he did not immediately lower himself to the ground, he, Roda, would strangle him with his own hands and break the damn machine. Jacek could not understand it, but Mataret was afraid that the master, possessed by fear, would commit some madness.

Then, he grabbed Roda with one hand and hissed through his teeth: "If you don't calm down at once, I'll throw you out to the ground. You are not worth anything more anyway."

There was an unyielding threat in his voice. Roda fell silent at once, and only his teeth chattered when he looked with a dumb and terrified look at his former pupil who now showed so little respect for him.

Jacek was still smiling, looking at them kindly. "We're about three thousand meters above the sea," he said. "Now we'll start flying straight home."

Saying this, he turned the machine north and, bringing it to a horizontal position, stopped the operation of the batteries with a push of a lever. The propeller growled for a few more minutes with its acquired momentum, but its movement became slower. After a few moments one could see its spinning propellers until it hesitated and stopped. The plane was now like a kite or a huge bird with its motionless wings. It was flowing northward by the very action of gravity on an inclined plane, strictly defined by rudder planes.

Vibrations, caused by the movement of the propeller, ceased completely, and because there was not even the lightest wind in the air, it seemed to the flying travelers that they were hanging motionless in the abyss of the sky.

But that illusion did not last long. As the rush increased, the air cut by the wings of the descending plane started whipping their faces like a violent wind. When Mataret looked down again, he noticed that there low, low below, the world behind them was escaping with a crazy haste, while rising towards them at the same time. The sun, like a huge blue-red sphere, lay on the left side somewhere on the sands of a distant desert. The night was coming toward them from the east.

After checking the position of the wings, the rudder and the direction of the magnetic needle once again, Jacek lit a cigar and turned his face to his companions. "We'll be at the Mediterranean Sea before night," he said. "Now we have time to talk."

He said it in a quite friendly way with his usual smile, but that sentence filled Roda with a sudden fear. He thought he heard some terrible and threatening mockery in it. He was afraid that Jacek, guessing the truth, would now demand, between heaven and earth, a report from him, and he would be thrown into that abyss already darkening with the evening shadow under their feet.

"Mercy, my lord!," he shouted. "I swear to you in the name of the Old Man that Marek is the Conqueror and King on the Moon, and we have done no harm to him!"

Jacek looked at him with surprise. "Calm down, Mr. Roda. You are too edgy from the arrival on Earth, and maybe by the experiences of the last days. Should I repeat that I have no bad intentions towards you, gentlemen? Rather the opposite. I am grateful to you for this heroic journey through the starry abyss at the request of my friend, though I do not conceal that I would prefer to see him here. After all, now that he has sent his vehicle with you, he will have no way to return ..."

His last words calmed Roda down a lot. He thought that if Marek could not return from the Moon, everything was all right, for it would never be discovered that what he was saying was not true. He immediately gained self-confidence, and after adjusting himself in his seat, began to tell Jacek about his friendship with the Conqueror, careful not to look down, because it made him dizzy every time.

"Marek," he said "has no intention of coming back. His life on Earth was never as good as it is on the Moon. We made him our god and king, and he bought a lot of young wives and took the best land for himself. He also has a lot of dogs. In the letters which Hafid had stolen from us, he was just writing to you not to wait for him here ... He could not find the willing messengers to go to Earth for a long time, until we agreed to do it. We wanted to do something for him ..."

A slight breeze from the west rocked the plane, which suddenly interrupted Roda's fabrications. After a while, when the balance was restored, he asked Jacek if they were in danger, and having received a reassuring answer, he began to say again: "Our trip was very unpleasant and landing, as you know, very dangerous. I think that they should pay us here on Earth properly. I am a great scholar, and my companion is not stupid, though he speaks so little. However, we have no excessive requests. It's enough for me if I get a more prominent position..."

Jacek interrupted him with a question about a detail regarding Marek, and Roda was lying even more terribly.

After some time, Jacek no longer doubted that he was dealing with a fraudster who was knowingly hiding the truth. But what does this truth look like and how to bring it out? He pondered about it. Probably nothing good happened there when Marek sent the missile and messengers ... Maybe he is calling for help? But why did he choose these lying people for his messengers, and why are they lying? Did they really lose Marek's letters, or did they not have them at all? Could Marek be in some danger and had no ability to prepare letters?

Then, Jacek thought that maybe his assumptions were too dark. Maybe this curio was really happy on the Moon. After all, it is quite probable that he became the king there and was ruling the society of the midgets.

The evening was already falling. They flashed over the pyramids which glowed below, as usual illuminated with electric floodlights for the admiration of onlookers, and now sailed under the stars over the expansive Nile Delta. The plane lowered significantly to the ground, because Jacek, by turning the propeller several times, accelerated the speed, and still maintained the altitude reached in Aswan ... Although they were now a few hundred meters above the ground, they could see nothing below except for small lights sometimes unexpectedly appearing and disappearing quickly ... They were electric lamps, indicating landing places for the planes flying at night, or villages and cities whose names marked with light loomed from above like small, bright snakes cast on a black earth.

Jacek was silent, and the lunar travelers slowly began to doze off. Only sometimes, when the propeller set in motion and jerked the light aircraft or the wind blowing from the desert tilted the wings, did they opened their eyelids. Then they became terrified again, not being able to realize at first where they were, and what they were doing suspended here in a black night. After some time, the tireless plane began to wobble more and more and sway sideways. Mataret noticed that they were fighting the wind, rising up again along an invisible winding path. He looked down. The dim lights below disappeared somewhere without a trace, but he seemed to hear a steady, wide, continuous rumble in the dark ...

"Where are we now?," he asked involuntarily.

"Above the sea," said Jacek. "We will fly across it at night when it is the quietest above. We're just getting out of the coastal whirlwind..."

Soon enough, when the plane was climbing higher, the swaying stopped suddenly, and only the metal skeleton joints were quivering from the whirl of the propeller turning and, cutting into the night air. When after some time, and apparently at sufficient altitude, Jacek stopped the propeller, the plane began to sail in a quite silent sky, over the sea, from which, on the right side of the travelers, the late, red and incomplete moon was beginning to peek.

PART TWO

I

There was a faint knock at Robert Tedwen's laboratory.

The old man lifted his head from above the paper where he was scribbling some symbols and columns of numbers and listened for a moment ... He heard it again. Seven knocks: four slowly following each other and then three quick ones. The scientist pressed a button in his desk, and the door opened silently and disappeared in the wall. Jacek slid in the room through heavy draperies.

He approached the elderly man sitting on a highchair and bowed silently. Recognizing him, Sir Robert Tedwen extended his hand. "Oh, it's you ... Are you coming with something important?"

Jacek hesitated. "No," he said after a moment. "I only wanted to see you, my master ..."

Lord Tedwen looked inquisitively at his former and still loved student but did not insist with questions. They started talking. The old man was asking what was happening in the world, but when Jacek was answering him, he was listening with indifference. He obviously did not care about anything that was happening behind the always closed door to his laboratory.

And yet, once he used to hold the very fate of this busy world in his hand, the existence of which he hardly remembered now. Sixty years ago, when he was almost thirty, he had already been the elected president of the United States of Europe, and it seemed he would become its lifelong autocrat.

He had that stunning administrative and practical genius associated with iron determination and steadfast will. He was capable of instinctively finding a simple and fast route to his chosen goal. He boldly changed the existing laws, determined the fate of nations and communities and did not step back. In the enormous mass of office workers (and who at the time was not an official or in any social profession?), he had fierce enemies of his arbitrariness and ruthlessness. They murmured widely and sometimes even loudly, but when Tedwen ordered something, there was no one who dared not listen. It was said that he was striving for unlimited power, and that it was necessary to remove him not only from the helm, but in general from any involvement in the government. It was also understood that if he chose to put on his head a royal crown from a museum, everyone would bow down before him.

Sir Robert Tedwen, himself, gave up his position. So suddenly and for no apparent reason from one day to another, he quit. Then people could not come to grips with that fact for a long time and were guessing wrong and complicated reasons.

Heedless of all useless speculation, Lord Tedwen started working. He was one of the best naturalists but specialized in biochemistry. Thanks to his expansive mind and unheard-of general knowledge, within not more than a dozen years after his resignation, he managed to give people a handful of stunning and blessed inventions.

After some time, people forgot that he used to be the president of the United States of Europe. They only knew that thanks to his method of reviving tissue, diseases ceased to exist. It was also known that by influencing atmospheric electricity and controlling the weather and warmth, he was determining the crops and feeding the starving people ... and many more wonderful things.

It was the second stage of Robert Tedwen's life. He gave it up before he reached his fifties. As surprisingly, as he once abandoned his position of power, he now left his "smithy", from where new inventions went into the world every year. After abandoning the practical application of knowledge, he decided to become a teacher and was preparing students selected for the most-important task of carrying forward the achievements of human thought.

Jacek was one of his favorite and most gifted students. They met when Tedwen was old, and he worshiped him not only as his teacher and the greatest thinker, but also as his friend who, in spite of that great difference in their age, was always ready to share in his life with thought and heart ...

But those times, when the old man was an educator and, in a way, the father of the "those in the know," all belonged to the past now. With age and time, he accepted fewer and fewer students and was stingier and more miserly in sharing his bottomless knowledge with them. A day eventually came, when even his last few students found the door of his house locked. Lord Tedwen stopped teaching.

When asked for a word of knowledge, he just shrugged his shoulders and answered with a sad smile on his lips: "I don't know anything ... I have squandered nearly eighties years of my life, so now I have to use the last days to work for myself."

Indeed he was working. His powerful mind, not weakened with age, dug into the secrets of existence, and spun general and frightful theories. He discovered the naked truth or a truth so dreadful, that although he rarely shared it with only the most trustworthy people, shivers passed through them, and their heads spun as if they suddenly looked into an abyss.

Legends began to flourish around the giant, silent, old man. For the longest time nobody believed in sorcery, but he was avoided with fear as if he were a sorcerer, when haughty and pensive, he was taking his daily walk on the seashore.

He did not receive anybody in his house except for the members of the great society of scholars he was the president of, giving in to the requests of his former students.

Jacek rarely visited him being terribly busy with his own research and the office position typically obligatory at his age. However, each time he did visit, he could not resist a strange feeling that the old man was getting younger than ever, as if his thoughts were gaining more and more fearful clarity and courage with age.

At the same time his sight, calm and cool, which peered through people's affairs as he tried to pretend that they were interesting to him, always fell somewhere in an inescapably close but unfathomable abyss. It opened for him, behind a spoken word or a shimmering ray of light suspended on a pollen spore in the air, just behind a vibrating particle of the so-called matter. It was behind the simplest coupling of the incomprehensible phenomena named energy, and running all the way beyond the stars, beyond the end of all existence, equally embracing both human souls, boulders, and nothingness.

However, Lord Tedwen would never let you feel that something was indifferent to him or unworthy of his attention. While taking time off from his mental work, he seemed to talk equally eagerly with a passer-by on the seashore, with a child collecting shells, or with a member of his society of scholars ... It even seemed that in rare times of rest, he preferred to turn his attention towards minor, simple everyday matters.

And now, sitting with Jacek in his quiet study, he changed the subject of their conversation from the world events to more personal news and to their acquaintances. He was asking about his former students who were still alive in his amazingly sharp memory even if some of them were dead. He remembered with a smile some minor circumstances accompanying this or that event.

Jacek, facing the window, when he heard only the sage's voice, was under the impression that he was really interested in answers to his questions. However, when he accidentally turned around and looked into the scholar's eyes, he involuntarily stopped his insignificant story... The old man's open, motionless eyes were similar to two bottomless abysses or to strange rays running from infinity. They were looking beyond all that was happening now, and what they were talking about. They were looking for something in the endlessness, instead ...

He felt embarrassed and felt like his words were pushed back in his throat. There was a brief silence. Lord Tedwen smiled. "What has brought you to me, son?," he repeated. "Talk about yourself now. I am really interested."

The young scientist blushed. He was really going to talk about Grabiec, and about that underground movement, the inevitable beginning of which he had sensed. He wanted to ask this old man, but a former ruler for his advice and his opinion. But now he understood that all this might be as meaningless to this strange old man as a dry leaf perhaps falling from a tree in front of his house at this moment. On the other hand, it could matter to him a lot as his wizard like eyes could see beyond the surface of it. He might see the mystery of being manifested both in a grain of sand thrown by a sea wave, as well as in the greatest social revolutions and world upheavals, or in the most splendid flash of thought.

He bent his head. "I really wanted to talk about some matters, but I see how small they may be ..." "There are no small matters," responded Sir Robert. "Everything has its value and its meaning. Speak."

So, he started talking and told him about his meeting with Grabiec. He spoke about the struggle, or the uprising he wanted to stir up on the Earth which had been at peace for a long time. He was talking about his plan to draw them, the wise men, and scholars into that vortex, so they might attain their due position as the brain of the world.

The old man was listening in silence, his head bowed slightly, looking from under his bushy, high raised eyebrows, his eyes fixed straight ahead. Sometimes, a fleeting smile ran around his narrow and pursed lips and quickly faded in thought.

"Father," Jacek finally spoke ending his story, "that man simply summoned me to help him with putting the power behind our knowledge on the line ..."

Lord Tedwen turned his piercing eyes at Jacek. "And what was your response?"

"I said that all the power of our knowledge had already been gifted to the mob, and that we don't have anything else besides the highest truths which couldn't be hammered into gold or iron ..."

There was a brief silence. Robert Tedwen nodded several times, whispering to himself more than to his student listening to him: "Besides the highest truths ... Yes, yes! The problem is that we don't know any more about what the meaning of the word 'truth' is, since everything we call this name is such a nothing ..."

He lifted his head quickly and looked at Jacek. "Please forgive me that I involuntarily return to my thoughts, but what you have just told me is very interesting."

Jacek was quiet. The old man looked at him closely. "What are you thinking about?"

"I lied when talking to Grabiec."

"Ah!"

"We have that power ... I have that power." He corrected himself.

Lord Tedwen did not say anything. His slightly absent-minded eyes ran over Jacek's face and his lips moved strangely ...

"You have the power...We have the power...", he whispered after a moment. Something like a smile flashed by his lips.

"Yes." Jacek said thoughtfully. Sitting with his head lowered, he did not see the smile on his teacher's face. "Yes," he repeated. I have made an appalling discovery. I am physically doing what we only treated as theoretical research up till now. I disengage the "matter" and quench it in the same simple way as if I extinguished a burning candle with a blow. If I wanted ..."

"If you wanted ...?"

"I could use fear to enforce complete obedience for myself or for the one I would give my invention to ... With a movement of one finger placed on a device not larger than a camera, I can annihilate cities and destroy countries in such a way that they would perish without a trace of their existence ..."

"And so, what?," asked lord Tedwen not taking his eyes off him.

Now, Jacek shrugged his shoulders. "I don't know, I don't know!"

"Why did not you give your invention to Grabiec?"

Jacek raised his head quickly. He stared at the old man's face for a moment, wanting to read the meaning and intention of his question, but Sir Robert's eyes and features were both as expressionless as the seemingly indifferent tone of the question asked.

"I don't know that either." He finally said. "I thought that I should keep it to myself and probably destroy it before my death or use it... in case of an ultimate need ... only once ..."

"Destroy your device today. Why should one make any effort to blow away a phantom called matter, if sooner or later it will inevitably fade away by itself? "

"Meanwhile everything is bad ..."

"And so, what? So, are we supposed to physically do, what you say, we can do at any moment with our thoughts, without actually knocking our fellow man out of a state that could ultimately be the best for them? Remember, that when we free ourselves from our physical fetters through so-called death, the action of our thoughts will be the only reality for us ..."

"We need to believe ..."

"Yes. We need to believe." Tedwen repeated seriously.

"And what about this world, this world around us? Should it go in the same direction as it is going right now?"

The old man rested his palm on Jacek's shoulder. "Your invention won't get it on the right track."

"If only the best of us could govern ..."

"Do you want power?"

"I have not joined Grabiec. I do not know if I could execute power. I feel pity for the world I live in. But ..."

"What?"

"It seems to me that I willingly and clumsily stay out of the mainstream of life, and I sometimes feel ashamed for it."

Lord Tedwen was silent for a while. His wide-open eyes seemed to wander somewhere among the past years which were now coming back vividly in his memory. He finally shook it off and turned towards Jacek. "What can one do for this life, or rather for people's coexistence? You know that I held power perhaps greater than anybody else ..."

"Yes."

"And I gave it up. Do you know why?"

"It did not give you satisfaction, master as you preferred working for your own spirit ..."

The master shook his head slowly but firmly. "No. It's not about that. I had only found that nothing could be done for the social system. Society is not a rational product, and therefore it will never be perfect. All utopias, from the oldest Platonic ones, through the course of centuries to the present days, to the dream of your Grabiec, will remain utopias forever as long as you read about them in the books. It is an edifice built of cards without respect for the law of gravity. However, when you start acting on it, you will see a new evil appearing in the place of the former one just removed. A perfect coexistence of people and an ideal political system are problems impossible to solve by their very nature. Any harmony is an artificial, invented concept. In nature, in the universe and human society, there is only struggle and the passing seeming balance of opposing forces. Justice is a seductive and extremely popular demand, but it actually means nothing from people's position. Everyone can understand it differently, and rightly so, because there should be different justice for everyone, while society has only one or at least wants only one - justice. After all, it does not matter if the people or the tyrant rule, the chosen sages, or a crazy bunch of shouters. There will always be someone oppressed, someone who is always unhappy, there will always be some harm done.

Someone will always suffer. In one case a majority suffers, in another case only a small group, and even if only one victim suffered, the one who was told to be "equal" when he happened to be born an autocrat. Who will judge when the greater harm is done, and who will enforce the law that everyone brings into the world with them? Devotion to one principle is a violation of the other, no less "just", and always so, without an end.

He fell silent for a moment and moved his palm on his high, wrinkled forehead.

"It does not mean", he continued again turning his eyes at Jacek "that I believe one does not have to try to improve relationships that exist at times. But it can only be done or must be done by people who have such illusions, and who believe that what they do will be better than what was. There will never be a shortage of such people, as it is already human nature."

"You thought this up yourself, master?", Jacek interrupted.

Tedwen nodded. "And that's not the right way. Inventions, discoveries, benefits, and amenities are used primarily by those who are well-off even without them, and who are the least worthy in the community: the vast majority of whom are, lazy and thoughtless. Inventions only enhance these"advantages" of the mob ..."

"So, do you think, sir, that one should not make them, that it is not worthwhile?"

"I thought so myself no more than half a century ago when I was still young … And later, after losing this faith, I thought again that when you cannot please everyone and can't create ideal "fair" relationships, then at least there should be as many goods as possible to share … You know that for many years I "was making humanity happy" with my inventions, until I finally understood that this was nothing as well..

"Hawel hawolim, omar koheleth, hawel hawolim, hakol hawel"…. "Vanity of vanity, said the preacher, vanity of vanity, all vanity!" And it is not the right way. The inventions, discoveries, benefits, and amenities are primarily used by those who always had everything they needed, and who have the least value in the community. They constitute the vast majority of lazy and thoughtless people. Inventions increase such "advantages" of the crowd...

"So, you think, sir that there is no need for greater knowledge?"

"Would they appear less often if I said there was no need for them or sense? There will always be people whose thoughts struggle with nature and learn to put it at the service of man. They are useful, and they are very special people. I thought they mattered the most and maybe only those who are the brain and soul of a human community. I was old when I started teaching. I wanted as many righteous, thinking people as possible to be in the world. You know me from those times, and you listened to my words, my beloved son."

"We all bless you, teacher."

"Unjustifiably. I have to quote the preacher again: 'The one who multiplies knowledge, creates suffering as well.' I am looking at you, the flowers of humanity and the light of the Earth, and I see you as proud but sad. You are entangled in secular events, straining your spirit for the so-called benefit of the crowd separated from you by an abyss. It is my fault that you see and feel this abyss. I feel guilty that your weary thought flies over the final emptiness, unable to find rest, like an eagle on its wide wings, astray over ocean waters ...

So what have I given you in exchange? What indisputable truth? What knowledge? What power? Indeed, I myself know too little to be a teacher ... Everything I told you about the universe and being was only to tear apart the reality that your eyes see, and unfortunately, I could not give you the final answer to any of your "why?".

That is why one day I closed myself to my students, wanting to find wisdom for myself in these last days of my life. Today, I am close to reaching a hundred, and I have been working in solitude and concentration for twenty years."

"And what do you have to say to us now, teacher?," Jacek asked.

Lord Tedwen seemed not to hear his question. He rested his high forehead on the palm of his hand, and looking out the window at the wide sea swirling in the summer wind, he slowly said almost whispering: "The hardship of life and every effort that a human thought could bear is are already behind me. I ascended the highest peaks, where the distant world totally disappears, and there is only emptiness around you. I descended to such depths where I found only emptiness around me again. I never shied away from any idea, and I did not consider any existence untouchable, examining its last roots, tearing at its very first fibers..."

538

"And what do you have to say to us now, teacher?," Jacek repeated persistently.

The old man turned his quiet, wide open eyes at him. "Nothing."

"What do you mean by nothing?"

"Everything I have discovered is just looking at the world we know from close up, from the inside of a drop of water, from the inside of an atom or a vibrating electron particle, or from such a distance that the details and differences disappear, and the being merges into one even sea. I have not gone beyond experience, I have not answered any of my 'whys?' And therefore I have nothing to say to all of you today."

"But what have you discovered? Tell me!"

Jacek's voice carried a note of urgent human curiosity, which, striving for a high and inaccessible mountain, meets on its way to a traveler, just returning from the top. The old man hesitated for one moment. He reached out and scooped up the papers in front of him. For some time, he was still looking through columns of numbers and signs, and small notes hurriedly made on the edges of pages...

"Nihil ex nihilo...," he whispered. "The sensual world is really and literally nothing." He raised his head. A brilliant explorer and a teacher were waking up in him ...

"The centuries-old theory of the so-called 'ether'," he began to say "collapsed against the principle of relativity of movement, unable to deal with the second phantom of human thought, which is matter ... Today, school children already know that light will spread with the same speed in all directions, regardless of whether its source is in motion or at rest ... If we wanted to marry this fact with the existence of ether as a guide of vibrations, we would have to take not one, but as many all-encompassing, incomplete and boundless ethers, as there are bodies in the universe changing their relative location ... Yet there must be a medium through which the waves of light and heat and electricity go from star to star, when one celestial body gravitates to another..."

He stood up and started walking around the room with his hands on his back. He suddenly stopped before Jacek and put his hand on his shoulder.

He started again: "Ether exists regardless how we name it, but it has no matter. What our senses have considered for centuries as the only reality is not even a concentration of energy, not even a permanent condensation or dilution of the ether. It is only a funny illusion, only a wave which goes through the ether like a sound wave through the air. Nothing is really permanent or material. There is no solid or important thing. Both the suns and sun systems, as every particle, every atom and electron are only a wavy movement. That waving is a non-autonomous phenomena rushing through the ether, which in the face of human investigative thought dissipates in one all-encompassing and infinite nothing ... Matter is still less than nothing."

He sat down and propped his forehead in thought.

"Everything flows: 'Pantha rei...' Like a gas flame that shimmers before our eyes despite the fact that it consists of separate carbon particles combining themselves with oxygen! When a flame leaves a trace in the new body connection, a wave of matter passes through the ether without a trace. Every minute, every second and a hundredth of second, the Sun rushing through space keeps creating itself from other vibrating ether particles which give it some shape. If this vibration were stopped, it would disappear without a trace like a rainbow when the ray of light fades. The principle of the indestructibility of matter and energy is a lie invented by our thought which is in a pursuit of solid value, but everything turns into nothing and everything arises from nothing."

"So where is the truth? Where is the absolute being?," Jacek whispered with paled lips.

Robert Tedwen dropped his palm on the open, old book on the table. "Here. Look and read."

In the darkness of the falling evening. Jacek bent and started to read from the yellowish page:

'In the beginning was the Word, and the Word was with God, and the Word was God.

It was in the beginning with God. All things were made through him, and without him nothing happened that happened.

In him was life, and life was the light of the spirit.

And the light shines in the darkness, and the darkness has not overcome it ... '

He lifted his eyes from the page and looked at the silver sage's face in surprise.

The sage's lips were moving slowly as if repeating the sentence from the book: In the beginning was the Word..."

"Teacher ...?"

He turned his head towards Jacek. "That is what it is. My whole knowledge, to which I devoted my life, showed me only one thing: there are no obstacles to believing. My investigative thought dispelled all those ridiculous visions. Those "obvious facts" which supposedly oppose the Revelation disappeared like a feverish dream in a sultry dream at night: I stood before the emptiness, the inconceivable emptiness, the all-indefinable emptiness, which the Word can fill and fertilize ...

The spirit is the only truth and reality among the flowing wave. Everything came from it, for it and through it. The Word has become flesh."

"Amen," a voice answered from the door.

Jacek lifted his eyes. A young priest with a skinny, frozen face was standing under the heavy curtain covering the door leading to further rooms off the private study. In his white hands, he was holding a small book with a cross in the middle and a silver fitting on the corners. He nodded and pointed to an open window through which the sound of a bell could be heard from a distance.

Lord Tedwen stood up. "Here is my teacher," he said. "In my old age I found a source of Wisdom and Truth that God sends into this world through the lips of the humble ..."

Jacek looked at the priest, and although it did not seem to him at all that this priest, with the blunt hard features, was a humble servant of the Truth, he did not say a word, and only lowered his head slightly.

Meanwhile, the old man, was hurriedly saying goodbye to him. "Forgive me, but I have to be left alone; it is the time for my daily prayer..."

Darkness was already falling when, pensive, Jacek was walking along the seaside on the way to his plane. Only now, he realized that his old teacher neither gave him an answer nor dispelled the doubts troubling him. He still did not know how he would behave towards the movement stirred up by Grabiec, that was about begin ... He remembered that he had more questions to ask, and that he wanted to tell his teacher about the arrival of these strange messengers from the Moon. He wanted to share his news of Marek and talk about that inconceivable magician Nyanatiloka, but he somehow ran out of time. Anyway, all got lost in his consciousness in that old man's presence.

He thought for a moment whether to return or wait until the next day to talk to Sir Robert one more time. He smiled to himself and shrugged. "What for? What for? He will not answer me anyway. He is already so old and overcome with his age ..."

He was saddened by the recollection of the young priest whom he had seen there, at the door of the scholar's study. It was apparent that he had indisputable power over the soul of that once great teacher. "He is old, and his thought weakened ...," he whispered again.

But at that moment he remembered what the old man had told him about his discoveries. He remembered the manuscript he was holding with pages covered with rows of numbers. He thought about the courage of the old sage's spirit, which did not hesitate to articulate a seemingly crazy and improbable theory. He pondered upon the persistent sharpness of his clear thinking that pursued it to the last detail. He saw with his own eyes that this old man undoubtedly supported it with an undeniable proof by his math, and he felt that he did not understand anything anymore ...

He sat on a stone bench on the shore and, supporting his chin in his hand, stared at the darkened sky above the sea where the stars were beginning to flash...His thoughts were persistently circling around one point: "This priest, this young, frozen, unknown priest who took possession of the famous sage's mind".

He was chewing on this unbelievable puzzle in his soul for some time, when suddenly like a light, rather a hunch ...No, it was not the priest! Not this or that flawed and imperfect man, but something enormous, something inexpressible, which the human brain does not want to agree with, but it remains in human souls, longings, and desires: Revelation ...!

What? Whose? Who are they given to? Why this one and not others? And perhaps, it does not matter?

The grayed-hair sage said that all his science and knowledge only managed, as its greatest deed, to break up the alleged obviousness, which seem to be an obstacle to Revelation and faith ...Maybe, in fact, science never does anything else besides dispersing the network of perceptions created by our senses so that light can penetrate it? The creative power is deeper, and one cannot know what it creates, as one can only believe in it. It creates the human spirit and the spirit of the universe ...

'In the beginning was the Word, and the Word was with God, and the Word was God.'

The words, the most negligible nothingness of the ether, waved into energies, flared with light and heat, shook with electricity, and shivers of matter began to go through it: electrons, atoms, particles, converging into cosmic dust, into stars and suns, and systems of the suns... and in cluster systems, in milky ways, in the universe.

"The Word!"

"All things happen through it, and without it nothing happened that happened."

Blessed are the ones who believe! Certainly, blessed are those who did not see but believed!'

How can one spark the inner flame that always says 'yes', the only one able to create and give the true power and peace?

Faith and deed are beyond thinking and knowledge, but it is so difficult, so difficult, so difficult to reach them from the outside with our hands if they have not awakened in our soul by themselves. And anyway, maybe all this is ridiculous, and they are just longings of an awakened fantasy, which should not be given access to ourselves? Then he threw back his head.

Over the rocking sea, in the sky among the stars, he spotted a streak of giant light, a fountain of white fire, disappearing with a diffused fog somewhere at the horizon, almost resting its bright head on the horizon in the west ...

The comet, which appeared unexpectedly a few days ago, and in a few days, having brushed by the Sun, will disappear from its vicinity for eternity, for eternity, for all eternity! It is a glowing nothing, thrown into millions of kilometers of space, a symbol, and a vivid picture of the whole world ...

In spite of himself, he remembered how comets were feared centuries ago, and that they were viewed as heralds of misfortune or war, and at that moment Grabiec came to his mind ...

Was it his comet ...? He, who wants to go into the world with action, proudly disapproving of all that is thinking only? Comets supposedly once led Alexander and Caesar, Attila, William the Conqueror, Napoleon ...It just was a play of shadows, a fight of shadows, and victories of shadows...Spirit is the only truth! He was thinking about it, hiding his face in both hands.

II

Benedict was just sitting in his office at the desk, covered with Aza's photographs, when the automatic instrument, which had for long time been replacing the awkward and expensive butlers, told him that someone wanted to see him.

The noble old man was not happy about the intruder. After that unfortunate incident in Aswan, he was forced to break all relations with the singer who did not want to see him again. For some time, he totally could not cope with that. He was too used to leisurely traveling around the world and accompanying the diva. She was never overly gracious to him, but being accustomed to seeing him next to her, she often sweetened her mocking him with a friendly smile. He just did not know what to do with himself now and with his own time, which he began to have so much of at once. He valued himself enough to be convinced that sooner or later Aza would miss him. She will acknowledge her mistake, would feel remorse, and humbly call him to her side. But meanwhile weeks of anticipation were passing, and the singer gave no sign of life.

Finally, he ran out of patience and decided to take revenge. "I will get married," he thought, "and I don't want to hear about her again."

Who knows why he thought it would make her upset? He rubbed his hands with satisfaction. He had not made a choice yet, but it was the smallest thing. There are so many young and poor girls, forced to work hard or perform on some small stages. They will be happy when the rich pensioner offers them a place beside him ...

He immediately got to work on his plan, that is, he decided to inform Aza about his decision ...He asked at the central address office about her whereabouts and bought a quarter of melancholic, lilac letter paper. It occurred to him that he should have returned Aza's photographs along with the letter. He was not just sure which of them he should send. There were those which he had received from her at different times, and a lot of those he had bought in stores. He proudly decorated the walls of his study with some and filled the drawers of his desk with others. After some thinking, he decided to send her all of them to make a stronger impression.

The box was already ready, and he was saying goodbye to those photographs thinking about contents of the letter he was planning to write to her when a guest was announced.

Benedict cursed silently but no less severely. There was no way to hide the scattered portraits. Putting them back into drawers would take too much time, and he did not want them to be seen by the visitor ... He fidgeted awkwardly for a moment, until suddenly a genius idea came to his head. He took off the patterned cover from the sofa standing near it and covered the entire desk together with all those photographs. Then he went to the door and opened it while pressing the button to set the electric elevator in motion.

In a few moments Lachec stood in the hall door.

"Ah, it's you ..."

"Yes, it's me."

They both smiled sourly.

"I haven't seen you for a long time."

"I haven't seen you for a long time either, uncle ..."

Lachec came to Benedict with the desperate thought of asking him for a loan. After that unfortunate game in Aswan, he only had enough money left to return to Europe by the cheapest train. He also disappeared so suddenly that neither Halsband, not willing to let him out go of his grasp nor Grabiec who was looking for him, could find out when or where he had gotten lost ...

Some inner, stubborn, peasant vigor saved him from those suicidal thoughts caused by his exasperation then. Now, he was far from such thoughts as that moment of depression gave birth to the idea of a new composition, victorious, triumphant, full of power and full of laughter of gods. Since the first creative outlines loomed in his mind, he was no longer able to think of anything else. Everything disappeared from his eyes except for one great desire: create, write, hear!

A few weeks, a few months of peace! A little opportunity to concentrate and work, without the necessity to remember that you have to eat, live, and earn!

He knew that at that moment generous Halsband could give him a small sum in the form of an advance. He also knew well that in that case he would not have any peace of mind, as he would be still haunted by : "What are you doing?," "Will you be done soon?," and "When will you resume working on my things?"

He thought about Uncle Benedict as his last escape and decided to pluck him at all costs. The thought of this necessary procedure did not please him. He was deeply and painfully disgusted with any humiliation, pleading, expressing gratitude, and through the bizarre "consequence" of his human soul, he felt hatred towards his uncle for his intention of borrowing money from him.

Now, sitting across from him on the other side of the office, he was looking at him with rage not corresponding with the intent that brought him in. He was grinding his is jaws as if he wanted to grind the good old man in his teeth without mercy.

"How are you doing?," Benedict spoke after some thought.

"Very bad."

Benedict wanted to say something nice to his nephew, "I liked your music written for Ms. Ada.

Lachec jumped in his chair.

"I heard you had made a lot of money."

"I lost it all."

"Oh!"

He raised his eyebrows and was looking at his nephew for a while, nodding his head with sadness and reproach. Then he said unexpectedly: I am getting married!"

"Uncle, have you gone crazy..!"

He broke off half-word and blurted out kindly: "Congratulations! And to whom if I may ask?"

He bowed his head to hide a malicious smile, and at that moment his gaze fell on half of Aza's face, looking at him from under the cover on the desk. In suspicion, he grabbed the cover with both hands to remove it, but Benedict was watching. He pressed the fabric with his hands, and they struggled for a few moments until the musician finally won. From behind the torn rag, photos fell on the floor in a pile. Mr. Benedict, flushed like a youth, bent down to pick them up, and Lachec turned pale. He fixed his eyes on that face, from hundreds of pieces of cardboard looking at him, and grunted in a muffled voice:

"To whom? Whom are you marrying, uncle?"

"I don't know yet! Have you gone mad? Are you crazy! Why did you break them up? I must send them back ... I will marry in the coming days, but I don't know who yet."

Lachec burst out laughing. "Oh, that's different!"

"How's that different?," the pensioner panted, flushed from the effort. "Help me pick them up. Has the devil brought you here, or what? I have to send them back!"

The musician suddenly became confused and intimidated ... He knocked his chair over and got down on his knees. He started to awkwardly scoop up scattered photographs while mumbling some excuses to the still grumbling old man. Finally, the work was completed.

They sat down opposite each other again and started a strangely interesting conversation during each of them thought something different than what they said. Benedict was still freaking out in his head, why on earth was his nephew haunting him at this inadequate time, and Lachec, telling some imaginary story, was playing a game in his mind with words: "will lend or won't lend".

Finally, he could not stand it anymore. He broke his sentence in the middle and asked unexpectedly: "Uncle, I'm destitute. I need help..."

Benedict fell silent. He stared at the guest for a time, moving his white eyebrows and nodding seriously, until Lachec got tired of it.

He spoke again: "Couldn't you help me, uncle?"

Benedict did not answer right away, now. He stood up, walked around the room and grunted a few times, "My dear," he began "I should properly reproach you for being reckless ... Indeed, it was not necessary to play in Aswan, but save the penny earned there so unexpectedly ..."

Lachec stood up to leave. Benedict noticed his intention and took him cordially by the arm. He even smiled kindly. "Sit, sit down! I am not refusing you! I told you I was getting married, so I would like to do something nice for you."

He went to the desk and pulled out one of the drawers. He was flipping something long until he finally got out a few small pieces of the saved paper. He ran his eyes quickly through them

"You owe me two thousand one hundred and sixteen gold ... Here are your I.O.U.'s"

"Yes. If only such an amount now one more time ... at least half..."

"Swapping it for a current silver coin, we will have ..."

"If only a quarter of this now ..."

"I've already told you I'm getting married. I would not like to have something like that between us at that moment ... Your mother was some kind of cousin ..."

Benedict was really touched. He swallowed and opened his wet eyes wide. With a heroic and cordial movement, he held out his hand with the I.O.U.'s towards the astonished Lachec.

"Have them! From now on you owe me nothing! I am gifting you two thousand one hundred and sixteen gold pieces. Keep it for the memory of your mother." His voice quivered with emotion.

Lachec was dumbfounded, completely stunned by such an unexpected turn of things. He saw that his uncle was standing and waiting for him to throw his arms around his neck or at least thank him. He said something incomprehensible and slipped his own I.O.U.'s back into his pocket, as if they indeed had some value for him and began to get ready to leave.

Benedict moved impatiently. It was obvious that he was amazed at the nephew's cool behavior towards his generosity, and he still wanted to say something ... And indeed, he kept him on the doorstep.

"Listen,' he said, giving a somewhat mysterious sound to his words - you have not paid me any interest for three years ... I am giving you the capital ... but the interest ... you see ... I am getting married now, I will have considerable expenses ... If you do not have it with you, send my overdue interest in a few days. Let's call it even now."

He hugged him warmly and returned to the room. He could not understand at all why Lachec was not happy, but yes, standing up, he looked at him as if he could kill him. Benedict sighed deeply and painfully over people's ingratitude, smiled tearfully at his own nobility, and sat down at the desk with a feeling of doing some good by writing a letter to Aza.

Meanwhile, Lachec, having left his uncle's house, began to roam the city streets without thought and purpose.

Huge electric lamps, dimmed with blue glazing, flooded the wide pavements full of crowds taking their evening strolls ... The old and ridiculous ban on opening shops at night had long been lifted. At present stores were closed from eleven to five in the afternoon. Then until midnight and longer they shone with illuminated exhibitions, full of movement, bustle and gold still pouring together with people. Indeed, gold was falling everywhere, flowing in a river, splashing sideways, like drops of water, then flowing in another place into one wider channel ... Its sound could be constantly heard at the entrance to huge, numerous theaters, concert halls, circuses, and bio phono-stores. You could hear it in the door of a café in breaks between the voice of a phonograph (Halsband and Co, Ltd.), shouting alternately the last news and arias of the most fashionable singers. You could also see it in apparently modestly clad, yet disgustingly naked dancers kicking their legs in black, mesh leotards. Banks full of it, were working the most intensively now. Brothels decorated with incredible splendor and therefore higher than all restrictions of the police of public morals were filled with it. Yes, it was present everywhere, everywhere, where you could turn your feet or eyes.

Lachec was walking aimlessly here, knocked by a circling crowd, pushed off the sidewalk and again giving way to numerous cars in the middle of a bursting street. He did not know at all what he was doing, and what he would do tomorrow. He could not even think about his situation anymore. Through the buzz of conversations, screams, calls, the sound of sirens and the screaming of car horns, the snoring of disgusting jukeboxes and the grinding of braked wheels, crumbs of Lachec's own music fell into his ears. Those detached scraps of his music seemed to explode from his soul, surrounding for a moment his tortured head with a good wave ... Then he stopped in the street crowd for a moment, his thoughts hundreds of miles away. Still, he caught the sounds passing by, before they died, before the victorious crackle carried them away and drowned them out. But here again someone hit him, and someone screamed the name of a new daily in his ear. A public order officer told him not to stop and block the traffic, so he resumed his gait again and walked on as if he was really going somewhere in this confusion.

At last, he stopped in the recess of a gate, not quite knowing why he was standing. He had the impression that he was somewhere in a well-known place. He raised his head. Before him, on the other side of the street, there was a huge sign, decorative and somewhat flirtatious with colorful lights arranged: "Halsband and Co, Ltd. - Improved Phonographs".

He snorted like a horse who was suddenly frightened by a firecracker bursting underfoot. A terrible cacophony of hundreds of instruments was coming from the windows of the huge building. It seemed like they were set in motion as some form of a test. Each of them was playing something different. Some were singing, others in which some imprisoned orchestra repented, moaned desperately, as if asking for mercy over their own destiny. There were others simulating the voices of animals or the drunk screams of arguing workers in the suburbs.

Lachec's hair stood on end. He wanted to run away from this miserable hell and his prison, when suddenly his own Hymn about Isis fell into his ears victoriously from the throat of some powerful instrument. He recognized Grabiec's words, dignified and strong, and the storm of his sounds, and Aza's voice ... distorted, battered in a tin jar ...

His eyes darkened, and he leaned his back against the wall and began to look at the house with such menacing hatred, with such hostile passion that his lips trembled over his exposed teeth and his hands curled into fists, hard, harder and harder to pain ... Various thoughts flashed through his mind like lightning. They were terrible and impossible ideas like blow the building up or smash all the instruments, cut Halsband's throat or put the loudest of these roaring machines in his ears and yell him to death ...

Suddenly he felt all his powerlessness and nestled his head between his high shoulders, as if embarrassed. His eyebrows narrowed, and he was looking grimly ahead now with a dull, worried look ...

He stayed like that for some time without thought when he suddenly felt someone's hand on his shoulder. He turned around.

He saw Grabiec standing next to him: "I've been looking for you for a long time ... Please come with me."

Lachec listened to this commanding voice and followed Grabiec without a question into the less lit network of side streets. They walked in silence for a long time. Having passed the swarming and bustling galleries, full of shiny shops, they were just reaching the huge factories on the outskirts of the city, boiling with work night and day. The roads and courtyards here were mostly unpaved but only covered with crumb and coal slag to a certain height. The soft lights from downtown were replaced by unshielded arc lamps that looked like tall stars hung on gallows. In their bright cold glow, black shadows fell from factory chimneys; from the wagons moving briskly along the rails, from the people moving about. The enormous windows of the buildings divided into small panes, cloudy from eternal dust, blazed with embers of light, like some hell furnaces.

Grabiec and the still silent Lachec stopped in a wall recess. It was the time when workers in one of the factories changed after the usual two-hour shift, giving way to fresh replacements. A wave of silent people, dressed only in linen gray uniforms, flowed in through the wide-open door. They were clearly visible as they spilled over the huge hall, standing ready just behind the busy workers at the machines. This one and that one rolled up their sleeves, rubbed their hardened hands... The first bell sounded, and the faces of the waiting ones took on a blunt and watchful expression.

At the second signal, a hundred or so suddenly left the machines, and at the same moment, without a second pause, a hundred new hands fell on the levers, grabbed the handles of the regulators, pushed the lowered plugs. The freed ones, gathering in the middle, were stretching their tired muscles slowly and lazily now, as if awaken from a cataleptic dream. They were throwing words of broken conversations to their comrades and becoming people again. New mannequins were standing by the tireless machines.

The wave of people started to spill in the huge courtyard. Grabiec was checking out the passing workers and suddenly approached one of them. "Yoozva!"

The big, red-haired man turned around and stopped. His young eyes were filled with stubborn determination. "Is that you, Grabiec?"

"Yes."

The worker looked at Lachec with suspicion. "And who is this?"

"A new comrade. Not important. Let's go."

They stepped through the group of young people passing them and turned their steps to a large tavern nearby where at night the workers gathered to rest and have fun.

The spacious rooms were crowded and noisy. Lachec looked with interest and not without certain admiration at these faces and firm, strong, bulky figures. They looked so different from those he had seen all his life downtown, in the theater, on the street, in clerical offices and in cafes. Over the centuries, the gulf separating the working masses from the rest of society had grown so ardently and inconceivably that there was almost no knowledge of their existence "in the high places" of the civilized mob ...

They sat in a corner at a separate table. When Yoozva left them to give orders to a server, or talk to a friend, Grabiec spoke to Lachec, pointing at the crowd:

"Do you know what it is?"

Lachec looked in his eyes.

"The sea which needs to be rocked, loosened up, bloated to flood the world with it ..."

In Lachec's still dazed head, something suddenly flashed, and he thought he was beginning to understand ...

"And you want to ...?"

Grabiec nodded, his eyes never leaving him.

"Yes."

"And you've summoned me ..."

"Yes."

"To get rid of Halsband, record players and pensioners?"

"Yes, that is what it is. To make everything that is there disappear and leave only a great sea absorbing the dirt of the earth, and gods ruling over it."

Yoozva came back and slumped on the chair heavily. They began to talk, tilting their heads toward each other. At first, Lachec bewildered by what Grabiec had said to him earlier, could not understand the pieces of their conversation. He was just looking at these two heads tilted towards each other, so different, and still joined by one thought. Yoozva's eyes opened heavily when he began to speak, and stayed still, open, persistent, and hard. He spoke slowly, separating each word, with the seemingly most complete, almost indifferent calm. Still at times it was visible that an inexorable hatred and power vibrated beneath them, kept from exploding with an enormous will power...

The man's face, with low forehead under the round skull, seemed blunt and unpleasant at first sight. However, after a few moments when Lachec had a better look, it occurred to him that this man could not be just a worker ... He began to pay attention to his words.

"Grabiec," Yoozva started as he supported himself with his two fists on the table, "do you think that my reason for joining the workers and spending ten years of my life doing this stupefying work was to grant someone's wishes today? Listen Grabiec, I do not care about anyone's good, I don't write utopias, I don't dream about the future. I just know that it is necessary, that sometimes what has been on the bottom for centuries should move to the top for the underground fires to explode outside ... What happens tomorrow, tomorrow will show."

"Still, you are not refusing to go with me, are you?," interrupted Grabiec.

A slight smile ran through Yoozva's wide lips. "There is no reason to refuse," he replied. "For now, we have a common goal. But you want to use us, the mob, as you call us in your mind, as a tool, and I laugh at this and you. It is best to make it clear and open. In your opinion, you, the wise men, scholars, artists, and those like you will benefit from the victory received with our help. And I tell you that we will not serve you, but you will serve us later, if we really want to use what you can give us.

"Time will tell. We don't want to take advantage of you."

"Yes, you do, but never mind. You are right that time will show everything. There is nothing to talk about at the moment. Now, for us and you, there is only one thing: the destruction of what is there, depression of the center of power throwing its weight around, time for an upheaval. We will go together ... We will leave debris, ashes and blood behind us."

Lachec was listening with bated breath, and some new thoughts, similar to strong wine were coming to his head.

III

It was already afternoon when Jacek's plane, returning from Lord Tedwen, landed on the roof pad of his house in Warsaw. Jacek quickly jumped out of his seat, and after calling the mechanic to take over, he ran downstairs. He was overcome by an anxiety that he could not explain as he rushed to get to his study. He felt as if something had happened there in his absence ...

This tormenting thought came to him at some point on the way, when high above the ground suspended in the air, he was trying in vain to spot his native town in the eastern parts of the horizon. From that moment on, he was rushing at a dizzying speed, the fastest his flying vehicle could attain. The growl of the straining metal shaft frantically tearing the air apart with its propellers was joined by the constant whistling of the wind. Jacek had to put on his mask to be able to breathe at that unheard off speed ... Blood was throbbing in his temples, they ached from the accelerated pounding.

He was relieved when he saw that his house was standing unmoved in its former place.

In his large porch, covered with asbestos rugs of great colors on the floor right at the door of the studio, he met a servant who rushed out of the distant rooms at the sound of the plane.

"What's up?"

"Nothing much, Excellency. We were looking forward to your arrival."

Jacek felt his pocket, where he kept the key for his study door.

"Nobody asked about me?"

"No. There has been no one during the past two days."

"What about our guests from the Moon?"

The servant smiled. "They are doing fine. Only the disheveled one ..." He stopped.

"What?" Jacek interrupted.

"Your Excellency told me to have all their wishes satisfied. The disheveled one constantly gives orders. We cannot manage. At the same time, he speaks in a strange language that has extraordinarily little Polish in it and is angry that we do not understand it."

Jacek dismissed the servant with a nod of his head and now, postponing meeting with the dwarfs, put the key in the secret lock. A few presses and turns and the door suddenly slid to both sides, opening the darkness behind it. The metal curtains on the windows were down. Jacek felt with his hand for the button in the door frame and pressed it after inserting a little key. A wave of light came through the suddenly exposed windows, blinding him.

He passed the first circular study with the desk he usually worked at and opened another metal door hidden in the wall. Behind it, there was a narrow corridor that led to his private laboratory with no other entrance but through his study.

As he stepped through the threshold, he gave a slight involuntary shout. A motionless man was sitting there bent over the device which contained the terrible secret of his invention ... Jacek got to him in one jump. The man stood up slowly and turned towards Jacek.

"Nyanatiloka!"

He stared at the Buddhist's face for one second, then without even asking how he got here through the iron-clad doors and windows, he bowed his head over the instrument ... One of the wires carrying the electric current was cut. Jacek looked at the clock, the current, and he froze! The wire was interrupted just at the moment when the current, for some unexplained reason, increased to such an extent that the device could have spontaneously exploded ... Another split second, and not just his house, but the whole city would have turned into a pile of rubble on uprooted dirt.

"The danger has been avoided," the Hindu said smiling, "The current is interrupted."

"How have you done it?"

Nyanatiloka did not answer. He grabbed Jacek's hand and slowly led him to his study. The scientist let himself be led like a child, almost incapable of thinking. The chaos was boiling over in his head, but he was simply afraid to ask the Tri-worldly what had happened. It all seemed to him so unbelievable and upsetting any order of human thinking.

Only after some time, when seated in a comfortable armchair in front of his desk, he awoke from the daze and began to look at Nyanatiloka with wide open eyes as if awakened from sleep. He wanted to reach out and touch his burnous to check if this man was really standing in front of him, but some embarrassment stopped him ...

It was hard to tell if Nyanatiloka saw the beginning of his movement, or if he just sensed his thought ...

"Do you think," he said, "that the sense of touch is truer than the sense of sight? You can see me with your eyes."

"How did you get here?"

"I don't know," answered the Hindu quite honestly.

"Why don't you know? It is absolutely incomprehensible! At the moment I was locking the studio two days ago, I knew for sure that nobody was here ..."

"Yesterday, I was on Ceylon island in the company of my brothers ..."

"Nyanatiloka! Please have mercy on me! Tell the truth!"

"I am telling the truth. Today, an hour or maybe two earlier, while praying, I suddenly felt that something terrible was happening in your studio. Despite the greatest effort, I could not understand what it was, so I could not stop the disaster from a distance, and I felt that there was no time to lose."

Droplets of sweat appeared on Jacek's forehead:

"Talk, keep talking!"

"There is not much left to say. I closed all my senses so that the appearance of the outside world did not distract me, and I wanted to be here. When I opened my eyes, I saw the wire of your instrument in front of me, and I cut it."

"If you had hesitated for one quarter of a second, you would have been vaporized by the explosion with the whole house simply turned into nothing.

Nyanatiloka smiled looking Jacek into eye.

"Don't you believe me?" Jacek scoffed.

"Could the explosion of your machine change the spirit, the only existing thing, into nothing?"

Jacek got silent. He rubbed his forehead with his white hands several times, stood up and began to walk around the room. After a while he said: "I can't talk to you. My head is all mixed up, and I am tired of thinking ... I already had a strange conversation last night, which I still haven't thought through."

He paused and stopped, and then turned quickly towards Nyanatiloka. "Listen! Tell me what a spirit is! I can still hear this word ... I know a lot, but I have no idea about this one, although this is the closest one, although it is me! And nobody knows it, nobody has ever known it! Is it really always necessary only to believe in what is the most essential substance of man?"

"It is not enough just to believe," whispered Nyanatiloka looking straight ahead with his eyes wide open. "It's necessary to know for sure."

"And do you know?"

"Yes, I do."

"How?"

"Because I want to."

Jacek shrugged his shoulders with a disappointed face. "We are entering a vicious circle. My and your way of thinking are so different that apparently, we will never reach an agreement. Can knowledge depend on the will?"

"Yes. It depends on the will."

There was a moment's silence. Jacek sat down again and rested his head on his hands. "You are saying strange things. It is hard for me to accept the results of reasoning that is so incomprehensible to me. And yet I am attracted to all this, your peaceful and certain knowledge based on the act of will. Tell me, what is this spirit for you?"

"Spirit is what it is. Everything happened because of it, and without it nothing that happened, happened."

Lord Tedwen's big gray head bending over the Gospel of Saint John loomed before Jacek's eyes. "So, you, too, and you the same ...," he whispered

Nyanatiloka seemed not to hear him. "The world arose from the spirit," he went on "The spirit is the light of life and its only truth, and everything around it is only seemingly drawn from it, and it passes for the time being. The spirit has become a body ..."

"And if it dies with the body?," Jacek involuntarily interjected.

The Eastern sage smiled. "Are you able to suppose such a perverse thing even for a moment?"

"I do not know anything. I can openly confess to you that I do not know. There are people who claim that the so-called body, no matter what it is, is not the beginning, but the last phase of the spirit that cuts into it, to finally free itself from its resilience and die with it."

"The spirit does not die. Something that is true cannot die."

"So, what happens to it after the body dies? After it loses the senses that let it see, feel, after it loses the brain that it used for thinking?"

Nyanatiloka kept his eye on the speaker. "It is free then."

"And then what?"

"It is. Then it draws the only truth from itself, instead of succumbing because of those senses to other spirits' truths or dreams."

"I do not understand."

"And it is not necessary to understand, only to know. What do you do when you close your senses?"

"I dream."

"When the spirit is left alone, it dreams as well, but then its dream is the undoubted and the only reality for it because nothing opposes it from the outside. How do you suppose that this life in which we both are now, can have another foundation? That it is something ... less than the spirit's idea, for it is the highest! Maybe in some other life, when we were getting rid of a different appearance of a body also dreamed up by the will, our last thought became the seed of this life, which lasts ..."

"Let's suppose so. But why do we all think the same and create a similar reality in spirit for ourselves, because you and I see the same?"

"Because in principle, it is one spirit that strives for its ultimate unity through various changes. It wants to become the same as it apparently was once in the beginning, although I do not know if this beginning can be understood in a temporal sense.

"And that future life?"

"I know that it will come, as long as we do not free ourselves from the last illusions, from the insanity of will, greed for variety, but I don't know in what sense. Perhaps we will imagine our life for ourselves with our last thought before losing our senses. Then everyone will have what they believed in it, what they wanted, expected or what they were afraid of ... Think of what a beautiful, and terrifying thing it is at the same time, to be able to create a new life from your last thought, expand it, fulfill it, make it come true! It is also terrifying because you need to watch this last thought, so that it is not a vile fear or torment, because that, will make you plunge in an irrevocable hell!

"And liberation?"

"Not to want anything! It is a sacred and great word all too often sacrilegiously abused and encompassing all being. It is an unchanging, full, significant, ultimate bliss. It is the closure of the ring of change: Nirvana. God is an abyss, the abyss is God, and we will return to God!"

After a moment's thought, Jacek stood up and snapped out of it.

"I needlessly talk about these things with you today," he said. "Thinking is tiring me now, and it exhausts me to the last. I have the impression that I have temporarily lost my judgment ability as your words put me in a strange state. Do not tell me, don't tell me anymore. I am scared! I have to turn my thoughts to other things now ... and my head is stunned, impotent ..." He rubbed his forehead with his hands.

The Hindu stood up. "I am leaving," he said. "I will visit you some other time."

Jacek vividly protested. "No, no! Stay. There are a few things I want your advice about ... but I need to calm down now."

He pressed the button to call the servant. "We have to eat something," he said with a forced smile.

The servant appeared at the door, and Jacek stopped him there with a gesture of his hand. "Prepare a breakfast for us and ask the messengers from the Moon to join us here."

After the servant left, Nyanatiloka looked at Jacek. "What are you going to do about that news of your friend, Marek?"

Jacek was already accustomed to the fact that this incomprehensible man could read his thoughts before they appeared in his words, sot he was not even surprised that he knew about the events of recent weeks. He just shrugged and spread his arms wide.

"I do not know yet. I am suspicious of these midgets. I think that I will need to build a new vehicle and travel to the Moon ..."

A thought flashed. "Listen, you can tell me what is happening to Marek..."

'Bhikkhu' shook his head in negation. "I don't know. I told you that the human will has no limits in its capability, but our knowledge is limited, and our consciousness cannot reach everywhere. It learns the deepest rules to the whatever extent possible, but many details are hidden from it, because they come from foreign sources."

"Yet you usually know what I think."

"When you talk to me with your thoughts, I know. You hit my spirit with your will." He put a hand on his shoulder. "Let's put it aside now. You yourself said that you were tired ..."

Jacek felt that under the Buddhist's influence his thoughts were getting mixed up and something, like a sweet fog, was enveloping his whole being ... It occurred to Jacek that he was putting his will to sleep, so he jerked away with an internal rebellion. He wanted to scream, run away, but suddenly a shroud seemed to envelope him, smothering his consciousness into a small, tiny spark, only glimmering with the feeling that it still existed in that shadow ...

He lost all sense of time and place where he was. This state could last for both a second and a millennium ... He did not want anything, did not know anything, did not feel anything from outside of himself.

Slowly, slowly some sound, some fog, at first so thick and gray that it hardly differed from the darkness, then becoming brighter, silvery, and dispersing into an indefinite wrapping of puffy cloudiness.

A childish, selfless, almost impersonal curiosity began to arouse in him. Something flashed before his eyes like the outlines of a dead landscape: green fields, lighted by the low hanging sun ... After some time, he noticed that he could not quite determine the place where he was, but he saw an extensive valley. It was scattered with round ponds surrounded with banks filled with unknown vegetation. A ring of gigantic mountains with jagged, snowy peaks closed the valley on all sides like a ring.

He started wondering where he was, and what he was doing there. It bothered him that, apparently absorbing those impressions with his eyes, he could not see or feel himself, his own body, as if he were something weightless and altogether intangible.

He was thinking about it, when he suddenly realized that in spite of his immateriality, he could perceive impressions through his hearing. A sound reached him, something like the pandemonium of a battle: shots, moans, cries. Now he noticed that there was a city in the middle of the huge valley on a high crag. There really was a fight boiling around. A handful of people were defending their position from an assault on them from everywhere, from the air and from the ground, swarms like birds, like winged amphibians ...

Four-eyed monsters on widely spread membranes floated around in flocks, showering bullets from above at the people firing back ...

Suddenly Jacek seemed to hear a familiar voice. With a sudden effort of will, he threw his consciousness in that direction:

"Marek!"

Yes, he saw him quite accurately as he was running at the head of the ranks - strangely gigantic compared to his dwarfed companions. He had a weapon in the shape of a long saber in his hand and was pointing with it at the city walls, red from the last sunny rays ...

Jacek wanted to shout, he wanted to call to him. Noise, confusion, the rumble of something like a black lightening of a crumbling world absorbing everything.

He opened his eyes. He was still in his study and Nyanatiloka was sitting on the other side of his desk starring at him. "Was I sleeping?"

"Yes brother. You fell asleep for a moment. What did you see?"

Jacek suddenly understood. "Was I on the Moon?!"

"I wanted you to be. I do not know if I succeeded. You are not a lifeless object but a conscious spirit like I am. A spirit can never totally submit to another spirit, and it will always fight it ..."

"That's it. I was on the Moon. I saw Marek. He was conquering a city there from evil monsters. Maybe he is indeed a king. But I know little, extraordinarily little! I woke up too soon. Couldn't you keep me in this condition any longer?

"I couldn't. Especially since I had to take care that you would not stop thinking in your own way, to look with your eyes and not through mine."

Jacek wanted to answer something, but at that moment the door opened, and the servant announced the arrival of the dwarfs.

They came in looking distrustfully at Nyanatiloka. Roda got seriously scared as the Hindu's clothes resembled those of Hafid's, who carried them in a cage. Jacek did not encourage him to calm down. Fully awake now, he briskly approached the lunar people and simply asked:

"Why were you lying, saying that Marek was peacefully reigning over the lunar people, when at this very moment he is fighting monsters inside a great ring like a chain of mountains?

Roda paled and began to shake all over his body. "Honorable Lord! He is actually fighting a war ..."

He stopped as it occurred to him that there was no way Jacek could know what was happening there on the Moon, so there was no reason to tell him about the true state of affairs. He pouted his fleshy lips and threw his head back hard.

"It hurts me, my lord," he finished the sentence, "that you call me a liar without a thought." The king's duties and regular duties include war, so how strange would it be, if Marek were actually on an expedition now, which neither you nor we can know at the moment.

Jacek looked at the dwarfs in silence for a moment, and then he spoke: "I wanted to tell you that I decided to follow my friend to the Moon in a new vehicle. Would you like to accompany me?"
The momentary confidence of the hairy "sage" disappeared in a moment of dread. His legs trembled again, and he mumbled some incomprehensible words ...

Oh! Yes, to the Moon! Oh, how he would like to return to the Moon to the city by the Warm Ponds, among his pupils and among his admiring members of the Brotherhood of Truth! That's what he missed since the first moment when he stepped on the Earth, but now he shivered at the thought of being in Jacek's company, and maybe of other people's who would soon know all his lies and tricks ...

He did not know what to do, how to answer, when he suddenly noticed that Mataret, who was standing behind him, was moving forward. A terrible premonition of something bad gripped his throat, and he wanted to signal and stop his companion, but it was too late.

"Sir," Mataret said seriously looking up at Jacek, "it's time for us to tell you the truth."

"Silence, silence!" Roda shouted in despair.

Mataret did not pay any attention to him. He was looking bravely in Jacek's eyes and was saying: "Marek did not send us here at all. We used a trick to get control of his vehicle and arrived on Earth unwittingly."

Jacek suddenly turned pale, "And what about Marek? Is he, is Marek alive?"

"As you guessed sir, I don't know how, he is fighting the Sherns."

Then, he started telling him what happened after Marek's arrival. The lunar nation immediately greeted him as the Conqueror who was foretold of by their prophets, but they considered him an impostor and started fighting against his dominance and gathered a group of like thinking companions. He talked about the battles with the monstrous aborigines, the Sherns, and about the defeats and victories. Finally, he told him about the fact that they took over the vehicle with the thought of seeking help from the inaccessible side of the Moon, from where they thought Marek was, but never planned to stop him from going back. However, he did not mention that it was his plan only, and not Roda's who wanted to oppress the hated newcomer.

"We unexpectedly fell on Earth" he continued, "and you know the rest as well as we do. We lied, in fear that he would be avenged here. We are weak compared to you, helpless and lonely. Now, you know the whole truth. Do what you think is appropriate, but if you really intend to go to the Moon, then do it hastily as Marek may really need help."

Jacek listened to this long story in silence. His eyebrows slowly narrowed above his eyes until they were arched in a hard and motionless arch. He pressed his lips together, squinted his eyes and unfocused gaze in front of him ...

"You will go with me to the Moon," he said suddenly addressing the dwarfs.

Mataret nodded his head in agreement, and said "Yes, sir, we will go."

Roda also bent as a sign of agreement, but swore in his soul that he would use all means rather than voluntarily accept this plan in which he would be in the power of a man who could take full revenge on him. A short stay on Earth was enough for him to understand that here he was protected after all, by equal law for everyone, and no harm could happen to him, until someone could prove his guilt. He would never fly back through that abyss in a trio that included his enemy's friend! ...

Meanwhile, Jacek's thoughts were flowing swiftly in his head. He involuntarily looked behind at Nyanatiloka, but he disappeared somewhere, silently slipping out of the room. Then without having someone to talk to, he took his temples in both hands and pondered deeply on the fate of his friend, on his intended journey, on what he would be leaving here, and what he could expect to find there.

The turmoil that he felt would break here any moment! He did not want to take an active part in it, and yet he had a premonition that he would leave here, fleeing into space as if escaping from a fight, from potential danger, from the final struggle of forces ...

What if he is needed here? If it comes to the worst here, and if not wanting to give the weapons he is saving for himself to strangers, he will have to fulfill that terrible deed, but he would not be here to release the hellfire...

"Why should I care about all this?," he whispered quietly to himself. I will leave. Let whatever happens, happen. My only friend calls me there ..."

He had just stood up when a servant appeared on the doorstep with a letter on a tray.

"From Ms. Aza," he said putting the envelope on the table. He quickly tore it open and ran his eyes swiftly over its content, forgetting about the presence of the dwarfs who were looking at the change on his face with interest ...

Jacek slowly sat down in his chair and put the paper in front of him. Aza informed him that she would be soon coming to Warsaw for a longer time to relax after her performances and triumphs...

"I hope to find that you will be at home as well my friend," she wrote, apparently having forgotten the fleeting, recent misunderstanding, "because I want to talk about many things and spend time only in your company ... Maybe a lot will change in my life, and you will be the first to know about it ..."

"I still have time," he said to himself after a moment, almost loudly, "before they build the vehicle for me, and then ..."

He stopped and gave a sign to the servant, that he should take the dwarfs away. He walked to the window and put his thoughtful and sad forehead against the glass.

IV

"Madam, you must get Jacek's secret at all costs. It is indispensable to us." Saying that, Grabiec removed the hand, which Aza's hand had just touched. The singer noticed this movement and stepped back. Her eyebrows narrowed over her eyes. She was offended by the dry, commanding tone of his words.

"And if I don't want to get involved in it all?" She said defiantly.

Grabiec shrugged. "Too bad. I will find another way to have that invention, and you, Madam, will just continue to sing ..."

He paused and began to look for his hat and gloves. Finding them, he bowed quickly to the silent woman. "Goodbye, Madam ..."

"No! Don't leave yet, sir!"

Suddenly, she came closer to him, her eyes sparkling. "Sir! Let's put all of our cards on the table. What will you give me for ... this ... secret?"

He backed away slowly from the door and sat down in the nearest chair. "Nothing, so far. I've already told you. I don't know what I will have ..."

"So, why should I put myself at risk?"

"Because you want to. You are intrigued and attracted by everything that will happen, whatever can happen. In fact, you would like to take part in this biggest and possibly final fight, which could be gut wrenching."

Aza laughed. "Is that all? You are attempting to persuade me that I am asking you for permission to do you the greatest favor?!..."

"It does not matter how you take it. You want to rule, and you know that only in our ranks and on our side, there is the place for kings."

She sat down opposite him, and resting her elbows on her knees, rested her chin on her open hands.

"Don't you think I could ... use Jacek's invention ... for myself?"

"I did not think it and I won't think it. I have too good opinion about you to suppose that you have such impractical intentions. You can't do anything alone."

"So maybe I will partner with Jacek?"

Grabiec looked at her with involuntary concern, but he smiled right away. "Try it. Maybe he will agree." A slight sneer sounded in his voice.

She stood up, hurt again, and took a step closer. "Do you think I have no other way to control the world and you except by stealing a recipe from someone for an explosive?"

He looked at her coolly and searchingly. He was silent for some time, his eyes on her face, arms, hips, as if he were evaluating and pricing her. "Yes," he finally said, "you are beautiful and therefore you seem ... No, my dear lady! So far, Madam, you do not rule, but serve people with your beauty."

She scoffed suddenly. She remembered that she had heard the same sentence recently from Jacek. A choked laughter twitched in her throat. "And yet, everything I want happens! And you came to me with your request ..."

He interrupted her with his hand gesture. "Madam Aza let's leave those discussions alone for now. I have little time as they are waiting for me. So, the last word: Will you attempt to get Jacek's secret for nothing but to have the right to stand on the same side with us?" Saying this, he stood up again, half turned toward the door.

She hesitated for a moment. "Yes! Because you will all serve me in the end."

Grabiec smiled. "Perhaps. Thank you for now. The choice of means naturally depends on you." He turned back in the door. "You must hurry," he said. "Jacek is ready to fly away" ...

She looked at him questioningly.

"Don't you know he's building a vehicle ...?"

"A vehicle?"

"Yes. To go to the Moon, following that Marek, who had just sent those messengers. There is no time to lose."

He left with a slight bow, leaving Aza alone with her thoughts. Since the arrival of the dwarfs from the Moon, she had only once asked what news they brought from Marek ... She was told, based on the newcomers' lies at the time, that he was doing well and was not going to return to Earth ... She still wanted to ask if there was a letter or word for her, but her proud shame and her pride made her clench her teeth.

She felt at this moment that she hated Marek just as badly, and even worse, than she hated all of those people, who were creeping around her legs, glancing lustfully at her inaccessible body. She despised him as much as she despised those artists and poets, who, like her lied about art, even when using it as a means for fulfilling their ambitions for their own exaltation, gaining power and wealth. And she thought Jacek was a hideous man with a powerful brain, and a soft heart like a woman, unable to demand and conquer, and have ...

However, Aza could not despise Marek as much as she did those others. She now fought the idea that she once really loved him. And she sneered at herself and at him for his ridiculous star dreams and forgetting about her. She couldn't understand that he chose a funny kingdom on the Moon, over the highest happiness and greatest pleasure. She called him a fool and a narcissist, but she still could not resist the feeling of admiration that he managed to do all that and went there from her, for eternity ...

Something like desire for indefinite revenge was bursting her chest. "I will be a ruler here!," she was thinking, "I will be on Earth, and you, you should sit there like Twardowski on the Moon."[5]

She had always had an overwhelming desire for power and reigning which now found a new motivation in this thought. It also became, in a sense, the reason that, despite hesitation, she joined Grabiec's supporters, believing that sooner or later she would see everyone at her feet. Although she soon realized that haughty and cool Grabiec did not really care for the role of a subordinate, she continued in the conspiracy, especially when she learned that Jacek did not want to join him. She had the impression that, apart from other things, it was still a game between her and this young sage beautiful like a girl. Although he was always nice to her, she wanted instinctively rather than reasonably to teach him a lesson at all costs.

On Grabiec's instruction, Aza organized meetings of the congregation at her place, and whenever she could, she also took part in the preparations, without even wondering why she was drawn into it all. She understood that she was only being used as a tool to gain Jacek's jealously guarded power. At first, she was outraged, and she almost withdrew from further complicity. She strained her strength to entrap Grabiec with the thought that once she had him, she would laugh in his face with a mocking and contemptuous laugh and walk away, but that plan failed. She began to believe that this unshakable and confident man was indeed ready to control the world. It would be bad to prematurely break up with him.

So, she agreed to trick Jacek, in order to "tear off his sting" as she called it, believing that he was too feeble to ever use it himself.

"You can choose the means to accomplish that." Grabiec had said.

Aza smiled at the thought. Yes, sooner or later, she would find the means. Now, she understood why Jacek was silent for so long without even answering her letters! Like Marek, he decided to escape from her to the Moon! And although she did not care about Jacek, much as she did about Marek, she wanted him to stay and serve her.

---

[5]Twardowski was a legendary figure who made a deal with the devil for knowledge and magic. When the Devil came to take him to Hell, he prayed to the Virgin Mary, who made the Devil drop him on the Moon.

In the blink of an eye, she had a flashing thought to cast away this vain and confusing life here on Earth and fly to the stars with Jacek, following the path of her only royal lover ... She closed her eyes, and her lips twitched with a true and sweet desire to fall under his mighty feet, to see his laughing face again...

Aza quickly recovered from this "childish weakness". A predatory smile wandered again on her red lips, the hard gaze of eyes went far beyond the present moment, ahead to events of a future day ...

She called out for her servant to help her change when she was told that Lachec had come. She looked at the clock: it was four o'clock. "I forgot completely," she whispered.

Without completing her dressing, she only covered her underwear with a wide, home dress made of shimmering silk. Then she hastily tied her luxuriant hair in a knot, and she went out to the guest.

She had not seen Lachec since that brief meeting at the casino. However, she heard about him often and listened with increasing amazement to what was reported to her. At least seemingly, Lachec stopped dealing with music. He disappeared for a time, and no one knew what he was up to, until he suddenly surfaced at one of these people's assemblies that were increasingly taking place around the world... He spoke fierily, wildly, inspiring crowds. He called for the overturning of everything that existed to create a new order on Earth. When reading about it, Aza thought at first that it was someone else with the same name. When the news came for the second and third time, with the clear addition that the instigator was a musician, holding a modest position at Halsband's publishing house, she could not doubt it anymore. She did not know all the members of the conspiracy as Grabiec was too cautious despite appearances of proud and scornful carelessness. That is why she only guessed that the musician's appearances were related to what was happening in the world.

The government of United States of Europe had been accustomed to patiently disregard all the "riots" and "anxieties" which had have no serious consequences for centuries, and it disregarded Lachec for a long time. It was only in recent weeks, that more attention was paid to him. He was too widely listened too and gained too much influence, but what he came to the people with was not pleasing to the government.

Finally, a police order was issued to imprison him. Here, however, the unexpected happened. The people who trusted and respected the seriousness of the government security service so much that they would never dream to obstruct them in their activities, resisted openly this time, violently snatching Lachec from their hands.

It was already worrying. But, for the sake of maintaining its authority, the government had to win at all costs. It was decided to capture the dangerous musician at the earliest opportunity and punish him as an example, but it turned out that it was easier to decide than to do. The warmonger had disappeared and would only appear suddenly from time to time in unbelievable places. He spoke, muddled, instigated, and disappeared again before the "hand of justice" could reach him.

Aza was tracking the news of that dangerous "hide and seek" game with the powerful government of the European United States with interest. In her mind, the humble musician slowly took on the shape of a fabulous figure. She involuntarily shivered when yesterday she unexpectedly saw him in the street. Slipping through the crowds, he recognized her first and bowed deeply. Aza immediately stopped her car, slowly moving among the crowds. The musician noticed it and stopped. He hesitated for a brief moment. After all, he was endangering himself in case he was recognized ...

He got to the vehicle in one leap. "What did you want to ask of me, Madam?

But she understood the danger that she put him in. "Sir, come tomorrow at four!"

She gave him the address of her apartment, not even knowing at the moment why she was ordering him to come, nor what she would tell him when he came. The musician disappeared into the crowd, and she soon forgot about the meeting, busy with other matters. It was only now when she was going to the living room to greet him that she vividly remembered that scene. She was a bit embarrassed, and she did not know how to receive him, what to say to him. With her own imagination, she put him on certain heights of heroism and uniqueness. Now, she was afraid that this once funny, though brilliant artist would want to talk to her from these high places. She was almost angry with herself that she did not know why she had invited him.

Aza stood in the doorway with a haughty and cool face, slightly frowning. The musician jumped up from the chair and approached her quietly, his head bowed. His abyss eyes, frightened like before, expressed a silent plea and gratitude that he was allowed to look at her, to be with her ...

"Welcome, sir."

He did not hear those simple words. He dropped to his knees with a spontaneous motion and put his face at the bottom of her dress. She backed away, really scared. "What are you doing sir? Sir! ..."

He looked up at her sadly and slowly stood up. "I'm sorry, Madam. I was wrong. If you tell me, I will leave immediately."

He spoke with some bitter humbleness. His lips were trembling, and he was nervously, and awkwardly pressing his hands to his chest.

A shadow of disgust ran over the dancer's beautiful lips. She looked at him long and coldly. "So, do you speak at the assemblies?"

"Yes."

"Are they looking for you?"

"Yes."

"What are the possible consequences?"

He shrugged, "I don't know. I suppose imprisonment, maybe for life, in some work camp"

"You put yourself at risk coming here at daytime ..."

He hesitated for a moment. "Yes. I know that. They watch me."

"Why did you come?"

Lachec raised his head at once, as if startled by that cold question. The earlier timidity disappeared from his face, and he looked at Aza proudly and defiantly. "I could answer because you called me," he began slowly, "but that wouldn't be true. I came because I wanted it so much, because I wanted to see you at all costs, even if I had to pay with my life ..."

Aza smiled contemptuously. "That's a strange way of speaking to me. I can make you leave right now ..."

Lachec suddenly became afraid and became humble again, but his eyes were burning hot and fierce. "I love you," he said in a subdued voice "I love you without even knowing what kind of demon woman you are, Madam, or what you will do with my love which you don't need! I am saying this because I need to say everything ... I don't know how long I will live and whether I will see you again ..."

"Why do you love me, sir?"

"Why such a question? I am not asking you for anything..."

She cut him off. Careless cruelty played in her eyes. She slumped slowly into the armchair and from under her eyelids, slightly lowered, she looked at him, her mouth slightly parted with a smile. "And if I were ready ... to give you ... everything?"

The musician took a step back with the highest amazement and madness reflected in his eyes. However, he immediately bowed his head and said quietly, as if begging for forgiveness in that tone with the content of words: "I'd leave here ..."

"Would you leave? Would you snub me?"

"No. That would not be snubbing ... I know that you just asked me as a joke, but I will answer seriously ... Will you let me speak, Madam?"

"Tell me," she said either with a real or pretended interest.

He sat on a low stool near her legs and began to speak, staring into her eyes. "You see, my whole life has been one persistent struggle to be able to create ... Why repeat, what I experienced, what falls, what calamities, what humiliation! It's all beyond me. And now ..."

"And now you've given up music," she interrupted.

He shook his head and smiled. "No, Madam. I haven't given up music, but my eyes were opened. Was it the man who gave me a hand or was it an accident? I really don't know. I understood that I was following the wrong path. You don't have to work and die to create, but to live!

"Live ..."

"Yes! I won't explain it to you any better. I can't, or I don't know how. All I know is that for me this struggle with being deprived of glory is over. I am dying from hunger now, I am falling from fatigue, I am chased like an animal in the woods, uncertain of the day or hour, and yet the heart in my chest laughs with joy! I once rushed up and was kicked, now I have come down and I am rising up! I was among "civilized" people, and they did not understand me, and I did not understand them. Today, I hang out with the "mob" and feel every twitch of their hearts, rushing towards the light through fire and debris, and I know that they are listening to my voice! A great, great song is being born in my soul now! If I survive these coming days, I will roar with it over the destruction like a wind, I will roar with such a hymn of triumph over the whimper of human misery that human hearts will burst with an excess of life, and with an insane pleasure!"

He stood up, and his wide opened eyes flamed: "To hell with theaters!," he shouted "to hell with back stages, with make-up, with artificial light and with this soulless orchestra, too learned and too cowardly! Nature must play for me: the sea, winds on the rocks, thunder in the sky, resinous forests, and steppes! My lady, I want to live to this song, I want to create it! I am already creating its listeners. I am cleansing the world, so that it can swing wide after it runs out of my chest ...'

He clenched his fists on his chest, his white teeth glistened from behind his wide lips parted with a smile ...

Motionless, Aza was looking at him calmly from under her lowered eyelids "Sir ..."

He came to his senses and bowed his head. "I'm sorry, Madam. I speak too loud ...".

"Come closer here. Yes. You are a strange, strange man, sir. A spirit is burning in you. But tell me at last what does all this have to do with me? Why would you ... run away ... if I reached out my hand ...?

Lachec's brightened face suddenly saddened. "I love you."

She laughed loudly. "I already know this."

"No, you don't know. You cannot know what it means. When I think about you, the whole world disappears from before my eyes. Oh! It is so good that I cannot have any hope!" He hid his face in his hands and stayed silent like this for a while.

"Keep talking. I want to know everything."

"Well. You should know."

He turned his eyes on her again, insane with his fanatical love, and he spoke quickly and urgently: "I don't know if love is always like that, but I hate you at the same time! I don't fear you so much, but I fear myself. I feel that if I put my lips to your hand once, it would be the end of everything, I would not be able to tear myself away from it.

"No worries. I would have pulled it away if I had to."

He flashed his eyes weirdly. "I would kill you."

"Some people speak like that." She was beginning to play with him like a cat playing with a mouse.

"No, Madam. If I say ... Ah! If only you could know how many times, I thought about it, looking at you while hiding, absorbing you with my eyes!"

"To kill me?"

"Yes. You should be killed, Madam. You came to this world to people's misfortune!"

"I can also give happiness. Oh! What happiness!"

Sudden shiver shook Lachec's body. "I know, I suspect it, and I feel it. That's why ... Insane happiness that breaks, destroys ... Be strong enough, accomplish it: wrap my fingers around your white neck and squeeze, squeeze until your last breath escapes! And not even touch your lips before that..."

Strange, almost painful pleasure shuddered Aza's back. "Why ... wouldn't you ... touch my lips...before? Don't you see ... how bloody they are? Can't you feel from afar how hot they are?"

Lachec, exhausted by emotion, leaned back against the wall, and looked at her in silence with unconscious eyes.

"What would happen if I kissed you, sir?"

"I do not know; I do not know. I have to go now," he jumped up quickly.

"Stay ..."

"I don't want to."

"You must."

"Please ... please ...".

"Look, look at my lips. You say this is a doom? Let it be. Do you feel that my one kiss is worth more than the salvation of all these ridiculous people, these fights, these great words and deeds, all art, even life? Don't you feel that?"

"I feel it, and that's ... that's why ... I'll leave ..."

"No. You'll stay. So long as I want you to!"

Lachec felt her eyes burning in him and staggered at once. He felt that his muscles were all collapsing, everything went dark before his eyes, his head was buzzing, and he was overcome by inertia ... With his last choked effort, he shouted: "I'll leave ..."

She laughed loudly, triumphantly, and before he could see what was going on, fell on his burning lips with her ravenous lips, which could so divinely pretend to love.

V

The pale dawn was rising above the Tatra mountains ... Nyanatiloka was sitting motionless, as if frozen, facing the waving moon. His eyes were closed, and his hands were braided around his knees. The cold morning dew covered his half-naked body and glistened, dripping down his long, black hair. Several spreading spruces were swaying over him in the wind sometimes blowing from the crags, whose peaks were already blushing in the first rays of the sun rising somewhere behind the rocks. The silence was perfect, and it was embracing the whole world. It seemed that even a distant stream had fallen asleep in it, not daring to disturb this strange hour of grace with a murmur.

With closed eyes, Nyanatiloka was slowly moving his lips as if praying to the essence of all things.

"Hail to you, heaven," he said softly, "Hail, to my earth and my soul, which you are all one, created by thought, alive in thought ...

Thank you my soul, that you feel heaven and Earth. Thank you, that you understand your beginning and know that you will never end! Everything returns to the sea, to abundance and power, and no drop is lost, even if it fell on sand or rocks, but its path is long and its work is arduous.

The circulation of worldly things will not be shortened, because time is nothing, and life is erected above it. So, the burden of work and torment will not be reduced, because the spirit searching for its beginning is not looking there.

Oh, my soul, be praised in your eternal, indestructible, and overwhelming being, that you have learned to look beyond the time and the agony of being, towards the sea and the source of everything in one!"

Somewhere, a stone broke off from the top of a rock and fell into the abyss, pulling an avalanche of boulders with it. A distant echo rumbled and receded in the ravines. The sunlight was falling lower and the fields of scree above the halls and the tops of the highest limbs were already gilding in it. The brightening sky and golden pieces of mountaintops were mirrored in the depths of the purple pond ...

Nyanatiloka slowly opened his eyes. Jacek, wrapped in a coat, was sleeping at his feet next to the expired fire. His curly hair was scattered on the moist moss. His bent arm was covering his eyes, but not his mouth, slightly pale from the cold and parted in a sleepy breath. The Buddhist stared at him for a long time with a sour, sad cordiality in his pensive look.

"If only you could get beyond your body," he whispered again, "if you could understand what your path is ... I think I found your soul like a pearl, but I should change it in a drop of pure water, like fog dissolving in the sun into the universe. I know, my duty is mostly to take care of my own development, but I feel sorry for such dimmed beauty and hidden supreme power ..."

On the high rocks above them, rock sparrows were awake pecking at the ripe seeds of the mountain herbs. A sharp, quick whistle of a marmot hidden in the grass sounded somewhere on the opposite slope.

The lips of the Mystic were trembling for some time, as if they were supposed to accompany and echo his prayer thoughts, until he reached out and lightly touched the arm of still sleeping Jacek.
Jacek jumped up quickly and sat up, stretching his stiff limbs. Suddenly, he looked around with supreme amazement. "Where are we?"

"On the slopes of the Tatras. Look, the crags of Mieguszowiecki are looking at themselves in Morskie Oko..."

He was already standing. "How did I get here?"

Something like a dream loomed in his memory that yesterday evening in his own home he was talking with Nyanatiloka about his beloved Tatra forest ... He pressed his forehead with his hands. Yes, he remembers well! He had the feeling that he was falling asleep on his desk, and then he dreamed of fire burning in a resinous forest and the moon flowing above the peaks ... He was dreaming about it ... and now...

He looked at himself. His coat fell off his shoulders. He was dressed like yesterday when he returned home in casual city clothes ... He glanced around to check whether his plane was there, which the Hindu could use to carry him in his sleep. No, it was not there. There was emptiness around them. Autumn herbs covered with cold dew were standing evenly. There was no sign of being stepped upon, as if they, coming here, had not touch the ground with their feet.

"How did I get here?," he repeated.

"We were talking about the Tatra mountains yesterday." Nyanatiloka said modestly but evasively. You are cold. Let's go towards the lodges below."

Jacek did not budge. "Is it enough to talk about something?"

"No, only to think of it. The spirit creates the environment it wants. Thinking is the only truth.

"Did you move me here with your will?"

"No, brother, I don't think I did that. I think, we are still where we were. Only the reality of our senses has changed ..." Saying that, Nyanatiloka began walking briskly, pushing away the lush herbs with his bare knees and shaking the dew from drooping twig branches with his forehead. Jacek was following him in silence and was involuntarily searching for some sort comprehension or a trick. How could he convince his mind about this inconceivable transference from the distant plains of Mazovia into the heart of the Tatra mountains that happened without his knowledge? He struck his forehead several times to make sure he was awake, and he tried to tie together logical and subtle thoughts that required total sobriety.

He heard a voice say to him: "Brother, don't you want us to remain here? Yesterday, you told me in your study that this is the only place where you could be and think, and live for your own sake ..."

"I am afraid I am not ready for that," whispered Jacek. Fear grabs me at such a thought ..."

He saw everything very clearly with his eyes, and yet, he was surprised that when he opened his mouth, he heard his voice as if it were coming from somewhere far away ... He felt that Nyanatiloka had stopped and was looking at him now. He felt embarrassed, as if this sorcerer could read his secret thoughts with his eyes ... He bent to hide his face and tore a branch of gentian covered with dark-blue flowers which he saw at his feet.

"Aza visited me today," he thought "that is what she wrote in her letter ..." He felt sorry for himself that he was not in his studio now, although yesterday he wanted to escape from the announced visit.

He straightened up the stem of a broken flower in his hand and raised his eyes. A staggering, frightening wonder, bordering with terror caught his chest. He was in his room, in front of the table, piled with papers, in front of his books and paintings.

"Nyanatiloka!"

Nobody answered. He was alone. The morning light was coming in the room from under the raised blind, the bustle of the already awake street came from below.

"I was dreaming!" Jacek whispered in relief and raised a hand to his forehead. "I apparently fell asleep in my chair yesterday and ..."

He jumped back. He saw in his own hand, at the level of his eyes, a blossoming stem of the gentian still covered with fresh, glistening dew drops ...

He spread his fingers in shock, and the flower released from them fell on the carpet next to his feet, dressed in soaked and muddy shoes. The tiny blueberry leaves were still stuck on them, glistening with dew together with dried spruce needles ... His clothes had a sharp smell of resinous smoke, like after spending a night at a fire with mountain dwarf pine burning in it.

He stepped toward the armchair and sat on it slowly, resting his head on his arm.

"What is everything we see?," he thought, "Everything we see, what is the so-called reality of life, if I'm sitting here right now with a mountain flower in my hand, and I just don't know what happened and how it was possible ...?" Nyanatiloka told me (I was not dreaming !?) that we are not moving from place to place in this case, but that our spirit creates its surroundings with its own will. Still, it was not just my spirit in the Tatras just a moment ago, but my body and these clothes were there too. Now, they are covered with dew and pieces of forest weed, soaked with resinous smoke of the fire started for the night ...? Is there any theory in the world that could justify this confusion and disorder in these events? Lord Tedwen had proved the existence of the physical world as something seemingly illusory, but he did not take away the steadfast law from what was happening. He did not free our souls from beliefs about the order of existence and coming into being... I know nothing! I don't know anything!"

He squeezed his head in his arms and remained silent for some time, trying not to think about it anymore.

A metal box in the wall behind him clanked, which meant the morning mail was sent from the central office directly to his home. He stood up to distract his thoughts and touched the spring closing the box. A pack of papers spilled onto the table. They were usually small cards containing a name, a number and the time when the sender would like to talk to His Excellency by phone ... Jacek flipped these cards quickly, not thinking about what he was doing. Against his will, his thoughts were coming back to the events of last night, unable to focus on the more or less important reports he was holding in his hand.

Finally, one thing caught his interest. It was a report sent to him by the manager of the plant, where he had ordered a new "lunar vehicle" for himself to be built according to the strictest plans. The director reported that the work was proceeding slowly, but surely, and he expected to give Jacek a ready vehicle in two or three months.

Two or three months! He twitched impatiently. Waiting so long is simply impossible! If Marek needed his help there on the Moon, it may be too late, and at the same time ... what will happen here before he could leave! Is there no other means besides this vehicle, thrown into space by compressed gases?

He looked behind him where Nyanatiloka silent and peaceful as usual was sitting in an armchair. Jacek had gotten so used to his unexpected and sneaky appearance, in various places and most often when he thought of him, that he was no longer showing surprise. He approached him intensely, and said without preamble:

"You once said that there are no smaller or bigger obstacles for our will, that if it has traversed one millimeter of space, it can do it over thousands of miles ..."

"I think so, brother."

"We were in the Tatras at night, not moving from here ..."

"I think so."

"We were really there. A stalk of gentian is lying on my table, covered with fresh flowers ... I am sure that I broke it off this morning on the slopes of Zabie ... Nyanatiloka!"

"I'm listening to you, brother."

"I want to be on the Moon today! Be there in an hour, immediately! Be there not in a dream, but in reality, as I was in the Tatra Mountains, so I could act there.

"I don't know if you can do it."

"You do it! Help me!"

"No."

"Why? I want it, I am asking you for it!"

"No. Not now ..."

"So, you apparently can't do it! Obviously, all your wisdom and power consist only of making pranks and creating delusions. He paused. He was embarrassed by what he had said, so he looked at Nyanatiloka with fear. The Buddhist sage looked at him indulgently and smiled slightly.

"Forgive me!," Jacek whispered.

"I have nothing to forgive you for, my brother ..."

"I got mad ... It's funny," he added after a while, sitting down slowly in his chair, "that I am talking to you as if I were angry with you, that you can't work miracles ..."

He fell silent quickly, remembering that what this Buddhist had done many times before his eyes was a miracle ..."I do not understand!," he said aloud, although he was only talking to himself.

Nyanatiloka grew serious. "And yet, you could understand it so easily, brother, if only you wanted to ..."

"You make miracles!"

"No. I make no miracles. Nobody makes miracles for the simple reason that dominance of the spirit over appearances is not quite a miracle and it does not go beyond the scope of the laws of the eternal Being ... And if I refuse you ..."

"Yes, why are you refusing me?" Repeated Jacek.

"Listen to me."

Nyanatiloka sat down next to him, and resting his both hands on the arm of the chair, began to speak, not taking his eyes away from Jacek's face: "You want to follow your friend to the Moon immediately as a result of the news. I helped you once to be there in your thought and look at your friend's actions with the eyes of your soul, but you are not satisfied. You would like to be there wrapped in this vain shape, which you call your body. You would like to have the possibility of sharing and making certain movements. You would like to accomplish all that in the way you still understand action at this moment. I am not sure that it would be necessary, and that it would help your soul, but that is not the point."

"Yes, it is, because it is for my friend who needs my help."

"What will you help him with? Will you take your deadly machine with you and destroy the whole Moon to save him if he is in danger? Do you know what's going on there? You spoke in my presence with the dwarfs yesterday. You infer from what they said that your friend Marek, with intention or against his intention, unexpectedly got involved in the fate of the lunar people and is influencing their life. What do you want to do now? Stand by him and help him make things happen more quickly on the Moon in the same way as it is on Earth?! Do you think that what we have here is really good?"

"Perhaps I could save Marek from danger," Jacek interrupted evasively.

"Why? And what if it is the fate, he had already taken upon himself? Don't interfere with his death as perhaps this is the fate he needs. Are you so sure that your friend can accomplish more alive and alone, than some kind of legend that will follow him through generations? Do you want to stop it at the beginning? Annihilate? Prevent?"

He approached Jacek sitting there with his head down and put both his hands on his shoulders.

"Listen to me! Don't think about the Moon or the other globes which you will come to know soon enough! Don't interfere with whatever is happening, even if you had the power! You do not need to interfere with anything, because it does not matter what is happening around us, only what we are striving for within ourselves ..."

Jacek raised his head. He felt Nyanatiloka behind but did not look back at him. Instead he focused his eyes thoughtfully on the opposite wall where several portraits hung.

"How do you know that I would not do it for myself?," he said. "Maybe I just want to run away?"

"You can't run. You have to face everything and experience everything without turning around. Without effort, even without joy. To be yourself."

He bent even more. Jacek was not sure if heard his voice or just the rustle of his own thoughts strangely excited by the sage.

"One achieves everything only when one does not demand anything, and when one does not want anything. It's necessary to become as dispassionate as the universe, as carefree as light; as knowing but, not searching like some Deity!"

Jacek's thoughts were wandering off towards an indefinite and diffusing distance.

Knowing but not searching! To be a creator of your own truth, which is also the truth of the universe closed in man. Instead of a seeker of other's wonderful truths, which turn out to be nothing, but emptiness and illusion, find your own, and faith is such truth! It can be any faith, but creative, strong, created in spirit and undoubted, and because of that being the unshakable truth!

It means to know, but not to examine! To create, not to seek. To think, not to doubt. Not to give up but to feel; not to desire but want! How can one find such a miracle?

Nyanatiloka once said: "You need to learn to be alone among crowds and noise - even more alone than one could be in the wildest of forests."

He said it at the Nile bank as Aza was finishing her performance in the ruins of the temple...

"Excellency ..."

He was startled and jumped up intently. The servant stood in the doorway motionless and up right.

"What's up?"

"We were worried that the Excellency did not go down to his bedroom for the night ..."

Jacek waved his hand impatiently. "What's up?"

"Ms. Aza ..."

"What? Has she come?"

"Yes, sir. This morning by a separate train. We wanted to wake your Excellency up as instructed, but your bedroom was empty, and we did not dare to come here."

"Where is Ms. Aza?"

After the servant's departure, Jacek turned his eyes to face Nyanatiloka. He stared at him meticulously, as if to find out how impressed he was about the arrival of the famous singer, but his face was calm, serene, and frozen as always. The usual smile did not even leave his lips, there was no indignation, sadness or even indulgence in his eyes...

"Are you going down right now, brother?," he asked, in a quite indifferent voice.

Meanwhile, Aza was waiting in the dining room, making herself comfortable, as if in her own home. She changed from her traveling clothes into a light dress and now, she was sitting in a deep leather chair with a scented cigarillo at her mouth. The silver tea tableware and crystal vases with fruit and sweets were standing in front of her on the table, covered with an antique linen patterned tablecloth. She pushed away the cup with unfinished tea, and with her head on the back of the chair, was staring with half closed eyes at the blue smoke slowly drifting toward the carved ceiling. She rested her ankle on the knee of the other leg. Her slender and firm calves in black, shiny stockings and small feet in golden booties were visible among the scattered folds of the light color silk.

Since Lachec's visit and his unexpected death, Aza had completely given up her former apartment in which she was only a guest in between her world travels. All this made a strange impression on her. People died for her more than once, either under her door and far away as if running away from her to the edge of the world. They died quietly, without a word, without complaint, without reproach or with lengthy letters announcing the time of their death. Some were blaming her or blessing her dishonestly in a jester manner for the "painful happiness" she had given them. It did not bother her much, and she got used to it ... but not this time.

She couldn't get over Lachec's death. Each time she was leaving her house, it always seemed to her that she saw his shrunken corpse on the threshold. She couldn't forget that terrifyingly white face, twisted in death, and couldn't understand why they brought him to her ...

That memory shook her even now. She knew that he died for her and because of her. Her thought, rebelling against indefinite remorse, began to snarl. After all, she did not do any harm to him. What could he want? Well, her crazy kisses made him insane, and at the last moment, when he dared to reach for her, she pushed him away like a dog? Why would someone take his life over something like that?! Or even worse: to challenge death so voluntarily and visibly?

His eyes were staring at her in her memory, at first mad with amazement and fear, and then so terribly sad as if fading away ... He was lying with folded arms on her knees and stretching his hungry lips to her face. He almost looked beautiful at that moment. She made him curse his art and his rebirth by the act he bragged about. He had to deny everything he had dared to say against her. She made him repeat clearly that he was nothing to her and nothing mattered to him except her single kiss ...

Ha! She did not even push him in the chest when he wanted to embrace her in the highest moment of passion. She only struck him with her eyes and those cold words: "What are you worth to me. You are as miserable, despicable and powerless, like all the other boastful ones ...?"

And he said, leaving: "I stopped believing in myself not because I did not possess you, but because I kissed your lips ..."

A bizarre story!

She tossed the burnt cigarette and stretched her feet out on the fluffy carpet. She was angry at herself that she was still thinking about something so trivial and unworthy. In this way she was confirming her weakness, hidden somewhere at the bottom of her soul, when she just needed to be strong and unrelenting, like a forest lynx reigning over the whole forest while hidden in the branches of a tree.

She turned to the rustle of the door opening. Jacek was standing on the threshold, a bit pale, and bowed deeply to her, apologizing for being late. Without getting up from the chair, she stretched out her left pampered hand with long pink nails. Leaning, he touched it with slightly trembling, hot lips, and at that moment Aza, looking down over his head, saw the half-naked Buddhist figure in the door. She twitched in a freezing unexplained fear and opened her eyes wide ... She seemed to her know this face from somewhere, so well, so well known ...

She rose slowly and while Jacek, surprised by her behavior, moved to the side a bit, she strained her eyes and memory ...

Something like a vague reminder when she was a small girl: a giant hall, crowded with people, the stage glowing in the lights, and on it the same figure, the same hands with long, subtle fingers that now hangs on the door handle, and this face with long black hair ...

And the magic violin singing in a living chorus of angels turned by the touch of those hands. She feels bated breath in her chest: he plays, master above masters, incomparable violinist, lord of strings and gold, and hearts, adored, famous, powerful, beloved, rich, beautiful...

- like a god ...

"Serato!"

The Three Worldly slightly bowed his head. "Yes, this used to be my name once." He said without a trace of uneasiness in his usual, calm-sounding voice.

VI

Day and night, Roda thought about how to avoid the danger he would be facing soon. He did not want to go back to the Moon in Jacek's company and decided to do everything he could to prevent it. He realized that he had extraordinarily little to say in this matter, and he trembled at the thought of appearing with Jacek in the city at the *Warm Ponds*.

He was not even bothered by the fear of the scientist's revenge for Marek, although he was not buying all his nobleness. What worried him the most was the shame he would have to bear on the Moon...

That would really be an irony of fate! He, Roda, the chairman of the Brotherhood of Truth, who throughout all his life fought against the "fairy tales" about their earthly descent, now returning from Earth and forced to testify that it is inhabited and in terms of devices is more advanced than the Moon.

For Roda became an especially passionate admirer of the technical culture on Earth. He learned a lot about it, at least from his superficial observations. Jacek, unwaveringly intending to take both "messengers" with him back to the Moon, wanted them to make the most of their stay on Earth before they go, and he hired guides with whom they visited various countries and cities, looking at stuff and learning more every day.

At first, he traveled with Mataret, but later he managed to beg Jacek to free him from his companion. From that fateful day, when Mataret unnecessarily confessed the truth, relations between him and the master were so tense that they could hardly speak to each other, except to accuse each other. This condition worsened a lot while on the road, as if that were possible at all. Mataret, recognizing the whole miracle of earthly progress, never ceased to be an old skeptic here, who also had his eyes open on the "other side of the coin". While Roda constantly admired and complimented everything, he, getting to know the earthly world more and more, often smiled sneeringly and shrugged his shoulders when asked if it was not better and not more perfect here than on the Moon. It led to fierce quarrels between both members of the Brotherhood of Truth, which eventually became so unbearable that they had to split up.

Deprived of his compatriot, Roda felt a bit lonely, but in the end what he saw and heard absorbed him so much that he rarely felt that lack.

He used his time very well and was learning a lot. Clever by nature, he quickly understood the forms of earthly devices and soon realized the relations there. As he was still disturbed by the thought of returning to the Silver Globe, so undesirable at the moment, so he was looking everywhere for the most convenient way out. He had no clearly defined plan yet, but he had some vague ideas in his mind that could potentially mature into something better over time.

From his stay in this world, he learned more and more clearly and solidly about things cooking under the surface. He also noticed in his guardian's home, that there was somehow core to those things here. He did not need much time to guess that there was a terrible and powerful secret, which would provide its owner with impunity, power, and advantage.

He understood that the extraction of this secret was the goal of Grabiec's several visits and also of Aza's prolonged stay in the scientist's home.

Contrary to his usual habits, Roda was silent, he was just looking and waiting.

"My time will come!," he thought. "As I mastered taking the vehicle over from the other one, I will also try at the first opportunity to steal this machine."

Indeed, everyone wanted this machine. Grabiec, touched by Lachec's incomprehensible death and thus weakened in his arrangements, urged Aza even more to hurry ... He wanted to have that awesome destructive power in his hands to make demands of society and the world and win without a fight.

Despite everything in moments of peaceful thought, he was still overwhelmed by the fear of the storm he was unleashing. He moved underground powers, threw a fire at the enormous masses of workers frozen in physical labor, but now before the explosion he became even more fearful while observing the rising and swelling of that wave. He planned to put this "sea" on a leash and let it loose on the hideous civilized flock in the service of the world's know-it-all individuals. However, he soon realized that once unleashed, no one would have power over it, once it ruffled and rocks, no one could ever push it back behind the broken dams.

One autumn afternoon, he and Yoozva had flown over several parts of the country. In a couple of hours, they visited the centers of the movement, stoking the fire already burning and averting it elsewhere. After that he lowered the plane on the empty, sunburned hill above the Eternal City. They talked for some time about other matters on the ever-widening conspiracy, but the words were falling lazily from their mouths, until they both fell silent, gazing at that strange city under their feet.

The bright, golden sun was hanging in the sky, and the air was saturated with a light dust that almost blinded their eyes. Grabiec's beloved city, eternal, royal Rome was sleeping silently under that blue and golden cress, under a transparent and opal cloud, which blurred the edges of the horizon and absorbed it.

There, far north, east, and west, were two centers of life, two hearts of the European land pulsating with red and gold blood: Paris and Warsaw. Those two monstrous hubs of all networks and roads were two centers of what the crowds commonly called culture. They were like giant polyps which were drinking the juices of the whole Earth with its thousand arms. They were the capital cities of governments, merchants, and industrialists. They were the seats of sin, meanness, and mediocrity. The other former capitals, of former European countries, were following the example of these two largest cities, and they also grew and transformed. They were always huge, monstrous, busy, and yet pushed to a lower rank by these two "suns".

Rome remained what it used to be centuries ago: the only city. Somehow, it had saved itself from the barbaric hand of "progress" and "civilization". As in earlier times, the intact ruins were standing in the Forum. The gray cypresses swayed in the wind, and the blood red roses bloomed under the orange trees above the remnants of the golden houses on the Palatine.

As in earlier ages, the bells still sounded in Saint Peter's church, and the gray, old man in a triple crown was still blessing the empty yard with his white, weak hand. He was probably thinking about those times, when from there his predecessors lifted the nations of Earth with the mere movement of a finger, and bent royal heads into the dust ...

At the same time, the white statues, the long-forgotten deities, the pieces of marble dreams, the lush shreds of the past, were still standing on the Capitoline Hill, on the Quirinal, and the military palace of Saint John Lateran. They were in the gigantic remains of ancient baths, theaters, circuses, cloisters of basilicas, under the domes of the churches, in the buildings remembering the Renaissances dawn, in gardens, squares, and above fountains ...

Grabiec dreamed that this unique city should be the future proud spiritual capital of the renewed world. He bowed his head and looked at a hundred domes basking in the sun: puffing up into the sky and covered with the golden-green patina of centuries, at the old and soaring obelisks, at the chipped crag of the Flavian Circus. Calm and strong dignity emanated from this city, which had survived a millennia and did not consider it appropriate to change with the example of others. So Grabiec kept dreaming ...

Let there be great modern metropolises there, in the north, in the east or in the west. Let them be the centers of work, traffic movement, and all other everyday trivial cares. Let them be swarming like hives, let them roar like forges, but far away from here. Keep the buzz away from the edges of Campania, gilded by the sun and the autumn, and don't let it disturb the pensive silence under the cypress trees on the ruins ... Here will be the brain and the soul of humankind, the permanent temple of "earthly gods". It will serve as the home and the capital of those in the know who the kings of the world will be.

Once, when the Caesars lived in marble houses on the Palatine Hill, the world sent wheat, wine, oil, precious stones, slaves, women and even gods to this city. Most of the world served it and was subject to the will of Rome. It was allowed to exist for the purpose of maintaining this very city, securing its development, and adding to its splendor.

Now, it has to happen again. Whatever best goods and accomplishments all countries, lands, and seas can produce, they all should flow here. This place will be the center of the world again, its thought and its will.

The news about this holy city with access allowed only for the chosen ones will spread all over the world. Mothers will tell their children about it like a fairy tale from the East and that all power, all the beauty, light, wisdom, and life are there. Since the gates of its impenetrable walls are high, to get on the inside one shouldn't bend but rather grow to fit their size. Oh, my dream city, my beloved city!

Yoozva's short, hard laughter pulled Grabiec out of his thoughts. He turned his head vividly and looked at his companion. He was standing there with his forehead bent and with his fists on an old, already broken sarcophagus covered by weeds.

"Yoozva, were you laughing?"

The leader threw his head back. "So, what if I was?"

He made a wide circle in the air with his hand. "After all, it's funny to think that after our storm, this place here will be only debris without shape and stones, on which the weeds will grow, and the bushes, and then the forest ... We can do it, oh! We will give it to these edifices that have survived for centuries, these old vaults patched with cement, these columns tied up with iron bars. Oh! These domes will fall to dust, and there will be an earthquake that no one has ever seen since the creation of the world!

He laughed again fervently, and then, turning straight to Grabiec, added "Listen, Grabiec, you are hiding something ... What is really the matter with Jacek's machine? "

Grabiec did not feel like answering. The last glares of the setting sun, so similar to the royal aureole surrounding the city, suddenly changed in his eyes into a fire. It seemed to him that he saw the eternal Rome, irretrievably collapsing into rubble. He pictured the wild mob scarier than the old hordes of barbarians, going through its ashes and through the rubble, so unstoppable, and so crazy ...

Only when Yoozva repeated the question more urgently for the second time did Grabiec turn his eyes to him. He hesitated for a moment. Is he to tell him the truth that if Jacek's terrible invention falls into his hand, it will serve him first to put down the rampant flock of today's human society, and to keep in check in a new slavery, the working masses unleashed for one day only? Should he have to tell him that so honestly and brazenly? And also add that as long as he, Grabiec is alive, everything else will fall apart in the world, before one stone from the top of these old columns falls down?

He looked at Yoozva and thought how he would react to that. Yes, this man, upon hearing this would not even be outraged or indignant. He would probably only laugh with his wide mouth, revealing his white, predatory, and strong teeth. He is so sure that the ultimate and invincible power will be the annihilation and destruction that he is going to deliver.

"I've sent Aza to Jacek," Grabiec said seemingly calmly and indifferently looking away. "She will do whatever is possible..."

"Nonsense!" Yoozva hissed contemptuously. "I don't understand these half measures and why is this woman, a comedian, involved? What can she do? It would be better to demolish his house in Warsaw and take what is needed by force."

"You shouldn't forget that he can defend it and explode almost the whole city with one finger."

Yoozva's eyes lit up. "Oh, yes! That would be a beautiful beginning. Warsaw and Paris would be first and then we would take care of those other smaller ulcers on Europe's infected body ..."

"It wouldn't be possible," Grabiec spoke as if to himself. "If Warsaw perished, Jacek's secret about that frightful machine would perish with it."

"So, what can be done?"

"He has to give it to us by his free will, as we probably couldn't use it without his instructions!"

Yoozva stretched out his veined, powerful hands. "That's not necessary," he said after a moment. "Damn, the smart men with their machines!" I have at my disposal more powerful and live explosives! Let all of mine move, let them start the dance, and I can swear on my soul, Grabiec, that there will be no trace or memories of this beautiful world after that."

Grabiec was about to answer that, but he suddenly understood that it was all a futile exercise. He saw Yoozva's eyes, burning with fierce, implacable hatred of everything that was and is, just because it is, and only because it was, and for the first time in his life cold fear ran through his spine. For one twinkle, he thought about pushing his knife into that broad chest now, but he was not so mean and cowardly. That would mean crashing your ship before a voyage taking it to new countries, for the fear of a storm that could prevail over the helmsman's strength and wisdom ...

He was looking at Yoozva. After all, he was not a dumb or blind man, hating everything because he was accidentally born and lived in hard conditions, or because his fate condemned him to a manual and stupefying labor ... He went through all the grades of public schools and for his exceptional abilities was awarded a scholarship to study at the School of Sages when he suddenly disappeared.

Life went on, and nobody remembered Yoozva or knew if he was alive. In the meantime, one day, he realized that everything was bad. Then, he went deep into the search for strength and power, guided only by the insane desire to destroy ...

"How strange it is that I met him," Grabiec whispered to himself, turning his eyes to the bloody glare of the sunset over Rome.

VII

Nyanatiloka slowly shook his head and smiled. "No," he started looking away from Aza, and if he did not answer her question ... "I renounced nothing, I never failed, I was never embittered or disappointed."

Jacek shifted impatiently in his chair.

"So why ...?"

He stopped suddenly and fell silent, overcome with shame that he was asking what he should have already understood.

Nyanatiloka looked up at him with calm and clear eyes. "It was not enough. I went further, I wanted to live."

"Live ...!" Jacek whispered to himself, like an echo.

In an instant, he vividly remembered everything he had heard of this strange man as a young boy, and what he knew about him now.

"I wanted to live," said Serato-Nyanatiloka, whose name was once synonymous with life alone, unleashed power, happiness, pleasure, and power.

In those times, he was spoken of as an idol. Wherever he appeared with his black-violin, people became ecstatic and dropped to their knees before him, and he just did whatever he wanted with them. If one could ever say about an artist, that he ruled the crowd instead of serving it, then that was true for him. In his celebrated, incomparable, and unique improvisations, he shook his listeners like a coastal reed. With one movement of his bow, with a movement of one finger, he threw people from the madness of joy into sadness and depression. He whispered wonderful fairy tales to them, frightened them and annihilated them. He tossed them under his feet or in one moment, with almost miraculous power, he transformed average bread eaters into raging, gods of life rushing with the wind.

Jacek remembered what the now deceased bishop once said about Serato:

"If this man wanted, he could create a new revelation with his violin, and people would follow him, even if he led them to hell."

The priest said it with fear and drew a cross on his forehead, and in Jacek's eyes, a young boy at that time, the violinist grew to fantastic, super-large sizes, became a symbol of exaltation, dominion, royalty and anointing.

It was needless to say that Serato was rich, for this far too weak recounting did not clearly paint the power of the gold that flowed inadvertently through his fingers. There was no thought that he could not bring to fruition, or fantastic idea that he would not be able to bring to life. One concert brought him more income than kings and emperors made, while they still existed in Europe.

Beautiful, healthy, unconcerned about anything, roaring with life like a storm, he inhaled the delight of existence with his whole chest, and there was really nothing that fate would deny him. Women trembled looking at him, and he could choose among them like a sultan in the Arabian Nights. Like that sultan, he could be sure that none of them would reject him at whatever price they would have to pay for that.

No one ever saw Serato sad or depressed as his face was always lit with a smile. And when the news spread one day that this man had suddenly and inconceivably perished, a crime was suspected. Long investigation for its proof was conducted but to no avail. Nobody could have thought that he would voluntarily turn away from that life, which until then he had drunk in with a hungry mouth.

Notwithstanding his will, Jacek raised his eyes and looked at the face of the hermit sitting in front of him. And that's Serato himself...! Nyanatiloka, the Three-world-knowledgeable Mystic. Shirtless, calm, living on beggar bread, and still divine ...

"I wanted to live," he said. He wanted to live!...

So, what was, this frenzy of art, fame and love seething with power? Was it not it just the life that sometimes flashes like a fire passing through Jacek's brain so tired of wisdom? And one could throw everything so irrevocably and so lightly ...

"Don't you miss ...?"

The former violinist slowly raised his head. "Miss what? Looking at me, can you assume that I left something beyond me that I could miss in my current state? I did not withdraw from anything, I did not reject anything, I only went further and higher. What I had then might have been worth something, but what I have now is worth more than that. I had fame, wealth, and power. What does it mean to me, what others thought about me, then compared to today, when I don't need anybody's opinion to know who I am? I am richer than ever because I have no unfulfilled desires. Since I do not want anything that could only be fulfilled by others, instead of having supposed power over others, I have a perfect power over myself."

"And art," said Jacek, "don't you miss it?"

Nyanatiloka smiled. "What kind of external harmony, even the most perfect, can match the tuning of the soul I have now acquired? Compare any art to compare my present awareness that I created my whole world and can keep it for as long as I want?"

He stood up and approached Jacek. "Talking about it isn't necessary when there are so many more important things. One does not need to think about what one once was as then there wouldn't be enough time to think about what one might be. And everybody, everybody without exception can be who one wants to be."

Jacek laughed. "Anyone who wants to! Anyone who will muster the strength to give up everything at once like you did?"

Nyanatiloka interrupted him with a movement of his hand.

"How many times do I have to tell you," he began gently, "that I did not renounce anything. After all, to give up means to abandon something alluring, having value for a person. I only got rid of certain life forms that became vain for me the moment I got to know the better ones. The years of my spiritual work, made it more and more exciting with the passing of time. After years of seclusion and loneliness, which infinitely increase the power of life, I gained what we call 'the knowledge of the three worlds'. If it is not the highest level of wisdom, then it is undoubtedly the first one and the most essential. One never loses this kind of knowledge. I could go back to the forms of my old life now, join this society, be crazy like them. I could work unnecessarily, enjoy fame, wealth, success and still be in my soul, what I am now, but just thinking about it makes me laugh as there is no more charm in it for me."

He spread his hands and raised his head slightly up. "I live in the most perfect form," he continued, "personal and all-encompassing. It is possible because I learned to connect with the world and its spirit in the true unity, like it was at the beginning, before human consciousness was conceived. I do not need to look at flowering meadows, listen to the roaring sea and the storm because I myself am truly a growing land and a flower, and a river, and a tree, a wind, and a sea. I feel the harmony in the pulse of my blood and in the rhythm of my thought. And it is at its deepest level, hidden under a delusional phenomena, under what seems evil, unjust, or unnecessary to a man taken out of the world. All my long previous life, although not scanty for me, never gave me a single moment of happiness similar to this blessed state in which I am constantly now and without fear of ever losing it.

Nyanatiloka was speaking to Jacek, as if he had forgotten about Aza's presence, who cuddled up in a deep chair, chin on her hands resting on the arm of the chair and looking at him in silence with wide open eyes.

At first, she was listening to what he was saying, later his words became a meaningless sound to her that she did not even want to mind. All she could hear was a smooth, calm, and soft voice, and see his bare, slim, and firm arm from the side. It had the color of a ripe fruit coated with southern sun. Some young freshness and power were emanating from this man. His black and shiny, slightly wavy hair was falling on his bare, brawny, shoulders, and Aza seemed to smell his fresh curls, reminiscent of the scent of mountain herbs growing over a cold crystal stream. She was looking at his face from the profile: a convex line where his temple was connected to the frontal bone, the raised eyelid, one corner of the fresh, vibrating, and red mouth.

"Young, bright, divine," she whispered in her mind, "he was and then ...," She suddenly jumped up in horror; "Serato!"

He turned slowly and looked at her slightly distracted, obviously not happy with her interrupting him.

She was looking at him for some time, as if uncertain, or not trusting her eyes. "Serato?" She repeated with a hint of surprise.

"I am listening."

Aza was counting in a low voice, not taking her eyes of him. "Six ... ten ... Eighteen, no!" Twenty! That's it. Twenty years.

Nyanatiloka understood her and smiled. "Yes. I left Europe twenty years ago to, go to Ceylon.

"I was a little girl in the circus ... I remember ... It was said then that Serato was forty years old."

"Forty-six," he corrected her.

Jacek, who was listening to this conversation with a growing interest, now jumped from the chair. "You! Would you be over sixty now?"

"Yes. Is this so surprising to you?"

Jacek took a step back, not knowing what to think, his eyes fixed on the hermit's calm face.

"After all, he appeals to be a thirty-year-old young man," Aza whispered, as if to herself, in breathless amazement. "Younger than he was when I saw him twenty years ago. It cannot be."

"Why?" Saying that, he turned to face Aza for a moment, and his eyes transfixed on her with that calm cold look.

She suddenly fell silent, not even knowing why she was overcome with unexplained fear. She thought of an old fairy tale in which a corpse kept alive and young by a terrible spell, until it was broken and then, in a twinkling spilled into stinking mud around its own bones. She screamed slightly and stepped back.

Meanwhile, Nyanatiloka continued speaking to Jacek: "Don't you understand that with some refinement, our will may control all body functions, as it usually controls only some movements? After all, the fakirs of the lowest ranks, as far from the true knowledge as the Earth is from the Sun, manage to stop the heartbeat and nerves, and thus put themselves into a state of apparent death for some time."

"This is about life and your unexplained youth," Jacek interjected. "

And isn't it all the same, in which direction our will go? Ultimately, it is about a certain state of our organs and about their functions, as you here in Europe speak in your learned language, or, as we would say, about freeing a form from time and putting it above it."

Jacek squeezed his head with his hands: " I am completely mixed up. So, could you actually live forever?"

Nyanatiloka smiled. "I can live forever because the spirit is immortal, and I am a spirit like you are, like all of us are. As for the body, which is nothing else than an external and temporary form of a spirit, it is not worth keeping too long. As long as it is needed, it is better when it is young and healthy and able to obey all your commands, than if it were withered and weakened, but when it fulfills its task, the man with this knowledge can loosen up the will that keeps it alive ..."

He paused and changed his tone at once, reaching out to Jacek: "Come, I don't know why we're sitting in this stuffy room. The sun has already set, and I would like to look at the stars from the roof. We will ponder there together and then talk about the existence on this and that side of the stars as one continuous and unbroken thing."

Aza did not even notice when they left the room, though it seemed to her that she was watching them all the while. She sat there for some time as if numb, completely stunned by what she heard. She was unable to place into any category of human reason the history of an eternally young violinist, who was now standing before her in the form of a Buddhist saint.

Suddenly it occurred to her that she must have been wrong, that this man was not and could not be Serato whom she had known twenty years earlier. He apparently assumed the name she had inadvertently blurted out and covered himself with it, as if for an unexplained reason, he did not want them to know who he really was. "He's a fraud."

She jumped up automatically; she wanted to call the servants, call Jacek, shout that this man should be imprisoned, and not allowed to be called that name ... She rested her hand on the table.

Is it possible, however, that she would not recognize him, mistake someone else for him? Is it possible that anyone could be like him? She lowered her eyelids slowly and a scene from long, long ago loomed under her eyelids. It felt like a long-forgotten night dream but still lively and clear ...

Then, twenty years ago Serato had crazy ideas. He sometimes ignored urgent telegrams and his friends' pleas begging him to perform in first class theaters for tons of gold.

At other times, he performed where he would be the least expected, and with his presence changed a roadside inn for a long-remembered concert hall. It also happened that, like a wandering musician, he walked with his violin along a dusty road, leading into the fields crowds of city dwellers possessed with him ...

Aza, a little girl in the circus, heard about it from her older colleagues, saying his name with a strange trembling of their lips. Then, she dreamed of the magical violinist, pulling the heart strings of his admirers into other worlds with his bow. They worshiped him as a divine presence, or as an embodied divine power. She did not even need to see him, as her childish imagination painted him so vividly. When it was dark, and she was sitting tired in a corner, she was invariably telling herself the very one and most wonderful fairy tale:

"He will come... It will be a dream that is unlike any other, brighter, and sweeter when he appears and takes her hand and tells her to follow him into the world, under some rainbows, on the clouds outstretched like some gates ...

He will certainly come. He will free her, poor little Aza, from the scary jester, who demands an incredibly disgusting thing from her. He will take her to the meadows, to those fields that are supposedly outside the city walls. Then she will listen to him singing on the violin and she will forget about the circus. She will forget about the line on which she had to dance, so she wouldn't be beaten, so people would clap."

She smiled bitterly at the memory of those funny children's dreams. She was not so naive, and she knew all too well, what the eyes of the elderly gentlemen from the first rows of chairs meant, ogling the leotards stretched on her slim, childish body, and she knew what the jester wanted.

And yet...

Yet, in those moments of hidden dreams, her prematurely acquired day after day cynicism would entrap her, like a turtle shell or a frog spell, in which the enchanted princess from the fairy tale was imprisoned. Then she kind of emerged from herself as she was in the depths of her soul. She was still a child, looking at the world with amazed eyes and dreaming about a bright, wonderful thing ...

And he came. Indeed he came one day, or rather one evening. She was very tired then. She was ordered to run up on a tightened, sloped outstretched wire rope onto a platform, from where she was to jump on a swinging trapeze, then to the second, and on to a third, to spin and dance in the air. She dashed the first time and half slipped off the wire rope, painfully falling on her side. She heard a few muffled screams from the audience, which were soon drowned out by the dissatisfied hisses. The director of the show came up to her and, having checked if she was all right, glared at her with evil eyes.

"Run, you bitch!"

"I'm scared," she whispered in a sudden attack of fear.

"Run," he hissed threateningly through his teeth.

She stepped back obediently, her body trembling all over. She jumped, and suddenly she felt, as if an invisible force kept her in place just before the beginning of the rope. "I'm afraid!" She almost moaned, "I'm afraid."

The audience was getting impatient. The posters for this evening heralded "an extraordinary spectacle, the only original air princess, a flying sorceress," while meanwhile the sorceress was standing there frightened, awkward, with red eyelids and lips childishly shrinking to tears.

"This is a scam!" People were calling from further rows. "Return the money! Stop this show!" The merciless crowd, demanding only fun for their penny, was scoffing at her, called her names, laughed at her, and loudly made indecent comments.

"Run!"

She heard the manager's angry voice, swollen with rage, as if in a dream. Gathering all her willpower she backed up once more for her sprint. Her eyes darkened, the noise in her ears was unbearable, her knees were trembling, as she felt that she would fall before reaching the end of the rope.

She jumped, took a few steps with her eyes closed, and suddenly felt that someone was grabbing her arm just as she was about to touch the stretched wires. She looked back. A sophisticated man, with black wavy hair, apparently coming from the audience, was standing beside her, and holding her back with a white, soft, and strong as steel hand. Wait a second.

She did not even have time to laugh or be scared as she was overwhelmed by the unspeakable sweet feeling that she was being looked after. The headmaster jumped pale in anger, but before he opened his mouth, her guardian said in a calm and commanding voice: "Give me a violin, please!"

"Serato! Serato! The whole amphitheater roared.

Serato! She turned her head abruptly and stared at him avidly and greedily as her heart almost stopped beating.

Fairytale, dream, golden fairy tale came, will take, lead ... No! Something else shuddered in her, something she couldn't even understand at first. She could feel his fingers on her bare, childish arm, and a heat engulfed her under his glimpse, but when he touched her face, something broke in her chest. She wanted to weep and get lost in oblivion. She wanted him to crush her with his hands or put his foot on her chest, and at the same time she wanted to run, run away...

Silence suddenly enveloped the theater. She heard some other-worldly, strange sound, like some silver crying. She was almost wondering where it came from, but it was Serato's playing.

Nobody was paying attention to her now. She was sitting a bit out of the way and watching. Some sound in her ears was muffling his music. She could only see his white hand pulling the bow and his lowered eyelid, slightly parted wet and blood red lips in his shaved face. A shiver ran through her from head to toe, and for the first time in her life, she had a strange feeling that there were kisses and embraces in the world, and that she was a woman. She stopped being a kid in that twinkling. It made her dizzy, and for a second, she was consumed with unconscious desire: to feel his eyes, his hands, feel his lips on her.

Awareness awakened in her again. Calm, she almost looked defiantly around. He, Serato, was not looking at her. Immersed in his strange improvisation, having changed the violin given to him by the orchestra into a miracle instrument, he certainly forgot about her existence and about his reflex of pity that brought him to the circus arena for her salvation.

He was playing for himself and people were listening.

The silence in the amphitheater was almost inconceivable. Aza scanned a series of rows, and she saw the listeners changed into statues. Some were taking in with their eyes the royal figure of the violinist. Others were listening with their faces hidden in their hands, and others were looking into the distance with glassy pupils from which the spirit ran away to sway somewhere behind the music on the waves of air.

A Sudden anger filled Aza, that he took pity on her but did not care about her now. Now, she also felt jealous and sad that he spirited away the audience, who usually clapped for her. Before she could think about what she was doing, just at the moment when the violin strings could barely be heard singing, a sacred, quiet dream began, she gave a startling circus shout and with one lurch ran onto the taut rope, and jumped straight on the trapeze suspended a few meters below the next one.

Her crazy jump was noticed in the amphitheater and people began to call, shout, clap, point fingers at her. Nobody was listening to Serato's music anymore as they all were looking at her, throwing herself forward from one bar to another from one rope to another one like a real bird.

Bitter, fierce feelings of triumph filled Aza's chest. She had never been so crazy, so audaciously promiscuous in this air dance, where one false step, one single millimeter miss of balance meant death ... She was bending and flexing her body, showing her small shape to the mob with the most painful pleasure. She did not know where it came from, but she was provoking lascivious looks and grinning in a cheeky smile at the people whose eyes were undressing her.

She tried not to look at the violinist, but painful curiosity was crushing her ...

Slightly, slightly, so that he wouldn't see the move, she raised her arms, and bowing her head quickly glanced underneath her ...

He was standing next to the abandoned violin in the arena and smiling while applauding with others.

She jumped off the swing and rushed into the dressing room, hiding a devastating jerky sobbing, which she could not soothe for a long time.

At that time, she saw Serato for the first and last time. However, every feature of his face, the look of his eyes, the expression on his lips were so embedded in her consciousness that after long years he stood in her eyes as if alive and often haunted her like a nightmare that is impossible to ward off.

No! She couldn't be wrong! This is really Serato himself. He is this inconceivable man, forever young thanks to a spell, who is now coming here by some magic incomprehensible to her, with superhuman and frightening powers ...

A sudden shiver took her whole body. A moment similar to the one that she had experienced twenty years ago, when he laid his hand on her childish shoulder, only that fire hit her with a more powerful wave ...

Aza folded her arms and stared straight ahead. Her thoughts were playing: "I am stronger than all the powers of the world; wisdom, art, and even revenge! I will be stronger than your holiness..."

She felt the deliciously sensuous tickling of blood in her breasts thrusting forward, the mist in her eyes obscured her vision for a moment, her lips opened slightly: Come on! Come ...!

VIII

They were sitting in silence, their heads bowed, listening intently to the arguments of one of the "knowledgeable brothers" in the gathering of the wise men, who was just elaborating for them, a new theory about the beginning of life.

A short man, with a large round head and sharp looking eyes, was speaking in a dry monotone, as if he were giving a learned lecture, quoting numbers, names of scholars, facts, and discoveries. Only occasionally his face twitched slightly when suddenly, in a short, thunderous, and unbelievable sentence with one flash of thoughts, he tied together observations of generations of researchers that, which were contradictory until now.

It seemed to the listeners that this paltry man was building a transparent pyramid in front of their eyes. Its base was as wide as the world, and each of its separate stones was connected to others by a bold and airy arch. Each arch was supporting a firm new floor, ever more compact, swifter, rising higher and higher to the sky, above the peaks already looming in one's thoughts, the final keystone, from which one could embrace the whole structure with one glance. Everything that had been done so far, discovered, invented, the effort of reason gained or created, became a brick and granite block for this sage with gray eyes. Sometimes, it seemed that in one word, as if with a certain and efficient blow of a hammer, he was chiseling a shapeless boulder of experience that could not be dealt with before, and extracting from it a nucleus uncannily adjusted to that structure.

The listeners, accustomed to ascending into the clouds and looking at the world from the lonely towers of their thoughts, rose with the speaker without dizziness to the heights where he led them, confidently and boldly.

He finished the long lecture, his gray eyes lit up, and his words came alive. He flung his arm outward, as if pointing to and embracing the walls of his pyramid, where each individual brick and stone had already melted, all in one, perfect, intact, and so strangely simple for the open eye to see.

"We went through," he ended "the maze of wonder from the simplest plasma, apparently trying to remain latent under its inorganic guise, from the embryo, and even from the initiation of that embryo before its first division happened. From there, we moved to the change in the brain accompanying those proud human thoughts. We saw everything, and we know that it is possible to tie together and derive one from another, as a strict mathematical formula, error free, reliable, and inevitably leading to one result. By tugging and juxtaposing the material of experience of tens of centuries, I identified this pattern, which is like a mysterious word in a spell, forever sensed, yet unrevealed.

Then we observed life in all its mechanisms from the simplest to the most complicated. We already know that it follows one rule everywhere without exceptions, transitions, without options, imagined by a human eye not able to look deeper. We have also undoubtedly learned that life is not the purpose of existence, and not the result of some development unimaginable without it, but its beginning, alpha and omega of our being and its whole and the only asset. Once, centuries ago, scientists persistently and arduously tried to understand the creation of an organism from unlimited existence. Today we not only know that there is a fundamental and primary necessity in it, but that it is governed by one principle, or indeed, by a firm mathematical formula."

He paused for a moment and turning around, he pointed to a series of characters written on the black board.

"This is the mystery of existence," he began again with a bitter irony in his voice "solved and brought to the banal nakedness of digits. We are really magicians, and we could create a new world, a new being, a new and arbitrary reality, if only we ... Ah, yes! Such a small thing stands in the way of fulfilling the power of this illusive secret. You see, gentlemen, that the equation I have written here has a mathematical integral in its essential part. Like every integral, it needs to be supplemented by a certain fixed value, the C for mathematicians, the matter for physicists, the eternal vitalism for biologists, namely: it is something you don't know about in this case, and you won't ever know it, because this formula does not lead to such a conclusion." He bowed his head and spread his arms helplessly.

Jacek, as silent as the others, was listening with his temple resting on his hand. The scholar's final words were not a surprise to him. When he saw the magic equation written on the board, he knew already that human wisdom, trying to penetrate the deepest secrets of existence, hit an impenetrable obstacle. It faced the same, ever-repeating puzzle, the same Nothing, which is also everything equals everything.

"And the Word became flesh," sounded in his ears again. Despite his will, he looked up at Lord Tedwen's haughty figure visible to everybody from his presidential seat.

The old man was sitting upright, his hands folded on his desk, eyes staring straight ahead from under his reddened eyelids. Only a slight twitch in the arch of pursed lips testified that the frozen face was still alive ... Jacek thought that Sir Robert would speak after the scholarly speaker finished his lecture and was impatiently waiting for his word. He was wondering how he would develop, for the smartest audience on Earth, the necessity of a dogma, as a necessary complement to knowledge, which meant nothing without it. However, Tedwen remained silent, and everyone around them remained silent. Jacek ran his eyes through the congregation, looked at the elderly sages with furrowed foreheads and at men in the prime of life, with strange, worldly sadness in their strained eyes. He also looked at the people who had just emerged from their teenage years but were already stooped under the burden of knowledge. He was looking for a mouth that would voice a demand for a word, or a revelation ...

Deaf silence said all too clearly, "we don't know." So, this was the moment, when the physical riddle of existence, development and life was put into a mathematical, clear formula. After long and arduous palpitations, the final understanding of the mechanism of the world was reached. Yet, at this pinnacle moment, a terrible sentence: "We do not know!," was in the look from pensive eyes of the wise men, their pursed lips sealed, and their high, furrowed foreheads, covered with mist.

Jacek looked insistently in the lord's cold eyes. "Speak," he begged him with this look, insisted, ordered "speak, speak, save us with bright suns from this nothingness in which we engage in our thoughts, save us, if you yourself are saved ...!"

The old man understood. He moved his head slowly, looking around to check that no one else demanded their voice be heard, and when under his gaze everyone's forehead was bowing, shrugging helplessly, he raised his white hand ...

He stood up tall, serious, and dignified, carrying almost a century on his broad shoulders. He stood silent for a moment, as if hesitating.

"The knowledge ends here," he said finally, "we have gained everything that could be obtained, we've heard everything that could be endured with a rational mind. I told you what I had accomplished in my lonely and apparently last years of my mental work. Others have spoken for me, the perfect sages, the light of the Earth, my friends, or my disciples, for I have no master yet, being the eldest. We have reached the nucleus of all things, and maybe at this moment I should dissolve this association of researchers, because we can go no further. We should abolish our order of believers because we will decide nothing more. We are now moving in a wrong way, like fish around an impenetrable glass ball. The sun is far behind us, and the cold is overwhelming us. We had the courage to reach this far, let us also admit: the knowledge ends here."

"Not true!"

Jacek flinched at this voice. He had almost forgotten that with the lord's permission, he brought a guest, Nyanatiloka with him to the annual assembly of scholars. So now he looked at him in amazement, almost anxiously, hearing the hardness in his response to the old man.

Sir Robert was silent for a moment. Like a fast wave on the sea, a wrinkle ran down his forehead, but at the same moment he only smiled with a lofty indulgence ...

"Our guest," he said "not understanding my words well, contradicts this obvious and unfortunately final, truth, that we have come to the end of human knowledge, and we will not be able to take any further steps. Our guest, fed with the venerated wisdom of the East, does not quite completely comprehends the difference between knowledge and faith, that is to say recognizing as certain, axioms not proven by reason ... Truth is the object of both faith and knowledge, but these truths have different origins which cannot be mixed. We are at the end of the knowledge; I repeat there is only room for faith beyond this point."

The men in the audience started to nod seriously, admitting the truth of their grandmaster's words. Jacek, looking around, saw pensive faces with a half-smile of resignation on their lips, and others distorted with painful irony despite their will, and yet others, only sad ... He knew all these people, the wisest in the world, and knew what each of them was thinking. He could point his finger at those who clung to faith with all their effort. They were those few Catholics who obeyed the Church and obeyed all its commandments since Catholicism was the only religion that survived the ages. Others created their own religious doctrines which were more or less mystical for themselves. They did it to fill themselves with an empty and impenetrable space, that knowledge couldn't penetrate and crush like waves hitting the sea on the shore of the Arctic landmass. Most of them were pantheists with the highest flair of spirit. They would take their eyes off the mathematical formulas of their knowledge to embrace with a loving look the world in which, according to their belief, the most holy Amor Dei Intellectualis was revealed. However, there were also those cool rationalist deists, theosophists of all sorts and mystics of all shades, including the people, who, despite great science and enormous knowledge stuck to sometimes funny and ominous superstitions.

Jacek thought, "Horror vacui" when looking at these people, who at all costs sought the positive metaphysical content of life and the world, even if it was difficult to resolve with what their perplexing research was dictating.

For one moment jealousy overcame him, when in his thoughts, he compared their faith, even the most fragile, with the state in which he and his kind found themselves, and those listening to Lord Tedwen with the greatest sadness. It was caused by the feeling of nothingness, the most terrible, terrifying emptiness, and this deepest conviction that if one is to live, that emptiness must be filled with something. At the same time it was allowing, a deepened inability by some, the failure of a sense of self-preservation, the lack of something or its excess, or not allowing to believe it, or to believe anything if only to believe something...

A few fanatic skeptics also emerged from this painful cluster. They were sitting before him with deadly desperate eyes and contemptuous smiles on their pale lips. Similar to madmen tearing apart their own wound, they were stubbornly probing the sense of being with their clever brains and finding nothingness. They did not want to admit that they too would like to see something else in their souls. They would welcome even a poor illusion, which they could crush within the next hour, but it would be a diversion from the exhaustion and terror caused by their continued looking at the crystal void.

Jacek covered his face with both of his hands and became lost in thought, he did not pay any attention for a moment to what was happening around him. Only when Nyanatiloka's strong voice hit him again, he looked up and not quite shaken from his own thoughts, began to listen.

The Buddhist was standing on a podium summoned there by Lord Tedwen. With a jerk of his head, he shook back the hair falling on his forehead, and raised his dark arm.

"Because I am not of this faith", he said ending his earlier started sentence "nor another new belief to add to a thousand already existing, which would only increase confusion, but I am bringing you the knowledge. With all my consciousness and courage, I repeat to you, the wisest of people, that there is knowledge beyond the range that you have pointed out here, that is to say, righteous, joyful, and empowering knowledge ...

They were moving their heads in disbelief, listening to those words, more with indulgent kindness rather than with significant curiosity. Jacek understood that Nyanatiloka was given the floor only because he was his friend. The thought stung him unbearably, as if it were an insult to this strange hermit. He felt a sudden disgust at this gathering of wise men who would undoubtedly listen to the newcomer if he appeared before them as a miracle worker and promised a new revelation to them. They did not believe or did not want to even assume, still trusting their own unsatisfied wisdom, that someone in the world could choose other ways than they did and manage to go further than they had.

He stood up compulsively and wanted to take his friend home, but Nyanatiloka, noticing his movement, gave him a sign to remain there. After which, ignoring the smiles and signs of impatience in the listeners, he turned towards the black board on which the speaker had written his previous mathematical formula of life, and pointing his hand at its unknown and constant part, said freely, as if he were touching something insignificant but not the deepest secrets of existence:

"Don't you think that we should start from here instead of helplessly ending here? I want to tell you about this constant and incomprehensible quantity in the equation of being, which is both its material and regulator. You all know that this is a spirit ... No, I said it wrong! Rather, you all believe it more or less strongly, and it is not enough that you only believe. I am looking at you, the wisest, and I see sadness on your foreheads, dilemma in your eyes, longing for the inexpressible thing in the painful parting of your lips. Your great knowledge does not satisfy you. Even the strongest faith does not calm you down because you are too wise to see the end in the fragmentation of existence. You are too accustomed to cut all data with your sharp thoughts to surrender to faith without reservation and have no moment of doubt. You are standing at a crossroads. Forgive me for telling you this, but I also once walked your path and like you believed that it was the only one."

He paused and turned to face the gray chairman of the assembly. "Don't you recognize me, master?," he asked. "When you began to teach, I was one of your first disciples forty years ago, before I quit the research to seek harmony in art, in life, and finally in the deepest, non-penetrating but creative knowledge, far from here in the East."

Lord Tedwen shaded his eyes with his hand and with the stunned face whispered: "Is that you? Is that you?"

"Yes, it's me. I am Serato, the only one you were futily trying to keep with you, even when being accepted to be your student was such a great honor. I am standing in front of you after forty years, and you see that I am not even older than when I was leaving you with a violin in my hand. I thanked you then, that you wanted only my good but involuntarily showed me the way which one should not take ... or at least not before attaining another kind of knowledge. I mean the knowledge coming from the depths of the soul that allows you to look at all nothingness in temporal existence with a smile. The goal you are striving for in vain, in a desperate longing, should be just the beginning. Look at me! You have discovered the undoubted formula of life and put it in algebraic symbols written on the black board, and yet you are standing helpless in front of it! Without dwelling on it, I hold my material life in my hand and don't allow it to wither, and I don't use any other means than my knowledge and my will!"

Anxiety overwhelmed the audience. Indifferent until this moment, they were rising from their seats, giving each other the familiar name of the odd man who was speaking to them in this way. Some squeezed closer, others shook their heads in disbelief, talking lively. Only Sir Robert, after the first moment of amazement, recovered his composure. As he looked at Nyanatiloka in silence, who then stopped speaking, he began slowly and emphatically:

"If this is really you Serato, it seems a miracle, however, but to act in spirit and knowledge is not the same. Every animal creates a new life without having a clear awareness of its own existence. All knowledge is always and only, research, nothing else.

"And why shouldn't it be creation? Nyanatiloka replied. "Forgive me, wise men, that I dare to say you forget for the moment that, for you also, research is only a means of leading to the desired goal, which is the full realization of being. That is what knowledge is about, it is the truth coming from nothing but the knowing of a conscious being. And if the whole universe could be created, with its life and all its forces, as a self-determining spirit, why not create the most important truths in this way? Why not illuminate the secret, while still in the spirit when it is fully and perfectly contained there? After all, you also know the word 'intuition', and you know that it is always at the beginning and must examine the path for every test. Why not, instead of killing it after the first twitch by calculations, let it develop into a lush flower? If the will removes external obstacles and brings the spirit to appropriate perfection, that is, freedom, then intuition will give us the truest knowledge undiluted by details, because it was created in the same way as the being was and its direct conscious equivalent. "

He raised both hands and held them out above the heads of the wise men. Jacek had never seen him like this, although he heard his teachings many times. His eyes were lit as if by the sun and his uncanny, youthful figure radiated with brightness.

"Brothers!," he cried in ecstasy, "accept me as a messenger from your own spirits, who is bringing good news to you. I have come to tell you about all that is asleep in your consciousness, asleep without knowing how to get outside, like fragile beliefs: about eternal reign of the deity, about immortality of souls, about lasting knowledge, about what gives the only value to life!"

A sudden laughter erupted near the door, Jacek turned his head to see who dared to break into the sanctuary of the wise men and disturb its seriousness. Raising slightly in his seat, he saw Grabiec's bald skull over his companions' shoulders. Someone there at the door, decorated with the eternal Egyptian symbol of the winged earth, tried to stop or ask him by what authority he entered here, but, without answering, he removed the doorman with one movement of his hand and walked straight towards the president's chair.

Lord Tedwen's eyebrows converged, and he looked at the newcomer with severe haughtiness.

"Sir Robert" shouted Grabiec, boldly enduring his disapproval, "Sir Robert, once ruler and lord, stop listening to the ridiculous fables of the Eastern beguiler, because it is not the time to renounce anything or seek happiness behind the world when it is so close ..."

"Who is that?," asked Lord Tedwen briefly.

"I am the power! I am not bringing you the kingdom of God in the fogs, I am not going to preach to you about the immortality of souls, but I am giving you your own kingdom. I will immortalize the race of the great! All those who want to deny life should get out of my way."

He looked defiantly at Nyanatiloka thinking of him as nothing more than one of the ascetic hermits from the East wandering around Europe at different times ... He seemed to be waiting, above all, for a word from him, to ridicule him in the eyes of the wise men, but Nyanatiloka did not show any desire to engage into a discourse at all. He only smiled mysteriously and stepped down from the podium, taking his old seat next to Jacek.

So Grabiec, not paying attention to the roar in the audience, walked with a lively and bold step on the podium and turned directly to the wise men sitting in wide stalls.

"I am not even asking you," he began, "for giving me a voice, I'm not sorry that I got in here without permission." Some of the gathered here know me well and know that what I want, justifies me more than enough ... I came to the gathering of wise men because it is not enough for me to speak with some of you, and it is not to get support of some of you. I want to address all of you and have each of you behind me!"

"Sir, speak to the point and briefly," said the chairman, to whom in the meantime someone whispered Grabiec's name. "We do not have much time."

Grabiec bowed his head slightly to the old man and began to explain the plan with which he came to the association of the wise brothers. His steady voice, restrained by his willpower, was flowing evenly, but it was obvious that he was full of the highest anxiety. It was the anxiety of a man trembling for the fate of his cause, to whom he devoted his life. In the moments when he stopped talking to take a breath, he looked around the huge hall, checking the impression made by his words, but from the calm faces of the listeners he could not read anything.

"I've told you everything," he finished finally. "Now, you know what I want, so give me an answer. It is up to you to become lords of the world or die in the turmoil that is about to break loose like a windstorm before the rising chariot of your power."

Silence fell after these words. All eyes turned slowly to the face of Lord Tedwen, who stayed silent, his eyes closed, and a slight smile on his old, wrinkled face. His mouth merely quivered nervously, and the hand resting on the desk twitched involuntarily ... It seemed that he was reliving his past in his mind, that he remembered the thorny path from the heights of power, voluntarily thrown away, to the foot of the cross, hidden jealously in his heart, so deeply that the blade of his own thought would not even disturb him ...

Meanwhile, those more impatient among the audience, especially those who had already agreed with Grabiec and had accepted his thought as a good one, began to urge the president to give an answer...

Lord Tedwen rose. He was pale now as the fleeting blush disappeared from his parchment face, and from beneath his anointed eyebrows he looked at the audience with his steel eyes.

"What do you want?"

"Action!" Shouted Grabiec.

"Action! Action," a choir shouted. "One action can save us! Break free from the vicious circle of our knowledge! Free us from the burden of our wisdom!

"There is only one action: Go in the depth of your spirit!"

He was not even listened to anymore. They formed a circle around Grabiec, and inquired about the details of his fight, then various ideas were developed ... Only a few of the oldest and saddest skeptics remained on the sidelines of this confusion and bustle.

Jacek looked at Nyanatiloka involuntarily. He was sitting calmly, arms folded on his chest, looking ahead with a strained eye ...

"Speak up! Say something!"

Nyanatiloka shrugged. "It's not time. I only spoke for the love of you. Now, nobody would hear me ..."

The noise was indeed increasing. Unfriendly voices against Tedwen were heard as they urged him to speak his mind.

Sir Robert was standing motionless for some time. Only when the buzz of mixed voices faded away for a moment, did he look calmly around, as if counting those who did not share in the general confusion. He found only a few of them and smiled bitterly.

"What do you want from me?" He repeated.

Grabiec turned to him, "Lord," he said, "you heard me speak, and you see that almost everyone is happy to answer my call ..."

"I have never followed the majority ...".

"Follow yourself, lord! You were once a ruler, the most powerful in centuries, so aspire to become him one more time ..."

Lord Tedwen straightened up proudly. "If I wanted that, I wouldn't have come down from where I was. I threw off the cogs and involvements of the Commonwealth because it was too common. It's not the time for me to influence it now!"

"That's what it is. That is the goal" Grabiec said urgently, "to save the world from commonplace..."

The old man laughed. "Illusions! This is what I wanted to do and save at least the best, creating this brotherhood half a century ago. I wanted to save those who think from a universal source of food in the cedar ark, and now I see that you yourselves are chopping up the ship..."

"We will raise it to the top of Mount Ararat, from where we will command the world!"

"You will sink!"

"Is this your last word, Lord?"

"Yes."

Grabiec turned to the wise men scattered around the room. "Who among you is with me?"

The vast majority began to gather around him. Only a few remained with Lord Tedwen ...

Jacek wanted to step forward, but he felt Nyanatiloka's strong hand grab him and hold him in place away from both camps. "Listen, look and understand!"

Grabiec looked at the old man with a defiant, proud face. "See?"

"I see." Lord Tedwen replied, and taking the golden book in both hands, in which the names of all members of the brotherhood were written, tore it in half before the eyes of those gathered.

IX

"If I have not beaten that one, I will certainly crush this one!," thought Roda, stalking like a cat toward the closed door leading from Jacek's office to his studio.

Anxiety overwhelmed him in the dark with every imaginary rustle, though he knew he was completely safe at least at the moment. He succeeded brilliantly in the first part of his brash plan. At the moment when Jacek with his unbearable guest with black and terrifying eyes, was going to the annual meeting of the wise men, Roda, using his distraction and his own small posture, managed to hide under the armchair and stay in the office. He heard the grinding of the metal shutters fastened by pressing a button, and the slam of the closing door at night.

He was alone. However, he did not leave the hideout for several hours, fearing that Jacek, noticing his absence accidentally, might still come back and look for him here. He was sitting huddled in the most uncomfortable way, choking in the almost complete darkness, without counting the passing of time.

Finally, when it seemed to him that Jacek should already be on his plane beyond the tenth border, if there were still borders in Europe, he came out slowly and carefully and straightened his stiff limbs. A piece of paper, knocked down with his outstretched hand, fell off the table to the floor. Roda curled up like an animal in danger, and a long hour passed before he realized that there was nothing to threaten him. The door separating the study from the rest of the apartment did not let voices through, and nobody could open it until Jacek came back. He had two or three days of free time ahead.

He succeeded, he thought, but this was only the third and easiest part of the task. It was now necessary to get to the studio, take that terrible device, and then wait patiently for Jacek to return and sneak away unnoticed when the door opens. "

He knew that Jacek had hidden the keys from the passage and spotted the secret symbol, that would allow the door to be opened. He began feeling around in the dark with his hands. Sitting for so long under the armchair standing in the middle of the room had the effect that, when he came out, he totally lost all orientation. He was moving slowly and carefully. Well-known furniture, which he accidentally encountered, seemed strange to him now. Instead of figuring out where he was and where he should look for the desired door, he was getting even more lost, unable to determine his location at all. He had the impression that he was somehow moved in the dark to some other strange and mysterious building ...

The desk saved him when he hit his head on it. He walked around it and found the chair where Jacek usually sat. In an instant everything was unraveled in his conscious. He could now press a button on the desk and turn on the light himself, but he did not do it because of caution or foolish cowardice as he knew well that with the doors and shutters closed, no light would get outside.

Besides, he no longer felt the need for light since he had found that familiar landmark. So many times, he thought about how he would find himself here in the dark, and he memorized all the details of the device that he could now move confidently.

In a few moments he already had the keys, pulled from a secret and long-spotted cache, and began working around the door leading to the scholar's proper workshop. And it went surprisingly easy. The lock sprung away without a rustle, and Roda had a narrow hall in front of him, at the end of which a weak, blue crackle of always burning electromagnetic light loomed through the windows in the long glass door.

Roda was all at once pleased by this unexpected brightness. He was afraid that in the studio he would have to move in the dark. It could ruin his whole idea, because he did not know it as well as the office in which he often sat with Jacek. He then went forward quickly. The glass door was closed again, and this was an unforeseen difficulty because he did not have the key.

He could easily push the glass out and get inside through the door framed hole, but he did not want to do it and expose himself to any additional danger by leaving an unnecessary trace behind. If his plan were to succeed, no one should know that he was even here.

He returned to the office and began groping around looking for the key, trembling at the thought that Jacek could have taken it with him and in such a simple way ruined his plan so well started. However, he vainly checked all the caches he knew. The key was not there, or at least it was not in a place accessible to him.

Tired, and already hungry, he staggered back to the door, almost losing hope that he could open it. Mechanically, thinking of something else, he looked at the lock with a faint light behind the glass, which, however, was enough for his keen eyes, and already accustomed to the darkness. Terrible uncertainties started to rattle his thoughts, thoughts like Jacek might for some reason return early and open the door to find him in this suspicious place. It worried him all the more that he did not know how much time had passed since he was locked up here. He had a prepared excuse for such a possibility, that he accidentally got trapped, falling asleep in a corner in an armchair, and threatened with death by hunger (he could not know when Jacek would return), now was looking for all possible passes to get out, but he himself did not very much trust the effectiveness of this defense.

Roda at once gave a slight joyful shout. He accidentally glanced at the narrow gap between the door lock and the recess in the frame and noticed that the latch was not filling it. He took the knife and carefully slipped his blade into the crack. The knife passed without resistance, apparently the door was not locked at all.

Roda grabbed the door handle with all his might, but the door did not move. There must be a hidden latch in the mechanism that had to be found. He started to work. With his nimble fingers, he examined every screw, touched every ornament on the door, inserted the knife blade into all the gaps and holes he could feel, all that in vain.

Discouraged was about to step away from the door, and give up, when he noticed that it was closed with the simplest in the world "screw cap" that had been widely used for a thousand years. His rage overwhelmed him that he had wasted so much time. After all, it was foreseeable that at the end of the corridor, protected from the burglary on the other hand, doors with thin windows, not showing a serious barrier, would no longer have any peculiar lock. The cap was too high for Roda's small height, so he brought a chair from the study and opened the door.

He was now in the longed-for scientist's workshop. At first, he stood stunned among the multitude of instruments and containers so inconceivable to him, simply not knowing how to look among them for that terrible machine he wanted to take. After some time, he suddenly remembered what he had heard from Jacek's conversation, that it was supposed to be a small black folding box, similar in appearance to a handheld camera. He began to look around, carefully sneaking among the instruments, fearing that he would hit and damage them, or, worse, hit the infernal machine, causing an accident.

In the center of the studio, there was a large metal drum of a darkened copper color, from which bundles of insulated wires ran towards the wall, getting lost in the hole punched in it. Two thin golden wires, made of a peculiar alloy, connected this drum, closed from everywhere to a small box on a tripod, which probably must have been the device in question.

Sweat appeared on Roda's temple. It was necessary to take this box, which could not be achieved without cutting the wires connecting it with the drum, and not cause an explosion that would not only kill him, but also destroy the entire city. Fear momentarily filled him so much that he was ready to renounce his bounty. Helpless and trembling, he looked at the device like a mouse at a piece of bait in a trap. Fortunately, he remembered Jacek saying on some occasion to Nyanatiloka that for some time he had never left a charged machine in the studio.

He took out a knife and laid it on the wires to cut them, but his hand was trembling so much that he could not manage it. As he was standing there, terrified, unsure of what to do, his eyes fell on a second box, quite similar to the first one, which lay separately on the sidelines. He leapt towards it in hope that it was a second device that he could easily carry with him. However, the box was empty. Apparently, Jacek was going to build the second one, perhaps with the intention of taking it with him to the Moon and had prepared an outer shell for it still waiting to be filled.

Roda did not think again. He returned to the camera in the center of the studio and, with his eyes closed, was cutting the wires. He heard a slight hiss, and the fear froze the blood froze in his heart, but it was nothing more than a whiz of wires that, when cut, twisted immediately like snakes.

In a few moments Roda was returning to the office, carrying the precious loot with him. In the place of the device he had taken, he put the empty box and connected the cut wires in such a way that someone entering, even Jacek himself, could not immediately see the change. He carefully closed the door behind him and tied his loot to his chest with a headscarf. In the darkness, he searched for the cache and put the keys back in it. Then, he groped towards the entrance door, where he hid to wait for Jacek's return.

Snuggled into the folds of the door curtain, he pressed his large head against the marble door frame and lurked there like a cat to slip out with one leap when the door opened. Drowsiness began to overcome him, compounded by weariness and weighty emotions. He tried ineffectively to fight sleep, repeating to himself that falling asleep now meant that he would be discovered almost immediately if Jacek entered unexpectedly. Some images filled his mind, and the blissfully heaviness overwhelmed his limbs. His consciousness was slowly fading away. It seemed to him that he was on the Moon, and that long night he was waiting for the arrival of friends and students plotting with him.

Suddenly…

He did not know what to think about the light he saw through the folds of fabric. He tried to remember where he was and what had happened, what was a dream, and what was reality when he had accidentally touched the box on his chest and in a flash remembered everything. He had fallen asleep without realizing it. He wanted to jump up, but suddenly a terrible fear paralyzed him. If there was light in the room, it meant that there was someone here, meaning that Jacek had returned.

And now he heard his voice :"There is no time to waste. Pure madness has overcome these people ..."

Then silence again. He could not understand at the moment whether Jacek was talking to himself, or if there was someone else in the office, and he did not dare to open the folds of the curtain so as not to be discovered by the movement. He could hear the quick pacing muffled by the soft rug and deaf knock of the sliding of the chair. He could tell that Jacek was walking around the room, upset by some news or event.

At last the pacing stopped, Jacek must have stopped there. Roda heard some words vaguely cast, and he gasped. With one hand, he pressed the box tighter to his chest, with the other using extreme caution he slightly opened the gap between the door and the curtain so that the voice would reach him better.

"What can you do? I am telling you again, give up all this and go with me into the far away world, and soon you will see that there was nothing to worry about or be bothered about."

In an instant a cold sweat covered Roda from head to toe. He recognized Nyanatiloka's voice, whose acumen he was instinctively afraid of more than Jacek and all the people on Earth. It seemed to him that the hermit's terrible eyes were already piercing the meager curtain he had hidden behind. He instinctively wanted to scream and run away, but fortunately his muscles refused to obey him. He heard his heartbeat so loud that he was afraid that it would disclose his presence.

"I can't go with you now," Jacek said, hesitantly. "I have to be here."

"What for?"

"Whatever, it is my duty. For this reason, I am even delaying my trip, although maybe there my friend needs me."

Roda could not hear the rest of the conversation. Apparently, they moved away from his hiding place, and were whispering now as people often do when they have very important things to say and not raise their voices even when they are convinced that no one is eavesdropping on them.

Roda was catching a broken word here and there, which accidentally resounded in the speaker's mouth. Grabiec's name was the most frequently repeated word. He also heard the names of Aza and Marek twice or three times ... Then Roda thought that he was talking about the Moon, about him and about Mataret.

"You will have the Moon!" He whispered in his soul and, despite his internal fear, smiled maliciously. The clatter of the sliding chair let him know that Jacek had risen again.

"Wouldn't it be best," he said loudly to Nyanatiloka, "to end it all immediately and radically?"

He laughed quietly with some awful laugh that cut the blood off in Roda's veins. "You know," he went on, unable to suppress his voice any longer, "that I could go beyond that iron door and connect those two tiny hands together ..."

"Yes. And what?"

"Ha, ha! The funniest thing you can imagine! It was not in vain for the government to entrust me with the position of director of telegraphs throughout Europe. I ordered universal wires from the wire network to be taken to my studio ... For experiments. Ha, ha, delicious experience! We cannot create yet, but we can destroy. Oh yeah, it is enough just to let one spark from my device into the main wire ..."

"And what?" Nyanatiloka repeated calmly.

"Lightning. A thunder that has not been cast by a conscious being since the beginning of the world. The whole of Europe, literally its whole, entire cities, lands and mountains are connected by a network of telegraph wires. All of this will turn into a monstrous explosive mass, every atom, loosening into primary particles, acts like a dynamite cartridge, water and even air..."

"And what?"

"Don't you understand that such a terrible explosion would release the Moon, and it would go into space, and who knows what celestial body it would run into. The solar system's balance would be disturbed ..."

"And what?"

"Death."

Roda Frozen with fear, seemed to hear Nyanatiloka laugh.

"There is no death. After all, you know well that there is no death for that which really exists. You would only dispel the miserable illusion and for no reason, when so many ghosts created it with so much difficulty and made it into this reality. Why would you bother to change it for others when you can destroy this illusion for yourself with the assertion of your will. But you have not even matured to this level yet. It would be an unnecessary act, like that of a child, who extinguishes the light so as not to see the scary image, and then gets even more afraid in the dark."

The conversation died down again. After some time, Roda heard a clearer sigh, and then Jacek's words muted, though louder again "I really have nothing to do here, but I can't follow you until I know that I won't miss what I have never had and will never have. You went through life like a fiery storm, and you did not need to regret anything at the moment, you decided to close in on yourself and began to create your new world. I sometimes have an impression that I am a clumsy child who would like to see his golden fairy tales dream yet."

Further words dissolved in a whisper that apparently only Nyanatiloka could hear. Roda did not care much about the conversation If he listened, it was only because he was eager to catch a word that could be a clue to him when the door would open and when he would be able to free himself from the trap. He was uncomfortable, and at the same time he was still afraid that maybe he was not well hidden, and the folds of the curtain were revealing his shape. To top it all, after all he heard, the device tied to his chest filled him with hellish fear. Only a vague sense told him that in order for it to work, it had to be connected to some force from outside and have an outlet, as he could see in the huge drum, standing in the studio, but that did not calm his nervous anxiety. There were times when he felt like fainting and trembled so that Jacek might really notice the movement of the curtain covering him, if he looked in that direction ...

Jacek, however, was sitting sat at his desk with his face hidden in his hands, not even thinking about looking at the door. Nyanatiloka was standing before him confident and calm as always, but instead of his usual smile, a shadow of sad reverie was wandering on his face.

"Worlds are collapsing here," he said, "and you do not have the courage to stand up and leave with me and not even look at what is necessary and inevitable, and ... so indifferent, although it looks so terrible. I pity you. I am sad for the first time since the old days, sad as if I were dying. Even sadder because I know the source of your hesitation. You are fooling yourself; you find various reasons not to admit this one thing: you are afraid that if you left, you would never again be looking into the eyes of this woman ... You think that leaving here and possibly finding yourself, you will not desire her at all."

Jacek raised his head. "Don't you think that I can be afraid of that very thing, that following you I will not want to look into her eyes anymore? What if this desire, which is my passion, or maybe a curse, is also my only happiness?"

He pondered in silence, but then he stood up abruptly and began to shake his arms around his head, as if chasing away swarms of obnoxious wasps.

"I have to save myself!," he shouted, and I have a path to salvation, I have, I have, I want to have!"

Three-worldly looked at him questioningly.

"My friend needs me," Jacek said. " I have been waiting too long. I will go to the Moon. It is my duty. The vehicle should be ready this week."

Then he looked at Nyanatiloka with a slightly forced smile.

"If I come back alive, no matter what I think about here, I'll follow you!"

Nyanatiloka nodded his head slowly, then, looking Jacek in the eye, he motioned at the closed door of the studio with his hand. Jacek hesitated for a moment.

"I will destroy this deadly machine before leaving," he said finally. "I do not want it to get into anyone's perhaps crazy hands."

Having said this, he called the butler with a nervous haste and, changing his tone, turned to his still silent companion:

"I will have my plane ready to see to my lunar vehicle. Meanwhile, please stay here. I will come back in a day or two and say goodbye to you."

The moment the butler opened the door, Roda slipped unnoticed from the office and ran down the stairs, not even looking behind.

X

Since Jacek's sudden departure, she was only thinking about how to fulfill her task of getting hold of his deadly machine as soon as possible ... She naturally did not guess at all that Roda's disappearance had anything to do with it, and she would never have thought that he could snatch that trophy so valuable for her.

Deaf sounds of the "earthquake" announced by Grabiec were coming from the world. A strike broke out, short-lived, but organized, ending the same way it arose apparently without reason.

"Grabiec is training his army," Aza thought as she read the news, "and measuring his strength." In fact, it was so. By all means, she should not waste any more time, if she wanted to play a role in the beginning of that movement, and not just be trampled by this rough wave of people, much like the sea, starting from vast depths, hitting the shore impatiently and foaming there ...

Against all her expectations and assumptions, she failed to win Jacek over. Usually sensitive to her every word, every smile and movement, surrendering like a boy to her will or even a whim, he became inconceivably hard and inaccessible when she mentioned the most important matter for her now.

So, she had to find another way. Her thoughts involuntarily turned to Serato. Admittedly, when she considered that option, this strange sage, and miracle worker seemed to her even less accessible than Jacek, after all being under her influence. Still she had to try....

Her feeling for Nyanatiloka was very strange. At times, there was a sensual desire to win the man who once unintentionally awakened a woman in her. It was now reinforced by the perverse desire to break his holiness ... She was ready to give herself to him, if only she could accomplish it. She was imagining a certain delight, that at the moment of passionate bewilderment, that the will holding his youth would weaken, and then she would push him away like a decrepit old man, like a rag.

"Victory!" Her predatory lips were smiling, losing the usual childish expression of a child, a victory greater than that which Grabiec can achieve over the whole world ...

As she was thinking about it, she had almost forgotten that the incredible task of overcoming Nyanatiloka was only one means of achieving her goal, obtaining some miserable and, in fact, not so interesting, deadly device. Now, she was panting with a wondrous desire to try her strength, a fight, and a victory...Grabiec, and even Jacek himself seemed insignificant and almost not worth the effort compared to this holy man ...

It was difficult for her to reach Nyanatiloka. The sage spoke to her whenever she wanted, but as indifferently as if she were not only a woman, not even a human, but only a talking machine. His gaze absentmindedly glided over her, and it was obvious that he was forcing himself simply out of respect for Jacek's house, where she was a guest, to notice her, listen to her and patiently tolerate her. When she once mentioned to him their meeting in the circus twenty years ago, Nyanatiloka said, "I remember," so calmly and indifferently, that she twitched with a sad feeling of humiliation. She wanted to determine if he would somehow avoid talking about that event, which would prove to her that she was not indifferent to him. However, he spoke to her when she wanted to with that cool and polite indifference with which he answered her sly questions about his past life, relationships with women, love, love affairs ...

All this, however, instead of alienating Aza, excited her even more, so that soon she could no longer think of anything but the possibility and method of defeating this superhuman and wise man ...

Meanwhile, Jacek had not yet returned from examining his vehicle. In addition to an extensive letter to Serato, there was only a short letter to Aza, in which he apologized for leaving her alone at home. He was blaming it on the troubles he had with the factory striking from time to time, and the need for his presence there to supervise the work himself.

Aza pondered upon reading this cursory card. How differently this Jacek used to write to her until recently, even when hurt by something, wanting to break free from her pull on him, he tried to be cool and indifferent! She understood that this was Nyanatiloka's influence, possibly just accidentally. Then even stronger stubbornness overwhelmed her against the man who had appeared here probably to ruin all her plans.

"If it were not for him," she reasoned, "that violinist turned into a Hindu wonder, everything would have gone easy." Jacek alone would not have had the strength to resist her charm. Sooner or later, she would do with him whatever she pleased. He would undoubtedly give her the secret of his invention, perhaps he would not even hesitate, and instead of giving its benefits to others, he would only to share his power with her and then they would control the world themselves. She would be a queen, without the need to look at Grabiec or anyone, anyone in the world ..., if Nyanatiloka had not ruined it for her it.

"I will take revenge," she was saying to herself. "You alone, you alone, old sorcerer, must give me Jacek's power. When I want, you will betray your friend like Judas, and you will die, you will die before my eyes like so many other fools ..."

There were, however, times when she herself did not believe in the success of her plans for this most-unusual man. It occurred to her then, that perhaps it would be better to leave it all alone and move to another world ...

After all, Jacek was going to the Moon. If she wanted, he would take her with him to Marek, who is undoubtedly the king and ruler of the entire silver globe ...

Then she closed her eyes and daydreamed of the familiar smile of the mighty man who would surely greet her on the Moon. She imagined he would be glad for her surprise arrival and thankful that she remembered him and risked the dangerous and crazy journey...

She almost missed him and not so much his smile, not even the look of his eyes and touch of his hand, but rather this masculine and calm power filling her with peace. In no way was it like the cool, haughty, and introverted indifference of the Mystic, which was taming her, like the eyes of the slayer hypnotizing a wild panther.

Such moments of "weakness," as she called them, lasted briefly, but they came quite often, so she had to fight with them and defy these fantastic ... gusts with all the coldness of her mind ...

Once in such a disposition, she wrote to Jacek, answering the card in which he informed her about the extension of his absence. She did not tell him about her fleeting plans directly and did not yet demand that he would take her with him. In any case there was a note of longing and deep, friendly cordiality in her letter, so rarely sincerely appearing in her.

Her letter found the scientist in the mechanical workshops of a large factory where his lunar vehicle was being prepared. He was impatient with the unexpected slow progress of works and constant obstacles, especially since he knew their source and was seriously afraid that coming events would stop him. The decision to take off to the Moon, which at first was only an impulse to help his abandoned friend, became for him a kind of lifebuoy or shield that he was using or trying to use against the growing confusion around him and in him.

It was the easiest way out of dilemma. He would fly away and know nothing about anything and get out of the obligation to take a position in the storm that was starting, with or against Grabiec. It would help him avoid having to choose between Nyanatiloka and Aza. It would provide him with this excuse to himself that he was performing an important act by risking his life for a friend ... Jacek was quite aware that what he was doing was rather dictated by weakness and indecision. Still, he also understood lunar that this was the only thing he could do without remorse or doubt whether he should have done otherwise.

His only fear so far was that everything around him could happen faster than he would like. He sensed that fighting would break out before he could set off on his space voyage and his flying away would not happen in an unfinished vehicle ... So, he prevailed upon both the management of the workshop and the workers working on it, watching with despair how the work was slowly moving forward. Aza's letter brought him a new dilemma. He sensed from it or read between the lines that Aza might be ready to fly with him from the old Earth into starry spaces, and at first, he shivered with strange joy.

Yes, yes! Fly with her away from this life, from suffocating relationships, from depressing society, and from the threatening struggles, break her away from her past on the Earth and start a new fate ...He laughed bitterly. "Yes, handing her over to Marek!"

For the first time, he felt something, like a rush of hatred for his childhood friend. At the same time, he thought he was in a very funny position. After all, it was obvious, he reasoned, that she had arrived at his house and now was giving him the thought of a common departure to the Moon for the sole purpose of joining Marek! She just uses it for the instrument of her will. She does not even tell him directly what she wants but is waiting for the proposition to come from him. If he suggests it, she will probably shudder and makes him ask, as for grace, to do it, which she obviously desires above all else.

He had a moment when he was about to stop work around the vehicle. "I'll stay here," he said to himself, "Why should I care about the fate of some madman who was once my friend? Everything is vile, disgusting, and bad! The smart ones cannot even keep calm, and now they reach out their greedy hands with uncertain power. Even the greatest cannot be satisfied with the size of their spirit ... Enough of this, really enough! I should go home and put my hand on the small lever of my machine and destroy this world, not worth anything ...”

At the moment, he realized that after returning from that last meeting of the wise men, he did not go to his studio at all and did not look at the device left there, and it worried him ... He shrugged it off.

This is stupid! After all, nobody could get to my studio without me ... except for Nyanatiloka. He was at a meeting with me, but who knows if he cannot be in two places at the same time! At the memory of the sage, he pondered deeply again ... He was enticed by the thought of going with him into the loneliness of the Ceylon forests or inaccessible Himalayan mountains in search of the final knowledge. It would be so different from what he could find in Europe and among European-thinking people, but he was afraid that he would not yet have the peace of mind necessary to obtain it.

In any case, this thought helped him to shake the charm of Aza's letter and get rid of the anxiety that it brought him. He decided to write back politely, but coldly as if he did not understand and did not notice at all her wish contained between the lines to accompany him on his intended journey ...

No doubt, he must go on that journey! If only the vehicle were ready as soon as possible!

Finishing the letter hurriedly at the hotel, he ordered the car to be ready and immediately went back to the factory which he had left an hour earlier to write back to the singer. On his way there, he was distracted by some unexpected movement. He was passing people who, as he thought, were workers and should now be at work.

“Some unemployment again,” he thought. “Fatality is apparently weighing on my vehicle and the entire lunar journey!” He ordered the driver to hurry, hoping that his personal influence might be enough to stop the workers from giving up the job so important to him.

He met the director on the threshold of the factory., He was standing alone with his hands in his pockets and whistling through his teeth.

“What's up?” He asked, jumping out of the car.

The director shrugged his shoulders without even greeting him, though he usually treated him with polite courtesy.

“Workers ...?” Jacek asked.

"They left," the director replied calmly.

“Unemployment again?”

“Yes!”

“When will it end?”

“It won't end.”

“How's that?”

"Oh yes. They went away, and they are gone. They say they will not come back. I am getting tired of it all. To hell with such a job!" Having said this, he turned on his heel and walked away, leaving a surprised Jacek on the stairs.

Now, when Jacek looked back, he saw that some people were standing a few feet away from him and were studying him and whispering something between themselves. He recognized some of them. They were factory workers, older masters, but he had never seen others in this area. For a moment he wanted to ask them what they were doing here, and why they were looking at him so, but in the end, he did not care!

Depressed and helpless, he began to descend the stairs, heading for the plane waiting below.

At the last step, one of the workers who knew him blocked his way. "Wait, sir!"
Jacek looked at him with surprise. "What do you want, my friend?"

The worker did not answer, but blocking his path with one hand, he was signaling with the other. Jacek looked in this direction in spite of himself. A huge man with a grim, stubborn face under a crop of disheveled hair was coming from behind the corner. "Are you master Jacek?" He asked, approaching the scientist.

"Yes. But I don't know who you are."

"It does not matter, but I am called Yoozva ..."

"Oh! Grabiec once mentioned you to me ..."

"Maybe. He also told me about you. You have a machine with which you can destroy cities and entire countries ..."

"Why is it of any interest to you?"

"It interests me. I need this machine."

"You won't have it".

"Oh, yes, I will!"

He beckoned to the workers who immediately surrounded Jacek in a tight circle. "I can order to have you killed immediately!"

"Yes. And then what?"

"Or we will keep you here, and meanwhile have your studio in Warsaw searched."

Jacek smiled involuntarily despite the horror of his position. He looked down at Yoozva from underneath his eyelids. He wanted to ask him if, by opening the door of his studio to take the deadly machine, he would also be able to get inside his brain to reveal the secret of its application, without which it would only be a miserable, unsuitable shell.

Jerzy Żuławski

At that moment, a man came to Yoozva and gave him a card with a few lines ... The leader glanced at it and smiled, then signaled to the workers to leave Jacek alone

"We don't need you anymore," he said. "My friend Grabiec is reporting to me right now...," he paused, then finished with a polite, mocking bow, pointing with his hand at the car standing nearby: "You can go home freely. I recommend that you guard your treasure ... well."

Jacek shrugged, got into the car, and told the driver to take him back to the hotel. He had nothing to do here. Manufacturing had apparently stopped for a long time, and he had to give up thinking about the imminent finishing of the vehicle and for now at least forget about traveling to the Moon. At the hotel, he ordered the plane to be ready for the evening as he wanted to return to Warsaw as soon as possible.

Meanwhile, in his home, Aza was bringing the game to an end. The evening was steamy and stuffy. There seemed to be a storm in the air. A storm was also felt everywhere. The storm or revolution was beginning. People were on the streets of the huge city. With the advent of darkness, the lights went on as usual, but after a while, entire streets began to sink in the shade, as if a sinister hand ripped wires and damaged the electric machines. Still, the traffic did not stop for a moment, but instead of the usual pedestrians who were hiding in the houses now for some reason, unknown crowds appeared downtown, and no one could tell where they came from.

A calm, chubby and unconcerned inhabitant looked on with amazement at those people with gloomy, fierce faces dressed in simple work clothes. He knew of their existence only by hearing, almost taking it for a fairy tale, that there were people like these who lived somewhere like he did ... An angry murmur was moving through the streets, although everything still looked calm. Aza heard it from the roof of Jacek's house, where she went out to find relief from the stuffy air of the rooms, which even the fans working with full force could not refresh. She was sitting on the flat terrace, stretched out in a folding chair, and looking down from under her lowered eyelids at the chaos down below, lit by lanterns still burning in the immediate vicinity. Further, the night was impenetrable, and it felt like only the crowd was rolling there, ready to light it up at any moment with exploding mines and fires lit to those magnificent houses ... The singer knew what it meant. She was sitting motionless for some time, inhaling all the joy of this electric tension of rebellion and struggle that was already in the air. Her nostrils swelled vigorously; her lips froze in a lustful half smile. For a moment, she had the impression that she could smell the irritating scent of a wild animal moving from the thicket ...

Suddenly she shuddered and stood up. After all, this is the last moment to act! If the uproar starts tomorrow, and she does not stand before it like a fiery angel, with the terrible tool of death and destruction in her hand!

She quickly ran down the stairs to the lower floor and went straight to Jacek's office. She knew that Nyanatiloka would be there.

Standing on the threshold, she looked against the light of the lamp burning on the table, which replaced the usual streams of electric glow, already dimmed due to broken wires.

The wise man was sitting in a chair with his head bowed on his chest and one could have thought that he was asleep, if it were not for his wide-open eyes with which he was staring at the empty space in front of him. He was naked to the waist, with only a woolen scarf around his hips. His long black hair flowed in calm strands over his shoulders.

Aza stopped at the door. For a moment, she was overwhelmed with intimidation, and then suddenly an unexpected surge of an insane yearning to free this man from his stillness and constant balance, to strip him of his sanctity, to force him into a passionate thrill ... At that moment, she almost forgot that it was not her goal and that she was only to trick him into opening the passage to that door behind him.

"Serato!"

He did not move, did not turn his eyes, did not even flinch at the sound of his name.

"Yes," he said in an ordinary, calm voice ...

All of Aza's wise plans, which she had been making long before this decisive struggle, became confused and fled at once from her thoughts. Pushed by her instinct, she jumped towards him and stuck her lips to his bare chest, her hands wandering around his face, grabbed his hair, slid down his shoulders... In a voice interrupted by insane kisses, she began to whisper the words of inexpressible delight, talk about the unspeakable pleasures he probably did not feel in his whole life nor could imagine, call him, ask him to embrace her, because she was dying for love ...

She did not even know at the moment whether she was saying what she was thinking and really felt, or if only playing a terrible comedy that captured her ... She only felt that she was losing consciousness with the last flash of awareness that she had thrown everything at once with one card.

Nyanatiloka did not move. He did not push her away, he did not move away from her kisses, did not narrow his open eyelids. It seemed that he was not a living man, but a terrifying wax figure, were

618

it not for the slightly contemptuous smile that had swept his lips.

Aza, suddenly touched by fear, moved away from him.

"Serato, Serato ..." she uttered out of her tightened throat.

There was no sign of a blush on his face, dark as ever, the blood in his veins did not pulse any faster.

"What do you wish, madam?"

"How is that ...? You ask that! I want you, you! Have you not felt my kisses?"

He shrugged slightly. "I felt them".

"And ... and ...?"

He looked straight into her face now with his eyes bright and calm. "And I'm surprised that people find them pleasurable ..."

"Oh!"

"Yes. And even more, that once they gave me pleasure."

Aza's eyes suddenly fell on the sharp brown paper-cutting dagger lying on the table next to him. Before she had time to realize what she was doing, she grabbed the knife and pushed it into Nyanatiloka's naked chest with all her might. Blood spurted on her face and her dress, she still saw how the hermit jumped up, stretched out and leaned back...

With a cry of terror and dread, she rushed to the door to escape. In the vestibule, she ran into Jacek, who had just dropped his plane on the roof of the house and was hurrying to his studio. He stopped dead when he saw her. He saw the blood on her face and her clothes.

"Aza! What happened? Are you hurt?"

She pulled back her hand that he tried to take. "No, no ..." she said as if sleepily, looking unconsciously in his face.

"Don't go there!" She shouted suddenly, knowing that Jacek had turned to the office door from where she had left.

"What is this?!"

"I ... I ..."

"What?"

"I killed ... Nyanatiloka."

With a cry of terror Jacek rushed towards the door. At that moment, however, Nyanatiloka stood on the threshold. He was pale like a corpse, there was no blood in his whitened lips, which instead flooded his body and his hip wrap with an abundant, hardly dried wave. He had a freshly scarred wound on his chest, under his left nipple.

Seeing him, Aza staggered and leaned back against the wall. The cry stopped in her throat.

Jacek took a step back. "Nyanatiloka ...?"

"Nothing, nothing, my friend. I was close to death ..."

"You are covered with fresh blood; you have a scar on your chest!"

"There was a wound here just a moment ago. I could have died because the knife passed through my heart ... But at the last moment of consciousness I remembered that you still needed me. With the effort of dying will, I grabbed the still burning spark of consciousness and began to struggle with death. It was the hardest fight I ever had. But in the end, as you can see, I won."

"You are unsteady on your feet ...!"

"No, no! He smiled wanly. It is the rest of the weakness that will pass soon. I am fine. I was waiting for you, knowing that you would come back tonight ... We would leave ..."

Jacek suddenly jumped up. "And my machine!"

The wise man stopped him with a wave of his hand. "It is not there anymore. It was stolen from you. I did not sense it earlier. Maybe it is for the better. After all, can use it without you?"

"No ..."

"So, it is good. We will leave here forever, forever ..."

Aza was now awake. Some frightening brightness burned her brain. With one thrust she leaped forward and fell to Nyanatiloka's feet.

"Forgive me, forgive me!"

He smiled. "I'm not angry at all."

He wanted to move, but she embraced his feet with her hands around his feet. Her golden hair, loosened in a violent motion, spread in front of him on the tiled floor, her fragrant lips stuck to his bare legs...

"You are truly a saint!," she called out. "Have mercy, have mercy on me, godly man! Take me with you! I will serve you like a dog! I will do what you want! Take me and purify me!"

He shrugged indifferently. "Women cannot acquire the grace of the knowledge".

"Why? Why?"

He did not answer her moan. There were roaring shouts outside the windows, the crowd boiled, roared ... A bloody glow hit the windows; Nyanatiloka put his arm around Jacek's shoulders. "Let's go!"

Jacek did not resist. As if in a dream, he could hear behind him Aza's crying, dragging herself behind them on the ground, heard her words with which she begged the hermit not to repel her, threatening that if he did, she would fall to the bottomless pit of crime, vice, and vileness ... He looked at the master. He seemed to move his lips, as if he were saying: "What do I care? After all, a woman has no soul ..."

EPILOGUE

After eight days of debilitating fear and uncertainty, Mataret finally dared to crawl out of his hiding place. The deafening bang, which pounded day and night on the locked heavy door of the vaulted basement and made the thick walls shiver so hard that cracks began to appear, had finally ceased and there seemed to be peace in the world ...

Mataret hesitated for a long time whenever he approached the door to push away the forged bolts. He remembered that terrible night when before his eyes the city began to collapse. Then, he was again overcome by a wave of fear similar to the one that had dumped him here in the deepest dungeon of Jacek's house.

Perhaps he would have remained in this basement for much longer if not for the hunger, threatening him with death. In his hurried escape, he did not even think about stocking up. All his food during these eight days was a loaf of bread grabbed by chance, when he ran by the door of the bakery located at the bottom of this large house. He had no water at all, he had to be content with wine, which was standing in great abundance here against the walls in squat barrels and in bottles arranged into rows on shelves.

He did not think at all what accident blessed him with that open basement, and that he could hide in it. As he dropped in here, he slid the bolts behind him and sat down in the darkness, frightened, not daring to even move in the first few hours. When his thirst tormented him, burning his palate, which was already dry with fear, he began to blindly look around, at first in the thought that maybe to refresh his mouth he would find moisture leaking from the wall ...

The basement was dry, and he found no moisture, but he came across barrels and bottles. At first, he was afraid that those might be the supplies of some chemical liquids Jacek needed for scientific experiments. Despite his increasing thirst, he hesitated for a long time before he put the first broken bottle to his lips.

The first sip of wine spread through his veins in an instant, and it refreshed his strength. He wanted to continue drinking, to oblivion, but his mind prevailed, warning that this unique and salutary drink could become lethal in the event of abuse. So, he got a grip on himself and decided not to drink more than enough to just quench his thirst.

Everything was fine at first, and the wine turned out to be a great drink, which not only watered and strengthened him physically, but also, excited his mind, uplifted him spiritually and cheered him up. However, after two or maybe three days, he could not count the exact time in the dark, his constant and forced intoxication began to bring fatal effects. His stomach, cheated by a scanty bite of dry bread, could not bear such heavy drink anymore. Painful dizziness and general weakness overwhelmed him, and they were becoming more oppressive with each passing moment. He preferred to suffer thirst, rather than take even one sip of wine, to the point that even the thought of it filled him with disgust.

The last day spent in this accidental prison was already an unspeakable torture. The lack of food meant that the wine, to which he returned involuntarily, poisoned him more strongly and, conversely, wine poisoning caused a more violent feeling of hunger.

At times he fell into a dream state filled with delirium, lasting who knows how long. At that time, he was hallucinating, and various terrible things were appearing to him: bloody riots, monstrous mines, crumbling cities, and some sort of fighting, with some human like creatures or like the malicious lunar Sherns... Then again unexpected relief would follow. He dreamed that he and Jacek were standing on a hill above the city and listening to stories about new, happy relations on Earth. Jacek smiled kindly at him and said that everything was happily over, that now the best and the smartest were ruling, and that he would soon go to the Moon to help Marek in establishing an eternal order.

And again, that bright dream was lost in the feverish terrible chaos.

The sunny city below suddenly turned into a pile of smoking debris. The glow of fire reached the bleeding sky, deathly moans were coming from everywhere, and the monstrous, devilish laughter of somebody, grown out of immensity, which had Yoozva's face and his powerful fists ...

Mataret jumped from sleep in terror and wanted to shout and call for help. The silence and the night around him were infinite, and his hunger grew worse, more and more consuming his intestines and pushed him desperately towards the exit.

Despite this, and although the sounds of the struggle had already been quiet for quite a long time, he shuddered, sliding open the bolts of the heavy door to step out to the world. In the dark and narrow corridor and still on the stairs leading up, he stopped every few steps and breathed heavily, as if to take courage with each gulp of fresh air inhaled in his suppressed chest.

He imagined what he would see when he stood on the street and prepared himself in advance for this sight.

"There will be debris around," he thought. Probably Jacek's house no longer exists, and he will probably find obstacles from stones and iron beams that may have already buried him alive, while he did not even know it ... And if he succeeds to leave, he will undoubtedly find himself in a terrible and final emptiness. The city is probably gone, and there is rubble everywhere and among it there are corpses and there is fire crawling over debris, digesting what can still be digested in these piles of boulder and iron.

The door at the end of the stairs was open. He went out into the wide hall; the house was still visibly standing, or at least its lower floor was intact. However, dead stillness was everywhere around him. "Apparently, the household members had fled or maybe had been killed", Mataret thought, sneaking along the marble walls toward the wide gates leading to the street. At a light push, they opened without a rustle, and he stood in the blinding glare of the sunlight and was amazed.

The city had its usual, everyday appearance. It was hardly noticeable that here and there a store was closed, or there was a broken window or a broken door. Some walls had fresh holes as if struck by shots. Further in a distance, Mataret seemed to see a house knocked down or destroyed by fire ... That is all. People were roaming the street as usual, maybe there were fewer of them, but nothing in their behavior indicated some unusual events.

Two policemen stood in front of the house, as if the symbol of a lively undisturbed order.

At the sound of a light click from the door, closing by itself behind Mataret, one of them turned quickly and grabbed the weapon at his side. "What are you looking for there?" He boomed angrily.

Mataret got scared. "I was just hiding ...," he began shyly.

Meanwhile the second policeman approached. He studied Mataret carefully, then turned quietly to his companion: "Excellency..."

"No," said the other. His excellency Roda is not bald. I saw him. It must be his companion or servant with whom he came from the Moon. He came toward Mataret. "You can't enter this house," he said.

"But I've always been here ..."

"It does not mean anything. So much the worse for you. Who knows, bird, if you are not a partner..."

"We have to tie him," said the other policeman.

"Yes," confirmed the first, "and take him to the precinct or straight to his Excellency ..."

Because the handcuffs turned out to be too big for Mataret's small hands, they tied them with a rope and thus was led by them. He did not resist or ask anything. Weakness overwhelmed him, he merely shuffled his legs, his eyes dim. Finally, the police noticed that he could not go any further, so on a street corner they put him in a car and took him to a magnificent building, which he had not noticed before in his wandering around the city.

Here he was led into a large waiting room where he waited for an hour before the door finally opened. A servant in livery summoned him before the face of excellency ...

Mataret staggered into the office and was suddenly speechless. In a room decorated with splendor, Master Roda in expensive clothes was sitting in a chair in front of the desk.

"Is that you ... are you?" He uttered out after a moment.

Roda frowned. "I go by the title of Excellency, please do not forget about it."

Then, beckoning to the servant to leave, he allowed Mataret to come and sit down.

"Where were you hiding? He began in a harsh tone.

"Give me some food," moaned Mataret, "eat and drink ..."

His Excellency graciously agreed to feed him, and when Mataret, refreshed a little, stood up again, he greeted him kindly and immediately promised to take him to his side if only he would obey him.

Mataret, looked at the former master and then his companion of misery with an astonishment bordering on distrust of his senses. He did not trust his eyes and ears and could not understand whether Roda was serious or just mocking ...

"But tell me what happened," he finally muttered.

"I told you I have the title of Excellency."

"Where from? How?"

"I saved the world!"

"What?"

"I saved the social order!"

"I do not understand."

"Naturally. You have always been dumb ... If it were not for me, this city would no longer exist today."

"So, the revolution?"

"Crushed! Crushed thanks to the tiny device that I heroically carried, risking my life, from the house of this damned Jacek.

"How is that?"

The old oratory flair awoke in Roda. He forgot his new seriousness and, leaping up on the chair with his new habit acquired on Earth, started speaking lively and waving his arms:

"Yes. Yes! I have always been resourceful. I stole from our venerable guardian, or rather I forced out of him, an infernal machine that could blow up the whole world! I carried it here on my chest, and I felt that I was carrying the fate of Earth, you understand? The fate of this Earth, which for us, people from the Moon, was our eternal mother, was in my hands ... My heart was trembling more vividly. Apparently, God alone brought me here, that I might save it and the human tribe..."

He paused for a moment, noticing that apparently such words in his mouth must seem strange to Mataret's ear, accustomed to completely different sentences, he used to proclaim.

However, he soon resumed not abashed at all: "Anyway, never mind. You will not understand it. In the end, everyone wanted this device. I could have taken it to Grabiec and even had that thought at first."

"And what did you do?"

"Wait! I wrote to Grabiec only that the machine was obtained, so if it were necessary, he would think that it was taken away from me by violence ... I could have also given it to Yoozva or for a reward, as if torn out from the enemy, return it to Jacek as its rightful owner ..."

"What have you done?"

"Ah! How impatient you are! I did what was best in this case. You know that I have always had respect for legitimate government..."

"Ha, ha!"

"Yes, don't laugh. I value it. That is why after more mature reflection; I went to the representatives of the government ..."

"And they ...with the use of this device?"

Roda laughed widely. "Yes. Using this machine."

"Did they kill and murder their opponents?"

"No, it was not so bad ... Anyway ..."

He jumped off the chair and, lowering his voice, said to Mataret's ear: "Anyway, I'll tell you in confidence: one couldn't shoot from this stupid device at all."

"How's that?"

"It just was not possible. Apparently, something was missing in the device I brought. When the door to Jacek's studio was broken down by force to take the rest, it turned out that he had destroyed everything before his sudden disappearance."

"So what?"

"Nothing."

"I do not understand."

"Because you are stupid. After all, no one except the government and me knew that the device was useless. Everyone had heard for a long time that Jacek had a terrible weapon ... It was enough when the news spread that this killer device was in the hands of the authorities..."

"Ah! I understand, I understand ..."

"You see. It was broadcast immediately that the wires of the entire telegraph network were connected to this innocent box. The government said: if we are to die in a revolution, let the whole world die! Scientists chickened out first. Then came the workers and all the mob that was afraid to lose the Sun...

"And Grabiec? And Yoozva? And so many others?"

"The government ordered to hang Grabiec. Yoozva was killed by his supporters because he did not want to surrender, desiring that the world be blown up, which they did not want at all ..."

"And in the end, you are the Excellency?"

"Yes, that is the way it is. I have the title "Guardian of the Machine" and "Savior of the Order."

Roda walked around the study with an inexpressible seriousness and stood in front of his former companion again, arms folded behind his back.

"Have I not always told you," he began, "that I can manage?" Who would have thought, when we were locked up here in a cage with a monkey...?"

He paused and looked around anxiously for anyone who could hear. Then he patted Mataret kindly on the shoulder. "I will not forget about you. You have suffered with me, so although I could complain about your slandering me in front of Jacek as if I were a liar, I will forgive you everything and try to ..."

He fell silent, because at that moment Mataret spat in his face and, turning on his heel, left the office.

There were no more policemen in the halls, so nobody stopped him. He slowly dragged himself down the wide marble stairs and joined the crowd. Many of the pedestrians passing by looked at the odd dwarf. Some knew him as a stranger from the Moon, so they stopped to look at him, but usually no special attention was paid to him.

So, he was walking like someone lost in the regular traffic, without a purpose, almost without thinking about where he was going. Sometimes his eyes fell on a house ruined with shots, from which workers were hurriedly removing the debris. He sometimes encountered a small group of people talking more vividly about the events of the last days, but besides that he did not notice any trace of the dangerous storm that had passed over the world. The most visible change was only the increased number of municipal guards and policemen who were following passers-by with their suspicious, ruthless eyes ...

Mataret was thinking about Jacek. Where could he have gone so suddenly? Was he not killed in the riots? Is he imprisoned? In spite of his will, he was recalling all the moments in the company of those scientists, conversations about plans for a new lunar expedition, to help Marek ... Or maybe Jacek flew to the Moon, leaving him here?

He raised his head towards the sky, where the crescent of the Moon could be seen in a blue, milky, dim glow in the midst of feathery and windblown clouds.

He was distracted from his thoughts, stopped by a crowd of people standing under some huge sheet of paper stuck to the wall. They were reading aloud the announcement printed on it. There were shouts of amazement, and more often words of recognition and praise for the government that issued the ordinance ...

Mataret approached curiously and pulled himself happily to the pedestal of a streetlamp, and read to himself ... The word grew dark in his eyes. Actually, he should not care, and yet he felt shame overwhelming him, a barbaric stranger from the Moon, for what was now beginning to dawn on Earth.

The announcement of the Government of the United States of Europe read as follows:

Citizens!

In the face of the unheard of and extremely deplorable events of the last days, the protective government, caring for the common good of the society it is entrusted with, is forced to put an end once and for all to the evil that society unfortunately bred on its own breast, with its own sacrificial blood.

Scientists, discoverers, and inventors were once indisputably a blessing of mankind. To some extent, we owe them our prosperity, flowing from the mastering of the forces of nature. It is true that we built factories and established economic order with our own hard-working hands, but it must be admitted that they with their inventions often gave us impulses to this fruitful work. The society aspiring to attain knowledge and progress contributed to general education by building millions of schools and undertaking education in our own hands. Still it cannot be denied that the smartest men played a significant role here, helping with their research to open new areas of thoughts.

It was a fair payment to society that allowed them to develop and create their work in the conditions necessary for peaceful and rewarding studies.

In the end, however, everything we needed was invented and far more was learned than we could need. These scientists, who proudly named themselves "knowing it all", became too expensive for us and society worshipped them only by remembrance of the merits of their predecessors.

However, a terrible thing has happened. Those smart men, living by the grace of society, conspired against it and, together with the darkest mob, tried to shake centuries of the Earth's established order.

Citizens! We do not need the smart men anymore! What we have gained so far is enough for us. For the benefit of humankind, the government, must put an end to their rampant conceit and troublemaking.

And therefore:

1. The association of scholars, existing under the name of the Knowing Brothers, is dissolved today.

2. All salaries until now paid to scientists are abolished, leaving them the freedom to earn by their own efforts if they want to live.

3. All establishments devoted to the so-called pure science and sterile research are also abolished, leaving only institutes of social benefit and economic value.

4. It is strictly forbidden and under severe penalties for the future to keep private laboratories and to publish works whose manuscript would not be deemed useful by a separate censorship commission.

5. While keeping the existing vocational schools fully operational and subsidized, once and for all we close any universities, the so-called philosophical or general universities, and above all The School of Scholars financed so far by the government

6. In order to prevent circumvention of the above regulation, any private teaching is strictly forbidden, no matter under what pretext.

Citizens! The government believes that you will gratefully accept the above ruling.

Mataret slid down the lamp post, and leaning against a wall was looking ahead with dumbfounded eyes, as what he had read appeared so unbelievable and monstrous. His relatively short stay on Earth and constant contact with Jacek taught him to value above all the achievements of human thought and its free flourishing, so now he had the impression that some terrible suicide was going on before his eyes.

He raised his head and looked sharply at the crowd. He was looking for people who would twitch in the same way as he did, indignantly, he was listening for a word of rebellion.

But the pedestrians, stopped for a moment before this announcement, so momentous for the fate of humanity, made only a few remarks more or less indifferent. Most of them expressed their appreciation to the government or at most wondered at its firmness and went on unconcerned, talking about common things, and inserting here and there only a word about the incidents of the last days.

Someone mentioned Jacek's infernal machine as a proof of the scholars' incredible malice, for which they are rightly punished now. Another mentioned Roda's name as a savior, expressing his appreciation for the government, which gave him a high honor as a reward. From the side, he heard an older gentleman telling two younger companions that the famous Aza who had not appeared on the stage for a long time was to appear again in the theater in the coming days. That news, thrown by accident and delivered from mouth to mouth, soon electrified the whole crowd, so that the ordinance concerning the smart men was forgotten. They asked if it was true. Where did the news come from? In what progressive role can the divine actress appear now?

Mataret did not listen anymore. Slowly, he dragged his feet forward, with his head bowed on his chest, and with sneering and contorted lips.

"Earth," he whispered, "the old Earth ..."

Behind him, in front of the poster proclaiming the death of knowledge, people are still talking about Aza, the famous singer and an outstanding dancer.

Jerzy Żuławski

The End

About the Author

Jerzy Zulawski (14 July 1874 – 9 August 1915) was a Polish literary figure, philosopher, translator, mountaineer, and nationalist who wrote The Lunar Trilogy between 1901 and 1911.

Starting with his first book of poems in 1895, at the age of 21, to his final World War I dispatches in 1915, Jerzy Zulawski created an impressive body of work—seven volumes of poetry, three collections of literary criticism, numerous cultural and philosophical essays, ten plays and five novels. He was considered an important and influential intellectual figure in the early years of the 20th century. Stanisław Lem credited Zulawski's with inspiring him to become "a writer of the fantastic" and describing the time he spent reading The Lunar Trilogy as "one of the most fascinating and life-changing experiences" of his youth.

Jerzy Zulawski was born into a strongly patriotic Polish household in the village of Lipowiec, in then Austrian Galicia, separated from Poland in the first partition. Jerzy's father had participated in the 1863 January Uprising against Czarist rule in the Russian portion of partitioned Poland and had a great influence on the writer's thinking. After attending school in Galicia, he received his Doctor of Philosophy from the University of Bern 1899. Zulawski returned to Poland in spring 1899 to co-edit the literary magazine *Krytyka (Critique)* and became a schoolteacher in Jaslo. After his marriage he published a number of his essays in the Kraków-based *Zycie*. He was a leading light of the Young Poland movement (Młoda Polska). He was concerned with the issues facing modern folks and the solution to dealing with them.

Zulawski devoted his full-time to writing by 1901 which resulted in the first volume of *The Lunar Trilogy, On the Silver Globe*, was serialized in the literary journal *Głos Narodu (The Voice of the Nation)* between December 1901 and April 1902 and subsequently appeared in re-edited form as a 1903 book in Lwów. Between 1908 and 1909, installments of a sequel entitled, *The Conqueror*, appeared in the *Kurier Warszawski (Warsaw Courier)*. It was published in book form in 1910. In 1910 the first installments of the final volume, *Stara Ziemia (Old Earth)* were published. *Głos Narodu*, published the installments of the final volume in spring 1911, with a re-edited book version coming out later that year. The first edition of the complete three-volume set was first published in Lwów in 1912 and was a staple of European science fiction from then on.

Jerzy Żuławski

At the outset of World War I Zulawski joined Piłsudski's Legions to fight for the cause of regaining Polish independence. Because of his literary reputation he was given a position on the Legion's staff in Łódź, where he edited and wrote for their newspaper *Do Broni (To Arms)*. At the end of 1914 he was given a position on the Naczelny Komitet Narodowy (Supreme [Polish] National Committee) in Vienna and, in April 1915, he served at the Legion Headquarters as a liaison to the First Brigade command. During a visit to the front in early August, he contracted typhus and, after a few days' illness, died at a field hospital in Dębica. He was 41 years old. His third son, Wawrzyniec, was born six months later, on 14 February 1916. His eldest son, Marek, was born as he started on *The Conqueror*, to become the namesake of the epic tale's tragic hero.

His three sons also gain some measure of fame in the arts and served Poland during World War II in the regular army and the resistance.

Jerzy Zulawski in the uniform of the Polish Legions in the early stages of World War I.

About the Translator

Elzbieta Morgan was born in Poland and is a Polish to English translator. She is a 1980 graduate of English Philology Department at the Jagiellonian University in Cracow, Poland and a retired American High School and college teacher of English as a Second Language from Jamesport, NY. She is an avid reader, a fluent speaker of four languages, a devoted teacher and a passionate translator who in 2015 revisited the dreams of her youth of becoming a translator. Since that time, she has collaborated with well-known companies translating hundreds of medical, legal and financial documents from Polish to English. She has often been hired for proofreading and editing of other translators' work.

This publication has been supported by the © POLAND Translation Program

Jerzy Żuławski

Look for more books from Winged Hussar Publishing, LLC – E-books, paperbacks and Limited Edition hardcovers. The best in history, science fiction and fantasy at:
https://www. wingedhussarpublishing.com
or follow us on Facebook at:
Winged Hussar Publishing LLC
Or on twitter at:
WingHusPubLLC
For information and upcoming publications

Other books that we have published in conjunction with the Poland Translation Program:

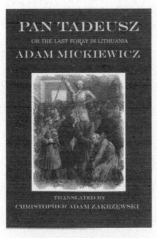

Antoni Lenkiewicz